I STARED
AT THE NIGHT
OF THE CITY

Bakhtiyar Ali

translated from the Kurdish by Kareem Abdulrahman

periscope
www.periscopebooks.co.uk

I Stared at the Night of the City

First published in Great Britain in 2016 by

Periscope
An imprint of Garnet Publishing Limited
8 Southern Court, South Street
Reading RG1 4QS

www.periscopebooks.co.uk
www.facebook.com/periscopebooks
www.twitter.com/periscopebooks
www.instagram.com/periscope_books
www.pinterest.com/periscope

1   2   3   4   5   6   7   8   9   10

ISBN 9781859641255

A CIP catalogue record for this book is available from the British Library.

*This book has been selected to receive financial assistance from English PEN's
Writers in Translation programme supported by Bloomberg. English PEN exists to
promote literature and its understanding, uphold writers' freedoms around the world,
campaign against the persecution and imprisonment of writers for stating their views
and promote the friendly co-operation of writers and free exchange of ideas.*

www.englishpen.org

This book has been typeset using Periscope UK,
a font created specially for this imprint.

Typeset by Samantha Barden
Jacket design by James Nunn: www.jamesnunn.co.uk

Printed and bound in Lebanon by International Press:
interpress@int-press.com

TRANSLATOR'S ACKNOWLEDGEMENTS

Many people have supported me in various ways throughout the translation of this book. My work would not have been possible without their help. I wholeheartedly thank them all, and apologise to those whose names are not mentioned here. Their input greatly improved the work, but I alone remain responsible for any flaws.

My friend Melanie Moore has been very generous with her time, reading two drafts of the entire book and making a significant number of corrections and suggestions. She also acted as a great sounding board; I cannot thank her enough.

Suzanne Ruggi and Beth Newton read the first draft of the opening fifty pages, and made useful suggestions.

Choman Hardi helped me with the translation of a considerable number of words and expressions. Marie LaBrosse refined my translation of the six ghazals used in the novel. Shaun Whiteside provided great feedback on one of the chapters, and was on hand to help with any queries I had.

John Peate and fellow translators on the brilliant Emerging Translators' Network (ETN) helped me pin down a number of expressions and sentences. Sarkar Ezat placed his sharp sense of the nuances of Kurdish words and idioms at my service.

Ros Schwartz's and Georgia de Chamberet's advice on finding and approaching publishers was very useful. Special thanks to my meticulous editor Ana Fletcher, who improved the text with her numerous suggestions. I would also like to thank everyone at Garnet Publishing and its new imprint Periscope – especially Mitchell Albert, Marie Hanson, Arash Hejazi and Sam Barden – for their support and enthusiasm for this book.

This translation is the outcome of close collaboration with the author, Bakhtiyar Ali, who was always happy to provide detailed answers to my queries. The author would like to thank Ako Wahbi and Fakhir Tayyib warmly for their support for the English translation.

Last but not least, my family: my wife Margot and daughter Fery were great sounding boards, and read a large chunk of my first draft. They are due special thanks for the patience they showed when obliged to share their lives with a sometimes very stressed translator. I also sought the help of other family members to untangle Kurdish words and idioms, especially my mother and my brother Karzan.

I dedicate this translation to my mother, who acted as the guardian of the many books in our home, even though she herself could barely read them.

A NOTE ON TITLES AND NAMES

The following list explains the most frequent titles and honorifics used in the novel. Most of them occur widely among the various nations of the Middle East, but are not always used in exactly the same way. The following definitions relate to their usage in Iraqi Kurdistan. Transliterations are from Kurdish.

Titles

Agha: A title often assigned to a tribal leader.

Beg: Another title for a tribal leader, one who often resides in the town and is educated.

Kak: An honorific preceding a man's first or full name.

Khan: An honorific placed after a woman's name; it is also another title for a male tribal leader.

Khanim: A woman's honorific used irrespective of rank or position, unlike the related Persian 'Khanum' or Turkish 'Hanım'.

Khwaja: 'Sir' or 'Master'; an honorific used for a great teacher, referring originally to a Sufi master.

Mirza: A son or descendant of a prince.

Mamosta: An honorific title before the names of an educated person or a Muslim cleric; it also means 'teacher'.

Mir: Prince.

Mam: An honorific placed before male names and denoting affection; its literal meaning is 'uncle'.

Names

The suffix *i* is sometimes used in Kurdish to join a first name to a nickname or occasionally a surname. It is preceded by a hyphen in English to make it clear it is not part of the first name: Ja'far-i Magholi; Hasan-i Tofan; Yaqut-i Mamad. (Both Magholi and Tofan are nicknames.) On official documents, the *i* is dropped; in some cases both forms of the name (i.e. Hasan-i Tofan and Hasan Tofan) are valid, and are indeed used in the Kurdish text. For the sake of simplicity, a single form has been adopted throughout the English version.

'The world was lost in a garden, and in a garden it was saved again.'

Attributed to Blaise Pascal

A STORY WITH NO BEGINNING

In the beginning of the spring of 2006, a slender, dark-skinned man set out for a village in the rugged mountains of the North on a highly confidential mission with a specific task to perform. He had been given a special and dangerous order to carry out a job no other human being could.

He was one of those cunning and misleading souls who always act the innocent. His deceptive smile was a great help in assuming a thousand different guises. He was one of those rare clowns who could play mischievously with every heart and toy with every soul. His smile, and the ability to feign a look of sadness, were his lethal weapons. Had the Devil seen him in that condition he would have been very pleased to have spawned such an artful creation – a man who dances to every tune but, deep in his soul, remains a loyal servant. The man himself would not be shy to admit it: 'I'm a loyal servant to those who feed me and give me my power.'

As he ascended, the man with the devilish scheme was taken aback by how harsh and inaccessible the area was. He climbed the long slope for eight hours, whistling contentedly and carrying a small bundle of food. It was his first visit to the area. Despite his wickedness and history, his fear of failure meant he had wanted to avoid this task. He knew something about the nature of those he was visiting, and they in turn knew something about his nature and obsessions. But there was still an opening, there was still a way, and he hoped that he could successfully complete his mission. He had left their last encounter with a good impression, and he held on to that good impression during the arduous climb.

Walking up the proud and rugged mountain, he was certain that although his life had been chequered with bad deeds and cowardly ruses, he himself was neither cruel nor mean-spirited. Despite all his evil deeds, there had been good moments in his life. There had been moments when he had wanted to be something else, wanted to snatch his soul out of the Devil's hands and wash it clean. But he knew his spirit had never been free, and he was not afraid to admit it. 'I am not a free spirit,' he would say.

The village he was walking towards, small and invisible, was sunk between the mountains. It was like a prison or a place of exile. Only three men lived there, in one of the villages destroyed in the 1980s. The village used to belong to Sahar Agha, whom, of course, we all know today as the Baron of Imagination. The Baron had abandoned the property because of the rough terrain, its remoteness and barrenness. In the end, at the Leader's request and once an amnesty had been declared, the Baron – one of those broad-shouldered men who has had a hidden impact on many things in this country over the past fifteen years – assigned the rebuilding of the village to the three men, who had nothing else to live for but memories.

They were to rebuild the village. It did not matter how many years it took them. It did not matter how many houses they built. It did not matter how they designed the buildings, the walls or the windows. All that mattered was that they kept on working. Once a month, a truckload of stone, cement and other construction materials was unloaded on the asphalt road at the foot of the cold, foggy mountain, and the three men were obliged to transport the materials on three old mules to somewhere up near the summit, and set to work there. They had to work day and night. Three men with dishevelled beards, covered in grime.

The day the new and unusual man arrived in the village, he was first received by the Real Magellan, whose given name was Zuhdi Shazaman – a man with long, grey hair and a long beard. If Christ had not died very young, but had gone on to gain in years, he might have acquired a similar look. Although Shazaman was old, he was solid and powerful, one of those men who could charm women more in his old age than in youth. He had been his city's finest bricklayer. He considered the guest with suspicion, and then led him to his friends. This was the beginning of the curious game the cunning and mischievous man had to play. He had to get inside the souls of the three men, carve them from the inside and rewrite them. And in order to succeed, he had to be a clown, sly and merciless, an impostor …

The man, who regarded himself as a close friend of the Devil's and a loyal brother to the Angel, possessed these evil traits in abundance. Our book is the story of this devilish, deceitful man's spiritual delving into the lives, memories and imaginations of the three men. It is his long journey in pursuit of a secret known only to these three. A trickster of his calibre is extremely rare. This book is the outcome of many months spent in those harsh mountains, until the beginning of the spring of 2007. It is also the story of some of the events that happened after that spring.

You need to know that the man with the cunning soul did his work meticulously. What he did not glean from delving into the three souls, he searched for in his own way. What did not come out of their three mouths, he completed by buying information and imagination. He employed different means and sources to enlist cunning men like himself to gather information. As he himself played an important role in the events at a certain juncture, he has deliberately highlighted certain angles. As to how these men ended up in these mountains – well, that's a story you cannot understand unless we go over the entire account from the outset. Once we have finally done so, however, we will see that this story does not have a beginning, that its roots go back beyond the births of the protagonists.

Despite the depth of these curious roots, our story does have features that are more or less from our own age. For instance, the soul of the clown, the trickster, who wrote all these pages, has no match in any other age or time. Each age has its own Devil and Angel, and in every age the Devil and the Angel play in a manner that is different to the way they do so in all other eras. During the game, they swap places. The most curious thing about the Devil is that he has to play like the Angel to win, and the Angel, to avoid being exposed, must – like the Devil – alter his appearance and be seen only through a haze.

Unfortunately, this story cannot be told chronologically. When the security chief was dismissed at the end of the summer, one of his colleagues smuggled some important secret files out of the department and circulated them in political confrontations with his opponents to avenge his underprivileged and beleaguered friends.

How these files had reached the security chief in the first place, I cannot fathom. I don't think His Excellency or any other person read them from start to finish, especially considering that in the spring of 2007 they were occupied with all the bother of hunting down Islamic terrorists. Besides, as you know, files had acquired a unique significance in our country after the 1991 uprising. So much so that we speak about the 'Golden Age of the Files', an era that will go down in history as the start of the worship and disclosure of files, an era in which the line between truth and lies became so blurred that the two could barely be separated.

The aggrieved colleague who spirited the files from the locker in the security department's basement happened to be a close friend of Shibr, the handsome, blond man we shall come across many times in these pages, a man you will certainly like and will want to meet after reading this book. What Shibr then passed on to us was a muddled bundle of papers, audio cassettes and documents – thousands of pages the cunning man had written in different styles of handwriting in order to mislead and deceive.

Now, after organising the stories in such a way that we understand where everything began, we have begun classifying the myriad papers and documents at our disposal so that they make sense. We have compressed, abridged, organised and, as far as possible, dated them. In places where we felt the truth had not fully emerged, we have done our own research.

Because retaining the complex and opaque language in which the entire report is written would be confusing for everyone, we first needed to refine the language of the ill-intentioned report writer and to neutralise his tones, which are so equivocal and oblique that we are yet to make out his aim in places, and have still to discern the games he is playing with certain words in others. To produce clear writing and achieve our purpose, we had to translate the sentences into language that was not so complex, deceitful or ridden with secrets, to change the words from something with the reek of a report by an evil soul to one that smells of life; to a story told in a clear voice, its style, outlook and viewpoint visible from every angle. And in doing so, as God is our witness, our sole aim has been to arrive at the truth.

Right from the beginning, we wanted to tell a story that was an exact replica of the events that metaphorically started with the bizarre and extraordinary birth of Ghazalnus ('Writer of Ghazals'),[1] and that continues to the present day and is still not at an end.

The chapters pertaining to the Baron of Imagination are the work of a close friend of his, who worked for another wing of the Party. He recorded everything the Baron said on small cassettes, thrown in at random with the files.

Our intention in publishing and exposing this story is partly to inform the world about this curious tale, in which most of the sad and dangerous events take place after the spring of 2004. It is also a detailed journey into the treacherous and bizarre events that thwarted the construction of a mythical district in our city, which could have made this ugly and un-majestic municipality home to one of the new wonders of the world. To comprehend the precise, profound and genuine reasons for the collapse of this project, we need to examine the details because, contrary to the proverb that says 'the Devil is in the detail', we believe that generalisations are the Devil's work: it is the angel who pays attention to the detail.

THE MEMOIRS OF THE
BARON OF IMAGINATION

Even if I don't tell you my name, you will all know who I am before too long. Like a wind blowing over a vast steppe, like a small golden wave in a huge pond, I ebb and I flow. My name is not very important. The night I embarked on this, I decided not to reveal it but to listen and remain anonymous, like any person of ill intent. But friends, I swear to you that everything I am going to tell you is accurate.

Sight is related to the workings of all the other senses. I could see through my heart and through my fingers. With the aid of my soul, with the aid of my hearing, of the powers of smell and touch, with the aid of all the men I had dispatched and the eyes I had set free like doves, I was able to be in all the places I was meant to be. There was just one place that was out of my reach. My whole life is a yearning for that place, is the grief of being denied access to that home, that idyll.

Listener, if you wish to accompany me from the start, pay heed to my conditions. You must be like an engineer working on the foundations of an ancient, ruined palace. You must not feel bewildered by that world. You must not judge me in terms of vice and virtue. You must be willing to look at a simple architectural plan, shut your eyes and imagine all the grand palaces that might have awakened from that slumbering piece of paper. You must have such powers that when you look at a ruin, you can understand that it once glittered with life, or when you look at a skull, you can penetrate its dreams, find out its hopes and the evil and good intentions it houses.

You must be an expert in all forms of travel and be able to respect plans and maps. You must look at plans and maps as symbols of a new world. All types of maps: engineers' maps, geographers' maps, the map of the winding paths of the psyche. Unlike the Imaginative Creatures, I have always worked from plans and maps – that's the difference between me and those who have only imagination. So then, if you wish to come with me, you must understand the significance of maps; you need to teach yourself the rudiments of cartography.

I'll do my best to help you, provided you genuinely want to learn. I'm fed up with liars who say they want to learn but make no effort. They drive me mad, out of my mind. At moments like that, you see, I lose it, and may do things you wouldn't expect. It's always been this way. Someone makes me lose it, and I behave in a way I didn't want to. I'm telling you right from the start: I much prefer idiots to people who want to understand but make no effort. If you're one of those, leave me be. All my life I've suffered because of you, and I don't want to endure that suffering any more. I am angrier, more cunning, more perplexing and ill-intentioned than you could ever imagine. If you wish to come with me, I shall narrate everything so that you can see for yourselves, and deliver your own verdicts.

Do not treat me as a virtuous storyteller. Do not seek to understand me or have pity on me. My task is too daunting for me to be virtuous. I am like a ship's captain, dispatched by the Devil onto the sea of bleak and impossible hopes. I take pleasure in seeing you and your ships lose your way. I take pleasure in seeing you fail to reach the destinations of your dreams. Often, I picture myself as a merciless swimmer, standing on the edge of a pool with a smile on my face as I watch a younger swimmer drown. Just as you take pleasure in seeing me drown, so I take pleasure in seeing you drown. But you must not think that every time you drown and do not resurface, it is my fault. I'm sure that we often get it wrong because we are supposed to get it wrong. Making mistakes is a part of life; the question is when and where we make them. It is imperative that we don't know when we've been deceived or mistaken. It's for our own good. If humans came to know all their mistakes, they would go mad.

I am an honest person, and so you should know from the start that in this story my intentions are not honourable. I, of course, know where to begin and where to go next, but you know nothing of this – and that gives me infinite delight. And you must be magnanimous and let a poor wretch like me have this pleasure. Oh, evil pleasure, how many more times will we cross your path, how many more times will we blame you for our bad deeds! Anyone who boards a ship with a guileful and wily person should be aware that pleasure has a vital role to play in the game. The pleasure of incarcerating you within my maps and making you walk the roads I have appointed, the roads I sought to escape for years and years. Nothing is more pleasurable than having a map in which you incarcerate all God's creatures, a map that can reach the territories of the imagination and reality, a map from which only one person can escape, and that person is you.

Now that almost everything has drawn to a close, I think the story is like a war between the pleasure of power and that of the imagination;

the pleasure of taming and reining in the world versus the pleasure of wildness and the alienation of a sad imagination that does not want power and beauty to come together at the same table, that wants man to be forever alienated and alone; an imagination that does not want to forget the old world, that does not want to forget the darkness of the present for the sake of the future's light. Oh, do not ask me. The pleasure of power is a way of forgetting a disease, of abandoning the humdrum day-to-day. It is the steady burial of whatever reminds us of the ugliness of our hands and hearts. Imagination is not something you look at and understand. Imagination is something you have to taste – with your lips, with your hands – and that is real pleasure.

The maps, too, can be real and controlled, or maps of an imaginary world that defy control. The map I'm talking about isn't a piece of paper you can spread out on a table and read. It's not something we draw up before a journey, or lines we go over with a pencil. It's something you find yourself in. You look and see that you're halfway along an extended path, at an unknown spot, faced with evil trickery, but you have to keep going right to the very end without stopping. Oh yes, maps, which make life easier, can also be fatal, are indeed fatal when you want the roads to go in a direction they refuse to take. My dears, while at times the maps resemble witless mules that dig in their heels and refuse to budge, at others, the strange places you wish to plot on the map are themselves so obstinate, so out of reach and so untrodden that no map can tame them. It feels like standing by a door you can't open. You understand that to go forward rather than backward, you have to embark on destruction and devastation. Unlucky is he who heads towards a city he never reaches, like I do. Unlucky indeed. Ill-fated is he who has a dead-end map in front of him, just like I do. Ill-fated indeed.

But it's deceptive and unsophisticated to think I am merely an unlucky explorer who has not reached his destination. No, the stories, the maps and the fantasies have this in common: they are made up of a number of tight knots, elaborate plans, infinite complexities. None of us has a map in our pocket as we walk along. Rather, we have a jumble of tangled maps in our heads; the psyche is nothing but a patterned landscape on which we draw maps every day. We often draw new maps on top of old ones, and the lines become so criss-crossed that we cannot easily tell them apart. But now, oh blabbering and ill-speaking mouth, keep quiet, do not reveal anything you're not meant to. Keep quiet and tell your story, it should reveal everything …

A ball is always rolling. It doesn't matter whether you can see it or not, just like a billiard table on which invisible balls seem to roll alongside the real ones. My God, that game drives me mad. Have you noticed that when good players play, it's just as if there were imaginary balls on the table. As if the ball that you and I can see, the white one propelled by the cue, were only the shadow of other imaginary ones that we can't see, that move like magic around the cue ball. Don't hold it against me if I ask, 'What is life but billiards played with real and imaginary balls?' Each of us a solitary ball, or two or three or four of us in a corner, in a square, when all of a sudden a moving ball, a mighty ball, a real ball, with a degree of imaginary force and some imaginary followers, comes and scatters us, sending us each in a different direction. And then we wait until another force, another ball, comes from the opposite direction and moves us again.

In this country, a man is nothing but a billiard ball, waiting and looking to see where he rolls. I've watched this all my life. I see those balls hitting one another, being scattered, coming close, dispersing, rolling away and disappearing into a black hole. Some don't come out again, some do. I have enjoyed the rolling. All my life I wanted to look like the white billiard ball, to become that ball. And no, I'm not so foolish as to want to become the cue. No, I'm the ball. Not the player, but the thing being played with.

Almighty God, help my soul, assist me in virtue and in vice. Judge me not for my virtues and vices, but understand me through Your greatness and wisdom.

THE IMAGINARY MAGELLAN SEES
THE FIRST CORPSE

MAJID-I GUL SOLAV, SPRING 2004

I couldn't stay and wait any longer. For as long as I'd known Bahman Nasser, he'd always been late, and every time he had an excuse that shut me up. I couldn't fall out with him, and after years of working together I should have forgiven him his small mistakes. Sometimes I waited for him no matter how late he was because he came along eventually, opened his little bag and had something new.

Nothing killed my imagination like waiting. I even wished once that I'd never met him. One day I was teaching the blind children, and when I turned round there he was at the door, listening with a smile on his face. When I finished, he put his hands on my shoulders and said, 'So, it's not for nothing that you're called "Magellan". You have seen strange things on your journeys.'

Timidly, I replied, 'Journeys? What journeys? I haven't been anywhere. All my stories are fiction. I've never left this city. I've lived here since I was born. I haven't left this city since the day I was born.'

Back then I didn't know he was called 'Ghazalnus'. I'd seen him around, but didn't know who he was. He introduced himself and said, 'Trifa sent me to meet you. You and I should become friends.'

And we did, we became close friends.

For a few years now, Bahman, Trifa and I had been working with the Notebook-Keepers on the big book. I was younger and less experienced than them when we began, although we were all part of a mightier legion, a huge army of imaginative beings, and I, like a madman diving into the sea, plunged with great gusto into the project of writing that big book about the recent history of death in the city.

No one outside of the legion knew about the book project – in fact, no one had asked us to write such a book. It was a mania, an obsession that entered the heads of Ghazalnus and Trifa Yabahri first. Later, we all worked on it. Ultimately, as with most of life's toils, all our efforts were in vain.

We each went by a different name. Mine was 'the Imaginary Magellan'. In the beginning, they merely called me 'Magellan', but after the appearance of that magnificent globetrotting traveller Zuhdi Shazaman, who became known as 'the Real Magellan', they renamed me to distinguish me from that tall lover, and also to present me to the world as his antithesis. Trifa was a delicate, dark-skinned girl, with long black hair and breathtaking black eyes. And the entire city already knew Bahman Nasser by his pseudonym, 'Ghazalnus'.

When we became friends he was already a big name, and had friends and like-minded followers everywhere in the city, boasting a long history of swimming in the sea of imagination. He was a king without a throne, and the fantasy-rich men and women of this filthy city looked up to him as a kindred spirit. As I was the only solitary, friendless soul among them – and there was no other group that could shelter me – they accepted me as one of the writers of the book so that I wouldn't remain companionless.

However, Ghazalnus was often late and could never manage his time. One minute he was in a rush and a muddle, the next he was slow, listless and absent-minded. As if unsure of himself, he oscillated between simplicity and greatness, imagination and truth, but there was something in his face akin to the solemnity of the masters and the look of the Sufis.

That day, for the first time, I decided to simply walk away and leave him. I took my briefcase and was trying to cross the ugly street when he, confused and panicked, got out of a cab, calling out, 'Don't go, for God's sake don't go, I'm coming!' As always, he was badly dressed and his hair was unkempt, but he had a charming smile and a deep expression in his eyes.

Furious, I stopped and said, 'I'm not working with you any more. You have no respect for anything. Nothing at all. Why should I wait for you all the time?'

In typical fashion, he said, sweetly, 'No, I know you wouldn't do that, I know you. You have a big heart. You'll never fall out with your brother Ghazalnus. You shouldn't fall out with unlucky Ghazalnus. If you do, you'll never come across another unlucky Ghazalnus as long as you live. Things like this won't come your way every day. It doesn't happen every day that people get to know an unlucky Ghazalnus like me. Anyway, I have something that will calm you down. Last night something happened, something important … do you want to hear about it?'

In those years it was my job to copy out the notebooks that Trifa received from the Notebook-Keepers. But ultimately I yearned for something full of life, fear and secrets. Sad and powerless, I looked at him, unsure of what to say.

Not waiting for my reply, he said, 'Darsim Tahir isn't lying, you see. You can keep saying he is, but, my dear Magellan, you're wrong. Darsim Tahir isn't lying. You harbour suspicions. I've never seen you expect anything good of anyone. Your dark thoughts have the upper hand – I told you this a long time ago.

'My friend, you need to change a little. My God, what a poor opinion you have of people! I sometimes wonder how your suspicion-ridden head can live with your kind heart. How can all your suspicions live with your vast imagination? How can your imaginative and pure side tolerate your conceit and vanity? I just don't understand.'

Right from the start, I had worried about extending the range of our tasks too far. Trifa Yabahri and the rest think I'm a faint-hearted sea captain, but I'm not faint-hearted. I just don't think we can mix imagination with life in that way. Obviously, I know we can't separate imagination from life, but the most important thing is the rules that govern their fusion. The rules matter.

Ghazalnus's eyes were very truthful that day, but his hair was so unruly that a couple of times I wanted to reach into my pocket, take out my comb, beg him to stop talking and comb it. It was a bizarre scene: me in my milky-white suit, my black, collarless shirt with the small, gold buttons on the cuffs, my hair like Johnny Depp's in *Finding Neverland*. I wore it parted on the right, flattening it with a shiny gel. Carrying a black briefcase, I stood calmly like someone waiting for a train on the platform of a remote station. And there *he* was, in his navy blue trousers and olive-green shirt with the short sleeves, as sad and romantic as ever, with his small glasses and long, unruly hair. He personified disorder, but it was a beautiful disorder. Grey strands were appearing in his hair. His only possession in life was his nickname: Ghazalnus.

I didn't dare talk to him about the ins and outs of my own life. He was one of those people who somehow forget to live for themselves. In the past five years he had been so overwhelmed, I could see him disappearing. That evening, when we were about to cross an ugly street in this ugly city, he said, 'When darkness falls, I'll take you with me and show you something you've never seen before.'

From the very first day I met him, he told me that a big part of his life was a continuous journey through certain secret worlds.

He was a man unable to reveal himself. Like the flowers and birds, he did not understand the enigma of his own being. What made Ghazalnus a complex person, impossible to interpret, was that he tied his secrets to the secret of the world. And yet he worked so carelessly and fearlessly that I was left surprised and anxious. In an ugly city like ours, anyone who is full of beauty will, whether he wants to or not, come face to face with people who'd like to inspect the deepest corners of his soul and circumscribe his very existence, who regard the secrets of his beauty as a great threat to the security of everything else. So since I've known him, I've been worried about his indifference. Although he and his ghazals filled our lives with courage, he himself seemed cold and careless.

Trifa Yabahri was a courageous woman who worked on women's issues. I think my sister, Nawras, played an important part in introducing Trifa to that world. Their journeys had such complicated outcomes that to this day, I cannot dissect their secrets.

Initially, Ghazalnus worked with children – he was both educator and minder. He wanted to devote his entire life to them. I came into the fold by accident. Before that, I had organised a small class for blind children.

My head was full of fantasies. God alone knew how many stories were born and perished in my head every day. I'd always liked nice clothes. I liked my hair to be done properly and I liked to be well-dressed, to put a book under my arm or carry a briefcase and roam the city from one end to the other. Since childhood I'd had a burning desire to travel, but lack of money and human support tied me to this ugly city. Damn this city. I'm afraid I must state my hatred and revulsion whenever I speak of it ... humour me, please.

Over the past few years, all my friends had gone abroad. I was the only one left. I thought perhaps I could travel in a different way and I drew myself an imaginary map, the map of a fantasy land, a map that exists only in my head, the map of a land covered by a huge network of rivers, streams and seas. I spent months dividing that land into its fantasy regions – I had to create it dunam by dunam, acre by acre, in my imagination. For a long spell, my relationship with that land was stronger than my relationship with life; I devoted my time to the labours involved as a worker bends to his task. Some days I would be drawing trees until late in the evening.

I stuck the huge map on the wall of my room, building its realms inch by inch. That period gave me a thorough grounding in cartography. I learned the differences between the geographer's and the geologist's styles of mapping. I looked at old explorers' maps; checked the imaginary atlases of ancient travellers; and an expert taught me the old and new criteria of mapping. I spent hours every day enlarging my map, and the remainder of my time building a massive, imaginary ship upon which to cruise the rivers of the fantasy land. So that I didn't stray too far from my ship, I made sure the river criss-crossed the imaginary realm with many branches and tributaries. I filled my nights with skies to match the new lands. I was so immersed in creating cities, towns and peoples on the map that I dropped my evening walks; I forgot about my friends and my family, until I could no longer recognise my own relatives. I looked at whomever I came across as a fabled creature of the towns I had created. I suffered endless insomnia, hallucinations and daydreams.

One day, when I sensed I was on the brink of insanity, the border between life and fantasy blurring, I had just enough of my wits about me to think of a way back into the world. One morning I went to the Organisation for the Blind and timidly knocked on the door. Back then I knew nothing about the organisation, but I had seen their office during my walks. When I went in, a young manager received me and listened to me patiently. The gist of my idea was to hold a small class for blind children in which I would take them on imaginary journeys. I went on to say that, because the blind have not experienced the world in the way we have, they have fewer fantasies; but on the other hand, because they are not as absorbed in the world as the rest of us, they could more easily accompany me on an imaginary journey.

Because my listener did not quite know what I meant, he said shyly, 'Are you saying you would like to take some of the blind people on a journey?'

'Yes,' I said, 'but my journey is a fictional one, it's a journey through a story. I'll tell stories of my travels and they'll assist me, as if we were roaming an imaginary land along the shores of a long river, of which nobody knows the source or the mouth. I will be the pilot and they, the crew and passengers. We'll discover forests, mountains and towns that can only be found in the imagination.'

He looked at me sadly and said, 'As if you were Magellan?'

I nodded contentedly and said with a big smile, 'You've got it. As if I were Magellan.'

My smile betrayed surprise and foolishness in equal measure. The man understood my idea, but only with great difficulty. I wanted to carry out my fantastical journeys across imaginary maps accompanied by a group of blind children because they needed to travel. A world that we, the sighted, can't see with our eyes, and that is the same for all of us – blind and seeing alike.

The idea that we, the sighted, would travel a world in which we couldn't see so moved the young manager that he wanted to bring all the blind people in the country into a single room together right there and then, so that I could lead them into an unknown land.

I told him from the outset that waiting kills my imagination, so I didn't want to wait too long for an answer. He quickly dispelled my fears, saying, 'I'll sort out everything as soon as possible and you'll become the sardarbashi of a new ship.' The word 'sardarbashi', or 'captain', was new to me, but I was happy to be called it.

Although the man had initially seemed rather dull and lacking in imagination, my idea brought him to life and he said, happily, 'Sir, we can make it a mobile class so that the blind can feel the movement, as if they were cruising a bottomless river.' The man was thinking of buying a caravan and attaching it to a small pickup truck, which a driver would steer at my command so that the blind felt the restless movement of the waves.

I warmed to the idea too, picturing myself sitting with the blind as if we were on the sea. I imagined them asking me, 'Admiral Magellan, how far can you see?' and myself declaring in a loud voice, 'No rush ... hey, don't rush, we'll reach land and inhabited places soon enough. A patch of green has just appeared on the horizon ... we're almost there. Land ahoy! Row slowly now, to the right.'

Unfortunately, like most Kurdish officials who planted their backsides in the seats of power at the turn of the twenty-first century, the man was a liar. He neither bought us a caravan nor gave us so much as a muddy turnip. He provided us with a room in his organisation and never got back to us.

I, of course, didn't take it to heart in the slightest. Don't forget that we were living in a region of the world I called 'Mockistan' on my imaginary map – a place where lying didn't make anyone feel uneasy. For three to four thousand years, lying has been part of the daily routine. The fictional history I wrote for Mockistan was full of mock caliphs, lords and barons, full of mock sword fights between emirs and kings who pretended to be fighting, dead or victorious, when they had neither died nor triumphed. It was full of bizarre civil wars in which the victims were genuine martyrs, but all the battles were made up. Mockistan is certainly worth seeing. Even if you're living in a country very far away, it's worth saving up to come and visit, especially as, in the last few years, the region has been swarming with mock airports and people can buy tickets from mock airlines, board mock airplanes and spend a mock period of their precious lives there.

But let me get back to the evening when I was waiting for Bahman Nasser and he didn't turn up. I was about to leave when, at the very last moment, I saw him emerge from a dirty cab, confused, his hair dishevelled. That night I had my first real encounter with fear. Bahman and I whiled away the evening in the teahouses, on the pavements and in the parks. As night fell, we left for the suburbs. After an hour's stroll breathing polluted air in the darkness of a filthy district, we greeted a late-night grocer, whose small oil lamp was keeping a gloomy street corner awake. We found Hasan-i Tofan sitting on a filthy box beside the quiet grocer, eating grapes that were covered in dust.

That night was one of Mr Tofan's quieter ones. He was often too bubbly and talkative to let anyone else get a word in edgeways, and would normally blabber incessantly in a nasal tone redolent of old age. That night on the corner of the same alley, Darsim Tahir popped up. The spitting image of a cross-eyed lizard, he bent before the romantic figure of Ghazalnus, kissed his hands and led us away before any of us said a word to him. A small, fat, young man only slightly taller than a dwarf, he walked unusually fast, to all appearances like a sphere circling in an unknown orbit. For a dignified man like myself, proud as an aristocrat in my English suit, it was an embarrassment to be following such a bizarre creature. His nose was so large it made his head heavy, and he found it hard to lift his face and look you in the eye. I had never seen such an enormous nose.

The night was dark and cold. We walked for so long, we were exhausted. All I could see was the darkness. Until that night, I had thought of darkness as a meaningless space, devoid of secrets and mysteries, but that night a lot changed inside me. Familiar with the roads, and like a creature who has spent his life in the shadows, Darsim jumped over potholes and kept on walking without looking back at us. Ghazalnus had to stop him every now and then so we could catch up. Tofan was a night creature and, like an owl, was used to different degrees of darkness; as for me, a secret guide inside me lit up the night. But Ghazalnus walked at a more leisurely pace, and more than anything I was impressed by his nonchalance.

After a half-hour walk, Darsim, like a well-trained dog, started sniffing the earth. I said to myself that this fucker had benefited a great deal from his big nose. There are many people with big body parts they make no use of.

To wind him up, I called out, 'Hey, Big Nose. You're putting that fucking conk of yours to good use. What are you sniffing at? Why are you sniffing the earth with your arse in the air like a dog?'

'Big Nose,' I said, 'your father's fucking body isn't here. So, why have you brought us to this dump?'

No reply. He paused his sniffing from time to time and, as if gazing at a huge map in his mind, carefully counted his steps, measuring them against other imaginary points we couldn't see. Before long he paused at a particular spot and started digging with his small, powerful hands, like a frightened rat. Two workers shovelling dirt could not have kept up with him. He was cutting through the earth in such a way that I could scarcely believe my eyes. I was expecting a chest of gold to appear; what I saw was anything but gold. Rather, he unearthed the upper part of a body and said with satisfaction, 'This is it.'

It was the first time in my life the smell of a corpse came over me. It was the first body I'd ever seen exhumed. The corpse looked fresh, and actually seemed to have been buried fairly recently. Not bothered about getting my clothes dirty, I got closer and looked at it by the light of the torch. The sight of a corpse, like that of a painting or a unique pearl, is never forgotten. Man forgets many memories, bitter or sweet, forgets many a beautiful woman's face, but it's very rare to forget seeing a corpse.

In most of the people I know, seeing a dead body leads to philosophical reflections and questions about the meaning of life, but in me, right at that moment, it stirred nothing, nothing at all. I blurted out, 'Leave him in his peaceful sleep.' I didn't know myself what I meant.

From the very first moment I saw the corpse, I felt a sort of affinity with it. That night the four of us exhumed the body. It was a young man wearing a pair of jeans and a short-sleeved orange shirt. One bullet had entered his head through his mouth. Another had gone in through his navel and come out through his back.

When Tofan saw the two enormous wounds, he said in a loud voice, 'This is Magholi's work. Only Magholi does this. He's the only one who shoots them at close range. This is his work, gentlemen, I swear to you. This is Ja'far's signature, Ja'far-i Magholi's. He used to be my friend, but ... hang on a minute, as far as I know, he migrated to The Netherlands seven years ago. Seven years ago. Friends, can you check whether he has any other bullet wounds?'

Big Nose tossed the body around a few times, but couldn't see anything. Tofan himself took a closer look, moving the dead man's head a few times. He touched his chest several times, calmly running his hands over the body, but to no avail. He stood up, wiped his hands on his sharwal and said, 'God Almighty, what's going on? If Magholi's back, it's definitely him.'

Ghazalnus's eyes brimmed with tears, but I restrained myself and asked, 'Do any of you know him?'

Ghazalnus said in a distraught, broken voice, 'It's Murad Jamil. Murad Jamil has been missing for a few days now. He was a restless, imaginative lover. You know the type.'

Ghazalnus spoke as if he knew the victim very well. I didn't know who Jamil was. I'd never heard of him. Calmly, I asked, 'How long do you think he's been dead?'

Tofan sniffed the body and said, 'Three, four days at most. It's fresh.'

Gently, I said, 'Let's inform the security department. They should know about this.'

'The security department can't do anything for him,' Tofan retorted, shaking his head. 'They might even implicate us in the matter. I think we should keep it quiet for the moment, until we've thought it through properly.'

'What do you make of all this?' I asked Ghazalnus.

I knew he couldn't answer. I could tell he was very sad and exhausted. I put my hands gently on his shoulders and said, 'Try not to let it get to you.'

He put his head between his hands and said, 'My heart cries out to him. He was very young.'

I took the torch from Hasan-i Tofan and looked closely at the victim's face. He really was very young.

IN THE BEGINNING WAS
A LINE FROM A GHAZAL

In the previous chapter we heard Magellan tell part of his and
Ghazalnus's story. On this journey, we will pause every now and
then to listen to the hopes and desires of the protagonists – those
who are writing this book with their stories. This book, which
begins simply with Magellan's story, is in fact more intricate, more
multi-dimensional and more interlinked than might at first appear.

I ought to tell you from the beginning that Majid-i Gul Solav,
whom we know in this story as the Imaginary Magellan, is the polar
opposite, the very antithesis of the Real Magellan, a man who plays
a major role in parts of this great epic and received his share of the
punishment for it.

I ought to make it clear right away that the Real Magellan of our
story is not in any way related to Magellan, the renowned sailor who
circumnavigated the Earth and was killed in a battle off the Island
of Mactan in the Philippines on 27 April 1521. Magellan's name is,
rather, a metaphor for a widely travelled man who has seen many
countries, who has spent plenty of nights with a variety of women
on peculiar remote islands, who has brought back the smell of many
races and strange tribes; the scent of many unfamiliar plants from
his mythical dreams has spilled over into this story. In short, the Real
Magellan, unlike the Imaginary Magellan, made journeys with real
people using real maps.

All these different stories and characters and many others, right
from the beginning, make our book into a compilation of a whole
set of other books. Sometimes it's a novel, while at other times it
may look like a painting by a great master. Sometimes it's a voyage
through a fantastical geography; at others it's a manuscript buried so
deep in the dust of time that it has acquired something of the spirit
of the ancient gardeners as well as something of the obsessions of a
modern architect. Ultimately, however, this book is a multifaceted
creature. It is story and painting at the same time. It is order and
disorder. It is truth and dream. It tells the story of multifaceted

people, people who settled down and people of no fixed abode, the happy and the sad, those who exist and those who don't, the loyal and the fickle.

I have to say that it is a book of sadness and unhappiness, a book that brings grief and old age to its authors and deep, genuine sorrow to its readers. It is a book that, once written, makes us feel we have bidden farewell to many angels and demons in our own souls and opened the door to dark storms, to gardens filled with secrets and the untrodden roads of the darkness in our hearts.

We start this book with the story's complex man: Ghazalnus, whom we can't easily describe or introduce because sometimes he shines brightly but at other times he is more like a silhouette, very mysterious. There was a mythical element to his birth. He seems like someone trying to outrun the devils of his childhood. Now, when I say 'the devils', please don't leap to imagine a religious story, the story of a prophet pursued by sinners while he, a sacred soul, carries his purity from one land to another. No, what I mean is the real story of a real child, a week after whose birth a huge number of devils, jinns and ogres were born.

The tale of the birth of Ghazalnus is simply mind-blowing. During the week Ghazalnus was born in the late Fifties, dozens of other children were born as well – all of them deformed, disfigured, repellent. The midwife who was supposed to deliver him had told his parents before his birth that the child might be lame or devil-faced, because for a whole week neither she nor any other midwife had taken a normal child from the womb of a woman in the city. But by divine exception, by the mercy of God, Ghazalnus, bearing the face of an angel, was born inside the amniotic sac. He was the sole normal child in that season unusually full of deformed children. As if the Devil had slept with all the women of this city; as if, on one of the coldest nights in the region when the women were looking for something to keep them warm, the Devil, by one of his flying tricks, came and injected his sperm into the wombs of this dear homeland's women, women who seem to have borne only mischievous children for many years.

Astonished by the bright eyes and unblemished face of little Ghazalnus, the midwife did not, however, show the slightest expression of pleasure at this unexpected event. She did not beam with happiness. Baffled, and as if considering the future, she carried in the tiny baby and told his mother, 'This is a perfect human being. Look after him well. Beautiful boys end up sad, unlucky men.'

'A perfect human being.' Those were the first words and the first description Ghazalnus heard in those first moments of his existence. An expression that was to follow him like a curse and become his main preoccupation in life.

In short, the season in which Ghazalnus was born was one in which ogres and semi-humans were born. Today I believe that the little Ghazalnus was the only perfect child of that season. But when his parents first looked at him together, they saw something on his chest that made them uneasy, something that looked like an inscription or a long scar. The mullah who cried his name into his ears as he christened him said, 'Bismillah', in the name of God, as he held the tiny infant. When he opened the blue, swaddling blanket where the brownish, agile baby was kicking his tiny limbs like a frightened rabbit, he saw a long line on the infant's chest, which he only managed to read after lengthy reflection and with the help of his glasses, a mirror and a special mixture of coal and salt.

After much effort, the mullah muttered the line of poetry that was inscribed upside down and back to front on the child's chest. Nowadays, they say the poem was a ghazal, one with such deep philosophical connotations that only religious men could understand it; a ghazal that soon sank beneath the child's chest, like a ship going down at sea. It disappeared into the infant's flesh and blood, only to gush forth years later from his soul like a great surge of love.

Those who see the grown-up Ghazalnus – the tall, messy-haired, bespectacled guy in his trademark olive-green shirt, pale jeans and the gleaming white trainers – have all forgotten about the ghazal that connects this dreamy, tender man to the time of the classical poets, to a time when love of God and love of humanity were fused in such a way that blasphemy and faith could live side by side without either knowing that the other existed.

Today the image of Ghazalnus as a young man, engrossed in a number of major and yet commonplace human issues, has completely overshadowed the image of the infant – seemingly the last messenger sent by the classical poets to revive the bygone reign of literature. Nowadays he has the demeanour of a far-sighted sage or serene poet, though this is not to suggest that his looks don't make you think of other possible professions. In other words, if we look at him differently, he might appear to have the look of a calm, dignified young doctor, one of those pleasant doctors occasionally encountered outside hospitals. But however we look at him, his demeanour is not without the charm of the profound meanings that have accompanied him since childhood.

But before I get to say anything about the life of Bahman Nasser Saeed, alias Ghazalnus, you have to help me answer this question: What does 'a perfect human being' mean?

Don't forget that our book is full of digressions, of untimely questions that force us to retreat to our rooms, lock the doors and mull them over by the dim light of a candle. And some chapters of this book *should* be read in dim candlelight; not because of the classical style and composition of the writing, but because reading them will make us disbelieve and doubt the things we see and the very world we live in. They force us to retreat to our rooms or behind locked doors to ponder how much our understanding of the world is rooted in reality and how much in fantasy.

When I finished writing and compiling this book, I started to question myself and was forced to revisit the meaning of my life, childhood and youth. Please forgive me from the outset for being merely a nameless storyteller who will not take off my mask and reveal myself. No, I'm not comparing my role to that of the storytellers in Brecht's plays. My role is more like the new electronic devices that allow you to pause a film at any point and not let anything escape your attention, devices that allow you to rewind or jump ahead, to slow the scenes down or fast-forward through them. I have a wish that one day, storytellers will be able to act like a universal remote control that can switch many devices on and off at the same time, to pause and restart the action; but they're not going to be able to reach such an advanced level of mechanisation and absolute authority. I try my best to work as mercilessly as a machine, to organise the pages in front of me and order what are often erratic written, taped and oral accounts. I have a lot of work ahead of me, and am only too aware of its significance. I'd like to pay just enough attention to my technique that I neither lose the truth nor succumb too much to fantasy. Despite all these headaches, there are few moments when I forget my role and get carried away by all the mysteries and the questions.

Now that I feel you understand me and can relate to my concerns, I wonder if any of you have, in this brief interval, thought about what a 'perfect human being' is. I'm obliged to ask you this difficult, indeed unanswerable question, so that you know what thoughts preoccupy me. You must know this isn't easy to explain, so please be patient while I find a balance between my techniques and what you want.

While I do just that and make some progress in the telling of this bizarre and complex tale, why don't you think about it – about what makes, and who is, a 'perfect human being'?

Ghazalnus was born at a time when children of bizarre or animal-like appearance were the norm. But if Ghazalnus's birth was extraordinary, it was not because of his perfect features and immaculate human form, but because of another fantastical and inexplicable account that he heard many years after the true story of his birth.

On a cold, damp, foggy morning in late March 1975, the year in which the collapse of the Barzani-led Kurdish revolution saw tens of thousands of hopeless and dejected fighters cross the Iranian border, four people carried a sick man on a makeshift stretcher made of tattered blankets and the thin branches of a plane tree over the border to an Iranian hospital. The ailing, long-bearded man, suspected of having tuberculosis, was vomiting blood and experiencing frequent bouts of shivering. Two of those carrying him were his sons, and the other two were close, loyal relatives. They had come a long way through snow and storms and had asked everyone they ran into on the road for pen and paper, but under such conditions and in such a region these were not so easy to come by.

The patient seemed to be wrestling bitterly with death as he sought to acquire a piece of paper on which he could write down a very important piece of information. Neither his sons nor the close relatives understood the secret of his strange request; the four knew that the sick man they had been carrying for days through rain and snow had not touched pen and paper for years. The sick man was Mullah Gharib-i Hajar, who had published a collection of poetry titled the *Gharib Ghazals* at some point in the Thirties and Forties, at a time when printing machines had just arrived in Kurdistan and newspapers were beginning to emerge.

No one knew the real identity of the man who, under the pseudonym of 'Sukhta' (an advanced Islamic theological student), achieved some fame among the mullahs, *Gulistan*[2] lovers and hafizes,[3] but the poet and his poems soon faded into oblivion and slipped into the margins with the advent of a new literary wave. After quitting poetry, Hajar laid down his pen and lived like an ordinary man, but as with all ordinary men something unusual remained in his soul – namely, the ability to fall silently in love.

At the age of fifty-five he started to admire one Baharbanu – a shy woman with fair skin and full breasts. Mullah Hajar would see Baharbanu in the evenings when she was making up the bed for her husband on the roof of their house, and in the mornings when she went shopping. The mullah belonged to the category of men who love silently, the category of men who burn with love for years but do not allow anyone to see it, the category of men who can shut the doors to their souls very tightly and not let anyone smash them down from the outside.

In an era when concealing love was a virtue, and patience in the face of the temptation of the loved one a sign of a gentleman's strength, Mullah Hajar used all the will in his body and mind to stifle the untimely and silent love in his heart. He went back to performing strict religious rituals and became madly obsessed with the mosque. To punish his body and murder his fantasies, he would sometimes go outside the city during the day in his old clerical cloak carrying a sharp adze, a long file and a knife with a wide blade, and would inscribe verses of the Qur'an on the trees and write down his penance on the rocks as he sought to exhaust his body in futile, aimless activities.

In that season, the mullah's self-mortification brought him close to death, but some loves can find mythical routes to their object of desire when the natural path fails. They are stronger than faith and superior to reason. Their light goes beyond the confines of the human body, creating a prism that illuminates its surroundings, a light that is at times the torch of happiness and at others a dangerous ray of sadness and disaster.

Mullah Hajar's fell into that unique category of love that can take leave of its owner and operate outside his powers. One night, when he was looking at the stars through a window on the second floor of his house, a handsome young man opened the door to the room, gently put his hand on the mullah's shoulder and said: 'Don't be scared. I am part of you. I'm the love you've stifled inside your soul and seek to kill.'

After a lengthy philosophical discussion, the mullah understood that his love for the shy, fair-skinned woman was out of his control, that it had reached a different level of being, one governed by laws incomprehensible to him. That same night he started chasing the man through the quiet alleys of the city, but couldn't catch him. The man he pursued was an adventurous creature born in the dark corners of the mullah's imagination, an unreal creature who had escaped his obsessions and the secret chambers of his existence, who dwelled in places the mullah had been terrified of all his life. Many a night the mullah, with angry eyes and a will of iron, as if hunting a dangerous animal, chased him with a thick rope through the alleys – through the dark streets near Baharbanu's home, in tucked-away bars and amid the throng of nighttime gamblers.

He caught him many times, and tied him to electricity pylons, trees or the pillars in the bazaar, beating him with a shepherd's crook or the whips of carriage drivers. As if dealing with a rebellious animal, he put a string around his neck and dragged him along. The unruly young man was constantly reading the ghazals of Kurdish, Arab and Persian poets; intoxicated and entranced, he swam in the seas of the literature of love. The more the mullah hurt him, the more he wept for him. The more he chained him up, the more he longed to set him free. After all their long battles, their confrontations and wrestling bouts, the mullah, defeated and powerless, released the young man's chains and told him, 'Go away. Go away and never come back.'

But one night the wild, fearless, ghazal-stricken lover returned with Baharbanu, the shy woman intoxicated by the ghazals, who was wearing a dress of purple chiffon. She had given in to the imaginary young man, who both was and was not part of the mullah. The mullah couldn't believe what he was seeing; yet there was no doubting it was she, the fair-skinned and dazzling Baharbanu. She stripped naked before the mullah's very eyes during a ghazal-reading ceremony and made love to his in-love half, a lovemaking that was nothing like the conventional intercourse of the men and women of that era, who barely pulled down their trousers before clambering on top of each other, their clothes still on. This was a type of lovemaking that lasted for hours; two human beings stripped bare, trying out every position in the *Kama Sutra*. After that night, this scene was repeated umpteen times.

And then one day, Mullah Hajar saw the timid Baharbanu in a dusty alley, pregnant now and with a new expression in her eyes. Baharbanu gazed at the mullah in an odd way, as if she were aware of the nightly game her fantastical half played with the mullah's fantastical half: a mysterious and mythical game, the fruit of which was a real child, which Baharbanu now showed the mullah by removing her cloak and exposing her belly.

When Ghazalnus was born, the mullah paced frantically up and down near Baharbanu's home like a madman. The story of the infant with a line of ghazal inscribed on his chest further reinforced the imaginary realm of his life, but he kept it secret and no one heard anything about it until he was on his deathbed. Baharbanu named her son Bahman; his father, Nasser Saeed, a seasoned employee of the education department, held his son in his arms without any sense that something fishy was going on, or any doubt that he was holding a child of his own flesh and blood.

After Ghazalnus's birth, Mullah Hajar was not rid of his ghazal-poet half; there were many nights when the wild lover haunted him, reading him dazzling ghazals and epic love stories. He put the mullah under immense pressure to compile his new poems for him in a book, but Mullah Hajar, angry and exasperated by such overwhelming love, decided not to take up the pen until he was close to death. To resist his situation and put it out of his mind, he moved to a faraway town with his children, where he plunged headlong into the treacherous ocean of politics – the best place by far for anyone who wants to stifle his heart. The fight for Kurdistan, coupled with relentless battles against the communists, kept his mind so busy that when he finally awoke he noticed that he had aged and forgotten his once-anguished in-love half. He had deserted the ghazal-reciting poet of his soul. The two never met again until his death.

Towards the end of 1975, when Mullah Hajar, saddened by the collapse of the armed Iraqi Kurdish revolution, contracted a terminal illness and was being carried through the storms to Iran, he resolved not to take the story of the phantasmic young man to his grave. All the way, he searched for pen and paper to write down the story of Ghazalnus's birth before his own demise. The men carrying the ailing mullah on a stretcher during those dark, rainy days stopped at a lonely hamlet on the border. They took him into a house and began searching for a pen and paper. After some time, they returned with four notebooks and several pens. As he hung between life and death, 'Mullah Hajar' sometimes listened to the thunder and rain, and sometimes to the call of death. Under these harsh circumstances, the mullah tried to inject some energy into his aged, worn-out bones. He placed a large pillow under his arms and, by the light of a small oil lamp – which, like him, had barely any life left in it – he embarked on the writing of a long and dangerous letter to someone he had never seen or met.

THE BEGINNINGS OF JA'FAR-I MAGHOLI
AND HASAN-I TOFAN

I, Hasan-i Tofan, along with Ja'far-i Magholi, grew up in the Party's network. The day Mamosta Shawboyan called us and told us the good news that we had both been assigned to a clandestine cell involved in purges and killing, we were over the moon. If my memory serves me right, Magholi was a hundred times happier than I was that day. In front of Mamosta's walrus moustache and wild gaze, Magholi – a diminutive, thick-lipped, wide-nosed man – stood as still as a statue or a soldier receiving an important order from his commander. He had his dirty, chequered headscarf wrapped around his neck. His erect posture made him look like an overgrown mouse abnormally planted on its two back feet. He was ecstatic, as if he'd just been crowned King of Persia.

Ja'far-i Magholi used to say he was born to kill. He believed our acceptance into the assassination squad was a launch pad to senior positions. Back then, he thought – and still does – that people who were not adept at the art of killing, purging the ranks or overcoming barriers would stay at the bottom of the pyramid until they rotted to death. Talentless as we were, we had nothing in common with those affected, limp-wristed intellectuals who joined the Party and soon became all-powerful; we had no assets other than our stupidity and our pistols, invaluable assets seldom given their due value. I've always maintained that an idiot with a pistol can climb to the rank of President of the Republic in this country. I have often been proved right.

Magholi and I were both idiots, but we knew how to capitalise on our stupidity. We had become friends after haggling over a lamb with a local old man, who had several beautiful daughters. We were both young – and we were both there to look at the man's coquettish daughters. When we discovered our shared motivation, we became friends.

Our association dates back to when we worked for the assassination cells, which Ja'far-i Magholi, with his vulgar language and simple mind, called 'The Finishing-Off Sports Club'. At the time we were apprentices of a well-known Party cadre, whose nom de guerre was Sabir Tarano. He was one of the leaders of the clandestine struggle and a methodical politician of the Eighties who had developed his own comprehensive school of thought. I ought to say that he was one of the fathers of the revolutionary violence practised at the time, a time I regarded as a dark era but which my colleagues thought was full of life. Back then, different methods of killing were employed in the country, but no one rationalised it as neatly as he did.

Tarano was a weak, bespectacled man with a wrinkled face. He'd never killed an ant nor slaughtered a chicken in his life. He described himself as the theorist of the revolution. Although I couldn't make out much of what he said then, I do remember him saying that this life, indeed this world of ours in its entirety, was based on something called 'silence'. There were two approaches among the politicians then. I called one the 'smear school', as the essence of its political propaganda could be summed up as dishonouring opponents. I called the second approach, which was more dangerous (albeit more respectful) the 'silent killing method'. Its followers obliterated their opponents very quietly and in mysterious circumstances, leaving many unanswered questions, loose ends and unexplained secrets. They created an atmosphere in which a murder turned into a mystery, so that no conclusions could be reached with absolute certainty.

I, who consider myself one of the shapers of that era, spent the early years of my political education in the hands of Tarano, one of the prominent leaders of the politics of silence. Magholi and I worked for him, took part in the obliteration of fascists and meted out the people's punishment to a large number of traitors and hirelings. We were behind the disappearance of some of Tarano's opponents in the Party and we killed many cadres from other political parties for him, all in complete silence.

Throughout his many years in the national struggle, Tarano had a tailor's shop. He would bend over his sewing machine like an innocent soul, his poor eyesight attracting the sympathy and kindness of his guests, customers and passers-by. He was so frail and feeble that no one could have imagined him being behind all those intricate and bloody operations. He looked gaunt and ill. If you saw him, your heart would ache for him and you would marvel at such an unlucky person. Because of his wretched demeanour, he escaped the eyes of the regime's spies and informers even during the most difficult of times.

I have to say that even then, our teacher and guide, Sabir Tarano, was very impressed with Magholi. Ja'far-i Magholi had his own style of killing: he would stand very close to the victims, speak and even joke with them, and then pull a gun on them and kill them. He always carried his pistol in his pocket. To this day, I've never known anyone else to do that. He would find an excuse to draw close to his prey and shoot them in the belly button at point-blank range. Just as the victim fell and opened his mouth to groan, he would fire another bullet into the mouth. Magholi's style was very different from mine. I would take aim with my powerful, steady, unshakable arm and shoot the victim in the chest from fifteen to twenty metres away. I don't remember ever having shot a victim anywhere else except in the chest, and I never missed my target.

The art of killing is not about shooting at just any visible part of the prey – that's the hallmark of inept and cowardly assassins. Killing is about hitting the enemy in the chest: the chest, and nowhere else.

There were many other styles as well as Magholi's and mine. Shibr, for instance, only took aim at the forehead. Those who were hit in the forehead in the late Seventies and mid-Nineties all died at the hands of Shibr Mustafa. Taqsim riddled his victims with bullets in a straight line running from head to toe. Bezhing, or 'the Sieve', would pepper his victims with no less than fifty bullets – hence his name. Fara-i Tunchi fired from behind, usually hitting the victim in the nape of the neck or the shoulders.

Around fifty of us worked in this field. Our work was to erase one another, the Party's opponents and our nation's enemies. We each had our own path and worked for a designated cadre with a specific objective. Magholi and I often carried out tasks together. He always wore a pair of large leather gloves. His menacing expression was in sharp contrast to his delicate, pleasant voice, which helped him draw close to his victims and talk to them. When you heard his gentle, melodic voice, any doubts you had would be dispelled, and you'd feel reassured. Sometimes he became quiet, and when I looked at him I couldn't believe such an enchanting voice could come from someone with such bulging eyes and crooked lips, and such a swollen face.

We shot our victims alternately. I was the fastest of the assassins. As soon as my target appeared and I saw his or her chest, I would have everything done in the twinkling of an eye, wasting no time at all. I don't remember having ever startled my prey or made them experience any doubt. The greatest sin is to allow the victim to think about death. In that short breath, nothing is left – no politics, no hatred, no revenge. The only thing connecting you to the prey is death. For me, the most important thing is that the prey dies without having time to be scared, without having to go through the long interval between the certainty of death and death itself. Unlike me, Magholi made no distinction between hunting a partridge and hunting a human being. He believed that just as a partridge calls his or her friends to their deaths, so a man should draw his victim into the ambush with a special song. And when both sides realise they are inside a storm controlled by the killer on the one side and the prey on the other, both will see the game through to the end, having accepted their fate.

I was a member of the killing cell for as long as a year after the uprising. One day they sent us a long list of women we had to pick off, one by one. I hadn't yet killed a woman. They dispatched me to kill a gorgeous woman living with her very young husband in their shabby home. My several years in the Party had taught me not to enquire too much about the victims. It's not that I wasn't curious, but I had learned from experience that familiarity with the victims only caused a headache. Too much information about them, and your hands would begin to shake. You would become hesitant and unable to hit the target. Furthermore, neither knowledge nor absence of knowledge could make any difference to the task. I knew that even if I didn't kill them, Magholi, Tunchi or Fazil Qandil would. There were some among us who wanted to dig deep into the stories. They wanted to know the reasons for a killing, establish its justification and kill out of conviction. Most of them lost their lives in dubious accidents on foggy nights. If one day you become a murderer, don't try to find out much about your victims. Extra information about the victim only makes the job harder and the consequences more dangerous.

On the day I set off to kill that gorgeous woman, my whole body was shaking as if I'd never killed anybody before in my life. I can still see her: a tall, graceful beauty. When I stepped inside the house, she was hanging the washing on a nylon line, wearing a thin Kurdish dress. I could see her black slip underneath. Throughout my life, I had never been particularly preoccupied with women. Nevertheless, killing such a woman didn't sit well with me. I saw a small child sitting on a staircase, holding an empty bowl and crying. As I took out my pistol and aimed at her, for a moment – a moment shorter than the flickering of an oil lamp, or a heartbeat – I hesitated. For the first time in my life, I wanted to drop my pistol and not carry out a Party order. Perhaps I wouldn't have killed her; but, unfortunately for me, at that very moment her young husband came out of the room and saw me with the pistol. The man's frightened look, the strangled cry in his throat, the panic on his face, all revealed my helplessness and weakness: I pulled the trigger and shot the beautiful woman in the heart. The blood spattered a long way, and although I was some ten metres away from her, I was soaked. The woman fell while I, shell-shocked, stood frozen to the spot.

Until that day, not a drop of blood had ever landed on me. Magholi always smeared himself in blood. He would soak a handkerchief in it and carry it as a keepsake. But I had always kept enough distance between myself and the victim to avoid being spattered. I usually left the scene quickly, fleeing like the wind and disappearing. I would leave so fast I was called 'Tofan', the Storm. That day, however, as if I were under a spell, as if someone were holding my legs, I didn't move for some time. The sound of the bullets was deafeningly loud and the smell of gunpowder filled the yard. I saw the husband coming towards me, weeping. I saw him on the staircase, screaming. Slowly, I approached the woman, who was drawing her last breath, soaked in her own blood. I saw her big green eyes, their empty, unquestioning gaze fixed on me. Drenched in blood, I left. Outside the gate, I saw Magholi; I was screaming as he pulled me away.

That was my last day working for the Party. That same evening, I gave it all up. I stopped playing the game. After my departure, it was Magholi, Tunchi, Dansaz and Haji Kotar who did everything. In less than a year, they had killed a large number of women across the country. That marked my first separation from Ja'far-i Magholi. I would not see him again for thirteen years, but when I did, I felt that even though the world had changed a lot and time had come full circle, he hadn't changed one bit.

KHANIM-I SHAMS'S PROBLEM WITH HER ADOLESCENT DAUGHTER

EARLY WINTER 1992

'Khanim-i Shams, Khanim-i Shams, you've got to understand that this girl has no imagination. I've been trying for days to get just one single point across to her: that some organisms are tiny, too tiny to be seen by the naked eye, while others are too big to be perceived by our natural but imperfect senses. I want to make her understand that there are plants that can eat humans – yes, they can, they really can – but your daughter's problem is that she is lacking in imagination. Khanim, listen to me, all last week I was trying to prove to this girl that some organisms can reproduce without copulation. That's right, without copulation. My God, no matter how much I tried, your daughter simply couldn't understand how that could be. She put me in such a state I uttered words that are not appropriate for a man like me to use in front of a respectful, modest girl like her. And we've got harder lessons coming up. If Mahnaz Khan doesn't understand how tiny sea creatures reproduce, I don't know how, come tomorrow, she will comprehend the reproductive system of fleas or the circulatory system of crocodiles. How will she understand the skeletons of birds that lived fifty million years ago? My dear lady, I'm sorry, but that's how it is.'

Several years before the day Majid-i Gul Solav, Darsim Tahir and Bahman Nasser unearthed the first corpse, Saeed Bio, the biology teacher, spoke thus to Khanim-i Shams, the wife of a senior official. The teacher was in his early fifties. The man appeared so miserable and helpless you'd have felt sorry for him if you'd seen him. He was agonising over Khanim-i Shams's beautiful daughter. Anything related to knowledge, learning and thinking was beyond Mahnaz – a girl unique in her beauty, unique in her lack of intelligence, unique in her quietness. No one knew how she had even reached Year 11. Some teachers swore to me that she still didn't know her times tables, knew nothing about geometry theorems, and in biology, she could just about tell the difference between a camel and a rose.

Khanim-i Shams looked at Saeed Bio with great concern, unsure of what to say. Although she deeply hated the surly teacher, this time she knew he was in the right. Her daughter knew nothing other than how to dress up, put on her make-up and watch TV.

Finally, she put her hands on the table in front of her and asked the teacher, 'So, Teacher, what can we do? What's the solution?'

Sitting back in his seat, Saeed Bio said, 'Khanim, I told you, she needs a teacher to teach her imagination. Someone to make her fathom those things that are not happening right in front of her, to make her relate to things she doesn't physically or mentally experience. In other words, one doesn't need to be a flower to understand how flowers die. One doesn't need to be an ocean creature to understand living conditions underwater. Khanim, I mean it, really: you need to look for a specialist tutor of the imagination. Your daughter does not have an imagination.'

Khanim-i Shams, who had no idea what Teacher Saeed was talking about, said, 'Do you know anyone who teaches imagination? Because I've not heard of such a discipline.'

As he reached for his tea, Saeed Bio accidentally nudged the plate of pastries, glanced at Shams's white knees – which her tight, black skirt did not cover – and, clearly ill at ease, said, 'Everyone has some imagination from birth. No student I've tutored has gone away without showing improvement. As God is my witness, two years ago, twenty-three of my students got into the College of Medicine. You know, Khanim, if Khanim-i Mahnaz, your innocent daughter, doesn't get through because she fails biology, it would damage my reputation. It would make me look bad. You're a well-known family. Anything that happens in your household will get out. People will say: "Look, Saeed Bio visited Sayfadin Maro's house for a whole year, he spent ages there with Shams and her daughter Mahnaz, and still she failed the exam." So how can we explain this? How? My dear lady, I've never come across anyone as lacking in imagination as your daughter Mahnaz Khan. I'm grateful for your tea and delicious homemade pastries, but sadly I have to tell you that I won't be coming here again, because it isn't making the least bit of difference. Why should I charge you for nothing? Why?'

Khanim-i Shams was a little alarmed by the teacher's last few sentences. After her husband became a senior civil servant and had won the trust of the Leader and the high-ranking party cadres, they had suddenly struck it rich. She was worried that her daughter would fail in school, and her close female acquaintances would say she was too mean to find a good tutor for her daughter. The thought made her shudder. She must do whatever it took to ensure that no one could say such a thing. Her daughter did badly in all her lessons. Her highest mark had been in Kurdish, in which she once got 53 percent. Apart from this, she had never passed a test in any other lesson. She should have been a third-year university student by now.

Shams and her husband had provided everything for her: she had her own room and her own balcony; her female friends were allowed to visit; she was engaged; she was allowed to go out, within reason; she listened to the songs of Simon and Bülent Ersoy. And yet she failed in school.

This was the first time she had heard someone tell her, 'Your daughter has no imagination'. Sayfadin Maro, her husband, who with his big, bald head and potbelly looked like a basinful of dumped fat, was always roaming round the house in his long robe saying, 'This girl has no brains. Don't waste money on her. You can't buy brains.'

Poor Shams didn't know what the difference was between a human being with no brain and one with no imagination. Deep in her heart, she thought Teacher Saeed Bio's words were more accurate. The girl *did* have a brain. She was cunning enough. If she wanted, she could be shamelessly coquettish. Shams even had suspicions her daughter might have something going on with another man behind her fiancé's back. Just who that could be, she didn't know. Generally, she was no different from other girls her age. And Shams's main concern was that she herself could not be found fault with. When she heard Saeed was the best biology teacher around, she called him and begged him to give her daughter private lessons. But now, for the first time in her life, she was being forced to look for a teacher of the imagination. An imagination teacher. She'd never heard of such a thing.

When Saeed Bio left, she went to her room, put her head in her hands and began to cry. There was nothing worse than living with an ugly man like Sayfadin Maro, and on top of that she had a child who was not very bright. As she'd aged, and with the passing of time, she'd got used to Sayfa's ugliness. She consoled herself by saying he was a senior Party member. But she couldn't get used to her daughter not achieving anything. In this life, there was nothing worse than your child failing at school. Nothing. She often said this to her female friends. She wanted her daughter to make it to university on her own merits. It didn't matter which university. What mattered was getting in on her own merits.

That evening, when Sayfadin came home, a storm was in store for him. Even before he could begin to enjoy his position as a senior

Party official, his life had started going from bad to worse by the day. Why is it that no sooner do you relish the prospect of something – a victory, say – than something happens to spoil the experience and ruin your life? That evening as he stepped into the house, Khanim-i Shams poured out the entire story before he even had chance to sit down. Sayfadin had already quarrelled with Shams over this habit of hers. As soon as he appeared at the gate, the woman would inundate him with all sorts of bad news before allowing him to take a breath. Sayfadin would sometimes get into a rage and sometimes laugh or cry. On other occasions he would simply look at her without uttering a single word.

The problem of finding a teacher of the imagination was a new one. He'd never even heard of such a problem before. He had long left the issue of the children's education to his wife, but now she was insisting they should find an imagination teacher straightaway, that very moment.

After a disturbed and argumentative evening, Maro called Sarkawt Nazmi late at night, imploring him to find him a teacher who could boost his daughter's imagination. When the phone rang, Sarkawt Nazmi was in bed with a big towel wrapped around his head like an Indian maharaja, watching an Arabic film on video. Sarkawt didn't have a specific job; he was a jack-of-all-trades. If you were looking for the latest model of car, he'd find you one; if you needed a rooster from the Levant, he'd get you one; if you needed a plumber, he'd track one down within a few hours; and if you asked him for a good physics teacher, he wouldn't let you down. He'd spent all his life in the bazaar, but had never heard of an imagination teacher. However, he didn't want to come across as an ignorant man, and he badly wanted to win the heart of a newly promoted official, from whom he knew he'd need a favour sooner or later. Betraying no sign of panic, he said, 'No problem, my dear sir. We'll find an imagination teacher tomorrow.'

Had Sarkawt Nazmi not said that, things might have gone differently. This whole story might have taken a different course. But Sarkawt promised Sayfadin Maro he'd find an imagination teacher without even knowing what one was, and that was the beginning of the first crazy game in our book.

A CONTRADICTORY AND IMAGINARY TWIN
TRIFA YABAHRI'S BIRTH IN THE LATE 1960S

One day, Jawhar Zahir Yabahri, Trifa Yabahri's brother, decided to become a millionaire without resorting to either his mind or his body. By this he meant that he would lead a very comfortable life and want for nothing – not the fanciest of cars, nor largest of mansions. He would marry the most beautiful woman, wear the most expensive clothes and work in a plush office – all without applying his mind or moving a muscle. I must say that before the 1991 uprising, no one could have entertained such dreams. Not a single soul in our country would have dared to make such a decision. However, with the rise of the ever-glowing sun of freedom, our country teemed with men who could realise their dreams without engaging their minds or making an effort.

Jawhar and Trifa were not twins, but they were introduced to the world as such. No one so far has got to the bottom of the story of Trifa's birth, a complex and ambiguous tale that defies any explanation and cannot be fathomed or disentangled on the basis of the available data. We do know that on a mosquito-ridden night a few weeks after the July 1968 coup, Fawziya, Zahir Agha Yabahri's wife, gave birth to Jawhar Agha under a rusty ceiling fan on a sweat-soaked and pain-wracked bed in an old, ramshackle neighbourhood. Everyone knew that Fawziya Khan – a respectable woman and a descendant of the Yasamis – had been childless five years into her marriage. Despite her best efforts during those five years, God had not brought happiness into her life through the gift of a child. After three years of marriage, she had started to see herself as a barren tree, a useless creature. Like all women who cannot conceive, she was grief-stricken, and the sight of an infant made her heart leap. Conceiving had become the greatest obsession of this decent, virtuous woman. When Fawziya Yasami finally conceived, fantasy became reality and a lifelong dream came true.

But Fawziya's deep sadness was not the only problem the Yabahri family faced in those five long years; the family's biggest problem was the extreme jealousy between Zahir Yabahri and his sister Samira, which dated back to their earliest days. The sister was hugely jealous of her charming brother. Samira was not the type of woman to resign herself easily to a woman's lot, to simply accept that affection and superiority had been enjoyed by the male members of the Yabahri family since its beginnings. This led to a furious row between Zahir and his sister, one that continued a number of old battles between the male and female members of the Yabahris. Zahir's deep hatred of his sister prompted his vow to ensure she never married, and therefore never bore or raised children of her own. From 1963 onwards, Zahir turned down all Samira's suitors. Meanwhile, Samira secretly resorted to amulet-makers for amulets and charms that would make her brother Zahir sterile. The family's life during those five years was hell. Samira, a fierce and aggressive girl, would often start vicious fights against the respectable Fawziya, who suffered in silence among the Yabahris.

When Samira heard that her sister-in-law Fawziya Yasami had conceived, she almost lost her mind. She could not sleep for many nights. Her jealousy made her think day and night about how to have children of her own, so that she would not be deprived of the Yabahri family's fortune. No one knows just what happened in that period, but on the summer night that Fawziya went into labour to give birth to Jawhar Agha Yabahri – at the same hour of that same night – Samira Yabahri went into a painful labour, too. Throughout Fawziya's pregnancy, no one had observed anything unusual in Samira. So, the night she went into labour, everyone thought it was merely another one of her evil tantrums. When an intelligent and scrupulous Egyptian doctor who had been living in the city for some time examined her carefully, he made a surprising diagnosis: Samira was still a virgin, her hymen still intact – and yet she was pregnant.

Human happiness is often accompanied by sadness and grief; Zahir Yabahri, who had been soaring on wings of happiness in the early evening and considered himself the luckiest man in the world as he looked forward to presenting another offspring to the Yabahris after so many years of waiting, was plunged into restlessness by the news that his ill-intentioned, jealous virgin sister was pregnant. True, Zahir Agha could not recall a day when he had felt he loved his sister, but this didn't mean he wanted her to stain the family's honour. This was an unparalleled disgrace, and would have tarnished the Yabahris for good. He had to do whatever it took to cover up the shame, and quickly. Zahir Agha paid a stupendous amount of money to the Egyptian doctor to attend to both his wife and sister in secret; to deliver their babies, and to take this secret to the grave. Which is how

Fawziya Yasami and Samira Yabahri came to give birth to two babies at the same moment in two adjoining rooms under two big ceiling fans in the scorching-hot summer of 1968. One of them was Jawhar Zahir, the other Trifa Zahir. They were introduced to everyone as twins, as a boy and a girl conceived in Fawziya Yasami's womb, and registered to Zahir and Fawziya Yabahri.

They could not be more different, however: one the product of truth, the other of fantasy. Jawhar was born normally, head first, while Trifa was born in the breech position. Jawhar was born crying, Trifa laughing; Jawhar was fair, Trifa dark-skinned and hairy. Jawhar had light-brown eyes, Trifa's were jet-black. Samira Yabahri was incarcerated in a room on the second floor of Zahir Yabahri's house from the night she gave birth until the day she died. Zahir kept the door locked during the first three years lest she escape, but in the fourth year the good-hearted and compassionate Fawziya wept for several days and finally persuaded her stubborn, spiteful husband to open the door and set his sister free.

Fawziya Yasami hadn't seen Samira for three years. She hadn't set foot on the second floor. When Zahir Yabahri opened the door, instead of the Samira she used to know, Fawziya came face-to-face with an aged, devastated person, a far cry from the aggressive, argumentative individual of old. She was now a vulnerable woman who took fright at the shadows, and at the scent of people. Samira Yabahri had forgotten many things in those three years, and had developed an overpowering inner fear that prevented her from leaving the room. For the next fourteen years, until Samira Yabahri quietly passed away on a cool, magical spring evening, Fawziya Yasami cared for her in that same room like a loyal and selfless sister. Throughout those years, Samira – half-mad, half-paralysed – inhabited an imaginary world. Ever since giving birth to Trifa, she had lived with a group of peculiar creatures only she could see.

Fawziya Yasami told us this interpretation of Trifa's birth to Samira Yabahri, an interpretation she seemed to believe in wholeheartedly. During that period, in those moments that Samira had her wits about her and their bonds of co-suffering and sisterhood were strong, she reassured Fawziya that she had not slept with a man to give birth to a real child, but that jealousy had made her sleep with men from her imagination at night in the hope of conceiving a child, at least in her imagination. Samira obsessively wanted to give birth to a child, and her obsession suddenly became reality – no one knows exactly how. 'Trifa Yabahri was born from the breath of fantastical beings,' as Fawziya put it. She was the product of an imaginary desire that was somehow fulfilled. Evidently, there will be some people who do not believe this story, although for centuries humanity believed that Christ was born of an imaginary breath. But I would say that, for a nation such as ours that has lived in fantasy for hundreds of years, its hopes realised only in dreams, it is perfectly easy to believe this kind of story.

As far as I am concerned, I have no trouble accepting Trifa Yabahri's story. Often, if people wish for something from the bottom of their hearts, regardless of how unreal or far-fetched these hopes might appear, something extraordinary, some mythical force, will emerge and realise those dreams. It has happened that in the heat of the summer, I have looked up at the sky and asked for rain, and suddenly the weather has changed and clouds bearing fat raindrops have appeared and a storm has broken. It has happened that I longed to see someone, and suddenly there on the corner of a street or an alley he has appeared, and I have embraced him as my wish came true. I would say that the problem of humanity is that people no longer have genuinely strong wishes that come from the very depths of their inner selves and force the world to pay attention. When people's hopes and wishes come from their very depths, they acquire such power that they can overcome the laws of physics and any other hurdles in their way. Hope is the only thing that can shatter solid matter, bend and break earthly laws and bring down the barriers of the world. However, if our hopes are not sufficiently strong, the world will be unmoved and will heedlessly keep turning. I believe Trifa Yabahri was the product of the fiery hope and volcanic desire in Samira Yabahri's soul, which was ultimately woven into the shape of a human being in the womb of that woman and became real. She was more like embroidered muslin on which the imagination could work its intricate stitching than a real girl to be controlled and tamed.

We should know that women's wombs are the mirrors of their dreams. Many women do not conceive, I believe, because deep inside, in the invisible darkness of their psyches, they rebel against something in this world – against a destiny, against an eternal duty that is tantamount to death and slavery; they no longer dream or burden their souls with hope. In short, women's wombs are not only an organ of their bodies, but also an organic area of their souls. Men have lost that important area of their souls, so it is their hands that produce their creative and spiritual work. Their creativity is less profound than the life-giving powers of women, like the difference between a naturally available product and one obtained through cultivation and much effort. So I can tell you from the outset that my understanding of the story of humanity is back to front. It's not women who are doomed to endure great pain during labour, but men who are fated to bring something into the world only through blood, sweat and tears. A woman's womb is a crucial part of her soul, but when it comes to us men, what is the crucial part of ours? What is it? What? That's why I think a woman is a more complete creature than a man; the only creature in the Book of Genesis whose body is the mirror of her soul and her soul, the mirror of her body. So I understand how Samira Yabahri's womb defied our mundane logic and simple understanding, creating a miracle, a miracle of her soul and of her hopes rather than a miracle of her body. Years later, Ghazalnus would jokingly call Trifa 'the daughter of imaginary sperm', and indeed she was – she was the daughter of invisible and magical sperm.

Even into adulthood, Trifa thought she had been born Jawhar Zahir's twin. An antagonistic pair, the outcome of clashes between two different worlds, they had been locked in a relentless and cruel war since childhood. The deep, inherited hatred between Samira Yabahri and her brother Zahir was passed on to Trifa and Jawhar, even though they were not siblings. They were exact opposites, two subjects of two incompatible worlds rushing away from each other.

Trifa Yabahri had been an imaginative person from childhood. She was still young when she took to leaning over a water barrel in the bathroom, gazing at creatures only she could see. She was always drawing intricate arabesque patterns on the walls, which, Fawziya felt, might take off and fly. One day Fawziya was terrified to see a rope, one end suspended in mid-air, the other in Trifa's hand. This was a girl who could skip along with people who were invisible to Fawziya. Later on, one of those imaginary creatures would hold her hand on the staircases to the second floor, leading her up to Samira Yabahri's room. Samira, with her tangled, tousled hair, would give Trifa a cold look, understanding at once that this child was her own real-imaginary daughter. Despite Samira's deteriorating condition, isolation and madness, she had her wits sufficiently about her not to reveal her motherhood, saving her daughter from certain distress. She knew it would achieve nothing other than to make the girl's life an unfathomable mystery.

Jawhar Zahir, on the other hand, was cunning, always scheming. His father was very impressed with his attention to detail and planning abilities. From childhood, he had an unrivalled desire to collect things and to accumulate expensive games. As the only male Yabahri offspring, he had a privileged life opening up before him, promising the fulfilment of all his dreams; like a hungry squirrel, he sought to control everything in his small domain. He was a red-skinned, pudgy child with a dimple in his chin, an angry face and wild, sparkling eyes. Zahir saw in his son many qualities of his aggressive, red-skinned

41

forebears, those blond-eyebrowed, covetous grandfathers who, in times past, like an army of white ants, attacked convoys transporting goods from Baghdad to the enchanting northern regions, convoys made dizzy by the heat and burned by the southern sun. As soon as they left the hot lowlands and entered the cool highlands, Yabahri gangs would rob them and send them back to where they came from, empty-handed. Jawhar Yabahri had something of the opportunistic, wealth-seeking spirit of these gangs, but I should also say that he had a certain amount of planning ability and trickery that was all his own, something inherited from our own times.

In short, Jawhar Yabahri was a soul devoid of imagination, immersed so deeply in this world and his transient desires that he was like a machine. Apart from his wild, vicious instincts, you could see nothing else at all that linked him to other humans. He initiated a long, cruel and spiteful war against his sister in their childhood. With his investigative skills and meticulous intuition, he very quickly arrived at two dangerous truths – although for a very long time everyone treated his views as the babble or delirium of a child, spoiled by too much attention, who oversteps the bounds of courtesy and speaks beyond his years. From a young age, Jawhar maintained that Trifa was neither his sister nor a real person, but rather a white bubble, wet foam, empty space that would one day disappear, bursting in the air or melting into a picture.

Sometimes children's lives are nothing but a reverse image of their fathers', the same performance on a different stage, the same text read by a different group of actors. And so it was with Zahir Yabahri, who, whatever way he looked at it, saw his own past life in his son's behaviour. He noticed that the eternal hatred between the male and female members of his sad tribe had resurfaced in Jawhar's relationship with Trifa. For years Zahir Yabahri, who was becoming softer and more kind-hearted as he grew older, tried to establish a bond with Trifa, doing all he could as he raised and nurtured her, but his daughter – indifferent and insouciant – lived in a world of her own. Deep in his heart, he was concerned that his son Jawhar would repeat his story. One day, out of sight of all his heirs, Zahir assigned a third of his fortune and properties to Trifa in the presence of a lawyer and a great many friends who acted as witnesses, lest his son Jawhar seize everything after his death and drive the unwary and powerless Trifa onto the streets. The reading of the will after Zahir's death led to a series of crazy events, with unusual and tragic consequences for all the characters in this story – something none of them expected at the time.

HUSNI MARDINI SHOWS ATTAR
AN OLD TOWEL

EARLY WINTER, 1993

The morning after Sayfadin Maro's phone call, Sarkawt Nazmi began the search for a teacher of the imagination. It was the first time in his entire life that he had looked for something without knowing what it was. Over the years he had been asked for, and had found, the most unusual, most logic-defying of items: a tiger's hide, a lion's tongue, a singing flower, a talking nightingale, a scented butterfly – the list went on. In the bazaar, he came to be known as 'Attar', and his work was indeed akin to that of a modern-day attar. Just as in olden times, people went to the attars to obtain unusual, hard-to-find items, so they now went to Sarkawt Nazmi and his kind in search of rarities. He regarded the nickname as a special honour. He managed to establish unusual connections on various sides. He had, in his possession, embassy stamps and brand-new passports for most countries in the world. Whatever he was trying to find, he knew what it was and where to look for it. That day, however, for the first time, he walked around quietly, not knowing where to go or whom to ask.

It was a very fine day. The hustle and bustle of the bazaar and the cries of the itinerant tradesmen could not disturb the cool air or soft morning sunlight, which spoke of late spring freshness rather than the cold of winter. But our friend Attar was not enjoying the fine morning very much. So mournful was his expression that whoever saw him knew he must be preoccupied with something particularly difficult to find. He wore a worried look like those of kings in the ancient stories. Most who knew him had learned to read his face. He had a big head, thinning hair, black eyes, a knobbly nose, dark, tattooed skin, a trimmed moustache and beard and a lingering smell of sweat. Whenever he got excited about something, two fat drops of sweat like dewdrops would fall from his ears. When he was uncomfortable, his ears would be covered in sweat. His close friends called him 'Dew-Ears'.

On days such as this, when he was restless and aimless, the knobbly skin on Attar's nose would thicken, his face would become even gloomier and his eyes would bulge. Although to date he had not been known to do anything terrible, when he was in a panic he looked like a murderer who had just stepped away from his victim. Like most people in this city, he had a degree of mercilessness, which at times he masked with silence and shyness and at others with anger. He had high hopes of becoming fabulously wealthy, and had succeeded in protecting his existing wealth and assets from repeated market falls. His life was soured, however, by his constant fear of defeat. He lived with the restlessness of a man who wants to protect what he has and increase it, which meant he learned new tricks and new ways of earning his livelihood. Day by day, he became more entangled in curious dealings with exceptional businessmen.

By around midday, he had begun to fear he was not a brilliant Attar after all, able to obtain anything under the sun. At the end of the morning's business, he had come up with only two names to approach: Husni Mardini, the owner of one of the city's biggest shops, and Galawezh Bahir, the wife of the owner of a handmade carpet factory where a remarkably imaginative girl supervised the designs and patterns.

He went first to Husni Mardini, a close friend and secret rival. Some people called him 'Husni the Imaginative', because he knew a lot of stories and had a rich imagination. Husni the Imaginative had a shop where he sold towels – nothing but towels. Some of the towels were not for sale, and you weren't allowed even to touch them; they were there just to be looked at while you listened to the long stories Husni so delighted in telling.

When Attar appeared outside Husni's shop, the latter noticed his sweaty ears and realised he was looking for something specific. He called out to him at once. 'Hey, Attar, come on in. I have a towel the Emir of Kuwait used to dry himself with. It's the original silk. There's nothing like it in the world. I bought it from the son of the commander of the Third Division. His dad has run away … haven't you heard? How come? The vile man has been with our lot for a week. Come in, it's worth a gander, come on in. What's wrong? Why don't you say something? Has the dew been dripping off your ears again?'

Ordinarily, this kind of thing would have been right up Attar's street. Husni the Imaginative knew just how to get to him; he knew that Attar would pay a lot of money for a towel like this. He had already sold expensive towels to Attar twice before. One had belonged to an Arab girl who used to present a youth programme on state-run

44

TV, the other to an Iranian actress who had risen to fame in the time of the Shah. After the death of the Imam and Khamenei's rise to power, she had seized the chance to leave Iran, but left her suitcase behind at the border. It contained some underwear and two towels. Husni the Imaginative had bought the lot for peanuts, sold each item individually and amassed a fortune.

Today, though, Attar was worried about something else entirely. In the deep voice so suited to his build, he said, 'My dear Husni, you must excuse me. I'm not here to look at towels today. I'm here because I need your help. I need you to find me someone like yourself, someone with imagination, who could be a tutor for a while. I have a friend whose daughter is not very bright. Someone needs to teach her a way of understanding her schoolwork.'

Husni laughed, his thick, white moustache moving up and down, and said, 'You were a sensible man until a week ago. What's happened? I'm a towel merchant. What do I have to do with teaching?'

'Nothing,' said Sarkawt as he dried his ears in front of a large mirror. 'All I am asking for is advice. Give me some guidance. Find me someone who can help. I don't have a lot of time and I don't know where to turn.'

It was the first time Attar had been so sad, so at a loss. Husni gave him some water and said, 'Have a seat. Tell me what it is you need.'

Wearing the expression of someone embarrassed by his own request, Attar said, 'I need an imagination tutor. I need to find an imagination tutor by this evening.'

'But what kind of imagination?' Husni said, after reflecting briefly. 'Imagination comes in many shapes.'

'I don't know,' Attar said, throwing up his hands in despair. 'How should I know what kind of imagination? I've no idea. Dear God, how could I know? An imagination that helps a girl who is not very bright pass her exams in school and understand her lessons. Her teachers say she can't understand a thing because she has no imagination. She has private tutors for all her lessons, but she doesn't take anything in. Now they're saying she needs to work on her imagination.'

Attar didn't know what else to say. He'd never thought about such things. He couldn't understand how Sayfadin Maro had become fixated on this. Besides, what is imagination, let alone a tutor of it?

If only the request had been to fix a TV set or recharge a fridge motor or install a water tank on the roof – such a thing would be easy. Now his last hope lay with this talkative towel-seller, whose wares told all the stories of the world.

Husni, in the way typical of all the patient and kind-hearted shopkeepers in the bazaar, shook his head, saying, 'Anyway, these bastards, every day, they come up with something new to make more money. Every day they invent a new story.'

'But it's true,' he added, after a pause. 'It really is. Imagination can radically change people. Imagination can turn human beings into something else. It can instill different desires and dreams.'

'I thought no one could live by imagination alone,' Attar said miserably. 'Until today, I thought no one could earn anything by the imagination. I seem to be wrong, don't I? Maybe I am.'

'There are fantasies that can kill people,' Husni said. 'They make people lose their connection to life. This type of imagination is closer to madness than reason. Then there are fantasies that bring people back to the world of the living. They save people from death and restore life to the senses.'

Attar shook his head, wiped his forehead one more time, and said in a surprised, high voice, 'My understanding was that imagination misleads us and prevents us from understanding the world properly.'

'No,' Husni said after a short pause. 'Often, people don't understand anything at all without imagination. My biggest fear is that imagination is dying out in this city,' he said calmly, lowering his tone. 'Day by day, I am aware that imagination is dying. My dear Attar, I realised this a long time ago. Are you honestly not aware of it yourself?'

'Husni, what should I be aware of? To tell you the truth, I don't even know what imagination is in the first place. You know, working in the bazaar means you stay away from fantasies. I can't recall ever setting time aside simply to fantasise and such like. You know, life is hard. Things are expensive. Currency rates are fluctuating. All these things affect the imagination. I've been in the bazaar since I was born. I opened my eyes among the butchers and greengrocers. But I know you can help me. Something in my heart brought me to you. You are the only person who might be able to help me.'

'You are right that the bazaar kills imagination,' Husni said, ignoring his friend's subsequent remarks. 'You're right there. And life itself is nothing but a filthy, litter-strewn bazaar anyway. All I'm saying is that imagination may save us from death and lift us out of this bitter life. Brother Attar, I have a story that might be useful to you. I know you are short on imagination, but you're still an intelligent man. Your mind works well. People whose minds work well can understand the imagination.'

Whenever Husni was about to embark on a story, it showed in his voice. His hand gestures changed, and the wrinkles disappeared from his face. Husni reached underneath a pile of towels and took out a small, rusty key. Then he climbed a short ladder to the upper part of his shop and came back with a big towel. He spread the towel

46

open in front of Attar. It was patterned on both sides, teeming with the designs Attar had seen on his grandmother's old chinaware. The Chinese script was unmistakeable. As a man of the bazaar, he was required to be familiar with foreign products and to recognise their brands. In recent years, ruthless Iranian merchants had filled the markets with cheap goods from China, South Korea, Taiwan, Hong Kong and Malaysia. They bought cut-price merchandise from around the world that had passed their sell-by dates and could not be sold anywhere else. They knew that unscrupulous Kurdish merchants would buy even rubbish and manage to sell it.

'The Chinese are just plundering all these poor, decrepit countries,' Attar would say whenever the conversation turned to this subject. He was crazy about Western goods, and would go mad when someone tried to pass off a useless bit of made-in-China as a German Siemens.

At noon that day, when Husni the Imaginative spread the towel open before him, Attar asked himself, 'Where does the son of a bitch get all this marvellous stuff?' Like everyone who worked at the market, he was ever-poised to try and ambush his fellow merchants. He was greedy and very jealous. He had known Husni for a long time; this man, who appeared to be so simple, friendly, sweet-tongued and hardworking, was both complex and mysterious in equal measure. God, where did he get all his wealth? Attar was involved in all sorts of trade, but it was never enough, and here was this bastard, this cheerful chap with his white moustache, living like a king without a fraction of the effort Attar put in.

When Husni spread the towel before him, Attar saw that it was a rare and astonishing thing. It was beautiful … a masterpiece. He wished he could buy it and keep it with the rest of his unique, extraordinary items, though he was sure Husni would not sell it. Evidently, it was no ordinary piece of craftsmanship. It was one of a kind, the work of an old craftsman. Time had laid a priceless layer of dust upon it. Whenever Attar saw that kind of dust on anything, he would fall in love with the object.

To stir Attar's imagination even further – and to prove that he was the one with the greater number of extraordinary items – Husni lifted up the towel and said, 'Brother Attar, look at this towel. It tells the story of an ancient battle. No one knows when or where it took place. I have kept it for many years. I don't know how many, but its story has always stayed with me: the story of a foreign army entering an old city; the story of a young king who doesn't know what to do, whether to continue as king or become a poet. A young king who is an immensely talented poet. Several times, he tries to give up his throne to begin writing poetry and, like literature's wandering dervishes of old, take to the mountains and dwell in caves and other places far from the masses, only to have his ministers and aides dissuade him.

'It just so happens that the young king enters into all-out war with another prestigious monarch, whose court is home to the most famous poet of the day. The restless and passionate young king decides that if he defeats his enemy and takes him prisoner, he will enter him into a simple contest with the poet to see which is better – to be a king or to be a poet. And to encourage the two to give their best, he tells his aides that whoever wins the contest will be pardoned, while the loser will be hanged in the centre of the city.

'So, dear Attar, consider this carefully. The story goes that a seemingly endless war ensues, a long and bloody war, and that after countless confrontations the young king, with God's help, defeats his most implacable enemy, triumphantly entering the rival king's fortress and fortified residence.

'When the greatest king of the day and the most famous poet of the day are taken alive and brought before the young monarch, a king and poet himself, he has a unique opportunity to compare the abilities of monarchs and poets. He tours the city with each of his eminent prisoners of war. He asks that each of the two describe in his own way the city in which they were born and raised, that each use his abilities and talents to offer him convincing evidence that will discourage him from destroying the kingdom and endear the country and the castle to him. My brother Attar, see what a cunning and scheming king he was. He chose a subject that mattered to their lives, to the lives of the people and the future of the country.'

Anyone who dropped in on Husni had to be prepared for this kind of story. Attar didn't know the connection between the story and his predicament, but he listened in spite of himself. No one dared do otherwise; Husni himself would say, 'Not listening to my stories brings bad luck. It will bring ill fortune upon you.' Although Attar didn't believe his friend's tales, he couldn't help but pay attention. Husni knew Attar had not yet understood what the story meant, and pressed on to get to the crux of it. He showed him one side of the towel.

'Look, dear cousin,' he resumed, 'this side of the towel tells the story of the tour of the city by the victorious king and the defeated king. You'd think, wouldn't you, that as it is the captive king's own kingdom and residence, surely he could describe the city better than anyone else – especially when it is his last chance to be set free and to recover his city? Of course, the king would put all his intelligence to work to outdo the poet and regain his crown and sceptre. That's so, isn't it? My brother Attar, look: the king and his prisoner of war, along with his companions and guards, start their tour from here. Look, my friend. You can see it all, just like on a map. At every stop on the tour, the king, his prisoner and his companions appear again, the defeated king pointing to a landmark. But in the pattern, all we can see is the location as straightforwardly described, meaning there is no imagination in the king's description. He describes things as they are. He calls a tree a tree, a garden a garden, a lake a lake. When he points to a house, he merely suggests it is a house and nothing more. The world in the king's description is poor and colourless. My brother Attar, he who is without imagination sees the world without colour. That's what the towel tells us. This side of the towel is short on patterns and pictures. There are fewer images, fewer colours, less beauty.

'But now look at the other side. It's the same city, but this time as described by the poet. It's the same map, but more colourful; richer, and with more drawings. The poet hasn't described the trees, but the birds that live in them. He describes the memories of the trees, and the lovers who are asleep underneath those trees. He does not describe the houses, but imagines the lives of their inhabitants. Look at this corner. See, here is a house where a family lives happily together. The whole drawing resembles an imaginary paradise, and looking at it makes you feel content. Here is another home where two lovers sleep serenely. Here is an orphanage for distressed children …

'Do you see, Attar? I am showing you this towel so that you can recognise the differences between two worlds: the world depicted by someone with no imagination, and the world depicted by someone with a vivid imagination. Now it's down to you to understand the end of the story. You ought to know who deserves to live and who doesn't.'

'Husni, you are a very good friend,' said Attar. 'We should, then, find Sayfadin Maro's daughter a poet. Poets are masters of imagination. Is that it? Have I got your point?'

'I do know someone,' Husni said, nodding. 'I know someone who might help with your problem. A very imaginative man called Ghazalnus. He has established a good reputation for himself in the city. Ghazalnus might be the only person who can solve your problem. I've heard he is very imaginative and unworldly.'

Attar pondered for a while, reflecting on Husni Mardini's words. He paused on the word 'unworldly'. It was the first time he had heard it used as praise. He should have known that people besotted with imagination are not overly involved in the world, that their imaginations take them to another world, that they fly away and loosen

49

their ties to our Earth. Now he understood what the imagination meant; *now* he did.

Late that same afternoon, Attar arrived at Galawezh Bahir's house with his big, sweaty head, growing balder by the day. A year earlier, in the process of buying a carpet for a senior Party official, he ended up at the small factory run by Abdulaqadir Niya and his wife, Galawezh. Attar had known Abdulaqadir Niya since childhood. 'Niya' was the name of the huge store where Sayyid Qadir sold antiques, precious glass and crystalware. He was known as 'Sayyid Qadir Niya' after the shop. Once business was booming and they had earned a lot of money, they bought the small, decrepit factory from the State, which was selling off some of its lower-value assets at one point during the war. They were a cheerful, friendly couple. During their breaks, they often played backgammon. On some evenings, they would doze off over the board.

I have to say that no one could outplay Galawezh at backgammon. As long as the dice were not stubbornly against her, on most afternoons she defeated all the men who gathered at the factory and spent their lives arguing over double-blanks and double-sixes. She was a small, skinny woman with straggly, salt-and-pepper hair that was combed only once in a blue moon, a tough, vigorous woman who had not worn make-up even once in almost fifteen years. She ran the factory in the mornings until two o'clock in the afternoon, when Sayyid Qadir was supposed to replace her for the afternoon shift. Even when he turned up, however, she often stayed on. She had lunch with the female workers, cleaned the place with the female cleaners and fed grain to the chickens, ducks and swans reared behind the factory. And in the evenings, she would either be playing backgammon with the older men or fanning the charcoal on the barbeque and preparing meze. That evening, when Attar knocked on the door, she happened to be in. She had come home in an old cab after her shift and was stretched out on the floor, flat on her back. When she opened the door, she was still not properly awake. Attar, with his peculiar appearance, seemed like the ambassador of a faraway country who had lost his way, and for a few moments Galawezh Bahir thought the tall, bald man at the door that winter evening was calling on one of the neighbours and had simply mistaken the house.

Whenever Attar spoke in the presence of courteous people, he displayed some of the bashfulness he had had as a child. That evening, his mouth dry with shyness, he said to Galawezh, 'Allow me to introduce myself, Khanim. My name is Sarkawt Nazmi. I am the son of Nazmi Beg, the merchant. A long time ago our shop was behind your section in the bazaar. Nazmi Beg was known as the "Sesame-eater". You do know who I'm talking about, Khanim, don't you? I am his son. Last year, I had the honour of meeting you in difficult circumstances, although it was only a short meeting. It was in relation to carrying out some work we were doing with you. It's fine if you don't remember me; you might not. I'm Sarkawt Nazmi; people call me "Attar". To tell you the truth, I am looking for an imagination tutor. I desperately need your help. You are my very last hope.'

There was enough innocence in Attar's voice for Galawezh not to feel at all suspicious of him. However, she could not make out much of what he was saying. She was the type of woman who lost her temper when she couldn't understand someone, but she kept herself in check and said, 'My son, do you know whose house this is and who you are looking for?'

'I do,' Attar said quickly to make up for his mistake. 'Of course, I do. You are the esteemed Galawezh Khan. There is no one who does not know you. Last year, I bought some carpets from you, a large number of them, for Shayda the Norwegian, the senior official who might become a minister in the next government. The carpets were for him. Remember that you said, "I will give you a carpet woven by pure imagination"? You do remember saying that to me, don't you? It was about eleven months ago, early last winter. You must remember, surely, Khanim. Back then, Shayda the Norwegian was in charge of a brigade. You didn't want to sell me the carpets directly. You told me to go to Rahim the carpet-seller, but I begged and said, "I want the carpets for Shayda and I will only buy them direct from the factory. I won't buy them unless they are directly from you in person. I don't want to be cheated." You didn't know who Shayda the Norwegian was. You got a bit cross and asked me, "What kind of pimp is this Shayda the Norwegian?" I said, "Khanim, how can you not know who he is? Don't you watch the TV news? The 8.30 evening news? Don't you read the newspapers?" And you kept saying, "Big-Head, I don't watch TV; I don't watch the news, I don't read the papers." I said, "Don't be so angry, Khanim. I'm a good customer." You didn't calm down until I promised to get you a backgammon set made from marble. But I couldn't get one, and brought you one made out of Japanese steel instead. You said you had never seen one like it, and you were very pleased with it. And then you had a change of heart, and things became easier between us. Later, we bought your beautiful carpets and left. Then you sent after me and told me that if I had any favour to ask, to let you know; that I was like a son to you, and so on – things that you know better than I do.'

Everything came back to Galawezh now. She remembered this man with his big head, who had been slightly thinner a year ago, his hair thicker.

'Last year,' said Attar, certain now that Mrs Niya recognised him, 'you showed me the girl who sat and drew enchanting flowers, designs and patterns in her imagination. You told me that the beauty of your colourful rugs and carpets owes a lot to her imagination. I need that imagination for a small job, for a short time. Basically, I'd be very pleased if you let me speak to that girl, because I am desperately looking for someone to become an imagination tutor for a short period of time.'

Galawezh appeared not to understand this tale of an imagination tutor. Attar had to tell the story of Sayfadin Maro's daughter from the very beginning, and to say that the issue was related to the future of a senior official's daughter. Like all those who utter the names of idiotic officials with a note of reverence, Attar altered his intonation when he mentioned the name of Sayfadin Maro.

It turned out, however, to be no easy matter. The girl in question was horrified of exposure. Galawezh Bahir was unable to make the decision. The girl herself had to have the final say. Therefore Galawezh set a time for him to come to the factory the following day, to speak to the girl there. I ought to say now that the girl working at the carpet factory, the girl whom Attar so desperately sought, was our very own Trifa Yabahri. Oh yes, my dears, poor Trifa Yabahri, the good daughter of an aristocratic family, had been ended up in the factory. The gist of the story is that, after the death of Zahir Yabahri, the situation went beyond the control of Khanim Fawziya Yasami – and Jawhar Yabahri became such a beast that no one could live with him. As a result, Trifa ran away from his home and lived in the little factory. If you're patient and don't rush me, soon I shall tell you the whole story. Soon.

A LETTER BEFORE DEATH
MARCH 1974

But what happened to Mullah Gharib-i Hajar?
Before he died in one of the hospitals in Urmia, Iran, Mullah Hajar entrusted a long letter and a handful of documents to an acquaintance, begging him to stop at nothing to deliver them to one Bahman Nasser. Mullah Hajar appears to have waged a lengthy battle to keep death at bay while he tried to write the letter the way he wanted. When he finished, he spent several hours gazing out the window at a huddle of sad doves in a tree, quietly took off his glasses and surrendered his soul to the angels with untimely and extraordinary delight. The mullah's friends and followers were greatly saddened by his death, coming as it did after he had survived a harsh and hazardous journey, but for the mullah himself, it was the calm after the storm.

The man who carried the letter to the mullah's hometown took a long, circuitous route. Exhausted after this difficult trip, he reached his destination and found where Bahman Nasser lived. As if keen to be rid of a dangerous burden, he did not rest until he had delivered the message to Bahman, who was in the schoolyard memorising the satirical poems Jarir and al-Farazdaq had written about their feuds.[4] The man approached the weak, bespectacled Bahman quietly, handed him the envelope and urged him to read it carefully. Bahman, ignorant of what was in the sealed envelope, took it and put it in his bag without a word. The handover was completed in a flash. It all happened so fast that later Ghazalnus was never sure whether the messenger had been real or imaginary, whether the letter had been delivered in reality or in a dream. Many years later, no matter how hard he tried to remember the face of the messenger, he couldn't recall a thing.

Bahman had always known that one day he would receive a letter from somewhere far away that would completely change his life. From early youth, he had dreamed every night of a message from afar that would shake up his world. Mullah Hajar's letter affirmed this belief. It contained the long story of the mullah's life, and was full of details about the mullah's past, his childhood, his falling in love and his old age. Evidently, Mullah Hajar had formed every letter of every word with the utmost conviction. After years of hesitation, deep in his soul, he had come round to the view that he ought to reveal everything, to keep nothing hidden. Every line of the letter gave off great awareness of fatherhood. He wrote of how he had once been a lover; every part of it exuded the strong scent of death, and a colour particular to the ishraq,[5] the illumination, at the end of life. Mullah Hajar appeared to have had great difficulty getting to the point of his story, and to his final words. It was, however, clear that in some places the mullah's concern was that of a man who wanted not to hurt his own son, but to reveal to him a secret in a calm and composed manner, a secret that could change his life and make him a completely different person.

Mullah Hajar used the language of someone who had loved words in the 1930s and '40s, someone who had pondered the secret of rhetoric. In the rhetoric of that time, he wrote a letter teeming with Arabic words, a somewhat contradictory peculiarity in such a hardline Kurdish nationalist. Somewhere in the letter, he wrote:

> It is difficult for an old man like myself who has one foot in the grave and is but a breath away from death to toy with another's life. Yet it is no less difficult to take leave of this finite world with you knowing nothing of me. In the end, I am, rather than a father, an apparition that comes to tell you a truth. I am an old man and my experience has given me a sense that great truths are close to fantasy. People see naught but the surface of this world. They do not apprehend the world as a great truth. They accept the surface of this complex world as the truth and yet man is merely a broken looking-glass, only one piece of which has fallen in this life upon the Earth. Where and in what world are the other pieces? That is known only to God and to His angels.

Mullah Hajar found a roundabout way to introduce Bahman Nasser and the story of his birth. He wrote:

> Our dear Bahman, I have come this far and now stand between life and death. This moment is impossible and I am very close to bowing out like the humblest of slaves. The world has sapped my energy and sadness all my power. Old age has gnawed at my flesh and bones for years but has not yet taken its last bite. My soul is empty, my body exhausted, my desires gone. There is a secret you must know,

a secret deeper than the secret of death and more infinite than the mystery of life. It is something that you may choose to believe in or to regard as the hallucination of an old man, breathing his last in a hospital in a foreign land. I have borne the pain of it throughout my life. Now that you are grown, you will understand that had I opened my mouth any earlier than this, I would have done so in vain, and all I have written would have been without meaning. The only living being able to understand this tale is he who understands love, that is, he who is able to reason. Only God knows whether you are indeed such a person. Only God, and He alone. Do I, who impose this difficult task, this strange duty on your newly awakened heart, do I myself understand love? Is there any human being who does? Or is love too divine a mystery, a holiness of so high an order it is far beyond the grasp of you or me?

Our dear Bahman. Eighteen years ago ... eighteen years ago, on a clear night, I was lost in contemplation of the sea of stars when all of a sudden into my room came a young man, his face and figure like the pictures drawn by ancient miniaturists on the covers of books kept by the kings and princesses. He was a strange young man who knew by heart every ghazal I knew, who could recite any poem I had written better than I could myself. His knowledge of metre was impeccable. He introduced himself as a part of me. He portrayed himself as my shadow, my other half. Like any handsome youth, he was arrogant and without mercy. He said: 'I am your other half, the half you have incarcerated inside a dark and dangerous cellar. I am your stifled and unfortunate half.' And I believed him.

I don't know how to open up my heart to you. We are created in such a way that the moment we come close to love we shatter something. Do not be shocked, therefore, or taken aback, if as the moment for the final handover draws near, my shaking hands and defeated soul succumb and shatter other things. My son, for eighteen years I have kept the secrets I am telling you now at the back of a shelf, as if inside a glass container full of them, placed behind other glass containers. Do not blame me, or criticise me, saying, 'What a shameless, sad old man.' It is my conviction that it is a coward who tells the truth only on his deathbed, yet that coward is still braver than one who takes his secrets to the grave. Doddery old man that I am, I must now climb a broken ladder, the ladder of my hesitations and cowardice, and from the top-most rung, the rung of the fears and apprehensions of my seventy wasted years, with my wrinkled fingers, I must throw the glass containers in the air one by one, and shatter things – break and shatter them.

At the moment of death, man should open up his box of secrets so that later he may have a proper understanding of the divine verdict. As he hands over his soul, man should have the courage to gaze into its darkness. If not, what will he talk about with the One, the Omnipotent? Now I must sharpen my eyesight, take down my book of secrets and open up my book of sins.

The young man who visited me that night was me, myself, when I fell for a shy, noble and most honourable woman. No one is unluckier than a man who takes a fancy to a modest woman. When I die, sick, bedraggled insect that I am, I will pluck up all my courage to tell the Lord of all creation that no one is so as unlucky as he whom God condemns to fall in love with a shy and honourable woman.

As I neared the end of my life, my sole purpose to increase my worship and consolidate my faith, God Almighty, He in whom all creatures take pride, inflicted upon me such an ailment that I still smart with it today, still simmer with a suppressed anger that boils up within me. One day I awoke and found myself in love, in love with a modest woman whose name was Baharbanu, who was your late mother – may her grave tonight be filled with more light than any other. Love is without honour. Love alone is above honour, the only thing to which both God and the Devil devote the same degree of labour … I beg you, do not see this as blasphemy or regard it as the godless sentiment of a soul without hope. Love, my son, has two faces; one painstakingly created by the Devil, who spent all his energy upon it, exercised his black arts and infused it with his magic; the other engraved by Almighty God. He toiled over it, imbued it with his mystery and made it pure. All loves in the world are so. God does not abandon even an iota of love. Nor does the Devil back down. God is the owner of one half of every drop of love. The Devil owns the other. And when they drink that drop, poor human beings cannot tell whether they have taken poison or drunk of divine nectar. Do not look at me as if I were a disgraceful old man with trembling hands and a soul still full of worldly greed. I never was the slave of my soul, but if a person keeps the door of the soul too tightly closed, something else, some other secret, will come his way. The soul has its own way, its own creatures and creations. What I had endeavoured all my life to slay crept from its dark cellar in the form of a human being, a young magician; a person who was both truth and imagination. It was myself and yet, at the same time, not myself. Yes, my son, you. You were born of him and yet, at the same time, not of him.'

In a great many long and jumbled passages, Mullah Hajar sought to interpret the emergence of the young poet and ghazal writer from his soul and, with great hesitation, wrote many pages about the strange, erotic experience connecting a fantasised version of Baharbanu with the fantasised half of himself. With a desire that should not have existed in an old man as he neared death, and with an appetite inappropriate to the soul of a shy man whose lifetime had been defined by modesty, he filled countless pages with tales of unreal, passionate nights in which two thirsty bodies and wild spirits met. Sometimes he apologised for speaking in a particular way; other times, he completely forgot he was talking about Bahman's mother. He forgot he was speaking about a woman whom Bahman had seen as pure, and without desire.

At no point did the mullah refer to a direct relationship between Baharbanu and himself. He lived in his fantasies, fell in love in his fantasies and slept with Baharbanu in his fantasies. It is a story the men and women of this country have lived for many thousands of years. For thousands of years, the women and men of this country have slept together in fantasy, have liked each other from afar, have fallen secretly in love without revealing their love to one another, like a hunter and a deer, neither wanting the other to know the secret of their heart. Century after century, stifled fantasies have piled up in the alleys and streets, in the rooms and on the verandas of this country. Century by century, this restraint and self-censorship have become a profound and secret science, producing its own sages and scientists; century by century, our alleyways have become a theatre for our imagination while the prayer mats and prayer niches of this homeland became the platform for such sighs and moans as even the heroes of Greek tragedies and the god of Olympus had not witnessed.

A large part of these fantasies seem to have come together in Mullah Hajar's dark psyche, heaped in the bottomless, locked-up cellar of his heart, the heart of a man who combined extreme shyness with extreme desire, extreme religiosity with extreme poetry, extreme submission to the conditions of the world with extreme fantasies. This deep contradiction, this endless division, appears to have riven Mullah Hajar so badly that his soul, like that of the age, was split between two creatures: one severe and inhibited, the other free, unashamed and full of poetry. One of them was grounded in this world, obedient to its terms and dictates, the other emerged from an imaginary world that heeds no orders.

In his classical style, Mullah Hajar wrote:

Man is a strange mix of different creatures. Inside, he is both beast and angel. I was neither beast nor angel, neither one nor the other, and yet I have spent thousands of nights in fantasies, for which God has apportioned no sentence, and which cannot be seen by my fellow men. Since my youth, I have presented myself as an ascetic and a mystic. From early morning until I slipped into bed there was nothing in my heart but the dhikr[6] 'Ya Allah, Ya Allah', but as soon as my head touched the pillow and I knew that the world was asleep, that none of my relatives, my friends or enemies could see me, as soon as silence fell and no creature made a sound, a dark lust would surge within me, the boards of a different theatre would fall into place and my soul would become the stage for something else. Any yearning I had stifled in the daytime, any desire or lust I had hushed, would surface in the shape of weird creatures. I had a feeling that a secret power was drawing me towards a different Earth and Heaven, taking me to another place where I saw strange sights, naked houris and ghilmans, women beyond human capacity to imagine, the food and feasting God has promised man only in Paradise. In those dark and secret alleyways, my appearance changed in front of every looking-glass, and each time I took on a different shape as if it were mine to choose, as if God had granted me the indulgence of seeking my own appearance.

Oh, my fantasies transported me to where I could assume whatever human form I wanted, could give my body whatever face I liked. It was on those nights that I became the author of an anthology of ghazals. When I summoned up the courage to have the poems published, no one could believe that such a shy and pious young man could have written such a book, a book that hinted at blasphemy and debauchery. It was the harvest of darkness, the harvest of my secret other life. I responded quickly, however, and denied it was mine then kept myself to myself, avoiding every kind of gathering. In both body and soul, I felt it was not I who had written those poems, not I who had drowned in a sea of ghazals at night. There was an estrangement between my self and the peculiar performances that took place in another world. My self, one part of which swam in one world and the other in another, was enslaved to a war in which I knew not on which side I fought, nor on which front I was supposed to stand. For a whole lifetime, lust tore me in one direction, modesty in another; propriety confined me while fantasy let me take flight. Honour imprisoned me in my body, while lust, like a wild beast, dragged me away. Day after day, night after night, I was torn into ever more pieces ... but who among us is not in pieces? Let him who does not contain a double-sided being and a many-headed soul step forward and stone me. We are all two-sided creatures. Many of us see only one side of ourselves because we dare not look at our other side. One night, the other creature within me simply emerged and, boldly and without shame, introduced himself to me. He said, 'I am you, your self and nothing but your self.' He was arrogant and self-centred. He was handsome but his beauty bore no resemblance to any other thing. I still wonder why I let him live. Why did I not put him to death? It would not even have been murder or have counted as a crime. Why then did I not do this? Every human being has experienced moments like this, where they have slain their own creature without hesitation. They have no regrets. They simply don their old masks once more and carry on, even, after a while, forgetting.

I, Mullah Gharib-i Hajar, however, with one foot in the grave, must now confess the truth and tell you that I could not kill as others do. Though the killing would have been justified. Failure to kill him results in guilt and a multitude of sins. I do not know what stayed my hand but I do know that there were countless nights when I held a dagger or a gun and could have drawn the dagger or aimed the gun at that damned apparition. I need not have followed his debauchery and yet that is a lie because his pull was too great for me ever to think of resistance. Like an ocean of secrets, it worked its endless effect and swept me away; often, neither my hands nor my mouth worked, and by the time I had recovered consciousness and realised how dangerous were the fantasies he harboured, neither my lash nor my stick were of any use. Each time I took the lash to that vile man, it was my own soul and body that I whipped. No matter how much I try to explain this to you now, it will avail nothing. But the history of man is the history of the apparitions and ghosts escaped from man's imagination. I swear to you that I spared no effort in punishing myself constantly. And still I was enamoured of your bewitching mother, and I had to make sure my desire to meet her was fulfilled, even if in that other life. I was drawn to her with every fibre of my being and such attraction surmounts both time and place. When,

on a moonlit night, that speaker of ghazals, that young man came
it was from my dark side. Had I the option, I would have chosen
to have his appearance and figure myself. It resembled a favourite
form of mine, chosen when I was on stage at night; his debauchery
was part of my own internal, secret debauchery. When one night
he appeared along with your noble mother, I was perplexed. I
found myself slammed against a wall beyond the power of my
reason and consciousness. My faith was in danger. I did not know
what to do. The magic of that encounter made me dizzy and all
this debauchery was beyond my body's strength. I was in heaven
but I was also in hell. As we say in Kurdish, I was drowning in fire
and in water. You are made from those nights. True, you were
born from the real womb of a real mother and you were born a
perfect creature made by God and you were born in a week when
imperfect and disabled children were born, but still, nobody knew
you were not a real child. You are imagination's son, the child of
my imaginary nights with Baharbanu. If you are not my son, what
explains the ghazal already inscribed on your chest when you came
out of your mother's womb?

> Oh, child of the day, night melodies conceived you,
> My secret, her secret conceived you,
> Love created you: kneel and prostrate yourself to no one,
> You who are conceived of imagination's secrets, of being's enigma

These are lines no other human being but me knows or understands,
the blasphemous verse recited by the ghazal-speaking youth on the
night he was drunk. They are the same lines he recited when sated
after intercourse. The mullah who baptised you was a religious
scholar and a friend. We fought over and debated matters of faith
and the hidden aspects of Sharia. He was a keeper of secrets and
knew something of the torments of my heart. I made him swear
that he would bring me the secret of that poem and write down
for me the lines inscribed on your delicate flesh. He was an adept
code reader, someone who could resolve mysteries. No one else
could have read the secret of that line. That day I was on fire from
morning to evening. I oscillated between fire and tears and, when
he arrived with the lines, I was in agony. He was astonished at my
tears and moans, and as soon as he said the first line, I recited the
full couplets to him. He bid me goodbye in great sadness for this
was a mystery he could not resolve. Who could understand it? Who?
You were my son and my evidence is the verse drowned in your

blood and your flesh. I am your father, an imaginary father. You are my son, my imaginary son.

The letter carries on in this vein, and ends many stories later. It is long, and copying it out in its entirety here would be inappropriate and impossible, but you really had to seem some for yourself. That letter shook Bahman Nasser's life to the core. It changed how he viewed himself. Bahman Nasser has been a different man ever since. However, it took a while for him to acquire the nickname 'Ghazalnus'. That, too, has its own story, which will be told when the time comes.

TRIFA YABAHRI AND THE CARPETS
1986–87

After Zahir Yabahri died, many unpleasant events occurred, forcing Trifa to leave home and head for the small carpet factory. After the death of Trifa's mother, Samira, the second storey of the Yabahri apartment became vacant. Trifa was preparing for the tough Year 12 baccalaureate exams at the time, and, on Fawziya Yasami's advice, had moved to the second storey so that she could apply herself to her studies in a quiet place, away from Jawhar's racket. As long as Zahir Yabahri had been alive, Jawhar had had someone in his life he considered important, someone he was scared of. The rules of the game changed radically, however, the night that Zahir's body was brought home from hospital. There was no longer anything to contain the beast who became head of the household after his father's death.

When Zahir Yabahri's will was revealed, Jawhar – already a hot-blooded, promiscuous young man, his eyes red and gaze devilish – acted like an uncontrollable madman. His wheezing and puffing recalled a crazed animal in a vast field fleeing its hunters. The news of his father's will struck his soul like a sharp axe. Only if his heart had been slashed with a razor could it have been similarly wounded and bled so much. Fawziya Yasami had been aware of her son's bad intentions from early on, but even she had not foreseen that one day he would become this ox, which, with all its might, would smash its horns into stone walls and iron gates, with no respect for anything human at all.

Fawziya had endured a great deal of pain at the hands of Zahir Yabahri for many long years. The sudden outbursts of her moody, short-fused husband had resulted in a deep depression that changed her from a pious woman into one who believed in nothing, and her self-confidence waned year after year – so much so that she no longer liked to look at her own face, in which she now saw infinite sadness rather than her former attractiveness. She was no longer the gorgeous Fawziya, adored by everyone for her beauty and elegance, but a woman destroyed each day by sadness, and robbed each night of sleep.

After her husband's death, events rushed headlong towards calamity. Jawhar Yabahri simply could not grasp that one-third of his father's wealth would go to that small, dark girl whom he had always treated with utter derision. He had never accepted her as his sister. Like all the Yabahris, he looked on women with suspicion as worthless creatures who did not deserve compassion or mercy. Nevertheless, despite all Jawhar's aggression and beastly qualities, things might have gone more smoothly had Trifa not exploded in his face and told him, in no uncertain terms: 'I am not your sister, and not related to you at all. I'm Samira Yabahri's daughter, and was not born to your parents.'

Samira had told Trifa everything just before she died. Fawziya had tried hard to stop her, to discourage her, but to no avail. Samira came to know her precise moment of death weeks before she passed away, something she attributed to a lifetime of conversing with extra-worldly creatures. Before she died, Samira had developed a profound desire to voice the truth and reveal everything – a human tendency we might call 'the instinct to tell the truth before death'. One night she summoned Trifa and told her she wasn't Fawziya Yasami's daughter, but her own. Trifa believed the story without delving into it any further.

Deep in her heart, Trifa had already known she was not Jawhar Yabahri's twin; her intuition was so strong that she could recognise such truths without being told. Meanwhile, Fawziya Yasami, despite having tried all her life to cover up the secret, was a gentle, guileless woman who simply could not lie when confronted with the truth; a graceful, respected person who could keep secrets, but not tell a lie herself. Thus, when the kindly Trifa asked her about the story and made her swear to tell the truth, she did so, in floods of tears, revealing at last the biggest secret of her life. 'You are not my daughter,' she said, 'but God knows ... as God Almighty is my witness, I love you more than Jawhar, and not for one moment have I thought of you as not being my own.' Fawziya Yasami hadn't needed to say this; weeping, Trifa embraced her and said, 'You are my mother forever, my mother ... and I have no one but you.'

Rather than go any further with this episode, I ought to say that the events of this particular night are so heart-rending and powerful that they do not really belong in our book, which is supposed to avoid strong emotional scenes. So let us summarise: Fawziya Yasami and Trifa agreed that the elderly Zahir should not know that their secret had been revealed, because his heart was too weak to bear such misfortune.

A week after Zahir's death, all hell broke loose in the Yabahri household. The revelation of Zahir Yabahri's will, legally watertight, drove Jawhar mad. The beast went so far as to raise a hand to his own mother, making nasty comments and ascribing insulting characteristics to the Yasamis, obscenities that no one had ever before dared to utter against such an honest tribe. Although the innocent and imaginative Trifa was physically much smaller than her brother, she had so strong a will and was so daring that she could face that great mountain of a man and stand up to him. And one day she said, 'What a brute you are, to dare to speak about heritage and money a mere week after your father's death. Only a beast could be like you.'

So merciless was Jawhar that he dragged her out to the courtyard by her hair, saying, 'Either you voluntarily give everything up, or I cut off your head. You've never been my sister. You're nothing but a dog, a thief whose time has come to an end!' There was a terrible din. The normally calm Fawziya screamed at the top of her voice as Jawhar, snorting like an animal, dragged poor Trifa to the oil barrel and, still clutching the frail girl's tresses, poured a jerry can of oil all over her, swearing he would burn her alive. As his helpless sister lay before him, the modest Fawziya screamed so much that the whole street flocked to the house, the neighbours smashing down the door. As soon as the heartless, disgraceful Jawhar let go of Trifa's hair to take a matchbox from his pocket, the unfortunate girl seized the opportunity to run away and screamed at him from the staircase: 'You beast, Jawhar! I'm not your sister! Your parents didn't give birth to me! I am Samira Yabahri's daughter, and you are an animal!'

Jawhar became even more incensed. The men and kind neighbours crowded around and restrained him, while Trifa, who had lost all control of herself, shrieked like a wounded bird and wept. The men ushered Jawhar out of the gate with a lot of pushing and shoving, and he bellowed again like a wild ox from the other side, prancing away then rushing forward, calling his modest, respectable sister a 'whore'. No one else in the city had ever been heard to use the words that came from his mouth against their own sister. The women from next door gathered around Trifa, who wept on the stairs.

Embarrassed and humiliated, Fawziya fainted, lying on the grass in the front yard. A woman shouted, 'Help, Fawziya has dropped dead. Oh, my poor dear. Such a virtuous woman!' The number of men among the gathered neighbours grew and grew. Together, the whole lot of them dragged Jawhar Zahir to a neighbour's house, from which his groaning reached the sky. He struggled free of the men, but this time he did not head for the front of the house. The men gave chase, and he disappeared. The women hurriedly removed Trifa's oil-soaked clothes; Fawziya Yasami regained consciousness and, upon seeing herself in such a state, disgraced and a failure, went into the house with the women's help, speechless. What was a respectable woman like herself to say in these circumstances? But her only son, once the source of her delight, refused to give up. Several hours later, he returned with a pistol. (God alone knows where a boy of his age got hold of something like that.)

Before entering the house, he started screaming and showering the door with bullets. The noise awakened the entire neighbourhood. Once again, some daring men leaped into action, followed by a great commotion as people hurried back to the scene. Fawziya and Trifa both locked themselves in their rooms. Jawhar barged into the front yard. The men arrived, begging him to lay down his pistol, while he threatened everyone around him like a wild ox. A wild ox? What am I saying? A devil who had lost his head and attached a mule's in its place, more like!

Among the neighbours was a mustashar,[7] who, along with his guards, reluctantly joined the action. Fawziya wept inside the house, while Trifa shouted from behind a window. Jawhar shot at the walls, doors and windows without any hesitation. By God, who knows what might have happened had not the mustashar, who had betrayed his homeland, intervened in the unfortunate events of that evening. Perhaps the decent girl who constitutes part of our story would have fallen victim to the unbridled Jawhar. The thick-necked mustashar, looking for an opportunity to flex his muscles, charged into the front yard accompanied by his bodyguards. Nobody knew why he had been fully armed and ready for action at that late hour of the night. Displaying the demeanour of a man who seeks to put fear into the heart of his opponent, he admonished Jawhar: 'Hey, you – what's all this commotion? A real man doesn't shoot at his sister or mother! Disarm him and arrest him! At once!' The bodyguards pinioned him and took him away briskly and efficiently.

This marked the end of an important night in Trifa Yabahri's life. From then on, Jawhar Zahir became a dangerous spectre, hot on Trifa's heels. The days that followed proved that Jawhar was an obstinate, threatening person whose sudden outbursts were not to be underestimated. Fearless and unperturbed, Trifa and Fawziya Yasami stayed at home for a few days, trying to view the horrible events as a scene in a violent play on which the curtain has come down. One day, however, when Trifa and Fawziya went to shop at the bazaar, Jawhar Zahir popped up outside a cloth-seller's, wielding a big knife in his hand; but before he could grab Trifa by the hair, she screamed and ran away. The decorous Fawziya could never have imagined that she would one day be so humiliated right in the middle of the bazaar.

Jawhar Zahir chased Trifa through the qaysari,[8] holding the huge knife, while Trifa ran faster than a deer. Bystanders merely watched and laughed. The two of them were running so fast, nobody could work out what was going on.

Just picture the scene: in the midst of the big bazaar of this greedy, shameless city, a girl in tight blue jeans is running, screaming, falling over sacks of chickpeas and buckets of yoghurt and hearing some women say, 'Shameless hussy. Her brother caught her *doing it*.' Picture this delicate girl as, just to escape her pursuer, she bursts into a mosque, enters the filthy men's toilet and locks herself in there for three hours, the smell from the backsides of the gluttonous men of this city as they come and go in groups washing over her; she hears their hands splashing water, their farts. It was such a bitter experience that she would remember it until the day she died. Later, she would tell the story to the girls at the carpet factory hundreds of times. Galawezh Bahir, the owner's wife, would ask her: 'Trifa, tell us the mosque story.' Trifa had to tell it from scratch to every woman who joined the factory, and they would all be dumbfounded upon hearing how a girl like her ended up in the mosque toilet.

But when she reached the part when she returned home in the evening, tears would gather in her eyes. She would tell them how Fawziya Yasami wept because of her only son – 'his parents' favourite', 'the favoured among all the male members of the Yabahris'. She would recount how Fawziya was so grief-stricken that her mouth became almost permanently crooked; how she took Fawziya to hospital in an old, worn-out cab; how the doctors said that if they had not come so quickly, Fawziya could have died. Then she would tell how Fawziya cried unceasingly for three days and nights. Trifa told this story to everyone of goodwill, even Hasan-i Tofan, who would smile at her words. Whenever she reached the point at which she said, 'So, I decided to leave my childhood residence and bid goodbye to the Yabahri home,' tears would pour from her eyes like spring rain.

Where, though, could a girl like her turn, in search of a place where her life and dignity would be safe?

That Trifa landed in Abdulaqadir Niya's factory is down to a good brother of Fawziya's, an old friend of Qadir's; they had played games of mahbus and gulbahar together a few times several years back. This good man rang Kak Qadir, but Galawezh answered the phone. They spoke for around an hour. It transpired that Galawezh was an old acquaintance of Fawziya Yasami's. They had met dozens of times at memorial services and pashtelanas, post-wedding feasts. When the two women spoke on the phone, Galawezh said, 'Weren't you the one wearing a knee-length quilted purple coat with sequins at the party held by Akram's wife, Aftaw, sitting at the far end of the room? Wasn't it you sitting at the funeral service of Othman, Shafiqa's cousin, next to Mullah Gurun? Or who brought a set of silver when Inayat's daughter graduated? Wasn't that you? Yes, it was.'

As it happened, everything went smoothly. Galawezh Bahir knew Trifa's family well, and when she learned that the poor girl had been about to sit her Year 12 baccalaureate but had abandoned everything to protect herself, she became even more soft-hearted and affable. When they told her the whole story, she said without hesitation, 'Let her come. I'll look after her like the light in my eyes. Here, she can do whatever she likes.' She was a kind woman. She spoke in such a friendly manner that Fawziya Yasami could hardly credit it. Poor Fawziya suffered so much during that period, she had almost come to doubt that good people still existed. You have to remember what she had witnessed from her son at first hand. When she hung up the phone, she said, 'Thank God Almighty that there are still some good-hearted and pleasant-speaking people in the world.'

The following day, Trifa Yabahri went to the carpet factory. And as soon as she arrived and saw the first carpet, she had an unusual idea.

As soon as Trifa saw the first carpet, she understood what she could do. In her very first hour at the factory, she introduced herself to everyone as a designer of carpets. She told Galawezh and her husband, Sayyid Qadir, 'Making normal carpets is of no use to you. You have a small factory and work in a region renowned throughout the world for its carpets. Famous princesses and actors come and buy carpets in this region. The most beautiful rugs and other floor coverings are transported here from the other side of the border. The carpet-sellers prefer the work of the masters of Kashan, Tabriz and Kerman to those made here. Your output is small and your scope is limited. Therefore, you should do something exceptional, something that stands out and can be easily distinguished.'

Sayyid Qadir and his wife were pleased to hear Trifa's idea, as it was what they, too, had initially thought, but had not known how to carry out. Now the imaginative Trifa Yabahri told them, 'I would like to offer you my imagination. From now on, our carpets will not resemble carpets from anywhere else; not the ones from the Tehran factories, nor the ones from Khorasan. They will be a departure from the old, classical designs reproduced over hundreds of years. From now on, we will make unique carpets and rugs, so that anyone seeing them anywhere in the world will think of the Niya factory.'

Trifa was so bold, and had such a strong character, that she raised her voice above everyone else's; but she was also so gentle and friendly that the others knew she wasn't the type to want them as her subordinates. And her suggestions were so reasonable that no one could argue with them. The instructions in her plan were that the big looms and other essential machinery should continue working as normal while she would be in charge of a carpet that was her brainchild. Galawezh was a sceptical person – the complete opposite of Sayyid Qadir Niya, who would let the floods carry him away without asking where he was being taken, as the proverb goes. After much thinking and hesitation, she said, 'Give me a sample and we'll take it from there.'

That night, Trifa Yabahri designed her first carpet. In it, a girl like a princess sits by a lake reading a book; opposite her, a handsome man on a winged horse is looking at her. The sky above the young man is full of great stars and mythical trees; the lake is full of golden fish, staring at the pair in astonishment. The small space between the young man and the woman appears infinite and eternal, with the colours conveying a sense of separation; each scale on the fish is a different colour, the young man's robe is edged in glittering brocade, all the creatures have dreamy eyes. A strong wind is playing with the young man's hair and the horse's mane, while the atmosphere around the woman is calm and still; on the horizon, the same wild wind is also playing with a sad sunray.

That, in summary, was Trifa's idea for the carpet. They needed to complete it in a short time; Trifa put all her imagination into the work, and her colourful vision filled the fingers of the girls weaving the carpets with desire. Those working with her felt intoxicated, as though a wind had awakened inside them. They worked with incredible speed, as if pushed and pulled by the tide. Trifa's meticulousness astonished the female weavers. It was as if everything had already been woven onto an imaginary board, and she was transferring it centimetre by centimetre onto the carpet. She would close her eyes and know what the machine should do, line by line, which threads the weavers should pull and, to the scale of a pinhead, which colours should go next to one another or which lines should crisscross. As if she had been the seasoned apprentice of the Armenian masters or the famous rug weavers of Turkmenistan, from the very first she assessed the subject matter and colour combinations so astutely that skilled rug weavers and experienced carpet-sellers could find no flaws in her designs. Her inspirations came from the pure imagination she lived in at night, even in her sleep.

She would not allow anyone to see the carpet while she was still working on it. 'As with lightning, for true beauty to strike and deliver a blow conditions should be ripe,' she would say. 'My dears, it is not as if beauty is water and you drink it in sips. Beauty is like a sharp spear: it strikes when you are least expecting it. And that's how we should hit Mr and Mrs Niya.'

Trifa was not beautiful by the criteria of the men of this city, but she was delicate in a way that would attract anybody. Trifa's arrival at the carpet factory had made everyone happy. She often had the unfortunate female workers in stitches, giggling and laughing ceaselessly. 'Before you came, we never laughed,' they all said. After much toil, the carpet was finished. On the morning they were due to display it, they all put on their best clothes and stood before it. Trifa appeared rather pale and distracted.

Abdulaqadir Niya was to be the first person to see the unique carpet. When he stood before it, he was lost for words. The carpet was extremely beautiful; he had never seen its like before. Although he had been in the carpet business since childhood, it was the first time he had seen such intricate drawing on a rug. He saw this carpet as a tiny piece of fabric born from an angel's imagination rather than from the fingers of these simple, sad girls. He touched it and turned it over many times to establish whether what he saw was real or imagined, a drawing or a carpet, an intricate embroidered muslin or a real rug. He paced around the carpet a few times without saying a word, shaking his head and taking deep breaths. Finally, he left the room without uttering a word.

Galawezh's state was no better than her husband's. She said, 'Oh dear God, oh dear God,' a couple of times, apparently so dizzied by the carpet that she could not speak. As if she had a sudden fever and a headache, she put her hands to her head and let out a sigh, then left without saying anything more.

A whole day passed, and no one spoke to Trifa. That night, she could not sleep. The following day, Galawezh and Abdulaqadir called her and had her sit on a leather chair in front of them. Abdulaqadir spoke first. 'My dear Trifa, I know you want our opinion on the carpet now. We are both aware that you put your heart and soul into it. We have no qualms about you or about the carpet's beauty. But there is something in it that does not resemble a normal carpet ... something unusual that we can't put our fingers on.'

'There's something in it that isn't suitable for the market,' said Galawezh, holding her forehead. 'It's more like a drawing. A carpet is something else. You can't have a carpet without arabesques. Plus, it's extremely beautiful. So beautiful it scares you; so beautiful you don't know how to put a price on it.'

'I am sure it is suitable for the market,' said Trifa in tears. 'Put it out there and see. There will be people who want to buy it.'

'Trifa, you've misunderstood us,' said Sayyid Qadir, putting a hand on her shoulder. 'We know there will be a demand for it, and that it will sell. But what will the consequences be? Have you thought about that?'

Trifa looked at Galawezh and said, 'Dear Khanim, I don't understand. Really, I don't.'

'I am sure they will ask for more carpets,' Galawezh said. 'I am sure the senior officials, the mustashars and statesmen, will be after this sample. They will keep coming here and ruin our lives. Qadir and I don't want them here. They bring nothing but trouble. Besides which, you won't be staying here forever. You're not going to sit in this filthy factory and make carpets for me for good. You have to go away and worry about your own life, help your poor mother. What's more, the carpet has something about it that reminds me of opium. It makes you dizzy; it drives you into fantasy, into a different world. Oh God, I don't know what to say. My dear girl, not everyone can endure those fantasies.'

Trifa laughed happily now that she was sure the carpet's problem wasn't that it was distasteful, but that it was beautiful and unique.

'That's easy, Khanim!' she shouted with all the passion of a teenager. 'Believe me, it's very easy. We won't sell the carpets here. We'll put up a sign outside saying: "No carpets sold here." We'll appoint an agent. Whenever someone turns up, we'll tell them we don't have any carpets for sale. We'll put a high price on them, even higher than the market price. Khanim, believe me, it's easy. Let's try this for a while and see.'

Galawezh and Sayyid Qadir Niya didn't know what to say. They wanted to expand their market, bring in new items, sell more and buy newer machinery for the factory. But they worried that they would risk being exposed to the thieves and liars who thronged the city. After a few days of deliberation, after they had shown the carpet to a few carpet-sellers and some expert friends had given their opinions, they concluded that they would set Trifa's hands free and let her make carpets as she wished.

Everything went well. Sales went through the roof, and demand was very high. Their products reached distant lands. For many years, they believed it was the best and boldest decision they'd ever made. But not so. A few years on, three near-identical, well-dressed men, all sporting black moustaches, pulled up outside the factory in a vehicle and stepped out. That evening, Galawezh and Qadir Niya understood that the decision had been the biggest mistake of their lives.

BARAN SHUKUR'S LAST LETTER
SUMMER 2004

One day in August 2004, a man stepped out of a taxi with an old suitcase outside the Snow and Mirage Hotel. He was over two metres tall, slender and clean-shaven with long, white hair. He wore a pair of trousers covered in dust from the road. Despite his dirty, dishevelled clothes and skinny frame, something in his appearance brought ancient kings and princes to mind. It seemed as though the cityscape had made him dizzy; when he emerged from the taxi and took the suitcase from the boot, his eyes were as wide as if he had just encountered some dreadful sight.

Exhausted, he hauled his suitcase into the hotel as if dragging a dead body. It was the first time he had been home in twenty-four years. When he gave his British passport and driver's licence to the hotel owner, he made a sad sound – a short, stifled murmur. The owner was a small man with a truncated pencil moustache, like a short sentence on a sheet of paper. He raised his head and smiled unpleasantly, as if looking at a foul, abhorrent creature. There was something disagreeable about his appearance – deceit mixed with suspicion and jealousy. Whenever he saw one of these Europe-based Kurds, he couldn't resist this kind of smile. He considered all of them stupid people, their minds something he could play with. He loathed them. He would tell his friends, 'I fleece them for as much as I can. Why not? What are they? A bunch of good-for-nothings who've made a fortune without lifting a finger.'

It seemed he had never seen such a tall and feeble man, such a long-haired, pale-skinned person. The guest had a confused look, as though he had just emerged from an encounter involving heavy weapons. Although from his general appearance and complexion he seemed young, his hair was completely white. Until then, all the returning Kurds who had stayed at the hotel had been arrogant, all wanting to be regarded as rare birds. But this one seemed more confused, more complicated. Despite his tall figure, mysterious serenity and his strange air of authority, he seemed wild and impatient.

'Welcome back to Kurdistan,' said the hotel owner sarcastically. 'We've missed you. Where have you been all these years?'

'Give me a quiet room, please ... a quiet room,' the man said in refined Kurdish, paying no attention to the unpleasant smile. He gave the owner a serious look.

'Why, certainly,' said the owner, slightly taken aback. 'I'll give you the quietest one I have.'

'Take good care of my passport and driving licence,' the man said after a pause, in the same deep, sad tone, and levelling a finger at the owner. 'If anything happens to it, I'll hold you responsible. I've never lost my passport anywhere in the world, you know. I wouldn't want to lose my things here.'

His voice was so powerful, and his look so calm and authoritative, that the owner hid his smile and stepped back a little. He was obviously regretting his manner.

'No one's items are lost here,' he said politely. 'You can keep the passport and leave the driver's licence with us. You'll have to excuse us. We don't want anyone's items, but the security forces come and check the papers occasionally at night. They make it a requirement. Anyone without the right papers won't be allowed to sleep at the hotel.'

'Tell the security people,' the man said, without looking at the owner, 'that God's domain is vast enough for those without identity papers to sleep in.'

The owner was certain this was not an easy person to deal with. He had never had such a guest before. Very politely, he took his suitcase and led him to room 213, the best room in the hotel. The windows were big, the view wasn't bad and it was less exposed to the roaring of vehicles and buses.

'Please feel free to take a rest now, sir,' said the owner as he brought the suitcase in. 'There is hot water; you can take a shower. If you need food, I can order some for you. There are many good restaurants in the area.'

Without answering, the guest looked at the room and touched the walls, and said under his breath, 'That's okay, you can go now. You can go. I want to be alone. I don't want anything to eat.'

The owner closed the door quietly and left him. When he had gone, the guest calmly took off his shirt and sat on the edge of the bed. He closed his eyes for a short while and took a deep breath, like a yogi. 'How much time will I need to find her?' he said out loud. 'How much time? A week, a month, a year?'

He slowly unzipped his suitcase, and, from under a well-thumbed atlas he had carried with him for more than twenty-four years, took out a thick, blue file. He opened the file, took out a letter and then closed it again, unhurriedly. It was a plain piece of paper. Someone had crammed an immense amount of writing on it in a minuscule hand. As on all previous occasions, he turned to the last page first. He looked at the name on the back of the page – 'Baran Shukur', the name of his sad niece, the only daughter of his sister Gulistan Shazaman. She alone wrote him letters from home. In the past five years, she had written him thirty-three letters. She always began with the words, 'My dear uncle, boredom is nearly killing me.' That was how all thirty-three letters started, and they all ended with the following words, written in the final empty corner of the page when there was hardly any space left: 'Your unhappy niece, Baran Shukur.' She always put the 'n' on the 'a', the 'k' in 'Shukur' going up while the first 'a' in 'Baran' rose as if flying. She had unusual handwriting, and he would have recognised it anywhere. He had received the last letter five months earlier, and since then had heard no word from her. In those five years, he had only written three very short letters to her, and wasn't even sure they had reached their destination. She, however, wrote with depth and sincerity, as if she was certain her correspondent was listening. When he was sure he was no longer going to receive any letters, he decided to return home and search for her.

But for reasons he could not fathom and out of deep fear, he kept putting his journey off. Some days he would walk along the seaside from morning to evening, waiting for another letter. In the evenings, he would climb to the top of a large rock and speak to the ocean. He had learned, in those twenty-four years, to speak to all sorts of things – rocks, flowers, birds. He had lost all connection with Kurdistan before the letters, absolutely all connection. He didn't want to hear anything from back home, and didn't have even one Kurdish friend.

In times of great catastrophe, he had sat in front of the television, shocked. He had seen people's immense suffering, and empathised with every single one of them. But he always went out at night and got drunk in the free air, under the clouds and stars. He had done nothing. He had not let any suffering from back home wound him deeply or pierce his soul sharply. What could he do? Nothing. Out of profound conviction, he had decided not to be sad about his homeland. Like many who spend interminable years in exile, he felt there was no place he could call home. All his life, he had ridiculed patriotism. Home was wherever he happened to be living; it was the second he took a calm breath. He washed his hair most days, shaved his moustache and beard, wore leathers, rode a motorbike and drove like a madman along the endless motorways. Home was the smell of the trees, carried by the wind from the seaside onto the long, snaking roads.

To him, Kurdishness meant growing old as a gypsy on the streets and highways of the world. Kurdishness meant a fear of walls, an eternal flight from barriers. Kurdishness meant driving your motorcycle like a man possessed, never looking back. It meant putting your foot on the pedal and, like a prisoner escaped from Hell, never having to ask what had happened in the Hell you left behind. Kurdishness was tantamount to a disease in which you spent your entire life trying to forget Hell. And he had done everything he could to do just that.

When, five years earlier, he received Baran's first letter, he had not contacted his mother or sister for nineteen years. He wanted the whole world to believe he was dead. He wanted to live the remainder of his life as a crazy traveller, to buy and drink beer and flatten the cans under his feet, and tell himself, 'I'm happy'; to put on a red motorcycle helmet, and, like a missile being fired, head with the wind towards the unknown; to get off his motorbike and onto a ship without asking where it was going. The important thing was to feel that he was leaving Hell further and further behind. He would go where there was nothing to remind him of the old country, the Kurds or home. His happiest moments were when he knew he was still running away, still moving forward, surging forth at a gallop like a wild horse. To him, Kurdishness was a relentless charge, a leap into the unknown. All that mattered was that he was free, with no walls to imprison him, no chain on this planet that could drag him inside four walls and force him to sit and think, to ask: 'Who am I? What am I? Where did I come from?'

And now, after twenty-four years, he had ended up in this strange little corner of this filthy hotel. Oh God, who is Baran Shukur? Who is to say that there isn't some fatal mistake in this whole game? Who is to say that he even has such a niece? But the question of Baran Shukur's identity is not important. What matters is why she hasn't sent him any letters for five months now. In great confusion, and as if seeking to understand something, he read the final letter aloud to himself:

My dear uncle, boredom is nearly killing me. In my previous letter, I explained everything to you. Things aren't going well. I can sense that my husband knows everything. Things are taking a dangerous turn, even though I burned all the letters from the young man, even though I did eventually tell him that I didn't want to see him any more – although there isn't a woman in the world who could say to him, 'I don't want to see you' and mean it. Last night, I was aware that my husband had brought some man along, one Murtaza Satan. Oh God, Uncle, you have no idea what a bad man he is. A girlfriend of mine told me that whenever that ugly mug of a man appears in a house, disaster strikes. That was the second time he had come to our house. Yesterday, he greeted my husband Saman obsequiously with an unpleasant laugh: 'Baron of Courgettes, I will faithfully carry out whatever you tell me, whatever orders you give.' I wanted to find out what they were talking about, but I couldn't. They closed all the doors and windows and pulled down the blinds. I couldn't hear even a murmur. They might as well have been whispering. Every now and then I heard Murtaza Satan's laughter. He often laughs for no reason.

For the second time, an unknown person had brought me a letter saying: 'Go away, Baran Khan, go away. The baron and Murtaza Satan want to kill you ... go away.' Uncle, you don't know what a dangerous man Murtaza is. I have seen him at lots of parties and dinners, laughing for no reason. My dear uncle, at the last one, he just kept looking at me. It wasn't a good night. We had to go to the Namam Club. It's a big club, run by a filthy Turk. Neither he nor his wife look like the Turks I see on satellite TV stations. A friend of mine has been to Turkey. I mean, she got married and they went to Istanbul. I don't know what happened out there, but one day she came back, crying, and gave her ring back to the young man's family. She says that unless the Turks wear make-up and contact lenses, they don't look beautiful.

Oh God, there I go, bothering you with trivial stuff as usual. But, here, among these men and women, it's all I hear. The other night a huge fight broke out over whether the Turks or the Iranians were more beautiful. God Almighty, the men were all whispering and laughing; we, the women, knew what they were saying. Then, we, the women, started whispering and laughing. I looked around and didn't know what to say. There was a woman who said, 'What do you know? I've lived in Teheran. I swear to God that Persian men are the most handsome.' So as not to look stupid, I compared two old Iranian and Turkish singers. A girl said: 'Silly girl. Just how ancient are you? They are so old hat. It's Mansoor and Arkan nowadays.'

I can rarely find an intelligent person to talk to here. They all say girls don't need such things. They all say that I'm the luckiest woman alive, that my husband is the richest man, and yet boredom is nearly killing me. The other night at the party, Murtaza Satan stared at me often, laughing every time he did. His protruding yellow teeth scare me. At first, he was sitting at a different table.

Even then, he was looking at me a lot. 'God have mercy upon you. Murtaza is looking at you a lot,' the girl next to me whispered in my ear. All the women at the table were whispering to each other that Murtaza was looking at me. One of the women put her hand on her heart and said, 'Please, for God's sake, don't say that. Maybe it's nothing. That old dog's teeth mean no good.'

I didn't want to have to look at him all evening, but he joined our table after a while. Without any sense of modesty towards my husband, he said out loud, with his unpleasant smile, 'Baran Khan, you are very beautiful tonight.' Dear God, this isn't Europe. No one can just tell someone else's wife out loud, 'You're beautiful.' Even if I am, it's not appropriate for a man to say so in public. My husband said nothing, nothing at all. I thought he would get angry. He does get angry at small things. Instead, he said, 'She has indeed become beautiful, and why not? She is about to begin her studies. She will go to England or Germany.'

Everyone was stunned. They all looked at me. I didn't know what to say. As God is my witness, I wasn't aware of any such thing. It was the first time I'd heard speak of it. Murtaza laughed out loud, gave me a mocking look and said, 'There is nothing that the wife of the Baron of Courgettes does not deserve.'

I got very upset when they referred to me as the wife of the Baron of Courgettes. I felt as if I had a lump in my throat. They all looked at me and laughed. I nearly burst into tears. So as not to cry in front of them, I took my bag and went to the bathroom. When I stood up, people at every table were looking at me. When I passed the drunken men, each of them made some sexual comment about me. In the toilets, I didn't worry about messing up my make-up or my expensive chiffon dress, I just cried. I cried a lot. When another woman came in, I controlled myself so she wouldn't hear me sobbing. I wiped my eyes and touched up my make-up so that no one would suspect I'd been crying. But anyone who looked closely could tell.

I didn't say another word that night. When we went home, my husband was drunk. He's better at telling lies when he's drunk. All the men here are. All the lies they can't tell when they're sober, they can tell when they're drunk. He told me in the car, 'Dearest, I will send you to Germany. That's how things are. It's what they all do. They send their wives and daughters abroad. Why not you? You're not inferior to them in any way. Didn't you say you have an uncle abroad? What are you doing? Go to him for a while.' I knew he was lying. I asked him, 'Why are you lying to me? Why? I'm your wife.' He looked at me sweetly and said, 'Ah, my dear baby. How could I lie to you?' Then, he drove fast, as fast as if he were angry, as if he weren't taking me, or what I said, seriously. Suddenly he stopped the car, then shouted at the top of his voice: 'How can you lie to me? How can you?' I began to cry, and said nothing. I didn't know if he or I was telling the truth. That night we slept separately. Since that night, I've been scared.

My dear uncle, I wish you were here. I'm scared of him now. I will write to you as soon as I know more. I hope you're not angry with me. I know you'll come back, I do. What matters is that I get to see you and hug you. Don't worry about me. Don't worry about your sad niece. Although sometimes I feel weak, at other times I feel very strong. Although sometimes I'm scared, at other times I feel as if I'm not afraid of anything.

You must take care of yourself. Here they say that Europe is very cold. I sometimes watch your channels on satellite TV. I say, 'Oh God, it's so nice! That's where my uncle lives, in those lovely places.' Take care of yourself for my sake. I will write to you very often, but don't worry whatever happens. Promise me you won't worry. Okay? I kiss your eyes.

Your unhappy niece,

Baran Shukur

He had read the letter hundreds of times. There was nothing all that important in it. It was a simple letter written by a simple woman. It was a letter like all the others in the world. But every time he read it, his heart sank. It was through her letters that he found out his sister had died. Baran was alone in the world; she had no parents, brothers or sisters. Maybe it was the lack of relations in her life that prompted her to turn to him. But why hadn't she sent any letters at all for five months? What was going on?

He stood up and looked out at a small view of the city from the window. It was nothing like the city he remembered. It was another city. He touched the walls again and decided to sleep for a while. He was extremely tired. He had not slept properly for over thirty-six hours. He had spent all his life travelling, but couldn't remember having ever been so tired. He didn't know how he managed to fall asleep. When he woke, he saw that he had been asleep for three hours. In his dream he had been working on an endlessly long wall. He said in his heart, 'I should start anew from here.' Night was falling slowly, and he had to get up and leave. He felt he mustn't stay still. But he didn't know where to go, or what directions to follow.

AFTER THE REVOLUTION,
A RETREAT INTO PRIVACY IS RECOMMENDED
HASAN-I TOFAN, THE POST-UPRISING YEARS

After I quit the Party and went home, one of the senior officials of our rival party (we'd been killing their members, they'd been killing ours) came to see me one day and said, 'Hasan-i Tofan, you are the best shot and bravest gunman in our country. We know how well you have served this nation; we know you have killed many people on behalf of our adversaries; we have the name of every single person you shot. Now, our party proposes that you join our ranks. And we will happily meet any demands you have.'

That was the beginning of an age that Shibr later called 'the age of buying humans'. I told the high-ranking official, 'I've decided not to kill people any more. I am no longer of any use to politics. I want to stay in my own home for a few years and do nothing.' The man tried hard with me, tempted me with ambitious proposals, mentioned a sum that was a mind-blowing amount of money at the time. His words also contained a few minor threats. However, I said, 'Boss, I have no desire left for the job. The scene is now full of youngsters who could behead a whale in the water for you for less money. You shouldn't play with the Party's budget like that. After all, killing is killing, and I'm not such a rare asset. There are many who are better than me. It's only fair that you look for those people. I want to give up this sharwal and spend two or three years in pyjamas.[9] Ever since my childhood, I have wanted to take off my sharwal, like everyone else, and spend a few years putting on another set of clothes in the evening, to rest a little bit and make rosewater with my mother.'

'Hasan-i Tofan,' the man said, 'you are a true gentleman, and your mother's rosewater is unique in this city. We know that murderers are two a penny, but we also know that you are a man of great conviction, and your signature is unmistakeable. Your trust and your reputation mean a lot to us. Every murder is like creating a puzzle. It is a question that should elude easy explanation; it is a secret whose mystery should not be cleared up, a knot that cannot be untied. Yours is a job that requires reason and thought. We have big and complex jobs that can't be done by youngsters. Killing calls for feelings and reflection. It is like painting a picture or writing a poem. It is a series of puzzles and traps.'

The man went on in this vein, but his words fell on deaf ears. He couldn't understand why I had suddenly changed and given up everything. I was shocked, wondering how it was that, seemingly out of the blue, the price of an ignorant murderer such as myself had gone through the roof, and why I was being treated like a diamond. Later I learned that, regardless of the groups we'd originally belonged to, we pre-uprising assassins all developed a certain sadness after the uprising. All of us felt our parties had sold us short. Seeking an alternative, a number of assassins and gunmen from the other side crossed over to ours, which prompted the leaders of the other side to take revenge by trying to buy *us* at a high price. We were the pawns who never had a permanent place in the game. We were the carpenters who made thrones for kings and bilwers[10] for children's cradles. Poor tailors who made a donkey's packsaddle one day and a nobleman's robe the next. We didn't care who killed whom. What mattered was that the profession remained alive and the job got done.

I didn't know at what moment our profession became disconnected from everything else. But I quit and quietly bid goodbye to everything, and went home to my mother and sat by her rose-filled pots with a skimmer in hand. During the years of the civil war in the mid 1990s, instead of fighting and killing people, my mother and I made the rosewater to sprinkle on the dead. I was pleased that I was finally doing something good for the martyrs. I used to say that if I could go back in time, I would dedicate myself only to making rosewater with my mother.

During the civil war, the price of some of my friends soared so high, and their political standing went up so much, that someone like me could not easily reach the doorstep of their offices. Some of them were implicated in awful things, such as the killing of dissidents from other countries who took refuge in our city and country. Some of them stayed where they were and became cheap assassins who killed simple and innocent people for very little money.

During the civil-war years, sometimes I felt down, and at other times happy. I spent a lot of time with the old women who visited my mother and brought us roses from imaginary gardens and lands to make rosewater. I benefited a lot from their wisdom. Whenever I felt depressed, they found herbs and prepared solutions for me that immediately brought back a smile to my face. The smell of the roses tied me to our home in a very unusual way, which, unlike the smell of the outside world, was magical and wrapped itself so tightly around my heart that it did not allow me to move. The pleasant smells and the magical flowers turned me into a domesticated animal. My mother and I made little money, but were completely at peace. On some nights, ignorance got the better of me, and for no good reason I would start telling the stories of my murders to my mother.

'Don't make up such falsehoods,' she would say as she brought out her head from under her blanket. 'What are these big lies you are telling an old woman like me? Shame on you.'

My mother had considered me an inveterate liar from childhood.

Shibr visited me three times during that period of isolation, and brought me news of my friends. I was so detached from everything that I didn't know what was going on in the world. When I quit the Party and abandoned everything, I gave away my TV set and radio, and decided not to listen to the news any more. Half the troubles of this world are caused by the news. Take away news reports, and you will see what a lush oasis and peaceful place this Earth would become. People's misfortunes start on the day they listen to the news for the first time. That was my life's main malady. If my late father hadn't bought a radio, I might have become a doctor or an engineer or taken up some other important job. Listening to and following the news, and a strong emotional attachment to current events, turned me into an assassin.

As soon as you see that desire for listening to the news born within you, understand that you are done for. Bid goodbye to happiness. It will no longer matter what is going on in the world. What matters is that you will be forever unhappy, and die of grief over trivial things. To cure this malady, I became so detached from the outside world that I no longer knew who was winning or losing in the civil war. Our city was seized and freed several times. I always heard the news very late. My only source of information was the old women who visited my mother every day. I understood belatedly that some of them were detached from this life, and lived inside their fantasies. The events they told of were events from other epochs. They confused me so much that I couldn't put anything back in its proper place later on.

When the women came, I asked them, 'What's the news?' They spoke about King Ghazi's death. They told of Rashid Ali's rise to power as if it had happened that very day. They informed me of Queen Alia's illnesses. They spoke about the looting of the 1940s. They told the story of the migration of innocent Jews to Palestine in minute detail. They wept for the Shah of Iran and for Dr Mossadegh at the same time. They cursed Bakr Sidqi. I, who knew nothing of history, fell victim to the unusual and imaginary events the old women related to me. While the world outside was living in the present, my mother, her friends and I were busy with stories from another era.

Shibr Mustafa visited me three times. All three times the Party had sent him to take me out of my solitude and bring me back to work. He would arrive outside my home in the latest Land Cruiser models, but I received him in my tattered pyjamas. On one such occasion, he was wearing a dark brown katafi – baggy trousers and a jacket; under his jacket, he wore a very fine white shirt. He was short and his moustache was shiny blond, just as in the old days. His hair was backcombed in the fashion of the time.

When he saw me with the skimmer, he said: 'You have become a housewife. Next time I come, I'll bring you some darpe-i kudari.¹¹ I'll tell the Party to buy you some henna and woad.'

If anyone had spoken to me like that in the old days, I'd have killed him. No one would have dared to say such things to Hasan-i Tofan. All the murderers of this country held me in high regard. However, that's over now. No one is scared of me.

'The Party should buy itself some darpe-i kudari,' I said coldly to Shibr. 'It needs it more than I do. I have a small job, and make a living out of it.'

Shibr gave me a genuine embrace, and said: 'You are in our thoughts. We are not happy that you are so isolated. Sabir now holds a very senior position in the Party. He appreciates your value. He can cover you in gold.'

In fact, I didn't understand why everyone wanted to cover me in gold. I was too unskilled and ignorant to be covered in gold. Some time later, Shibr himself explained everything to me and said: 'That was when they started buying and selling human beings. Each group prepared a long list of names and put prices on them. Their middlemen would come and ask for your price. It was very important that your name made it onto that list. Some people paid a lot of money for someone to put them on that list. It was a market like the old one for buying and selling slaves. It was a new and very profitable business. All that mattered was to find someone to buy you. The lists were full of disparate names. At that time, the Party needed everyone. They wanted to accumulate an enormous amount of human capital so that they could invade every nook and cranny in the world. Eventually, invading everywhere was just what they did. There was nothing else left to buy except for the imagination.'

Shibr brought me the news that some of our old friends had been killed. He was also the one who told me that Ja'far-i Magholi had travelled to The Netherlands after sustaining a light injury. Shibr's attempts to take me back to the old world were fruitless. I insisted on staying at home. Humans live more at peace the narrower they can make their world. In fact, I had a happier life compared to the old times; but even being at peace is something we get bored of quickly. Sometimes, I missed my old pistol badly. Some nights I brought it out and smelled it. I placed it on my chest. I imagined shooting at dangerous creatures waiting to ambush me in the dark. I missed the days when I lived in danger. It made me sad, the feeling that being at peace was gradually making me more stupid.

Despite all of this, however, I was not ready to go back to my old life. For more than six years, I locked my door with a huge iron lock and didn't allow much about me to leak outside. Now, I say that I wish all my friends would do the same: go home like that and close their doors with a big lock. Although I know my opinion doesn't count for much, I think that after a revolution a man needs a few years to get used to the new era. I knew from my limited and worthless experience that those who tear down and destroy one era cannot build another. Just as weapons can't suddenly become flowers, a killer can't suddenly turn gardener. I needed more than six years of solitude to take myself out of history – my personal history, and the history of those bloody years, scenes of which were constantly being replayed in my head. The elderly flower-sellers who befriended my mother, who brought their flowers from imaginary gardens, helped me a great deal to forget about those bloody times. Regardless of how competent and honest humans are, they can only live in the spotlight of history for a short time. After that, they need to go home.

'Shibr,' I said, on his second visit, 'we are like brothers, you and I. Let me give you a piece of advice. Listen to me. Go back home, lock yourself in for a few years and don't come out. If we want to become normal human beings again, we need privacy. A revolutionary is someone who goes home after the revolution and tries to forget about it all. The day I killed that woman and returned to Ja'far-i Magholi's home, I was soaked in blood. That day, I said: "I can't build a happy or beautiful era." I said: "Now it's time to go home and rest." I changed my clothes and went home to my mum. You can't build the future in a bloodied sharwal. Shibr, you are like a true brother to me. Listen to me. Go home and build yourself a private world.'

He didn't listen. Six months after that, an unidentified person opened fire on him on a dark night, leaving him paralysed from the waist down. He is confined to a wheelchair now. I often go to see him and take him to the bazaar. 'I should've listened to you,' he says and weeps. 'I should've quit earlier.'

He was a handsome young man. His life was ruined very early on. When his sister is busy, I go with him when he gets paid. Once, while

85

waiting in a queue, he got to talking to a woman with green eyes who was also in a wheelchair, and who had been brought by her own sister to collect her salary. They liked each other a lot. Shibr could not marry her, and she could not get married, but a great love was born. That made Shibr forget about the world for a while, and turned him into a gentle person with no interest in the Party or politics. When, in later years, I re-entered the world and became friends with Ghazalnus, Shibr really helped us to understand those days and months immediately after the civil war.

SEARCHING FOR MURAD JAMIL

MAJID-I GUL SOLAV, SPRING 2004

Excuse me. It's me, the Imaginary Magellan. I'm the one who told you about Murad Jamil's body at the beginning. You're bound to have forgotten the poor man, dead as he is. You've been so immersed in the details of this story that you're ready to overlook the poor guy's body altogether. That's not how it's meant to be. What kind of readers are you? Are you impatient and shortsighted, or do you just forget things from one chapter to the next? I would have never imagined you capable of reading about Murad Jamil's body and then assuming he had merely been mentioned in passing.

After the night that Ghazalnus, Hasan-i Tofan, Darsim Tahir and I unearthed the body, I couldn't sleep. Ever since, I have felt as though the corpse were close to me, constantly walking beside me. That night, as we got further and further away from the scene of his death, I had a vague feeling deep inside that it was my own dead body I was leaving behind. Until that night, and in comparison with my friends, I had led a sheltered and unexciting life, pathologically engaged in my imaginary travels through rivers and forests. But seeing the body brought me back to Earth and filled me with a worldly sadness much more painful than the imaginary version.

For someone like me, walking around the city with the swagger of an English lord in my long jackets, seeing the face of that young man killed my imagination for a while, forcing me to suspend my classes with the blind children. In my dreams, I was always wherever the corpse was. I would tell myself that our punishment for disturbing the helpless cadaver and taking it from its resting place should be to do something for it, rather than ignoring it. I wanted to put myself at its service to ward off the effect of its form and smell and its authority over me.

The day after we found the body, we all met in the presence of Trifa Yabahri. I was completely powerless. I didn't know what to suggest, and anyway, it wasn't as if anybody ever accepted the suggestions I did make. I can't remember a single case where anyone attached any worth to what I suggested. That day, Trifa, unusually for her, was wearing a red skirt, red boots and a red jacket. She had even put on red lipstick. I thought she was doing it on purpose, to destroy my imagination. I was the type of person whose imagination could be killed by the colour red. I sat quietly that day, pretending I didn't find the issue very important. I can do that sometimes, pretend to be disinterested and unconcerned, to be someone who asks questions merely out of cold curiosity or gentle indifference.

That was the first time the story of a corpse had been the subject of our discussion. Hasan-i Tofan – previously employed as a killer, as you know – looked at things more keenly than everyone else. He was an aggressive man. He spoke in a nasal twang and expressed his fears honestly and extremely well. Killers like him are wonderful human beings once they renounce their past. They make so fine and beautiful an entrance that anyone who sees them says deep down, 'God, why am I not a penitent murderer so that I, too, might be reborn so beautifully?' That day, he told us, 'If Ja'far-i Magholi had a hand in the matter, we might as well give up any hope of finding clues. It will be too complex a knot for a bunch of inexperienced people like us to try to undo. It would mean that there's someone more important involved. Ja'far-i Magholi has never killed anyone for personal reasons. He's harmless. He has no problems with anyone.'

Hasan was not one to give up easily. His interests had changed in a way he himself couldn't believe. From being an efficient murderer, he had turned into a well-meaning individual. He was much less erudite than me, or even Ghazalnus and Trifa, but his talk was not entirely devoid of philosophical insight. I don't know why, but that day Mr Tofan proposed that I should gather information about Murad Jamil. No one would have paid any heed if I'd put myself forward, but because it came from Hasan-i Tofan, they all accepted it. I had the impression that Ghazalnus really wanted us to follow up the story of this death. However, despite the feelings conveyed by Ghazalnus's hand gestures, his gaze and his state of shock, he didn't utter a single word; nor did he ask me anything.

Back then, I didn't know that this story would take each of us back to our roots. As a matter of fact, I didn't know where or how to start, but, like a debtor obliged to live with a feeling of gratitude towards his creditor, I had to do the job come what may. It was what I wanted: to be involved, at long last, in a story that was bigger than myself. For ages, I had longed to be part of an issue like this one, something that would turn my life into a beautiful film. I was very jealous of Hasan-i Tofan and his stories. The lives of all the others were fuller and more vibrant than mine. Whenever I sat and watched the films of Tom Hanks, George Clooney, Jim Carrey, Tim Robbins and the rest, they would reduce me to tears. I wondered whether a director might want to make a film of my life – but what was there to film? A young man who believes he looks like Johnny Depp? Someone who portrays himself as handsome and pro-Western, his suit always immaculately pressed, as he walks aimlessly day and night along three or four dusty, dirty streets in a city at the end of the world? My life needed to include something dangerous to be like the lives of other humans.

That day, as if he wanted to take me out of my daydreams and show me the way to another world, Ghazalnus gave me some insights into Murad Jamil's life, from which I was meant to glean more information about his death. Thanks to that information, I soon became acquainted with Murad Jamil's cousin, who looked very like Kevin Spacey in *American Beauty*. He was forty years old, courteous and shy. He knew a lot about Murad Jamil and was quite happy to share his knowledge with me. He even brought me some of Murad Jamil's clothes and said, 'These will fit you. You're the same height.'

I sat facing him, listening to his stories in my small glasses, with my goatee and briefcase, just like Johnny Depp in *The Ninth Gate*. I initially introduced myself to Murad Jamil's relatives as the representative of an international organisation working on missing people. I said, 'Our job is to understand why some people leave home and never return.' To avoid talking about Murad's death, I described death in a roundabout way. I said, 'Our organisation investigates missing persons around the world. We are convinced there is a secret link between certain people and certain creatures. They use highly sophisticated techniques to take away our loved ones and imprison them in a different world so they cannot come back to us.'

Murad Jamil's relatives did not realise that what I was doing was describing death, albeit from a different, slightly spiced-up angle. They saw my story as some sort of hope, and me as a saviour who might be able to free their son from these creatures and bring him back to this world. The way I talked, my sophistication, appeared to make these people – powerless in their bereavement – believe I had extraordinary powers and superhuman abilities.

Through my enquiries, I discovered that Murad Jamil had been unusually good-looking, and, what's more, had put this handsomeness to good use as a Casanova, recklessly entering into liaisons with dozens of women across the city with no thought for the potential risks. According to his cousin, Murad hadn't lived a single day without a romantic adventure, going from one dangerous story to another, restlessly jumping out of one controversy into the next. In his fantasies, the poor guy had been the kind of man who thought he could love all the women in the world. He was so full of passion, he thought it would stretch to all the women on the planet. He was the type who could stand among the young women of his city and tell them, 'I can love you all and still have passion to spare.' From his pictures, he appears to have been so handsome that the woman who could say no to the love of this angelic youth simply didn't exist. 'The only ones who don't, eventually, find him attractive are the ones who can't imagine he would ever take an interest them,' his cousin said.

I took this information back to my friends. To my surprise, Hasan-i Tofan became angry and said that my remarks were taken from an imaginary report, written under the influence of films and books, and were of no use to us at all for interpreting the complex conditions in which Murad had been killed.

'Clearly,' I said, 'I need some time to look at things as an intelligence officer and to distance myself from the views of a romantic film director [which had always been part of my character].' The second time, things went more smoothly; this was after Murad's faithful cousin made a huge archive available to me, which included hundreds of letters and pictures from different girls and women, which Murad had left in the care of our Kevin Spacey before he disappeared. When he brought me the archive, Murad had been missing for three weeks. Initially, I thought the archive useless. There were no names on most of the pictures and no dates on most of the letters. The names the girls did give were often fake, and the letters themselves were written in clichés that did little to express the intensity of their love. In my early youth, letters like this had made me give up on love forever. I loved two girls, both of whom bombarded me with such letters. They were so similar and so full of tired formulas that I lost all interest. There are few people in the world able to write genuine love letters, and Murad's lovers were not among them. I didn't know any of the women in the pictures, and didn't remember ever having seen any of them. The sad cousin appeared to know some of them, but fear prevented him from saying who they were. When I took the letters and pictures to my friends at another meeting, Hasan-i Tofan was more jovial and received me more pleasantly.

'This archive could tell us a lot,' he said. 'Perhaps the secret of this young man's death lies in one of these papers.' Hasan looked at the pictures carefully. He was more experienced than Trifa and me, and knew more people, but because he had been something of a recluse for six years, his memory had faded. He tried very hard, but couldn't recognise any of the faces in the pictures. Ghazalnus, for his part, didn't utter a word. Hasan then selected some of the pictures and took them away. He had a friend who knew even more people than he did, a handsome, blond-haired young man who went around in a wheelchair. I often saw Tofan pushing him between the second-hand market, the cotton-beaters' street and the film-sellers' street. He always wore clean clothes. He looked as if he'd once been a contented chap. I didn't know his name, but one day I overheard one of the radio-sellers in the second-hand market say, 'Shibr, Shibr, Tahsin has set a tape player aside for you. Come and collect it.'

When Hasan took the pictures, I was sure he would be showing them to Shibr – but I acted as if I knew nothing.

THE LOVERS' CHAMBER

MID-1970S

At the time Ghazalnus read Mullah Hajar's letter, he was an intelligent and quiet adolescent with big glasses, black, curly hair and a pure white complexion. He was tall and thin. He had a certain kind of handsomeness that would attract mainly intelligent people. He was the sort of young man who, if you saw him, you would think, 'I bet he's very good at maths.' His hands were slender, as were his fingers. He talked little, but when he did, he gesticulated as if searching for something just above him or planting words in the air. There was nothing about the young Bahman Nasser to suggest that he would one day become Ghazalnus, writer of ghazals. Rather, his appearance resembled that of people who are brilliant at natural sciences. He looked neither like his father nor his mother, Baharbanu, and there was no physical likeness to Mullah Hajar, whose pictures in the archive of the September Revolution show an old, white-bearded man with thick lips and big eyebrows.

When Ghazalnus received the letter, his mother had been dead for five years. Bahman grew up without a mother, in a vast house with many rooms. Such a house was too big for a boy and an old man. His father was in charge of the education department's warehouses, which supplied school laboratories. The smell of the acids and shining colours of the rare metals had weakened his eyesight. He was forever drowning in paperwork, in long lists of chemicals distributed to schools, in chlorine and iodine, and had no time to spare for his son. Bahman, left to his own devices, was a lonely child. He took to doing his homework on the walls of the house. When his father finally realised what was happening, he was amazed to find all the walls, floor to ceiling, filled with answers to mathematical questions, geometry theorems and chemical equations. There, too, alongside the logarithms, the Arabic sentences and English vocabulary lessons, were vast gardens and colourful flowerbeds.

After the arrival of Mullah Hajar's letter, Bahman went through a stage of deep reflection. He suddenly began to ignore all his lessons, and decided to leave school. The change was so fast and unexpected that no one could believe it. Mullah Hajar's letter appeared to have set in motion something already present in his mind, or that his soul had expected all along. When he read the letter, he didn't think it revealed a moral wrongdoing. He didn't say, 'I am the result of my mother's illicit relationship with another man.' Instead, he happily set about preparing for a different lifestyle, one in keeping with the spirit of this new story. He needed no further convincing that he was the outcome of an imaginary love. Rather than wasting his time on useless science, he dedicated his life to bigger things. One day he wrote a letter to his teachers and told them all he was leaving school. At that time, children only left school if they were very poor or not very bright. No one before him had ever left with a letter like that one. The letter displayed maturity and the emergence of awareness in a young man searching for meaning in his life. In it, he wrote:

Dear Sirs,

School numbs my soul. It makes me feel like a useless human being. Over the past few years, I have wanted to learn something useful from you, and from the subjects taught in school. I have wanted to learn how to enjoy life and become more open. I have not been negligent in preparing for my lessons, or in memorising and understanding my subjects; I have diligently carried out every task that was expected of a student, but day by day, the value of the sciences dwindled before my eyes. I would, therefore, like to pursue a science that I trust, one I know is useful to a human being.

When Ghazalnus wrote these lines to his teachers, he didn't yet entirely understand their meaning. He didn't know what science could be more useful than the ones he had studied at school.

If we take a close look back at the dark events of that era, we can understand why Ghazalnus turned away from the real world and reached the point where things become pure imagination. Dangerous events took place the year he left school. The Kurdish revolution collapsed. Failure took root in everyone's souls and found unusual modes of expression. One spring went by without anyone seeing a single bud; life was redolent of its own end, and the earth smelled scorched. A colourlessness and a silence akin to the silence that follows the burning of a wheat field prevailed over the land. Human imagination had perished, and a barren land was born. Hundreds of thousands of people saw the revolution's failure as their own personal failure. A generation emerged that wanted to bounce back quickly, and any generation that wants to bounce back quickly from failure is a dangerous one. The result was a unique blend of blood and dreams.

Ghazalnus wanted to come out of the war unscathed. Mullah Hajar's letter gave him a strange opportunity, an escape route through which he could resort to his imagination. For the following year, he simply thought about things. He believed everyone should dedicate a year of their lives just to thinking, in order to redraw the images and alter the state of matter of their innermost selves, even change their spirits. During that year, he wandered through cold, meaningless alleys like a madman. Everything before him seemed so faded, so soulless, that he couldn't help but see the world as one huge hell. He felt he had no roots anywhere in this city, as if he was hanging, unsupported, in the air. From then on, he began to look for a different environment, somewhere to which he could escape so that he wasn't suffocated by the profound sensation of being lost. During that year, through intensive training, he managed to change his perception of the world. With his imagination, he painted all the trees, introduced other smells and forms to the districts, bazaars and doorsteps; he filled the streets with different colours. He drew a map of a different city, and built it in his mind. He recorded each and every alley of that city until he was able to walk the streets according to a different map, to another version of the world. Of course, he was too intelligent to allow this process to reach the edge of madness. He developed an inner faculty that allowed him not to lose touch with the real world. He held two worlds simultaneously, and two perspectives. He could enter his imaginary world but also jump back to this one, to the unpleasant smells, to his home with its dull colours, to the dark shadows and the ruins of the Earth.

One evening, he was wandering around his colourful world with its mauve sky, azure earth and yellow horizon. Suddenly he was brought up short by the sight of a sad young man, who appeared distressed and yet had an angelic smile. His clothes were like the ones worn by noblemen in the 1920s, but his long hair and wide sideburns followed the fashion of the day. He resembled the restless, educated men who become obsessed with women and fame. He appeared just when Ghazalnus was being carried away on his sea of colours, eagerly repainting the world. He pretended to be waiting for someone else, idly twirling his chain in one hand. When Bahman approached, the young man asked in a clear, deep voice, 'Did Mullah Gharib Hajar's

95

letter ruin your life too?' He so startled Ghazalnus that the colours before him vanished, and the beauties he was gazing on took flight. The sky acquired the dull shade of the clouds, the earth its own rich brown and the horizon the colour of night. The young man had a deep voice – a dangerous one, but full of imagination.

'Who are you?' Bahman Nasser asked with trepidation.

'Your friend,' he answered.

As if he were in a dream and someone was dragging him along by a thin rope, he followed the young man, who, with all the politeness of an old-time intellectual, invited him to take a walk. He was slender, and apparently happy as he walked. His body parts moved in harmony and with rhythm. He may have hurried, but not out of confusion or any lack of certainty. He seemed to be someone with very clear knowledge of his goals. The young man didn't take Bahman too far, only opening the door of an old house in a nearby alley.

As soon as Bahman stepped into the house, he was struck by the odour of a different age. They entered the dilapidated front yard together, and were in a world that smelled of wet soil, crumbling walls and things from an older time. He saw battered, faded clothes on a washing line. They seemed to have been there for years, exposed to the rain and then dried in the sun, over and over again. An untimely wind darted wildly around the yard like a caged swallow.

The young man looked at him and said, 'This is the old house of Mullah Sukhta, your real father, the great lover; he lived and died here. Many years ago, Mullah Gharib-i Hajar and your father confronted one another in this yard. It was the first time Mullah Sukhta had explicitly stood up to him. They stood face to face under that great tree, and he defied him. Back then, Mullah Sukhta had a plan to kidnap you and raise you here, under his roof. But Hajar swore that, if he did, he would punish him by burning all the ghazal books in the world, that he would smash the tombstones of all the lovers, that he would kill himself and Mullah Sukhta too.'

'But who are you?' asked Bahman in a low voice, as he looked at the ruined world in astonishment. 'Why do you talk as if you were here on that day? Where do you know Mullah Sukhta from?'

'Your late father, Mullah Sukhta, and I were friends,' he said with sadness in his voice. 'He spent his last fifteen years here in their entirety. He didn't leave this house after Baharbanu's death. He recited ghazals here all his life. He read them day and night. I was a child when I met him. One day, I came to this yard after a ball. He was sitting on an old chair in the middle of the yard, reciting poetry like a bearded, homeless dervish. I listened to him for about an hour.

His voice didn't resemble that of any living being. Never before or since have I heard anything remotely like the tone of that voice. He was unaware of me. I looked at him, astounded. May his memory live forever, he had lost all connection with the world around him. He lived constantly in another world. That day, when he saw me, he offered me a bowl of water, telling me to drink if I was thirsty. As I drank, I was mesmerised. I became a bundle of warm emotions. I thought I had a fever; my body was pure sensation. I was a child. My body was weak, and my soul was young. When I drank from that water, I became aware for the first time that I had a body, and that my body was full of desire. That's how we became friends. I came and worked for him. I wrote down his ghazals. The cold water that tasted of the wine of Heaven was my only reward. Whenever I drank the water, I would be calm and full of hope as I sat and listened to his deep, warm voice. He didn't tell me his own story until I grew up. The first secret he told me was yours.'

Bahman Nasser looked at himself as he stood rooted to a spot that threatened sudden collapse. He didn't know where he was, or what the young man was talking about. He inspected the rubble of the house with concern. 'Mullah Sukhta died in hospital in Urmia a year ago,' he said.

'No,' The young man said, 'the one who died in Urmia was Mullah Gharib-i Hajar. Mullah Sukhta died a short while afterwards, in the hospital here. They were one soul but became two different people, and so their deaths were one death; they just occurred in two different places at two different times. They were doors on opposite sides of the same hallway. Mullah Sukhta was aware of everything to do with Mullah Hajar. I should say that the letter he sent you made him very angry. It was as if Mullah Gharib had denied Sukhta's existence until the very last moment. Until his very last breath, he had hoped Hajar would come to his senses and realise that no man can be different from what he is.'

'Mullah Hajar has explained everything to me,' Bahman said.

'Understanding those two is not easy,' said the smiling young man. 'I wrote down Mullah Sukhta's ghazals over the last few years. At the very moment that Mullah Hajar began writing a letter to you, Mullah Sukhta did the same. You should hear his letter, too. He saw the story differently.'

'Do you have the letter?' Ghazalnus asked. 'Is that why you're here now? To give it to me?'

The young man led Bahman Nasser to the pleasant-smelling ground floor, which contained nothing but a chair and a bed. It was deadly quiet, and had no windows.

'My name is Sarab Bahjat,' he said. 'My father was killed fighting in '67. Our house is now in the alley behind your house. No one knew Mullah Sukhta lived here except me. He was always alone. After you were born, the battle between Sukhta and Mullah Hajar intensified. Their treatment of one another was uniquely hurtful. One day, Mullah Hajar concluded that he should leave the house. Sukhta pursued him for a while. He wanted Mullah Hajar to kill him and set him free. He lost any desire to live. But it was obvious Mullah Hajar couldn't kill him. Killing isn't easy.

Lost and hopeless, Sukhta returned one night, and from then on he lived here. He spent most of his time on this ground floor. On some nights, he would go to the first floor and not come down until dawn. Up there was his and Baharbanu's imaginary bedroom. But he didn't allow me to go in for even a moment. I wasn't to open the door, even after his death. When I did finally go up and open the door, I realised what a fatal mistake I had made. I understood why he hadn't allowed me to go up there for years. He was a merciful man. Before three friends and I put him on a stretcher and took him to hospital, he accosted me again and warned me not to enter that room. The only person allowed to enter it was you. But my great curiosity and greedy imagination got the better of me. A day after his death, I went upstairs. I opened the door to the room quietly, as if opening it to a calamity. A cool breeze swept over me. I felt as if something powerful were slicing through my heart, a force shaking me to the core and drawing me forcefully towards it. Bahman Nasser, whoever enters that room is doomed to be alienated forever. For in that room, a breeze steals upon him and dooms him to the magic of ghazals.'

'Mullah Sukhta must have wanted me to catch that sickness,' said Bahman, taking his glasses off in the damp air of the basement. 'He must have.'

'Mullah Sukhta never read his ghazals to anyone in his entire life,' the young man said, raking a hand through his hair. 'The ghazals were part of a huge sea that ebbed and flowed in his heart. In his last years, he felt he was a failure. He was sure Mullah Hajar had defeated him and made the world forget him. His ability to be in love was his only capital. He had nothing but an eternal love, and he wanted to leave that behind to you as his legacy. He wanted the comfort of knowing there was someone who, after his death, would assume that pain, and reflect on the meaning of his ghazals. I believe that he knew no one adequate to the task but you.'

'But the house is about to fall down,' Ghazalnus said in a low, fearful voice, putting his hand on Sarab's shoulder. 'These walls and roofs can't last. The whole place smells as though it were about to collapse. I think it's had its day.'

'It's been neglected for over sixteen years,' Sarab said. 'The clothes on the washing line are from sixteen years ago. Early one morning, Mullah Hajar simply moved out. In all the years Sukhta lived here, he never tampered with a thing. There were many questions he couldn't answer. After Sukhta's death – just a few months ago – Hajar's sons came and smashed down the door. The house is registered to them at the Property Office. They came back again, two weeks ago. I was determined to approach them no matter what, and to ask them about their intentions. I learned that they were planning to demolish the place in a few days' time. I think they're right, as it's no longer fit to be lived in. Before the house is demolished, however, you were meant to come and see it. That was his very last wish in his will. He also asked me not to give you the letter too soon. We were both sure you would need plenty of time before you could understand everything.'

'I want to see the room,' Ghazalnus said. 'I have to see it. This whole story started in that room. From the day Mullah Hajar looked at the sea of stars from the window of the second floor.'

'Don't rush in to write the story before reading Sukhta's letter,' said Sarab, leading Ghazalnus inside. 'You have to read both stories carefully and compare them. As you're the owner of them both, you don't need to rush your decision.'

Sarab went ahead of him calmly. Slowly, he opened the door to the enchanted room. He took the first step inside ahead of Bahman, as if stepping into a perilous ocean. Ghazalnus rested his hands on either doorjamb. A heavenly smell assailed him. Without knowing how, exactly, he found himself in the middle of a cool breeze and a storm of rosewater.

THE REAL MAGELLAN AND THE WALLS

When I arrived at the Snow and Mirage Hotel and once again walked these streets and alleys, a voice in my heart told me, 'Go away. Pick up your suitcase and leave. What are you doing in this filthy city?' But I decided to ignore my mind's whispering. A man should be able to tell his own heart, 'Be silent, heart', should be able to shout at himself and say, 'Be silent, consciousness.'

My long experiences on land and sea, my lengthy journey from one end of the Earth to the other, across immense islands and small empires, had instilled in me the belief that I was a unique person in a unique world.

'Stop! I'm asking you to stop!' No, not you, I am not asking *you* to stop, I'm talking to these walls constantly closing in on me. You might find it strange for someone to be shouting at the walls and telling them to stop, but walls are the planet's greatest affliction. They move more than the wind, and advance more swiftly than the waves. Without walls there would be no propriety, no morals, no property and no war.

Don't blame me. I know it's not the logic of a reasonable man but it is a simple and oft-forgotten fact that we humans have brought countless miseries on ourselves just to avoid being caught in a mild drizzle or rainfall. The walls don't stop, though. I can see them closing in on me. Not for a single day have I believed in the silence and immobility of things. All creatures and inanimate objects move. They do, believe me. They all move. Listen, I'm not talking about change, but about the restlessness of things. I, more than any of you, have traversed the Earth from end to end. I have travelled more than any of you. Fretful, restless and homeless, I have wandered this planet for thousands of nights. Aimless and companionless, I have been outside hundreds of times in the rain and in storms from dusk till dawn. And still, I fear the movement of things and the vigour of creatures that appear unchanging and listless, which seem not to be moving. I am scared of all things that don't move.

Even now, I don't know what I was avoiding or seeking when I went on my travels around the Earth. Oh, my heart, my restless heart, after so many long years, so many distant oceans and continents, after all my journeys, calm or fraught, I still don't know whether I am running away from something or chasing something running away from me. Wandering and running away – that is my life. At a time when no one thought of freedom, I linked liberty to a crazy leap into the beyond ... the beyond of everything. Oh, my heart, like a madman appealing to a sea even madder than himself, since my youth I have been yelling, 'Jump, madman, jump!' Like an idiot who closes his eyes and leaps off a precipice into the raging ocean, I jumped. My friend, life is merely a mad leap. There is no such thing as a great life that does not include a blind leap. Those of you who can hear me, who are happy to see me suffer, to see me in agony and confusion, those of you who delight when a hapless Kurd returns home a failure after twenty-four years: if your lives lack such a moment, make haste to embellish them with a mad, blind leap. Man's greatness lies in jumping from a height he hasn't measured, not knowing where it will take him or where he will end.

I remember that, twenty-four years ago, I used to run away from the walls of this city. Running away from these walls was a real disease I suffered, a disease the cold of the stormy nights and the heat of the dangerous summer days could not stamp out. I am running away from walls, in vain, all the time, but that is what humans do. One day in a distant city, I came across a huge carnival. As I gazed about me, drunk on the endless beauty of life, and danced, glass of wine in hand, and sang along loudly to a Julio Iglesias song in front of an extremely beautiful black girl, I felt suddenly dizzy and almost lost my balance. For a fleeting moment, everything went dark and I thought I was going blind. Then awareness returned all at once, and at that moment I realised that all this running away was futile, in vain. Life itself, with its great beauties, its happiness and freedoms, is a colossal, endless wall, and man a frightened deer that runs alongside it. In all my long travels, I have encountered many wanderers, people like myself, all of them running away from the walls of their own houses, their own cities, their own homelands. Man runs away, thinking the wall in his alley is worse than all the other walls in the world. But when you have travelled the Earth long enough, when you have touched other walls and spent a lifetime examining them, you come to realise that the walls in your alley are, in fact, just like all the others. They are no worse, no more evil or more dangerous. No, I assure you, they are no worse. A wall is a wall, nothing more. Build them, then. Be silent and live within them. When I took my hands from that woman's waist, I saw in a flash of dark ishraq that life is full of strange and invisible walls. It is as you dance and feel completely free that you gain the fullest understanding that wherever you go, the walls will come after you.

My friends, don't look at me like that now. I've come back to my childhood town after twenty-four years of relentless wandering. I am wearing a long-sleeved shirt; I've let down my white hair, long and straight, like that of the old sailors. I've shaved my moustache and beard and I am taller now than when I left. Don't be surprised if I tell you that, against all the laws of nature, I kept on growing until I was forty-five. I've stopped now, at two metres. I look thinner and sadder than I once did. I speak many different languages, and am very knowledgeable on many subjects. I have visited most of the world's major cities. I was twenty-four when I left here. I was betrothed and in love. My only real fault was that I was a bricklayer. I became a bricklayer at the age of eighteen. When I left school, I lost interest in speaking to others and pretended to be mute. I didn't utter a single word to anyone. Even the poor girl who loved me liked the fiery letters I wrote to her. Indeed, she liked them so much that it didn't matter to her that not a word came out of my mouth, and besides, a quiet lover is a hundred times better than a talkative one. My later experiences taught me that women sometimes prefer a taciturn man to an angry and voluble one.

Feigning muteness would end in a big ordeal for me. One day, the great dictator's men came and dragged me away to build a secret prison. At the time, it was very difficult to find a competent bricklayer who couldn't speak. What they wanted was someone who couldn't tell stories or expose the design and location of the prison to other people. It seemed they had scoured the country for mute bricklayers and workers. They arrested me on a black night. I thought they were going to kill me, like all the other innocent people. However, that same night, they transferred me, together with five other mute workers, to an unknown, secret location, where my journey as a prison bricklayer began.

From the very first night, I knew they were going to make me build dark, dangerous buildings. That same night I cursed my hands, but I was too much of a coward to break one of my fingers or my whole hand or to jump off a high wall and escape. Back then, I didn't believe in taking the mad, intoxicated leaps I believe in today. They took the other workers and me from one town to another, wherever they needed to build a secret tunnel or basement. Official state documents called us 'the group of mute workers'. All those years I was afraid I would talk in my sleep, reveal my secret and get myself killed as a result. Fear prevented me getting much sleep, so I became ever weaker and more exhausted. At night they blindfolded us and took us to bases, military camps and security offices. They took us to the dark, frightening corridors of the Defence Ministry. They made us work like the slaves of old, and fed us like dogs.

I was an excellent bricklayer. Seeing me now, with my current physique, so well-groomed, you would think I was a European count or an old sailor from the Middle Ages, but you'd be wrong. Allow me to introduce myself. Me and my strange name: Zuhdi Shazaman. It is my real name; a meaningless, unrhymed and unmelodious name. Yes, I, Zuhdi Shazaman, was for a long time a mute bricklayer. Even I don't know how many secret shelters and dark prisons I built. This was what made me hate the walls.

One day the soldiers released me and brought me home in a green pickup. I was surprised to find my fiancée still waiting for me after four long years. She had saved her chastity and fiery passion for me. But I could no longer rest in any room. I had caught the disease of keeping my distance from the walls. Something in my heart told me they would arrest me again and force me to build wall after wall. The urge for freedom shook my life to the core. My fiancée was an unfortunate girl. On this occasion, I didn't want to explain everything to her in a letter. When the time came to bid her farewell and leave her for good, I told her the truth. I told her, 'There is nothing wrong with my tongue and mouth; I've always been able to speak. Always. I chose silence of my own volition. Now, I need to bid you goodbye in order to find myself.'

At that time, if you told someone 'I want to find myself', they believed you. It was a time when people went looking for themselves more often, not like nowadays when people prefer to get lost or to forget about themselves. My poor fiancée took everything I said on the chin and bade me goodbye with a gentle heart and a sad smile, saying she would remember me until death.

Since that small woman, I've never known another as simple, as guileless and as easygoing, and yet I don't once recall having felt sad to leave her. I don't recall having ever felt any great sadness for any woman in the world. I must tell you the truth: my deep fear of the walls had split me in two. My mind is always on something else. Although women occupy a big chunk of my imagination, my psychological state has always been so precarious that I believed there was more to my life than their concerns. I have always thought it will not be the wind that blows from the women's land that kills me but something else – some other secret that will suffocate me, something dark inside my very self.

After twenty-four years, I and my dark shadow returned. In those twenty-four years, I slept under many of the world's great walls; I crossed many seas. Although I have run away from walls all my life, I nevertheless visited many distant lands to look upon the famous and mythical walls they have there, to touch them and examine them. I mingled with many unheard-of tribes and nations; I drank a thousand different types of wine and slept with hundreds of women. Because I was always hurrying from one country to another, crossing from one ocean to another, I can't recall ever sleeping with the same woman twice. After that small woman, I never fell in love again. Instead, in the faraway cities and on the cold margins of the Earth, I always found a woman to sleep with me for one night, for one hour, for one memory. Until, that is, finally, in our dusty city, which outwardly seems not to have a single female skilled in the art of lovemaking, I found the amazing woman who changed my view of all women. Before then, I thought the secret lay in constantly changing the woman you take to bed, that success was the ability to melt many women's hearts. However, in our city, where it is not so easy to move between women or conduct multiple relationships, this astute young woman taught me that the secret lies not in change but in repetition. The greatest pleasure is not in the first time but in the second, third and fourth times. This delicate, masterful woman taught me that the first time is nothing but a small test, like dipping a toe in the sea. She taught me that the secret, the ultimate pleasure, is in repeating it in poetic circumstances. What a great poet she was. But here I must be silent, for I cannot tell you what happened between her and me. I simply cannot.

ATTAR AND DARSIM TAHIR
THE CIVIL WAR PERIOD

At the height of the civil war, Attar bought his very first big house. I can honestly say that he was among the pioneer builders of these vast mansions. He also invested a huge amount of his capital in purchasing plots of land that initially seemed of little value, but that he thought held great promise for the future. Attar's occupation as a great buyer of human beings dates back to some years after the afternoon he spent with Husni the Imaginative. Two years on, the man also known as 'Dew-Ears' was still a normal person, a trader in the same vein as his fellow traders, someone who had not yet violated prevailing market ethics. Attar's career as a great trader in human beings began with small steps. It was harmless and uncomplicated at first; there was nothing in it to scare anyone off. The brutal nature of his work only became clear once it was too late, once he had already become entangled in strange stories that it took the bazaar folk some time to believe.

You might find it strange that human faces could be someone's stock in trade, that he could sell people's looks. There was nothing, however, that Attar could not trade. The way a person looks is a commodity like any other, and it is up for sale. He began by finding some very special faces for an Iranian filmmaker who was seeking sad, unsmiling countenances. The director worked with amateur actors. He wanted a face that bore the shadow of infinite disaster. Our Iranian chap didn't know Attar like we do; he wasn't familiar with his talents and abilities like we are. He couldn't imagine that this big-headed, knobbly-nosed man with dull skin could understand what an artist like himself was after, what kind of actors and faces he needed. But Attar's forte was the ability to know precisely what you wanted.

On the evening Attar took the much-sought-after faces to the Iranian filmmaker, the Persian was ecstatic. He didn't know what to say. Had he been looking himself, he would not have found those sad faces even after many months. That was Attar's first transaction with a human face. From then on, he bought and sold human faces countless times. He sold some for a fabulous amount of money to a Greek photographer making a documentary about life without make-up in the East. He found dozens of hunchbacks within the space of a few hours for a specialist teaching the effects of sunlight on the natural development of the human body. No one knew where he had found so many shy, reserved hunchbacks who appeared not to have been exposed to sunlight for years. Eventually, Attar became a meticulous expert in human faces. Slowly, he came to understand the secret chemistry beneath a stare or a smile – a chemistry Attar could convert into a commodity and sell.

The dangerous facet of his business revealed itself the day he was commissioned to find a group of young knuckleheads to become bodyguards for a minister. From that day on, he established a reputation among politicians as an expensive trader in human beings, a competent individual who could buy and sell guards. He became a permanent fixture at their dinners. To begin with, he limited himself to the role of middleman between buyers and sellers, but one day he became fixated on the idea of buying people for himself. The first real person he bought was a child by the name of Shahryar the Glass-Eyed, who could see through walls. He bought the child from his grandfather for an exorbitant sum, and provided him with special accommodation. This child was the type of commodity he wouldn't sell, but would rent out for vast sums of money. One can only imagine how much money this child earned for Attar, who had not known how many jealous husbands and hesitant wives, deceitful politicians and devious merchants there were in this city until he acquired the boy.

Another time, he bought a small girl from her mother. The girl could tell you whether someone would or would not die in the following forty-eight hours. During the civil war, he hid her at a secret location and would only show her to people who paid well; at that time, the fighters desperately needed that kind of information in order to have the strength to fight. Far less glamorous was Darsim Tahir, a teenager with a big nose who could find and dig up a body on a large plot of land. It was he who would go on to tell us the stories behind Attar's children. He told us about the boy who could stop bullets; the girl who could make you fall asleep at the sight of one of her smiles; the boy who, instead of shedding tears, produced scented flowers; the girl who could change a baby's sex just by touching the mother's abdomen. Attar amassed vast wealth through these children within a few years. He bought unusual and exceptional human beings just as he collected antiques.

I have to say that Attar treated his gifted children well, in keeping with the spirit of the age. If the children didn't want to be separated from their parents immediately, he convinced them to accept a contract, which they had to sign in court. Then he would let them stay with their parents until he needed them. Everything was covered by a contract. The years he spent in the qaysaris, the local second-hand market and outside the cinemas gave him the necessary experience to buy any human being. He could soften up Party leaders, security officials and judges one way or another. Everyone, he claimed, had a weak spot you could exploit to get what you wanted. His dealings were legally faultless. The other children, the ones he bought from passers-by, he provided with new clothes, clean accommodation and a special yard to play in. He had acquired care and supervision licences from children's organisations and the juvenile courts.

More importantly, Attar was not a crazed or angry dealer. If, when haggling over an item, he noticed his opponent was obstinate and impatient, he would force a smile and say, 'My friend, don't be angry. The bazaar is synonymous with smiling. Slap on a smile, and you'll see that we can reach an agreement.' He treated his human commodities with respect. Money mattered to him above all, and a smile and respect brought money his way. He didn't engage in the ugly dealings of low and untalented men, such as buying and selling women, dealing in prostitutes under the guise of employing them as secretaries or dishonouring women on the pretext of finding them work. In that respect, I have to say that he was a decent man. He did, however, collude dangerously in many things, as you will see later on.

Although some of his deals led to disaster, deep down he believed himself innocent. That was life. He did his best to see that things went well, and to get out of any trouble in the easiest and most appropriate manner. Having said that, his children's gifts were so dangerous that he would not commit to certain jobs without setting out stringent terms and conditions. He knew the children had the capacity to unveil secrets that would lead to major disasters, which would only put all their lives at risk. In order to reduce the chances of danger and to make a hefty profit, he asked for such exorbitant fees that only a handful of the richest people could pay.

Darsim Tahir was the least profitable child, as well as one of the most obstinate he had ever bought: a big-nosed, ugly teenager who poisoned the other children's lives. Attar bought him from an Arab soldier in Baghdad in 1998. Darsim was fourteen at the time, and spoke Kurdish and Arabic fluently. He had been six years old when his father was killed in a tribal feud in one of the collective towns.[12] With his own eyes, he watched three angry men drag his father's body to the distant edge of a clearing – they had sworn to kill him and deprive him of a grave. Had they seen Darsim, they would have killed him too, but chance was on the child's side that night.

Darsim had no one in the world except for a covetous, money-grubbing maternal uncle. After his father was murdered, this heartless uncle kept him in a barn and refused to let him out for days. One hot summer night, young Darsim broke down the door of the barn and raced away to the dangerous, wolf-inhabited plains. His father was all he had had in this world. For days, he sniffed the earth in search of his body. That was when he learned he could sniff out the location of bodies underground from a great distance, then use his small hands to burrow into the soil and uncover the graves. He discovered a great many strangers' bodies over those two nights until finally, in a thorny ravine, he came upon his father's. When his uncle learned this, he realised that Darsim was a dangerous, cursed creature who would get both of them killed if he stuck around. He took him to an intelligence officer, Captain Qahtan Sabir, and told him the whole story. The captain had never heard of anyone who could locate bodies like that. He sent an urgent telegraph to the senior intelligence apparatus in Baghdad, setting out the whole affair. Baghdad responded the same night, and Darsim was bought from his uncle at a reduced cost. The greedy man handed his nephew over to the Arabs without so much as a goodbye kiss, before leaving the captain's room in his tidy turban.

Accompanied by a special armed force, little Darsim had to scour the border areas and front lines for the bodies of Iraqi soldiers temporarily buried or forgotten in the battlegrounds of the long war years. He did this for five years in different regions, and under different circumstances. He spent the whole of his childhood surrounded by the stench of the bodies of Iraqi and Iranian soldiers, as he inspected locations in the south, inch by inch. At night he was forced to sleep with the army's dogs and mules. He became someone with no sense of hygiene or aesthetics. He had no concept of humiliation, even though he was harried and hurt like a stubborn animal.

After 1993, the state dissolved the unit. Darsim remained in the service of a senior army officer, working as a groom. He lived and ate with the horses and didn't dare leave the stable because he stank of manure, a smell so overpowering that people simply couldn't bear it. By the time he turned fourteen, he felt no shame in revealing any part of his body. Like a monkey, he was oblivious to the notion of shame. In his torn Arab robe, he was capable of dreadful things, and was becoming a heavy burden to the officer. One day, through an aide, the high-ranking officer sent Darsim to the public baths, bought him new clothes, poured an entire bottle of perfume over him and sent him off in a special jeep to a station in the northern region. The man had resolved to sell him to a Kurd, even if for only a small sum, just to be rid of him. For two days they didn't meet a single Kurd willing to take this big-nosed, ugly creature, even for a pittance. On the third day, the unfortunate Attar arrived at the station on an errand after having taken care of an illegal shipment of carpets. The aide had been looking for his prey for two days, and finally, in Attar, he got lucky. After a long chat, the tired salesman enumerated Darsim's unique qualities, received a nominal fee, bade goodbye to both of them and left the station in his red beret, a happy man.

Attar hadn't known what kind of a child he had invested in. He consoled himself with the thought that the money he paid for Darsim was less than the price of a turkey. He knew that if the boy turned out to be useless, he could always pass him on to the children's organisations or the orphanages, or make up a story about him that would endear him to the head of the organisation dealing with people displaced by war. In fact, Attar would come to realise that he should have never bought Darsim Tahir in the first place, but by then it was too late.

Attar had set aside a very comfortable house for the children, where they were cared for by a loyal woman who said little. Whenever any of them had a problem, Attar would arrive at the scene. If they fell ill, he would bring along a doctor to treat them. In picnic season, he would bundle them into a van and organise a summer camp for them on the outskirts of the city. However, the arrival of Darsim Tahir – with his filthiness, nosiness, shamelessness, the lingering smell of manure on him, his unexpected and untimely pissing and his big nose, which tilted his head to one side – ruined the children's lives. Although he was bigger than the others, he was less mentally agile. He rarely spoke, and didn't know how to play. And when he did talk, he spoke of only two things: corpses and horses.

During this period, Attar tried very hard to find a use for Darsim. For a while he was constantly on the lookout for anyone who might want to locate a corpse. He asked around in the bazaar and among his friends, politicians and rich men. He was astounded to find that nobody in the country was searching for a corpse. The dead had died and then were ignored, buried and forgotten. Attar knew people were constantly getting killed in this city and the neighbouring towns. He knew that every year a number of bodies were secretly buried in shallow graves. His ambition was to diversify, to go into business finding and selling those bodies. Yet no matter how hard he tried, he couldn't understand the secret of the disappearance of the bodies or the world's indifference. People were more likely to hide the bodies or ensure the dead did not have a grave than to think about finding and unearthing them. Some of his friends advised him to knock on any door but that of death, because nothing was more dangerous than reviving the story of a corpse. 'Attar,' they told him, 'it's quite normal to take part in killing someone, but it isn't at all normal to wake that person up again.'

Attar understood what they were saying very well. After nine months, he decided to get rid of Darsim Tahir, to sell him on, but the decision meant nothing as he couldn't find a buyer. The only solution he could think of was to take him to Ghazalnus, who at the time was sheltering a group of homeless children in his house with the help of a foreign organisation.

One evening, Attar put Darsim in the front seat of his car and drove to Ghazalnus's, a mistake that a shrewd dealer of his ilk really ought not to have made. But what else could he have done with this big-nosed, good-for-nothing child?

THE BEAUTIFUL CARPETS
AND THEIR SAD WOMEN

After Trifa's arrival, the girls at the Niya factory wove many carpets that invited people to embark on imaginative journeys and mythical adventures. Trifa's carpets put the factory in the same league as other renowned manufacturers. They featured patterns and designs that had never before been seen. The most famous range, the one that introduced Trifa's trademark style to the outside world, was the 'sad sisters' series. These carpets caused such a ripple in the market that people from faraway countries came to buy them.

In one of them, a group of girls stands by the sea, their faces pensive as they weep; their tears are carried away on the wind, then turn into seagulls in the sky. In another, the same girls stand atop a rugged mountain, the wind teasing their hair, their tears turned to sparrows. In a third, the girls weep inside a boat, their tears turning to fish in the water. In another, they bend over books, their tears already butterflies in the air.

This series was followed by 'the girls and the cuckoos', 'the night princesses' and 'the intoxicated female huntresses'.

From 1990 to 1992 – between the invasion of Kuwait and the establishment of the first government in Kurdistan – sales dropped significantly, but the Niya factory never stopped production. On the contrary, during the looting that followed the 1991 uprising, Abdulaqadir Niya got his hands on some new machinery and parts and installed them in two newly built halls. During that period, Trifa and the other girls became obsessed with their work, virtual prisoners of their imaginations. They worked round the clock, as if hypnotised. Trifa's imagination seemed to bewitch the entire factory, propelling it forward; even the machinery appeared to have adopted the same rhythm and responded to the same magic.

For two years, Trifa and another female colleague slept at the factory. In those hard times, when people from central and southern Iraq fled to Kurdistan, Trifa's mother Fawziya Yasami was harassed out of her home by her son Jawhar and took refuge with one of her gracious brothers in Baghdad, where eventually she died. Initially, Fawziya had wanted to take Trifa with her; but when she heard all sorts of stories and saw for herself how the police and security forces behaved towards the women of that unfortunate city, she changed her mind and accepted that Trifa should stay in her job. The women at the factory worked relentlessly. Even during the uprising and the 1991 mass exodus that shocked the world, they never took a break from their work. That work took them out of history, as though they were living in a different land. It had been many long years since they had taken any pleasure in their weaving and their work, but the arrival of Trifa and her dreams put happiness back in their souls and their fingers.

No matter what historical era someone works in, if their work is devoid of imagination, they move closer to death. That is why Trifa, with her rich imagination, brought everyone closer to life. The carpets gave her a means of recording her wild gift. Before coming to the factory, she had seen herself as a patient, tormented needlessly by a dangerous delirium. She knew no use for the fantasies dancing in her head, with their many shapes and colours; there is nothing more painful. Before the death of her father, Zahir Yabahri, she had been to see a psychiatrist. True, the dark-skinned, cheerful girl could be open with strangers without going over the top, befriending them instantly, soon removing any barriers between herself and others. True, she was always charming. Yet, at home, she appeared lonely, sad and gloomy. She often said: 'The smell of my life is like the smell of an extinguished oil lamp; the smell of my body is like the smell of a fireplace that has suddenly gone out.'

There were times when the torrent of these obsessions and images overwhelmed her, and she took to her bed for weeks. She felt as if the bed were made of sticks, the sheets of ashes, as if she had been plunged into a huge barn full of hay in wet clothes and that her own body, from head to toe, was made of hay. She would run to the bathroom and look at her feeble body. In short, she was tormented by her fantasies. But at the carpet factory, she was happy. Her delirium shed its bleakness and took on a colourful appearance.

For all her cheerfulness, her carpets were full of sad girls. It was rare for one of them not to feature a girl in tears. In the factory, her understanding of her own imagination increased, and the charm of her ideas deepened as she grew closer to the poor factory girls. The experience convinced her that no human being lacked a profound imagination, but most people simply didn't have enough time to reach into their souls to discover the contents. Her female friends worked various shifts, but she was there all the time, relieving

Galawezh of a great burden: before Trifa's arrival, she had taken care of all the girls on her own. Most of them were sad women with tear-filled eyes. Their problems, however, were not the kind that could be solved. Most were the daughters of poor villagers who had been expelled from their lands, and now they had to make a living. What Trifa saw when she started work was a group of quiet, shy girls who wore hangdog expressions and kept their heads down as they moved their hands across the machinery. The fear in their eyes and their cowed expressions pained her, but the factory's cold atmosphere and its large, unfurnished space stirred nothing in the listless girls but sadness.

In the mornings, whether in the cold gusts of winter or summer's gentle breezes, they alighted from an old bus in their dirty scarves; in the evenings, they returned home with fingers bent and bloodstained. Their scarves and cloaks smelled of sweat and hunger. All they knew was working for Sayyid Qadir Niya and bickering among themselves. Trifa's arrival completely changed their lives. They treated her like a beloved sister and had nothing but respect for her, despite a touch of jealousy. None of them opened their hearts to her quickly, but then again, how could these vulnerable, unfortunate girls open their hearts to her at all? Did they even know they had hearts, or what it was to open them to someone else?

It took Trifa a long time to get to know them one by one, and to get to like them all; but slowly, she won their hearts, and after a year of their company she began to see the bottom of the ocean of grief that each one of them carried. We shouldn't assume that Trifa had planned any of this: imagination gave the girls the courage to speak. The imagination is as slow as a tortoise. It takes a long time to learn to move. As Trifa considered how to translate her visions into carpet designs, the golden drops of her imagination slowly fell like raindrops upon the girls. No sooner had they finished a carpet than they gathered around it eagerly, examining it closely and applauding. Although shy, they were impressed. Their trust grew day by day in this girl, who seemed to have come from another planet.

When she was at work, Trifa Yabahri would sit on a chair, shut her eyes and delve into her imagination. Then she would copy her intricate images, thread by thread, onto the carpets, telling the weavers what to do. She was like the composer of a symphony who had all the notes in her head. The girls found that they couldn't stop working, despite themselves. They became so immersed in Trifa's dream that it became their own. They all noticed that Trifa grew paler and paler in her chair, that she *became* imagination, that she became transparent. Those who worked the night shifts said there were moments when she disappeared altogether, that she ceased to have a body and became pure fantasy.

It is my belief that most humans are not daring enough to fantasise on their own. We need to be near someone rich in fantasy in order to reach out and open the door to their own store. Fear of imagination is deeply rooted in the human soul, because no one knows where their imagination might take them, what doors it might open. Our fear of the imagination is greater even than our fear of scorpions, dragons or ravenous wolves.

All the female workers at the factory were young, their ages ranging from fourteen to thirty. Three of them were unhappily married. One was married to a drunk who beat her at night, so she often turned up to work with a black eye. Another was married to a disturbed individual who rarely left his bed, convinced his enemies were lying in wait outside to kill him. The third had a decent, generous husband, but he had lost a hand in the war and could not work. Befriending Trifa took these unfortunate women to another world, where grief was not just grief but the thread that connected their suffering souls. On the cold shop floor, amid the squeaky machinery, they were now as addicted to Trifa's fantasies as an alcoholic to drink; they took flight with her, no longer feeling their exhaustion or their aches and pains, and forgot their domestic misery and poverty. Imagination provided them with a land of their own, a land you and I, poor things that we are, cannot see.

The carpets produced by the Niya factory were no longer contained sets of dizzying arabesques, symbolising ancient times and forgotten religions. Rather, they were works teeming with expectations and devoid of repetition.

As the years went by, the girls learned to tell Trifa their stories. They learned to dream not only about the designs in the carpets, but about their own lives and futures. At lunch, they would argue over who should sit next to Trifa to tell her their story. Trifa, with her broad smile and dark, hairy arms, would say, 'So, dear Shiler, tell me. What do you want to say?' ... 'My delicate Naznaw, what's bothering you? Why are you so sad? What are you thinking about? My dear friend, your eyes hold enough sadness to melt a stone. What is it, dear?' ... 'Gizing, when I see you, so quiet and shy, I wonder, "God, how does this girl cope?" Just open your eyes a little ...'

And eventually, they would speak – about the beautiful things they desired, the young men they longed for with all their hearts. They were no longer cold, dead people, suppressed under headscarves and shyness. Their relationship with life changed. After each carpet was completed, after each dip in the sea of imagination, they grew braver. Sayyid Qadir Niya was astonished to see the girls happier and braver in the space of only a few years. They never shed the facets of poverty, but now they could do things they had not dared to do before. Imagination is nothing but the extreme end of bravery, a bravery that could often be fatal.

MULLAH SUKHTA'S LETTER

When Bahman was touched by the breeze of love inside that chamber, a universal love was born inside him that stayed with him until his death. Very few people experience the moment they fall in love – not in the simple human sense of 'being in love', when you suddenly feel in thrall to another human being and are unable to do without them or to stop thinking about them, nor in the religious or Sufi sense of love as a profound relationship with the Creator, but rather in the sense of a great force that makes people care for others, makes them aware of a profound connection to all life and makes them weep for other human beings, whoever or wherever they may be; in the sense that we fall in love with human suffering and love others because they suffer, because they are eternal victims and forever alone in their suffering.

Ghazalnus would later interpret his entire life in light of the breeze he encountered in that lovers' chamber. He considered it the real moment of his birth. He believed that every human being has two birthdays: the day they are born, and the day they discover the meaning of their births. It was an experience beyond the limited ability of language to express. The air that entered his body felt as though it had travelled the far-flung reaches of the world; as though it had gathered up the hidden perfumes of faraway lands, then emptied them into his soul; as though it had brought with it gardens with deep roots and planted them in his heart; as though it had brought the sun and all its rays and hid them there. It was as though it reduced the ocean to a single wave and poured it into him; as though he was being given a new body, plunged once more into a vortex and born again.

It was a feeling beyond the power of words, something that memory could not retain, nor consciousness interpret; an experience the imagination could only retrieve or reconstruct afterwards. In the midst of the storm, Ghazalnus began to understand a great truth about his life. Until then, he had been just a simple young man, misunderstanding everything: a stupid, poor-sighted youth who thought repainting the streets would rid him of his boredom, and the world of its evils. He thought that repainting the streets and reconstructing the alleyways in his head would change his life. He was a fool. An utter fool. After a long night of deliberation, deeply intoxicated with an air that filled his bones with the bouquet of a magical wine, a dizzy Ghazalnus spoke in his agony and said, 'To have imagination is to understand the truth.'

That night, Ghazalnus read Mullah Sukhta's letter, the one written in the same style as Mullah Hajar's. It read as if it had been written by the same person in a different state of mind. For the sake of brevity, and so that you can experience this strange story first-hand, you ought to have a look at an excerpt from the letter. This is how it starts:

It is hard for an old man like myself, with one foot in the grave and but a breath away from death, to toy with another's life. Yet it is no less difficult to take leave of the finite world with you knowing nothing of me. In the end I am, rather than a father, an apparition that comes to speak the truth. I am an old man, and my experience has given me a sense that the great truths are akin to the imagination. People see naught but the surface of this world. They do not apprehend the world as a great truth. They mistake the surface of this complex world for the truth. Still, whatever else, man is a fine creature, and this world is his home. This world is home to this magical creature, his present and eternal residence. Without the presence of man, existence is like a sleeping animal. There is no absolute power to be aware of its infinity, and no Supreme Being to understand his own superiority. It is man alone who has awareness of the finite and the infinite, the high and the low, who places a high value upon gold and none at all on refuse.

Mullah Sukhta continues in the same vein, in the very words used by Mullah Hajar:

Our dear Bahman, I have come this far and now stand between life and death. This moment is impossible. I am very close to bowing out like the humblest of slaves. The world has sapped my energy and sadness all my power. Old age has gnawed at my flesh and bones for years, and has not yet taken its last bite. My soul is empty, my body exhausted, my desires gone. There is a secret that you must know, a secret deeper than the secret of death and more infinite than the mystery of life. It is something that you may choose to believe in, or to regard as the hallucination of an old man who could die at any moment. I have borne the pain of it throughout my life. Now you are grown, you will understand that had I opened my mouth any earlier than this, I would have done so in vain, and all I might have written would have been without meaning. The only living being who can understand this tale is a person who understands love; that is, a person able to reason. Only God knows whether or not you are such a person ... Only God, and He alone. Do I, who impose this difficult task, this strange duty, on your newly awakened heart – do I myself understand love? Is there any human being who does? Who understands that it is a divine mystery, a holiness of so high an order, it is far beyond the ken of you or me?

Our dear Bahman, eighteen years ago, on a clear night, I was lost in contemplation of the sea of stars when there came a knock at my door. It was a dour-faced old man, his gaze like that of the devils on the covers of ancient tomes that speak of Hell. He was a strange old man who knew by heart every ghazal I knew, who could recite any poem I had written better than I could myself. He introduced himself as a part of me. He portrayed himself as my shadow, my other half. He was stonehearted and merciless. He said: 'I am your other half, the half you have incarcerated inside a dark and dangerous cellar for thirty-five years. I am your stifled and unfortunate half.'

And I believed him.

I don't know how to open up my heart to you. We are created in such a way that the moment we come close to love, we shatter something. Do not be shocked therefore, or taken aback, if at the moment of the final handover, my shaking hands and defeated soul succumb to this ailment and still more is shattered. My son, for eighteen years I have kept the secrets I am telling you now at the back of a shelf, as if inside a glass container full of them, placed behind other glass containers. Doddery old man that I am, I must now climb a broken ladder, the ladder of my hesitations and cowardice, and from the top rung of the fears and apprehensions of my seventy years of ghazals, with my wrinkled fingers I must throw the glass containers in the air one by one and shatter things.

At the moment of death, a man should open his box of secrets so that later he may have a proper understanding of the divine verdict. As he hands over his soul, he must have the courage to stare at its light. If not, what will he talk about with the One, the Omnipotent? Now I must sharpen my eyesight, take down my book of secrets and write my colourful letter.

The old man was me, myself, when I fell for a shy, noble and most honourable woman. There is no one unluckier. When I die, sick, bedraggled insect that I am, I shall pluck up the courage to tell the Lord of all creation that no one is so unlucky as he who is condemned to fall in love with a modest woman.

Although by then I was no longer an adolescent but a young spirit, love remained a major part of my existence. My entire soul was made up of praise of the beloved, the ghazal of her kindness. When that aggressive, sour-faced old man appeared in my room, it was a blessing from God Almighty and the Prophet that I still cherish to this day. One day I woke up and found myself in love with this modest woman, whose name was Baharbanu, and who was your late mother – may her grave tonight be filled with more light than any other night. Love is an immense honour. Nature bestows it only upon a select few. Nothing, no matter how great or infinite, can rival it in serenity.

Then, too, love is the one thing made by man alone, the one thing in which the Devil has no hand. Nor is God its starting point. God Himself is beloved, and the truly beloved does not create love. God is love's subject, not its creator. If He were its creator, He would be a false lover; it would be like my hiding a golden box among your treasure purely for you to return it to me. Only the ignorant and the uninitiated think love is created by God. God is not so unskilled a player as to bestow love so that He might be beloved by you … dear Lord, the idea is an offence against the Creator. Love is the one thing that lacks any contribution from both God and the Devil. In the latter's case, he is excluded from love: it goes not near his domain and remains apart from all his tricks. Whoever would allege a connection between the Devil and love is nearer to the former than the latter. The Devil exists. He comes to kill love. It is not that love exists and the Devil has a hand in it. Whoever attributes love to God or to the Devil, or sees things from such a perspective, merely uses an interpreter's skills to degrade man. Man's greatness or his smallness is made manifest in love. The power of love is the sole barometer of humanness, one greater than all the rest. Neither faith nor morality is the barometer of our souls. The power of love is the essence of man. Whoever lacks the power to love, lacks everything.

My son, do not look at me as if I were a disgraceful old man with trembling hands and a soul still full of worldly greed. I have always been a slave to the human within me. Unless man is such a slave, he cannot be the slave of God. And yet, we humans see ourselves as weak and worthless, because the Devil in all his danger whispers always in our ears: 'Ignore yourself, ignore yourself, ignore yourself. Dissolve in the Creator, vanish in the Divine love.' Because the moment man forgets himself, he becomes nothing. When man loses all love of himself, he becomes a wolf. His essence is lost, for his essence is love. No creature can come to God if he loses himself. Hence man must use his reason, for it is not God who asks us to dissolve in His love but the Devil. God immersed His own love in human love, so that human love becomes the prerequisite for loving God. And yet, when God blessed me with love, the doubting old man inside me, the one who reluctantly recited ghazals with me, lost all patience with me and my ghazals and emerged from his black cellar, both truth and fantasy. He was me, and yet at the same time was not me. Yes, my son, rest assured, you were born from me, and not from him.

Dear Bahman, I started out as a mullah. I received the religious education of the time. My real name is Mullah Gharib-i Hajar. Like most mullahs, I saw little conflict between being a mullah and writing ghazals. Ghazal-writing is an old art we inherited from the mullahs. When I chose my pen name, Mullah Sukhta, I was merely following a practice common among the poets before me. Until the point when I had written a good few poems and brought out my first collection. Thereupon my strange doubts increased to become an overwhelming fear, as if an invisible axe within me was chopping me in two. I felt I was being inwardly taken to pieces. I did not know what had befallen me. It was a force that pulled in two directions, so that I was obliged to live a double life. On one hand, like any pious mullah, I was married and cared deeply for my honour. On the other, I was enchanted by an incredible love, and, although I did not know what it was or where it had sprung from, it bore me away. On one hand, a being within me spoke ghazals like a bird singing; on the other, an earnest and serene mullah praised God with all the might of a true believer.

My inner struggle was not between good and evil, or love and hate. No, dear Bahman, it would be foolish to liken my internal schism to man's common division between good and evil. Deep within themselves, all human beings are riven by good and evil. It takes little insight to realise that good and evil are in conflict in the human soul. The conflict in my own was not between two creatures. Mullah Hajar and I differed in one thing only: that he was timid, while I was free-spirited. I have reflected on the people of this country for a long time. I have not come across a single human being who is so great a sinner, so guilty a spirit, that one might say, 'Dear God, this is the type of man for whom you created Hell. He deserves no less.' I am convinced that Hell is merely a metaphor, conceived with the sole purpose of underlining and understanding Heaven. Man is too pure a creature to deserve Hell.

Hajar was not a bad man. He had all my desires and wishes, but his fears grew year by year. The more poetry I wrote, the more in love I was, the more scared he became. We discussed at length whether I was forcing him to divide his world in two, or whether *he* was forcing *me*. Increasingly, he stifled me, laying undue claim to all I had. He went to my wife and slept with her. He believed all my legitimate children were his. He regarded me as a wild animal living in a rickety shed on his huge swathes of land. He saw himself as a garden of faith in which a single weed had not grown. On some nights, as a lover reciting ghazals, I would seize the opportunity and lie down with my wife. I slept with her as one skilled in all the arts of lovemaking. When he woke up, he acted like a wounded tiger, scratching me all over my body. I looked on as he had hurried, hasty sex, and said: 'Mullah Hajar, enjoy life's pleasures, take pleasure in your own body. Sex like this is an offence against nature.' And yet, day after day and year after year, he isolated me. Like a dog guarding a treasure, he drove me into such dark corners that had it not been for the light of love, I would surely have gone blind.

Fear and trepidation increasingly got the better of him, leaving him so overwhelmed, he could no longer see any light. Many a night he would weep on my shoulder, and his weeping made my heart go out to him. He wanted to live like me, to go out, to gaze upon beauty, to know pleasure, drink alcohol and sing amid the cupbearers and the wineglasses, but he could not. In those days, I secretly continued writing ghazals at night, but whatever I wrote at night, Mullah Hajar tore to pieces in the day. I knew we could not co-exist any more – a shameless writer of ghazals and an insipid, pious man have nothing in common. A time came when Baharbanu's love severed all ties between Mullah Hajar and me; Baharbanu and I found ourselves pitted against his will. We created you in opposition to his will and that of the modest, bashful Baharbanu, a condition that greatly tormented that passionate woman. My dear Bahman, we are each of us made up of different creatures. Man is a colourful entity, a ball painted in thousands of hues, and if you rotate it slowly, you will see that each tiny section reveals a different colour and characteristic. Only a fool speaks of human nature as fixed. Man is an army, comprising a multitude of creatures inhabiting a single entity.

The letter soon moves on to more recent developments:

After Mullah Hajar's death, I stayed in that house like a homeless ghost. My life was nothing but an infinite dance in praise of the beloved. Day and night, I paced that place. The smell of the nights I had spent with Baharbanu was stirred within me. The room had become home to the lightning storm of love. For years, I slept with Baharbanu in this house. It is a wasteland on the surface, but a heavenly garden underneath. I protected it like a security guard. I scared people away from this house of love, like a menacing phantom. Troubled by all the scenes of debauchery, Mullah Hajar fled. Baharbanu and I were two eternal ghosts, and this was our home. I would reach out for that very door and enter the room, barefoot and empty-handed. I would wait until she arrived. There is nothing more pleasant or more awful than awaiting the beloved. Before her arrival, all kinds of scents and fragrances brought by merchants from faraway lands would rain down on my soul. Winds from distant seas and the gentle breeze of the oceans that tame the wild ships bore me away. Flowers of every sort sprang up within me. Love is a kingdom with two gates: one for little creatures, which dip briefly into the ocean of love then emerge once more, the other for swimmers of a different kind, who dive into the sea of love and head for its bottomless depths, relentlessly and without respite, until death. I went in through the second gate.

For many years, I did nothing except write ghazals. Love was my only food, and loving words, my only harvest. My collection grew bigger and bigger – so big, in fact, that I imagined no other soul had written as many ghazals as I had, nor praised humanity and love as much. Now that I am dying, these ghazals are my only legacy to you: hundreds of thousands of couplets, which not only praise the beloved but extend that praise to the whole of the human race, to the endless beauty of humanity. What could an old ghost like me leave behind apart from ghazals? Ghazal after ghazal, all collected in massive volumes and placed in great sealed boxes. You are the only heir to these poems; you are the only creature made by God who can touch them. I am not an offspring of Adam; nor do I belong to the Umma of God's beloved prophets. I have been nothing but a ghazal writer.

So immersed was I in the sea of the beloved that I had no route to climb to the light and think about publishing my poems. My poetry was born in the sea of secrets, uttered by a soul that had lost its way to the world. I have nothing for you except a bundle of keys and dozens of ghazal-filled boxes. This is your destiny. You are the one who can introduce these ghazals to the world. You are the one who can disseminate my poems among the people.

Mullah Sukhta's letter is too long for this book. It is too profound, and too dark for every reader to fathom its secrets. When Bahman Nasser finished reading it, he put it down and looked at the sea of stars outside his window. He looked at the world with unrivalled love. He watched the breeze playing in a few distant trees; the scent of the faraway seas of love, which came from some other part of life, wafted over him. He put down his glasses and ran his fingers through his hair. He inhaled the moisture of the nearby gardens. He was aware of birds coursing through the sky like shooting stars. But these were all tricks of his imagination. He let out a deep sigh and placed his hand on his heart. He felt that even he was a figment of the imagination, a mythical scent carried on the wind towards an unknown destination.

FIRST ENCOUNTER BETWEEN GHAZALNUS AND TRIFA YABAHRI IN SAYFADIN MARO'S HOUSE

EARLY WINTER 1992

In the early winter of 1992, Attar and the white-moustached Husni Mardini, with his loud laughter and bazaar-merchant's intuition, arrived at Ghazalnus's house. Husni was sure their reason for visiting was as good as their intentions.

The idea of a 'tutor of the imagination' was new to Ghazalnus, though it was the kind of notion that was not alien to his realm.

This was Ghazalnus's first meeting with Attar. He couldn't recall ever having seen a man with such a big head. Although Attar acted the part of a small, shy man in Husni Mardini's company, in his heart of hearts he felt assured that he could demonstrate his supremacy if he wanted to; he could do extraordinary things, things of which Husni was incapable. Today, however, he needed to keep Husni on side. Whenever he needed something from somebody, he diminished himself in their presence; he regarded this as one of his many great tricks. He considered himself the master of all rare things, and believed he knew all the important people there were to know – so he was surprised he'd never met this Ghazalnus before.

Ghazalnus had been through a lot by then. He had long, unkempt hair and a thick beard. He was no longer the thin, shy poet of his earlier years, but increasingly resembled a lost poet or a desperate dervish. His gaze was that of a sad physicist struggling in a huge lab. There was calm, maturity and depth in it, something that set him apart from other people and was difficult to understand or penetrate. He was a complicated person, but to Attar he seemed so simple and easygoing it was as if there was something out of place. He had never seen such a simple person before, into whose eyes he could look and discern no worldly desires. The bazaar had taught him to understand every human gesture, to assess people by tone of voice and expression, but Ghazalnus's simplicity left Attar clueless. All the knowledge he had gleaned from the bazaar was futile here; the bazaar seemed completely alien to this man. Ghazalnus agreed so quickly to the idea of becoming a tutor of the imagination that it frightened Attar. If the bazaar and its transactions between customers and vendors all worked like this, life would be hell. He had spent all his days mastering the science of the bazaar; if it became worthless, he'd have no other skills. Haggling with Ghazalnus had been meaningless and disappointing. He felt he hadn't achieved anything, had failed to use his arts, that this deal had taught him nothing about this man who sat there in his olive-coloured shirt and jumper looking altogether content.

'A tutor of the imagination,' Ghazalnus said. 'A tutor of the imagination ...' Without making any enquiries, without asking who Sayfadin Maro or Mahnaz were, or what the girl's problem might be, he agreed to the offer as if accepting an invitation for a trip he had always wanted to take. Husni, who understood Attar's confusion very well, recognised that he was poised between two souls from opposite poles that would never meet: the world of the market and the world of the imagination. Husni laughed so loudly that the walls of Ghazalnus's bare room shook. It was an empty room, containing nothing but a few plastic chairs. He could hear the sound of children, their laughter and calls, coming through the wall. He hadn't, until then, been aware that Ghazalnus had any children, but he was more taken aback by the bareness of the room than the sound of them playing. Every time Husni laughed, the echo of his own voice startled him, and he looked with silent astonishment at the great empty space.

Nothing worth mentioning, nothing Attar could take credit for, had happened. Alas, it had all been so easy – child's play. Without asking any questions or complicating things, Ghazalnus agreed to accompany this man with the big head, who looked like an ambassador from Hell, to Sayfadin Maro's home the following evening after dusk.

Had he not had the strange encounter with Galawezh later that day, and had the sleepy woman not given him a light grilling, he would have felt he had wasted a whole day of his life.

The next day, Trifa Yabahri told Attar: 'I am overwhelmed by all the work to be done here. The carpet factory really needs me right now – the work doesn't get done if I'm not around. It's very hard to do anything else on top of it. But just a moment. Maybe on Fridays, my day off, I could give Mahnaz lessons in the evenings. Unfortunately, I'm not available any day but Friday. I've always got something to do, you see. There's just too much work at the factory; it doesn't leave time for anything else, especially right now when demand for our products has grown. I appreciate you thinking of me, but please don't be upset that I don't have any time bar Fridays. I'll come and give it a go, and if I like it, I'll do it.'

Attar only needed one tutor of the imagination, but to show the full extent of his versatility, he wanted to take on two. In addition, he wanted to know what kind of people these tutors were, and exactly what it was they did. He hid his satisfaction and agreed to take Trifa to Sayfadin Maro's home that evening, after dusk.

The first time Ghazalnus saw Trifa was in Sayfadin Maro's big living room. That scene – the red furniture, the smell of the perfume worn by Shams and her daughter Mahnaz – would never fade from either of their memories. For years, the waves of their imaginations would swell as the vision of that evening resurfaced. Many years later, as Trifa's hands lay in Ghazalnus's during a dark hour of farewell and she asked him about that evening, it would all come back to him: the combined scents of 'Tea Rose', 'Hawaii' and 'One-Man Show'; the smell of the plastic flowers in the corner of the room; the thin, orange curtains; the tiny golden flowers in the blue vases; the white light of the fluorescent bulbs that hung from the ceiling; the soft velvet of the sofas; the smell of the leather armchairs; Shams's white knees peering from under her tight skirt; Mahnaz playing the role of shy princess. There was nothing in that living room that they could not remember. They even remembered its two big paintings: one of a rabbit running towards a fire, heading straight for the blaze of a burning forest, the other depicting a dark night and an abandoned boat on the shore of a tranquil lake.

Shams was a pale, fine-looking woman, and Sayfadin Maro a bald man with a huge head. When he sat down, his body spilled over his seat like melting nylon, the bundles of fat sagging from the sides of his thighs and buttocks and drooping from his stomach to below his waistline. Mahnaz was an exquisite girl. There she sat, in a pair of black trousers and a white T-shirt. She had straight, blonde hair, small, pursed lips and light brown eyes set above narrow, white cheeks. She was so beautiful that neither Attar nor Ghazalnus spent much time looking at Trifa, who was not the type of girl to be hurt by such things.

But right from that very first evening, Trifa felt spiritually drawn to Ghazalnus. Ghazalnus, with his curly hair and small glasses, was not the type of man people fell for at first sight, but there was something about him, a special look, something you only find in certain people, a sort of attractiveness that has nothing to do with beauty. At times it's even stronger than beauty. It is like the glow of faith, like suddenly feeling you're in front of a sheet of clear glass, standing before someone who brings nothing but light.

The sight of Sayfadin Maro and his wife Shams, though, frightened Trifa. The minute she set eyes on the serene Shams and Sayfadin's strange eyes, she decided not to return to their house. Obviously, at the time, she had no idea how or under what circumstances fate would bring her back to these rooms. When she returned to the carpet factory, she tried to get Ghazalnus out of her head, tried not to think about him all night long, but to no avail. Trifa could not forget his presence, his looks, his posture. She had succumbed so much to the young man's appearance, his way of speaking and his expressions, that she nearly phoned Attar to ask for his address; but a deep feeling of womanly propriety held her back. She was aware that Ghazalnus had shown barely any interest in her, but that didn't matter. What mattered was that he seemed to be innocence personified. He looked like someone she already knew, someone she thought she could win over very quickly, someone she could reach out to no matter how far away he was. She was sure this man would play a role in her life, but what role exactly, she couldn't tell.

That day Mahnaz's fiancé was there too. He was a tall, black-moustached young man, the type who, if he wore suits in the morning, would switch to traditional Kurdish garb in the evening, and if he wore sharwal and mirakhani in the afternoon, would change into a pair of trousers and a shirt in the evening; the kind in whom frequent changes of the style and colours of his outfits revealed a deep feeling of insecurity. His posture and expression revealed the same self-doubt. He pretended to possess a certain aura of solemnity, which in fact he lacked. He held a long string of prayer beads. He looked at the guests from under his thick eyebrows, but said nothing. Attar knew him. His name was Najo Ashkani, and he was a veteran peshmerga who had come onto the bazaar scene after the uprising with a great deal of money. He mixed with a number of currency traders and powerful officials, clearly on the lookout for a big break. Handsome though he was, he was not very likeable.

Najo was one of many people to become very upset about this whole tutor-of-the-imagination business. He wanted to marry Mahnaz as soon as possible, but was held back by Shams's determination. Although he sometimes took on the role of a man who has the final say, he could do nothing in the face of Shams's determination, imposed with a woman's delicate touch. He was completely powerless. Shams wanted her daughter to finish university at any cost, and she made it a condition of the marriage agreement. News that a university would soon be opening had wound all the city's rich and eminent families into a frenzy. How could her daughter be the only one to miss out? It was unthinkable. She would rather die than be so humiliated. I have to say that Mahnaz had no special feelings for this fellow, who only knew how to talk to veteran peshmergas and money-men. Six months after their engagement, a veil of shyness and formal respect continued to dominate their meetings and outings. When they went to a new restaurant, a party or a picnic, most of the time they had nothing to say to one another. Mahnaz felt she had become closed and withdrawn. True, Najo had a virile handsomeness, but he was not the gentle-youth type who could quench Mahnaz's teenaged fantasies.

The two had first met at a party held on Nawroz, the Kurdish New Year, and Najo at once decided to ask for her hand in marriage. The presence of Party colleagues and acquaintances who knew Sayfadin had made the whole affair easier. Mahnaz said nothing when she heard about the proposal. Of course, she could have said, 'No, I don't want to marry him,' but there was something about his appearance that made it hard to turn him down. When her girlfriends saw his picture, they said, 'You'd have to be mad not to want to marry him! How many young men like him are there in the city?' Her father said he would have a bright future in the Party. Initially, her mother did not want her to marry this man, who, she said, still smelled of the village stable. It was true. When Najo wore a suit and tie, he looked very much the equal of the engineers and rich men of the city, but Shams was aware that he had no qualifications, was almost illiterate and lacked the appropriate manners for the public gatherings of our time. In addition, she would say, the city is full of beautiful village girls worthy of him; we have doted on our daughter and given her only the very best – she isn't right for him.

I have to say, Shams was right. Although Mahnaz was indifferent to the matter, if we bring suitability and compatibility into the equation, Najo should have married a cousin of his who was besotted with him. He, however, had an eye to the future. He had become close to a Party official and, by using his money, had rapidly found a foothold in the market. Marrying Sayfadin Maro's daughter would open another door. Moreover, she was as delicate as a flower. No matter how much he tried, he could no longer take an interest in the village girls, some of whom he had tried out in his years as a peshmerga. He had sworn that his future wife would be a jeans-wearing city girl – and the cream of the crop, to boot.

Najo Ashkani developed a grudge against Ghazalnus from that evening on. It was the type of grudge everyone experiences at least once in their life. There is no specific reason for it, and yet it is stronger, more lethal and longer-lasting than an ordinary one. Najo was the type of man who hated those who knew something he didn't know or understand. He was the type who frequented only one kind of get-together, who can only open up to certain types of people and only delight in a few subjects. His father-in-law had told him about the tutor of the imagination the day before. (As his daughter's fiancé, he needed to be informed about everything.) He had been well briefed about each of the private tutors they had hired previously, and none of them had stirred any fear or jealousy in him. Saeed Bio, Khasraw Algebra, Ala Squared, Maja Excellence the English teacher? No, none of them had the looks to make Najo Ashkani – the handsome chap from Brigade 133, the smartly dressed peshmerga of the hard days of the revolution – feel jealous, or to make him think of them as his match.

When he first saw Ghazalnus, though, he was startled. Needless to say, he considered himself handsomer and better positioned; he knew Ghazalnus could not compete with his physique, his moustache, his eyes or his eyebrows. And yet he saw something in him that he couldn't pin down – something he didn't even have words for. When they shook hands, he felt a pleasant coolness. He was sure it was a sensation that would move women. In addition, his outward appearance, his face and the way his voice perfectly matched his appearance gave him a unique quality that was impossible to ignore. Oh God, what could his real name be? Could there be someone whose given name is 'Ghazalnus'? Najo observed Mahnaz until the end of the encounter. He noticed how she looked at Ghazalnus, but saw no cause for concern. In fact, no one could detect anything in her expression. Her face was unreadable. Not even Attar, shrewdest of them all, read anything in it.

That evening, Shams went on and on about how she wanted her daughter to continue her studies, while Sayfadin, without much thought for his daughter's feelings, insisted she was too stupid to be expected to achieve anything. What astonished Trifa was that although the father's words were very hurtful, they didn't seem to upset Mahnaz. Although the whole meeting was dedicated to discussing her feeble intelligence, her expression didn't change for a moment. Trifa could not tell whether Mahnaz's calmness was due to lack of brains or extreme self-confidence.

Ghazalnus said, 'Imagination takes a long time to master – it's not all that easy to play with it. There are two types: one of them is harmful because it takes us further away from seeing the truth, while the other transforms human beings. It allows them to live in two worlds at the same time, helping them understand reality better.'

Ghazalnus did not intend to elaborate much further, as there seemed to be no one present who could understand such a lengthy explanation of the imagination. But, though she chose to say nothing at the time, limiting herself to one of her big smiles, these few words left a very deep impression on Trifa. Sayfadin deemed the whole matter of the private tutors a fruitless business stage-managed by his wife. Yet Shams continued to maintain that the girl didn't need a tutor to explain biology and physics to her like a parrot, but someone who could open up her imagination. After lengthy deliberation, they agreed that Ghazalnus would give her lessons twice a week – and that this would be the very last contribution Sayfadin made towards his daughter's education.

That night, none of those present at the meeting could sleep in peace. They all thought something had changed in their lives, without knowing exactly what. Ghazalnus's presence in the house had abruptly turned everything upside down, and now they all felt shocked, as if Ghazalnus had brought with him the air of a different world. Sayfadin, who for the past year had heard nothing except the blabber of Party officials and Shams's whining, was more unsettled than anyone else. He was worried that this imaginative man would erase what he had taught his family over many years of hard work. He had tried to impress on his family that life was a set of battles, of impositions, of having to grow accustomed to certain things. If Ghazalnus was to open another door to them now, God only knew what the consequences would be. Shams, on the other hand, felt that he brought an ease – an opening – that for too long had been lacking in her life. She wished a young man like this would marry their daughter. She wished her own life had not taken its current course, that she had not got involved with a man of her husband's ilk … although by now she could not even imagine her life without Sayfadin. It was as if they had been born together. He no longer resembled a husband, but a congenital disease.

Nobody, however, was as moved as Trifa Yabahri. Many years later, she would still liken her heart to a rock that had been moved by the winds that evening. Whenever she told the story of that living-room encounter, she spoke about the colour of Shams's dress and the smell of the furniture. She spoke about the emotions that the colours of the paintings, carpet and vases stirred inside her. 'That evening's wind moved my heart,' she would say. That very night, Mahnaz Maro dreamed a different dream quite unlike any she had had before. For the first time in her life, she awoke from a dream and felt a great thirst. She felt she needed air. She felt she should open the windows. And for the first time in her life, she enjoyed breathing in the fresh air and crying, as if everything in her life had changed. She felt very vulnerable. She left her room, went into the kitchen, put her mouth to the tap and drank with this incomparable thirst.

She splashed some water on her face, opened the door to the balcony and surrendered to the cold night air. For the first time ever, she felt that she hated Najo Ashkani from the depths of her heart, that she hated him very much. Very, very much indeed.

MAJID-I GUL SOLAV'S ONGOING SEARCH TO DISCOVER THE DEAD MAN'S REAL CHARACTER

SUMMER 2004

We had to understand the story of the corpse. That was our mission. Although the truth kills my imagination, I still felt driven to chase the corpse's story non-stop. There are two things in life that have a hold over me: what they call the truth, and what they call the imagination. History, politics, love, hatred and everything else in this universe is subordinated to the great conflict between the two. From the very beginning right up to the present day, this has been my understanding of life: man is just a creature who must live in the middle of this storm. He should draw a thick dividing line between the two worlds. Civilisation is nothing if not such a line drawn by humanity between the imagination and the truth. Science is that line; so are the arts.

It is difficult to believe that I, Majid-i Gul Solav, happy to go by the nickname of 'the Imaginary Magellan', was once obsessed with a seminar on the boundaries of imagination and truth in the arts. Would any of you believe it? Eight years ago, I wanted to hold a seminar on the subject. I hired a venue and hung posters all over the city, but not a single soul showed up. Not one. At those moments, only imagination can rescue you. Oblivious to it all, I filled the hall with imaginary young men and women who listened quietly to my seminar about the arts. 'Even the arts have drawn a thick line between the imagination and truth,' I told them. But I alone observed that line. Both Trifa and Ghazalnus were obsessed with blurring it. I felt torn, but was still happy to play their games. I'm someone who likes to discover the furthest end of both realms, to go as far as the place at which imagination meets its end and truth takes on its final form.

Everyone treats my perspective as that of an idiot, of someone who acts obstinately and merely likes to be in the opposite camp. *They* believe imagination is tantamount to approaching the truth, and the truth to approaching imagination. They maintain that unless man has one foot in this world and one foot in another, he will go insane. They don't see the contradictions and differences between the two hostile poles. This often drives me mad and makes me depressed and isolated. Despite my best efforts, I simply cannot think that way. When I'm Majid-i Gul Solav, I'm no longer the Imaginary Magellan, and when I become the Imaginary Magellan and board my ship on my imaginary map, I am no longer Majid-i Gul Solav.

To me, the lines matter. If man were to remove them, *then* he would go mad, and all the dangerous things in our imaginations, all our terrible unconscious games, would spill out into the real world. Have you seen the Robin Williams film *Jumanji*, or its sequel *Zathura*? If we don't maintain the line between imagination and truth, the world will plunge into chaos and confusion, as in those two films. Imagine a game you have to play in reality, like the dangerous chess game Harry Potter plays in the first volume of J. K. Rowling's novels. It is real and unreal; magic, and truth.

When I decided to take part in writing the book of the bloody gardens, I knew it would take me right to the heart of the truth. I was the lowest-profile member of the group. At the time, Ghazalnus was already known as a poet, Trifa was active with women's rights groups and Hasan-i Tofan was well-known in every corner of the country and shielded by his reputation. But no one knew who I was. Although I spent hours walking the streets of the city, nobody noticed me. I don't recall anyone ever greeting me when I was out and about. My only friends were the blind children, who couldn't see me either. I was excited by the prospect of becoming a visible person and enjoying the pleasures of taking risks.

The idea of a book about the dead was the brainchild of Trifa and Ghazalnus. They had already witnessed the painful experiences of a number of victims in a series of dangerous events. They told these harrowing stories so dramatically that I couldn't believe what I heard. I think humans are fabulists because they are so often keen to fuse the imagination and the truth. Trifa and Ghazalnus, though, regarded me merely as a disbelieving scribe who goes so far as to scorn human suffering.

The idea behind the book was simple. We had to record the stories of the deaths that occurred after the 1991 uprising, or, in other words, to write down what nobody before had dared to. For my part, I titled it *The Book of a Thousand Bodies*. Obviously, the title was merely a metaphor, but it stood for this and all the other cities of our region. Each one of us gave it a different title. Ghazalnus called it *The Garden of Blood*. Trifa called it *Hell's Notebook*. The book had three main chapters: 'Blood', 'Fire' and 'Water'. The chapter on blood was dedicated to those who were murdered, the one on fire to those who were burned and the one on water to those who were drowned. Our task was to collect a number of stories, delve into the reasons for the deaths and record the lives and dreams of the victims. If people live in a city rife with death, they ought to understand it. They cannot cover their eyes with their hands and refuse to look at the dead. It was crucial, however, that the truth did not kill my imagination or ruin my personal imaginary journeys. 'This book gives us the power to look at the dead of this city,' Ghazalnus would say. 'To look at the dead is to look at reality.' Ghazalnus wanted his long journey in the realm of imagination to end in the arms of truth, but I did not sail towards the realm of truth in my imaginary ship. Even now, when I am far from the ship, I don't think the ship – still sailing in the imaginary rivers and infinite world – has any destination other than that of the imagination. And there it will always remain, crossing from one body of water to another, or from one forest to another.

On the night we found Murad's body, we had already been collecting stories for several years. Our Notebook Keepers wandered through alleys, visited the families of the dead and brought back the stories of their deaths and farewells. However, we had not yet come across a sad corpse ourselves, one that would enter our dreams and ask us to do something for it. Today, I can swear to you that Hamlet did not lie. He really did see the apparition of a dead man, and I saw Murad Jamil's apparition many times during those nights. I saw him wandering around our house; I saw him calling to me from the other side of the road. Sometimes he walked beside me or came towards me on my walks. Initially, I thought this only happened to me, but later I learned that Ghazalnus and Hasan-i Tofan also saw the apparition all the time.

The day Hasan-i Tofan brought back some pictures was a strange day for me. He'd obtained the names of two women from the owners of the photos – two women I now had to track down and somehow glean information from. As I knew it was easier to extract water from the sands of the desert than to acquire information from certain women about previous love affairs, I tried to wriggle out of the task, and instead recommended the ever-smiling Trifa. Whenever I needed her, though, she would become as obstinate as a child, refusing to do anything for me. Trifa believed I was brainless; that I didn't understand anything about women and was nothing but a hopeless, arrogant man who sang the praises of his own handsomeness all too often, and that I had yet to understand that in these circumstances women believe men more readily than women – that is, they will open their hearts to a handsome man more easily than to a woman.

Although I was often hurt by what Trifa said, I didn't hold it against her. I was certain that, deep down, she loved me like a brother. She had told me in passing that she cared about my feelings, yet too often she forgot this and attacked me at the first opportunity. For four years, I had known no women but her. One day, I decided I would never again fall in love or suffer heartache over love. I grew very indifferent towards women. When Hasan-i Tofan put the pictures of the two girls before me, I pretended Trifa's harsh words had not affected me. My greatest strength was that I could conceal my feelings and not lose my serenity. At times I wept inwardly, but revealed nothing on the surface. I would not let my great serenity be disturbed.

They were two beautiful girls. One was called Salma Najib, the other Gulzar Khalid – two meaningless names, like those of the women who received their monthly food rations at my neighbour's grocery. I calmly collected the pictures and asked them to give me some time to find them. Then I left the meeting without letting anyone know how hurt I was.

Salma Najib was a secondary school teacher. I waited for her outside the school in my neatly ironed clothes, briefcase in hand and without a shred of embarrassment. With the poise of a beautiful woman, she arrived a few minutes before school started. I approached her courteously and introduced myself politely – something women rarely encountered in men. I told her that I worked for an organisation that was investigating the fate of missing people, and needed a few moments of her time. I spoke so politely she believed me and walked along beside me towards the staff room. I, of course, told her that we needed to speak one-to-one. Initially, she thought I had come to enquire about one of the female students; when she realised the questions were directed at her, she looked at me, shocked, and didn't know what to say. I didn't want the other teachers to know anything. Before we reached the noisy staff room, I took my opportunity and quickly showed her a picture of Murad Jamil, saying, 'Khanim, I want to talk to you about this man.'

When she saw the photo she turned pale, and said in a sad voice, 'Here? Right here? And now? No way.' Her voice took on a pleading tone. She resembled a trapped nightingale. Until then, I had never had the privilege of seeing a woman's hands shake out of fear that her secrets might be uncovered. I wanted to elaborate, but she told me, her voice trembling and her face pale: 'Please stop. I'm married now. Wait for me tomorrow evening at the bus station behind the big hospital. When I get on the bus, come and sit next to me. I'll give you a phone number, and you can contact me that way.' I was impressed by her quick thinking. God, women are so much smarter than men in these matters. In fact, when it comes to such situations, we're nothing but great big idiots compared to women. I had no intention of doing anything that could sully her reputation, so I moved away with an ugly smile, one suited to a man who had achieved an ignoble goal.

I waited patiently for the following day to come, then carried out her instructions to the letter. I sat next to her on a bus heading for a remote part of town. On board, she looked at me with a big smile and slipped a piece of paper into my hand. She seemed to be enjoying this adventure enormously; perhaps it reminded her of times past. I have to say that her gaze was not empty of a lover's emotions, of a woman's desire to plunge herself again into a new love story. When I disembarked, I said goodbye with just a look, like a man of great experience, and returned home via a different route. Scribbled on the piece of paper was a phone number and the time of day. When I rang, a female friend of hers picked up and quickly called her to the phone. Before I could say a thing, she started speaking in a coquettish tone that bore no resemblance to the voice of the frightened teacher who had spoken to me in the school corridor.

'I'm a married woman,' she said. 'I'm no longer interested in love affairs and such things. I don't know why you don't leave me alone. Why are you hassling me?'

The words were said in a way that implied: 'Get this – if you just try a bit harder, I may well join you in any fun activities the consequences of which only God and the Prophet know.'

I explained to her calmly that I only wanted some information about Murad Jamil; apart from that, I had no other aims.

'But I'm worried that if I talk to you about Murad, you might then ask for other things,' she said, almost disappointed. I reassured her that I needed nothing else, but she still kept talking as though I did.

Most of Salma Najib's words went into the big book about the dead. She spoke with the voice of a woman who had known many beautiful moments with Murad. Her voice faltered at her magical memories. She had heard nothing about Murad's death. I didn't want to make her sad, so I just told her that the poor guy was missing and we were searching for him. She was the first one to talk to me in detail about the stars Murad had left behind.

'When I first slept with Murad, I wasn't particularly impressed,' she said, without shame – something else I hadn't experienced with other women until then. 'But later on, a number of small stars appeared on my body, a number of real, shining stars. They were all over my body. Whenever and wherever he slept with a woman, he would leave a number of stars on them. Between their breasts, on their shoulders, anywhere else you can think of. Sometimes he even left stars on the walls, huge stars that would remain in the atmosphere of the room for a while. They didn't bother me. When I returned home, I would close the door of my room, take off my clothes and look at the stars. In some cases, if I was truly elated, the stars would stay on my body for days at a time.'

Salma seemed like an honest woman to me, someone who, had life not dictated otherwise, might have lived independently outside marriage. She told me that Murad had always been in danger, but also that he was indifferent to it and that he never thought about death; that he was a young man created by God solely so that his beauty could leave the sweetest memories in the hearts of dozens of women. Salma did not know what had happened to him since she had married. When I reported all this information back to Hasan-i Tofan, he didn't think it so important. What mattered to him was with whom Murad had had liaisons in the past few months.

'Murad's old stories aren't very significant,' he said stubbornly. 'What got him killed was a dangerous relationship he had in the last few days of his life.'

The person who opened the door to the mysteries for me was Gulzar Khalid, who was suddenly hospitalised for an emergency gallbladder operation. I seized upon her illness as an opportunity to talk to her in her hospital bed, tubes still in her nose.

'I know nothing, nothing at all,' she whispered to me, the sadness in her sick voice suggesting she hadn't forgotten Murad for a single moment. 'Leave me alone. Find the wife of the Baron of Chickens. She knows everything.'

And that's how I came to be the first person to discover the world of the barons, who created the realm of our incredible story.

THE IDLE MURDERERS' CLUB

HASAN-I TOFAN COMES OUT
OF SECLUSION IN 1998

One night, six years into my isolation, my mother passed away. Together with two or three of our male neighbours and a large number of older women, I took her body to the cemetery. It was the first time a deceased person had been taken to the cemetery by women rather than men. When she died, Pizo left nothing behind except her tools for making rosewater, and several handfuls of loose keys. I didn't know what the keys were for, at first; there was something strange going on. The deeper I put my hands in her pockets, the further they went. Each time, I came across more keys. Never in my life had I known she'd had all these keys. I didn't know what they were, or what doors they were meant to open. In the end, I put all the keys on a big iron ring and kept them in a secure place, the final memory and mysterious legacy of an adorable and imaginative woman. For many years afterwards, and even today, I maintain that every dead person's pocket contains a bunch of keys like that. If you use your hands skilfully enough, you can find and extract them.

The death of Pizo-i Gulaw, a great friend to the old women of this country, left a huge gap in my life. My mother's real name was Piroz, but when I was a little boy all I could manage was 'Pizo', so her friends and family called her Pizo-i Gulaw – Pizo of the Rosewater.

The day we buried her, the entire cemetery was covered in black. Hundreds of older women, all fragrant with my mother's rosewater, occupied the hills around the graveyard completely. After the men's memorial service, I spent exactly fourteen days receiving these older women, who had come from far and wide to offer their condolences. Some of them smelled of another place and time. They bore with them the displaced soul of bygone days. None of them knew me as 'Hasan-i Tofan'. They called me 'Hasan-i Pizo-i Gulaw'. They all told me that from now on, I would be their son, and they would be my mothers. Suddenly, I had discovered an infinite number of mothers who all comforted me staunchly.

Once the memorial services were over, I had nothing to do but get out of the house and resume normal life. Six years on, in the autumn of 1998, I went back into the world and became a normal person again. Initially, I received a small income after a friend helped me register as a retired peshmerga, for after my mother's death I had no desire to carry on making rosewater. I felt the six years I had spent making rosewater had done their work. They had changed me radically, had made another human being out of me. Wherever I went, the smell of rosewater was imprinted upon my imagination, taking me back to the moment I decided on my atonement. This made it all right to mix with people and pursue a normal life. Like someone burying his past, I took the pistol and the tools for making rosewater down to the basement of the house, locked them away with a big lock and prepared myself for a new life, eager and full of hope.

In the early days of my return, I wandered around the city as dizzy as a lost soul. I had forgotten many places in those six years, and many things had changed. At first I did nothing but wander the marketplace, asking how much things cost. Sometimes I would go into a shop and ask the price of each item. One day, at the herbalist's, I was busy assessing the various varieties of rosewater when someone put his arms around me and said, 'Where have you been, stranger?' I recognised his voice immediately. It was Fara-i Tunchi. Fifteen years earlier, we had shot a security officer right next to the fish-sellers. Fara went over to him and yelled, 'I killed the son of a bitch! I killed the bitch's brother!' I often heard those shouts. I relived them in my dreams, and often remembered them for no apparent reason. Fara was a man without mercy. It was his face I remembered whenever I thought back to the cruelty and mercilessness of that time. He did a lot of bad things during the days of the revolution, and I was very wary of him. He gave me an address and said: 'At night, all of us, the old gang, meet up here. You should come along as well.'

They met up in a club at a big hotel that served alcohol, on the outskirts of the city. An old man driving an old cab took me there. In the hotel parlour, a small, dark waiter with a big mole on his nose showed me to a side room to the left of the main bar. The first person I saw was Fazil Qandil, who received me with a glass of beer. I'd never seen such a strange place in my life. It was a big hall, full of people who had been active in the assassination cells. I'd got to know them all on different occasions in the Seventies and Eighties, not just the ones who worked for our party but those who had been our opponents too, who had opened fire on us and worked for other political parties. Tunchi, speaking to a fat young man with a black moustache, opened his arms when he saw me and silenced everyone with his loud voice: 'Guys, look who's here. Look. It's our great guru, our teacher, our wise man: Hasan-i Tofan.'

They all knew me. There wasn't anyone who had worked in the assassination cells for even a day who wouldn't have heard of Hasan-i Tofan; but I hadn't seen any of them for seven years and it was strange to see them all again, convened in a place like that.

They gave me a warm welcome. I felt like I was dreaming, for only a dream could bring all these old faces back together in the same room, all these enemies. They noticed that I looked dizzy, bewildered and nearly out of breath. To give me room to breathe, they pointed me to an empty chair. Tunchi and Fazil Qandil came and sat next to me. Their faces, too, had a dream-like quality. They sounded hoarse and slightly drunk.

'Brother Hasan,' Tunchi said, 'You don't know how happy I am to see you here. After you left, we went through many terrible days. Even as late as the start of the civil war, we still had some value. We had our jobs. But nowadays, we just get together in the evenings. Our only entertainment is this parlour, where we drink and wait.'

Fazil Qandil was indeed slightly drunk. While Tunchi spoke, with his drooping face, greying moustache and freckled nose, Fazil gazed at the ceiling. Finally, as if suppressing a great rage, as if keeping something to himself, he took a deep breath through his nose, put his beer on the table and said: 'Tunchi, tell him everything. Everything. Hasan-i Tofan isn't someone you and I would hide anything from. Tofan has been our friend. He's very dear to us. Tell him who they've brought to the Party, tell him about the limp-wristed queers who've risen to the top.'

Tunchi, as if he were about to give me the news that someone close to me had died, sat back a little, paused, took my hand and said, 'We've set up a club here – the Idle Heroes' Club, though some of us call it the Idle Murderers' Club just for a laugh. Obviously, some of us have got new jobs now, but the rest just sleep from morning to evening, then come in here for a drink. We laugh, we sing and we get drunk. Brother Tofan, we're all here. Make yourself at home. Think of us as your brothers. This place has started getting a bit of a reputation recently. If someone needs something done, they come to us – to Fazil Qandil and me. We sort it all out, allocate the jobs and the cash. We make sure no one's left out.'

'You mean you're still killing people?' I asked, worried. 'Is that it? Are you still killing people?'

'Not necessarily,' said Fazil Qandil, reaching for his glass. 'It's not like the old days. You can't kill without special orders. No, really, it's not like the old days. You have to have someone's backing, one of the big men, the really big chiefs. Otherwise, it's not so easy. The rules of the game have changed recently. There are jobs, but not many. And they're done very cautiously. The Party doesn't reach for its guns unless it has to. I mean it, really. Things have changed. They've changed a lot. None of us expected it to come to this.'

'So what do you do?' I asked, intrigued.

Tunchi rubbed his freckled nose and said, 'Some of us have been accommodated in other formations. Others have gone into the army. However, this is our main place. Nowadays, nobody can work for the Party. You have to work for individuals. You sit, drink and sing here until they come to you with a job. The Party doesn't have many jobs any more, but our colleagues in the Party still need us.'

Fazil put his arms around me and, in the tone of someone who is getting increasingly drunk, said, 'Hasan, you are as dear to us as our own eyes. Do you understand? You are dear to us, very dear. Whoever needs us will come to us, you know, but killing's on the way out. I know your story. I know you don't want to kill again. Don't ask me how, but I've heard it and I know everything. Things are easier now. There's no killing involved. Sometimes it's threatening someone, beating them up, turning them out of their home, firing shots over their heads. Some son of a bitch has a plot of land, and you go and take it off him. Another won't vacate a shop, so you apply a bit of force to get him out. Or an official gives you some other job, transferring a whole heap of money, say, smuggling an Arab out of the country, evicting a tenant or whatever else God sends us on the side. And there's money in it. It's changing too, slowly. Six months ago, you'd find only insects in our pockets. It's better now. It is. It's getting better day by day. There's movement on the market and it's cleaner than the old days, much cleaner. Hasan, let me tell you, I swear on the grave of my loved ones, I don't have a hidden agenda; I don't need you. It will just be nicer for us if you're with us too.'

I didn't know how to respond. I stood up and looked around. The air in the hall was so thick with the smell of smoke and beer I could hardly breathe. Faces appeared longer and weirder, and voices became more distant and echoing. I knew most of the people I could see, and yet at heart I felt I didn't know any of them, as if I'd been brought there on an alien wind. Too much noise danced in my head. Old age and grey hair had taken their toll on many of them. They had left behind a fruitless youth and were heading for an unknown destination. Some of them had learned to wear suits, but they looked awkward in them. They didn't look like the suits I'd seen before. Most of them were getting drunk and chainsmoking. The voices got all mixed up inside my head, turning into the banging of an enormous, tight-skinned drum, pounding to no particular beat.

Without a word and still unable to respond to Fazil, I threw a long glance at the two of them. A noise kept coming into my head that dominated everything else. It was all I could hear. My head was full of the sound of old shootings, memories of gunfire rattles and explosions I had repressed for six years. I could smell gunpowder from the bullets we'd fired. I looked at my hands and at theirs, one after the other. I could see the steam of a dead age and a bloody century between their fingers. I held on to the edge of the table and stood up. I was no longer aware of Fazil and Tunchi. Suddenly, the smell of rosewater washed over me. The smell of Pizo's rosewater called to me from afar, and carried me away. As if under a spell, I closed my eyes and walked. I could hear the noises following me. I couldn't understand a thing, as if they were speaking a different language altogether. I could see a young man at the gate of the club. I could see the waiter with the big mole on his nose. 'Take me home,' I said, almost begging him. I staggered, and someone grabbed hold of me. I knew I was going to fall. I would fall and remember nothing. Nothing at all.

When I opened my eyes, I was in Shibr Mustafa's house. I had fainted, and none of them knew my address. One of them called Shibr; he instructed them to take me to his place. I didn't know at that point that Shibr was in a wheelchair, and he'd had no news of me. When I came to and saw Shibr in that state, I put my arms around him and wept for him. He cried a lot, too. 'I was always going to end up like this, Hasan,' he said. Finding him in that state, I forgot about having fainted. Shibr told me a great many things about the Idle Murderers' Club that night. After the uprising, their workload had gradually declined. It was Shibr who had come up with the 'Idle Murderers' Club', both the name – for a laugh – and the bizarre concept itself: somewhere all the friends could get together and think about their future. With tears in his eyes, he ran a hand through his blond hair and said, 'I thought that at a club, we'd start thinking about our lives again, write down our stories, find jobs, help each other, speak out on political matters, ask poets to come and read to us, invite good musicians to play for us, become active in other organisations and support good causes. I wanted to bring painters in to give us lessons; to visit nurseries occasionally and learn from the children; to set up a fund to support one another when we got married and had a family. That was my dream. But it didn't work out because *they* poke their noses into everything. Everything.'

Shibr wasn't the guy I used to know. He felt he had wasted his youth and his life. There was great despair and anger in his voice. All the events he had witnessed had shaken him to the core. He no longer trusted his old Party pals. After his injury, they'd sent him cash in a white envelope on several occasions, but each time he had thrown the money back at them and asked them to leave him alone. Now he lived on a small disability stipend. For some time, he had been keen to set up an organisation for his old colleagues, most of whom were unemployed. But when he did, they took it out of his hands. That night, he was drinking alcohol, jittery in his chair as he spoke. He was tearful. I'd never seen him cry before.

He put his hands over his eyes to hide them, saying, 'Hasan, those people have even made a crying man out of me, you know. Nowadays, I cry at nothing. You know what they did? Just one week after we set up the club, they sent Tunchi round, the scorpion with his seven stings. He knows just what poison kills what person, and he uses it. The senior men in the Party, our leaders, sent Tunchi round. They don't want anyone but themselves to be able to breathe. They've ruined everything with their fine talk and great lies. They'll wait until the end of the world before they let anyone leave the game. They will. Either you go home for six years and the world forgets you, like you did, or they have their spiders weave their webs around you, bind your arms and legs and drag you to whatever lair they want. I'd been working there for less than a week when they sent Fazil Qandil round, then Hidayat Gurji, Rostami Aziz Awara, Khalil Kisal, even Fatih Majid Bajar. They took out anyone they could find in their box of poisons and used them to fight me. They turned the club into a place to look for work. Just as people who want to hire a worker go to the square where labourers gather, anyone looking for a murderer goes there. After only a month, I was thrown out into the street, in my wheelchair. Then they used to send me money with Lieutenant Shrimp. It's what they do when they want to win you back, send you money through Lieutenant Shrimp. They don't need murderers like you and me nowadays. The accountants do most of the killing for them now. Do you get me?'

'Shibr, all that matters is that they're not killing people,' I said. 'You know? So long as no blood is shed, nothing else matters.' I meant it, too. It was important for me that human blood wasn't being shed.

'So you say, and I don't blame you,' he replied. 'But bullets aren't everything. It's often kinder to be killed with a bullet. Also, don't assume they're not killing people. Don't assume that at all.'

Shibr advised me not to go back to the club. That night, as I slept in his living room, my breath was redolent of my mother's rosewater. I felt that the rosewater prevented me from falling back into my past. The following day, I took Shibr in his wheelchair to the bazaar. From that day on, he and I became very close friends, who could only be parted by death.

146

THE MEMOIRS OF THE
BARON OF IMAGINATION

A nd now it's my turn to talk again. They talk too much, as if I were out of the game, as if the map of this world were drawn by random men with no sense of discipline or purpose, as if Ghazalnus were the only person with a cue on the billiard table and I was just one of the balls rolling around in futility. No, don't forget, I am one of the key players in this game, one of the key balls. So let me have your attention for a while and listen to me.

In the early days of the twenty-first century, a story about a wandering notebook was going around, a notebook known in town as the Winged Notebook. It would suddenly and mysteriously appear in households that had suffered a tragic loss. It was an invitation for people to write about the death of a loved one in their own way. I heard the story from my own followers. Although I believe strongly in the power of the imagination, to begin with I saw it as one of the many things superstitious people in this city unashamedly make up on a daily basis. But eventually the story became too prevalent to simply ignore.

At that point, the heads of the Party security and intelligence agencies knew very little about the issue. I dispatched a few of my loyal aides to the bazaar to investigate. All of them testified to the notebook's existence. Through these same loyal individuals, I also met people who had seen the notebook directly and even written entries in it. My understanding of the whole story, in contrast to that of the ordinary people, was that there was more than one notebook travelling around the city in an organised fashion, as were some strange and unfamiliar people whose homes no one could easily identify. Their only aim was to collect stories about tragic deaths.

I spoke about the story of the Winged Notebooks at my own party's Politburo meeting and at a joint conference of Kurdistani parties, but as always, my colleagues gave me strange, cold, empty looks and said nothing. During that period, fears about the return of Saddam Hussein's forces or the deployment of Turkish army units from the north were so great that no one was interested in the existence, or lack thereof, of some notebooks. Yet as soon as the uprising was over,

I recognised the danger of neglecting these minor matters. Obviously, the issue posed no threat to our national security, and my party's Politburo saw the whole affair as child's play by some idle persons best left to get on with whatever they liked.

When we heard the story of the notebooks, I had just started searching for Ghazalnus's poems. Until then, I'd had no clear idea about the plan I had to draw. I didn't really know what I was doing, or what kind of creatures I was dealing with. However, one day His Excellency the Leader called me out of the blue to discuss a project I had been turning over in my mind, but had not had the courage to speak about out loud. Yes, the Leader summoned me, and told me he had a plan to set up a dream district within the next twenty years, something that would testify to a rich and fantastic imagination; something that could become the icon of 'Kurdistan's special democratic experiment', which we could show off to visiting foreign guests and say: 'Gentlemen, this is what Kurds are like. Given the chance, they will perform miracles. That's right, miracles!'

With all due respect to His Excellency, he didn't really know what he was talking about. He didn't know that for me, this was opening up old wounds. This all happened early in the twenty-first century. The district of Nwemiran, 'New Princes' District', was still under construction; some of the mansions were up, and others were still being built. I explained to the Leader about all the strenuous efforts I had made to ensure Nwemiran did not become just another fenced-off area.

'Our Chief and Great Leader,' I began, 'I wanted to build something different to the new districts going up, something fantastical; a place where, stepping inside, you felt as though you'd left Earth behind and entered a fantasyland. Right now I'm on the lookout for imaginative people to help and guide me in building such a city.'

Without a clue as to what I was doing, I accepted the task of thinking about building a dream district ... but the story of the Winged Notebooks left me uneasy. I won't hide from you that I understand the imagination as a force that helps human beings forget about death, suffering and darkness. I need the imagination to create a different truth, a truth unlike any I can see in this city at the moment: imagination as a substitute for reality. But the story of the notebooks caused me a lot of pain. It was the product of a different type of imagination – one that doesn't want to forget the real world. Meticulously, I started to pursue whoever might be behind the notebooks, to no avail. It seemed that those doing the job were Imaginative Creatures who couldn't easily be found. It's no mean feat to catch an Imaginative Creature to begin with, but if you succeed, then cannot tame it ... dear God, whatever do you do with it?

THE REAL MAGELLAN ENCOUNTERS
SOME PROBLEMS

SUMMER 2004

After a week's stay at the hotel, Zuhdi Shazaman had gradually become familiar with the streets and the bazaar again. The hotel owner tried to please him at any cost. For no real reason, he was afraid of this tall, long-haired man, about whom strange stories and speculation had begun to circulate. One story had it that he was the son of one of the men who owned massive amounts of property, and that he had returned because of disputes over his share of the inheritance. Another held that he was a very rich man who had grown weary of foreign women, and had come home to find himself a decent woman and take her to Europe. According to yet another story, he was a British spy there to carry out a secret mission.

The hotel owner snuck into his room a couple of times to rifle through his things, but found nothing. He brought out the file containing the letters, but all he could understand was that the guest had a niece by the name of Baran Shukur. He could glean nothing straightforward from them. His long career as a hotel owner had taught him to inspect his guests' rooms and examine all their things without leaving a trace. He tried repeatedly to befriend the man in an attempt to get something out of him, but his guest was too strict and introverted for that to work. He was the type of person who erected barriers between himself and other people that could not easily be breached.

The hotelier was dying to know who this man was, and what he wanted. But Zuhdi Shazaman himself did not know how long he would be staying, or what he would be doing: it was as though he was waiting for a miracle. He hadn't yet come across anyone he could ask about Baran Shukur. He had to tread carefully, to make sure she was safe and that nothing had happened. And what if something had? No, he couldn't think like that.

Returning to the hotel that night, one week into his stay, Zuhdi met the hotelier's wife, a petite, dark-skinned woman with black eyes. She was young, and looked at him eagerly. She wore a thin blue blouse and a purple skirt. Her appearance suggested she was more educated and more urban than the rest of the hotel staff. She was the type of woman who would rest her dark sunglasses on her head. She handed him the key with a smile. She was a beautiful woman in any case, but there was something about the way she wore her make-up that simply stunned Zuhdi. When he took the key from her, he felt that she had deliberately sought to touch his hand. His first thought was that she was just one of the female workers there, whom he had not met. Unusually for him – because normally he would say nothing – he asked, 'Khanim, do you work here?'

'I am his wife,' she whispered, as though telling him a secret. The way she said it made it seem as if she were sure that speaking that way would quickly break the ice and remove some of the barriers between them in their fleeting encounter. It was a delicate, husky whisper. In the past twenty-four years, he had never known a Kurdish woman to speak to him so directly. The unexpected tenderness made him tingle. In twenty-four years, he had only heard this tone of voice from a woman by accident. He had shunned all gatherings of Kurds. He didn't even listen to Kurdish music. But now that short sentence, that delicate female voice talking to him so intimately, changed something in him.

'I see,' he said. 'You're his wife.' He lifted his head, his face betraying no emotion.

Running her fingers through her hair, she said, in an even lower whisper: 'Yeah, I'm his wife. I'm the wife of the hotel owner.'

This is one of the few cities in the world with no nightlife, and yet, despite the empty, lifeless streets, it felt good to go out into the hot August nights. Over the past few days he had walked around with no clear destination in mind. He had gone to many places and sat listening in teahouses, but found no clues or anything useful at all. With his long hair, big, bright eyes, neat appearance and reflective gaze, he stirred suspicion and jealousy wherever he went. He was handsome, and his handsomeness was feared by the plain people of the city. That night, after tying up his long hair before going to bed, he put his head on the pillow and felt the whisper of the hotel owner's wife echo in his ears. His life was full of women's whispers, but this time it was different. Very different. He felt himself slowly drifting away, but could not fall asleep. 'Alien and unlucky man, where are you going? Where are you going and what do you want?' he asked himself with a sigh. In his many years of exile he had learned to talk to himself like this, but he was unable to answer his own questions.

Meeting the hotel owner's wife was a big reason for staying put. That week he considered changing his hotel several times, but her whispers held him back. Sometimes a beautiful, delicate woman is worth pursuing from city to city, continent to continent. Sometimes, because of a woman, a man becomes attached to just one place, one town, and forgets about the rest of the world. The short period he had spent in the city had not been pleasant. It was a city that had nothing but the noise of cars, the shouts of drivers and glimpses of buses. But there was such magic in the whispering of that delicate woman that it held him in place, as if through her whispers she was telling him that underneath it all, the city was like a deep, mysterious sea. Her bewitching whispers seemed to concentrate all the guile and tenderness of all the women in the world, whispers that could incarcerate you in that city.

Since he'd come to the hotel, he had felt too shameless to be able to live in such a 'moral' city. During his travels, he had avoided moral cities. Deep down, he was sure that the wildest, most intoxicating women lived in precisely these dusty, moral cities, but that finding them was very difficult, something that could only be done by the kind of man who was just as wild and lived by the same code of honour. He wasn't the type to seek out elusive women. He'd always looked for accessible, transitory women, the ones he called 'one-night doves': prostitutes, women who stood on streets at night to be picked up by passing drivers, women who took their annual holidays without men or friends and strolled the warmer parts of the world, their eyes revealing their search for a colourful night. Most of his experiences had been with women who'd been left behind in bars, or women riding motorbikes, as lost as he was. And yet he couldn't recall having ever heard such whispering. It was as though all his life he had been searching for a bewitching, beguiling voice like that one, as if he had been looking for a woman who was drunk not on alcohol, but on the game, the sheer joy of playing.

Until that moment, he had been content with his past, believing he had enjoyed life more than other men. After all, what else could a lost Kurd on a motorbike expect from life, except forsaken midnight prostitutes and women seeking to forget the suffering of life for just one night? 'A lost Kurd on a motorbike' – that image was a painful one. He felt he had reached an age when he could no longer afford to carry on like that. Sometimes he felt that he was lying to himself and hadn't returned to search for Baran Shukur at all, but that exhaustion, old age and an excruciating loneliness had brought him back, and that, as a Kurd, he had betrayed himself all his life. Now he was back to receive his punishment, which he knew had been awaiting him for a long time. What kind of punishment, he did not know.

Late that night, he woke up and went back down to the hotel's small parlour. It was the first night he hadn't felt the August heat. On the contrary, it was very cold. He didn't know if it was real cold or a mysterious feeling a man might feel at the beginning of old age. In the parlour, he saw the dark-complexioned, skinny guard with the unkempt moustache and weary eyes, sitting slack-jawed as he watched porn on TV. Unashamed, and without bothering to change the channel, the guard looked at him without a word. Shazaman was aware of the woman's presence still lingering in the room.

'Is the hotel owner here?' he asked the guard, his voice that of someone who wasn't very well.

'No, he's not,' came the curt reply. It was clear the guard had no desire to talk.

'What about his wife? Isn't she here either?' Zuhdi asked in the same sick voice.

'Do you mean Afsana Khan?' he asked.

'Yes, that's right. That's who I mean.'

'No, she isn't here tonight either.'

He had meant to find out her name. Now, he could ponder its mystery. That night, he fell asleep with great difficulty. When he woke the next day, his entire body was drenched in sweat. He couldn't remember his dreams, but he had a severe headache. After a quick shower he went back to the parlour, his hair still wet. There, waiting for him, was the hotel owner in an old, black jacket, his ugly smile made uglier by yellow teeth.

'There's someone from the Security Directorate here to see you,' he said, his tone of voice that of someone who takes pleasure in other people's suffering.

Zuhdi Shazaman looked around the parlour and noticed a small, thickset man in ironed plainclothes, an officer whose every feature was wide: his body, his head, his face, his nose, his hands and his backside. He was wearing a navy-blue suit and a red tie. The knot was so tight it almost strangled him.

'Bring us two teas,' he said unsmilingly, his handshake cold.

Zuhdi sat on one of the sofas and said nothing.

'I'm Captain Samad,' said the man, his voice lowered. 'From the Security Directorate. I've just got a couple of questions, and then I'll be out of your way.'

Zuhdi gave him a long look, but still said nothing.

As if scared of this fierce, Rasputin-like gaze, the man bowed his head and said, 'Kak Zuhdi, it appears that some people are suspicious of you. The reports we've received about you are not good. No one knows who you are, what you're doing in this city or what you're up to in this hotel.'

'My name is Zuhdi Shazaman,' he replied. 'I'm not doing anything. This is the city of my childhood. I was born and bred here. I've come back to revisit my memories, to smell them again. As I have no relatives left alive, and don't know a family who could put me up, I'm staying at this hotel.'

'What proof do you have that this is your hometown?' the man asked, as if pondering a profound matter.

'My proof,' Zuhdi said very seriously, without a trace of a smile, 'is how much I hate it. If you don't hate your hometown, you don't live in exile for twenty-four years. You don't leave it for twenty-four years. People who spend all their lives travelling hate their hometowns.'

'Do you have any other proof?' enquired the security officer after a short pause.

'Yes,' Zuhdi said. 'My other proof is that I've come back. You return to your hometown no matter how long you've been travelling. It's man's most terrible disease. They can't forget the cities of their childhood, and this is their most terrible ailment.'

'We want to inspect your room,' the security officer said with the customary arrogance of his kind. The way he spoke was as though he did not want to acknowledge his own words, or understand them.

'I've nothing but a suitcase,' said Zuhdi, looking at him in mild surprise, 'which has been inspected eighteen times since I crossed the border. Are you planning to write books about my underwear? Why do you need to take them out and put them back in so often?'

'It's our duty,' said Captain Samad with a frown, tightening his tie even further.

'If my underpants are dangerous,' said Zuhdi calmly, 'you'd better take my suitcase to the Security Directorate, and I'll come with you and put them on there.'

The officer wasn't listening. He whispered to a younger colleague who had just arrived, stood up without another word and headed to Zuhdi's room, accompanied by the hotel owner. After a short while, they returned with the file of letters.

'Kak Zuhdi, don't be downhearted,' said Captain Samad from the other side of the parlour door, as if he was addressing one of the pictures on the wall. 'We've got nothing specific on you. It's the Security Directorate's job to question strangers. We'll just send these letters off to be photocopied, and you'll be free to do whatever you like.'

'Those are private letters,' Zuhdi said. 'I haven't done anything wrong. What gives you the right to photocopy them?'

'As if you didn't know!' said Captain Samad, laughing as he walked out. 'The Security Directorate has the right to photocopy everything. Absolutely everything. And there's no one in the world who hasn't done anything wrong.'

Captain Samad didn't return that day. Zuhdi was certain his letters were gone. He also sensed there was something he wasn't quite understanding. Two days passed and nothing happened; but on the third day, two things occurred that would radically change his life.

GHAZALNUS AND THE IMAGINATIVE CREATURES
LATE 1970S AND EARLY 1980S

In that magical chamber of love, Ghazalnus found many boxes full of ghazals. One dark night, he moved them all to his house in a friend's car. There were dozens of boxes of ghazals, enough to spend the rest of his life reading and interpreting them.

In late 1975, Bahman Nasser retreated into his own world, accompanied by Mullah Sukhta's ghazals. For six years, he learned as many ghazals and books as he could by heart. In those six years, he had very little connection with the outside world; his father, without saying a word, without preventing him, without asking him any questions about the old, strange, dusty boxes, let him live in the house. Not once did he ask him why he never went out. He didn't ask about the whirlpool that had sucked him in, or about the odd books that so absorbed him. Rather, like a guard whose job was to care for an ailing hero in an old castle, he served him. Nasser Saeed's relationship with his son resembled anything but that of father and son. He was a quiet father whose one wish was for his son to complete his long journey with the books. All those years, the quiet father and the inquisitive son exchanged but a few words. During that time, Nasser Saeed's job was to find and buy any source Ghazalnus needed to better understand the ghazals. Over those six years, Ghazalnus became, as he himself put it, a diver in the sea of classical poetry.

Ghazalnus needed every one of those years to become an ashiq – a lover, in the sense that you set no conditions on your love for another human being.

It was a dark, dangerous political age when Ghazalnus came out of seclusion. Within the space of a few months, he fell in love with a girl by the name of Nergiz Furat, who was black-haired and dark-skinned, with full lips and blue eyes. She was his first love.

Without getting into too much detail, I shall say only that Ghazalnus first tried out the power of his ghazals on Nergiz, who, like most of the soft-hearted girls of this city, was not mentally or spiritually ready to understand their depth. Having learned how to love and

155

to immerse himself in literature in praise of the beloved, our friend Ghazalnus wanted somehow to follow the path taken by Mullah Sukhta and Baharbanu. As the incredibly imaginative offspring of two imagination-rich lovers, he believed that treading that path would be a straightforward matter. In short, Bahman Nasser, like most poetry lovers who truly enter the sea of love, had the spiritual strength and mental preparedness to inhabit a wild and magical devotion. Confronted with previously unheard ghazals, Nergiz went from not even knowing what such a thing was to becoming a genuine admirer of poetry. Then again, there is no woman in the world who wouldn't delight in ghazals. The only question is how much and for how long she might be stunned by them. Women who want love for its own sake are rare. To be fair, so are men. It is a bitter and painful truth for the various gods of love to discover that love is unsupported; rare is that love in the shape of a lonely knight with a book of ghazals, or of a horseman powerless but for the arrow of love.

Ghazalnus, who had inherited a vast literature on love, was himself one of these lonely knights, armed with nothing but love's power. It's hard for us to know whether or not there was ever an age in which love existed with no agenda other than its obsession with love itself. It appears that in olden times, when the world occasionally produced creatures like Las and Khazal,[13] there might have been a gap in the natural order through which such creatures stole into the world. Ghazalnus initially appeared like the classical knights who entered the battle of love with no other intentions. When he and Nergiz began courting, he had only love, nothing else, while the poor woman wanted other things as well: she wanted a home, marriage, children, a husband who would put her in the front seat of a car, drive her to other cities and show her other lands. These simple, practical demands bitterly disappointed Ghazalnus, who was wildly in love with her. Nergiz's alien demands brought Ghazalnus back down to earth, to the land of merciless objects, to the place where reality showed its face unadorned.

Ending his relationship with Nergiz also marked the moment Ghazalnus stopped reducing the love of human beings to the love of one person. Nothing is more dangerous than putting all your love at the disposal of a single individual, who might then look at all that love as a toy and throw it off a high balcony and break it. Love is a fortune of such value it should be stored in many places, objects and goals, just as we hide our gold in various locations. After reading Mullah Sukhta, after reflecting deeply on the meaning of love, after the collapse of his first love, Ghazalnus understood that what is true for the teacher is not necessarily true for the student.

Mullah Sukhta taught Ghazalnus that nothing on Earth is as diverse and multifaceted as love. Given that love has no divine or Satanic sources, it is something humans need to sculpt and mould with their own hands. Human diversity is, therefore, matched by the diversity of the colours of love. After his experience with Nergiz, Ghazalnus understood that a lover is not just someone who can love the beloved the way anyone can love someone else, the way anyone can be in love for a while. Even the most dangerous people might have loved once. What matters is how you switch from love for your beloved to love for your enemies. What matters is not how you give your love to one person, but how you distribute that love. Love is like an irrigation channel: the goal is not to direct water to a single tree, but to take it to thousands of trees around dozens of bends, towards thousands of withered flowers and bushes. Not all trees necessarily know how to drink the water of love; nor will love open every flower. Ghazalnus likened his relationship with Mullah Sukhta to that between a flower that bears the seeds of love and the wind that spreads them across the land. Sukhta was the huge garden that produced the infinite seeds of the ghazals and Bahman Nasser was the wind that would collect the seeds and spread them upon the earth.

The day Nergiz broke Ghazalnus's heart for reasons not to do with love, he understood that she could not be a wild wind, a storm able to spread love left and right. From that day on, Ghazalnus looked at Mullah Sukhta as the Euclid of love, his books full of the many theorems of love whereby he measured the different angles of the human soul and drew the intricate lines of the psyche. He saw himself as the engineer who would take those theorems and use them to build a city of love. And yet he had no idea how to go about it. If he was a wind meant to be carrying the seeds of love, how could he ensure they came to ground in the world? Very quickly, it had become clear that Nergiz was not the kind of land on which Ghazalnus could build the gate of the city.

Many years later, talking to Majid-i Gul Solav about a lifetime of spiritual change, Ghazalnus would say, 'I understood after the failure of my first love that I am not Mullah Sukhta in his eternal seclusion, I am Sukhta when he comes out into the world, Sukhta who has arms and legs and wanders the Earth.'

No one knows for certain who introduced Bahman Nasser to the bars for the first time, who made him a regular of the nightly gatherings of mediocre teachers and civil servants that represented his first way station on his journey into the world. After he broke up with Nergiz, he started to frequent these bars in the evenings with a friend, a short man with a protruding black moustache, a small nose and a yellow tint to the whites of his eyes. He looked like any inexperienced young man out to find a place for himself among those who consider themselves masters of everything. It was there, in that world of hopeless little people who spend all their lives drunk, that Ghazalnus first read one of Sukhta's ghazals in public.

He had spent his first few forays to these bars in silence. One night, influenced by the sound of torrential rain and the smell of wine, he began to recite one of the ghazals out loud. When he spoke the opening couplets, his small friend with the black moustache couldn't believe that Bahman knew such fine and extraordinary poems. They were so powerful, they would have woken the dead. They introduced the drinkers to fantasies the likes of which they had never known. That night, as the rain came pelting down, Ghazalnus read his poems and the lonely, intoxicated men entered a trance, became immersed in the words, moved their arms as if they were flying. Ghazalnus was like an unconscious adventurer who took delight in displaying his own inebriation and wildness, like someone removing an outer layer of serenity and trampling it underfoot. As he recited the fiery ghazals, and for no apparent reason, he left the warmth of the bar – nobody understood the method in this madness – and ran out onto the grass in the garden in the rain.

For a long time, he had wanted to try out his madness in the rain; he wanted to read his poems in the falling rain and see how his words intoxicated people. His black-moustached companion was the first to follow him out into the night storm, but gradually his voice drew out all the drunks. Even those who still had some awareness and serenity left were unable to resist, and followed. The drunks that night, the men in whom the poems stirred a love that God had planted in their hearts long ago, followed the sonorous, love-filled voice of the rain-sodden youth reciting a strand of classical poems they had never heard before. No one knows for sure which of these poorly paid drunks raised his voice and shouted, 'Keep going, Ghazalnus, don't stop! I'm willing to stand in the rain every night until dawn and listen to you!'

It was the first time someone had addressed Bahman Nasser as 'Ghazalnus'. Prior to that, not even he had heard 'Ghazalnus' used as a name. From that night on, no one ever asked for the real name of this eager man with a sea of classical poems in his breast. Out in that rainfall Bahman Nasser died, and Ghazalnus was born. The name stuck, and as time passed his given name faded like an old memory that only he recalled. I have to say that on a deep level, Bahman Nasser was sure, on this night when he accepted his new name from the drunk and wine-loving civil servants and teachers, that he was just another manifestation of Mullah Sukhta. From the day he left the mysterious love chamber, he had been certain that Mullah Sukhta, with all his vigour and might, had settled under his skin. In the six years he lived with the poems, he was so immersed in Sukhta's words and couplets that he no longer saw himself only as the guardian of his treasure trove of texts, but as the bearer of his soul as well. He was not Mullah Sukhta's son, he was Mullah Sukhta himself. He was not Baharbanu's son, but Baharbanu herself.

Among the bar's employees were men who happened to be experts in classical poetry, and upon hearing the extraordinary poems they became fixated on discovering the author. They began to search through old libraries, but found nothing. Later, a couple of samples of the poems ended up with university professors who claimed to be specialists in classical poetry. They, too, could not make much out of them. No one could believe that these profound masterpieces were the work of a young man like Ghazalnus, and they concentrated all their efforts on finding the source somewhere in the worn-out pages of old manuscripts.

Be that as it may, that night changed Ghazalnus into a displaced soul, distributing the heritage of imaginary lovers around the world. In that small civil servants' club, he thrilled them, night in, night out. Through his ghazals, the poor employees lived the imagined love they had not experienced in reality. The first listeners and lovers of the legendary ghazals were drunks, arrack drinkers, condemned by their parents and their families, treated as worthless by their wives, feared by their children, who were repelled by their smell. When they returned home late at night, ties askew, mouths drooling and eyes dazed, everyone looked at them as beasts who had forfeited all respect. And yet, among those doomed creatures were wonderful people who astonished Ghazalnus. The short period he spent with the drunken men was the beginning of Ghazalnus's complex treatment of the infinite images of the human being.

Most of these bearded, yellow-toothed employees, these untidy alcoholics who could look so dangerous if judged by their appearance, smell and tone of voice, were desperate, oppressed, failed human beings at heart; excited by the shortest ghazal, they would burst into tears at the slightest show of sympathy.

All through the eight years of the Iran–Iraq War, which changed the face of the world, Ghazalnus travelled constantly; word spread quickly about the famous gatherings where he read out Mullah Sukhta's ghazals. The poems were so powerful, they made people faint. Among the lovers of fantasy and poetry, he established a reputation as one of the greatest ghazal writers in history. At those gatherings, he made contact with imaginative people. (He was surprised to find that this horrible, unhappy city in particular had so many lovers of the imagination.) He mounted podiums with the collection of ghazals, and read them out. The poems maximised people's ability to love and to fantasise. On whichever podium he appeared, young and old lovers of the imagination gathered around him. He read his ghazals out everywhere: in forests and distant woods, aboard ships and among farmers. Wherever he read, mighty barriers to the imagination came crashing down and people saw things that had been invisible and unknown until then.

The power of the enchanting rhymes and words meant fishermen walked with greater ease towards imaginary waters, and dark forest paths became bright. All those who heard the ghazals construed them as a secret message from destiny, as though the fantasies found in the poems were divine calls or heavenly inspiration directed at them specifically.

During the war years, Ghazalnus travelled from one city to another, from one district to another. His mission was to find Imaginative Creatures, those people who gained nothing from the real world and set out for the bottomless ocean of the imagination. He created an extensive network of these rare souls, producing a mosaic of scattered stories from different periods of time, from different lands and imaginations. Sometimes he wanted to connect all the imaginary lands together, to make one region out of all the imaginary forests and gardens. He wanted to merge the smaller streams to create entire imaginary rivers. Imagination in that land dwelled in a group of scattered, varied and remote regions that teemed with fear. It was full of dark and undiscovered alleyways, full of secret desires governed by humanity's darker instincts. He wanted to convert all these into an infinite open road for all who wished to travel endlessly through the imagination. Mullah Sukhta's poems were like light from a lighthouse, attracting ships from every land and every age. The light was so strong it awakened the Imaginative Creatures in the remotest, darkest depths. But unless people had an imaginative soul in the first place, they could not understand Ghazalnus. The impact of his ghazals could only be felt by imaginative creatures.

Ghazalnus – with his full beard, curly, dervish-like hair, his light, olive-coloured suit and the bag that held copies of his collection of ghazals – became an itinerant. On the country's borders, he mingled with a battalion of imaginary peshmergas fighting for an imaginary

Kurdistan, a Kurdistan that existed only in their strange and vivid dreams. He got to know the sad martyrs searching for a garden that would be a home of eternal tranquillity. He read out poems to gardeners whose trees bore luminous fruit. All the souls he came across on these travels were people like himself, created half from the real world and half from the imagination.

One day, when he was reading out ghazals, he came to a lush plain. Like the ancient dervishes, Ghazalnus walked with a long crook and carried an old sack. His beard now reached his chest, and his curly, jet-black hair came down to his shoulders. Suddenly, an old woman blocked his path and asked, 'Ghazalnus, where are you going?'

'Grandmother,' Ghazalnus said after the fashion of heroes in the ancient tales, 'if you know my name, you must also know where I am going.'

'Follow me, then,' she said. 'There is a woman who needs your help.'

Ghazalnus followed the old woman for four days and four nights, in silence. They passed through places of great cold and great heat, through green, green gardens and withered, thirsty grasslands. They passed through villages blighted by drought, and villages that were flourishing. Finally they came to a quiet, neglected hamlet with a smattering of low-walled derelict houses. In one of them, Ghazalnus saw a small, sick woman lying in a rickety bed with a torn mattress and yellowing sheet. The edges of the purple brocade pillow under her head had begun to disintegrate. Everything appeared cold and drab and old.

'I've brought you here to help her,' said the older woman. 'She is ill, and gave birth only recently. You can tell from her complexion that she's dying. She gave birth to a bastard child a week ago. She's my niece. Her father died a long time ago. She has a married sister, and if her husband finds out, he'll kill them both. She had the baby boy seven days ago. She wanted to see you before she died. If I weren't afraid for her sister's life, I wouldn't have given this bitch shelter, ill-omened as she is.' With this, the old woman turned around and walked out the room, leaving Ghazalnus alone with the ailing mother.

Ghazalnus looked down at her. Traces of a fading beauty were evident in her face; hers was the type of beauty destroyed by hardship and sudden disaster. Although she was clad in the customary garb of a village girl, he later found out she was a poor woman from the city. She was dangerously pale.

'Ghazalnus, is it you? How can this be?' she said, lifting her head slightly.

She spoke as if she had known Ghazalnus for a long time. Slowly and with great difficulty, she sat up in her bed.

'I didn't think I would ever see you again,' she said.

Ghazalnus scrutinised her. He could see nothing but a sick, pale woman with no hope of recovery. She was so emaciated you could count the bones in her wrists and fingers one by one.

'Khanim,' said Ghazalnus, 'you are very ill. We must take you to a hospital. Why are you lying in this dark room?'

She had difficulty breathing.

'No, it's not possible,' she answered Ghazalnus calmly. 'I can't go to a hospital. I don't want to see a doctor. I'm dead already. I am quite sure of that.'

'How can you be so sure?' said Ghazalnus. 'No one should surrender to death so easily. There's no such thing as death as long as you're alive and breathing.'

The girl was trembling a great deal. She appeared weak and lifeless, as if she had not eaten for days.

'I'm glad you came, Ghazalnus,' she said miserably. 'I didn't think my aunt would be able to find you. I heard your ghazals at a seminar two years ago. They changed my life.'

'You are very ill – very, very ill,' said Ghazalnus. 'You must go and see a doctor. You mustn't say another word. You must get out of bed so that I can take you to the doctor.'

'Do you want to dishonour my sisters and all my relatives? And let the whole world find out I bore a fatherless child? Whether I go to the doctor or not, I'm dead. There's no longer a place for me in this world. If I lived any longer, I wouldn't know what to do. My only wish is to find a safe place for my son.'

'What are you saying?' said Ghazalnus, distressed, as he shook his dervish-like tresses. 'How can you speak like that? How can you have so little respect for your own life? You mustn't say such things. I can find the child's father and convince him to raise his son, to change his ways, to marry you so that you can live together.'

'Ghazalnus, I've already been dead for several days,' said the woman, pushing her purple pillow back slightly, 'but I didn't want to leave this world before seeing you. No one can find the child's father. No one. Because I made him with someone who isn't aware of him, with someone I've slept with in my imagination. Only in my imagination. He doesn't know. We loved each other for three years, but never slept together. Not even our fingers touched. I swear to you, we never slept together, but no one believes me. I imagined being with him every night. Every single night. This baby is the fruit of my imagination. I read your ghazals and thought about that man. Every night, I read the ghazals in bed. I've been dead for over a week. Don't touch me. I'm as cold as iron. If you take me to the doctor, you'll become a laughingstock. I am a corpse who bid farewell to the world seven days ago.'

Ghazalnus touched the girl's hands. She was indeed as cold and bloodless as a corpse.

'You've borne a child created by love, by great love,' Ghazalnus said in disbelief. 'Khanim, you are a great woman. You can do the impossible.'

She looked at Ghazalnus, moved her head closer to his, and said, 'Those ghazals drive people mad, make them fall wildly in love. Ghazalnus, only you understand what I am talking about out of everyone in this whole world. Only you can raise this child. He is the offspring of the ghazals. He's your child; you mustn't abandon him.'

Her voice was deep and pleading. He couldn't tell whether what she said was real or whether they were both in a dream, whether he had entered the woman's dream or she had entered his. He was, however, sure that one of them was in the real world and the other in the world of the imagination.

'Khanim, whatever could I do for this child?' Ghazalnus asked.

'I don't know,' she said sadly. 'But if you don't adopt him, he'll die. He has no one but you. He has neither mother nor father. My aunt made such an effort to bring you here in order to be rid of him. I ran away from the city four months ago, and took shelter with her.'

'She can raise the child better than anyone else,' said Ghazalnus. 'I can support her. I assure you, I can support her in this.'

'Be quiet,' she whispered. 'If she knows you won't take the child away, she'll strangle him. Do you understand? You'd better keep quiet. I've given that child a dead person's milk for a week now, imaginary milk from my lifeless breasts, to make sure he survives. If she finds out that you don't want the child, she'll kill him. She'll strangle him tonight and bury him. She's my aunt. She's been trying to kill me for four months now. Do you understand? Take the boy and leave. Take him and leave.'

'Take my pulse, Ghazalnus,' she said, reaching out as she spoke. 'Ghazalnus, come and take my pulse.'

'Good Lord,' cried Ghazalnus as he put his head on her chest. 'Khanim, you are a cold corpse.'

'You must save the child,' she said with some anger. 'He's waiting for you. I don't see why you don't understand. You have to see the child, you've got to. Auntie! … Auntie! … Auntie!'

She called for the old woman in a high-pitched voice that was nothing like that of a dead person. The bad-tempered aunt, who seemed to have overheard the entire conversation, entered the room holding a tiny infant. 'Take your child,' she said as she put him in her lap. 'Shame on you. What a mother you are. He's hungry.'

He was a tiny, angelic infant with a fair complexion, small eyes and soft hair. Unlike his mother, he didn't appear to be hungry or tired. He looked as if he had just been bathed in the waters of a pure river.

'Perhaps he came from a magical garden,' Ghazalnus thought to himself.

When he held the child, he had a strange feeling of déjà vu, as if Mullah Hajar's words had suddenly come back into his head. Quickly, he loosened the swaddling clothes. He wanted to see the boy naked, to touch the pale, delicate skin. When he saw the baby's chest, a deep, cold shudder ran through him. He didn't know if what he was seeing was real or not, if his eyes were deceiving him, if this was the result of great exhaustion and a long time without food. But no, he could see it quite clearly. A quatrain was inscribed on the infant's chest like a deep wound:

> Oh, child of the dark, you were a flower, I was ash.
> Oh, love's creation, from me love, from you your naked face.
> Imagination's flute and being's melodies conceived you:
> Bloom like a garden, gleam like a ruby

The young woman was aware of Ghazalnus's astonishment.

'Now you get it,' she said, looking at him. 'This is your brother, but you want to discard him. He's close to you, as close as you are to your own self.'

For a moment, Ghazalnus was in shock. He just kept looking at the sick woman, and said nothing. The young woman took the infant from Ghazalnus and began to dress him again.

'Now you understand, you are not alone,' she said. 'You may not have known it when you saw them, but there are other humans born from ghazals, just like you: children of the imagination, created by love. If human beings cannot sleep with their beloveds, there is a magical, imaginary garden where they can go to meet with them. Forgive me, Ghazalnus, but you'd have to be stupid not to realise this. There are brainless people, idiots, who think that just because two lovers don't sleep together in real life, it doesn't happen at all. That is a lie. All the lovers of the world sleep together in their imaginations. Forgive me, Ghazalnus, sometimes I think even you are an idiot. You've travelled so much and still, you haven't understood this. Everyone has a place where their wishes come true. I've been there. I was there for hundreds of nights, you know. But you're very tired, Ghazalnus. You've seen many places recently. Too much seeing wearies the imagination. You must take care of yourself.

'Now this child has no one but you,' she said as she raised her head. 'You can't sit and think forever. You must take your little brother and go. Don't forget, he has no one but you.'

Ghazalnus still could not utter a word.

'Too much thinking prevents action,' the young woman said. 'You have a long path ahead of you, and I have to go. I entrust this boy to you. You need to give him a name; the dead shouldn't name the living. But let me tell you, go to Afsana. Go to a woman called Afsana at the Snow and Mirage Hotel. She'll help you. She'll help, but don't forget: this is your child. He has no one but you.'

Ghazalnus took the swaddled baby and cradled him gently. A cold wind was blowing outside. A seemingly infinite night was falling. Without a murmur, he held the child close and left the room.

This happened halfway through the autumn of 1988. An unseasonal cold had arrived. Oblivious to the wind, the night and the roads, Ghazalnus returned to the city with the infant. It was the first child of ghazals he had ever seen, the first real child of his own kind.

PARINAZ EATS A POISONOUS FLOWER
MAJID-I GUL SOLAV, SUMMER 2004

I was the first to put the barons under the spotlight. Ghazalnus and Trifa Yabahri had heard the titles 'Agha', 'Mir' and 'Khoja' before, but not 'Baron'. I didn't know whether Hasan-i Tofan knew anything about them or not. I looked at his face as I uttered the words 'the barons', and thought I saw what appeared to be a shudder. The shadow of Murad Jamil loomed increasingly large in our awareness. One evening, together with the three greatest friends of my life, I decided to look for the barons – as if Murad Jamil were a sick king with three loyal sons who were taking to the road to seek out a rare cure. After a long meeting, we decided we would pursue his story to the end, that we wouldn't stop until we found his murderers.

It was at this point that Ghazalnus took to repeating the same words again and again: 'Don't put yourselves out for me. Don't risk your lives for me. Only carry on as long as you don't think you are in any real danger.'

At the time, I didn't understand why he thought we were investigating the murder for his sake. It was a pointless request that hurt us all. For me, working on the past of the deceased was a private and spiritual matter. It was like a hook that dragged me from one world into another. Initially, I had wanted to do everything on my own, but when I looked into my friends' eyes I realised the magnitude and complexity of the task at hand, and knew that I couldn't face it by myself. They all thought I was incompetent. They knew I was forever thinking about the films that had become such a big part of my life, about how I would go to Hollywood one day and have a beer with Morgan Freeman, how I would take a road trip from Texas to California in a soft-top with Cameron Diaz, or eat at a restaurant in Chicago with Julia Roberts. Though my task was to search for the barons, they knew I had no leads, that I didn't know where to start. I didn't have extensive connections to draw upon for help, either. In any case, I resolved to do my best in furthering our mission. I didn't want to seem like someone who only ever carried out simple tasks. That hardly fit the image I had of myself as someone with an adventurous soul, wild and untameable.

We were all overawed by the greatness and grandeur of the word 'baron'. The others had a deeper and more accurate sense of danger, especially Hasan-i Tofan, who could smell it very early on and knew exactly when we crossed the border into the danger zone, into territory that was off limits. Saying the word 'baron' was like approaching a strange, invisible terrain. The barons were a new phenomenon, and not to be taken lightly.

The name 'Baron of Chickens' was my only clue. I began with the chicken-sellers. I rarely went to the bird market. The behaviour of the poultry merchants always came as a shock: the way they reached inside the cage to take out a bird, the way they stamped on the animal's wings and slashed its throat with their blunt knives, the blood they spilled on the pavements. It all made for a scene I couldn't bear to watch. None of the chicken-sellers knew what the word 'baron' meant. I tried to ask them, in simple language, who the most famous poultry merchant was, hoping it might pave the way to a secret. In fact, no one knew. Most of them were junior vendors who bought their poor birds from a few private farms. One of them told me I ought to ask the vendors who sold frozen chicken, the major merchants in the market, rather than these small-time sellers sitting next to a single caged bird. After a long search, a turbaned shopkeeper sporting a motorcycle moustache – a cheerful man, very unlike the city's grim-faced vendors – told me: 'Brother, don't bother trying to find him. No one in the bazaar has heard of the Baron of Chickens. It doesn't sound like the kind of name the bazaar folk use; more like the moniker of someone who knows a bit about the world. Go and ask somewhere else.'

I went home that night disappointed, and clueless as to where else to go. Meanwhile, I could clearly recall Murad Jamil's beautiful corpse. It seemed to beg me to do something for him. I was certain my friends would return with more information. They knew other methods, other streets that I was not familiar with. And I wasn't wrong. I might not have got anywhere, but all three of them returned with important information.

The title 'baron' was a new one. In the early spring of 2004, when we found Murad Jamil's body, the barons were still in the making. Hasan-i Tofan, as always, had more information than anyone else, and, as always, he did not share all of it. All I understood was that the barons constituted a group of wealthy people – politicians, merchants and real estate tycoons – working together. Each of them was in charge of a certain sector. They hung out together most nights.

They drank together, worked together, picnicked together and ruled together. One way or another, the city was in their hands. Obviously, this information wasn't of much use in explaining Murad Jamil's death. I decided to take my revenge on Tofan.

'Esteemed, Hasan-i Pizo,' I said, 'I hope you won't be angry with me, but I don't feel that your information has any real value in understanding the untimely death of Murad Jamil. And as your esteemed self knows, what we're trying to do is to ascertain the details of his death, nothing more.'

I knew it drove him mad when I talked like this. He became so irritated he could hardly breathe. Sometimes he managed to control himself, but other times he would look up to the sky with tearful eyes as if facing great disaster and say: 'Oh God, what should I do with him now?'

'If we want to finish this book,' he said, after a moment's silence, pointing to the big, celebrated book that I kept updated in my nice handwriting, 'if we want to record the history of death in this city – the real history of death – we have to penetrate the barons' stronghold. Do you know what that means? It means we mustn't be afraid of death. We must find someone who isn't, someone who will step into the beast's lair.'

'I'll go,' I said without thinking. 'I am more reckless, more daring than any of you.'

'For this job,' Hasan-i Tofan said, 'we need someone who *isn't* reckless or daring, by which I mean, someone who *isn't* like you. We need a wiser man than you.'

Anyone else would have left the meeting at once.

'As you wish, Hasan-i Pizo,' I said, offended. 'Hurt me to your heart's content, yet I am willing to do this job the way you want. You shouldn't treat me as if I'm worthless. I am, after all, a person who can do great things.'

I needed the chance to prove that I was an adventurous, daring person.

'Gul Solav, brother,' Ghazalnus interrupted, 'we're not going to put you in danger. None of us qualifies for the job. The person who brings us information from the barons will have to be one of them, one of their own.'

Ghazalnus was right, but that was impossible. How could we find someone among the barons to provide us with information about them? It was, I thought, yet another example of Ghazalnus's wishful thinking.

In fact, back then, I didn't understand a thing. Back then, we were facing a closed door.

Sad and disappointed, I resumed my imaginary voyages on my imaginary maps. I felt that in the imaginary world I could compensate for my ineptitude in the real one. In the imaginary world, I was the captain of a huge ship that I steered through an infinite and magical realm.

Since starting my imaginary voyages with the blind children, I had felt more at peace and more focused than ever before. I had my own individual path, one that did not resemble anyone else's. I had my own ship, and I sailed freely along a river of infinite length. Its banks teemed with imaginary kingdoms, which I had woven with great effort. That day when I returned to the blind children, they were all waiting for me. We had interrupted our last voyage after reaching the edge of a city lit not by ordinary lights, but by a group of luminous birds that circled its skies. These birds, which flew out of the forests at night, shone like lightbulbs. They would circle non-stop, and land only when the sun rose. My children and I had become competent navigators. On a pitch-dark night, we dropped anchor at the edge of that magical city.

During our voyages, they all called me the 'Great Magellan'. I had three costumes, which I wore in turn. One was similar to Ray Danton's in *Sandokan Fights Back*; the second was like the one worn by Anthony Quinn in *Caravans* – a blend of Western and Oriental styles; and the third was like Gérard Depardieu's in *Conquest of Paradise*, which tells the story of Christopher Columbus's discovery of America. Yes, I stepped into the imaginary lands wearing those three costumes. In most of the cities we went to, I didn't reveal my identity, passing myself off as an ordinary tourist taking a group of blind children on a world tour. On our extraordinary voyage, which saw us sail the longest river in the world for the longest time, we came to many unusual places.

From my travels across the imaginary map, I came to realise that there are two types of cities in the world. The first are those you cannot penetrate. Even when you've entered this type of city, you are always on the outside, constantly circling its walls. You are always at a distance, never crossing its threshold. The other type, meanwhile, you can never leave. Once you enter, you remain imprisoned there forever. Wherever you go, you are still there. You might combine it with other cities or make it part of bigger ones. You can add cities to it, like adding another layer to a cake, but you can't get away.

That evening, my blind fellow sailors and I had reached a city of the impenetrable type. All elusive cities are circular, their streets winding dangerously. This kind of city does not think like explorers and travellers, however: While we move towards the centre as if along the coils of a spring, the opposite is true for the city in question. When you think you're going towards the centre, according to the city's logic you're on the way out. And because you can never enter it, you can't cheat and pretend you are making your way out so that the city will draw you in. As a result, you are always outside. This is the opposite of the stifling cities, the cities that imprison people – where you think you're moving outwards, but the city is actually taking you towards the centre. Therefore, the more you try to leave, the further inside you find yourself. My shipmates and I were moving around in an impossible geometry. On one hand, we had left one city for another without entering it; on the other, we were in another city without having left the first. It was a complex imaginary equation that my companions and I had to get used to. True, these cities that we visited so frequently existed only on my imaginary map, but it should be noted even so that a well-thought out, well laid-out fantasy follows a complex and impossible geometry. The mathematics of the imagination adheres more rigorously to terms and theorems than the mathematics of reality.

On board the imaginary ship, I realised that imagination does not mean absolute freedom. The world of the imagination submits to multiple conditions and to precise geometry. Before I started drawing my map, I thought the imaginary realms were lands of genuine freedom. That isn't so, however. The lands of the imagination are not places where you can do whatever you want. At times, the imagination is subject to a greater degree of predetermination than reality. I've often thought that we can understand reality with the help of the imagination, but not imagination with the help of reality. Right from my very first encounter with Ghazalnus, I was pitted against him. I believe the imagination is, at times, as dangerous as reality. Compared with the imagination, reality is a peaceful, less troublesome realm. My experience of the voyage along the banks of the infinitely long river taught me that the imagination was home to unusual creatures and unexpected people. Man knows the trees, birds and stars of the real world. We have learned a certain way of life and system of interaction, whereas in the imagination everything changes, and everything is alien. You don't know when you've entered the danger zone, or when you've crossed from the river of fear to the shores of happiness and certainty. Most of us pass through the darkness of reality easily, but rarely can we understand the darkness of the imagination. Every time we embarked on a voyage, my young co-sailors asked me, 'Sardarbashi, why are you so scared of the

darkness? Have you not created these imaginary lands yourself?'
Although the question was often asked, on every single occasion it
was cause for astonishment and reflection.

'My dear sailors, my imaginary rowers,' I told them, 'when someone
creates a place in the imagination, he draws only the outline to
begin with. He draws a simple line, then colours it in. My power
over my imagination sometimes stops at the line. What might lie
beyond it, I don't know. Some people are lucky. They have very
broad imaginations. They can see everything, right down to the last
garden and the last flower, but the imagination of your unfortunate
Sardarbashi is of a different type. It is darker and more complicated.
You can create everything, but a vast space will always remain for
invisible and unexpected things. The dangers of the imagination
cannot be defeated by reason. Imaginary things pop up unexpectedly.
I'm the kind of person who doesn't know in advance what lies
sleeping in my imagination. I can create a city with my imagination,
but I can't be sure how its every dark street and every alley will look.
I can create huge imaginary forests, but what creatures live inside that
forest, what happens there, how we can pass through its darkness,
all that has its own rules, something your unlucky teacher cannot
specify. Often, you don't know what you're looking for in your
imagination or what you expect to find there. In the old days, they
called this 'inspiration' or 'revelation'. Inspiration is an inopportune
and extraordinary feature of the imagination that suddenly comes
into play. At first we see only the exterior form of the imagination, but
no one knows its deep, dark contents.

'My brave oar-bearers, there are two types of passers-by on the
road of the imagination. One type cannot cross into the world of the
imagination. They are safe, but lack the beauty of the imagination,
the taste for its dangers. Whereas people like us board a sailing
ship but don't know where it will moor, what cities await us, what
unheard of and invisible forms we shall see or what emotions we
shall experience. No invisible object, regardless of the darkness that
surrounds it, can match the invisible inside our imaginations.'

I subscribed to the view that the imagination is a free force, and
that we should let it take us as it wishes, that we should succumb
to its secrets. Obviously, for people to cherish the imagination,
they need reason. Imagining is closely connected to our awareness
of the world and our power of reasoning; it is not a meaningless
exercise. However, to expect that reason can completely understand
everything about the imagination and its contents is to destroy the
land of imagination. From the outset, I made a distinction between
intelligent and imaginative people. I had an imaginative soul; I was

not a wise or clever person. Hasan-i Pizo was justified in his concerns about my lack of intelligence. For me to be a truly imaginative person, I ought not to know where the ship was heading – like that, I would always be at the mercy of the imagination, and those on board my ship should not know what awaited them either. Imagination shouldn't be like a story you have already heard, but one whose ending you cannot predict.

Now I think this was the biggest difference between Ghazalnus and me. From the very start, he could see the end of his life. I was more fortunate in this respect, as, like a blind man, I could see nothing. My voyages were substitutes for the real world. I often thought that Ghazalnus was more a lover than an imaginative person. 'It's like you have a train, Ghazalnus,' I often told him (not without irritation), 'a very long train that you have populated with Imaginative Creatures. We, the Imaginative Creatures, are all passengers on your train. Your train moves on two infinite tracks – one, the imagination; the other, reality. It needs both tracks to run. If you removed one of them, it would collapse. As for me, I'm a different type of person. I'm not the driver of a train riding along two tracks, like you. I'm a sailor, and my ship has no legs. It's an imaginary ship sailing imaginary waters.'

For as long as imaginary creatures exist only in the imagination, there is no danger; for as long as the realms of imagination and reality do not merge, everything is all right. But once you combine the two, disaster strikes. Although I took part in everything alongside my friends, I posed no threat to the real world. I fell into the harmless category. Fewer people boarded my far less intriguing vessel that night as the young, blind sailors and I circled the city; we couldn't find a way in. Imagination often circles around an empty terrain, in an eternal orbit, allowing you no escape. The luminous birds flew over our heads. The city denied us entrance. If an imaginary place doesn't let you in, you must retreat calmly. There's no point digging in your heels. Human beings can often find the truth through sustained effort, but that doesn't work with the imagination. Imagination is akin to a door that opens voluntarily. Otherwise, no power can force it open. I often resorted unsuccessfully to my own tornado-like powers to open those closed doors, but let me tell you, whenever a door resists being opened, don't smash things up. Just go away and never return.

Standing by the city's gates, which I didn't know how to open, I felt unable to employ the same persistence I was showing in unravelling Murad Jamil's mysterious death. True, here I was the sultan of the kingdom, but there isn't a single sultan who would stand his ground in the face of the inaccessible mountains of his domain. Outside the gate of that city, as we looked wildly for an opening, I felt that imagination can be every bit as elusive and inaccessible as truth. To my frustration over finding the truth behind Murad Jamil's death had now been added frustration at trying to break down the gate to this imaginary city, a city bathed in darkness except for its tall towers and shining birds.

Frustration and the death of the imagination are one and the same. That night, I moved away from the city's impenetrable gates so that the children wouldn't notice my powerlessness, so that they wouldn't say, 'Don't keep us here much longer', so they wouldn't ask me, 'Are you not the master of these rivers? Haven't you created this city on this wretched map? Haven't you created every inch of it? How, then, can you not enter it?'

If they had asked such questions, I would have told them: 'Dear friends of Magellan, you've got it wrong. Imagination is not like memory. It is reality. Man can never step into an imaginary city twice. Heraclitus's adage that man cannot step into the same river twice is a lie. You can step into the river of reality dozens of times, and it will still be the same river. What Heraclitus was talking about is the river of imagination.' My young, inexperienced apprentices and I have put this to the test dozens of times. We'd leave an imaginary city, and when we attempted to return, we could never find it again. Ever.

In short, I was using an enormous, detailed map – but I was the one following it. Imagination followed its own map, and the map dictated its own laws that were beyond my power.

That night, I withdrew my small army and boarded my ship again to avoid further disappointments. On board the ship, at times, we felt free and happy; at other times we were like fugitives trying to escape dangerous forces by river, or a group of prisoners escorted by imaginary guards. But we always felt ourselves the slaves of a large number of cities. The imaginary cities we had visited, and which had imprisoned us, were calling us: cities, as I said earlier, that grip and then refuse to release you; places you think you have left behind when in fact you've done anything but; places that attract you; places that trick you. You're heading somewhere new, to a different, unknown destination, when you notice another place summoning you, a place that exists in your head before it features on the maps. When you get closer and anchor your ship, you realise it is the same city that has been holding you captive and tricking you, a city that deceives you and appears in various guises.

All those who have wandered imaginary maps know what it means to become the captive of a place. Being a captive of imaginary cities does not mean you keep finding yourself in the same place. Rather, there is a clear sense that the place is playing tricks on you, changing colour to ensnare you, making itself lovely to prevent you from leaving. Even though you happen upon it in different places and different periods of time, it refrains from all repetition so that you have the impression of being on the move. Yes, being captive in the imagination is not tantamount to being frozen in a particular area; it is, rather, a strange feeling of being on the move when you are standing still.

That night we passed through a very narrow tributary. We were all worried about what might be lying in wait on its banks. More than once on our unusual journeys, we had been summoned by deceptive fantasies from the other side of the river. From where we were on the river, we could see lights. We anchored our ship in a tranquil spot. Although the blind children had seen nothing but darkness all their lives, whenever I mentioned pitch-dark forests or waters they were overcome with fear. I knew that the darkness of the imagination was different from other forms of darkness. The children were accustomed to real darkness, but they hadn't encountered the darkness of the imaginary world; they were as afraid of it as I was. That night, we disembarked and walked towards the lights of a nearby village. It was clean and dust-free, full of new houses. From the herd of wounded deer running past us, we understood that we were in a hunting ground, and that the village was home to hunters who lived alongside their prey.

The more we advanced through the village streets, the more hunters we saw wandering about, bearing long rifles and wearing exotic costumes. Most of them appeared to be sad. What struck us, however, was the wounded prey wandering through the alleyways – the stunned and bleeding deer, the maimed rabbits playing in back gardens, the murdered pigeons that landed on the hunters' shoulders. In that city, we saw most of the creatures ever hunted by humans. It was the first time my blind children had been able to see birds and animals so clearly, ones I had seen in films but which they had never seen at all. We were surprised when we realised that there were barely any creatures humans had not hunted, from fledgling birds to fierce lions and tigers. In that town we saw fishermen with nets, and fish swimming in huge rivers. We walked next to a bottomless body of water resembling the edge of an ocean, in which we saw sad whales raise their heads above the water to stare at us. Their eyes were so extraordinary, their gaze so unhappy, that it made my young sailors cry.

That's one of the biggest problems with these imaginary lands: you enter them thinking you are in a small place, but slowly they open up and teem with more rivers, more seas, infinite pathways. A place would be filled with bigger and more unusual maps, which cannot be seen on your normal map at normal times. That's why a journey in the imagination is never like it is in the real world: in the latter, you know your destination, whereas in the former the only thing you can be sure of is whether you are stationary or mobile. And even being sure of that is not easy. Well, nothing is easy on this kind of journey. Any journey through the realm of the imagination is slow. The time needed to see our entire world is thousands of times less than the time needed to see just one imaginary city.

That night, a group of old fishermen invited us to dine with them. I don't eat fish, but the fish in that world had a different taste. On the shores of the tranquil water, we ate the most delicious fish of our lives – food that you, reader, can never eat because you are unable to board an imaginary ship and accompany a Sardarbashi like myself on a journey towards the unknown. I should say that on the days we boarded the ships, my imaginative children and I would not eat any real food all day long. We were sure the ship would take us to where there would be imaginary food. We had eaten many imaginary fruits and vegetables on our journeys. In the imaginary world, there is always a dinner mat spread out on a floor somewhere, waiting for us to reach it.

That night, while we were eating the fish, little Parinaz – the only vegetarian in our group – nibbled on a few small flowers growing on a strange tree. It was a sad and solitary tree, as if the Devil had planted it there to trick us. Its white flowers resembled almond blossoms, only the tree was definitely not an almond tree. While we were busy removing the delicate bones from the fish, Parinaz developed an agonising stomach pain. I had always been terrified of the idea that one day a poisonous plant would kill us all, because I knew the forests of the imagination were rife with them. Powerless, I stared at Parinaz. She was in excruciating pain. We all thought she was going to die. I was overcome with fear, and couldn't do a thing to help. I was surprised to see the imaginary fishermen lift Parinaz in their arms and carry her swiftly to the ship on which we were to return. They ran, and we followed them. I came back to my senses then. I knew we had to take Parinaz to a hospital. I was responsible for the blind children, but to tell you the truth, I didn't think an imaginary poison could lead to real food poisoning. When we came to the ship, I turned it southward and headed back like a madman. You never know how or where you will leave the map.

Once we left the imaginary world, we noticed that Parinaz was indeed sick. I passed the news to her relatives through some of the other children and, carrying her in my arms, rushed her to a hospital, as frantically as a parent trying to save his own child. When we arrived, there was still life left in her, but no one could tell whether or not she would survive. I held her close in my arms and raced through the corridor of the casualty ward. At the height of my sprint, I became aware of someone else running beside me: a stranger, a man I had never met before. As we both raced along the corridor, the tall stranger told me, 'My name is Mir Safin. Some people call me the Baron of Dolls. Don't worry. I am with you. I am Parinaz's uncle. I'll help you.'

'Thank you for your kindness,' I said as I ran. 'I need it.'

I ran even faster, and could not fully make out what he was saying. Because of Parinaz, who was fighting for her life, I was unaware of what was happening. But the speed at which the man ran, and his bald head, shiny beard and melodious voice, all stayed with me.

That night, as I laid my head on the pillow at bedtime, I remembered his name suddenly – and it startled me. 'The Baron of Dolls, the Baron of Dolls, the Baron of Dolls.' I felt strong emotions stir in my breast, and then a force dragging me down with incredible speed towards a remote and dark spot ... a place I didn't know.

When I fell asleep I dreamed about the Baron of Dolls, with his shiny beard, talking to me as we ran side by side down the long hospital corridor.

SHIBR'S INFORMATION ABOUT THE BARONS

From the very first day I became friends with Shibr, we tried not to dwell on the past. Neither of us had an honest and noble past worthy of discussion. We both hated our past, but while renunciation and condemnation of it had driven me into strict isolation, dealing with it had somehow been less painful and troublesome for Shibr. He was loyal to his friends, and to the people close to him. He rarely lost contact with them. Having said that, some of his close friends had become senior officials in recent years, and none of them spared a moment's thought for the blond guy with pale eyes who now went around in a wheelchair. When it comes to political parties, you only need to drop off the radar for a couple of weeks before you're quickly forgotten.

Back then, I was happy to help Shibr. Helping him had become part of my life. On many a spring, summer and autumn day, in the happy evenings when the cool shade before sunset brought us hope, I would push him along in his wheelchair. He was a very amiable, outgoing individual, which won him many friends. People couldn't understand how I, with my sullen expression, could possibly be the friend of such a merry and gregarious chap, someone who stirred life in the lifeless. I had never seen anyone undergo as radical a transformation as he had. He had become open-minded and tolerant. Obviously, many people knew me in the bazaar. Most of them had, at some point, heard the name 'Hasan-i Tofan', even if they might not have known who he actually was. Now that era was gone forever, I begged those who knew me to call me 'Hasan-i Pizo'. I didn't want to be called 'Tofan' any more. I was in the midst of trying to change my image from 'well-known murderer' to 'quiet man with nothing to hide'. In fact, I rarely went near the heaving bazaar or other crowded places. In the evenings I would often accompany Shibr on his excursions, pushing the wheelchair to his destination and then leaving him there with his friends.

A great silence and tranquillity reigned over my life. I ambled around with the sense that no one in the city knew who I was. The people of my own age group with whom I had grown up had either been killed in the wars, emigrated or become rich and powerful, in which case they were no longer in touch with me. The silence astonished me. I wanted to deepen the calm as much as possible. I felt I had developed a strange faculty no one else had: I could open and close my ears at will. Just as people can speak or remain quiet at will, so I could choose whether or not to listen. I could shut my ears and become immersed in an infinite silence. I often sat in tucked-away teahouses, resting my chin on my chest and drowning in infinite peace for hours. In those moments, all I experienced was the scent of the flowers around me. There were many days when I wished I had someone to talk to – but I didn't. Shibr had more friends than I did. He knew more about the world and was still very keen to know what was going on in it. I saw myself as someone who had been dropped from a plane with only a parachute, and who had landed in a city he couldn't befriend. When I say this, I don't just mean that I felt alien in this city. In fact, I am alienated from the whole world. I am alienated from all human beings. I am alienated from myself.

After my mother's death and my return to society, I was still quiet and alienated. You might well ask repeatedly how a murderer like me, a good-for-nothing, useless creature in the shape of Hasan-i Pizo – small, dull-skinned and ugly with a nasal voice – became friends with such gentle souls as Trifa Yabahri and Ghazalnus. I am well aware that I am nothing but a rusty gun left over from another era, nothing but a political party's worn-out ex-assassin. Shibr and I spent many nights talking about this: we were blunt knives in a closed museum, implements used in a crime and still stained with the blood of their victims, as no one had washed it away. You have every right to say so. I was too dreadful a person to deserve their kind and gentle company, yet that's how my life panned out. Pizo's magical rosewater bore me away until I came down among those pure creatures.

I became one of the Imaginative Creatures without even realising it. In fact, no one ever knows how they become an Imaginative Creature. One night, a group of cheerful, older ladies came to me and said: 'Hasan-i Pizo, your mother was a great teacher of the art of making rosewater. She held the keys to many of the inaccessible gardens of the world, and she left those keys with you. Whether you like it or not, you now own the keys to dozens of gardens whose flowers would die without you. Those flowers are now in season, and it's time to extract the rosewater from those gardens. If you don't open those doors to us, dozens of imaginary flowers will die.'

I understood nothing of what the cheerful older ladies in their black clothes, black headscarves and black silk shawls had to say. One black night, I followed these smiling, joking ladies to an unknown destination. I believe that all strange journeys begin with a step in an unknown direction. To become an Imaginative Creature, you first need to take such a step and to follow a route without knowing where it goes. I had every confidence in the old women, but I didn't know the secret they harboured. The meaning of the keys my mother had left behind made me toss and turn in bed. I knew that apart from these older women, no one else could uncover this secret for me. I had to pluck up my courage, take the key from its hiding place and follow these wonderful women.

That night they took me to a district that, until then, I hadn't known existed in the city. It was called Hazarbagh, or 'One Thousand Gardens'. I hadn't heard the name of this district before. It was huge. It was full of older women extracting rosewater day and night. Its alleyways gave off an intoxicating scent. At the entrance to the perfumed alleyways, another group of older women received me. They all resembled Pizo-i Gulaw in some way. They took me to a great garden, where I saw flowers so rare they could only exist in Paradise. Some of them I had seen in my years of isolation, but because I was not a lover of flowers and had spent my life far from these beautiful, colourful gardens, it never occurred to me to ask Pizo where her flowers came from. That night, for the first time in my life, I understood that I had another home I could turn to outside my ordinary life. I was so astonished by the sight of the magical, moonlit gardens that I never wanted to leave. And whenever you find yourself in a place you don't want to leave, you have crossed into the realm of the imagination.

The women led me to a few locked gates, which I had to open with my keys. I used them to open all the locked doors in that imaginary garden. The women and I entered the winding paths of that vast rose garden. I saw extraordinary flowers beyond the dream of any poet. The gardens were so magnificent; you could walk through them till death without ever feeling tired. There, I forgot about my past. Before that, I hadn't thought that such immense gardens would open their doors to me, Hasan-i Tofan.

That night was the beginning of my meanderings in the gardens of the imaginative women, the gardens of the honest old mothers who had created a secret paradise for themselves from which they made enough rosewater for this city and the neighbouring provinces. That night I became friends with these solemn women who walked me around the flower and rose gardens. Each night thereafter, they helped me open a gate, and each time they made me water a certain type of flower. These same sweet-tongued old ladies introduced me to Ghazalnus. He was one of the rare men who had made his way to the garden. That was where I got to know him, and where I became his friend.

In his busy life as the most famous ghazal reader in the country, Ghazalnus had known a considerable number of Imaginative Creatures, one of whom was Gulistan Khan, the woman in charge of these gardens. She had an extremely beautiful daughter who worked as a hospital nurse. An extraordinary fragrance of rosewater emanated from the younger woman's hair and breath, the kind of fragrance that would make any passing man fall in love with her, a fragrance that cured patients of one disease only to give them another. Her name was Sabri. Her loveliness and the scent of her hair and breath became a key motif in the songs sung by singers from the region. A number of people fell so madly in love with Sabri that they wanted to die at her feet and to sleep on her doorstep like sentries. The girl became confused. She didn't know how to run away or hide from them. To free herself from the curse of all these lovestruck men, she hid for a while among the flowers of Hazarbagh. The older women forbade their children from going to this neighbourhood, because any youth who walked its gardens would become so infatuated with the flowers he or she would forget real life altogether and ignore the outside world. However, in their compassion, the women saw Sabri – who had contracted the fragrance of rosewater in her mother's womb – as an unfortunate girl paying the price of her beauty. They sheltered her amid the imaginary flowers in order to hide her from the innumerable singers, poets and lovers for a while.

So powerful is the magic of those gardens, however, that anyone who spends long enough in them becomes unable to tolerate the sight of ordinary things or return to a normal life. Sabri, who spent a long time in the gardens, could no longer leave. She had become a part of them. She also happened to be an only child. Her immersion in the infinite sea of flowers left her mother inconsolable. Like any mother, she wanted her daughter to marry and have children. All Gulistan's efforts to take Sabri out of the flowers of Hazarbagh were in vain. Sabri strolled endlessly about the gardens, repeating: 'I will never get married.'

Eventually, the older women tried to lure Sabri out with something more extraordinary than the flowers. The only things that could match the beauty and magic of the flowers were Ghazalnus's poems. The rosewater-makers, determined though they were to protect the secret of the gardens, were forced to reveal their identity as Imaginative Creatures to Ghazalnus and to take him to Hazarbagh. Ghazalnus was astounded when he reached the gardens. Like me, he had passed

Hazarbagh hundreds of times during the day and, like thousands of others in this city, didn't know that when the world went to sleep at night, the district normally known as Sebagh – 'Three Gardens' – became an immense garden. It was there that Ghazalnus met Sabri for the first time. Until then, he had thought she was merely a product of the folk singers' imagination.

The story of Ghazalnus and Sabri is a long one that will be discussed again later. The point here is that on a cool summer night towards the end of the twentieth century, as I took a long walk through the imaginary gardens, I stopped at a corner in the rose garden and overheard one of Ghazalnus's poems as he read it out to Sabri under the moonlight. Hearing the poems among the flowers, I felt a deep change in my life. Listening to Ghazalnus gave me an opportunity to come to know my soul. I had never been sure the soul existed until I heard the ghazals. That night, I listened to them in secret until late. At dawn, I revealed myself to Ghazalnus and told him I would remember that night until my last breath, that I would live under the influence of the ghazals for the rest of my days and that their magic would never leave my heart. Obviously, you will all be surprised that a murderer such as myself, who'd had very little contact with poetry, could be so influenced by these ghazals. In fact, Ghazalnus's poems, the fragrance of the flowers, the moonlit night and the summer calm of the garden all made up an enchantment that I was too weak, too powerless to resist. Later, I thought that Ghazalnus's poems had absorbed all the magic from their surroundings. In that moment, the flowers, the moonlight and the calm could only be felt through the ghazals.

From dawn of the following day, I became friends with Ghazalnus. That very same morning I told him my story from scratch. He was so shocked that for a long time he didn't believe me. He hadn't known any murderers before. He couldn't believe I was someone who had killed women, but I had to tell him everything. I decided I wouldn't hide my past from a person with such a pure soul. From that night of the ghazals onwards, the sad young man with the curly hair was my closest friend. Today, I would say that if Ghazalnus hadn't known the truth about me, it would have been impossible for him to choose me – out of so many Imaginative Creatures – to take part in writing the book about the history of death. The night we unearthed Murad Jamil's body, I really felt he considered me one of them, one of the true Imaginative Creatures. Once I entered their fold, I soon realised that despite his thorough knowledge of the city, Ghazalnus desperately needed me. He looked at the life of this city as a book whose front cover was the real world, its back cover the imagination. Although he was very well versed in both worlds, he didn't have the power to penetrate the place in which the death machines operated – while I was a true son of that world. I had grown up there. I knew each and every bolt in the machines. I knew how and when they operated.

Ghazalnus had more life experience than I did, but the world he had seen didn't resemble the one I knew. Not once had he even been among Kurdish politicians. I believe that at one time he had even regarded them all as honest, patriotic people; but after the uprising, like tens of thousands of others in this country, he was bitterly disappointed. After the uprising, he searched constantly for an imaginary realm. I believe he wanted the whole of Kurdistan to be like the winding paths of Hazarbagh. For my part, I don't understand how the intellectuals of this country can harbour this obsession with the idea of a Hazarbagh popping up in every corner of this dilapidated city, home to people like Fazil Qandil and Tunchi, how they can expect to come across a flowerbed which, as Ghazalnus once put it, 'produces sufficient rosewater for all humanity'. I've always said that intellectuals can be the stupidest people in the world. If they knew Tunchi and Hidayat-i Gurji as well as I did, they wouldn't expect anything good from this city. When I saw Ghazalnus in that garden, the first thing I told him was: 'Don't try to bring the calm of this garden into the real world.'

In this respect, I was more like the Imaginary Magellan, the arrogant young man who dresses like a smart English lord and goes on about an imaginary ship cruising a world removed from our own. I got to know the Imaginary Magellan, or Majid-i Gul Solav, very late. True, he was full of himself – like all this country's young intellectuals – but there was a time when we sat together and I told him the stories I had written in the book of the history of death, page by page. He would edit them and write them down in his beautiful handwriting. He was a poor, harmless young man, who boasted only about his imagination. His handwriting was so elegant that just looking at it could induce daydreaming. As a joke, I began to call him the 'Baron of Handwriting', but he kept pleading with me to address him as 'Sardarbashi'. Although he was the loneliest and most isolated of us all, we were constantly criticising him … and yet now I believe he was the truest Imaginative Creature in the world. He was more real and more imaginary than even Ghazalnus.

The day Majid-i Gul Solav came back with 'the Baron of Chickens' scribbled down on a piece of paper, I felt that we were entering a dangerous place. The name immediately reminded me of the skinny Tarano. In the mid-Eighties, our mamosta Tarano gave me a folded letter to deliver to one of the senior leaders based in the mountains. As was my habit, on the way there I opened the letter and read it. At the top, it said: 'To our great baron, Kurdish and revolutionary greetings.' It was the first time I had ever heard the word 'baron' in my life. Thus, when Majid-i Gul Solav handed me the piece of paper, I sensed grave danger. Obviously, I had to be careful not to let it show and thereby spread my hidden fear to the others. I didn't know what the word 'baron' meant and I didn't ask anyone to explain, so that they wouldn't find out I'd opened the envelope. When I heard it again after all those years, the fears of that time and the shadows of the old days I had been running away from all came back to me.

Even though it was in the imaginary gardens that I got to know Ghazalnus, for some inexplicable reason I still felt I was not an Imaginative Creature. I thought I was too evil to become one. I had to follow a tough road to redemption. When one night I swore to Ghazalnus, Majid-i Gul Solav and Trifa Yabahri that I would take part in compiling and protecting the great book of the dead, I knew it was the only way, the only opportunity to make me feel I was their true friend. We all had to help each other gather the data. Then the child with the big nose came along and complicated everything. When we unearthed Murad Jamil's body, I knew that corpse's story was not going to leave us in peace. And as soon as I heard the name of the Baron of Chickens, I became obsessed with finding out what kind of person he was and what his wife had to do with all this.

My only hope when faced with those difficult situations was Shibr. Shibr kept a close eye on the world. There was very little of importance he hadn't heard about. The day I broached the subject of the Baron of Chickens with him, we were sitting on the clean white veranda, he with a blanket over his legs, listening to a very old Selda Bağcan song. When he heard me mention the baron's name, he switched off the tape recorder and asked me: 'The Baron of Chickens? Where do you know the Baron of Chickens from?' I couldn't tell him the truth. Shibr knew nothing of my connection with the Imaginative Creatures or my travels through the flower gardens of Hazarbagh. So I said that a friend of mine had a problem, and an acquaintance had advised him to approach the wife of the Baron of Chickens for support.

'I am surprised the barons' names have spread,' he said, 'because the title is an exclusive one, used by a limited number of people only among themselves.'

'Shibr,' I seized the opportunity to ask, 'what does "baron" actually mean? I've never heard the word before. I know nothing about its origins.'

'Well, Hasan-i Pizo,' he said with his bright smile, '"baron" is a title for great men, a European title. They used it there in olden times. It's used by aristocrats. The word entered our world in a pretty unusual way. In recent years, as wealth increased, the people running the country began to address each other as "barons". To start with, it was just used for a laugh. Tofan, you know they laugh at everything, absolutely everything. First, they addressed each other as "Mir", "Bag" or "Mirza". And then when this became common, when they gathered at night and started telling jokes about one another, they addressed each other as "barons" in jest.

'The first person to be given the title was Ghani Kirmanj. Do you know who that is? You do? Good. After the uprising, when the civil war broke out, he started importing flour through highly secret, private channels from Turkey. The Party protected him, and he had partners in the other parties too. He earned millions of dollars within months. So when they gathered at night in groups and got drunk, his friends would call him "the Baron of Flour" for a laugh. As far as I know, he was the first person to be called a baron. I've known Ghani for a long time. He is a resentful man. That title might have stung him a fair deal, especially as it was known at the very top. Some people say that the Leader himself addressed Ghani as "Baron" at important meetings. Anyway, the name spread like fire through a hay field and by and by became a real title. As the number of wealthy men increased – those who hold power in the Party, the government and the market at the same time – they created the Barons' Club, a restricted club open only to a group of senior party men, company owners, chief executives, members of parliament, ministers and no one else.

'Brother Tofan, it's not easy to enter the world of the barons. You might stumble upon it once, knock on one of their doors to ask for help, seek a favour from one of them or ask another to pull strings for you. But it is not easy for poor people like us to fully understand what's going on in their world. It would be easier to reach Waqwaq Island or climb the peak of Qaf than to penetrate the world of the barons and reveal their secrets.'[14]

Shibr's last words frightened me. I felt he knew something, had got wind of my secret and was warning me off, calmly and politely. I looked into his eyes. There was deep sadness there, as if he were indeed warning me, as if he knew what was on my mind, as if he sensed that – like thousands of other people in this country – I, too, was desperate to climb and peer over the wall, into the barons' secrets.

'Shibr,' I said, 'we're friends. Tell me, how do you know all these details?'

'Tofan,' he said, as he tightened the blanket around him and looked up with a friendly smile, 'I know this guy who works as a servant for the Baron of Flour. He's been running errands for him, washing dishes and setting his table for years and years. You see, they have created an extensive network of servants, watchmen and bodyguards around themselves. Hasan-i Tofan, you may not believe it, but the army serving the barons is ten times bigger than the one you and I know. Do you think we live in this city? No, Hasan. We are two decrepit clowns, out on the margins of the world. If you and I go into the heart of this city or this country, we won't even recognise it. Many evenings, I'm pleased when you leave and head off to sit in a corner of some teahouse on your own. I want you to be far away from these stories. You and I are no longer from this city. Every evening when I go out, I have a sense that the city is not the same as it was yesterday, that it changes day by day. The alleyways are changing. The streets, the houses, its creatures – they are all changing all the time. Hasan, listen to me. I'm not an educated man, but you know that in my youth I was a radical Marxist. I haven't read any books for many years now. Most of my friends and I have given up reading, but I can tell you a few facts. If you should one day mix with that world without me and find yourself in big trouble, just remember that tens of thousands of people in this city serve the barons. They are friendless people like you and me. If you want my advice, keep away from that world. Stick to your isolated lifestyle. They aren't afraid of me any more, not in this state – but you're still standing, Hasan. You haven't fallen yet.'

I could tell that Shibr sensed something, that he knew I was about to step into a world of danger, but despite my uncertainty, I didn't say a word. I was sure that if I did, he would scare me so much it would affect my work. We had to understand the secret of Murad Jamil's death. That evening, I walked Shibr around the bazaar. It was a cool and pleasant evening, but he seemed upset.

'Take me to Shahab's,' he said. I didn't object, and pushed his wheelchair to Shahab's bootleg liquor store. When Shibr was sad, he became lighter, less charismatic. That evening, for the first time in his life, he bought two bottles of Turkish arrack. I had known him to drink the occasional beer, but for him to act like a heavy drinker was something new. I knew his health couldn't take it, that his body couldn't handle too much alcohol. That day I didn't say a thing, but I knew he was very concerned about my fate. It was the first time I felt that anyone was worried about my survival. Carrying the bottles, he took me to a district on the outskirts of the city. I kept pushing his wheelchair and didn't grow tired. It was a beautiful evening. A cool breeze was playing with Shibr's blond hair. He was a very handsome man; no girl could fail to notice his handsomeness. When I pushed him through the old alleyways and streets, people beckoned to each other just to look at him. I didn't know he was crying. I stopped on the way to buy him a soft drink from a shop. When I handed him the Pepsi bottle, I noticed he was crying. On that wonderful evening, Shibr pitied both of us.

'Don't cry. It's not worth it,' I told him as I wiped away the tears.

'Hasan, life is unfair, very unfair. Isn't it?' he said.

'Dear Shibr, life is very unfair. Mankind is very unfair,' I told him as I kissed his head.

That evening, I became certain that Shibr genuinely wanted to protect me. He knew there was a big, dangerous machine of which I was ignorant, and that my image of the world was still the old one. Shibr wanted to tell me: 'Hasan-i Pizo, you are mistaken. The world has changed in a way you don't understand. Gone is the machine that you and I used to operate, the one we were inside. Now, a giant, more curious and intricate machine is in operation in ways that you don't understand.'

Shibr didn't want to tell me these things directly. His tears made me aware, gave me more than a hint.

LESSONS OF THE IMAGINATION
ARE NOT LIKE ANY OTHER LESSON
WINTER AND SPRING 1992

'Lessons of the imagination are not like any other lesson, Mahnaz Khan. Imagination is among the most powerful forces in the world. A person is born when the imagination is born. The truth exists first in our imagination.

'Mahnaz Khan, do you think man grew gardens right from the outset? Of course not. Everything in this world is the fruit of the imagination. If there is no imaginary garden in our head, we can't plant a real one. Before creating them in real life, man first builds a house and invents machines in his imagination.

'Mahnaz Khan, in the beginning, science is a thing imagined; in the beginning, war is a thing imagined; in the beginning, love is a thing imagined; in the beginning, even God is a thing imagined. There is nothing that has not first been imagined. Even before there are words, there is imagination.'

Ghazalnus was speaking thus to Mahnaz in the garden of Sayfadin Maro's home. In her pale yellow shirt, Mahnaz blended in so well with the grass that she could hardly be distinguished from the withered lawn. The poor girl had never had a lesson like this before, one that – right from the start – freed her from boredom and re-taught her the basics of life, things that were so simple but which nobody knew, the very things Mahnaz had wanted to learn from childhood without knowing how.

'Mahnaz Khan,' Ghazalnus said, 'human beings first need to learn simple things in order to then learn about the imagination. For humans to be able to imagine, they need to be able to see, smell and touch. There is nothing harder than the act of smelling a flower properly. Achieving it means we have learned to use our imagination. The first great outpouring of a sense is also the first outpouring of the imagination.'

From her very first lesson, Mahnaz became aware that something important had been missing from her life. She felt that up until then, she had not begun life on this planet at all, that her days had been wasted. She felt that her inability to grasp school subjects was on account of her inability to understand the simple things in life. Her failure in biology, physics and mathematics was because she hadn't understood the garden of their house, the small tree in their front yard, the lonely children on their street, the hungry sparrows by her window. From that very first lesson, she felt that her life so far had been absurd, that she had been living in a world in which she did not understand the meaning of the things around her.

'Mahnaz,' Ghazalnus continued, 'to understand, you must recall the simple truths through your imagination. You can't see the flower in your front yard through your eyes alone. You need imagination, too. Truth oversimplifies things, makes them one-dimensional. When I talk to you about imagination, don't try to fly too far. At first, imagination only means landing in the garden of your own house, next to the first blade of grass or the nearest house sparrow. And then these smaller things will take you far away.'

Ghazalnus's influence on Mahnaz was astonishing. She blossomed dramatically after only a short while. The change she displayed in her lessons was incredible. Saeed Bio considered the girl's progress a biological miracle. Mahnaz opened up quickly now, and displayed a rare talent. The imagination lessons were also lessons about reason, emotions and feelings. Not only did she make swift progress in the difficult subjects, she also spent a long time looking at gardens, nature, clouds and the sky.

And not only that. Mahnaz Maro was in love. Wildly, secretly, quietly, she fell for this rare and wonderful tutor of imagination who always turned up wearing small glasses, a mad head of hair and a black, dervish-like beard, bringing with him a sea of surprises. From the first night she saw Ghazalnus, Mahnaz fell for him with the crazy passion of a teenager who feels that a unique, poetic moment has been thrust upon her. From that same night, when she opened her bedroom window and the doors to her balcony, she began to develop a hatred for Najo Ashkani. She felt the roots of this hatred might be attributed to her incipient feelings for Ghazalnus. True, she was not very bright, and true, everyone considered her an idiot, but from the night she first saw her wonderful tutor of imagination, she understood her own feelings.

She had always been hesitant about her decisions, but this time she knew what she wanted. From that night on, she spared no opportunity to pick a fight with Najo. Her mother, Shams, was as bewildered by her daughter's attitude as anyone else. She knew that if the poor girl had had a change of heart, she could hardly reveal her new feelings on the subject given the overwhelming pressure from her teachers, parents and relatives. That she now felt able to fight with Najo was a novelty, a sign of genuine change, the direction and destination of which were not yet clear. After ten imagination lessons, it was not only Mahnaz's school results or her way of thinking that were changing. Her whole character was being completely transformed. Her style and appearance changed. The great attention she once devoted to her hair or to ironing her clothes was suddenly replaced with extreme shabbiness. Then one day Mahnaz came home from the neighbourhood hairdresser's with her hair cut short. She no longer wore typical women's clothes and, unlike her peers, she did not bother with the latest fashions. In the space of two months, everything had changed. From a chic young lady the local boys described as 'the girl from the style catalogue', she became bold, a rebel, unconventional in the way she dressed and in her behaviour.

Sayfadin Maro was astonished by this imagination tutor's work, but did not know how to assess what was going on. On one hand, the girl's sudden sharpness was pleasing. On the other, he detected a sudden wild, if quiet, change in her, and could not predict where it would end. For some inexplicable reason, however, he kept the story of this tutor of imagination from his friends. In contrast to Shams, who spoke proudly of her daughter's progress and newfound insight, Sayfadin thought Mahnaz was changing so fast that the final outcome remained unknown.

Najo was more hurt than anyone else. With the arrival of this imagination tutor, his fiancée had completely changed. On most of their outings she would stare at him, bored, not saying a word. When they first got engaged, he had felt she was rather cold and reticent, but overall she had not seemed averse to marrying him. Their long silences and extreme shyness had prevented him from getting closer to her. Before Ghazalnus's ugly mug appeared, he had felt she was happy to see him when he visited her at home. When she bought a new item of clothing, she would ask, 'So, Najo, does it look good on me?' If a new restaurant opened, she would say, 'So, Najo, would you like to take me there?' Now, without consulting him or taking his personal tastes into account, she had had her hair cut short like a boy and would not even ask for his opinion. What's more, Mahnaz's disregard for him contrasted with her unfailing attention to the bearded imagination tutor. She wanted to be intelligent for *his* sake. She knew that unless she showed progress, her mother would not allow her to see Ghazalnus again – and it was evident that whatever Mahnaz did, it was precisely in order to see Ghazalnus again. Najo, with the intuition of a wounded lover, could tell.

Mahnaz wanted to be brave now. 'To imagine, you need to be brave,' Ghazalnus kept telling her. 'Imagination and bravery are the same thing.' And now bravery meant telling Najo Ashkani: 'I won't marry you.'

Her imagination expanded in a very short time. Not even Ghazalnus could believe it. In those years, a number of women had loved him, but never had he thought someone like Mahnaz Maro would. After all, he was her tutor, she was engaged to be married and she was many years his junior. The slightest mistake would have ruined the poor girl's life.

But Mahnaz hated Najo's black moustache, military physique and clumsy language as deeply as she loved Ghazalnus. Now, thanks to her great imagination, she could transform the world into something else. At night, her room became an infinite garden. She populated the house with bulbuls and curious creatures she created in her mind. 'The hardest thing is the first imaginary bird,' Ghazalnus often said. 'Once you can create that one, the rest is easy.' Mahnaz created her first imaginary bird very early on. She was so addicted to her imaginary universe that had it not been for her longing to see Ghazalnus, she might never have returned to the world of real things.

She knew herself better than anyone else did. She had never been a stupid girl – they all just thought she was. That's how she had presented herself, and they all regarded her as beautiful but brainless. Yet over the past year, and especially since her engagement to Najo Ashkani, she had lost all desire to learn anything. All desire will die in a girl convinced that her life resembles a picture other people have already completed. Her life before Ghazalnus arrived was like a table set for dinner: all she had to do was come to the table, eat and take her leave. She did not need to listen to Saeed Bio or Maja Excellence. Not anymore, though. Now she felt her life had been very limited and poor, as though she had never really seen flowers, birds or gardens. Now she wanted to learn, and she wanted to learn it all. She hated her old image, that of a beautiful, smartly dressed girl in well-pressed clothes, chic and delicate, engaged and secure, her only function to greet her parents' guests in a sweet and artificial tone; a girl who was supposed to accompany Najo Ashkani to every party, every outing, every function, picnic and dinner – until her death. Ashkani, a man whose greatest achievement in life was boasting about her long, golden hair. At every opportunity, she would have to present herself as the woman who'd managed to catch the well-dressed, wealthy businessman. She had thought that this was all she could expect from life; but Ghazalnus's arrival had shown her something other girls could not see.

Once she'd been introduced to the realm of imagination, she could no longer bear a person like Najo Ashkani, who had nothing to talk about except food, money and politics. On any night that she thought about Najo, she had to open the window for air. She then began to open the windows at night out of habit. She felt that imaginary beings were in the world outside the window. At night she would step out onto the balcony. She didn't phone her friends or listen to songs. All she did was think about Ghazalnus, about her imaginary flowers, about the magical bulbuls that sang in her head. She was certain now that she could never live with Najo Ashkani. If she married that man, her imagination would die. There was nothing more certain to kill it than his black moustache, black eyebrows and 'political poise', which was how her mother, Shams, described his stiff bearing. On the days she met with Najo, she found it difficult to get back into her small, imaginary room.

It took six months for Mahnaz to become one of the Imaginative Creatures. 'She was one of the lonely Imaginative Creatures, the type who is born spontaneously and does not blend into any group,' Ghazalnus would say years later when he spoke about her. In those six months, he tried many times to introduce Mahnaz to some of the Imaginative Creatures he knew, but she couldn't form attachments to any group. Her imaginary world was her room. 'There are some imaginative humans whose imaginary realm does not go beyond their homes, and Mahnaz was one of them,' Ghazalnus would add.

As she started to prepare for her key end-of-year exams, Mahnaz told Najo one evening that she did not want to marry him. They had gone to a dinner party hosted by one of Najo's relatives, and while he held forth about the permanent conflict between the country's two major parties, Mahnaz – much to everyone's surprise, as they had grown accustomed to not hearing her voice – said: 'Najo, don't you know about any other matters? Is there nothing you can talk about other than this political nonsense?'

Najo was so shocked by these direct, harsh and insulting words that, for a moment, he didn't know where to look. It was hard for him to bear such humiliation before his relatives, in an environment in which he cared about his dignity more than anywhere else. That night, as he drove Mahnaz home, he was so angry he almost crashed into several lampposts and trees by the side of the road; but Mahnaz sat serenely in the front seat as though his anger had nothing to do with her. She sat with such an imaginative air about her that she appeared bathed in a divine light. When they arrived at her door, Najo was sweating, but Mahnaz calmly put her hands on his and told him: 'Najo, listen. I'm not the one for you. When I am with you, I cannot fantasise. You have to forgive me; but if you leave me, you will be happier too.'

Mahnaz Maro had never been so brave in her life. They had all treated her like a coward, but now she could be brave to the point of death. She had made up her mind weeks earlier. Between death and Najo Ashkani, she would choose death. For weeks on end, she had found herself waking up at night, going to the balcony and thinking about death – a death that would free her from her father, Sayfadin Maro, and from Najo.

For too long she had been forced to listen to her father and Najo in her imaginary garden, to their endless, repetitive conversations about politics. Now, whenever she heard political conversations, she felt sick to her stomach. Apart from Ghazalnus, there was no one in her life who spoke about flowers, about souls that matured at night under the moonlight and died in the morning. Apart from Ghazalnus, there was no one who could teach her the art of drawing closer to the birds. How strange it was to see Ghazalnus persuade the cuckoos to land on his hands. She knew Ghazalnus couldn't be with her forever, and that was the greatest source of sadness in her life. How could she live without these imaginary gardens and curious birds! How could her feelings revert to what they had been before she met him!

Twice she had gone out with Ghazalnus – with Shams's permission, but behind Sayfadin's back. She met two groups of Imaginative Creatures, each of them versed in a specific strand of the imagination. But she was a solitary soul. She had no one but her mother Shams, and had no desire to mingle with the other imaginative people. She had a world of her own, and was afraid she might lose it if she left home. Despite this, she did all she could to ensure that Ghazalnus remained in her life: everything. A few days before telling Najo Ashkani they should end their relationship, she had spent a whole night thinking about what it would be like to sleep with a man like Ghazalnus. It was the first time in her life that she thought about a man's naked body. The idea of Najo's hands touching her skin enraged her. She would rather die than be naked before him. But what about sleeping with Ghazalnus? What magic and fantasy that must be like!

She knew she had to call everything off with Najo before the start of her final exams. She also knew that Sayfadin would never accept it. She knew that if she talked about it with Shams first, things might get so out of hand that they would be impossible to put right. But why shouldn't she test herself? Why shouldn't she put her bravery to a test she had to undergo sooner or later? She had to decide now. She had to go to Sayfadin and say, 'I'm not marrying Najo Ashkani.' To hell with whatever happened next.

Sayfadin Maro was on the phone late into the night. The country's first-ever serious election was just around the corner. The Party had asked him to take part in drawing up the list of candidates. He was as diplomatic, well-mannered and soft-spoken outside the home as he was stiff, impatient and volatile inside it. Mahnaz waited many a night, but her father did not have time for anyone or anything other than politics. One night when he had been on the phone for hours, Mahnaz, oblivious to everything, went into his private study – the room from which he spoke to Party leaders and new election candidates, from which he persuaded doctors, engineers and lawyers to stand 'in the first free elections in the history of the Middle East', as Sayfadin proudly labelled them when he talked to Najo and Shams.

It was the first time in many years that Mahnaz had gone into her father's study so late at night to discuss a personal matter. Sayfadin Maro had enough political experience to know when someone had something important to say. He could not recall a single occasion in the past few years when he had sat with his daughter for a friendly chat. Mahnaz's aloofness and quietness were more to blame for this than his busy schedule. When it came to family life, he considered himself unfortunate. He always felt that his wife was a boasting chatterbox rather than a supportive problem-solver, while his daughter appeared dim-witted and naïve. He consoled himself by saying that all children were like that nowadays.

Sayfadin did not like the tutor of imagination. He found Ghazalnus a rare type of man, whose kind he had not met before. He wasn't like the politicians, doctors, engineers, bazaar folk or even singers. He wasn't like the intellectuals, either, as he understood them: most of them succumbed to small financial or material support, and the most prominent among them were gobbled up by the Party. Since being put in charge of the parliamentary candidates' selection committee, whenever he met someone he wondered whether or not they would make a good candidate. He was glad his would-be son-in-law would make a good parliamentary candidate for the next term, or the one after. His physique, face, posture and aura of respectability were all made for parliament. Sayfadin was very pleased with Najo, and believed him the ideal husband for Mahnaz. When Mahnaz entered his room that night, he had not the slightest inkling of what she was about to say. He could not believe this young girl could stand before him and so fearlessly say that she did not think her betrothed was worth getting naked before and sleeping with. It was the height of rudeness.

That night, Sayfadin could not sleep. He shifted positions in his bed until morning. By contrast, Mahnaz left Sayfadin's room happy to be relieved of a great burden. She had had to articulate things clearly, to say that she wouldn't marry Najo Ashkani. For too long, she'd kept the decision buried inside her. She hadn't even talked about it with Ghazalnus. But now it was all over.

Strangely, the arguments and commotion did not come until the following day. Her decision had been like lightning, like a sudden curse causing speechlessness or even paralysis. Yes, Shams had initially opposed the marriage of Mahnaz to Najo. No, she didn't like the sight of him. Yes, she thought her daughter deserved someone better. But they had been engaged for a year now. They had appeared together at many functions. They had been out walking together, and had come home late at night. The young man had done everything right: provided a full set of gold jewellery, prepared a home and accepted each and every one of Shams's conditions. There was no excuse for a change of heart; none whatsoever. On top of everything else, what would people say? What about all the stories that would circulate, all the questions they would face, all the shame brought upon them? No, Mahnaz could no longer change her mind. Things weren't that easy. They had all grown used to seeing Najo, to his evening visits. Plus, Mahnaz could offer no convincing reason. Shams had absolutely no idea what Mahnaz was talking about – that the sight of Najo 'killed her imagination'. She didn't understand what imagination actually was, let alone that it could be killed by the sight of Najo!

That day, Sayfadin had to spend the entire day and late into the evening on the phone with the candidates. He had a meeting with the Leader's aide for election affairs, and another meeting with the Party's media chief, and had to speak to two women about the female candidates. It was a packed day – but even so, he could not stop thinking about Mahnaz and what she had said. His daughter's change of heart after a year-long engagement would have adverse effects on his position in the Party. His opponents would use it to sully his reputation. Najo would become his enemy, and people would slander his daughter in public. He had to save Mahnaz from her sudden, meaningless and irrational desire at any cost. He was sure now that the bastard imagination tutor was a bad influence. He should never have agreed to allow this complex, strange and seditious young man into his house. He should have had more sense than to let a 'tutor of the imagination' darken his door. When Sayfadin left home in the morning, he knew what a commotion there would be when he got home that evening.

Shams, meanwhile, was certain Sayfadin wouldn't want to lose a young man like Najo Ashkani so easily, and would use everything at his disposal to ensure that Mahnaz changed her mind. She had decided not to stand in his way. 'Even if your father wants to cut off your head, I'm not getting involved,' she told her daughter bluntly. 'All I have to do is bring him the knife.'

'If he gives me away to Najo Ashkani,' said Mahnaz fearlessly, 'he won't need to cut off my head – because he will have killed me anyway.'

Mahnaz refused to give in. No force in the world could make her change her mind.

'One evening I went to Mahnaz Maro's home,' Ghazalnus would recount to Majid-i Gul Solav years later. 'I went there like I had all the other evenings, completely unaware, oblivious to any concerns. I just went. Shams received me in the big parlour. For decency's sake, she made sure her knees were covered by a towel, and sat opposite me calmly. She said, "Mamosta, excuse me, but as of today there will be no more imagination lessons. Sayfadin and I believe that your lessons have had a bad effect on the girl. Her father thinks her decision to leave her fiancé is connected to the lessons she has with you. It's like she's jumped into another world. She's losing all awareness of herself; she's always saying odd things."

'I didn't say a word that day,' Ghazalnus continued to Majid-i Gul Solav. 'I knew that anything I said would be in vain. Neither Shams nor Sayfadin Maro would have understood. They were not imaginative creatures.

'Two days after that, late in the evening, a girl brought me a letter from Mahnaz Maro, a letter from a young and devastated heart. She had written to me in tears, saying that she loved me and had left Ashkani because of me; that she couldn't live without me and that I should save her at any cost, because her imagination would die unless she saw me. I didn't know what to do. Nothing is worse than being the object of an adolescent girl's love. No pain on Earth can match it: to be a man, to be loved by a beautiful, delicate girl and to be unable to love her back for thousands of reasons, because of thousands of obstacles. At that moment, I envied Najo Ashkani. I didn't know what I could do for the girl. I didn't know how to help her. You shouldn't take the feelings of a young woman lightly. Back then, I didn't have much experience.

'That evening, a resentful Najo Ashkani turned up at my house with bloodshot eyes, like an enraged wild animal. He accused me of misleading Mahnaz, of flouting my position as a tutor and deceiving her. I dismissed the accusations very angrily, and told him that I wasn't aware of a thing. But he had a copy of Mahnaz's letter to me. The same girl who delivered the letter to me had sold a copy of it to him. It didn't matter to me what he did or didn't know. All I could think of was Mahnaz. I told Ashkani, "Leave the poor girl alone. I am sure she doesn't love me, but she still hates you. She hates you so much that she's looking for someone else to support her. Unless you want to cause her a great deal of trouble, let her find herself again slowly and peacefully."

'Najo Ashkani didn't even hear me out. He was one of those people who are not gifted with even the tiniest amount of imagination, the type who made things happen by force. After that, I knew nothing at all of Mahnaz Maro for some time. During that period I tried to find her through the arts of the imagination, but to no avail. I knew they had even stopped her from going to school. So I lost Mahnaz in this real world forever, and never saw her again.'

Ghazalnus's distance from Mahnaz Maro had fatal consequences. In a short space of time, everyone learned that she was madly in love with her tutor of the imagination. Saeed Bio greatly regretted suggesting the appointment. But who could have known it would all end up like that? Mahnaz's love for Ghazalnus was so strong that she said she would agree to marry Najo Ashkani if they let her see Ghazalnus. But neither social norms nor reason allowed it. Against Mahnaz's expectations, her mother and Sayfadin Maro decided that that she should get married and move into her own home as soon as possible rather than sitting her final exams and going to university. Sayfadin made the final decision, and Shams reluctantly accepted.

No one knows what happened during Mahnaz's final days. Her parents talk about utter loneliness and a deathly silence. She did nothing and said nothing. Four hours before Najo Ashkani arrived at their house, with his military bearing and thick moustache, wearing the old peshmerga outfit he had saved specifically for his wedding day, she set herself on fire in their garden.

Afterwards, no burned bone, charred body parts or ashes could be found, as if the air had borne the body away, as if her body had become imaginary and taken flight. Shams and Sayfadin had seen her set fire to herself in the middle of the garden, but could neither smell scorched flesh nor find any ashes when the fire had gone out. Everyone thinks the story of Mahnaz's self-immolation is nothing but a lie to cover up a bigger disgrace, and some rumours even have it that she ran off with some other man to another country. But that's not what the events that happened after Mahnaz's death suggest.

A few days after the memorial service held for her, fantastic flowers began to blossom and spread in every direction throughout Sayfadin's house. Birds no one had ever seen before flew through the rooms; the sound of unusual creatures was heard, their songs echoing in the parlour and other rooms, while wild grass covered the floors. No matter how much Shams and Sayfadin tried to remove the flowers from the walls, expel the birds and pull up the various types of grass, it was useless. They eventually put the house up for sale, and the first potential buyer to come and see it was Attar, who was astonished by all the plants and birds. He backed away quickly, as if worried that the house was cursed. He did not even name a price for this strange place.

In a short space of time, Sayfadin Maro's house went through such a complete transformation that it became uninhabitable. The family moved to the other end of the city. At first no one wanted to buy or rent their old house, but before too long a strange customer came forward and bought it for a hefty sum.

A STRANGE DAY IN THE REAL MAGELLAN'S LIFE

AUGUST 2004

Zuhdi Shazaman woke up earlier than he had on previous days. The sun had not yet emerged fully. While still in bed, he felt a strange movement of the curtains and an air too cool for the time of year, inconsistent with the night's sweltering heat. He felt as if a powerful current were wafting through the windows, bringing with it the cool, magical air of morning.

He drew the thin, white sheet over himself and remembered that before going to bed the night before, he had closed the windows so that the air conditioner could keep the room cool. When he raised his head, he felt something strange, as well as a deep silence that did not resemble that of previous days, a silence that felt as if it had been imposed by the presence of something else, something huge. He started, as if scared of some giant creature.

He pushed his hair off his face and sat up. There, in a chair facing the bed, sat an ugly, lanky man he had never seen before, with veined and elongated hands. He had never been in a situation like this. He felt a sudden fear. Within a few seconds, a cold sweat broke out across his body. Had it not been for that, he would have thought himself still asleep, seeing one of the horrible creatures that occasionally crept into his dreams.

However, he could clearly hear the man's warm, contented voice, saying, 'Honourable Zuhdi Shazaman ... don't be afraid. Don't panic. Please, don't. Everything's fine. Really it is. Just like a spring morning, isn't it? Look out the window, it's so cool. Just like a spring morning. Such beautiful mornings don't happen often, mornings when the air is magical and the city is quiet, when coolness delights the heart. Feel how pleasing the cool air is to the heart.'

'Who are you?' Zuhdi asked, pulling himself together with some difficulty. 'How did you get into my room without my permission? What is this place, a hotel or a madhouse? Who sent you? Can't you see this is a single room, for goodness' sake?'

The man laughed a strange laugh, as though he hadn't heard Zuhdi. 'Ha! Zuhdi Shazaman, what are you saying? I like Friday mornings a lot. I am mad about them. I like this strange silence. I do. I do not need sleep. I like the mornings. I really do, especially when it's so calm, when the air is clear, the streets are empty and no one can be seen. Friday mornings in August. Friday mornings. You don't know how pleasant they are, really, how very pleasant!'

'Who are you?' Zuhdi asked. 'I don't care about the mornings. I want to know what you're doing in this room.'

'How could you not care about the morning?' the man said. 'One lives for the sake of a few pleasant mornings. Oh, if there were no pleasant mornings – ha, oh my, oh my – life would become Hell. Everyone lives for something. I live for Friday mornings. Friday mornings are the best moments of my life. If there weren't any Friday mornings, Friday evenings would have no meaning.'

'You'd better get out right now,' Zuhdi said angrily. 'I like to spend the morning sleeping. Whoever you are, just get out. If you need something from me, drop by later. Right now, I just want to sleep.'

'Sleep?' the ugly man said. 'Honourable Zuhdi Shazaman, sleep? On a day like this, on such a pleasant morning, at such a quiet moment?'

'You must have been sent by the Security Directorate,' Zuhdi said, astounded. 'If that's the case, just tell me. I want to know who you are and what you want.'

The man stood up. He was very tall – similar in height to Zuhdi. Both were very slender, but Zuhdi wore his hair long and tidy, while his visitor's was short and messy. The man had an unsightly, bendy body. One bend made his body even more unsightly: he was a hunchback. One shoulder drooped in an odd fashion. Anyone who saw him would have thought one of his arms was longer than the other. His protruding yellow teeth had gaps between them, and his short upper lips pulled back to reveal red gums.

'Zuhdi Shazaman, I know you need me,' said the man with the strange laughter. 'You've come back from the other side of the world to look for me. Haven't you? You've come back to find me.'

'If you don't tell me your name,' Zuhdi said in frustration, 'if I don't find out what your job is, I'll leave this room and this hotel right away. I don't understand what's going on in this hotel. What sort of life is this?'

'No, no, I don't want to hurt you,' continued the man. 'I am Murtaza. Murtaza Satan. Aren't you looking for me?'

'Murtaza Satan?' Zuhdi paused and took a good look at him. 'So, you're Murtaza,' he said after some reflection. 'I'm sure that stupid security officer has given you all my letters, hasn't he? Has he? This is ridiculous.'

Zuhdi appeared more serious now. He tied his hair back and said, 'Anyway, who says I'm looking for you? I'm not looking for you. I'm looking for Baran Shukur. What do I need you for? Who are you, that I should be looking for you?'

Murtaza Satan sat back in his chair.

'If you don't find Baran Shukur, you'll look for me, will you?' he said, as if deliberately messing with Zuhdi Shazaman's head. 'I read all the letters, the beautiful letters from Baran Shukur, wife of the honourable Baron of Courgettes. She was having an affair with a handsome young man. Ha!'

'Do you know Baran's whereabouts, is that it? Do you?' Zuhdi said.

'Say that again and I'm going to get cross with you – very cross, Zuhdi Shazaman,' Murtaza said, with his unholy laughter. 'You're a reasonable man, aren't you? You are, aren't you – or do you really not understand anything?' He swayed in his seat and repeated the words several times over.

Zuhdi looked at him and realised that he was dealing with a deceitful creature, a dangerous fool. 'Murtaza, tell me the truth, have you read Baran Shukur's letters?' he asked as he stood to face him. 'Have you? Honestly?'

Murtaza paused, screwed up his face and said: 'Ha ha! I am a very good reader. I like reading a lot. Sometimes, I visit my friends at the Security Directorate and open the locker where the files are kept and read offenders' testimonies. Ha! Zuhdi Shazaman, there is nothing nicer than listening to offenders when you're innocent. Ha ha! I don't like reading books, but I do like reading files – at the Security Directorate, in the courts ... oh dear, oh dear. It is such a nice day, a very nice day. As far as I'm concerned, it is nicer than ever.'

'The letters say you are an animal, a dangerous person, a foul creature,' Shazaman said as if trying to provoke him, or else dampen his spirits. 'And looking at you right now, I think you're even worse than your descriptions. Certainly much uglier.'

'My brother Shazaman, listen,' Murtaza said, unperturbed. 'Everyone tells me that. Baran Khan saw only the worst in me too. All the women speak very negatively about me, but I like the fact that certain people are scared of me. I do, really. What matters is that I am honest and I am innocent. That's what matters, you know. Ha! When you're honest, everything else is fine, isn't it? Everything else is fine.'

'I still don't know you,' Zuhdi said. 'I don't know you, so I can't say. But there is something animal-like about your appearance.'

'You don't know Murtaza. Murtaza is a butterfly,' Murtaza Satan said as he stood up and let out a rumble of laughter. 'I've never been bad. Never.'

'You know Baran's whereabouts, don't you?' Zuhdi asked.

Murtaza's voice changed suddenly, sounding warmer and more serious. 'Zuhdi Shazaman, I am here to ask *you* where Baran Shukur is. I swear by this beautiful, cool Friday morning, by the sheer beauty of the morning, that I am here because a good man sent me. I'm not one of those impolite people who intrude on others in their sleep at six in the morning. Ha! A virtuous man forced me to come here. Do you know who I mean? You do, don't you? I mean the Baron of Courgettes. He came to see me last night and told me that I had to come. He made me promise. He was restless. Since the day his wife disappeared, he's looked like a dejected bird. He lies to everyone. He tells everyone, "I've sent Baran to Germany." Ha ha! He has lied so much, he feels sorry for himself. If people find out that you, Baran Shukur's uncle, are here now, the city will be flooded with rumours. God only knows what turmoil there will be. The poor man has told everyone, "I've sent her to live with her uncle." He's lying, poor man. Of course, he is. He's told so many lies, he can't look himself in the mirror.

'You know what a disgrace it will be if they find out his wife has run away or disappeared. You know the kind of furore it will create in the city if the wife of the Baron of Courgettes has eloped. The poor guy has the patience of a saint. I've named him the Baron of Patience, the Baron of Endurance, the Baron of Will ... but when he came to see me last night, he looked like a dejected bird. No one knows the Baron of Courgettes better than I do. I know him. I know him well, really well. The poor guy has no luck with women – just like me. A man who has no luck with women is unfortunate. Even if he is the Baron of Courgettes, even if he is a king, he is still unfortunate.'

Murtaza Satan was all movement. Both his long, crooked arms danced in the air. He appeared to be speaking in earnest for the first time, but it was impossible to tell whether he was telling lies or the truth.

'So where's Baran Shukur?' Zuhdi asked sadly. 'Where is she?'

'Her poor husband looks like an injured bird,' Murtaza continued, waving his arms around. 'He looks like a house sparrow attacked by a sparrowhawk. The poor guy is out of his mind, and has been for months. Ha! He has an uneasy conscience. He feels guilty without having committed any crime.

'When I came by Baran Shukur's letters, I immediately took them to him. I didn't so much as pause for breath; I got the letters from the captain and delivered them to him. Ha ha! I know the captain. Almighty God, I feel I know the whole world. All of it. If only you'd seen him when he opened the letters and looked at them. If only. He sniffed at the papers, and looked like an injured bird. Like a woman, he had tears streaming down his face. Ha! And by Friday morning, I swear, he was bawling like a woman, too. He was sniffing the papers and saying, "Dear Baran, where are you?"

'There's no one like the Baron of Courgettes, you know. There isn't another man like him in this world. He is a real angel, an angel without wings who has fallen from the sky. He knew Baran had had a liaison with that young man – ha ha! – but he was patient. When I took the letters to him, it didn't matter to him what was written in them. Baran's cold and humiliating words didn't matter. What did matter was being able to smell the letters, to look at her writing and kiss her name … I swear by all the companions of the Prophet – ha! – that poor man lifted Baran's letter and kissed it. He kissed her name thirty-three times. He kissed each of the thirty-three letters in Baran's name one by one. Ha ha! I was looking at him furtively and laughing. Anyone else would have spat on those letters, but because the Baron of Courgettes is an angel, because he is of the same order as the angels, he kissed the name of his adulterous wife thirty-three times. He has pinned all his hope on you knowing her whereabouts, on you saying: "I know where Baran Shukur is." He lives for that moment. The poor guy looks like a bird with a broken wing. If you say "Baran Shukur is with me", he will give you half his wealth – more than half, ha ha! I am not as good as him, but he is not of Adam's race. The angels of Heaven would love him if they saw him, but Baran Khan hated him. Ha! When I saw the letters, I immediately took them to him – Captain Samad is an acquaintance of mine. He nearly went mad. I had to hold him up; I took his hands. I said, "Baron of Patience, control yourself … Baron of Endurance, stay on your feet, don't fall. Everything will be fine." Ha ha! He's a strange man: when you say "everything will be fine", he immediately feels it *will*. That everything will be fine.'

Murtaza Satan stood up, his figure stooping to the side. His body was like that of a contorted animal; a curved line began in his upper back, reaching its lowest point at his waist. His entire body was an uneven zigzag, but his voice was clear and powerful, amply conveying the spirit of a deceitful soul. Zuhdi Shazaman had not mingled with this particular kind of creature for a long time. Not even his vast experience of the world was sufficient to separate the truth from the lies in what Murtaza said.

'Can I see the Baron of Courgettes?' he asked, as if taken in by Murtaza. 'I want to see him. I don't know anything about Baran, anything at all. I've never even seen a picture of her, you understand? I don't know why, but she never sent me a picture of herself. Sometimes I think there is no one in the world by the name of

"Baran Shukur". That she's just a meaningless fantasy, a nightmare, a dangerous shadow of the past chasing me.'

With a false smile, Murtaza Satan looked at Zuhdi Shazaman sitting on the edge of the bed, speaking as if to himself.

'I told him so – I spent all last night talking to the Baron of Courgettes,' said Murtaza, who seemed to be stepping his deceitfulness up a gear. '"My dear Baron," I said, "my cherished Baron, this Shazaman is an innocent man. He isn't dangerous. Perhaps he's come back to see the summer holiday resorts, perhaps he wants to revisit the places of his childhood memory. Perhaps – ha ha! – he's come to see a woman. It's hard to forget a beautiful woman – ha! I, for one, just can't, ha ha! I really can't forget. If only humans had no memory, eh? But for memory, what a good life they would have."

'Who knows what you are here for! If it wasn't for the letters, if the damned people at the Security Directorate hadn't been so curious … That captain from the Security Directorate will check you right down to your underpants if you've come from abroad. He likes to man the checkpoints, go to the hotels, rifle through the suitcases and look at people's pants. He's a sick man. Ha! On my honour, I swear he's sick. The Baron of Courgettes doesn't know a thing about this world. Recently he's become afraid of everything. He looks like a house sparrow attacked by an eagle. I tell him. I tell him, but he doesn't listen to me.'

'I want to see the baron,' Zuhdi Shazaman said. 'I want to see him. I've come back in search of Baran Shukur, not to see the resorts. That's all I've come for. All I want to know is where Baran Shukur is. The baron is Baran Shukur's husband. He must know where she is, surely. You've read the letters. You know why I'm saying all this.'

'I swear by all the stars in the sky,' Murtaza said as he muffled his laughter, 'I swear by the high orbits in which all those strange celestial bodies move. I swear by – ha ha! – by the light that comes from afar, by the rays from a source that no one knows, I swear by August Friday mornings, the Baron of Courgettes knows nothing at all. Nothing at all.'

'I don't know either. I don't,' Zuhdi said. 'But someone must, mustn't they? Drop this damned laughter of yours. It reminds me of ill-omened birds. It's this laughter that makes you look like an ugly jinn. Can't you stop laughing? And tell me, can I meet the Baron of Courgettes or not? Well?'

Murtaza seemed overwhelmed by a great wave of ecstasy. The laughter was stuck in his throat. Then he dropped down and rolled on the floor with it; he rolled about in the middle of the floor, giggling. His uneven legs kicked the air and his hands waved backwards and forwards, and he looked like a beetle that had fallen on its back. Zuhdi looked at Murtaza as if he were a clown; he had no idea what the man was laughing about. Finally Murtaza crept away, making his exit on all fours. He disappeared without making any promises to Zuhdi.

Zuhdi felt that the laughter of this foul creature was a strange, hellish laughter, redolent of Satan himself.

Zuhdi didn't immediately know what to do, whether to follow Murtaza or let him go. Some instinct said to let him go. He was sure the man would be back. He had no explanation for his strange and sudden appearance. The whole scene had been like a waking dream. He had never seen such an ugly creature before. He didn't know what kind of human being Murtaza was, and yet he was certain his own journey had entered a new phase now.

That day, he walked around aimlessly until evening. He walked through the whole of the old market and the new qaysaris. He had tea in many small teahouses like a man deprived of attention, a man with no plans or hopes. All his life, he had been just such a man. All his life, whatever route he had taken had been just like all the rest. Now he had to stop and wait. From the day he'd arrived in the city, he had had a strange feeling that things would come to him eventually. All his searching was futile. He had to stop and wait for things to come to him.

When he returned to the hotel that evening, the owner's wife was talking to another woman. Zuhdi pretended he hadn't seen her. Calmly, he took his keys and headed to his room. Before entering it, he heard Afsana's magical whisper behind him: 'I want to talk to you.' Her voice still held the same magic, the same allure of the first time she had spoken to him in the hotel lobby. No other woman's voice had ever affected him like that.

'Please, do,' he answered, showing no sign of his internal agitation.

'May I come in?' she asked, in the same low voice.

'If you like ... why not?' Shazaman said.

Inside the room, Zuhdi Shazaman was struck again by her beauty, her slim figure and black eyes.

'Excuse me,' she said, her voice even more deliberately tender, 'I heard that Murtaza Satan was here this morning. I heard it early this morning. I wanted to come and see you then, but you weren't here. I'm really worried about you. I wonder whether you know this man or not.'

What Afsana was saying was strange. She spoke quickly, and her voice revealed a degree of concern that was worth dying for. Zuhdi had never in his life met a woman who was concerned about him. Now this voice could leave him dizzy. He felt slightly panicked, as if this were the very first time he was speaking to a woman. No matter how much experience a man might have with the opposite sex, there is always a chance he will encounter a woman able to take him right back to square one. The game men play with women is like a pointless game of snakes and ladders. No matter how experienced and confident you may feel you are, a woman can suddenly take you back down to the very bottom. That's the state Zuhdi Shazaman found himself in when faced with the hotel owner's wife. All he had learned of women until then meant nothing. He simply had to start all over again.

'Khanim, where do you know Murtaza Satan from?' he asked in astonishment.

'My name is Afsana,' she said. 'And it doesn't matter where I know him from. What matters is that you must be on your guard against him.' She lifted her hair coquettishly, seemingly aware of the impact her presence had on Zuhdi. 'You're definitely not his friend. I know you're not his friend. You're no one's friend in this hotel. I pity you. You deserve to be somewhere better.'

She always spoke in whispers.

'Khanim, where do you know me from?' asked Zuhdi as he sat opposite her. 'Who says I deserve a better place? I don't want to go to another hotel. At least here, one sees a beautiful woman like you. What is there in the other hotels?'

'Murtaza Satan is the barons' top man, you know,' Afsana said in her magical whisper. She ignored his last remark, and that only made the tension between them thicker. 'Any woman who knows the barons will know him too. I don't know him very well myself, but I know people who do. They say very strange things about him. You may not believe any of this. There are many things those who return from abroad don't believe.'

'But I don't even know who the "barons" are,' Zuhdi said. 'My information about Kurdistan doesn't go beyond what is generally discussed in the news. And I'm not very keen on politics. It's such a quagmire.'

'I knew you wouldn't know them,' Afsana said, crossing her legs, 'I knew it. Even here, not everyone knows about them; and yet everything in this city is in their hands. My husband works for them too, you know,' she said, lowering her voice further. 'This hotel isn't his.'

'Do you know the Baron of Courgettes?' Zuhdi asked her.

'I've heard the name, but I don't actually know him,' she said, shaking her head. 'If you want, I can ask. I can do that.'

'I'd like you to help me,' Zuhdi said after a pause. 'But I'd also like to know why you want to help me.'

'Because you are a stranger, because for days now everyone's been curious to find out what you're up to,' Afsana said quickly. 'You don't know what city you've come to, do you? It's been a very long time since you were here, isn't it? A very long time ...'

'God only knows how many years ago I left,' said Zuhdi, exhausted. 'To tell you the truth, I feel as if I never even lived here. All I can remember is the feeling of touching the walls with my fingertips.'

'The walls? Why the walls?' asked the woman with the utmost tenderness.

'Because I have a strange relationship with walls,' Zuhdi said, shutting his eyes. 'I'm scared of them. I feel I've returned to see them.'

Afsana asked: 'I've heard you're looking for Baran Shukur. Is it true?'

It was the first time her voice had conveyed such seriousness. There is nothing in the world more beautiful than a delicate woman who suddenly becomes very serious.

'How do you know Baran Shukur's story?' Zuhdi asked in surprise. He was becoming more captivated by the minute.

'I overheard Captain Samad speaking to my husband,' she whispered. 'I overheard them talking about Baran Shukur. I was surprised, because we're looking for Baran Shukur as well.'

'"We?" Who are *you*?' Zuhdi asked.

'I knew you didn't know me,' Afsana whispered, moving even closer to him. 'I knew. I did.'

'How could I?' Zuhdi said. 'I'm a stranger. I don't know anyone. No one at all. I am much less familiar with this city than you think.'

'I belong to a society of distressed and forlorn women,' she said. 'And we are Imaginative Creatures. When I first saw you, I thought you were one of the Imaginative Creatures.'

'But why are you looking for Baran Shukur?' asked Zuhdi, leaning back in his chair as if he was afraid of something. 'What do you have to do with Baran Shukur? Almighty God, what is this girl's story? I'm really starting to fear the worst.'

'How can you say that?' Afsana asked, in the same low voice and simple words. 'Baran was one of us. We'd accepted her in the group recently. She was the wife of one of the barons. I was initially opposed to taking her on board – I hate the wives of the barons. They all try to pretend they're sad and unfortunate, but they're lying. At first I thought she was lying, too. She hadn't been in our group for very long – I didn't know her very well – before she disappeared without a word of warning to anyone. We've been searching for her for some time now. One of the group's requirements is that the women take care of each other.'

'Can you tell me what these "imaginative creatures" and "distressed women" are? I've never heard of them.'

'I know you haven't,' Afsana said simply. 'Don't worry. It's nothing bad. We're a group of sad women brought together by our love of the imagination. Each of us lives our own imaginary life alongside our miserable real lives. Do you understand? We all hate our husbands. Most of us are sterile. Do you understand? Most of us can't have children with our husbands.' She dropped her voice very low and said, in the most delicate whisper in the world: 'Because we don't want to have the children of those beasts. Baran Shukur was like that, too. We are a group of sterile women who wished to have children with imaginary men.'

This was all far stranger and more complicated than Zuhdi Shazaman had expected.

'You're a beautiful woman. You're the wife of the owner of a big hotel. Why are you unfortunate?' Zuhdi asked. He felt as if he were in the midst of a dizzying array of subjects he couldn't understand.

'Because he's not the man I want to spend my life with,' she answered seriously. 'This isn't the street I want to work on. These aren't the friends I want to care about. This isn't a place I like being in charge of. The parks I want to go to don't exist here. The books I want to read don't exist here. Here, I am just a corpse bobbing in the water. I have to be an upright woman twenty-four hours a day. There is no reasonable human being who can be upright twenty-four hours a day, but here we're all condemned to just that. Do you understand? Do you understand what it means for someone to be condemned to being upstanding all their lives? What's worse than living in Hell all your life and having to maintain a dignified front, having to pretend you're happy? I know there are people more unfortunate than me. But I am unfortunate, too. Any woman condemned to live with a man she doesn't want, in a place she doesn't want to be, is unfortunate.'

'You're too beautiful to be unfortunate,' Zuhdi interrupted her.

'It doesn't matter what I am,' Afsana said hurriedly, as if afraid of something, as if she felt he was exaggerating. 'I'm not here to talk about my being unfortunate. Believe me, that's not why I'm here. I just want to know whether you're looking for Baran Shukur or not.'

'I don't need to hide anything from you,' Zuhdi said. 'Baran Shukur is my niece. There's been no news of her for months now. She has no relatives but me. I've come back to search for her.'

'You have to excuse me,' Afsana said, standing up. 'I don't have a lot of time. It was important to find out how you are related to Baran; I had to know. Later, I'll tell you what we should do. That's for later. I must go now. I really must.' From the doorway, she said: 'Please don't lock the door at night. Whenever there's an opportunity, I'll come to see you. And if you want to leave the hotel, let me know in advance. Don't leave without letting me know.'

After she left the room, Zuhdi wondered whether or not he had actually come back from the other end of the world in order to meet this woman. This charming woman, in this shabby, filthy hotel. At that moment, he had a strange desire to read Baran Shukur's letters again. Unthinkingly, he reached into his suitcase to take them out. Only when he opened his case did he remember that they were now with the Baron of Courgettes.

THE MEMOIRS OF THE
BARON OF IMAGINATION

The whole world is a dangerous conflict between the imagination and power. That's how I had come to understand it. But lately, quite suddenly, I have developed the crazy notion that this definition is wrong. Don't laugh at me, lest I lose all seriousness in your eyes.

The imagination is power, and power is the imagination. An imagination without power is nothing but cold, white foam swept away by life once and for all, while power without imagination is cold governance devoid of visions. Power without imagination resembles a dreaming slave. Both lack real force, and cannot work effectively on their own.

Whether you understand it or not makes no difference. I needed to harvest the minds of all the Imaginative Creatures. If you wish to build something beautiful on Earth, you mustn't be too proud to bow before those gifted with imagination.

One day I visited Husni the Imaginative, the jovial towel-seller with the extraordinary towels. One night when I was drunk, the wicked Attar had recounted the story to me of the wretched towel that tells the tale of the imagination's triumph over power.

Swallowing my pride and dignity, I begged and pleaded with the towel-merchant to show it to me. I didn't introduce myself as one of the city's noblemen, although I am the son of a respectable agha and have been one of the country's leading politicians. Back then, it was unlikely anyone would have recognised me in public. Genealogists would have heard of my name, but the man on the street didn't know me at all. Disguising my appearance was my secret, and my great desire. In this city, you cannot live with just the one face. I swear that if there were no masks, human beings would be disgraced. Since my youth, I've learned to wear masks rather than display my true self; to appear under different names, in different costumes. Often I chose to dress in such a way that no one would recognise me, blending in with the crowd as a horse trader or a smuggler.

On the day I went to see Husni the Imaginative, I introduced myself as an antiques dealer. I managed, albeit with difficulty, to convince him to show me the towel. I told him I had come from a faraway city and was writing about imagination in ancient literature. He showed me that piece of imaginative work, but wouldn't let me take a photo or make a sketch of it. It was an extremely beautiful towel, striking and magical. The night Husni the Imaginative showed it to me, I was pitched once again into the tumult of questions that had tormented me since my youth, plaguing me like a chronic ailment.

Power or imagination? This is my eternal and dangerous question.

The day Husni the Imaginative showed me that extraordinary towel, I had a different interpretation of the story it told. I felt that the great war it depicted had never happened in reality. The entire conflict had occurred only in the imagination of the king – who was also a poet – in which the king's poetic half murdered his authoritarian half. But what happens if one is poet and king at the same time?

That towel could ruin my life forever. I had struggled and suffered with these questions for ages. Slowly, day after day, I understood that the imagination had meaning only when it worked as part of a huge plan. What is imagination after all, if it isn't backed by great power?

I had to work calmly. There is nothing more torturous than drawing up a detailed plan or map, but someone who seeks great power must make meticulous plans. He must be gentle and patient, hard-hearted yet sympathetic. Ultimately, I needed a plan within which everyone would have a place.

Please don't assume that the son of a noble family must be free from pain. Like a madman, I covered my face and walked through the city. I asked the wise men, the teachers and the poor: 'What would you do if you had power?'

It takes imagination to answer this question. Remove imagination from power, and the latter becomes like a blind person, not knowing how to proceed or where to go.

One day I told a Party plenum: 'Comrades, colleagues, we are blind not because we can't see but because we lack imagination.'

Don't you misunderstand me, too. Don't assume I'm infatuated with the imagination. The wealth of those who believe in imagination without power is useless. They have a power that destroys themselves alone. I have no sympathy for those with a rich stock of imagination who don't invest it in a superior power. I have more respect for the Sultans' magicians, for the fortune tellers and astrologers.

On its own, imagination might save someone's soul once in a blue moon, but with power it can build Paradise. That's right, Paradise. Almighty God, help me and support me. The scent of

Paradise on Earth drives me mad; if man seeks it, he will go crazy, utterly and forever.

When I first saw the towel, I knew what a dangerous story it told. What can be more dangerous for the world than a king and a poet engaged in a fight from which the poet emerges triumphant, and the world survives without the king – the great symbol of power? When I pondered the deep meaning of the story, I forgot about the beauty and magic of the design. I thought about it for a whole week, leaving it to my conscience to decide. Finally, I was ready. Yes, my dears, I was ready for anything.

One evening I went back to Husni the Imaginative, in the same guise of an antiques dealer. I had decided to kill him if he refused to give me the towel. I had the energy to do it, to put dozens of bullets in his pale body and big head. I had the energy to send him to Hell and set fire to his towel shop.

To begin with, we spoke as two salesmen who couldn't agree on the price of an item. He didn't want to sell the damned towel. He just didn't want to. He pretended he wanted to keep it with him until death. I handled him with my well-known patience. First, I raised the price 1,000 dinars at a time, then 10,000 dinars. I tried to entice him with properties, travel and beautiful women, even young prostitutes. Nothing worked. I didn't want things to get so out of hand that I had to show my pistol but my impatience, anger and madness all surfaced. This dangerous towel shouldn't be allowed to remain in this man's store until doomsday for everyone to see. As for the towel-seller, he appeared to take my keenness as a youthful prank.

'Master of imagination, know where you stand. Do not become confused,' I told him in the heat of the moment. 'This isn't a game. I want that towel at any price.'

He looked into my eyes and understood that this was no ordinary transaction or mere game.

'Give me 100,000 dinars and take it,' he said fearfully, placing his hands on the towel.

Had he asked for even more money, I would have paid it. I had to take the damned towel away and hide it. What a great sin it is for poets to kill kings!

No, my dears, my dream was of the king and the poet sitting together, exchanging whatever was in their imaginations. That night I took the towel and hid it in a safe place, a place that only I knew about.

THE STORY OF THE BARON OF DOLLS
SEPTEMBER 2004

In the days that followed my visit to the hospital with Parinaz, I got to know the Baron of Dolls better. I saw more of his soul, with its strange contradictions. I began to think that he represented a strange, irrational aspect of our world, the part that eludes language and interpretation no matter how ardent the attempt to explain it.

'Multifaceted' is the only word I could use to describe the baron. He had a strange multifaceted soul, one that epitomised a large number of the barons' strange qualities. On one hand, he resembled the kings in Shakespeare's plays; on the other, a forest dweller. I should also say that he had something of the spirit of the ancient Kurds of bygone centuries, who knew nothing but forests, mountains and hunting. Yet, he also had the solemnity of those skilful merchants encountered on long-distance journeys by sea, and the imagination of the bold men who put themselves in jeopardy in the search for gold, diamonds and other hidden minerals.

In the course of his life, he had fought on very different fronts. He had served in the Iraqi army's artillery unit for some time, but had also risen to prominence among the peshmergas. The baron was a poet, too – not in the sense that he published collections of poems, but in the sense that he talked and lived poetry. When I first encountered him, I couldn't have said whether he was like a Kurd left over from the army of the sad Kurdish emirates or a dangerous post-uprising businessman who could disguise himself in thousands of ways behind thousands of words. His presence among the barons struck me as unusual. At first I thought it was a grave error, so I was shocked to discover that he genuinely loved them. He came from a family of aghas, and considered himself an offshoot of the great Kurdish emirs. His views were like those of an agha, and he had a patriarchal spirit that I slowly came to know and understand.

One day the baron invited me for dinner, and I was happy to accept. He was one of those fearless, wealthy men who could invite

217

anyone to dine with them. On that first occasion, he provided a lavish feast – far more than was needed for two people.

'Mir Safin, I would like to know why you are called the "Baron of Dolls", I asked him. 'Why have they given you a name like that? Who are you, and who are the barons?'

He was wearing a silk suit and a shiny blue shirt. He was a well-dressed individual whose white beard and bald head didn't prevent women from admiring his composure and conversational skills.

'Souls are like butterflies; bodies roam. The soul of man is the same as that of an innocent bulbul,' he said in his melodious tongue, with a degree of solemnity I had only ever seen in Laurence Olivier.

'A bulbul is a bulbul, whether caged or flying freely in the skies. That is how it is. It is fate, and we cannot tell whether it will be good or bad, white or black. When the Earth rotates, so, too, do our fates. Each of us must stop somewhere and die somewhere. We are forever tossed upon the storm. Tonight, the Earth turns and we are set down upon one road, the next night upon another. Today we dine at one table, tomorrow at another. Now it is we who eat the meat of others, tomorrow it is they who eat ours.

'Man does not choose his own place in this universe. It is the universe that allots us our place. Whether I am the Baron of Dolls or a sad dove flying over withered gardens, I am a wandering soul like all the rest. The helpless ants and I are the same in the eyes of blind, infinite Nature. To the universe, there is no difference between a savage beast's roar and the sound of the most beautiful ghazal. Pay no attention to names and play your own game. This is what I always say: *Play your own game.* Sit and eat at whichever dinner table is the closest. Should you find yourself among the barons, be a baron; should you find yourself in a jungle, be a warrior; should you find yourself at sea, be a sailor; should you have wings, be a bird or an angel. Wherever you are, just be. You did not go there of your own accord; a hand deposited you there.

'Right now, you and I are in a similar position, and physically close to one another; yet we are also very far removed from one another. Humans interact; their destinies do not. There is no force in this universe that could make you the Baron of Dolls and me Majid-i Gul Solav. There is no force that could smash open my lock and place your soul inside my body. You and I meet the way two brainless, placid, unimaginative birds meet – but our lives do not. If we are destined to be at war, let us kill one another mercifully. Man has complete control over one thing and one thing only, and that is mercy. Should you find yourself in battle, what choice do you have if you are not a fighter? Should you fall in water, what choice do you have if you can't swim? Should you find yourself in the market, what else to do but trade? Should you need to kill so that you are not killed, then do so, my friend, but do not forget about mercy. Kill, but don't forget to weep for the slain. If you can avoid inflicting pain, do so. That I die now and you do not, that you die and someone else does not, that you are the victim and I your killer, that I am the hunter and you the prey – these things are not determined by you and me. They are the turning of a great wheel, a whirlpool that flings each of us onto a separate square. Just as a pawn on a chess board may not ask why he is not a bishop, a king or a knight, likewise I may not ask why I am a baron and you are not.'

I knew that I couldn't swap places with any other person in this world, but I didn't think that if a human being should find himself among the brutes, he, too, should howl.

'But it isn't fate to kill a young man who has a liaison with a woman?' I said, practically giving away my secret with the first sentence I uttered. 'Human beings can refuse to submit to such destinies.'

The baron stroked his dignified beard and looked at me suspiciously.

'We would be unlucky if we became like doves who believe the forest is Paradise,' he said. 'We would be unlucky if we didn't understand that a long trail of blood has been shed. Unlucky is he who tells man not to kill and not to be killed. All our duty is to love man, but to say to him "thou shalt not kill, thou shalt not sin, thou shalt not steal, thou shalt not lie" is to share the perspective of the gods. Why do you make the same requests of me as the gods do? God did not create man like the angels, and yet that's what He asks us to be. Why are you asking the same thing? Majid-i Gul Solav, I have entered wars and killed people, but I have also sold dolls and made children happy. I don't believe in innocence. There isn't a thing on this planet that is innocent. Here there is no such thing as a criminal or an innocent person – there are only winners and losers.'

I knew that it was not easy to fully understand the Baron of Dolls. I thought at first that he was not a genuine baron, and I was tempted tell him my plans to my heart's content. On that first day I saw only his angelic side, but after meeting him several more times I felt that Mir Safin was a genuine mir, endowed with all the clout and grandeur of a lord.

His was the first large, expensive car I had ever been in. Until then, I had only ever ridden the city's buses. Don't forget that I was a great walker. I have no doubt that if I totted up all the ground I've covered in this city, my total mileage would be greater than the distance covered by *Marco Polo* or any other explorer in the world. Just as a small bird jumps from one side of its cage to the other, I too had been hopping from one street to another in this city my whole life. I was surprised that the Baron of Dolls gave me a lift in his car. It was the first time anyone had offered me a lift. The baron was astonished that I'd never been in a car before. He couldn't believe people like me existed in the world. He shook his head several times, not knowing whether to believe me or not. When he learned that I had never left the city, he was even more astonished.

It was my knowledge of cinema and unique insight into the world of film that led him to become my friend and to enjoy my companionship. I was so erudite when it came to cinema that he thought I was lying to him, and that I had spent part of my life in Hollywood or else studied at a film school.

When I got into his unusual car, I understood what it meant to be a baron. I understood why, when someone entered that world, he wouldn't want to leave it. In my relationship with the baron, I had to stay on the sidelines and not break down the barriers between us too quickly. I also thought that I shouldn't attempt to get too close to him, lest he grow suspicious of me. I wanted to become his friend without making him feel I was pursuing some personal goal.

'Honourable Baron, I have very fine handwriting – the finest in the world,' I told him. 'I also have some limited skill in accounting. Why don't you hire me as your bookkeeper?'

'I have three girls doing my bookkeeping,' he said, laughing. 'Their handwriting is very beautiful, and they themselves even more so. Why do I need you to do it? If you want us to become friends, don't even think about working for me. Anyone who works for a baron becomes his employee. I'd like you to be my friend.'

He talked about those working for him with great disdain.

'When you are a baron,' he said, 'your workers have to show you all the respect due to someone of your standing. If you worked for me, my image of you would change before my eyes.'

I said nothing. What mattered to me was that I should gain access to the world of the barons and get to know the Baron of Chickens. Then I could try and find a way to speak to his wife about Murad Jamil. That was my biggest goal.

'Baron, tell me, are you the only baron, or there are others?' I asked him.

'The barons are the summit, the very peak of society,' he said, giving me a sidelong look. 'They hold the torch, and they can burn you with it. If you like, I can take you to them. They're friendly, cheerful, pleasant company. They're no different from anyone else. They laugh, they swear, they get drunk, they betray one another. The difference is that they have more wealth and power. The weak, by nature, hate those with wealth and power, regarding them as a species that did not grow in the garden of humanity. The weak hate force, and the solemnity of force. I am the son of princes. I wanted to become an artillery officer, to fight, to see the fire of battle, to attack. My motto has always been, "Test your power, oh son of Adam." Majid Solav [for this is what he always called me], if you can't find yourself a place among the greats, don't be ungrateful. Let the greats cherish their greatness. Let them be. Don't ask how they got where they are. That's a weak person's question.'

I said nothing. I was surprised the baron held such strange views. I didn't want to come across as someone with political views that would upset the barons.

'Honourable Baron,' I said calmly, 'you speak so beautifully about the barons. I would love to get to know them, but I don't know if someone like me is fit to sit at the table of such great men.'

'You look like a real baron,' he said, as if enjoying the game. 'I swear, you have the appearance of a nineteenth-century baron. You have greatly benefited from watching films. None of the barons has your solemnity. I am sure that, given your appearance, I could introduce you as a baron to the others. What do you think? I could call you "the Baron of Narrative".'

A shudder of joy rippled through me, but it was only a few seconds before he began to laugh and said: 'Such tricks wouldn't go unnoticed by the city's new princesses. Such ruses would not go undetected by the princes and aristocrats of any city or country. You are not a baron. The barons have a strong intuition about that sort of thing. They know who is genuinely a prince, and who isn't. It is not just a title someone acquires. It is also the attitudes and behaviours that grow inside your soul ... so, no, I won't do that; I'll introduce you to them as a guest, as a storyteller who can astound us with your stories. But you must think about it carefully before agreeing. He who enters Nwemiran does not leave so easily.'

'It would be a great honour to enter that world,' I said, unhesitatingly. I couldn't know the true meaning of his words back then. 'An insignificant person such as myself would be proud to step into your world.'

'It will become evident further down the line whether it is an honour or a curse,' the Baron of Dolls said as he drove. 'Don't say anything now. Empty rhetoric and soulless letters cannot express what hasn't yet been experienced. How does a dove perched on a treetop know whether a bullet awaits it, or light? Sometimes, it takes a long while for water to recognise dead fish; it takes a long time for night to find its sleeping stars. Do not hold dark intentions in your heart. I say the same thing to all my emir friends: "My brethren khwaja and knights, tell those to whom you open your doors not to hold dark intentions in their hearts." There are people who enter the world of the mirs as beggars and leave as barons, and others who enter as barons and leave as beggars. Power and wealth are like beauty; they make you both happy and crazy. There are many tricksters who sneak into the barons' fold and end up dying like dogs. This is a war; yes, a war. He whose hands tremble during wartime will end up on the losing side. When you mix with the barons, there is no one to protect you or take pity on you. Only you can do that. Among the barons, you must take pity on yourself.'

'Baron of Dolls, take me to them,' I said. I didn't know what I was saying – I hadn't understood any of what he had just said. 'Take me to them. I feel that I was born into this world by mistake.'

'You should have been born among the barons, but you weren't,' he said with a sigh. 'And unless you're born into the fold, you're not a mir. Just don't forget that. Don't let such delusions enter your head ...' After a brief silence, he said: 'I have to find you a suitable way in. You must be patient.'

'I'll be patient, honourable Baron, I will,' I said quietly.

222

GHAZALNUS, AFSANA,
ONE THOUSAND GARDENS
LATE 1980s

In the late Eighties, Ghazalnus's father Nasser Saeed died of one of the unknown illnesses of old age, leaving his huge house to his son. Ghazalnus returned to his late father's house with the infant, whom he named Khayalwan, or 'Fantasist'. The first few weeks of raising him seemed simple and easy, but Ghazalnus didn't forget what the child's pale, sick mother had said about a certain Afsana who could help him. A month later, he left the baby with a female friend and went to the Snow and Mirage Hotel. It was a small, two-storey hotel built in the late Forties to attract farmers who came from the villages to have their tobacco crop inspected and to experience the mystery and magic of the city. It had been renovated in the early Seventies, when it began hosting Arab tourists, and then expanded and modernised in the Eighties with the arrival of frontline soldiers returning home on leave.

When Ghazalnus walked into the hotel that evening, Afsana was folding freshly laundered pillow covers with one of the hotel maids. At the end of 1988, Afsana, who had been married to the hotelier for nearly five years, was twenty-two years old. Anyone fortunate enough to see her on two different dates – the evening when Ghazalnus visited her, and the evening she met Shazaman – would have observed that in those sixteen years she had shown no signs of ageing, and become still more beautiful and enchanting. From their first meeting, Ghazalnus called her 'the lady of the enchanting whispers'. She had seen Ghazalnus before. Without a trace of shyness, she took his hands and led him through to the guest dining room.

'We know. We all know Nashmil has died,' she said in whisper. 'Don't tell me what happened. Don't give me any details. The child is in your care. I know that. I am concerned about such a young baby, Ghazalnus. Tell me, what have you called him?'

'His name is Khayalwan.'

Afsana thought it a unique name. She went on to tell him the story of how Nashmil had ended up on her deathbed. She portrayed herself as one of the young mother's closest and most supportive acquaintances.

'Years ago, Nashmil invited me into the society of forlorn women,' she said.

That was the first time Ghazalnus had heard of the society. Afsana explained how they held weekly meetings to talk about their suffering, and about the knights who rode through their dreams on horseback; to speak of magical places, beautiful moments and romantic regions they wanted to visit and live in. That same day, Afsana invited Ghazalnus to recite his ghazals to the women of the society. From then on, he began to mix with these sad women, with their rich imaginations, their sighs and hopes.

Over the years, Ghazalnus recited ghazals for the society on many occasions. Through it, he also came to know the fantasised children who were born of the imaginary and illegitimate relationships of the city's women. Fretful little Khayalwan was not the last child of the magical generation to be born with a line of ghazal inscribed on his chest. Many more fantasised children would follow.

The society of forlorn women was the biggest association Ghazalnus had encountered. Over the years, he had met scores of small, imaginative groups; he had travelled through many gardens, and climbed many high mountains whose peaks ended in the imagination. All across his homeland, he had met people full of desire and imagination. He had met small groups of young people, poets and lovers. However, none had as many members as this one. Some of the women in this society were the mothers of fantasised children born of failed loves. Some were in a position to raise their fantasised children, while others had to put their infants in the care of other women to save them from death. Through various means, via various gardens and alleyways, Ghazalnus soon became the carer of some of these fantasised children. They had nowhere else in the world to go but his home.

When, years later, he met Mahnaz, he was the adoptive father of three fantasised children created by unidentified girls and their unidentified lovers. All the illicit children were the fruit of the sad mothers' surrender to, and immersion in, imaginary, infinite moments of love. Ghazalnus found it strange that women who could not bear children by their husbands could give birth to such beautiful children.

One day, he walked around with the lady of the enchanting whispers and felt as if he were searching for his mother Baharbanu – as if, through his encounter with these women, he might access his own past. He wished he could understand why there was no force except love that could make some women in this world bear children. Afsana showed him some families that had adopted illicit and fantasised children.

'Hatred makes men kill each other and go to war, but it makes women sterile and sad,' she said in her customary whisper. She had been married to the hotelier for five years, and from the very first night she had intended to kill him; but she couldn't.

Through her, Ghazalnus saw sad women on the verge of madness, women who, at meetings with their fellow sufferers, had no fantasies but those of love. Some of them hated their husbands so much they experienced hallucinations and harrowing nightmares. Ghazalnus was the only man allowed to listen to the secret conversations of the women of the city. They always met in dark rooms and neglected corners, places where no man could hear their secrets.

Most of them were so pale they seemed extremely ill, and smelled of death. The women were very different, ranging from the wives of very poor men without so much as a day's supply of provisions to wives of the powerful and wealthy; from illiterate women to poets and actors. They were all sad women who, for just a few moments, could discuss their true desires. When he was among them, Ghazalnus understood that he lived in a part of the world where the simplest things were at the same time among the most unattainable.

During their closed meetings, everyone sat in a big circle around a candle. Some of the women bared their faces while others wore headscarves or niqabs, and they talked about their darkest desires. Some came in their best clothes, others as if attending a special ritual. Some of them couldn't speak. Instead, they danced or cried. Imagination was their last refuge. Had it not been for their fantasies, they could have become people with evil hearts, capable of killing. When the women had finished speaking about their suffering and uttered words prohibited in daily conversation, the last item on the agenda was Ghazalnus himself. He would come forward as a great energiser, and read out his enchanting poems. The ghazals generated even stronger desires and abandon in the women, as if taking them back to their origins, into the only world they sought. They became so intoxicated by Ghazalnus's poems that they came to see him as the spiritual representative of the knights they had dreamed of in childhood.

Although the world of these pale women appeared poorer, more secretive and more closed than others, as far as Ghazalnus was concerned it was the remotest and most unusual garden on the planet. There, more than anywhere else, he could see women's grief-filled hearts, understand how they surrendered to magical moments of love and opened up their bodies to the breeze of the imagination. Afsana spoke about the dark part of women's souls that would not come out into the light, except in the safety of the secret society; the part of their souls that was full of love and unaccountable hatred, suffering or joy; the part that did not obey the same rules that governed the visible part. In her whispers, which sounded less like the voice of a hotelier's wife than of a woman whose throat had been used to read nothing but poetry all her life, Afsana spoke about the secret garden each woman harboured in her heart, the dark infernos and the deep pain inside the labyrinthine corridors that were locked inside them, to which there were no keys. Ghazalnus slowly came to understand that apart from great love and great sadness, there was no other route to the outermost edge of the imagination.

In those same years, a certain Gulistan took Ghazalnus to Hazarbagh, where he fell truly in love for the first time in his life. In Hazarbagh, he got to know Sabri, the imaginary woman confined to the infinite gardens. Generation after generation of singers had proclaimed her eternal beauty, refreshed each night by the scent of the flowers in the magical gardens. She had entered the gardens out of fear of her infinite lovers and had never since left.

Ghazalnus visited the gardens one night with the intention of bringing her back to the real world. He read out his poems with a view to making her so infatuated she would feel a pull back into reality. He hoped that the ghazals would slowly lull Sabri into a magical slumber that would allow him to lead her out through the gates of Hazarbagh. But night after night, ghazal after ghazal, the magic turned on the magician – and now it was Ghazalnus who could no longer ignore all the beauty. In a short space of time, he found himself in love with her.

Although he was the greatest ghazal reader, and everyone who heard him believed that what he read came from the bleeding hearts of all the lovers in the world, he had never really been in love until the moment he met Sabri in Gulistan's flower gardens. It seemed he was destined, finally, to love a woman whom the flowers had long since rendered an imaginary person, in an imaginary garden outside this real world of ours, a woman with whom he would never be able to share a home, sit in an arbour, walk under the sun of our cities or through the alleys of our sad districts; a woman who was so immersed in the tulip beds, moonlight and flowers, that life outside the imaginary gardens was unthinkable to her. Ghazalnus understood from the first night that Sabri lived only in this garden, that she was nothing but a mirage beyond its conjured flowers. She epitomised the imaginary girl you would never meet, the one who would always elude you. Night after night, he returned to read poems to this gazelle-like woman, who was at times docile, kind and amorous and at others wild, elusive and restless. Sometimes Sabri was captivated by the ghazals; at other times, less so.

Ghazalnus looked for her in the many streets of Hazarbagh. For the first time, he understood what it meant to burn for a woman. Late at night, he would tuck the children into bed and head for Hazarbagh, returning in the morning before the sun rose or the cock crowed.

The keys to the imaginary gates of Hazarbagh were held by the sad older women clad in black, who watered and gathered the roses and then extracted rosewater from them. Sabri was the only woman the gardens did not expel during the day, the only one who, when the sun rose and Hazarbagh disappeared, also vanished with the flowers, re-emerging when night fell again. Her beauty was beyond description, and was not subject to the harsh rules of ageing. Despite all the vigour of his ghazals, Ghazalnus could not tame her; he suffered the excruciating agonies of love. The man whose ghazals caused women to faint in the real world fell in love in the realm of imagination with an eternal and elusive beauty, with someone his ghazals could not reach. There he suffered all the pains of love.

The ghazals he declaimed in Hazarbagh were not the ones he had learned by heart from Sukhta's books. For the first time, he began to write ghazals about his own love. Initially, he couldn't believe it, thinking the poems he found himself reading out like a mad lover in the streets of the eternal flowers to be Sukhta's compositions. When day broke, he quickly referred back to the books, comparing his poems to Sukhta's texts, and noticed that his words in the flower gardens were not in the books: they were creations of his own heart. During those nights under the moonlight of Hazarbagh, he came to understand that there was a hidden writer of ghazals – a ghazalnus – in every person.

SEARCHING FOR THE BARONS
HASAN-I TOFAN, JULY—AUGUST 2004

One day, I revealed everything to Shibr. I told him I was part of a group of people known as 'the Imaginative Creatures', who each had a piece of land – a special place – in another world that existed in our imagination. I told him about Hazarbagh and its magical flowers. I told him about Ghazalnus and his enchanting poems with the power to enrapture anyone who heard them, making listeners set out towards unknown destinations. Then I spoke of the imaginary rivers of Majid-i Gul Solav, who took a group of blind children with him to the realm of imagination.

Shibr initially thought I was joking, and that I had merely come up with the imaginary world to keep the conversation going. Unperturbed, I told him, 'Our job is to rewrite the history of death over the past ten years.' I spoke about the thousands of women who had lost their lives to fire, the thousands of youths lost or drowned on the long journey to Europe, those killed in the civil war and the many sudden murders and suicides that occurred in this city. Shibr was surprised that someone like me, with my sharwal and salt-and-pepper hair, should be drawn to that beautiful world. I pleaded with him for more information about the barons, the ruling elite and their role in the bigger picture.

To begin with, Shibr thought my words were merely a fantasy to overcome my futile and prosaic daily life, but I explained to him in detail that we were working on the mystery of a corpse belonging to a certain young man named Murad Jamil. I also told him that one of the clues we held had led us to the barons.

When I began to speak about the barons, Shibr paused for a moment and said, with concern, 'I've noticed for some time now that you're putting yourself at great risk. You're entering a battle beyond your abilities.'

'Shibr, we aren't entering a battle,' I reassured him. 'We're writing a book that won't be finished before the end of the world. It will never be published. Even if we dedicate our whole lives to it, we won't be able to recount even a tiny fraction of the death stories. Who can write down the stories of all the women who have been or are being burned? We can only write down a few stories, a few cases. What we are pursuing is fantasy, and the book we're writing is a book that will never be completed. What's more, it is only for us, for our imaginative creatures, for our children, for the girls who will be born free in a hundred years' time – so they know that thousands of women in the twenty-first century bought the freedom they enjoy with fire. Don't worry, Shibr. It's not a new project. Ghazalnus began it, then Trifa Yabahri. We're not aiming to make a name for ourselves or to talk about the murderers or put their names into the public domain. The book is just for us, for the imagination-loving generations after us whose imaginations will often hide the truth. It is being done so that the imagination doesn't make us forget the truth.

'Truth and imagination are part of the same circle. Regardless of the starting point, the one leads to the other. Truth springs from the extreme end of imagination, just as imagination springs from the extreme end of truth. Whichever route you follow to the end will take you to the other. We want to complete the circle. If we don't write the book, it means we will have stopped halfway along the route of imagination, that we haven't completed the circle.'

It was the first time Shibr had heard me speak like this. He knew that I had learned some of these words and ideas from a more intelligent person. Although Shibr could see the risks, and although what I said sounded strange, it caught his interest. At one moment he appeared to be asking why he wasn't one of the Imaginative Creatures.

To dispel his sadness, I said: 'Shibr, you are the only person in this world to whom I can speak this truth and reveal this secret. You've just become the only person who is not an Imaginative Creature, yet knows our story. I'm telling you this so that you know what a great friend you are to me, and how much I need you.'

This pleased Shibr.

'Hasan-i Pizo,' he said calmly, shifting a little in his wheelchair, 'do you think I am scared for my own life? Brother, since the day I landed in this wheelchair, I haven't really considered myself alive. I didn't realise how small we are, how insignificant, until I became disabled like this. They use us for some time, then cast us aside. Pizo, I'm worried about you. Let me tell you something. Think about it carefully. You know that I worked for them for a long time after the uprising. I killed for them; I fought for them. They like two things very much: their own power, and their purity.

'They no longer look at power like they did in the old times. Back when we were peshmergas and worked in the network cells, power was something else. It was dealing a blow to the enemy, recruiting people for the revolution, ridding an inch of Kurdistan from the filthy fascists. Yes, power then was something in that vein.

'Pizo, nowadays power to them means owning everything there is to own in the world, from beautiful houses to massive shopping centres, from the small towns they're building right now to the grand resorts; it means owning the vehicles, the beautiful women of this city, the poets, those who play musical instruments and those who write. Everything, Hasan-i Pizo. Everything. Let me tell you this: they want *everyone*. They're willing to buy everyone. Absolutely everyone. Hasan-i Pizo, I worked for them a lot after the uprising. They want everyone, from imams conducting mass prayers to prostitutes, and they put random prices on human beings.

'This country must be theirs; from newspapers to stadiums and swimming pools, from printing houses to restaurants, from hair salons to universities, from lowly musicians obliged to entertain them at their parties to university professors, from the clowns they have set up to make people laugh to the tears of the martyrs' female relatives – it must all be theirs. They want everything, Hasan-i Pizo. They want the prostitutes they bring from other countries; they also want the local virgins and chaste women, the mullahs' cloaks and the dancers' bras. They buy a murderer like Tunchi, and the gentlest musician. That's the only way they can survive and make any sense. It's a lifestyle and mode of organisation that you and I don't understand. We don't know how it works, but that's how it is, Hasan-i Pizo.

'But they also value their purity a great deal, Hasan. They're obsessed with going down in history as pure and beloved fighters. I know them. You stood aside and went away after the uprising, but I *know* them. They won't forgive anyone who might blacken their reputation. They believe they've created a vast paradise for themselves and for us. They won't let anyone tamper with that image.'

I didn't know how accurate this picture was. I felt like a clueless outsider. Although I had been walking the city's streets again for over six years, I didn't understand a thing. I wasn't very keen on pondering its secret life. There are people who wander around a city's hidden backstreets, and others who want to walk its imaginary alleyways. Shibr was of the former type; I was of the latter. He didn't believe very much in the world I lived in, and I didn't believe in his, but now we were obliged to find a meeting point somewhere along the way.

The day Shibr and I spoke, I hadn't been to the Idle Murderers' Club for six years. Sometimes I would happen upon an old friend from the past. We would greet one another politely before carrying on our separate ways.

'We must go to the Idle Murderers' Club,' he said, despite his reservations, when I said we needed to find out more about the barons. 'That's the only place we can get the information – but we mustn't appear to be going there for that reason. Do you understand? Absolutely not. You must be patient.'

The Idle Murderers' Club had changed enormously in the space of six years. The place was decorated extravagantly. A lot of money had been spent on the décor and furniture. Night had not yet fallen when Shibr and I arrived. We couldn't see anyone, save for a couple of people drinking in a corner. A young woman received us, saying that we would only be allowed in if we had special ID. She wouldn't relent until we said that we were close friends of Tunchi and Haji Kotar. Relaxing music played in the background. They had named the place 'Swaran-i Zozan': 'The Knights of the Highlands'.

'Hasan-i Pizo, the world has changed a lot in the past few years,' Shibr said in a low voice. 'They all listen to music now. Some of them have their own singers. They spend stupendous amounts of money bringing over singers from abroad. Some of them have their own exclusive music bands.'

'To Hell with what they do, to Hell with all of it, as long as they're not killing anyone,' I said.

I kept saying this same, strange sentence. That evening, the place gradually filled with old friends and acquaintances. They all gave me a warm welcome. They were so astonished at our visit that they couldn't believe their eyes. They had all changed a great deal, and become dangerously fat. Most of them wore black suits and white shirts. All the tables were full. I saw lots of people I had not seen or met before. I let Shibr gather information for me, with his pleasant talk and jovial bonhomie. A beer bottle in hand, he moved from one table to another in his wheelchair. He talked to everyone, and laughed loudly. Sometimes he hailed me from afar, shouting across the tables, 'Hasan-i Tofan, are you aware of this? I swear by my honour, this place is Heaven on Earth. Swaran-i Zozan! Listen to this poem by Khila the Insect: "This is home to the Knights of the Highlands, where the hot-headed women of the hot country are. It is the night on which we serve wine, don't send the thunder and storms."'

I'd known Khila the Insect for many years – he was an old man who grew up with the revolution. His long record in the armed struggle had done nothing for him. He had a talent for producing meaningless poems. Ultimately, these ludicrous poems made him famous, and he had secured himself a special place at the gatherings of officials and politicians. Sometimes he wrote poems for a vast amount of money. In the space of ten years, he had become richer than all the Kurdish

232

poets from Baba Tahir Hamadani to those alive today combined, as Shibr put it. Khila the Insect spent his evenings getting drunk at this club, writing eulogies and satires. His poems made me want to vomit.

That night, I bumped into many creatures like Khila the Insect, people I hadn't seen for years. As if he had a magical key, Shibr was able to simply slip back into the fray. Disability or no disability, he could still charm everyone. Tunchi showed us every possible respect, although I knew that, deep down, he had questions and doubts. Shibr called our first night 'the night of fun'. I didn't move from my chair. I ate nothing but a bowl of pistachios and chickpea soup, but Shibr gave no thought to the amount he was drinking. By the time we went home that night, I hadn't discovered anything, but Shibr said, 'They were there, the barons. The Baron of Honey and the Black Baron were both there. That means they were up to something. They never go there alone, or without some purpose. Most of the jobs, most of the deals are done in that wretched club. Damn the place. Damn it.'

'Shibr, tell me,' I said, 'why don't they use their own men for the jobs? If they want something done, who are they afraid of? They've got their own men, their bootlickers. Isn't that so? What you're saying doesn't make sense, does it?'

'Hasan-i Pizo, since when have you been so stupid?' Shibr said. 'No one uses their own men nowadays. Don't you understand? They're not so shortsighted and brainless as to show their hand. A secret force carries out the big jobs in this country. One thing is sacred in this country, and that is secrecy. They often pretend that everything they do is open and transparent. Sometimes they show us a glimpse of their backsides and say, "Look, we have no secrets." Hasan, son of Pizo, they pull down their trousers a little bit and say, "Look at democracy. That's democracy. Can't you see it?" But for thirteen years now, one religion has towered over everything else: the worship of secrecy. There is a huge network. It's like a whirlwind; it prevents any major crime from being exposed. Go to the prisons. Go on. Then you'll know what I'm talking about. Apart from petty criminals, apart from those who commit crimes of a lower order, there's no one else in there.'

Shibr was so furious about people keeping secrets that I was afraid he would be angry with me too, but as he spoke I realised that the secrets of the Imaginative Creatures were very small and insignificant compared to the secrets of the barons. Shibr hated them so much that if he hadn't vented his anger, he might have died of it.

'Why are you so angry at the Party?' I asked him one day. 'They actually respect you. They would pay you good money. Help you make a home. It's your own fault.'

'Who says I'm angry at them?' he said, laughing. 'Who says so? Hasan-i Pizo, I am too insignificant to be angry at them. I am angry that I killed people for fifteen years, thinking I was serving a cause. Do you understand? *That's* what I'm angry about. I worked for them for fifteen years, and then realised there was no cause. One day I lost respect for myself. Hasan-i Pizo, when you lose respect for yourself, you're dead.

'You're a strange creature, Pizo. I swear, there isn't another person like you in this world, or on any other planet perhaps. I really don't know what you are. You think I don't know that I have my rights, my entitlements? Do you know what I mean? Do you think I don't know that it is within my rights to have a home to live in and a salary so I don't starve? I don't get it. Do you think I'm an animal? But *they* don't see it that way, do you understand? When they pay you your salary, they don't say, "This is the fruit of your efforts." They think they've bought you. Hasan-i Pizo, that's how they think.

'When they pay you your salary, they don't say, "That's the reward for your struggle on behalf of your people, your nation,"' he continued, as if my silence frightened him. 'They say it's the price of your hands, the price of your legs, the price of your mouth, which should stay shut and say nothing.'

I felt that there was no force – none at all – that could make Shibr embrace the Party again.

We went to the same club a few nights in a row. Shibr played the same game every night. He went to all the tables and spoke to everyone. He drank beer and got drunk.

'Hasan-i Pizo, Ja'far-i Magholi's here,' he said one night after we had gone home. 'Do you understand? Ja'far-i Magholi! I learned tonight that Ja'far-i Magholi has been here for a long time.'

It was the strangest news I'd heard in months. 'Shibr, I want to see him!' I shouted. 'I need to see him!'

'How?' he said, laughing. 'He lives among the barons. Do you understand what that means? In Nwemiran. People like you and I can't even visit that district. It's an exclusive place that poor people like you and I can't access.'

Shibr was right. No one could get into Nwemiran easily. But finding Ja'far-i Magholi now became my greatest obsession. From that night on, I was sure that sooner or later, I would meet Magholi again. But how and where, I did not know.

WHAT A BEAUTIFUL GARDEN YOU HAVE, MAHNAZ KHAN

GHAZALNUS, WINTER 1993

After Mahnaz's death, the smell of her burning body stayed with Ghazalnus. Night after night he woke up repeatedly, with the cold, dangerous odour of singed human flesh in his nostrils. Wherever he was, the smell would linger around him, leaving him restless. Despite closing the doors and windows and drawing the curtains, it still disturbed him, as if a mighty secret force was beckoning him to pass on a message. He knew the smell was nothing but Mahnaz's burned soul haunting his own life. To try and understand its secret, he visited the city's hospitals when they opened their doors on visiting days. He walked into the burn unit and wandered through the old, dirty wards. Every time he took this distressing journey, he saw dozens of girls in excruciating pain on their hospital beds.

At around the time Mahnaz Maro died, Ghazalnus inherited two big houses from his grandfathers, which he now owned in addition to the large house his father had left him (and where the fantasised children lived). Six months after Mahnaz's death, the tale of the enchanting garden that forced Sayfadin Maro and his wife Shams to leave the house was one of the unusual but not infrequent stories circulating in the city. Ghazalnus learned about it by word of mouth. The house was widely rumoured to be haunted. No house in the wealthy districts of the city had been talked about in these terms before because educated people of means lived there, who thought they had overcome superstition. However, the transformation of the house into a wild garden was certainly not a lie. It was there for everyone to see.

Sayfadin, who appeared shattered by his daughter's death, was surprised one late winter evening in 1993 when he found himself obliged to receive the bearded and bespectacled Ghazalnus – who turned up unannounced – in the living room of his new house. In his heart, Sayfadin held the sad imagination tutor accountable. The whole world knew now that, before her death, Mahnaz had been in love with this dervish-like maverick. Deep down, he wished he didn't belong to the civilian arm of the Party, which talked about peace and basic civil rights. He wished he belonged to its armed wing, which believed only in revenge. He wished that, one day, Najo Ashkani would take revenge on the man who had opened the gates of Hell before his family.

Sayfadin Maro didn't want to be seen as an extremist in the eyes of the advocates of democracy or the Party supporters. He restrained himself reluctantly and concealed the pain in his heart. He received Ghazalnus with the grace of a man who was adamant that reason should not desert him, nor emotions get the better of him.

I must say that after Mahnaz's self-immolation, Shams – in contrast to Sayfadin – blamed all her family's miseries on Najo and Sayfadin's mercilessness. For the first time in her life, she thought about leaving Sayfadin and retreating to a quiet corner for a few years to mourn her daughter, but she was dissuaded by pressure from relatives, the entreaties of female acquaintances and the proscriptions of the mullahs and sheikhs.

After Mahnaz's death, the Leader offered Sayfadin a mansion – a rare thing in the 1990s. The potbellied Sayfadin established a prominent place for himself in the Party. Gradually, he took charge of almost all Party funds. He personally discussed customs revenue with the Leader, and directly supervised the Party's ever-expanding property portfolio.

During that period, Sayfadin only bought properties for himself and for the Party. He never sold any. He was surprised that Ghazalnus had come to buy his old house from him. For six months he had been looking for a buyer, to no avail; now his ugly enemy, this maverick in his olive-coloured shirt and small glasses, had come to buy it. He didn't know what to say. He knew he couldn't easily find someone else. No buyer in the world would want a house where the rooms were alive with bushes, trees and birds, where the windows couldn't be closed and the walls smelled of wild forests, where the whole place was riven by a mixture of sunbeams and moonlight. On the other hand, he hated Ghazalnus so much that it grieved him to sell him anything at all. He thought to himself that Ghazalnus didn't want to buy the house, but had come to buy the dead Mahnaz from him.

At the end of their meeting, he bid Ghazalnus a friendly goodbye without making any promises. He offered a diplomatic smile and said that he would 'seek a consensus' with his wife, Shams. This phrase, 'seek a consensus', had only recently entered the vocabulary of Kurdistan's politicians, and Sayfadin Maro had taken to peppering his conversations with it. He was one of those men who listened to nothing but the Party media, and had decided to believe only it. As a result, whenever a new word entered Party media jargon, he was the first to use it.

When Ghazalnus left, Shams decided that she would pay with her life to ensure the house went to him. If the girl had been unable to meet her lover while alive, she would do so now that she was dead. She was certain that by buying the house, Ghazalnus would put right the fatal error he had made in Mahnaz's final days by ignoring her and thereby delivering her up to her dark fate. An adolescent girl in love, driven mad by a hopeless passion, had died – and no one in this world had understood her. No one.

After Ghazalnus had left, as if readying herself for war, she went to Sayfadin. 'You are going to sell the house to that young man,' said Shams, as if uttering a final and dangerous order. 'At least he is thoughtful and fair enough to want the memories of your daughter not to go to someone who doesn't know their value.'

Without saying a word, Sayfadin slowly got dressed to go out. Standing before the bedroom mirror to fix his tie, he wept inconsolably. He wept involuntarily. The wound of Mahnaz's suicide had never healed. Since her death, the whole world had been nothing but a lie. Sometimes, when he was sitting with the Leader, Mahnaz would cross his mind, or he would see her image momentarily, killing any joy he took in this world. Recently he had taken to going back to the old house furtively, without Shams's knowledge, to stand outside Mahnaz's room and picture her in his mind. He would stand there amid the trees, birds and grass, and weep. Come what may, he should sell the house to be free of this new obsession. He was sure that killing Ghazalnus would not bring him peace. Had he thought otherwise, he would have done it. He was certain he would not be at peace. And yet, he still wanted to kill him.

On a cold winter evening, he went for a drive by himself. For two months he had not gone out without his bodyguards, but now he wanted to be alone. He had become increasingly obese, and had begun to feel sudden pains in his heart. Often he would break out into a sweat in the car, feeling he might faint. Exhausted, sad and only half-awake, he drove as if the car were an old carriage pulled by a few sick horses. That day, as if surrendering to his fate, as if running away from everything, as if certain that he could not free himself from the illusions and absurdities of life, he had decided to sell the house to Ghazalnus and live as if he had never had a daughter called Mahnaz. Politics had taught him how to push ahead. Now, as he wept, he wanted his short, fleshy, slowing legs to carry him, with his ugly potbelly meted out to him by fate, to where he could become someone with a different past.

Two days later, he handed the keys to Ghazalnus and decided to dedicate his life to the Party for good. Ghazalnus, meanwhile, sold his two newly inherited properties, received the house keys from Sayfadin and moved into the old Maro house one evening in the winter of 1993. He had passed through dozens of inaccessible places, imaginary streets and mysterious canyons unafraid, but now, standing in the front garden of the house, he was overcome with awe. Outside, a strong wind played with the world; all at once, he felt as if a hand were pulling him, and a powerful gust swept him inside.

The dining room was now home to grass and trees. He saw many untroubled birds slumbering among the branches. These were the same imaginary birds he and Mahnaz had created during their lessons; the flowers, too, were the same huge wildflowers whose enchanting scent had ultimately lured Mahnaz to an unknown destination. The staircase leading to the second floor was covered over by a wild creeping plant, and a faint ray of light from an invisible source illuminated everything.

He trod through the undergrowth and climbed the stairs to Mahnaz's room. Months earlier, it had been a room like any other: the delicately decorated room of a girl who had just left the realm of childhood and entered the world of adults. Yet what a reception those merciless adults, who didn't understand what youth or childhood was, had given her! The tutors had persecuted and belittled Mahnaz, and paralysed her faculties. When Ghazalnus opened the door to her room, he was met instead by an illuminated garden, isolated from the world and rife with enormous pink flowers. It was a place of unrivalled beauty, expanding infinitely: the garden of Mahnaz's enchanting imagination, left behind when she died. As Ghazalnus walked around it, he wondered if Saeed Bio and the other teachers could ever have known that such a thing existed in Mahnaz's heart. How many others must there be who, like Mahnaz, seemed ungifted on the surface, yet harboured such magical gardens in their souls!

Ghazalnus strolled around the sad, imaginary garden all night long. He felt the house to be worth all the properties on Earth. Here he could live alongside Mahnaz's soul. He could gaze forever on her beauty, left behind in the form of a garden. He was certain she had left the garden for him. He hadn't felt at peace since the day she set fire to herself. He deemed it his spiritual duty to be near this garden. It was his, and this enchanted property was the biggest gift anyone had ever given him.

The idea of a book about death first came to Ghazalnus among those huge, pink flowers and broad, green, scented leaves. It was there that he felt he had to write down the story of Mahnaz and the garden.

He was certain now that every person had a garden like this inside himself or herself, but that only very few could leave their garden behind for someone else. Mahnaz had shown him the extremes of both reality and the imagination. She had asked him to keep her garden, just as he had kept the odour of her death. He felt that through this garden, she was telling him: 'Ghazalnus, look. You talk about imaginary love, but I am showing you real love'.

He was sure now that it was impossible for a person to travel from the imagination to the real world, and from the real world to the imagination, without love. For a long time he had searched only in endless, imaginary lands. Now he was standing among the flowers of Mahnaz's enchanted garden and, under the influence of the strange magic that imagination left inside his soul, he decided to do something for this world. He had to complete the path that had begun in the imagination; he had to write down the truth of this garden. But where should he start? He didn't know until the night he met Trifa Yabahri, when they decided to write a book together – the longest book in the world – a book about death.

A NIGHT WITH AFSANA

THE REAL MAGELLAN, AUGUST 2004

I was waiting for Murtaza Satan to reappear, but he didn't. Five quiet, depressing days passed. He seemed to be playing with my heart. *Oh, patient heart, be calm.* I was certain that they didn't know who I was. Except for the information the hotelier had given the Security Directorate, they didn't know anything about me. It was better that way. In this country, no one can be respected unless they appear to be harbouring a great secret. Without a secret, everyone sees me as a little, shameless man and looks down on me. And yet, except for the voice of the enchanting woman whose whispers still rang in my ears, I had no big secrets.

But Baran Shukur could be a secret, couldn't she? I didn't know. I knew and understood nothing. In those five days, I met Afsana twice in the lobby of the hotel. On neither occasion did she speak to me. Every night I left the door of the room open and waited for her, but nothing happened. Is there anything in this world more dangerous than a standoff between a man and a woman, than that period of time when nothing passes between them? It is the end of the world. Something has got to happen. Anything. It doesn't matter what. I told my patient heart to wait. I tried to convince it that *something* would happen. It would.

On the sixth night, at around three o'clock in the morning, she opened the door silently and came in. She had a captivating scent. Nowhere in the world had I come across a woman with such an extraordinary and arousing scent. She didn't turn the light on, but came and sat on the edge of my bed. I lay there half-naked, waiting for her. I felt her delicate hands on my shoulders; they were the hands of a woman who could turn anything she touched into a fragment of the imagination. When she touched me, I sparkled as though I were made of stars. What I felt was like a surge of magic in my soul, as if she was the first woman on the planet to lay hands upon me. Coolness and relaxation spread through my body.

She was exceptionally calm as she took my hands. We were both silent. All those versed in the ways of women know that silence. They know it is the hardest moment between a man and a woman. Something other than the man and the woman speaks in that silence. Sometimes, I say it's the very secret of existence that is suspended in that silence. Other times, I say no, it's the distance between us, apprehension and shyness, that leave us tongue-tied. Any couple able to survive this moment can go far. Very far.

I was willing to go very far, far beyond the point lovers speak about. I would have gone to Hell in pursuit of that woman's breath. This country had been lost to me for a long time. I didn't know what was wrong and what was right, but I had no opportunity to think about any of this before I sensed that she'd moved so close to me that I could hear her breathing.

I don't know which of us shifted that little bit closer to pave the way for the first kiss. There is nothing on Earth more magical than a first kiss. With the first kiss, all the fearful legal systems and constitutions of this world fall silent. Everything stops. The innermost part of human beings, the depths of their hearts, their real desires, speak out. The first kiss between Afsana and me was the kind that changes lives into 'before' and 'after'. I thought, 'Oh, heart, be quiet; oh body, shout.' I am not talking about the tenderness of her lips, or the cold shivers that bound her soul to mine. I am not talking about her slender hands, and the fingers she raked through my hair. I am talking about the fact that the first kiss is the first test of two bodies. In that kiss, it becomes clear how much they can merge into one another, how much closer to each other they can get.

There was only a very short space between our lips, a space that couldn't be measured in time or distance – where lips have touched, yet not touched. For me, that space is the distance between two souls, when the flesh of two people has not yet been fully joined, but their souls either move towards one another or draw away at great speed. At that moment, I felt a very powerful pull. I was certain I had been brought all the way back from the other end of the world for this kiss.

Putting it into words may well be the hardest thing I've ever done. I know you think I'm exaggerating this kiss, that I'm making a normal kiss in the dark out to be a miracle, but you're wrong. In all its long history, humanity has failed to speak about the first kiss in any depth. The world's great writers, its mythology, the magic of film – none have conveyed the mystery of that moment in any real depth.

It was night. We kissed. We committed an act of betrayal. The feeling of infidelity is the most enthralling sensation for any human being. She knew what she was betraying; I didn't. She was betraying her marriage and her purity; I was betraying the whole of my strange past, in which there had been no bridges between body and soul. Throughout my life, whenever I had slept with a woman, my body had been in one place and my soul somewhere else. I had always told my soul, 'Be gone. Be gone, and don't come back just yet.' Until that night, I had not slept with any woman in the world with my soul present. All my life so far, I had never allowed my soul to be there with me. This time was different.

My first kiss with Afsana was the sort that leads to self-discovery. If I had met this woman twenty-four years earlier, I would never have left the country. For twenty-four years, I had travelled the long roads of this world on my motorbike in search of a homeland and a woman. That night, when I kissed the hotelier's unfaithful wife, I felt that I had found the woman I had been seeking for an eternity. I felt that God had created this small and tender woman for me, that the ugly hotelier had stolen her from me. I felt she was my closest friend, and he had kidnapped her.

You don't know what I am talking about. She was a woman whose gentle touch concentrated the allure of all the women of the world. The merest touch of her breasts was like being in contact with the magic of the universe. Her whispers arose from a slightly hoarse throat imbued with the most extraordinary music. Suddenly, I didn't know how human beings move on from kissing to other manifestations of love. No matter which woman I'd slept with, I'd been alert. I had felt awake. If you remain alert and aware in bed, the glory of the first kiss has not left you so dumbfounded that Earth and Heaven are as nothing. That night was the one time in my life that I forgot even myself in bed.

All I know is that, slowly, in an elaborate ritual, we undressed. There was something deeper than love between our bodies, something that resembled a colourful whirlwind, a vast and mighty vortex. We were drawn to each other by a colossal desire, and each of us abandoned our body completely to the other.

In my state of rapture, I could see her form in the dark. The desire that bound our bodies was stronger than love. I, Zuhdi Shazaman, had never believed in a one-dimensional physical or spiritual love. Love is something neither the soul nor the body can achieve alone, the one thing in which both dangerous forces within a human being should fuse completely. In the act of love, unless the body enters the soul's game, the souls will be lost and unable to come together. If the soul doesn't enter the body's game, the bodies become disenchanted and begin to grow apart. Love is not tested until bodies meet. The soul alone lacks the power to sustain love. It is wrong to think that people engage only the soul when they embark upon love and move on to the body. Quite the contrary, in fact: the body must speak first, so that the souls can build bridges and draw closer to one another.

I think the biggest enemies of the soul are people who hate the body. That night, when I got undressed with Afsana, when I touched her dark skin, when my lips reached the most inaccessible places on her body, when the flavour of her beauty poured onto my fingers, when I carried her as calmly as one picks a flower from a sleepy branch, I felt I was carrying the moon, that I was touching moonlight and that my fingers touched the greatness of the Creator. She was naked and full with a woman's untamed desire. It challenged reason, and shone from her eyes. Nothing in this world is deeper, more exquisite or more serene than the imagination that pours from a woman's eyes during lovemaking. Nothing is more rapturous than the desire that suddenly wakes in your fingers, demonic in its strength. Nothing is more inexpressible than words born between thirsty lips and a willing, open body.

These are things that can't be conveyed by any letters or sounds in the world. No matter how hard I try to tell you about the taste of that whispering woman, to convey the magic and desire of the hotelier's unfaithful wife, I can only deceive you. She and I made love in a manner no language on this planet can describe. It was the first time I had felt that touching a naked woman raises you to a higher state, beyond the spiritual. Her body was like silk, coloured by the perfume of a faraway garden. You would have to smell all the flowers in the world to find her scent again. Her soft, husky voice made me want to listen to all the music of the world to see if any instrument could produce such a note.

I felt this was the first time I had slept with a woman. Whatever I had done before had been mechanical discharge, lovemaking that left the soul unmoved. Now, with the unfaithful wife of the hotelier, I travelled to the edge of the imagination and stepped off into a place that no one else had ever seen. *Oh heart, be calm. Oh tongue, stay calm, be patient.*

When we had finished, her shudders continued in my body for a long time. When it was over, the unusual sheen of sweat on her body made her features appear bronzed. She slept peacefully next to me like a small, exhausted animal. She resembled a person asleep after a sacred battle, or simply intoxicated from a powerful drug and sleeping it off in the dark grass of a garden. She had placed her hands over her heart. I was scared that day would break and her husband would find her in my bed like this, but I couldn't bring myself to wake her. I would rather have died. Unable to help myself, I captured some of the delicate drops of sweat around her navel with my lips. I wanted to taste the sweat of her body, the fruit of her desire. I wanted to cherish her pure exhaustion. Until day broke, I gazed at her body, examining its glittering beauty centimetre by centimetre. None of the countless bodies I had seen until then could match the elegance and harmony of Afsana's fragile, naked, passionate body. All I wanted to do was to look at it until I died.

The feeling of being deep inside her, in the liquid of life inside her, made me feel rather proud. When I caressed her waist gently, when I ran my fingertips calmly over her thighs, when I parted her knees with my big hands, I longed to be able to write down the full story of that night with the hotelier's unfaithful wife, to recount it to the whole world. Yet, I knew it would be impossible to find the language, to explain the self, to put the moment in writing with all its shudders and eruptions, its taking flight. No sheet of paper in the world could contain such descriptions without catching fire.

After a good hour of sleep, she woke up. Without saying anything, without panicking or showing fear, she dressed very slowly. She put on her underwear – pink silk panties and a bra. Her hair was unusually tangled. She stood before me now, half-naked. As if she could read her own effect in my eyes, she kissed me serenely and said, in her husky voice: 'That's how it was meant to go.' I didn't know her meaning. She said nothing else. She finished getting dressed, combed her hair with her hands several times, opened the door quietly and left. I slept as if drugged or knocked unconscious. When I woke up, the sun had set. A whole day had passed since my time with Afsana, and my body still carried her warmth. I took a shower and went down to the parlour. She was there, wearing a new and extremely elegant, expensive outfit. She had put her hair up like a crown. Seeing her thrilled me again, as it always did. It was the first time I felt I was verging on madness, that madness was very, very close.

TRIFA YABAHRI AND GHAZALNUS
1995–96

One day, Trifa Yabahri and Ghazalnus happened upon each other in the city hospital. That encounter was the beginning of their real companionship. Trifa hadn't heard anything about Mahnaz Maro's fate until then. The death of the poor girl saddened her deeply. Speaking in a tired voice, like someone eaten away inside by a secret pain, Ghazalnus told Trifa his troubles one by one. He told her about the unusual smoke, and the odour of singeing that was always with him; he talked about his weekly visits to the hospitals and the burned women he visited. 'In this country, politics, love, thinking, hope and honour all end up in the hospitals. Here, the final destination of the human journey is a hospital bed.' He said this gloomily, which only served to make him appear even handsomer and gentler.

Trifa, who was visiting a sick female weaver, was thrilled by the sight and sound of this man. It was like being pierced by a sterilised lancet. No one knows how they started visiting burned women and other patients together. By then, Trifa had often experienced her extraordinary ability to bring tranquillity to the distressed – so why should she not now be able to bring peace to all these patients? She was impelled to draw closer to the young man. Trifa invited him to see her imaginative carpets before shyness could get in the way. Ghazalnus said nothing would please him more.

When Ghazalnus first went to the Niya factory, he was astounded by Trifa's fantastical images and designs. He felt that on many carpets Trifa had drawn creatures and places that he had seen or visited in his imagination. He found it only natural that her carpets were the most expensive in the city, more expensive even than authentic Persian Kashan carpets, woven from silk by the very greatest masters. The carpets gave Ghazalnus an even greater impetus to try to understand her secret. Despite his wide-ranging travels, he had never seen their like. When they sat together, he understood that Trifa's customers were wealthy men and political leaders. He thought it a shame that the individuals who sat upon her imaginative carpets should be among the most unimaginative people in the world.

This was the first Trifa had heard about the world of the Imaginative Creatures. She didn't know that Ghazalnus was friends with people made up of two halves – one that inhabited reality, the other the imagination. As she spoke to Ghazalnus about making the carpets, describing the environment in which they were made, Ghazalnus looked at her, astounded, and said: 'Khanim, you work in a factory of the imagination.' The sentence came as a shock. Until then, she had considered the factory to be a perfectly ordinary place that was part of the real world. But she saw things change as if her eyes had been opened to a dangerous truth. From the image of the guard Simo Agha – an agha in name only – to that of the sad workers constantly immersed in their futile fantasies, she started to see them as a group of imaginary people.

Trifa looked at Ghazalnus's sad eyes, his dervish-like hair, his black beard. Like a woman experiencing the glow of love for the first time, she said, 'Ghazalnus, what are you doing? You're making me forget about the real world.'

That sentence was the bridge between these two humans, melding them. From that very moment, they began to dream one of the most impossible dreams since ancient history, the dream of all the great men and women of the ages, all the poets and prophets: how to live as an imaginative human being without forgetting about the real world.

They met again many times, and Ghazalnus revisited the factory on several occasions. Together, they went to see hundreds of troubled women, and dozens of incurable patients in their deathbed agony. When Trifa touched them, their pains would diminish, even if only for a short while. This was the beginning of the complex, mysterious relationship that forms the basis of this story. I feel that it was then that Ghazalnus fell in love with Trifa: from the moment he saw the kindness and sympathy in her eyes, and observed the peace that patients experienced from her hands and fingers. He had no option but to love her.

As for how Trifa and Ghazalnus came to live under the same roof for such a long time, I'll tell you that right now. For seven years, Jawhar Yabahri had searched everywhere for Trifa, and finally discovered where she was living. (Fawziya Yasami had visited Trifa once or twice a year; those were Trifa's best moments back then, as in Fawziya's kind arms she rediscovered her childhood, her lost paradise.) In those seven years, Jawhar, too, had been transformed into someone else. He was no longer the uncontrollable madman of old who attacked others like a wild ox. Mingling with the new businessmen and profiteers, coupled with his great desire for success and advancement, had calmed him down. He knew now that a composed demeanour, patience and sweet talk produced better results than anger and aggression. The day he came to the factory, he had no evil intentions. He was no longer the same person who had drawn a knife on his sister in the middle of the bazaar. Now he was a fox who played more complex games, and engaged in bigger business. When he heard about Trifa's carpets from his friends, he wished to find out how much fear he still aroused in her. From the moment he had started interacting with politicians, the first lesson they taught him was that intimidation was more effective than killing, that instilling fear in people bore fruit faster than bloodshed.

During those seven years, Jawhar had amassed a huge fortune. Yet he constantly had his eye on the few dunams of land his father had left to Trifa. He was part of a large network that smuggled arms and military hardware from southern Iraq to Iran, while at the same time transporting huge shipments from Iran to southern Iraq. He and his cohorts had the backing of the major players, and travelled in brand-new vehicles. When he appeared at the factory one evening, he wasn't expecting to gain very much. He was merely casting a net upon the water, as he had learned to do from his frequent involvement with the politicians. When Trifa first saw him that night, she was deeply shocked and felt a strong impulse to run away, but an inner voice said: 'Trifa Yabahri, what are you afraid of? What do you have to lose?' Her long years immersed in imagination had given her a different outlook. What's more, where could she have run to other than the factory? She had nowhere else.

Everyone knew that Trifa had a big estate, but that its poor location and her own vulnerable situation did not allow her to make any use of it. Now it was the images on the carpets, rather than any physical plot of land, that had become her real home and property. Trifa was one of those rare creatures who felt that no amount of wealth could give her the freedom she experienced when she was weaving a carpet. All the wealth in the world was not worth the key that opened her eyes to another land and time.

The day she saw Jawhar again, she felt a powerful force surge within her. She had always been strong, but that strength had been accompanied by a constant fear of death, of brutality, of a sudden dagger in the dark. That night she looked at herself in the mirror over a sink in the factory. She was tired, yes, but she was no longer someone who could be paralysed by sudden sadness or confusion. She was no longer a pessimistic woman who suffered from epileptic fits and was prone to excruciating headaches and a sense of malaise.

Among the greatest tragedies for human beings is not knowing what course of action to take, always waiting for life to deliver clues to follow or footsteps in which to tread. Now, Trifa knew what she lived for, and that was more important than anything else. She lived for the unfortunate factory girls, the poor female workers who had no shelter on this Earth. She lived for her imagination, which could engender a deep, constant happiness in these sad women. If Jawhar wanted her land, he could take it all – provided he left her with enough money to buy a house. One house, nothing more.

When Jawhar returned to the factory a second time on the pretext of buying carpets, she invited him without fear or hesitation to speak one-to-one in the small room that belonged to the factory owner's wife. They hadn't looked each other in the eye for seven years. They were great enemies, opposite poles that no force could bring closer together. Like two adversaries who sit at a table after a long war to reach a final agreement, they sat facing each other and settled their disputes. Everything went smoothly and easily. In return for the price of a big house, Trifa gave up all her properties, which – had she allowed enough time – might have sold at a much greater profit. But at that moment, she desperately needed a large amount of money in one lump sum.

Naturally, it wasn't an easy decision to give up her properties. It was as if she had betrayed the long-standing dream of her mother Samira, who had brought Trifa into the world to protect the share of the Yabahri tribe's women. It was as if she had announced that the women of that tribe had given up. But despite her great fears and accumulated apprehensions, she was sure she could recover the endless strength of the women of the Yabahri tribe in a different way.

Buoyed by his triumph, Jawhar left the factory and withdrew from Trifa's life. They never met again. Even at the funeral of their mother Fawziya in the capital, no one could reconcile them or bring them together at the same dining table. However, the disappearance of Jawhar Yabahri's shadow from the life of the slight, dark-skinned girl of our story does not mean that other, similar men, men who wanted to own the world, would also leave her alone. Years later, when Trifa and her female friends found themselves face-to-face with Wusu Agha's gunmen and Shahryar the Glass-Eyed, she understood better that the Earth teemed with men who were each other's shadows, all of them intent on completing the pursuit her brother Jawhar had started in her childhood.

Perhaps you are asking now what made Trifa abandon all her wealth so easily, why she was willing to take her life out of the dangerous reaches of Jawhar's claws for such a small payment? Throughout all the years Trifa had worked in the factory, she had heard nothing but stories of women's pain, loneliness and homelessness. Men's greatest strength lay in the fact that they had invaded every inch of the city. Alleyways, homes, streets – they all belonged to men. Since realising this, Trifa had longed for a house that she could put at the disposal of the hopeless women who had no refuge. As soon as she received the payment from Jawhar, she bought a big house with the help of Sayyid Qadir Niya. Trifa did a lot of work in the house so that it could accommodate women who had nowhere else to hide. Through Sayyid Qadir's wife Galawezh, she contacted women's organisations and put this private house at the service of vulnerable women who had fled their husbands or their families. Her long experience with the carpet weavers had given her a deep conviction that she should dedicate her life to just such a mission.

It is worth remembering that the fame of Trifa's carpets spread so widely in the world that, thanks to her golden imagination, the products of the Niya factory were much sought-after despite the country's economic downturn and rising poverty. Notwithstanding her initial efforts to try to maintain anonymity, Trifa's imagination had reached the guestrooms of sultans, presidents and princes without her ever wanting it to happen – and it was her reputation among them that led to the factory's self-destruction. Soaring carpet sales and the wealth they generated after 1992 brought great misery rather than prosperity. One late spring evening in 1996, Sayyid Qadir was looking out of the window of his new factory office. He saw three wealthy, influential officials from the city emerge from a new car and head towards the factory. At that very moment, he realised that he shouldn't have allowed Trifa Yabahri to bring her fantasies into this small, insignificant factory; but it was already too late. Judging by their steps, their gentle pace, the artificial grace in their strides, he could tell what these officials wanted. They were high-ranking men who had come to perform an important task.

When they entered the office, they ordered that no one should be allowed in, and that the doors should be closed because of the confidential nature of the discussion they wished to hold. They acted like three people who had been well-trained to show respect. The way they sat, and their choice of words, carried something of the attitude of modern gentlemen as well as of the old aghas. All three sported black moustaches and each had a slight bald patch at the front of their heads. Their smiles, hand gestures and gazes were very similar. Had it not been for the shapes of their noses and chins, they could have been taken for triplets or portraits of the same person done by an incompetent painter. They addressed Sayyid Qadir with utmost respect. They praised him as a great patriot, all using the same words – as if they had swallowed the same tape recording. Sayyid Qadir knew that death in this country began with just this type of tune. He was very familiar with the world of the bazaar. He counted as friends most of the city businessmen who had made serious money. He had known for a long time that the bait that men like this attached to their rods was sweet. First, they show you the bait; only later do you notice the rod.

He listened with great apprehension and sadness. Before the uprising, he had been concerned that the Baath Party's security people might fabricate charges against him, and that would be that. However, since the uprising and the 1992 elections, he had imagined this moment time and again. He knew that one day, sooner or later, officials would show up, get out of their cars, walk into the office entirely in step – moustaches, elegance and all – and ask him to close the doors and windows and listen. He had had recurring dreams consisting of just such a sequence of events since the spring of 1992, but had never shared his fears with Galawezh. Now he found himself facing the men who had featured so often in his dreams. In roundabout, ironic words, they told him that the Party was aware of everything going on inside the factory, but that there was nothing in the factory to concern him. He was sure they were playing a game, a difficult art that takes a long time to master. In other countries, people study it like a science, but here they learn it from long experience.

'The Party knows everything,' one of the three men said. 'From the purchase of the wool, the yarn and the dye to the design of the carpets, to every individual worker, to how you market the carpets and the routes you use to send them abroad. Everything is under investigation at the highest level.'

Sayyid Qadir knew that it wouldn't make a difference whether he talked or not. So he waited for their final words. After telling him a good many stories and beating around the bush, after mixing small talk with veiled threats, after relating the Party's efforts to improve economic infrastructure and expand local industries, they finally came to the point. The Party wanted to buy the factory and all that came with it: the workers, the machines, the building and the offices. Sayyid Qadir's friends had warned him long ago that he ought to sell his factory for a good price at the earliest opportunity, because sooner or later they would use the law to snatch it from him and he would not be able to do anything about it. Whenever he went into the carpet hall, however, and saw Trifa deep in thought, or the sad, friendless girls whose life and peace depended on this job, he would dismiss all thought of selling. The imaginative carpets, the excited staff, the passionate customers so dazzled by Trifa's carpets: all were good enough reasons for Sayyid Qadir to resist such talk. He didn't know what he would do, how he would live if he sold the factory. Very respectfully, he told his three guests: 'This factory is my whole life. I can't just give it up. I can't sell it.'

The three men were very experienced in buying and selling. They had been working for a senior Party official for some time. They never used hurtful or harsh language. They always coated their threats with kind words. Respect and politeness were at the heart of their work. When harsh words ultimately did need to be said, they would withdraw and let other people take the stage. They were well-versed in sweet talk, and always unruffled. They always told their interlocutors, 'It is better for you to settle the matter with us than with people who won't show you the same respect.'

They acted as if they thought Sayyid Qadir's words were only natural and that they fully understood his tender feelings, but they told him he should give the matter more thought because, they said, they were merely delivering an order from a higher and more powerful authority, one with other methods of persuasion.

When they left the office – quietly and politely – Sayyid Qadir was certain he had lost the factory for good; but he didn't want to give everything up just like that. A few days later, the men returned. They spoke in the same tones as on their first visit. They were polite and respectful.

'Kaka Sayyid, just think about it,' they said as they stood up to leave. 'The matter will be out of our hands in the next few days. Then nasty people will get involved, people who could damage the reputations of all concerned. Make up your mind tonight and, God willing, you'll come to the right decision and won't bring shame on either side.'

Despite all that had been said, Sayyid Qadir stood his ground. Ten nights later, unidentified gunmen kidnapped him outside his house, beat him up and left him half-dead among the trees and bushes south of the city. However, Sayyid Qadir had decided to fight to the last. He knew that no one would emerge victorious. A true fighter doesn't defend himself but a cause, an idea. Until then, his fights had never gone beyond games of dice, backgammon and such like. Now, it was time to fight for something bigger: for this small factory, for these girls whom he was expected to sell.

That was when he had one hell of an idea. This time, he would be the one confidently rolling the dice. One night, his head still bandaged and all his muscles still aching, he gathered his older friends – all the frail, white-bearded men who played endless games of backgammon in their ill-fitting suits, who passed countless winter and summer nights playing games and sipping tea. There were more than twenty of them. Some were retired, some housebound; they were older salesmen, shortsighted backgammon players or just old friends of Sayyid Qadir's. Each of them had, on numerous occasions over the years, come for picnics behind the factory or to enter the endless backgammon competitions. Sayyid Qadir was certain that while there wasn't a lot these old men could do, they could still help him in his fight.

That night all twenty men wrote a statement together, and the following day they made hundreds of copies and distributed them throughout the streets and alleyways of the city. The statement told the story of the Niya factory from its origins to the present day – the point where it was about to be seized. The men, with their hunched backs, rotten teeth and loose dentures, did their work thoroughly and with unexpected speed. As if borne by the wind or driven by energy of mythic proportions, they posted dozens of announcements on walls or slipped them into people's houses. On the following morning, the whole city awoke to the story of the Niya factory. Sayyid Qadir was certain that those in power would not forgive him. It was obvious they would show up at his place as soon as the news broke.

He summoned Trifa Yabahri beforehand and told her the entire story. He even revealed the names of all the white-haired elders and described them as great and truly loyal friends. A few hours later, unidentified forces removed Sayyid Qadir Niya to an unknown location. Within a few days, Galawezh, whose biggest hope was that he would be released in return for giving up the factory, reluctantly stamped the factory sale contract for the three black-moustached men, her face flooded with tears, and handed it all over for a pittance. But Sayyid Qadir Niya never came back.

Amid all this, Trifa and the factory girls felt as if a demonic force had kidnapped them and taken them to the very heart of darkness. The old men's efforts to release Sayyid Qadir proved futile. The group wrote and distributed many more statements, but the officials, as ever, denied any knowledge of the matter. That era saw the appearance of a new power in the market. Sayyid Qadir was one of the victims of a wave that swept away everything in its path. The three black-moustached men kept telling his wife, 'He shouldn't have made such a mistake. The people who sent us didn't like it. A good citizen is a reasonable person, and a reasonable person is a good citizen. A good party needs reasonable citizens, and good citizens need a reasonable party. A reasonable party should take part in educating the citizens.

A reasonable society cannot survive without a reasonable party. Therefore, the punishment of an unreasonable person is part of the process of creating a reasonable society, while the duty of a reasonable party is to protect a reasonable society, in which a citizen without reason must not be allowed to live in peace so that the majority can do so. The minority without reason may not live in peace. Galawezh Khan, this is all quite simple and straightforward, isn't it?'

'You're right, you're right,' she answered, although she hadn't understood a thing. 'But if you release him, he will become a reasonable citizen.'

'One must be reasonable before being arrested,' the black-moustached men said. 'Am I right or not?'

Galawezh felt she was going round in circles.

Sayyid Qadir's friends buzzed about in frenzied activity. No one could believe that these frail, wrinkled, vulnerable old men, with their drooping necks, big glasses and poor eyesight, could be behind such statements. They had been completely revitalised, and were driven to do this work. Yet their efforts, like those of so many in this city attempting to highlight a problem, were in vain.

The day the new officials took over the carpet factory, they sent for Trifa and said: 'Trifa Khan, you don't know how happy we are to see you. We did all this to establish what your imagination is worth in gold. We spent all that money to become the owner of your rich and beautiful imagination. Don't worry about money. Your imagination is priceless. Weave your enchanting carpets for us, and we shall ensure they reach the courts of mighty kings and princes. For each beautiful carpet, you will receive a significant bonus. We'll create a life for you that not even the wives of the Iranian kings and Turkish sultans experienced. You can have your own servants to work for you, here and at home. All we want you to do is to put your imagination to work and weave new and unique carpets for us.'

Yet from the very first day, Trifa felt unable to work. In the very first hour, she told the new owners of the factory that she simply didn't want to. Never before had she felt there were people who wanted to buy her imagination from her. She had discovered herself in the factory. In the carpets, she had envisioned the world's faraway and inaccessible places. Yet now she felt that her imagination no longer worked. Since the sale of the factory, everything had changed. Of course, this caused her endless pain. It was very sad to have to leave those poor, friendless girls with no shelter, and no other option but to work till they died. However, she felt that selling her imagination to these men would be the death of her: she would catch some dangerous disease; her head would fill day and night with brutal terrors that would not let her rest or even breathe. She was certain she could not live in peace under such conditions. She longed with all her heart to begin a new life. She moved into her new house with one of the friendless girls from the factory, and for several weeks did very little at all. She didn't know how to go on with her life, or what she should do.

During that same period, Attar reappeared. He introduced himself as the representative of the new factory owners. He had sworn to do everything he could to persuade Trifa to go back to work, and in the days that followed Trifa found herself under enormous pressure. Attar pursued her like a plague. At the same time, many more customers, factories and unknown men came forward seeking to monopolise Trifa's dreams and make use of them in strange businesses and products. To escape them, and to avoid tumbling into the dark pits that gaped wide all around her, she had to get away, to disappear from sight.

In 1996, when the civil war was at its peak and thousands of people were fleeing and emigrating, Trifa and Ghazalnus embarked on an exceptional journey somewhere between love and suicide. I shall recount the details of one small fragment in the coming pages.

THE DAY I BECAME A STORYTELLER
TO THE BARONS' CHILDREN
MAJID-I GUL SOLAV, JUNE 2004

My real story started the day I went to the barons' district with the Baron of Dolls. He came to pick me up in his swanky car at noon, and said he had found a job for me in Nwemiran, the barons' district. I had combed my hair as happily as the son of a king and put on my best clothes as if about to receive a young queen.

The baron was astonished by my appearance. I certainly didn't dress like anyone else in the city, to put it mildly. My suits fit my fine frame so well that I inspired envy in the best dressed of men. I won't hide from you that my indifference towards women was partly due to my fascination with my own good looks. True, my close friends always made me doubt myself, but whenever I caught a glimpse of myself in the mirror, I was convinced of my own charm and beauty. I was certain I could exploit my stylishness and good looks to gain entry into places others struggled to reach.

Nwemiran, which I called 'Baronistan', was a large new district in the middle of the city. Between it and the city itself lay a vast circular strip of barren land, devoid of flora and fauna. This flat, lifeless land lay like a thick wall between the barons' district and the rest of the world. It was encircled by a wire fence that separated it from the world outside. It wasn't the fence itself that stopped people reaching Nwemiran, however, but a fear of the place that had been instilled by persons unknown. Even before hearing the barons' names, I had known a few things about Nwemiran. People who went there became so infatuated with the lifestyle, the mansions, the size of the homes, the eating and sleeping habits and the love lives of its inhabitants, that they stayed for good and became workers and servants of the barons; or else they left, having gone half-mad from dreaming of attaining the same status as the residents of Nwemiran.

It was an extremely large district. You had to be inside to realise just how big. When I lived there, I saw hundreds of vast homes, arranged in such complex geometric patterns that they were hard to count.

Then there were the gardens, built identically in order to confuse anyone unfamiliar with the place. What made the district harder to enter was the sadness it generated in those who couldn't afford its lifestyle. In times past, it had been quite normal to travel between this district and others, but it made the barons uneasy that everyone who visited dreamed of becoming a resident. The beauty of its streets and its women, the design of its gardens, was too appealing; it was this great longing that forced the barons to separate Nwemiran from the world with a barbed-wire fence. It was also the barons who came up with the idea of the dry, lifeless circular strip of land that acted as a substantial barrier, keeping their world away from ours.

Since the year 2000 (the year in which I got to know Ghazalnus), Baronistan had become a different place, an independent entity; all its residents were now senior politicians, wealthy engineers and famous businessmen. Prohibitive land prices put ordinary people off that part of the city. They explored other areas instead. When ministers, members of parliament and government advisers began to move in, the district began to acquire enhanced political significance. As a result, protecting the district and fixing its boundaries came within the joint remit of the Security Directorate and the municipality. The stories they later circulated – about infiltrators catching scabies, falling ill and dying – were fabricated by Nwemiran's secret engineers.

The day the Baron of Dolls and I set off, my heart held a hidden fear mixed with a dangerous desire. My information about Nwemiran was vague and inadequate.

'It's not a difficult job,' said the Baron of Dolls in his deep, gruff voice. 'You will be telling stories to a girl, the daughter of the Baron of Shade. I've noticed for a long time that she is sad and friendless. This damned Nwemiran is not a nice place for children. It's nice for men. It's Heaven for women. But not for children.

'I still don't know what makes children happy. Although I've been selling dolls for twenty years and am the biggest toy merchant in the region, I still don't really understand what children want. To tell you the truth, I understood them much better before I moved to Nwemiran. People who live here forget their childhoods. I've observed this closely. None of the residents of this district remember their childhoods. Do you, Majid Solav?'

'Honourable Baron, I feel that I've never grown up,' I replied slowly and calmly. 'I've been the same from the day I was born until this very moment. By that I mean my worldview, not my height. When you are lonely, it's hard to tell childhood apart from adulthood, as children, on the whole, are lonely. Yes, Honourable Baron, humans are born lonely. To tell the truth, loneliness is the essence of man. Man's great miseries and misfortunes start when he grows up and wants to break away from that loneliness. However, because I am lonely to this day, I still feel I am a child who has not said goodbye to childhood. You see, Honourable Baron, as soon as we leave childhood, we become obsessed with love and other ridiculous desires.

'I know children very well. Just as a mechanic knows automobiles inside out, so I know the world of children. They are happy in their loneliness. Fear of loneliness is only for grownups. Yes, Honourable Baron, as a child one is not afraid of loneliness for long. Rather, it becomes the place where children feel most at home. It is the sickness of love that makes loneliness unbearable. Honourable Baron, love is an ugly disease. Being in love means we don't want to be alone. Take my word for it. Do not be concerned about lonely children. They are living their real lives. Don't be concerned about lonely men, either; they are still children, and have not grown up. Be concerned about those who are afraid of loneliness.'

The baron was wearing a white jacket, a black shirt and a new pair of brown shoes. He had the relaxed air of someone who had spent all morning in a sauna. He smelled of a perfume that was neither overpowering nor too faint. His enormous car was so comfortable I wished we could delay our arrival indefinitely, so I would never have to get out of it. When I was talking about children, he thought for a moment and, as if he had never heard such views before, asked: 'Children want to play, don't they? Is that what they want to do?'

These plain words were very un-baron-like.

'Children are alone even when they're playing,' I said. 'It is adults who insist they play in groups. Even when they're playing on their own, they enjoy it. The most enjoyable games are the ones human beings play alone.'

'As of today, you are the storyteller to Nwemiran's children,' he said, changing the direction of the conversation as if my insistence on loneliness had worn him out. 'Your job is to tell stories to them. Your stories must be so beautiful that they forget about the world and enter one of their own choosing. You must use your skill to make them ask for your magical stories every night.

'Majid Solav, I have showered you with praise among my fellow barons. The barons would only let a stranger enter their homes in an emergency. This child is depressed and introverted. She needs friends. So please, don't go banging on about loneliness.'

Nwemiran was a highly inaccessible place. I would never have had anything to do with it in my guise as the Imaginary Magellan, nor would I have even wanted to explore it – but I was obsessed with solving the mystery of Murad Jamil. This was just the kind of adventure I needed in order to feel that I was made of flesh and blood. I have been a resident of this almighty rubbish dump they persist in calling a city all my life, living on its filthy streets, and yet not a single soul knows me here. After leaving school I became an idle wanderer, but now I wanted to feel some zest about something I was doing, to feel as if I had at least the semblance of a life. Despite all the negativity about the district, despite all the iron, bricks and stones used in its construction, I felt Nwemiran was the product of an imagination; not the imagination of half-mad half-poets such as Ghazalnus and myself, but of people who were stronger than us, who had machines, cement, concrete, reinforced iron bars and asphalt, who had obedient workers and slaves and who could turn their brutal, crazed imaginations into real structures on this Earth.

When our car left the barren strip of land and reached the guards wearing their small caps at the entrance to Nwemiran, it was as if it had crossed a border between two countries. The kindly guards made no move to stop us; the baron was driving at such speed that I thought we would take off at any minute like the car in *The Absent-Minded Professor*. The baron didn't give me a chance to get a good look at my surroundings, and when we arrived at the houses in Baronistan I was the picture of bewilderment. Many people dreamed of visiting this very place. It was like reaching the enchanted realm of ancient kings. The doors and windows of the houses, rather than giving me the impression of a new city, reminded me of wonderful old film sets. It was very hot. Although I was struck by the attractiveness and unusual designs of the homes I saw, I still felt I didn't understand their architecture and aesthetics. I don't believe in looking at the world at high noon in the direct glare of the sun. To understand a place, I need to see it in the evening or at night, just before the false dawn or at twilight – not at midday. Strong sunlight kills the magic of a place, and its colours.

I am one of those people who doesn't much like sunlight. Everywhere in the world has a particular abiding sadness. Sunlight stops you from seeing it. All the nations that have survived a long time in strong sunlight find it difficult to distinguish happiness from pain. Has anyone ever wondered why the world's most romantic moment is at sunset? Because at that moment, the Earth is not at the mercy of the sun, nor beholden to the moon. Look at the trees, water, clouds and forests in that moment. Look at the cities, farms, orchards and streams. Only then does the world's sad, authentic face appear clearly. Sunlight is a kind of divine assistance so that we don't constantly see the sadness that is on every leaf, in every drop of water. For me to really see Nwemiran, I needed to consider it out of direct sunlight. I had to wait and see.

The Baron of Dolls allowed me the honour of visiting his house. Not until I entered his mansion did I understand why the place had a dangerous effect on people's imaginations. It had all the imaginative elements this country's engineers had ever devised. The Baron of Dolls led me to a huge parlour in which the world's largest chandelier hung from the ceiling. The parlour was round, and decorated with two sets of regal sofas. It was pleasantly cool, as if the engineers had created a duct through which the air of Heaven was conducted into it. At first I simply looked around for a while, without saying a word. I examined antiques and other extraordinary objects I had never encountered, even in my fantasies. A staircase led up from one part of the parlour; it resembled the magical staircases in Escher's paintings. It seemed to lead to a high ceiling with a dome-like structure at the top, and to finish in another circular parlour that occupied the entire floor and overlooked the whole city. This parlour, like most of those in Baronistan, was simultaneously a garden and a stage, a room and a museum. It was full of strange leaves I had never set eyes on before, fish tanks with hundreds of tiny, colourful fish, copies of marble and bronze statues from Ancient Greece and carpets so beautiful their detailed designs begged to be examined on bended knee for hours at a time. The baron held himself more erect and appeared more active in his own home. Just as the Real Magellan in me only materialised on my ship, so the Baron of Dolls only shone properly in his parlour. All human beings are like lions in their own homes, and so was Mir Safin in his huge parlour.

'What do you think?' the baron asked, as though reading my thoughts. 'Is it not like sitting next to an eternal spring and bathing in the cool air during the middle of summer, when the sun is so hot it can kill the flowers? Ignorant people suppose that when someone lives in such a wonderful tower he must be unable to see the world, that his heart is unaware of all the other creatures, that even his breath is different to that of his fellow humans. In fact, Majid Solav, you can see the world even better from here. This is my small fortress. This house is where I do battle with the world. He who fears the lion cannot tame or understand it. He who fears the water cannot swim in it. He who fears the light cannot love the summer. I am not afraid of this city. I do not ignore the world. Don't assume that if you live in a mansion like this, you will be unaware of the world, or free of its worries. I can't forget about the world. What would you have us do, just sleep here? Ill-starred and futureless is the baron who doesn't understand what's happening on the other side of our fence.'

I took his words as those of a man skilled in the use of rhetoric. He now sat opposite me, legs crossed. He lit a cigar and took long, deep puffs. He appeared tall, and positively oozed respectability. He looked old, but was more active than many young men; he was a man in control, a man whose comfortable and luxurious life had not sucked the energy out of him. He was like a strong, powerful animal that could be released from its cage for a big fight. Until then, I hadn't noticed all the gold rings on his fingers. Now I counted more than ten, each with a distinct pattern and adorned with a different type of stone.

'A clever, skilful engineer worked on this house, bringing all his art to bear,' I said, so that he would not be disappointed.

'It's always been like that,' he said with a smile. 'Life is unfair. Engineers reap the fruits of an orchard planted by others. Everyone assumes this district is the product of the engineers' imaginations, but it's not. New cities, unique palaces and tall buildings are born in our heads first of all, just as rain is made by the sea, not the sky. A palace is not built by an engineer's skilful drafts and plans, but by the dreams its owners have cherished since childhood. The fantasy of building a palace begins in childhood. Before this district was born on the engineers' maps, it had already been created inside our heads. I've been building this house in my imagination since childhood. To have a beautiful palace, you need imagination first.'

I was rather taken aback by all of this. I found it bizarre that the baron was speaking as an Imaginative Creature. I was still deep in thought when he invited me to see his birds and flowers. As I pondered how I would spend the evening, and as I listened to his praise of the flowers and the birds, I used the time to prepare for the unexpected. Noticing that I was tired and light-headed, Mir Safin said that he was going to take me where I could rest. He opened a door and said, 'This is my photo album room.' It was the first time I had ever heard of a room with such a name. It was a very big space. Large photographs adorned its walls, featuring the baron with the Leader, politicians and ministers. The room also had three long shelves holding dozens of photo albums. My knowledge of the baron was still superficial. I was very pleased he had honoured me by letting me visit a room that meant a lot to him and his family. Until then, I hadn't realised he was so keen on photographs. One of the shelves was devoted to framed photos of his family and other irreplaceable pictures, some of them dating back to the nineteenth century. The other two shelves displayed photos of the baron himself, from childhood to the present. Among them were dozens of bulky albums, all of them bearing dates.

In his youth, the baron had black whiskers and long hair. He had regularly taken pictures in the important cities of the region. As young people did back then, he had taken most of his pictures when drinking in bars. He showed me photos of his sons and daughters from his two marriages. His fifteen children were spread across the globe: some were in the US, some in different European countries and others in Australia. The baron and I had several cups of tea and coffee while poring over the photos. It appeared this was something he did with each new visitor. For the baron, sharing photos was a ritual that conferred respect on his guests. It was a sign of closeness. He was very proud of his life. He portrayed his past as something exceptional and his life as a flowing river, its days packed with great accomplishments, extensive connections and times when he had had to make big decisions. I soon realised that the baron was delighted by my praise and astonishment. He lived to astonish others. You were expected to show great respect and amazement, so that he wouldn't think you'd failed to appreciate his busy life and wandering soul. As far as he was concerned, his life of adventure, which had seen him grow from being the only child of a carpenter to a high-ranking baron, was akin to Sinbad's great voyages and deserved to be recorded.

'Honourable Baron,' I kept saying as I sought to worm my way into his affections, 'you have been through a great deal. You have worked tirelessly. Things didn't come easily to you.'

'Some people are made of gold, but fall and become dust,' he said, with all the serenity of a king. 'There are others made of dross who can turn *into* gold. Some are born with their hands full of gold, but when they die their gravestones are made of broken concrete; others are born hungry, yet in death they rest in gold coffins. I belong to the second category – the one that knows how to extract gold from a barren land.'

In the evening, the baron took me for a drive through Nwemiran. It was bigger than I'd expected. He showed me two big clubs at opposite ends of the district: the Namam Club and the Mirwari Club, both frequented by the barons and their families. He also spoke about several farms and summer houses he had built outside the city for holidays.

'Nwemiran is a big district,' the baron said. 'It doesn't have a precise boundary. Once inside, you find it's stranger and bigger than you can tell from the outside. It is a magical book – small when closed, but big when opened. Living in Nwemiran is like living inside a puzzle. Coincidences have a large part to play. No one can be sure what they will see when they open a door. All the doors are rather mysterious here. They belong to the world of secrets. Only people who don't want to solve the puzzle can be happy here. Just as you cannot unravel the mystery of the sky by understanding a single star, understanding a single individual or household won't unravel the secret of Nwemiran.

'We're not in Thebes here. Do you know where Thebes is? Don't assume that your friend, the baron, is stupid and unknowledgeable! I'm talking about the accursed city Oedipus visited, where he became engaged to his mother Jocasta. Do you recall the sphinx? It's a well-known story, of course. You, with your vast knowledge of films, must know who Oedipus is. Remember the sphinx, perched on a big rock, who asks a riddle and kills anyone who cannot answer it? My brother, this isn't Thebes. A different beast rules here, and the opposite is true: anyone who discovers the answers to the riddles will be killed. Anyone who tries to solve the riddles can be killed. There are places that live and thrive on their riddles, and Nwemiran is one of them. So what? There is no shame in admitting that Nwemiran is the home of intricate secrets. No one really knows its greatest secret. There is no happiness here for someone in search of a great secret: everything here is a small secret. In Nwemiran, there are thousands of doors, and thousands of mysteries behind each one. All these mysteries add up to something new, a different world. That's what Nwemiran is.'

I didn't understand why the baron was giving me all this information, but I sensed that he wanted to quash my curiosity and inquisitiveness lest I breach any taboos and get into trouble. During our quick drive around the quiet streets of the barons' fortress, he drove with one hand, smoking and gesticulating with the other.

'It's not the barons' fault,' he said simply. 'Wherever man is condemned by morality, the whole of life becomes a secret. Man is not made to be a moral creature. After a long life, I've concluded that secrets are not what you hide from others, but what you hide from yourself. The residents of this district hide things from themselves before they hide them from the world. That way, we're all happy.'

I had the feeling that the Baron of Dolls wanted someone from outside his world, outside his close friends and relatives – someone from the very bottom of the world's hierarchy – to hear his views. I often remained quiet as I listened, pretending to be a naïve youth delighted at finding an experienced man like him to listen to. I didn't feel that I either loved or hated him. His words about secrets were strange, and had a double meaning. I gathered that the barons' fear of their secrets being revealed had made them doubt everything.

'My dear Prince,' I said slowly and timidly, 'if that is the case, then man is the only creature who can lie to himself. Do you think there is any other creature with the ability to lie to itself?'

'Whenever a secret is revealed, man should look inwards,' he said. 'It's degrading to force humans to look at themselves. We all love those who stop us seeing what's inside ourselves. Friendship means allowing me to hide from myself even more. Whenever you make the fatal mistake of forcing a baron in this city to look into his heart, to look at the secrets within him, you should know that you are done for. You should go away, leave the country.'

I was very scared by the baron's last words, but I knew there was no going back now. The car was moving so slowly that windswept leaves were overtaking us. We passed a gardener watering a lawn. We saw a dove that looked unsure about landing. We saw a house sparrow looking at another house sparrow. After a short while, the baron stopped outside a magnificent, imposing three-storey house; its walls were made of white stone, and its windows were claret-coloured. Yet there was something aggressive about this dwelling, something you couldn't discern directly in the construction, as if Satan had had a hand in its design. The Baron of Dolls, in his gruff voice devoid of feeling, and as if showing me someone's grave, said: 'This is the house of the Baron of Shade.' I took my first step towards the door. I felt that our shadows entered the house long before we did.

The real name of the Baron of Shade was Mahdi Khudadad. He was one of those who had become wealthy after the end of the Kurdish civil war in 1997, when the economy stabilised and grew. He had started out as the attendant of one of the senior Party officials. He shopped for him, bought fresh bread at the bakery, washed his cars. Later he became the politicians' front man. He was a small, reddish fellow with a gnarled, fleshy face, and resembled Peter Ustinov in *Around the World in Eighty Days*. However, wealth had done little for Mahdi Khudadad. He wore a shiny black suit over an enormously protruding belly. He had straight, oily black hair, dyed so ineptly that anyone could see he was using the worst type of Indian or Pakistani hair colourant.

'They call him the Baron of Shade because some people believe he became a baron all too easily, coming from nowhere, making his wealth in the shade,'[15] the Baron of Dolls said. 'Unlike us, he didn't have to put a lot of effort into becoming prosperous; he hasn't sweated blood for it. Then again, others see him as a furtive man who operates stealthily, who works in the world of shadows and darkness.'

The baron received us warmly. He was very forthcoming. As soon as we were seated outside on the balcony, he and the Baron of Dolls started talking about the innumerable possibilities that had opened up after the fall of Saddam Hussein's dictatorship. From their conversation, I learned that some of the barons had obtained certain precious stones and extraordinary antiques from museums in southern Iraq, which they had sold to Iran for stupendous amounts of money. Then the conversation switched suddenly to a huge sewer system that the Baron of Shade and some other person wanted to construct.

I sat quietly, a shy listener, and didn't engage in the conversation but looked at the hands and legs of the Baron of Shade. He moved them about as he spoke. I had never before seen anyone move their legs as much as he did while talking. Most people move the upper halves of their bodies, but the baron was moving his legs about comically and, it seemed, involuntarily. The Baron of Dolls was calm, and sat opposite Mahdi Khudadad, listening alertly. The Baron of Shade didn't pay much attention to me at first. His conversation with the Baron of Dolls was mere chitchat, nothing urgent. Still, he moved his hands so fast, and spoke so passionately that you'd have been forgiven for thinking he was talking about something of vital importance to him. During breaks in the conversation, a young man with blue eyes and long, pale hair offered us hot cocoa, biscuits and some type of sweet made of dates, coconut and almonds. It was so delicious, it filled me with hope and raised my expectations. Some flavours make you so happy you want to live for a long time.

The balcony was tranquil, made especially pleasant by the song of the summer-evening bulbuls. I could have sat there forever, eating sweets and listening to the birdsong.

'Damn bulbuls,' said the Baron of Shade. 'Insufferable things. They've all escaped from cages. Once they're free, they make for the treetops and sing their heads off. They all come back to Nwemiran no matter how far away they fly. They fly away in spring. Then they sing and sing and sing – and then they die. I don't understand bulbuls, Honourable Mir. I don't understand bulbuls at all.'

I was surprised that a man like him didn't understand bulbuls. Later I learned that the barons on the whole didn't understand bulbuls.

'So, you're our storyteller,' he said, turning to me a good while later. 'What kind of stories do you tell?'

The question was sudden and unexpected. It took me slightly by surprise. You all know how ignorant it is. Only those who know nothing about stories ask it.

'Honourable Baron,' I said without really thinking, 'the story of the pure angels who come from the sky and stay on Earth for a while; the story of a black butterfly that ignites a huge war between two gardens; the story of a type of honey that changes the look and complexion of anyone who eats it, giving them an appearance closer to that of fairies; the story of a sick girl named Firmesk, who talks constantly to the ducks that swim in a pool of her tears. These, and hundreds of others.'

'Imaginary stories are good,' he said as he scratched his beard, 'but I want my children to learn to see the world, to learn good morals, to learn self-sacrifice and to love their homeland.'

At that moment, I had a strange urge to take off my shoes and hit him on the head. I hate men and women who talk too much about 'the homeland'. I learned as a child that those who spoke so much about the homeland were most likely to betray it, and to be cruel or unscrupulous.

'Honourable Baron,' I said politely, 'before children learn to love their homeland, they need to learn to love life; they need to learn to love butterflies, to like the sound of bulbuls. Honourable Baron, the homeland is made of a number of small things. If you don't love these, you won't love the homeland.'

My words appeared to sound strange and unfamiliar to the baron, and I felt I had made a big mistake; perhaps I shouldn't have stirred up such doubt in my very first meeting with him. Luckily, however, the man was too slow to understand what I meant. I was surprised that the Baron of Shade didn't have a bad word to say to me. Later, I understood that the barons were very afraid of people they described as 'intellectuals', and that he considered me one of them. It seemed that right from the very first moment, I had involuntarily portrayed myself as such.

The Baron of Shade turned away after our chat and started addressing Mir Safin. Speaking quickly, as if something was chasing the words in his throat, he said, 'Anyway, my children like all sorts of stories. Baron, there's no comparing our childhood to theirs, is there?'

That gave me yet another reason to dislike the man. People who compare their childhoods to those of others are dangerous. They might constantly lie in wait to take their revenge on the world. I wished they could swiftly introduce me to the children I had to tell stories to, but both barons continued to talk, oblivious to my presence. They mentioned politicians and businessmen I didn't know and, at times, the names of their companies. They were both sure that I wouldn't be able to make any sense of what they were saying.

As dusk fell, the fat baron led me to one of the upper storeys. His house, too, was laid with expensive carpets. A deep silence pervaded the mansion. He opened the door to a big room on the top floor, and we entered. At first I couldn't see anything in the dark; then, suddenly, we were flooded with light from a great many lightbulbs. I had never seen so many in one room. They continued to come on for a few seconds more. The light was so overpowering that, briefly, I put my hands over my eyes. I stood in the middle of the room and saw a girl in a white shirt and a pair of white jeans sitting on the edge of a bed. She seemed slightly angry and sad. She bore no resemblance whatsoever to her father: she had a narrow, smooth, white face and soft, black hair. Her clothes and face were so white that they made for a rather horrifying sight, but she herself looked peaceful enough. Her room was too luxurious for a child's room. It was full of expensive wooden wardrobes. Her bed had been made in the shape of a small dolphin. When she noticed the Baron of Dolls, she seemed to light up. From her expression, you could tell she had more faith in him than in her father. Although the former knew very little about children, they still loved him because of his toys and gifts.

The Baron of Shade introduced me to his daughter. Nawniga – her father called her 'Nawnaw' – was nine years old. She had big, green eyes that resembled the eyes of a black cat, shining in the dark.

'Kak Majid will tell you nice stories,' said the Baron of Shade, speaking in the manner of all the stupid men in this country who don't know how to speak to children.

The girl looked at me with her bright eyes, but said nothing. Neither she nor I had felt anything special. It is dangerous when children hate you from the very first moment. It is hard to rectify that later on. Children are not so pure and innocent. Most of them, one way or another, have preconceived ideas. When Nawniga looked at me, I was worried that she already hated me; but I didn't quite detect that in her look. I was surprised when the Baron of Shade told me, before bidding me goodbye, that Nawniga was not, in fact, his daughter but his wife's niece, that her father had died under mysterious circumstances and that, after his death, she had developed psychological problems – so she needed to be treated with the utmost care.

I was given two hours to spend with Nawniga. After a short while, the barons left the room. A heavy silence fell; the terrifying silence of the Baron of Shade's home was remarkable. As if momentarily paralysed, I merely looked at the girl and stood still.

'Is "Majid" really your name, or you are joking with me?' she asked after a while.

This calmed me down a bit. '"Majid" really is my name,' I said.

'How many stories do you know?' she asked.

'A thousand, maybe more,' I said as I went over and sat next to her. 'No one knows how many stories they know. Once we start counting the stories, we remember others that we missed out.'

'But I only know two stories – two and no more,' she said timidly. 'Auntie Narmin says that two stories for a girl my age are too few.'

'I'm sure you know more than two stories,' I said, stroking her hair gently.

'No, I only know the Cinderella story and "Awng, the King's Daughter",' she said sadly. 'Apart from those, I know nothing else.'

'No, you know more stories,' I said confidently, looking at her. 'People know many things that they think they don't, and they don't know many other things that they think they do. We humans are like that.'

She looked at me, astonished. Her eyes were breathtakingly beautiful. I had not seen such clear, pure and sparkling eyes even on my imaginary journeys.

'So do you know a story that I know but think I don't know?' she asked quietly.

I paused for a moment and looked at the doll lying next to her. 'Of course. The story of that doll, which is one of the nice stories,' I said. 'You know that, and yet you think you don't.'

'Do you mean Hiso?' she said as she looked at the doll.

'Evidently I do,' I said offhandedly, shrugging my shoulders.

She looked at me sadly. 'Shhh,' she said. Then, speaking softly so that the doll wouldn't hear her: 'Hiso's dad is dead. She mustn't find out.'

'Her dad died, did he?' I said. 'How did he die? Why don't you tell her that her dad died?'

'Her dad fell from a horse, you know,' she whispered. 'In a battle, her dad fell from a horse and died.'

'And what does Hiso do now?' I asked.

'She does nothing,' Nawniga said in a low voice. 'During the day, she sits by the window and waits for her dad. I won't let anyone tell her, you know. Even you are not allowed to tell her. Auntie Narmin isn't allowed to tell her, either.'

'I won't if you don't want me to,' I said in a low voice. 'But how long are you planning not to tell her?'

She put her arms around the doll. 'Forever,' she said.

I stroked her hair. 'Very well. We won't tell her, okay? We won't tell her. You and I will write letters to her together. You know, we can make her happy. We'll say, "These are letters from your dad." We'll send her presents. We'll say, "Your dad has gone to another country so that he can send you presents from there."'

'We say, "Your dad has gone to find gold, you know. Yes, to find gold,"' she said, with a big smile on her face.

I was pleased that she was warming to me.

'You see, you know Hiso's story very well,' I said. 'Auntie Narmin can't tell you anymore that you know only two stories. She just can't. Now you know three.'

'But the one about Hiso isn't a story,' she said, surprised. 'Hiso's dad really is dead.'

'I know,' I said. 'But when you tell it, it becomes a story. Whenever you tell an account well, it becomes a story. It doesn't matter if it's real or not.'

'But I don't want to tell Hiso's story to anyone,' she said, looking at me with suspicion. 'If Auntie Narmin finds out, she'll take Hiso away from me. Because she says, "You shouldn't speak to Hiso; Hiso is a doll, she's not a living thing."'

I didn't know what to say to that. 'Nawniga, listen,' I said. 'Tonight, I will teach you two stories. You can tell both of them to Auntie Narmin tomorrow. Every night that I come here, I will teach you two stories. After a while, you'll know more stories than Auntie Narmin.'

'Then I can tell Auntie Narmin that she smells of onions!' she said happily. 'I can also tell her that I know more stories than her. I can make her cry.'

'Yes, you can make her cry,' I said.

Most of Nwemiran's children were sad. Like Nawnaw, most of them harboured secret stories in their hearts. There was a mystery in their lives that they didn't want anyone to crack open. That night, I told Nawniga her first story.

That was how I became the storyteller for the barons' children. News of my stories soon spread. The children's boundless desire for stories opened the doors of all the homes of Nwemiran to me. It got to the point where I would spend the whole evening doing the rounds of the barons' homes. One baron's mansion was not like the next. A servant would always open the door and lead me through a long corridor to the top floor. All Nwemiran's children lived on the upper floor.

The barons' mansions were eerily quiet. I worked for many weeks, and didn't encounter a single woman in Nwemiran. I began to think that only children and men lived in this huge district. They planned everything in such a way that I would not meet any women from this neighbourhood, as if someone had meticulously drawn a map of my routes and hidden all the women from view. Until one night. The Baron of Dolls invited me to a party, where I laid eyes on the most beautiful women and girls of Nwemiran, and where I met the wife of the Baron of Chickens.

I STARED AT THE NIGHT OF THE CITY
AND SAW BLOOD

HASAN-I TOFAN, MAY—JUNE 2004

I first met Ghazalnus in the spring of 1998. By then, he had already been wandering around Hazarbagh for a long time. Ghazalnus never turned strangers away. After the uprising, he named his house the 'Children's Care Centre'. He didn't have much of an income, but he received financial support from several foreign organisations to help raise the children. Shortly before we began writing the big book, I visited him one evening and met his fantasised children. He was responsible for bringing up ten girls and boys with the help of a small, older man and an older woman. The fantasised children were the most beautiful in the world. They had an angelic look about them, and a touch of the perfume of Heaven. 'They have a pure imagination and they are loyal,' Ghazalnus would say proudly. In the mornings, a man driving a beat-up bus would pick them up and take them to school.

Because of the children, there was always a commotion in the house. I was surprised to see Darsim Tahir in their midst. Not only was he ugly and older than the rest, but he also gave off a foul smell. Now an adolescent with a big head, he appeared extremely timid. His gait, and his movements in general, were more like those of a horse than a human being. His nose was intimidatingly large. Ghazalnus's efforts to rehabilitate him had proved futile. He was unable to learn anything.

One day, a certain Attar had handed him over to Ghazalnus, and from then on Darsim had been in the latter's care. His only gift was his ability to locate a buried corpse and dig it up. Before he found Murad Jamil's body, none of us had trusted his skills. Even Ghazalnus had doubted his faculties. When he discovered the body, however, it marked the beginning of my strong belief in his unusual, secret gift. After we found the body, I asked Ghazalnus and my other friends to put all their efforts into attempting to unravel the mystery behind it. Our group was too small to pursue more than one story at the same time. What's more, the task was far more dangerous than we had first thought. On the night that Darsim dug up the body, I didn't think our lives would change as much as they did. Before finding that corpse, we had various cases to work on. However, death's dangerous façade only starts to show itself when you find an unidentified body.

There is nothing more extraordinary than an unidentified body. During my years of killing people, I never got close to the bodies of the victims. I always shot from afar, then fled like the wind. Although I had killed many people, I had never been face-to-face with a corpse. I preferred to run away, which is why they called me 'Tofan' – 'the Storm'. After finding Murad's body, I acted just as usual, but gradually I began to feel that the dead man had some strange hold over me. He entered my dreams at night. Some nights, I even went to Hazarbagh to escape the nightmares he and his terrifying image induced, but the dead man was constantly at my heels.

All humans die – that is our fate – but in the midst of that eternal torrent, one dead person will suddenly emerge whose death seems to be a mystery, as if it might contain all the secrets of the world. I've thought hard about this. All deaths resemble a box. Some are open: we can easily lift up the lid and look inside. We can reach into the bottom and take out all its secrets. Others are like sealed boxes: even if we break them open, we find more and more inexplicable secrets. True, I am a murderer and my guns killed a lot of people in the Eighties – some of whom deserved to be killed, or at least I thought so in the light of the revolutionary zeal of the time. Yet there were innocent people among them, too, people who just happened to have different views about life and the revolution. Still, I never thought any of those dead people would force me to pause and reflect.

After my mother's death, I was so immersed in the vastness of the flower garden and so busy opening and closing the secret doors of Hazarbagh that I nearly forgot about what was going on in the real world. Murad Jamil's body forced me to re-enter it as if it were my own corpse, as if it were my duty to find out who had killed me. Some deaths are like a mirror; when we look at them, we see ourselves. From that night on, I felt that I was in that dead man's grip. Sometimes the sight of a corpse has a bigger impact than reading a thousand books. From that night on, my worldview completely changed, and I began to maintain that we had to do something for the corpse.

I hope you never happen upon a dead body, but if you do, and if it is such a handsome one as this, you should not run away or condemn it. You should find out its story to the very end.

Some time had passed since the body had been discovered, but we were still without a breakthrough. I took it as our responsibility to move the corpse to a more appropriate place and bury it there in secret. That was the least one could do for a friendless body. One evening, I decided to transfer it to the city's main cemetery, to find a spot for it among the graves and bury it there, paying it due respect – all without Ghazalnus's knowledge. We had already given up on the police and security forces finding any clues. We were all convinced that unless Murad Jamil's killers died of natural causes or were struck down by other misfortunes, they would remain at large forever.

I revisited the spot where the dead man was buried, in a tucked-away ravine on the outskirts of the city. I dug where the corpse had been deposited in the ground, but found nothing. Nothing at all. I went mad. Like a desperate animal, I clawed the ground around me, to no avail. Clearly, someone had been there after us and had exhumed the body. I found small fragments of clothes and remnants of other things at the spot, left behind when the body was moved, and – crucially – a torn piece of fabric from his orange shirt. The disappearance of Murad Jamil's corpse was another great mystery in our story. When I told Ghazalnus, he looked at me with dreamy eyes, without paying much attention, and muttered a few things under his breath that I didn't understand at the time. I interpreted this as Ghazalnus being more concerned about solving the mystery of the murder than about finding the corpse itself.

The disappearance of the corpse became a dangerous obsession for me. I gathered that whoever had killed Murad had been unable to hide his body immediately, and so had buried him hastily in a shallow grave in that ravine. Later, for whatever reason, they had moved the body to an inaccessible location.

One night I took out my pistol for the first time in years, and roamed the open fields on the outskirts of the city. The few nights I had spent at the Idle Murderers' Club had led me to believe that dangerous things happened by night in the city – things no one heard about or saw, or if they did, kept quiet about. I walked towards the cold plains that surrounded the city. I was sure that if only I was patient enough, I would spy something. The first few nights, I walked around with Darsim Tahir, both of us inspecting large areas of the plains and the bare, dusty expanses near the city, but we found nothing. Darsim's hands quickly dug down like excavators in many spots. We found a few carcasses, dog bones and cow skulls, but nothing relevant.

During that period, I took Darsim out so often at night that his appearance began to show the telltale effects of lack of sleep and exhaustion. He was a young man who didn't know how to say 'no'. He did as he was told, spoke very little and was exceptionally obedient to Ghazalnus. I felt that he genuinely loved him. When

Ghazalnus was cross with him, Darsim would become angry, even infuriated, or very unstable. Because Darsim sometimes mistreated the other children, Ghazalnus would become upset with him and give him a tongue-lashing. On most days, he went to buy fresh bread or to do a bit of shopping for the children. During the period when I took him to inspect the outskirts of the city, he was obedient and taciturn. He did everything he was told. I felt that, inside, he had certain secret qualities that, if properly directed, would turn him into a different person. He might look like a giant machine when he was digging, but afterwards the exhaustion was apparent in his face. I often advised him to work slowly, but he was scared that day might break. I always took him back before dawn. When we arrived at Ghazalnus's home, he was so exhausted that he would sleep like a log all day.

Finally, I decided to head to the outskirts of the city without Darsim. I was driven by a dark and secret desire to understand this filthy city. I walked around in vain for many nights. I lay in ambush outside the city ring road. I didn't see much on the first four nights. On the fifth, I was awakened by the roaring of a vehicle after I had fallen asleep in a ravine. The lights were switched off as it came driving up the plains. It stopped around 200 metres away from me. Two people got out and opened the back door. One of them shouted: 'Get out, you son of a bitch, get out!' He shouted so loudly that I thought it was the night itself screaming. In the moonlight, I saw them drag out a young man and begin beating him.

Someone said from inside the car, 'Don't give us any trouble, you motherfucker, you whore sister! When I tell you to opt out, it means you *opt out*. Son of a bitch.'

For a moment, I lost sight of the young man. I was sure he was lying on the ground. I couldn't tell exactly how long the beating lasted, but it went on for quite a while. In the meantime, I could hear the sound of another man laughing and saying, 'My dear master, don't hurt him. I swear by this pure darkness, I swear by the morning sun that will soon light up the world, this young man will listen to us. My master, I think that he will listen to us. He's an honest and respectable person. He's very honourable and extremely polite.'

This was a tall man speaking. In the dark, his voice could be heard more than all the rest. He carried on laughing as he spoke more in this vein. He spoke a lot. He spoke about the beauty of the morning. He swore by bulbuls and nightingales. He swore by the fragrance of sweet clover and sweet basil. He surprised me with his delicate words. When the others swore at their victim, this man's words offered him consolation.

From time to time, someone would get out of the vehicle and give the battered guy a few more kicks. Then the mystery man would say, 'If you don't opt out voluntarily, I'll show you your sister's video next week. Get it? You only have two days to opt out and to persuade all the other partners. Get it?'

They beat the young man for a long time, but I didn't hear him utter a single word, not even a whisper. When they had worn themselves out, they got back in the vehicle and drove away. It occurred to me several times to leap into the midst of the scuffle, but I couldn't predict what would happen. I was concerned things might get out of hand, and the unfortunate young man might be killed. I waited for matters to take their natural course. Once they left and their vehicle was back on the main road, its lights on, I went over to the poor youth. He seemed to have been badly hurt in the head and chest. He was a small, fragile man, and I couldn't imagine how he had endured such a beating. He was astonished to see someone come to his aid so quickly on those barren plains. He seemed to have resigned himself to death and abandoned any hope of making it out alive. I pulled his head into my lap and asked him sincerely, 'What can I do for you?'

'Take me to your house, somewhere I can rest and get some water,' he said slowly.

I carried him on my back to the side of the main road. After a long wait, I took him home in a sleepy, early morning cab. He had excruciating abdominal pain and I wanted to take him to hospital, but he pleaded with me desperately not to do so. He said his wounds weren't life-threatening, and that going to hospital would mean big trouble. I asked no questions and just let him sleep. He was so exhausted that he slept for eight hours straight. When he woke up, it was two in the afternoon. I prepared some food, laid a modest dinner mat on the floor and helped him wash his face.

'Consider me your brother,' I told him. 'I'll do whatever I can for you.' He seemed grateful, and assured me that he would remember my help as long as he lived. Volunteering to tell me his story, he said that this was the second time he had received a beating, and that the perpetrators were 'Caesar's men'. According to him, Caesar was the city's leading businessman, very close to the ruling elite. He was friends with most of the senior politicians and, as co-partner to two very high-ranking officials, had bought an old section of the market for a nominal fee. It was the third area he had bought. He wanted to evict all the shopkeepers so he could demolish the shops and put up something new in their place. The young man and a few other shopkeepers had vowed not to give up their shops, but after his beating the night before, he was certain they would be killed if they didn't give in.

I didn't know how to advise him. 'Do you know the people who beat you?' I asked.

'It doesn't help whether I do or not,' he said. 'They're nothing. They're just workers. They do the job, they get paid.'

I bade goodbye to the young man with great sadness, then went to Shibr and told him the whole story. He was not surprised.

He laughed as he looked at me. 'Worse things happen every day – every single day. Hasan-i Tofan, it's a long time since you lived in this city,' he said.

From then on, I decided to keep going. I needed to know what was happening in the city. Murad Jamil's corpse drew me out to the plains repeatedly. At night, I felt as if his body was wandering through my life. I had to know, to see and to understand. Appalling things were taking place during the city's quiet, dark nights. On those nights, I saw a woman killed, and her corpse taken away; I saw a young man's head crushed with a concrete block and his body burned; I saw a group of children batter an old man to death with a rock; I saw other people come and weep in the desolate landscape; I saw petty thieves who hid small pieces of stolen gold; I saw fearful sex on the stony ground between men and women who trembled in the numbing cold; I saw young men and women sob on each other's shoulders, their hands kept chastely by their sides. On those nights, I felt I saw angels descending from the skies and ascending from the earth; I saw God himself come down to visit the city's sleeping districts and then depart again. I witnessed it all as a sad bystander. I could not get involved in anything. I could not change anything. I understood during those nights that the greatest cruelty and mercilessness in our world is that nothing can be changed without taking up arms. Yet I still preferred the ugliness of the world to that.

The use of weapons was nothing but another crime human beings had added to their list. During those nights, I watched the dangerous films of this world the way the Imaginary Magellan watched his fantasy films. Like him, I was the only audience member, but mine was a bigger, more shocking and more open cinema. Despite my toughness and my animal will, on some of those nights I became very sleepy. Sapped of energy as I lay in the dusty areas next to the wretched ring road, I would nod off, feeling as if I was seeing everything in a dream. But on other nights I would be so alert that the cool of the early morning and the cold of the night made me happy. When there wasn't a power outage in the city, I found there was nothing to match the beauty of its many lights – but seeing all the blood in the bowels of the night saddened me. I used to think this city was beautiful when it slept, but no longer. Now I think that even when it is asleep, it is filled with apparitions and black jinns; when it is asleep, it is filled with blood and sadness.

A REAL LOVER IN A FANTASTICAL GARDEN, OR A FANTASTICAL LOVER IN A REAL GARDEN?

GHAZALNUS AND TRIFA, POST-1996

When Trifa Yabahri disappeared in the spring of 1996, Attar believed she had left the country illegally with a group of emigrants. As he was very close to all the traffickers, he was aware that people were organised into groups at night and then dispatched to Istanbul. For several weeks, he questioned all the smugglers and their guides tirelessly, asking about a small girl with black eyes – but to no avail. No one knew anything. He knew the description was too vague. How many small, dark girls with black eyes were there in this city? A hundred thousand? Perhaps even more. On top of which, most of those heading to Istanbul had fake IDs, so no one even knew their real names.

All the while Attar was searching for Trifa, she was at Ghazalnus's. During that time they had been visiting hospitals together, taking flowers to friendless and lonely girls, flies swarming around their beds in the wards. Doing this had created an affinity between them, akin to the feeling of the early days of being in love. Ghazalnus's biggest problem was his profound love for Sabri, the queen of Hazarbagh, which he kept hidden; it was something he didn't want Trifa to know about. No woman in the world needed to know about his secret love for someone widely thought of as an imaginary symbol of ancient Kurdish songs.

The day Trifa left the carpet factory she was so lonely, so devastated, that everyone's heart went out to her. She saw herself as vulnerable, with no one to protect her. The men who had bought the factory were not going to let her get away so easily. She was terrified they might kidnap her as they had Sayyid Qadir, and force her to work like a slave. She was terrified they might eat her. (It was around this time that she had developed a dangerous ailment that would shake her life to the core: a phobia of being eaten. She often felt that a giant monster was staring at her out of the darkness, wanting to eat her.)

One rainy night, she went to Ghazalnus's. Even though she didn't know much about this bearded man who filled the world with his extraordinary, imaginative ghazals, there was nowhere else she could imagine feeling calm. She was not thinking about marriage. Unlike her peers, she had not invested a vast amount of time to pondering the characteristics of her future husband. She was one of those young women who barely thought about marriage, men or feelings. I ought to say that we live in a country teeming with such iron women – tough women who would rather die than let the slightest trace of emotion appear on their faces. However, the fact of the matter was that Trifa was not one of them. She simply hadn't encountered a man who could awaken her womanhood. (Most of the pale, cold women who wander our Earth like ghosts have never had anyone to awaken them in this way, and it is that which has turned their hearts into ice and their bodies into wood. Just as it requires a huge effort to help someone who has fainted to regain consciousness, so it is for a man who attempts to rekindle the dormant fire of womanhood in this sort of woman. Most men, though, lack patience, and want a woman who can undress on the spur of the moment and knows all the arts of lovemaking, without any effort on their part. However, we ought to know that these things are only attained with patience.)

At the factory, all Trifa had was her imagination. Instead of thinking about her body and of love, she was preoccupied with delirious heroes in the carpets, weeping with hope, happiness, loyalty and love. She was also concerned about her female colleagues. Their suffering overwhelmed her so much, she forgot about herself. Her time at the factory saw her draw closer to the pain of the young female workers who considered their tiring work at the factory Heaven compared to their Hell at home. She was always there for them, as confidante and guide. They shared their miseries with her, which left her with no time to contemplate her own life. Those who are swallowed up by the concerns of others are often unfair to the human inside them, but we all know that the fairest person is someone who is hard on herself. Even after Trifa walked out of the factory, her thoughts stayed with the sad workers. The day she wanted to run away from Attar, she visited a women's-rights activist.

'I need to disappear for a while,' she said after giving the woman the keys to her new house. 'I have some personal problems. Whenever you want to shelter an unfortunate person, here's the key to my house. Do as you see fit.'

Although she wanted to disappear, she didn't know where to go. One evening she visited Ghazalnus. She thought he might help her find somewhere. She was too scared to stay with Galawezh or the carpet weavers. Who knew what they were going through? What's more, Attar was cunning enough to find her there. Ghazalnus was her last and only hope. She was certain that no one could suspect this man. She had wanted to see his home since meeting him – not out of any ordinary female curiosity, but, on the contrary, a secret inner force that had germinated the seed of this desire in her mind. When she arrived at Ghazalnus's, she could not believe he was living in such a strange place. From the outside, his house appeared small, sleepy and dull. It was located in one of the city's oldest districts, where the dust of ancient principalities rose from the homes; the area was still redolent of ancient knights, plagues and Ottoman tax collectors.

When Trifa stepped into the alleyway, she felt as if she was travelling back to the olden days, the times of Muslim theological students in love and mullahs immersed in theology. She walked towards Ghazalnus's house, propelled by a strange force, greater than her. At his door, she glanced down at herself. She didn't look like an innocent person seeking help, but like a woman returning home. Despite her unannounced arrival, Ghazalnus received her warmly, as if in fact it had all been planned and organised by someone else.

Ghazalnus's house and garden were something quite different – they were magical. From the outside, you could see only a couple of trees, but from the inside, the flowers and trees displayed a certain regal serenity and splendour. As if the garden had made her shy, as if she had forgotten that she, too, came from an illustrious family, she sat in the living room shyly and in consternation. She was astounded by the angelic children running around her, shouting and screaming. When she saw them all, it occurred to her that Ghazalnus might have many wives, and had not told her the story of his life properly. Since meeting this man, she had had a strange and indescribable feeling, as if cold air had suddenly assailed her from within. Back then, she didn't know what love was. For her, love had been an ethical asset that she, as a young woman, had had to defend even though she had never been in love herself. It was a strange world in which people who didn't know what love was became its guardians, and others who were in love became its tyrants. She was certain something unusual was astir in her heart, something it would take time to identify for certain.

Obviously, love is like an illness. It is, in fact, closely related to illness. In the past few months, on the several occasions that she and Ghazalnus had met and looked at the enchanting carpets together, the same chill had stolen over her so that she longed to enfold herself in a blanket. When Trifa arrived in Ghazalnus's bare living room that night, she expected the mother of the children to appear and greet her; but there was no sign of her. Suddenly, she felt a sense of familiarity, as if she had been there before, as if she truly were coming back to her real home. My, how astonished she was when she heard the story of those children! She replayed the story of her own life in her mind, and understood that it was no mere accident that had brought her there, but the power of destiny. Sitting on a plain chair in Ghazalnus's living room, she listened to him with tears in her eyes. He recounted the stories of child after child, all the fruit of imaginary love. They were born to hapless mothers engaged in illicit, phantasmic loves. They gave birth to vulnerable children who might have been killed had Ghazalnus not offered them a refuge. Again and again, over time, he had provided the children with sanctuary in this lonely centre to save them from certain death. They were an illegitimate generation, made half from beauty, half from malediction. Apart from Ghazalnus, no one knew their true secret. Tearfully, Trifa listened to him, bending over his hands to kiss them and saying, 'You're an angel. You're not a member of the human race. You are not like us, you are without sin.'

Like a madwoman, she would hold and kiss one of the children. Like a madwoman, in tears, she would follow first one child then another, younger and older alike. She regarded herself as their sister. Gradually, she recounted her own story: her mother's pregnancy, her fatherless birth to a sick woman, her life as a friendless child in the same house as her brother Jawhar Yabahri.

Her stories animated Ghazalnus. Trifa had an extraordinary energy for narrative. He had never seen such an ideal young woman, one who was the outcome of an unsuccessful love and fantastical desire, desire that, instead of dying and becoming a mirage, had taken the form of a human being. That same strange night, Ghazalnus kissed her hands too and said: 'Trifa, marry me and become my life companion.'

No one ever knows where such a strange and unexpected proposal comes from. Is it rooted in the centuries-old culture that encourages a man to take the lead, to plant himself suddenly before a woman, ask her to enter into a relationship with him or marry him and demand a clear answer at the very same moment? Was it rooted in Ghazalnus's tremendous admiration for Trifa? Or was it a brave attempt by a true gentleman, wanting genuinely to save a woman from a dreadful plight?

All the children who witnessed Trifa's arrival still remember the details of that night very clearly. They all remember the moment when Ghazalnus kneeled down in front of her and said:

'The heavens and their extraordinary and invisible forces have sent you. You and I have not met by accident. It is not by chance that you came to my house tonight. I am the son of ghazal writers, you the daughter of unfulfilled fantasies. I will be your friend until death. I need you, and you need me. You are my imagined half who flew away and landed in a different corner of the world.'

For many long years, the children would repeat Ghazalnus's words, imitating his tone and delivery. The boys would kneel before the girls, and say in jest: 'Tonight the imagination has sent you, so that you can save me and allow me to save you.'

Regardless of how the events of that evening panned out, they indicate that Trifa and Ghazalnus realised right then and there that they could not live without one another. We all know that what connected them then was not love, but something greater, more complex and more profound – the force of the imagination. Love without imagination is akin to what happens when two shopkeepers agree to merge their shops. Their relationship was more enduring and robust. Ordinary love ages and dies quickly, but two beings with infinite imagination who feel they have long been travelling separate roads that were destined eventually to cross, two people each carrying a vast amount of pain as well as creative gifts they want to share with one another … these two immerse themselves in an endless sea that only death can interrupt.

When they met, Ghazalnus was more experienced and worldly, while Trifa had a wilder imagination. Yet neither of them knew where to take their lives from there. No matter how strong or boundless someone's imagination may be, he or she needs a truth to live for. That night was a meeting between two people, each seeking their own great truth in their own way. Trifa felt that in this house she had found a family, even a tribe. Fawziya Yasami's ageing and illness had left her isolated, but now she was certain that she had always been one of the Imaginative Creatures. Ghazalnus told her about his dangerous split between the imagination and reality. That night, he held her hands and took her to Mahnaz's garden, and together they opened the door to that fantastical house. Ghazalnus considered it his Kaaba. Trifa wandered among the pink flowers. She could smell the soul of the girl who had left behind an infinite flower garden. She perceived this reality assailed by the imagination. When she smelled the flowers, she knew that all imaginations must attack reality in one way or another, that each person must plant some of his or her imagination in the heart of reality whether in the shape of a flower, a garden or a fantasised child.

Ghazalnus appeared rather confused in the midst of Mahnaz's flowers, the birds and the moonlight. He didn't want his marriage proposal to be understood as concern for Trifa's life, or as prompted by fears that the life of a woman he considered a rare pearl might otherwise be in tatters. His decision to marry Trifa was mad – but all reasonable people who marry have taken a mad decision. Only opportunists and selfish types make careful calculations before resolving to wed. Marriage always entails a degree of madness, rashness and lack of thought; if people made thorough and careful calculations, nobody would get married.

Ghazalnus was a man who had lived most of his life without giving things much thought, an imaginative soul driven by sudden ideas and fantasies. His leaving school was mad; his six-year retreat with the ghazals was mad; his rise to reading poetry was mad; his travels through the domain of the imagination were mad; his adoption of the fatherless children was mad; his decision to become a tutor of the imagination was mad; his purchase of Sayfadin Maro's house was mad; his love for Sabri was mad … Everything he did was crazy, but serene; his craziness inspired hope. Why, then, should marriage and fatherhood not be crazy for him, too?

No, what pained Ghazalnus was his impossible, unsuccessful love for Sabri, for the flower gardens in Hazarbagh. Sabri was the greatest love of his life. She was an elusive night creature, her only link to the world the inspiration of the ghazals. Sabri was the imaginary woman every man pursues in his darkest, secret dreams, the fantasy woman whose various attributes men seek in all women. She epitomised the woman who does not love but is loved, and is not, therefore, possessed by any of her lovers. That was the great secret inside Ghazalnus's heart, which he had to hide forever. It is difficult to tell a woman that you're going to marry her because she has some of the attributes of the imaginary woman who lives within the garden of your soul. No man would say such things to a woman. Yet Ghazalnus was so impressed by Trifa's imagination, character and life that in her he saw the extraordinary attributes he had found in his ideal woman of Hazarbagh.

Trifa was the kind of person you immediately want to be friends with. She inspired calmness, trust and fascination; she could relieve your pain by laying her hands upon you. Something in her black eyes immediately washed away any sadness and invited peace. Other women with whom Ghazalnus had crossed paths had been beautiful and highly imaginative, but none had been able to alleviate the pains of his soul simply by looking into his eyes. Trifa was not a woman whose charm was distributed throughout her body; all her charm lay in those extraordinary black eyes that would suddenly display intelligence, excitement and concern, eyes as rare as they were stunning. Every time Ghazalnus had seen Trifa, he had noticed her eyes. He had also noticed her hands; whenever she placed them on someone's shoulders, they were so caring that they reflected her inner light onto the faces of the vulnerable people she touched.

During the months when they visited the sick, her hands, her elongated fingers, her eyes would be lit up with emotion, which made Ghazalnus painfully enamoured of her. He had met thousands of women in this city through the society of the distressed and forlorn women – women who were hundreds of times more beautiful and melancholy than Trifa. But he had never seen eyes that were so dreamy and yet so unloved, even as they showed the world nothing but love. Nor had he observed such hands. Ghazalnus knew other men didn't see those charms in Trifa. The men of this city go mad for a woman's face, skin, breasts or bottom, but it is rare indeed that they should fall in love with a woman's hands, her tapered fingers, the sparkle in her eyes.

Trifa was too intelligent not to understand that Ghazalnus was stunned by her, but not yet madly in love with her. The idea of marriage was both sudden and complicated, but also very exciting. She did want to marry Ghazalnus, but as if driven by a particularly female obstinacy, as if seeking something more profound and elusive, she did not say yes straightaway when he proposed. That night, they remained in Mahnaz's garden until late. Ghazalnus's efforts to win Trifa over proved futile. Although she had no previous experience of love, a deep feminine instinct made her say, 'Only lovers who do not meet are immortal.' It was an ancient Sufi conviction, and for Ghazalnus it enhanced Trifa's beauty, making it even more exceptional and unexpected.

Trifa felt that her understanding of love was more complex than his. She would have despised herself had she consented to his proposal that night; it would have damaged her sense of dignity and solemnity as a woman. If she agreed to marry Ghazalnus on a night when she had gone to him because she had nowhere else to go, it would appear as if she had said yes out of fear. She had had strange feelings for him since the night she had met him in Attar's car, and since then she had been hoping to see him again. Yet everything was now so easy that it could not but fail to excite an imaginative person. Yet a truly imaginative person would not accept such an easy love. Trifa wanted things to be more complicated, more difficult. Since childhood, when she had played with invisible creatures, she had been obsessed with the impossible. What love is stronger or better than that of an elusive lover searching for his or her elusive partner?

Thinking back to that day now after so many years, it is as if a secret power intervened to get Ghazalnus off to a tragic start. He had spent all his life with ghazals, and was certain that love died in victory and lived in defeat. His name as an eternal lover had spread everywhere. When we now think about his sudden and unexpected wish, namely, his proposal of marriage to such a girl on such a night, it is fair to wonder whether or not Ghazalnus knew from the outset that Trifa Yabahri was an intangible human being, a mirage. After all, he was a man who discovered and pursued mirages. I believe he ultimately wanted to surround himself with failed and impossible loves. Which is why he took Trifa to Mahnaz's garden that night – to show her the eternal magic and beauty that a failed love had left behind, the amazing garden it had created.

Ghazalnus did not want to reach the end when it came to love. His sudden madness, his unexpected fall at Trifa's feet, was a means of prolonging his ghazals, the expression of a desire to jump from one impossible love to another. Perhaps he was aware from the start that Trifa was playing the same game of hope and hopelessness. Both of them, more or less, knew the secret of the game. They knew they could only be together for good if they remained unattainable to one another. Searching for the impossible and imagined aspects of a lover is what makes love more than an earthly phenomenon; a love must look not for the real person, but for the imagined creature inside the real person. At first, love is about spying glimpses of that creature, observing its shadow moving behind a thin curtain. As love expands, the curtain becomes thinner and thinner; but when it dies, that curtain becomes thicker and thicker, until the imagined creature inside is no longer visible.

As they walked around Mahnaz's garden, they looked into each other's eyes and both clearly saw the creature they imagined inside the other. Couples are constantly searching for it in each other's eyes, but they seldom find it. Trifa was adamant that things should take a slower course, that they should stretch the game to its furthest point. Love is a game, but a difficult one. Those who oversimplify it kill it, was Trifa's take on it all.

That night in her sleep, she had a strange feeling of happiness and pain fused together. It was the first night in her life that she had slept in a big house with a man who was not related to her, sleeping somewhere in the house just as she was. She thought about Ghazalnus's odd, sudden proposal until dawn. She was certain that inside him was a creature she could both see and not see, which appeared and disappeared. It was this invisible and imagined person that she loved, not the flesh and blood man who stood before her. She had to reach that person. When she awoke in the morning, she told Ghazalnus all the thoughts that had run through her head in the night. From that day on, the path of the extraordinary relationship between Ghazalnus and Trifa was set, both of them waiting for that singular moment when the imagined person was revealed, a moment people can never say for certain they have reached.

Trifa stayed in the house and worked as the head carer of the homeless children. The foreign organisations that provided financial support for the orphans were pleased to have a woman in charge of the home. Only reliable, private visitors called at the tucked-away house. Ghazalnus, meanwhile, secluded himself for long periods in the basement. He now sported a longer beard; his hair had grown more dervish-like still, and his looks were sadder. Not only had he been learning ghazals, he was writing them, too. When he returned from Hazarbagh in the morning, he would write down the ghazals that had come to him the night before, secretly inspired among the tulip beds. Sometimes he would wander upstairs in his olive-coloured shirt to help, playing with the children until he was exhausted. At other times, he would read some of his ghazals to Trifa, leaving her dazzled and intoxicated. They were at once living near and yet far away from each other. That was the great rule of their friendship. Day after day, they felt a small fire growing within them; day after day, they felt something hurting them inside. They both looked for that pain, as it was the only sign that they were close to one another, that they lived for one another. It was a classic condition of love that they had inherited from their ancestors: unless love hurts very deeply, it cannot make you happy.

It was a long time before Trifa became aware of Ghazalnus's nightly trips to Hazarbagh. She checked on the children every night, tucking them in, bringing them water and stroking their faces. One night Miraw-i Awi – 'the Water Duck' – was ill. Mirawi was a small girl whose real name was Harmin, but everyone had called her 'Miraw-i Awi' since she was little. She was running a terribly high fever. Trifa searched the whole house for Ghazalnus to wake him, so he could take Mirawi to the hospital; but she couldn't find him. It happened again on other nights. Trifa was certain that Ghazalnus was going to a place unknown to her, that he disappeared into another imaginary realm. To his many secrets, the man had added another, darker one that Trifa could not fathom.

Day after day, Ghazalnus was torn between two superstitious, impossible and fruitless loves.

When we think about it now, it defies belief: a young man and a young woman like each other, one way or another, and yet for a long time they live together in the same house and work together without touching one another, without even their lips touching.

They enjoyed the distance, the inaccessibility and the pain. Clearly, their last hope was to reach the stage of spiritual union, to repeat the experience of the ancient Sufis. They didn't look like two souls from this age. They were two bodies alien to this city, even to this Earth. Ghazalnus smelled of the old ghazal books, the yellowed pages of Mullah Sukhta's collections, while Trifa looked like the girls from her own imaginative carpets, the elusive girls we fall in love with.

Today, so many years later, we believe that Trifa's desire for a love resulting in oneness might have been a spiritual reaction to an era in which the city gradually began to facilitate an easy life of pleasure; when thousands of farmers swapped their lives of honest work for cities and towns immersed in the roar of engines, where all they did was eat and watch satellite TV. People forgot about the land; nature lost its value, and work, its meaning. The multitudes lived peacefully under an authority that attempted to portray its own idleness as work. It was the start of an age in which an abundance of money and food seemed to rain down from the skies. It produced people obsessed with expensive cars, who went so far as to sleep in their cars at night. It produced others obsessed with the pornographic films that had only recently started arriving in huge numbers, to the point of heart attacks and even death.

Strange groups displaying previously unheard of behaviour were spotted in the city. A group led by an arrogant youth called Meezpasha, 'the Piss King', attacked libraries and urinated on the books. There was the Bulen Bulen group of singers with terrible voices, led by a bald guy in a cap: wherever they sang, hundreds of monkey-like souls danced around them. Clubs and restaurants opened where people could eat until they turned into pigs. The streets at night smelled of the vomit of drunks who treated the entire city like the toilets of their own homes. There, in that city, people ate and vomited, vomited and ate. At night, the southerly wind carried the smoke of the barbecues of drunks and gluttons from the mountains to the city. The air was stifling. In the evenings, tens of thousands of people headed to the outskirts of the city, where they sat opposite each other as if engaged in a dangerous contest to prove to one another just how much they could eat.

Trifa, for so many years completely engrossed in weaving her carpets, could not understand this new world. In the process of buying her house, she began to notice that wherever she went, people were stuffing their faces with enormous sandwiches: employees in the corridors of government offices or at their desks, or going back and forth between rooms to deliver tax forms and title deeds. The country – from the president's office to the parliament, from libraries to university lecture halls – reeked of food being cooked. The bodies of some of the country's leaders were so inflated you feared the wind might carry them up into the sky.

Eating was all the city's inhabitants thought about. Trifa was surprised when cab drivers steered with one hand and ate sandwiches with the other, and fat traffic wardens manned the roundabouts with huge rolls in their fists. The only art fathers taught their children was how to skewer meat and make wraps; the only art daughters learned from their mothers was how to cook and leave men overjoyed with the taste of meat. When Trifa went to the hospitals with Ghazalnus, she was surprised to see doctors enter and leave the operating theatres clutching greasy snacks.

All this eating meant that people forgot to water their gardens; the city dried up, and the trees suffered from unusual diseases. Everywhere, sumptuous dinners were presented, and dinner mats laid upon the floor. Wherever Trifa looked, she noticed this culture of gluttony. People didn't talk to one another, they ate each other up. Young men didn't love young women, they devoured them; wives didn't love their husbands, they feasted on them; vendors ate their customers, and customers their vendors. The day Sayyid Qadir Niya summoned Trifa and told her the story of the sale of the factory, she was sure that he, too, had been eaten. In the morning, when she went among the carpet factory workers and looked into the women's eyes, she was sure their husbands ate them at night. In those years, a small Islamic extremist group had emerged, headed by a respectable sheikh, and was beheading people and then eating their flesh.

It was around this time that Trifa developed her phobia of being eaten . When Ghazalnus proposed, she was still living with this fear. That night she decided to postpone marrying him. She wanted to retreat to an imaginary place, where she could look at the world without being eaten.

Trifa got used to the children very quickly. More than ten were living in the house by then. She was surprised that a man could raise so many children on his own. True, he was regularly assisted by a female worker and a jovial old man, but the amount of effort he invested in them was far beyond the normal capacity of a single person.

Right from the first night, Trifa told the children bedtime stories. Only three of the children had reached the age where they could talk and use reason: Khayalwan, Bulbul and Bakhan. Bulbul was blind, so everyone called him 'Blind Bulbul'. Bakhan was a fair-skinned girl with pale eyes who was so like a doll that everyone who saw her felt compelled to touch her skin to check that she was real. Khayalwan was a calm, sensitive child. His greatest weakness was a soul so delicate he couldn't endure the scent of a flower, and would faint after smelling one. All three established a good rapport with Trifa very quickly.

When the children were at nursery or in school, Ghazalnus would sleep late into the morning. He would rise around noon and take a cold shower to wake himself up properly. Come the afternoon, he would immerse himself in the sea of ghazals.

One night, he went upstairs to see Trifa. That night saw the first great fight between them, in what we shall call the 'war of ghazals'. He read ghazals to her on a daily basis – his own, written in the blood of his heart. Trifa was obliged to wage war day and night against the power of these ghazals. With each one, an urgent force pushed her closer towards the arms of that man. But she was not supposed to fall in love like other women. She had to resist the urge to be close to him, not because she didn't want to bring her body into their game, but because the beloved should forever remain a fabulous, even impossible, fantasy; all Ghazalnus's ghazals testified to this. Day by day, Trifa felt that Ghazalnus was playing the same game – the game of running away from her in body while drawing closer to her in spirit. Sometimes they went to Mahnaz's garden together, and made for the immortal pink scented flowers. Once, among the sad trees of that garden, Ghazalnus told her that he wanted to write a book about Mahnaz Maro and her imaginary garden and bequeath it to the children.

'But what about the thousands of others who die?' Trifa asked. 'What about those killed in wars? Or the Kurds lost in the dangerous sea crossings to Europe? What about those killed by sudden sadness, or those who walk the Earth, already dead? What about the hopeless patients lying in their hospital beds, for whom no medication is available? What about the old people who die without having understood anything about life? What about the young men who kill themselves for no apparent reason? What about the unidentified bodies discovered from time to time?'

It was in the garden that the idea of the vast book was born. It would be bigger than any other, and would never end; it would encompass the stories of every human being. Trifa was completely astonished by the idea of writing an infinite book, because there is always someone in this city dying a death not inflicted by God or nature but caused by other human beings. The idea was a pretext for distracting themselves from the pain of love. For days on end, they thought about the kind of team they would need to pull together for the project to work. They had to find people who could help them write the book.

Let me pause here and take you back to the beginning of this book, to where I asked you a question that I then left unanswered: 'What does a "perfect human being" mean?' I asked you to be patient so that I could arrange the chapters and the narrative in such a way so as to accommodate the answer somewhere in the book. I think this is a good place to pause for a short while, so we can ponder the answer to this eternal question that has, for so long, caused individuals and societies to agonise.

Whenever I think about the night that Trifa turned down Ghazalnus's marriage proposal, I feel that both she and Ghazalnus were victims of the search for the meaning of 'a perfect human being'. Everywhere in the world, when there is a decline, when standards fall, when people turn into ravening beasts, there are those who emerge seeking perfection more than ever, who practically overflow with love.

At certain junctures in history when the majority descends to the level of flies, pigs and wolves, when their lives are reduced to mere trivia, when they lose their imaginations, when their perceptions cannot accept truth and their eyes cannot see beyond material things – at such moments, some human beings are born who see perfection in being vast, limitless and versatile, in being capable of dreaming big dreams. These are people whose souls never stop flying, who soar ceaselessly along the winding paths of existence. They are creatures who respond to the littleness of human beings and the narrowing down of their interests by being everywhere in the world, by living at the extreme ends of imagination and reality, by roaming the margins of loneliness and mingling with those they find there; they want to be utterly themselves and to be there solely for others, to be alone and yet part of the world, to be both self *and* the world, a small tree on the bank of a canal and the entire forest. Ghazalnus was someone who wanted to live at both ends of the imagination and truth. He wanted to swim in imagination even as he bathed in truth. When he lived the extremes of beauty, mystery and all the vividness of the imagination, he wanted to see the extreme bitterness and bleakness of reality, its ability to kill life.

To Ghazalnus, a perfect human being was one in whom truth and the imagination could look at each other. I am not saying that they must live happily together, must not clash or fight, just that they must be able to *look* at each other. An ordinary person is someone within whom reality doesn't dare to look at the imagination, within whom reality can easily kill the imagination, in fact. Meanwhile, dreamers are those who dare not come near reality. They see the real world as a train station from which they travel to the imagination – they appear indifferent to the world. Whereas a perfect human being is ordinary, and a dreamer as well. To a perfect human being, the beloved is real, but can also become an imagined, ethereal creature. At the same time, the beloved is an imagined person who might become real. The perfect human being does not know whether the beloved is real or imaginary – whether she is here and can really be seen, or is only in our dreams. Hence the life of a perfect human being, the love of a perfect human being, is impossible.

At the moment that Trifa turned down Ghazalnus's love, she knew that if she became his wife, she could endanger her imaginative side, that she could become an earthly creature, a person made of flesh and blood. Trifa, however, was not the kind of young woman who could play the role of such a lover; she was intent on becoming an imagined beloved, which, among women, seems to be the highest station of belovedness.

THE MEMOIRS OF THE
BARON OF IMAGINATION

The day I saw one of Trifa Yabahri's carpets for the first time, I was stunned. I assumed at first that it had been made by virtuoso Iranian carpet weavers, but then found out it was the product of a small, hidden-away local factory.

As soon as I saw the carpet, I understood that its creator was a student of the imagination, someone trained in poetic reflection. I saw the hallmarks of those uncanny fingers in many other places. I saw carpets woven by those otherworldly hands in the home of many a wealthy man and eminent politician. I decided that the hands that made these carpets, the imagination that conceived them, the looms that weaved them, should belong to me.

I needed to collect all the imaginative minds of the world. I don't know when this obsession to become the first buyer of imagination entered my head. Don't try to tell me imagination cannot be bought. Throughout history, human beings have repeatedly sold their imaginations. One might say that the first thing humans *ever* sold was the imagination. Religious men in primitive societies had nothing but their imagination to begin with; religion was the art of selling the imagination.

When I saw those carpets, I realised that this city was in the grip of an accursed, imaginative soul. I had never before been overwhelmed by the power of the imagination like that. I had read many books about this city, from the memoirs of ancient explorers and travellers to more recent books by twentieth-century Kurdish historians. Neither the old nor the new histories of this city appeared to address the subject – and underneath a city that reveals nothing of its fantasies must lurk danger.

Don't think me an indifferent person making empty statements. I've walked the length and breadth of this city, street by street, alleyway by alleyway. On the surface, it does not show any signs of the imagination. I've always wondered where the imagination disappears to. Don't assume that I hold the imagination in such high esteem that

I want statues erected to pay homage to it. No, despite all my interest in and respect for it, I am scared of it.

There is nothing more dangerous than imagination when it becomes a secret force. I have talked to the Politburo, and one-to-one with His Excellency the Leader, about this dangerous issue. If we can't tell what people are thinking, a precarious future awaits us. A furtive fantasy becomes a deadly obsession, an illicit desire, with no one able to see how deep or how far it goes. When I walk around this city for a long time, when I see its domes, minarets and citadels, when I stroll through its cold and messy qaysaris, I can sense the danger of the hidden imagination: in this city, imagination always works furtively.

When I used to sleep with my tall, fair, beautiful wife at night, I had few fantasies. Her body appeared cold, devoid of imagination and without charm. I once slept with a loose woman, the wife of an old acquaintance from my youth. She didn't have even a thousandth of my wife's beauty, yet it was entirely different – pleasant, somehow. I visited a mullah I knew, someone whose honesty and piousness I completely believed in. I told him the entire story. I told him that fantasies drove humans to illicit, sinful thinking. This city had no imagination. I asked him where human imagination goes when it disappears.

'All these fantasies vanish, then re-emerge as lust and sinful desires, as something that cannot be tamed or controlled,' said the mullah. 'But stifled and concealed desires are better than those that are free and wild.'

The mullahs and politicians believe that this city, with its barren imagination, its timorous, ancient façade, is less likely to breed unhealthy obsessions and illicit desires than other cities with less restrictive ways. But I know that imagination does not die – like a horrible, untreatable cancer, it grows bigger and bigger from below.

I wanted to buy, know and befriend all the imaginative people, and if that did not work, to wipe them off the face of the Earth. It was I who dispatched three loyal men to buy the carpet factory, three people I knew would drive a hard bargain. The inflexibility of the unfortunate factory owner brought him considerable trouble. I don't subscribe to killing unless faced with someone acting as obstinately as a whickering horse. No, I don't subscribe to killing; but when it comes to someone behaving like that, I have no mercy in my heart. I lose all control, and then horrible things can be expected of me.

On what would turn out to be the very last time Abdulaqadir Niya refused to sign the sale contract, I began to cry in front of him; I wanted to let him go – I respect the lives of other people. I want to live in peace in a secure and orderly country, a peaceful Kurdistan for all of us. That is my wish. I've never wanted anyone to die. As man has a tongue as well as money, he can do everything he needs without killing. The more money a man is willing to spend, the less he needs knives and guns. Nothing has spared history from violence like money, but the commotion made by my witless partners and led some of the people in the Politburo who were aware of the matter (and feared that the rumours might end up tarnishing the reputation of His Excellency the Leader) to have Abdulaqadir Niya killed and buried in the secret graveyard.

On that occasion, I made my final attempt with Niya, to no avail. I said, 'You are now responsible for your own death. I've done everything I can.' After they killed him, my three loyal men had no trouble buying the factory from his shrewd, white-haired wife. She lost her mind after her husband's death. No, my real ordeal started when Trifa Yabahri fled the factory. Like a creature alert to traps near or far, like a wild bird that can discern a hunter or at a distance, she left the factory at once. I looked for her everywhere. Although Niya's death had made things easier for me, I cried before the Leader. I had to find Trifa Yabahri all the same. I had to see with my own eyes the imagination and force she used to make her miracles.

One night, I visited Attar and begged him to find her. I offered him handsome rewards. I knew what he was capable of. I told him, 'Avoid violence, hatred and cruelty; otherwise, do what you like.'

When I bought the factory, my aim was to purchase Trifa Yabahri's imagination. I did not expect anything from the soulless machines and ungifted weavers who merely followed catalogue designs and wove their carpets without imagination. Attar and I looked desperately for that woman. We left no stone unturned in our search – and yet, we failed to find her. Attar even employed Shahryar the Glass-Eyed, but without results.

By the time I found out where Trifa Yabahri was, I had already sold the carpet factory. Even so, I was still frantically keen on buying her imagination. I worked regularly on detailed plans. I wanted all the imagination of this city to feed into my plans. Daily, I pleaded: 'Almighty God, assist me both in virtue and in vice.'

HASAN-I TOFAN AND MURTAZA SATAN
EARLY SUMMER 2004

The early Eighties saw the beginning of my active involvement in the assassination cells. I was still a young man back then, guided by darkness, ambiguity and secrecy.

At the time, I didn't pay much attention to what the other killers looked like. To be honest, back then the appearances of human beings were not important or interesting. They seemed identical and charmless to me. As time passed, I contemplated the faces of my old friends more and more. There were some among them who were bloodthirsty in practice, but angelic in appearance. Some of them were terrifying in both aspects.

I myself didn't belong to either type. Ghazalnus told me that I was an imaginary killer. As I got to know him, his strange efforts to cleanse my soul began. At first, I only listened to the ghazals he read out to Sabri in Hazarbagh. At night, as I made my way to the flowerbeds, I would hide among the elaborate, winding paths of the garden. Listening to Ghazalnus was like travelling back to a more innocent time, when gardens were appreciated and poetry recited in them.

Listening to those poems brought out in me a strange desire for wine, prompting me to seek inebriation when I was already intoxicated. When dawn slowly brought the night to an end, I would come out of my hiding place and pretend I had happened upon those paths by chance. Ghazalnus believed that the ten years I had spent in the assassination cells were imaginary years, which I had created to hurt myself, and that I was nothing but an imaginary assassin. This fixation of his drove me crazy at first, but Ghazalnus believed that I had found my essence in this garden and should not lose it. He believed that I had been a rosewater-maker all my life, and that all the stories of murder, blood and cruelty were born out of the imagined and evil half of myself, which sought only to hurt my good half.

One day, when I was going out of my mind, I went to see Shibr to ask for his help. At the time, he knew nothing about Ghazalnus. There is an obsession in my heart that I must share with you,' I told him. 'Sometimes I feel as though I've never been a murderer, as if those ten years were just a fantasy, that in those ten years, I didn't hurt a soul or kill anyone … that I am only an imaginary murderer.'

Shibr regarded this as strange. 'Hasan-i Pizo, a man cannot change his past. He can object to it, but he can't erase it,' he said.

Still, the idea that I was an imaginary murderer helped me strike out in a new direction. The truth is, I couldn't hold on to the idea for very long. I would still take the pistol out at night and look at it. The pistol was my consolation. It always gave me the proof that I had been a real murderer. It felt so friendly and comfortable in my hand; it was as if it had missed my touch.

I couldn't understand how Ghazalnus gathered all that mercy, imagination and love together. I couldn't be like that. I couldn't love the world, the gardens, the light and the stars that way. He was someone who loved everything in this world with exceptional vigour. During the long period that I listened to his voice, I came to understand that the power of his ghazals was not only in the meaning and form of the poems, but also in their deep truthfulness, which came from his heart. Sometimes I thought someone from the heavens was talking to me, someone from the furthest part of the heavens. (Later, I learned that most of those who listened to Ghazalnus reflexively looked towards the sky.) Many times when we walked through the garden, I believed that he was right, that I really had been an imaginary murderer. One night I began to think that even Shibr had been an imaginary murderer, that he, too, was trapped in his own illusions. Although I had seen the bullet scars on his body many times, I told myself that those were scars of imaginary bullets.

After the disappearance of Murad Jamil's corpse, my life was divided between Hazarbagh, the dark plains and the cold streets of the city. As the story of the book had entered our heads, I had been doing a lot of work with the junior Notebook-Keepers, who needed my detailed planning and guidance to reach their destination without fear and return safely. I also took Shibr with me to the Idle Murderers' Club twice a week to look for the barons and see Ja'far-i Magholi.

One night I was talking to two old friends in the club's back garden. I overheard someone nearby say, 'Oh God, how poor and friendless he is! I swear by the taste of wine, he has drunk so much he has lost all his ties to this Earth. I swear by the tinkling of the wineglass, he's not aware of himself. Let's all pray for him. May God have mercy upon him and pray that he regains consciousness.'

It was the same voice that, a few nights earlier, had consoled the young man on the plains. His way of talking was unique, so unusual and unfeeling, that I recognised it immediately. I was certain I was not mistaken. It was him: the same man who had sworn by the bulbuls and nightingales in the dark. When I turned to look, I saw a tall man in traditional Kurdish garb, sporting an unkempt moustache. His thick eyebrows reminded me of some of the old assassins.

'That's Murtaza Satan,' Shibr told me quietly. 'He's one of the most dangerous servants of the barons. He has a special relationship with Awrahman Najib, who is now known as the Baron of Porcelain.'

The Baron of Porcelain was a powerful glass merchant. He had an office in Tehran and another in Dubai, and held a very high position in the Party. With the support of the likes of Murtaza Satan and the large network he controlled inside the parties, he completely dominated the country's glass market. He had crushed the smaller businessmen, sidelining them one after another through beatings and intimidation, and by subjecting them to strict trading conditions.

I was surprised to hear Shibr say that Murtaza was a close ally of Ja'far-i Magholi, and that Magholi was one of his strongest backers. He also spoke in detail about the heavy speculation that Murtaza might be behind the frequent killings of women in the city. Despite his joviality, there was something threatening in his voice, and in his appearance and his stare. Although nothing bad ever came from his mouth, although he laughed, he couldn't help looking like a dangerous beast.

According to Shibr, he had once been a successful theatre actor. Later on, during Saddam's dictatorship, he was imprisoned for six years for helping a friend stab his wife to death. After he was released from prison, in the strange club that brought together the worst of the city's creatures, amid the cigarette smoke, the smell of arrack and the wine-flavoured breath of these men who talked about money, women, senior officials and infighting between the government and wings of the Party, he found a place for himself thanks to his kinship with the Baron of Porcelain. Now they all saw him as the latter's favourite dog.

Murtaza was often found with the Billiard Group, and interacted with them a lot. To understand the Billiard Group, you need to learn a little bit about the internal divisions of the club. I had discerned that there was a secret division of labour, a hierarchical classification. The lowest men in the lowest level were known as the 'Castrated' – a group made up of servants, workers, guards, journalists and spies working for the barons. Anyone who entered the game started at 'Castrated' level and slowly made his way up.

'Hasan-i Pizo,' Shibr explained, 'when someone first joins the group, there is an elaborate process to castrate his mind, imagination and mercy. Later, they give him a grade and a name. That grade determines all his subsequent success.'

The next level up was 'Anise', a classification I initially found meaningless and strange. Later, I learned that the members of this group were tasked with looking out for unusual, often shadowy ideas popping up in the market. They recommended the names of original goods to their contacts abroad, and had items recommended to them in turn. They were not wealthy, but could sniff out profitable businesses. They listened and watched, touched, sniffed and tasted. As soon as they got wind of a unique idea or project, they quickly informed the barons, who, in turn and with the support of a few small groups, either became co-partners or completely hijacked the project through intimidation. Because members of the group were always in the bazaar, they began to smell of spices, ginger and aniseed – hence the group's name.

A third group, one of the most dangerous in the club, was the Billiard Group. Its members had a complex job: it fell to them to ensure that prices either skyrocketed or plummeted. They raised and dropped currency rates, tampered with the price of properties and real estate, increased and decreased the value of sites according to set plans. They influenced the price of oil, slashed car prices, closed and opened border crossings. They were among the most powerful members, and received orders directly from the Politburo, the Party's senior leadership and the influential barons.

'Most of those who go on to become senior officials, members of various councils and influential officers start from here,' Shibr told me. 'They emerge from this group and might end up as ministers, depending on their potential. These people see the whole country as a billiard pool. They can hit any ball they like. We are all, in one way or another, balls on their table.'

When members of this group came to the club in the evening, they showed much solemnity and behaved like politicians. Their politeness and grandeur were enviable. Yet, later on, they would drink so much that they would soil themselves. I was astonished that these men who smelled perennially of urine, cigarettes and arrack could play such an important role in running the city. Murtaza often sat at their tables. On some nights, when he became drunk, he would climb onto their tables and dance there. Every time I saw him, I remembered the scene from that night; the words I had heard in the dark rang in my ears. I was constantly looking at him with bewildered eyes. Sometimes our eyes met, and we exchanged smiles. I didn't know whether I was watching him or he was watching me.

One night I felt Murtaza Satan staring at me intently. I was certain that there was an overpowering fear in his eyes. From that night on, I sensed that he was running away from me, that he was avoiding me;

but I followed him like a sparrowhawk swooping down on a rabbit. I was not scared of his games, acting and disguises. Like someone keen to discover a chameleon's true colour, I followed him, my only hope to make him see the real colour of his own soul, to make him feel that he, too, was a billiard ball – one that I had come from afar to strike.

ATTAR'S RETURN

When Ghazalnus and Trifa were looking for volunteers to help them with the writing of the longest book in history, many unique people entered their lives. First came two brothers from a faraway land, who said they were looking for inspiration to continue their work. After a long journey through the northeastern regions, they had come to the city. They had a great ability to turn dry, barren lands green. If these two brothers stood in a field for any length of time, it would become lush with vegetation. The two men had power over nature. Wherever they went, they filled the place with greenery. Since the early Nineties, they had taken part in rebuilding many villages, staying in each one for a season. Their work was to look at fields and trees sympathetically, to sing for the plants and flowers so they would turn green again. It would take weeks to see the fruit of their labour, but the outcome was always certain.

An unidentified person had sent the brothers to Ghazalnus to receive more inspiration, so they settled at his place and began the work of reviving their surroundings, starting with the ruined villages, fields and farms on the outskirts of the city. When they first appeared at the house, dirty and tired, their beards overgrown, they seemed confused. Ghazalnus and Trifa received them, prepared baths and invited them over to the dinner mat. Ghazalnus read his poems for them, which gave them a fresh surge of energy. He led the visitors to a private, tucked-away room and invited them to rest and change out of their work clothes.

The sudden arrival of the brothers made Ghazalnus's and Trifa's lives very busy. For many days, the four of them would disappear into the plains, villages and farms near the city. They looked for the barren orchards and fields of poor farmers in order to revive them. Every evening, the two 'Green Brothers', known to all as the Dulbar brothers, would return to Ghazalnus when they had finished reviving an orchard, in order to rest for a while and listen to the ghazals that re-energised their souls.

At that time, Ghazalnus and Trifa thought they had wonderful friends. Many people came to them from around the world, the boundaries of their imaginative empire were expanding and their ghazals attracted people from nearby cities and towns. Over the same period, Trifa's house became a major women's refuge. As far as the neighbours were concerned, it was the home of an elderly married couple, but in reality it sheltered women who had fled their families and had nowhere else to hide. One of the independent women's organisations had assigned a woman named Nawras-i Gul Solav to be in charge of the refuge. She was an adorable, slender girl with light hair and bright eyes. Trifa first met her brother, Majid-i Gul Solav, there. The siblings were on bad terms. They lived with their friendly, jovial mother, but both mother and daughter regarded Majid as a layabout who spent all his time watching films and working on his infinite, meaningless map. There was another brother, too, who had lived in Scotland for many years. Every month he used a private postal system to send Majid a number of films and English-language cinema magazines. The family didn't have much money. They lived on their father's pension, Nawras's modest salary and a small contribution from their exiled brother. Majid-i Gul Solav did nothing except walk around dressed like an English lord. He had been unemployed all his life; a bit of a loner, he had never really had any friends either.

When Trifa visited Nawras at home for the first time, Majid had just started teaching the blind children. Right from the start, Trifa perceived him as an arrogant, selfish person who was nevertheless rather sensitive and charming. The young man's strengths were not limited to his exaggerated dress style and composure; he exhibited a certain charisma, a hidden appeal that was hard to pin down.

After a few friendly visits, Nawras-i Gul Solav and Trifa Yabahri became devoted friends who could confide everything in each other. One day Trifa and Nawras opened the door to Majid's room. Behind the door lay a whole other world. Trifa was stunned at the sight of it. A hand-drawn map stretched across all four walls, an extraordinary, eternal map that could be populated infinitely with imaginary cities, villages and plains.

The unusual, poetic place names dazzled Trifa: the Land of the Leopard; the Sea of Doubt; the Path of Dreams; the City of Waiting; Hope Mountain; Doves' Shore; Violinistan; the Blue Butterfly; the Garden of the Stars' Suicide; the Lily Pond; the Town of Blooms; the Stream of Sadness; the Tiger Garden; and many others. One glance at the map told Trifa she was dealing with an Imaginative Creature, one living aloof from the world and unaware of all the other Imaginative Creatures.

As well as the map, his room was full of hundreds of film videos and English, Arabic and Kurdish books, organised into an impressive library. The room was so clean and neat that it felt particularly inviting. When Trifa left, she was certain that she had seen a rare and exceptional world. When she arrived home, she began immediately to recount the story of the unusual map to Ghazalnus; he was so excited to hear about this young man with the inifinite map that he wanted to go and see it right away.

The following day, Trifa enrolled Blind Bulbul in Majid-i Gul Solav's fantasy school. Majid's serene, respectful way of interacting with women attracted Trifa's attention. His lessons involved travelling on an imaginary ship through an infinite realm. The first day Blind Bulbul attended Majid's lessons, Trifa waited impatiently for his return. No sooner did he walk through the door than she made him recount his experience in detail, but he was too excited and stunned by it all to be able to convey it: the child had genuinely travelled through another realm. For the first time, he felt he had seen things in the darkness of his blindness. He described, in detail, gardens, bodies of water and tulip beds. He spoke about fabled birds, multi-headed horses and talking snakes that existed only in faraway forests and imaginary lands. All this excited Ghazalnus even further and made him want to befriend Majid even more.

One day, he appeared at the door of Majid-i Gul Solav's imagination class. The two men took a long walk together, and realised they understood each other's language very easily. Ghazalnus read some of his ghazals to his new friend; they had such a huge impact on Majid that he put his arms around Ghazalnus and said: 'With the help of your ghazals, I could expand the boundaries of my map indefinitely.' That same day, without any hesitation, he invited Ghazalnus to see the map.

Majid had never before opened his bedroom door to anyone. No one had yet seen the map with his knowledge and approval. And yet he invited Ghazalnus in. Such an invitation was tantamount to a mutual vow, a declaration of undying friendship. The world Majid had created was hundreds of times bigger than the imaginary realms Ghazalnus had seen, but the latter was certain they had both passed through similar forests, plains, gardens and lakes. He was certain that the imagination was a real continent, that most of those who travel it see the same things without ever encountering one another.

After four years, Nawras-i Gul Solav invited Trifa to her home once again, into the midst of the sad girls who lived there in secret. The day she crossed the threshold, the house was full of the scent of tears, of ghost-like girls, girls being hunted by their fathers, brothers and husbands, daggers and other weapons in hand; a group of women who, apart from this secret house, had not an inch of land on Earth to shelter them. Trifa considered herself incredibly lucky to be in a position to save the souls of these, hopeless, terrified girls for whom the house was the very last resort. She started to visit them frequently, even sleeping over some nights. They were a group of prisoners forced to remain so for ever.

From the very first day, Trifa was keen to acquire a loom to teach the girls to weave rugs and carpets. She was certain it was the only thing that would make them, and her, happy. Nawras was astonished when she saw that, in a very short space of time, Trifa had had basic machinery installed in the basement, adapting the space into a workshop with looms and other weavers' tools.

The first year of the new century seemed calm and trouble-free. Many new guests visited their house, and the community of Imaginative Creatures was expanding all the time. Trifa's conscience was clear. She felt buoyed by her work. Her life consisted of constant play with the children, and a motherly concern to teach and protect them; then, at night, she spent hours talking on the phone to Nawras. She was happy that she had a busy life, that there was always something to do. Yet despite her peace of mind, her fears appeared to be increasing. She felt as if a monster was lying in wait, ready to attack her. On some nights, when she left her home-cum-refuge to make her way back to the children, this dark, primitive fear would so overwhelm her that she had to jump quickly into a taxi to get back home. Nor was her phobia limited only to her: she felt the monster also wanted to eat the children, to eat Ghazalnus, to eat Nawras-i Gul Solav and the fleeing women.

Her fears always took strange forms or emerged as sinister predictions. One morning she woke up and said to Ghazalnus, 'You must hide all the books of ghazals. You must take them to a place no human hands can reach. You must take them away from this house. I've had a dream. Do you understand? I've had a dream about these books, that they will be burned. I've had a dream. You should take the books to a place known to no one but you. Not even I should know about it.'

Trifa's request was so fervent that Ghazalnus could not ignore it. One day, he transferred all his manuscripts to an unknown place, somewhere only he knew about. Only many years later did it transpire how accurate and farsighted Trifa's fear had been.

Four years after Ghazalnus hid the contents of his library and several months before the discovery of Murad Jamil's body, Attar and his ugly mug reappeared. It was 2003. His head appeared bigger now, and his look even greedier and sadder than before. One evening, without prior appointment or notice, he entered Ghazalnus's home, leaving his new Toyota pickup parked outside. He was accompanied by a small, thin man who, many years earlier, had been a sickly novice butcher. Seven years had passed since Trifa had fled the carpet factory, and yet seeing Attar again startled her. He seemed to know many things, but finding Trifa in this house took him by surprise. His unpleasant, ironic smile horrified and stunned her. That day she understood that Attar would pursue her no matter how long she lived.

Ghazalnus had not seen Attar for a very long time. After taking Darsim Tahir from him, he had only run into him once – at Husni the Imaginative's home, where they had greeted one another cordially. On the other hand, he knew the small man accompanying him very well. He was Aziz the Castrated, who had progressed gradually from novice butcher to major property dealer. Now he was someone the top tycoons paid attention to. His knowledge of real estate, farms, gardens and agricultural regions was unrivalled. Aziz was one of those traders who provided a furtive front for the limitless wealth of a senior politician.

That evening, the two men seemed to be on a charm offensive. 'Brother Ghazalnus, great teacher of the imagination,' said Attar, placing a hand on Ghazalnus's shoulders, 'we've come to your house on an important mission. I hope you will not break our hearts. We bring the message of a man who doesn't like to be seen in public. This dear brother, Citizen Aziz, is in charge of the gentleman's wealth. I hope we can arrive at a price that is satisfactory to all of us.'

Attar had honed his buying and selling skills a great deal in the intervening years. He had cobbled together a private and secret network of informers whose influence and reliability could match that of the state police and the security apparatuses. As always, his ears were dewy, and there was a drop of black sweat on the tip of his nose. He had to take out a handkerchief frequently to wipe his forehead during negotiations, drawing attention to the fact that he was losing more and more hair with each passing year. It seemed that very soon, not a single black hair would be left on his head.

'We all know you have a huge library of ghazals,' said Attar with his customary insight. 'For many years now, you have been reading ghazals from this library, constructing beautiful fantasies. I've heard that, through poetry, you convert unhappiness to happiness and sadness into a type of rosewater that soothes the soul. I am incompetent when it comes to poetry and literature. In fact, I can make neither heads nor tails of literature; I don't understand its value. Clearly, I deal in anything in the world that can be bought and sold. Business, my friend, is life's engine, oh yes. In my humble opinion, business is higher even than love. Without business there's no bazaar, and where there's no bazaar, there's no life. I believe the bazaar, like literature, is a gauge. It measures development and progress. A nation that doesn't have bazaars or literature is a dying nation. Bazaars and literature are the criteria for everything else. You might have a different take on this, which I will very happily listen to. I've heard a lot about the reputation of your ghazals, and have even listened to a few recited here and there. Still, my friend, a goldsmith knows the value of gold, as the saying goes. Today we're here at the request of one of the gentlemen of this city: a kind and educated young man, an art lover. We're here to buy a section of your ghazal library from you. Yes, my friend, the huge, rare and unrivalled ghazal library, which I've heard described as a great national treasure, should be preserved in a special place. This is the proposal of a gentleman who would like to make you rich, and protect your literature from abrupt and sudden misfortune. He's a man who does not want to be seen in public or to be known to others for personal reasons, but we are all certain of his good intentions.'

Ghazalnus had never considered the notion of someone wanting to buy his ghazal library. The proposal was sudden, odd and suspicious. The books were not his property, so he couldn't sell them. Right from the outset, he had felt the ghazals belonged to all imaginative people, to the dwindling category of those who could still be intoxicated by poetry. It belonged to those who could shut their eyes and dream about another world, albeit impossible and unreal. The ghazals were his guide to this city, to its narrow and dusty streets, to the sad lives of its women and the dormant dreams at the bottom of men's souls. Without the ghazals, he could not understand the city's filth and blood and suffering, could not comprehend its disappointed sons, weep for its female lovers, befriend its white-haired, elderly men, or win the trust of its older women. What would happen now if the ghazals ended up in the hands of a trickster who only deceived and tormented these souls? What would happen if the ghazals ended up in the hands of someone who, assisted by imagination, made people forget the truth? The magic of the imagination lies in helping us understand the land we live in. What would happen if the ghazals ended up in the hands of someone who did not want to understand love, or a lover who was lying, someone who believed they were above love? What would happen if they ended up in the hands of people with more imagination than love or kindness?

For years, he had done everything he could to ensure that the ghazals helped people to fantasise with more clarity and come closer to love, to open their souls to their fellow man. What would happen if someone burned the ghazals, or usurped them, or used them to hunt down the Beloved? What would happen if they used the ghazals to secure power? For the imagination has the power to completely change the world.

How could he now make these people understand that they were asking to buy something that wasn't for sale? Ghazalnus had never in his life expected someone to want to buy the ghazals; but now he became convinced that an unknown person was after his imagination.

'My dear Attar,' he said calmly, 'I understand that you are an intelligent tradesman with many skills. I know that the bazaar of our city has become like a circus, and every strange person and moving creature can poke their nose in. The bazaar has expanded terribly. One almost feels ashamed not to be a shopkeeper. I know that everything is for sale in our city, from bottlecaps to human beings. But dear Attar, my fellow city dweller, there are things that cannot be sold, things that are connected to a person's sense of purpose. Would a novelist give his novel to someone who didn't know where his words and characters and their sufferings sprang from? The power of certain things lies in their sources, in the hands of he who wields them.

'I have no intention of selling the manuscripts of my ghazals, because they cannot be sold. All I can do is bequeath them – and only to lovers. The ghazal library would turn to dust if you touched it when you weren't in love. My ghazal library works in such a way that only I can reach its pages. It is a message from someone who made me responsible for it. So, my dear Attar, tell that innocent and honest gentleman that my library is rich in imagination, and is itself imaginary, that it isn't for sale. You may listen to its ghazals, but they cannot be bought. You can't buy ghazals, but you can live in them.'

It was impossible for the big-headed, dewy-eared Attar and Aziz the Castrated to understand Ghazalnus's words. They believed that the biggest problem any transaction in the world could face was two people not agreeing on a price. As far as Attar was concerned, there was nothing in the world that was not for sale, provided you paid the right price. Aziz the Castrated, dressed in a tight mirakhani, seemed to have been given free access to funds. He started by offering small farms, but in the face of Ghazalnus's resistance he progressed to large tracts of land measuring thousands of acres, safes full of money, vaults full of jewels and pearls – all to no avail. Aziz the Castrated looked rather like a sultan's emissary asking for the hand of a princess.

That day, taking their leave of Ghazalnus, they told him: 'The art-loving gentleman is so deeply in love with your ghazals he will pursue every avenue to pay for a change of heart.'

'Tell the gentleman that poetry does not belong to a single human being,' said Ghazalnus, putting his hands on the shoulders of the sad brokers. 'No one can own poetry. No one can register ghazals to his name, like real estate. All one can do is to use poetry, ghazals and the imagination to avoid losing the world and losing oneself.'

MAJID-I GUL SOLAV MEETS THE BARON
OF IMAGINATION FOR THE FIRST TIME
MAJID-I GUL SOLAV, SUMMER 2004

The party I'd been invited to by the Baron of Dolls was a big family affair, organised by the baron on the occasion of the return of one of his sons from Europe. Really, it was one of several gilded traps to force his son into taking a daughter of one of the high-ranking mirs as his bride. Back then, such parties were common. Families whose sons returned from Europe for a visit held them so that the young men could find a suitable woman to marry. Most of Nwemiran's women were there, all dressed in their finest, most elegant clothes.

Although I had lived in this filthy city all my life, I didn't know such parties were possible – even in Nwemiran. I arrived a bit late at the Mirwari Club, which was hosting the event, so that I wouldn't look like a fool or find myself in the limelight. When I arrived at the hall, it was full of perfumed women in sparkling clothes, but the servants had not yet started serving and the band had not begun to play. It was an unusual occasion for me. I had never seen so many beautiful women together in one place in my life. They sat serenely at their tables. Their make-up was still fresh, and their perfumes strong. The entire hall was suggestive of invisible sin.

When the Baron of Dolls saw me, he opened his arms and embraced me warmly. 'My son, enjoy the evening,' he whispered into my ear. At the time, I was secretly pleased whenever the baron referred to me as his son. I went to sit at a table at the back of the big hall like a hopeless, awkward person. There was only a smattering of other people by themselves, like me, as most men had come with their wives and daughters. Men who were there without women sat either at the very front or at the very back of the hall, as if to make it quite clear from the outset that we were unaccompanied. This was inhumane discrimination, a huge exclusion, but it did have one benefit: some of the women and girls paid us more attention. Because I had worn my best clothes and combed my hair for once, I stood out among all the young men in the hall. Before too long, another one of the loners took a seat next to mine. He introduced himself in an assured, harsh voice. He was called Pers – Pers the Engineer. He threw me a suspicious, unpleasant look.

'You're the young man with the stories, aren't you?' he said. I didn't know what he meant. But without awaiting an answer, he pressed on: 'I know you. I know you very well. The Baron of Lakes is my uncle. I know you tell stories to children at night. I know. No need to be afraid. No need at all.'

I looked at him with surprise. 'I'm not afraid. Why should I be?' I said.

'I'm not one of the barons either,' he said. 'I'm an electrical engineer. I work for them. Did you think I was one of them? Is that what you thought? I know it is. I'm not, though. I just work for them. I install and fix generators for them. I supply their electricity. I do all sorts of things for them. I'm like you; I am allowed to enter the homes of the barons.'

He smiled an off-putting, sardonic smile and whispered: 'I, too, can enter all the rooms. I can even go into the bathrooms and toilets. Consider me your brother; yes, a brother,' he added, putting his hands on my shoulders reassuringly. 'No need to be afraid of me. Me, of all people. Do you understand? Think of me as a brother. I hate them too, but you must be careful. Be very careful.'

I looked at him, but said nothing.

'Look, can you see the Baron of Parrots?' he whispered in my ear. 'I know you don't know him. You don't know anyone. You're new. The Baron of Parrots is one of the richest barons. He repeats everything the Leader says, like a parrot. That's why they call him the 'Baron of Parrots'. What about the Baron of Deer? I greatly admire the Baron of Deer. Do you know why he's called that? No? Because no one else in the world can hunt deer like him. He's the best deer hunter. He could hunt them as they run. I haven't seen it myself, but I have heard about it. It's said he can even mount and tame them, among other things.'

He wanted me to say something. To dispel any suspicion, I said, 'Where's the Baron of China? Can you show me the Baron of China?'

While we were chatting, the noise level and the sound of murmuring gradually rose in the hall. Members of the band occasionally tested their instruments. I couldn't fully understand what was going on because of the mild voices of a few girls and the laughter of two fat women in front of us.

When I asked Pers about the Baron of China, he scratched his head and said, 'Hmm, the Baron of China? I can't see the Baron of China.

He was the first person to open a trade route to China, but he's no good. He has grey hair and small eyes. He looks like a broken clay urn glued back together.'

I didn't care what he looked like. I wanted to capitalise on the evening to find a lead to the Baron of Chickens' wife. Pers went on to point out most of the barons over the course of the night. He knew what was going on in their lives. He knew how they had become rich, and the sources of their wealth. I never said anything that could have aroused his suspicion about my true intentions.

The party slowly got underway, and the earlier peace and quiet vanished. Calmly and with all the dignity of a prince, I took a sip from my beer. I was happy and alert. I needed to be careful not to do something that could cost me my place there. Serenity was not only my forte; it was the cornerstone of my life's philosophy. I felt that, as the party got into full swing, psychological barriers lifted and the curtain of shyness thinned. Many of the girls and women inside the hall were looking at me. Some of the men were so drunk from the outset that I didn't know how they would manage to regain consciousness. The sound of the music was so powerful and nauseating that only disorderly dancing was possible. The dancers seemed almost to shed their human skins altogether. Pers was drinking steadily, and growing sadder. It was evident that he was the type of bad-tempered drinker who would be overcome with sadness and, when drunk, could think of nothing but his life's ills. Despite all he had drunk, however, he remained very alert.

'Don't assume just because I'm the nephew of the Baron of Lakes, everything's fine,' he said every now and then. 'What use does a pimp like him have for me? I am nearly going deaf, spending all my time, day and night, with the generators, the smell of benzene and the roar of engines. Yes, the Baron of Lakes. Sa'ol-i Khila Ba Ron,[16] has named himself "Prince of Lakes", "Master of the Waters", "Baron of the Seas". He has an office. Ha! Sa'ol-i Khila Ba Ron has a secretary. To tell you the truth, I have fallen for his secretary. Should I point her out to you? Yes? Would you like to get to know her?'

He showed me a slender, extremely lovely girl, wearing a pair of jeans and a light red T-shirt. He said, 'That's the Baron of Lakes' secretary. Look at her and tell me what you think. I won't say a word.'

All the time he was talking, another girl, standing next to the secretary, gazed at me with warm eyes. She was slender and tall. She had short, blonde hair, lightly permed. She had pale eyes, the likes of which I had only seen in films. I swear, she was just like Jessica Lange in *The Postman Always Rings Twice*. The same look, the same erotic sparkle, the same magic that makes you weak in the knees. She was the type of woman I saw in my dreams. Her expression was so striking that I thought I could only have seen her somewhere in my imaginary realm. As the party began to heat up, Pers the Engineer and I moved from here to there several times – now standing, now sitting, leaving our spot and returning to it, going over to the buffet table laden with big plates of salad, disrupting the line of dancers as we went. All this time, I felt the girl was seeking me out, looking at me more than at anyone else amid all the hustle and bustle of the hall.

'Do you know the girl standing next to your uncle's secretary?' I asked Pers. 'The one in the pink dress and white headband?'

'You mean Tishkan Tahir?' Pers replied. 'She's new in the area. She's said to be working at the Baron of Civilisation's house. Take my advice, don't even ask about such girls. The Baron of Civilisation is the biggest womaniser of them all, you see. When it comes to escorts, prostitutes and loose women, he's the biggest expert you'll find in the whole region. He has his own women from Basra to the Bosphorus. He believes that sex is integral to civilisation and to appearing civilised. That's why they call him the 'Baron of Civilisation'. He's not married yet. As far as I know, Tishkan is the daughter of a friend of his. She's rumoured to be the daughter of a Kurdish businessman, one of those who settled in Baghdad after the uprising. Her father was killed by the Americans during the capture of Baghdad. She was his only child, and the baron keeps her as a nanny to his eight-year-old niece, whose name is Sewan. To be honest, I don't know if this is all true or not, but that's what I've heard.'

Sewan was one of the children I told stories to. At that point, I had been to tell her stories twice, but had not seen anyone else in her house on either visit. I couldn't get the beautiful blonde woman out of my head. As a distraction, I asked my new friend, 'My dear Engineer, is there anyone called the Baron of Chickens? Have you heard the name?'

'That's the Baron of Chickens,' Pers said with a smile, pointing. 'That's him.'

He was a very tall man with thinning hair, which, along with his moustache, was dyed such an excessive black that he resembled the wealthy men in old Turkish films. He was dancing hand in hand with several colourfully dressed women.

'Who doesn't know the Baron of Chickens?' Pers said sluggishly. 'He owns half this city.'

To escape any suspicion of harbouring ill intent, I said, 'To tell you the truth, I've heard that Baron of Chickens' wife has a reputation as a good and compassionate woman. I wanted to see her. That's all. Otherwise, I know nothing about that respectable family.'

All the drinking was taking its toll on the engineer. He lifted his head slowly and said, 'The Baron of Chickens' wife is the one in the blue dress, the woman sitting over at the other end with two younger women. She's wearing a padded, quilted coat with sequins.'

That was when I first laid eyes on her. From a distance, she appeared reserved and melancholy; she was several years younger than her husband. She didn't engage with the party as much as the other women. That night was my golden opportunity to make contact with her. There might not be another such chance for a whole year. Pers was drinking steadily. I told him a few times that he would become really drunk if he carried on, but he said he'd been drinking himself insensible since he was sixteen, and he couldn't stop now. I knew he would soon be incapable of coherent speech or thought, and gradually moved away from him to seize a chance to speak to the Baron of Chickens' wife.

Although I barely knew how to dance, I joined the dancers for several full circles. Each time, I placed myself next to someone new, never staying for long with any one person. I had a feeling that the Baron of Chickens' wife wanted to join in. The singer had such an unpleasant voice, and the songs were so dull and silly, that people tried to forget them by focusing on the dance itself. That's why we were all dancing manically, with people stamping their feet so vigorously that I was worried the chandeliers would fall from the ceilings. I felt people were benumbed by the hysterical dancing, so no one was fully aware of what was going on. During one of the dance cycles, I seized the opportunity and placed myself beside the Baron of Chickens' wife. As soon as she took my hand, I told her: 'Khanim, I have important business with you. It is related to the death of Murad Jamil.'

As soon as the words left my mouth, I felt her confusion. A strong shudder passed through her body. Her hands were suddenly cold, and she was speechless. Soon she left the dance floor and returned to her table. I didn't panic, but kept on dancing. I could tell she was looking at me with fearful eyes. At that moment I felt so bad for her that I wanted to calm her down any way I could, especially as she appeared to be an honest woman adorned with a tragic beauty. I was certain she didn't understand my intentions. Her fear was unwarranted. At the time, I didn't know anything about the relations between the Baron of Chickens' wife and Murad Jamil, nothing at all, so I didn't know the effect my words had had on her.

I was thinking about going over to her one way or another when two unexpected things happened all at once that utterly changed the course of my life. After another two cycles of vigorous dancing, I returned to Pers, who was slumped, semi-conscious, in his chair. Detached from the world, he was singing to himself in a deep voice. As soon as I sat down, the blonde who looked like Jessica Lange deliberately passed in front of me and greeted me with a discreet wave. In a quiet voice, she said: 'How are you, young man of the lovely stories?'

She didn't wait for an answer, but carried on walking. I understood that she'd simply wanted to build a small bridge, one we could easily work on and fortify later. I was still looking at the splendid white flower pin in her hair, lost in thought, when a young man appeared before me and said: 'Mr Majid-i Gul Solav, I'm sorry, but I must take you away from the party for a short while. The Baron of Imagination is expecting you in a special room upstairs. He is very eager to meet you.'

I don't know if any of you have ever experienced the sensation of stepping into a room and knowing your life and your fate to have changed completely. I am sure it's a rare occurrence; but that night, when I stepped into the Baron of Imagination's room, it was this feeling that grew in me.

I hadn't heard his name before. His room, which was on the upper floor, was so spacious that it looked like the captain's cabin on an imaginary ship. He owned the Mirwari Club. He was wearing a black silk suit over a dark brown shirt. He was younger and slenderer than all the other barons I'd met, with long, straight eyebrows. He had no moustache, but a mole above his upper lip made him exceptionally handsome. He looked like people did who had lived in the West for a long time before being lured back home by the prospect of a prosperous lifestyle. But I was wrong on that front, for despite his foreign-looking appearance and style, he had never lived in the West. Rather, as he put it, he was this city's eternal son.

That night, I sensed nothing. I didn't know how he thought, or what about. He was one of those souls who cannot be easily understood, regardless of whether they are good or evil. I first thought he had summoned me to talk about some of the stories I had been telling children in Nwemiran. He addressed me as 'the story writer of Nwemiran's children'. I was slowly beginning to be known by such names. Residents of the district called me the 'storyteller to the barons' children'. The Baron of Imagination received me so warmly, it was embarrassing.

'I've heard the reputation of your stories from Nwemiran's children,' he said. 'They all look on you as an angel descended from the sky.'

In fact, I was not even a good storyteller. I couldn't speak bravely and freely with anyone except children. Even now, I can say that what the children of Nwemiran enjoyed was sharing their secrets with me, rather than the stories. The Baron of Imagination introduced himself as 'Sahar Agha'. Some of the Party officials called him 'Mir Sahar'. He had inherited vast plots of land from his feudal grandfathers. He owned real estate in many parts of the city. He had a high standing within the Party. At the time, I didn't know why they called him the 'Baron of Imagination'. He said his biggest interest was reading stories of imaginary journeys, and seemed to be better educated than the other barons. We discussed *Gulliver's Travels*. He had read most of Jules Verne's *Voyages Extraordinaires* as well. We were both in agreement that *Forrest Gump* was the most wonderful Hollywood film of the 1990s, and that travel literature was one of the most fascinating branches of writing.

'You can read about your own truths in travel writing, though not necessarily in all your travels,' he said sadly.

Gradually, we moved on to speak about Sinbad the Sailor. In passing, he mentioned Magellan, his unusual voyages and his crazy obsession with circumnavigating the globe. 'In your view, how many more Earths are there for man to circumnavigate?' he asked in a serious tone.

'Your Excellency Mir Sahar,' I said, 'each human being has a secret Earth inside him, which he can circumnavigate in his own way.'

'Does that mean there is a distant and undiscovered continent inside every person?' he asked, with a dreamy look.

'I believe that's the case,' I said, 'As you put it, every person has a distant and undiscovered continent inside him. But a vast, dark sea always separates us from that continent.'

'Not everyone can cross that sea, though, can they?' he said with a sad sigh.

'That's true, Your Excellency, only a few people can cross it,' I said, letting out a sad sigh of my own.

'Can you help me cross that sea?' he asked me. 'Can you?'

At that moment, I realised that the Baron of Imagination knew much more about me than he had revealed. A moment of silence ensued, in which we looked each other in the eye. He stared at me, and I stared at him.

'Everyone needs someone to help him cross the dark sea inside him,' he said, to ward off my fears.

'Mir Sahar,' I said, trying to change the subject abruptly, 'there are many people who long to invade the sea inside other people's souls. If each human being pays great attention to the sea inside themselves, if they do that, everyone can find the sunken world within.'

As if we both understood each other's gestures, as if those few profound and powerful words were enough for this busy night, the baron calmly accepted my evasiveness and did not ask his unusual question again. He then saw me out with great politeness, excused himself and promised we would meet again soon.

'Mamosta,' he said before I went out of the room, 'I am also in charge of security in Nwemiran. If you need anything, don't hesitate. I am at your service, my dear.'

I didn't know whether the last sentence was a threat or a friendly gesture.

'Your Excellency, I won't hesitate, I assure you.'

When I returned to the hall, I was so confused and muddled up that I couldn't see anything clearly. Panic gripped me. My head was spinning, and I couldn't find my seat. I sat on the first empty chair I came across, and let the singer's dreadful voice torment me. A strange fear gripped me, as if I was under the watchful gaze of many people – all of whom knew my secret. I wanted to run away, to leave Nwemiran to them and their children. Suddenly the Baron of Dolls popped up in front of me and gave me a strange look.

'Are you tired? My son, are you tired?' he asked me.

'Your Excellency,' I said in a quiet voice, 'I've not been to parties like this before. I am not used to listening to such loud music until this time of the night. I would be very grateful if you would be so kind as to have someone accompany me out of Nwemiran. From there, I can go home, as I am familiar with the streets. You are very kind. Too many drinks have simply given me a headache. I feel unusually dizzy and unwell.'

'Too many drinks?' Mir Safin asked in astonishment. 'Too many drinks? Do you call two glasses of beer "too many drinks"?'

There and then, I knew I had been watched throughout the party. How else could the Baron of Dolls have known I had drunk only two glasses of beer, if not for a watchful informant? That night, leaving Nwemiran, I felt I had escaped from Hell. My limitless desire for adventure had waned. I felt the barons could see everything inside my soul, and read my intentions. I asked myself a thousand questions, none of which I could answer. Why had the Baron of Imagination summoned me? Why had he talked about Magellan? Why did he want me to help him see the imaginary sea inside his heart? What about the Baron of Chickens' wife? Could she have said anything to the Baron of Imagination or the Baron of Dolls?

Until then, I hadn't shared anything about my adventures in Nwemiran with my friends. That night, however, I believed the game was slowly becoming dangerous and complicated. The following day, we had a meeting at Ghazalnus's home. I told them proudly: 'My friends, I've been going to the barons for some time without your knowledge. I've found an important job in Nwemiran, and I have been mingling with the children of that district.'

I spoke so proudly that I was as astonished as they were. I pretended to be filled with pride and glory. I felt too ashamed to speak of my fears. I pretended I had no intention of leaving Nwemiran until I learned the secret of Murad Jamil's death.

But in the darkness of my mind, I wished I could run away and head to another place.

THE ENCOUNTER WITH THE
BARON OF COURGETTES

THE REAL MAGELLAN, SUMMER 2004

I can't ride a motorbike here. You need roads, real roads. The difference between an ordinary road and a real one is that the latter makes you feel as if you're up in the sky, that you're free, that there are no limits – just a road to travel on – that you can race along and nothing will get in your way. You feel everything lies open before you, stretching to the end of the universe. *Oh, you wide and infinite, you never-ending autobahns and long motorways – it was you who trapped me in the West.* For twenty-four years, I felt as though I was flying without a backward glance. I drove fearlessly. My dears, riding a motorbike is like listening to music – the same steady rhythm, the same breeze on the face, the same rises and falls, the same loops and often the same plunge, descent and death. But this unhappy city, with its narrow streets and thousands of old cars blocking the roads, holds onto you and won't let you move forwards. To tell the truth, all the cities in the world are ugly, but there are some that don't hold you back: they let you pass through quickly and get away. Passing through others is so slow and bumpy that you have to keep stopping and looking around.

But humans are unfortunate, and there is no escape: each one of us has something that holds us back. Nowadays, I think day and night about the body of the hotelier's unfaithful wife. I feel bound to this city by Baran's disappearance, and by Afsana's body. Everything comes down to these two women, one of whom I have never seen – I don't even know what she looks like. She is invisible and elusive. The other, meanwhile, unashamedly offers me the whole of her body, opening herself up to me completely. The two had me so tied in knots that they bound me to this land for good. Nothing binds men to a place like women. The curse of women and the curse of a place are the same thing. If it weren't for women, men would be bodies always on the move, never coming to rest.

Afsana's soft, smooth body, its slight imperfections that were so captivating, its uneven distribution of cold and heat, thrilled me. A mere look at her sleepy eyes stirred up all the light and dark inside me. Hearing a word spoken in her slightly hoarse voice disturbed my peace. Never before had I felt such a sense of reawakening with a woman; I never knew their bodies to light up such distant places in my soul. But with Afsana, the light in my life started to shift; some illuminated areas of my soul now appeared shaded, while new regions lit up. When we slept together, I felt that the wind of this city was being reborn in my body. The smell of the alleyways awoke. New creatures came into being; huge stars spun through my head and comets struck my body; the air felt like a hand's caress, the wind came to my rescue, the waves spoke right next to me, flowers whipped up a storm in my heart.

You shouldn't assume that these are the fictitious feelings of a man not normally interested in poetry but using it now to describe feelings that cannot be put into ordinary words. These were truths I *lived* with, and witnessed. I cannot describe my relationship with Afsana as one of 'love', as we never spoke a single word about love. Her body was home to the revival of my feelings. It was not love, it was the discovery of a new continent. It was like reaching top speed and feeling your motorbike rise up into the sky, as if you had taken off and found yourself hovering above a magical lake, oasis or city. Afsana was not love. A man like me, who has encountered hundreds of female bodies, cannot talk about love. I can only talk about fascination, discovery and bewilderment.

I have seen many cities, islands and beaches, but none of them smelled as extraordinary as that unfaithful woman. One night, when I slept with her, I felt I could smell a garden, a land with no walls: you would never reach its end no matter how far you travelled. To me, Afsana was not only a woman I could fall in love with, she was the soul of this place. She was the wings on which the sad birds flew over the hotel. Whenever I slept with her, I was sleeping with the throttled desires of this place; her body carried all the gardens, scents and touches that had been buried here for hundreds of years. When I slept with her, I knew I was realising the dreams of the thousands of men who, year after year, had passed through this hotel and seen Afsana. And when she slept with me, it was as if she slept with the thirst of all the men in the world.

The difference between Afsana's body and those of other women was that hers tasted like the discovery of a secret garden. Her body was a garden, and the more you opened it, the more you discovered its bewitching perfumes; when any garden has been abandoned for a very long time, it becomes home to unseen flowers and fruits.

During that period of waiting day and night for Murtaza Satan to reappear, I took to reading all the newspapers I could find. When it comes to understanding the spiritual collapse of a city, nothing can match reading a bad newspaper. Only then does it become clear how rife the stupidity and ignorance are. I don't particularly enjoy reading about stupidity, but I didn't know what else to do to pass the time. I rarely saw Afsana, and when I did, we were both quiet and didn't have much to say to each other.

I was at a strange crossroads. Her magic and the incredible pleasure I knew with her were too big for me to walk away from, but neither could I suggest that she run away with me and live in another country. I felt that what bound me to Afsana only worked, only had meaning, in this city. Before, as I walked this city's disorderly streets, I believed I was really seeing them. Through her body, Afsana showed me that the only real street in this city was made up of her stifled desire. Her body gave off the smell of this place; the smell of dormant fantasies rose from her breasts, her navel and her dark-skinned thighs.

If I had slept with Afsana anywhere else in the world, I might not have tasted that magic, that pleasure. Just as the specific prison in which a prisoner is held gives a unique meaning to his story, so Afsana's effect on me was tied to this place from which I had exiled myself. When I inhaled her body, I took in the sleeping gardens of the city.

One evening, Murtaza Satan finally appeared. He wore a grey suit and smiled his ugly smile. 'I can now take you to the Baron of Courgettes,' he said.

Happy and full of expectation, I followed him without further ado. He sang as he led the way, walking with an elegant gait and swaying as if on a tightrope. Sometimes he looked back at me and laughed aloud. He dragged me first through the bazaar and then through alleyways and streets, for a long time. He sang constantly to himself or whistled, feigning joyfulness. Despite the show he was putting on, he spoke less and appeared more enigmatic than the morning he had first sat in my hotel room. I felt he was singing to stop himself from divulging something if he talked. He was obviously thinking about other things as he sang.

When we'd been walking for an hour, he led me into a building, which looked like an old warehouse that had not been frequented for a long time. It was a mud-brick building with a sagging roof that seemed unlikely to withstand the coming winter rains. We went through many ruined rooms and into a long corridor, leading to two plain concrete rooms overlooking the back yard. In one of those rooms, the Baron of Courgettes was waiting for me.

He was a fair-skinned young man sporting a black moustache. His small eyes, tiny nose and thick cheeks gave him the look of a sad Mongolian. He had huge hands. I had never in my life seen a person with such huge hands. A tall figure, he paced up and down the room. His hair was short and straight. He wasn't at all like the image Murtaza Satan had painted of him. Baran had never mentioned in her letters how she had come to marry this man. In most of them, she referred to him simply as 'my man' or 'my wretched husband'. I had already painted many mental pictures of him, but none came even close to what he looked like. When I entered the room, the envelope containing Baran's letters was on the desk. He shook hands with me and gestured to where I should sit. He put a glass and a bottle of mineral water in front of me.

'So, you are Baran's uncle?' he said, and introduced himself before I could reply. 'I wish we had met under different circumstances.'

There was an artificial calm to his voice. Murtaza Satan wanted to leave, but the baron held him back, saying, 'Dear Murtaza, where are you off to? You're well aware I can't do a thing without you.' He added, with a hint of sadness: 'If Baran was here, she would be pleased to see you.'

'Your Excellency, I've come to learn Baran's whereabouts,' I said coldly. 'I've come back here from the other side of the world to find out where she is. I assume you can help me more than anyone else.'

My rather aloof start frightened the baron slightly. He looked around doubtfully and said: 'Me? I can't help you. I don't know her whereabouts either. Mr Zuhdi Shazaman, let it go. It's a black stain on my honour. Let it go. I don't know what to do, or what to tell people. I did have enough wits about me to say that my wife had gone to Germany to study. I had enough wits about me for that.'

I was certain he was lying. There was something about his voice, hands and looks that told me the Baron of Courgettes was lying.

'Baran was your wife ... you must know what happened to her. You must,' I said as I sat back calmly.

'I came home one night, and Baran had disappeared,' he said. 'I looked for her everywhere in this city and couldn't find her. She must've run away with that despicable man. She trampled on my reputation and honour. She must've sold my love for a cheating bastard who deceived half the girls and women of this city before he met Baran. So you tell me, Uncle dear, tell me, how I can find her?'

'Your Excellency, have you killed Baran or not?' I asked him blankly.

At that point, Murtaza Satan butted in.

'My dear Shazaman, how can you say such a thing?' he said. 'The baron, kill someone? The baron is an angel. Killing? Good Lord … *killing*? How could you think such a thing? Who says Baran Khan has been killed, in any case? Tell me, who says she's been killed? How could such a thing even enter your mind?'

I felt they were both putting on a big show.

'Look, Your Excellency,' I said fearlessly, 'if Baran had run away, if she had wanted to kill herself, if she had gone abroad, she would've let me know. Either she is being kept somewhere where she has no access to anyone, or she's not alive. Someone has killed her and buried her in a shallow grave. You must read the newspapers these days, and know how common these stories are. You see? These are the only two possibilities.'

'There is another,' the baron said. 'That your niece is having so much fun, and enjoying herself so much somewhere, that she has forgotten about us. That's possible too.'

'I am sure that's not the case,' I said angrily. 'She might have liked someone else, but you're not giving a true image of her.'

I deliberately wanted to anger the baron, but whenever I tried to, Murtaza Satan would interrupt and make sure the baron did not stray from their agreed path.

'My dear Shazaman,' Murtaza said. 'Now then, my dear Shazaman. You've been abroad. As God is my witness, you don't understand this city. You're too naïve and well-intentioned. You have such a good heart, you'll find it hard to understand the people of this new world. I swear by any white cloud passing over us right now that you've been living in another world and don't understand this city one bit. Khanim-i Baran … Oh, Khanim-i Baran. You don't know how much the baron loved that woman. You don't know how he protected her even from the air, and was jealous if the breeze so much as touched her. Good Lord, such awful things cross your mind. You don't know that the baron's love for Baran was such that he wanted to buy her weight in gold and give it to her as a gift. I still don't understand what misfortune befell this otherwise prudent woman for her to fall for the tricks of such a vulgar, tactless young man who had absolutely nothing but a handsome face and a silver tongue. Women sometimes bring misfortune upon themselves and their unlucky men. I still can't understand how she could compare the baron to such a tactless, undignified specimen. You don't know the baron. You really don't.'

'So you know the young man with whom Baran was in a relationship? What happened to him? What news of him, my friends?' I said.

The Baron of Courgettes blushed. 'He's also gone missing,' he said. 'I spent a long time looking for him but got nowhere. Nowhere at all.'

'May I know his name?' I asked. 'Can you tell me his name, so that I can look for him too? I don't know his name.'

'What use is his name to you?' the baron said. 'I myself, the security agency and his own family have been searching for him for a long time, but there's no news of him. He's missing. Since the night Baran went missing, he too has disappeared without trace. The story is crystal clear. They've run away together. They headed to another country, another city.'

'But Your Excellency,' I said, 'if I knew the young man's name, I might, just might be able to find him.'

'His name is Murad Jamil,' he said after a moment's hesitation. 'His name's Murad Jamil.'

He uttered the name of the young man with such hatred, I started to doubt him. He was about to say more, but Murtaza Satan barged in again and said, 'I swear by God, by the clean air, I swear by the sleeping flowers, he toyed with the reputation and honour of many noble families in this city. He is one of those cursed people whom God has endowed with a dark gift. I don't understand it, and I can't explain. He was a plague that took Baran away and left, as if sent by Satan's hand. Dear Lord, just like the dirty and ungrateful hand of Satan, who comes to your house and makes off with a precious object.'

I looked at them both with suspicion.

'Or perhaps someone killed Baran and Murad Jamil together. Just perhaps. That's a possibility too,' I said.

'Please, please, honourable Mr Shazaman,' Murtaza said, 'don't say such things in front of the baron. You know nothing about this man's heart. I swear by the sound of the bulbuls of the early morning, I swear by the heartbeat of cuckoos and doves – oh, my dear … my, my. You don't understand this man's love one bit. You have to excuse me, but even if it's only fair that Baran should die, that's not how he sees it.'

'Honourable Baron,' I interrupted Murtaza. 'I won't give up on my niece. I've come back from the end of the world to understand all this.'

I didn't know what else I could do, but I saw deep despair in the baron's eyes. I felt he had invited me there to play a game with me, but because of his ignorance and incompetence, because of his secret hatred, he could not see his game through to the end. He appeared to be a scared young man who wanted me to stay neutral on a dangerous matter. I didn't know Murtaza's place in the game, but I was very alarmed by the baron's narrow eyes.

That night when I returned to the hotel, I felt that someone was following me. I didn't know what the baron was capable of. I decided to start searching for Murad Jamil, but before I could do so, an incident occurred that drove me away from the city for a while.

THE MEMOIRS OF THE
BARON OF IMAGINATION

It is essential that no one recognises you, that you disguise yourself in such a manner that no one knows the sorts of fantasies you harbour. Getting around this city unnoticed isn't easy. Although it's a homogeneous city, the residents of which are all members of the same nation and follow the same religion, and although it's rarely frequented by visitors, and although the levels of crime, theft and vice are low, suspicious eyes follow you around wherever you go. I have the impression the people of this city all consider each other strangers. You rarely meet someone who puts his trust completely in others. On days when I disguised myself as a stranger strolling around the city, there was fear in my heart that someone would attack me in a dead-end alleyway and finish me with a poisoned dagger – that I'd die from a poisoned dagger like the Caliph Omar is a fear I developed as a child, an adverse effect, perhaps, of religion and history lessons at school. Although as I grew up I became a secular person and rose to a senior level in one of the secular parties, I won't deny that my imagination has always been thronged with religious fears and obsessions.

It wasn't any deep, philosophical conviction that made me secular, but fear of the mullahs' voices, the morning call to prayer, the cries of the evening prayers in the month of Ramadan and the morning prayer on the first day of Eid. My father was a religious man who hoped I would become a Muslim leader. He would have been very sad had he lived to see me among all these suited-up, well-educated, urban types. I have wanted to forget about him for a long time now. I often feel that if I don't dedicate myself to the imaginative projects in my head, I shall no longer be able to ignore the disappointed looks he casts me from the grave. I am sure my father – may he be bathed in the mercy of God, and may his grave be filled with light – still has hopes that I'll wake up, re-embrace my faith and become a well-known religious leader. The fear that someone will stab me to death in the dark was partly an extension of my soul's fear of my father.

On some nights, I would bring along bodyguards to accompany me at a distance. I deployed many eyes and ears on the streets to bring me news. The director of the security services, the director general of police and the Party's intelligence chiefs were among my friends, and I had their full support. Each of them wished I'd assign them a task. They all knew how close I was to the Leader, and how much he cared for me, but they couldn't understand what kind of news I was after. The world I was looking for, the land I was keen to discover, was darker and more dangerous than the most remote and inaccessible islands in the middle of an ocean. Through a young cough syrup addict, one of those willing to give everything just to earn enough to buy a bottle, I heard stories of eternal lovers who gathered to hold wonderful rituals and dervish-like dances to the sound of magical verses. Their fascinating if incoherent lines were so powerful and moving that they spurred me on to keep searching for more ghazals. I felt that these ghazals had a strong appeal from the outset. They made people want to hear more and more of them.

I had already heard Ghazalnus's name, but I didn't know what he did. Our statesmen and politicians have never understood the potentially huge role a poet or a man of letters can play. At first I avoided any encounter with him. It's wrong to show your face early on, when your intentions are not good. Far better to work towards your goal from a distance without making yourself known. After Trifa Yabahri's flight, I heeded a great piece of advice from the deceitful Attar, who told me we should have bought Sayyid Qadir Niya rather than his carpet factory. Now I've learned my lesson, and make a habit of buying someone close to the goods before the goods themselves, if at all possible.

On my first strange journey in search of the ghazals, I uncovered mind-blowing secrets. First, two strange people called 'Mamo' and 'Bamo' appeared. They told me they had a number of complete ghazals, the likes of which nobody else possessed. They spoke of Ghazalnus's appearance, and strange nights at the public employees' bar, saying that on those nights they had learned entire ghazals off by heart, and that these could not be found anywhere in the world except in their heads and Ghazalnus's own manuscripts. They put a hefty price on these, received their money and left copies of the poems. It was also they who alerted me to the presence of the Imaginative Creatures. I already knew that there were Imaginative Creatures scattered across the city, but my understanding was they were unaware of each other. However, as if revealing a dangerous secret, as if deliberately wanting to put Ghazalnus's life in jeopardy, they told me: 'Ghazalnus has dangerous fixations, he does. Dangerous fixations.'

They didn't know precisely what those dangerous fixations were, but I was certain that, of course, any human being with such great abilities would have 'dangerous fixations'. When I finally acquired the ghazals, I didn't sleep for several nights running. At first, I could only think about the beauty of the lines, the music of the rhymes and their profound meanings, but when I spent longer pondering them, I realised that their greatest magic lay in the fact that they encouraged you to look closely at the secret of life. Don't look at me like that – as if I were some ignorant fool fixated on the imagination because of my abundant wealth or the idleness induced by a peaceful life. The secret of those fantasies is that they prompt us to take action, to look to our inner selves, to discover the imaginary continent that lies in our own hearts.

After buying the ghazals from Bamo and Mamo, I became obsessed with putting Ghazalnus under surveillance and tracking him down. I felt I'd learned about his story very late in the day. I kept walking along the city's streets, wondering, 'Where's the imagination?' It's just not possible for a city to show no traces of it. It had to be hidden somewhere I couldn't see. In other cities, works of the imagination can be discovered very easily – in the designs of buildings and parks, in the statues adorning those parks, in the eyes of lovers, in libraries, in museums, theatres and opera houses, in women's clothes, in churches, mosques and temples, in the organisation of people's lives, their flowers and dinner tables.

As the result of my travels, I have come to the categorical conclusion that there are two types of city on this planet created by Satan. One where the imagination runs wild, prevailing over all the laws, and is free to do or say what it likes. Then there is a second type such as our own, one lacking in imagination; its streets and alleyways devoid of colours, the light of its stars like dust, its moonlight sad and lifeless. You walk around and see nothing but the filth of truth.

In these cities, humans pretend to be void of desires just so they don't appear to be imaginative. As soon as they raise their heads and your gazes lock, they want to hide their fantasies. Just as squirrels like to hide walnuts in the forest, the men and women of this city hide their fantasies, and never revisit them in later life. Have you ever asked yourselves why it is that despite all the hatred and cruelty that exist in this city, its residents seem so shy? Because shyness is the wall that prevents us from reading the fantasies secretly harboured by every human being.

I want to have power in such a way that the imagination won't run away from me. My biggest desire is to see people's imaginations, to cherish them and benefit from them – if they are dangerous, to tame them; if they are rebellious, to contain them, buy them, give them away, mourn them and scare them. I want to plan for the construction of a district reminiscent of legend; but in this repulsive city, as soon as you have a plan the monsters are all over you, wanting to know what you are doing, why you are doing it and whom you are doing it for.

When plots of lands in Nwemiran were being allocated to officials, members of parliament, ministers and big money men on the orders of the Politburo, I wanted to build an imaginative district. However, some Politburo members are so stupid that they can't tell the smell of money from the smell of imagination. To build a dream district is different from building one where the mansions evoke wealth. In fact, I myself didn't know what a dream district would look like, although I did know it must be something like Trifa Yabahri's carpets, something like Ghazalnus's ghazals. I also knew that such a place couldn't be built by people such as Trifa Yabahri and Ghazalnus. I can say from my own modest experience that most genuinely Imaginative Creatures hate power, without understanding that its pleasures are in no way inferior to those of beauty and the imagination. There is danger in people who don't want the beauty of their imaginations realised. There is danger in those who don't understand the need for force and a plan, and that each person, depending on their place, must contribute to that plan.

THE LONGEST BOOK IN HISTORY

The longest book in history was written in a large and unusual notebook. It was kept on a big table in a special room in Ghazalnus's home. You would never find another like it in any stationer's in the world. Ghazalnus had it tailor-made by an old, bespectacled bookbinder who sat surrounded by religious books as he bound the ancient manuscripts brought to him by the city's manuscript specialists.

At the turn of the twenty-first century, the Imaginative Creatures of this city began to collect and write down stories about death. I believe that this was a moment when our people's perception of death underwent a radical change. Perhaps the main reason for this was the decline in the number of wars between us and the countries invading our land.[17] Throughout the twentieth century, death in the struggle against oppression was perceived as a beautiful thing, but the uprising brought such ugly fatalities that death lost its romantic aura and became repulsive, dark and absurd.

Back then, there were many groups – 'The Imaginative Engineers', 'The Men Who Love Travelling', 'The Daffodils' Guards', 'The Book Worshippers', 'The Forlorn Women', 'Girls Who Talk to the Rain', to name just a few – and together they represented the vast boundaries of Ghazalnus's empire. He was the unappointed king of these imaginative groups, whose members knew him through his ghazals. They all played a part in writing the longest book in history. Most of them gathered information about the whereabouts of the victims' families. Their task was to discover the homes of desperate girls who had burned themselves to death, to identify casualties of the civil war, to find the parents of young men drowned in the Aegean Sea while making the crossing, to pursue the missing men and women who had suddenly disappeared and of whom nothing was ever heard again.

A seven-member group led by Trifa Yabahri distributed notebooks, which later came to be known as the 'Winged Notebooks'. Trifa, two young men and four young women ran the show. Their group was called 'the Notebook-Keepers', but the members' names will never be disclosed because their work may restart at any time. It is not over yet. Any mention of their names, or even indiscreet allusions to them, could put their lives at risk. The only thing we can say about the Notebook-Keepers is that they were rather like angels. Like angels, they simply appeared on the victims' doorsteps without prior warning. Back then, Ghazalnus and Hasan-i Pizo-i Gulaw often determined the time and manner of those appearances. They arranged everything so that none of the Notebook-Keepers could be caught in sudden ambushes. Pizo was the real architect of the plans, using all his knowledge about hiding, disguise and escape. What is still strange and hard to believe is Trifa's supervision of the Notebook-Keepers' rounds. As you will remember, she constantly felt she was being chased by a giant monster – so how could she commit to such a task, which was scarcely devoid of sudden fear or unpredictable situations? After much pondering, I have come to the conclusion that she had taken on such a job specifically to rid herself of her fears, to challenge her monsters.

At the turn of the twenty-first century and in the years that followed, the team worked hard on the book, gathering hundreds of strange stories of events that took place at the time. The Notebook-Keepers would return with their filled-in notebooks and hand them to Trifa. Then Majid-i Gul Solav, in his brilliant handwriting, would copy them into the huge book kept in the special room. When the friends discovered Murad Jamil's body, they had been secretly writing chapters of that huge book for more than four years. During those years, Majid spent one or two days a week, from early afternoon until late at night, copying out the notebooks section by section in fine handwriting that would be legible to all future generations.

For a long time, no one in the group felt they were in peril. Stories of death reached the book from all sides, but nothing happened in that period to put them off or dissuade them from their dream of actually writing it. Yet the stories themselves brought the smell of the alleyways, the damp air of the old houses and the smell of sadness from the city's friendless people into the book, so that as you opened it you felt a strange air, the hot exhalations of the deceased, the smell of the lives they had left behind.

As for Ghazalnus and Trifa's relationship, it grew increasingly sad. All real loves embody a considerable degree of self-inflicted pain, but for Trifa the idea of a Sufic love, its survival predicated on never reaching the beloved, became more extreme day after day and year after year. Following the teachings of the ancient Sufis, Ghazalnus and Trifa tried to learn how to bring about the metamorphosis of the real souls they encountered, transforming them into inaccessible, imaginary ones. Both of them subscribed to the Eastern school of love, which works to transform the beloved from a real being into an extraordinary one, as if there were two ways for lovers to meet – physically, in the real world, or in an imagined union. Fundamentally, they both believed that love's survival did not depend on physical union in this world, but on union at a spiritual level, somewhere else.

At first, only that liberating pain tormented them, but later on more real and dangerous threats emerged. Ghazalnus's name and extraordinary works became more widely known by the day. Another factor attracting too much attention to Ghazalnus's home was presence of the Dulbar brothers, now in great demand from all corners of Kurdistan as people sought to revive their barren lands and withered orchards. Their reputation had spread all across the countryside and its demolished villages, for they did not only revive trees and greenery, they created beauty as well. After reviving each farm, they returned to their small quarters at Ghazalnus's, smelling of wheat and barley and flowers. They sat in his library like two pure-spirited children, urging him to read ghazals to them.

Ghazalnus didn't sense any danger until the evening Attar appeared, keen to buy the ghazal books. He believed that his fantasies and wishes were no threat to anyone. All he had done was to prove that he and the other Imaginative Creatures didn't live exclusively in the imagination, but were residents of this world. A short while after Attar's appearance, they found Murad Jamil's corpse.

Many things occurred during that period that you should know about. While Trifa taught carpet-weaving to the women at the refuge, a number of similar safehouses were established in the city. According to figures I later read in a newspaper report, there were more than eight of these secret houses provided by philanthropists to protect the lives of helpless women. In the late 1990s, the first dangerous event occurred when an unknown person set fire to one of the houses in the early hours of the morning, reducing three girls and two women to ashes. After that, in another house, a woman who had fled from her husband and brothers many years earlier was murdered. Soon afterwards, two sisters were poisoned and died within the space of a few hours. Then an armed man raided another shelter, indiscriminately firing off a volley at the women, killing one and wounding two others. These incidents made the women running the shelters realise the extent of the danger. An active but unknown eye was behind the discovery of these refuges. According to the stories Nawras-i Gul Solav regularly brought back to Trifa and the other girls, some of the homes were about to close down. Over the following year, several of the women living in them fled, some reaching Europe with the help of activist organisations and some heading for Baghdad and other cities in the south. Others ended up in restaurants and hotels in Istanbul, while yet another group found nowhere to go but the top floors of the hotels of the Marja district in Damascus. The women left homeless when a refuge closed down were divided between the remaining shelters.

Trifa noted the deep and constant fear in which these women lived, and to help them forget it she felt obliged to immerse them in the worlds of imagination and carpet weaving. She herself grew increasingly quiet and sad. She wept and felt terrified far more often than before. Gradually, she returned to the world of her carpets. As Nawras told me later, Trifa and the girls constantly wove and then unravelled their carpets.

'Why do you unravel the carpets? Why don't you let people enjoy looking at your beautiful designs when you've finished?' Nawras once asked her.

'Dear Nawras, what we unravel aren't even carpets. They're nothing. They're just training exercises in preparation for the day that we weave the most beautiful carpet in the world. These girls and I are looking for a carpet in which we can express our lives and beings. We are looking for a carpet that, once laid out and set foot upon, will make you feel you are in an imaginary garden, that you are somewhere beyond the Earth, in a place where there is no fear or friendlessness, no walls or locked rooms,' Trifa said.

During that same period, the assassination of women reached the gated compounds of Nwemiran. The daughters of a handful of well-known, wealthy men and the wives of Party officials disappeared under mysterious circumstances; but no one dared broach the subject.

One night, a short while before the body was found, a stranger entered Ghazalnus's house. He wore a uniform that was rather like a priest's, had a strange beard and smelled of a pleasant perfume. He had on a long, white cravat. His eyes and eyebrows gave the impression that he had recently emerged from a jungle.

He took a seat in Ghazalnus's living room, greeting his host with contrived politeness and introducing himself as 'the hunter of literary masterpieces'. He began by talking about his father's will, and how he was spending all he had on collecting old manuscripts of classical poetry. He was very persuasive. From a small bag, he took out a rolled-up sheet of paper, unfurled it across the low table between them and calmly showed Ghazalnus what appeared to be the master plan of a city.

'This is the initial design of the dream city, a city that reflects paradise in both the divine and human senses of the word,' he explained.

'The dream city, oh … the dream city,' Ghazalnus said to himself as he looked at the master plan, baffled. 'And what are the differences between the dream city in the divine and human senses of the word?' he asked.

The stranger laughed, then said: 'Mr Ghazalnus, you are more competent and wiser than me. One of the mistakes of religion – all religions – is that it creates just one vision of Paradise. Each period has its own paradise. Each city views Paradise differently. I might even venture to say that each person has a paradise that doesn't look anything like that of anyone else. Mr Ghazalnus, to you, Paradise might be a garden, full of poets and great ghazal writers, or a library full of poetry books. Yet for someone who plays football, Paradise must have football pitches. For someone who plays chess, Paradise must be full of good chess players. Why is it that as soon as Paradise is mentioned, we think of houris and ghilmans? I don't know. Each person wants a different paradise. Man wants to commit in Paradise the evil deeds he can't commit on Earth. I wonder if we, the humans of this age, can picture a version of Paradise without computers, satellite dishes, aeroplanes, trains and giant ships. Imagine what a horrible place Paradise would be without cinemas, sports grounds and the Internet. On the whole, the fantasy of Paradise is a fabulous one. Man cannot do without it. I consider myself a believer, but unfortunately every age creates its own paradise.'

Ghazalnus was baffled by the sudden arrival of this stranger. He scratched his beard and asked, 'And you think the idea of constructing this district will bring us Paradise?'

The man, who had introduced himself as Jawahir Sarfiraz, said: 'I believe that the likelihood of creating Paradise on Earth is greater than seeing it in the afterlife. From what I've read in the ancient books, it is not a pleasant place. The only thing you can do there easily is mount houris. This image of Paradise no longer matches the fantasies of the people of this city. God Almighty drew an image of Paradise that was wonderful and fabulous for ancient man, but not for us, the people of this age.'

'But how can you transform this soulless master plan into a paradise?' asked Ghazalnus. 'How could you create Paradise from these dead lines? Tell me, how?'

Jawahir Sarfiraz looked at Ghazalnus sadly, and said, 'Mr Ghazalnus, that's the reason I'm here. That's why. I need the imagination. Paradise can be built only through the imagination. It is not some pleasant place where people get to satisfy their illicit desires. Man's understanding of Paradise is very flawed. Paradise is an imaginary place, Mr Ghazalnus.'

'I know it is very much connected to the imagination,' Ghazalnus replied, astonished, 'but I don't know whether imagination is Paradise, or Paradise is imagination. It's a difficult question – one I don't have the answer to. I wonder whether imagination creates it, or whether it already exists in an invisible location and we get there through imagination.'

'I think I know the answer to that,' Jawahir Sarfiraz said, adjusting his white tie. 'I know it better than the Imaginative Creatures. Yes, I do, better than them.' He gave Ghazalnus a wry look. 'I learned the story of the Imaginative Creatures a short while ago. Luck was on my side. One night, I was present at a gathering of the male singers who stir all sorts of desires with their wonderful voices. They show you the moon and the stars in the morning and the evening. They have embedded the dawn and the moonlight into their melodies. I heard your story through these singers with their magnificent voices, as well as from some troubled women. I heard the stories of your ghazals several times, and in various forms. I thought "Ghazalnus" was the name of an old poet I had never come across. Your name evokes another age. It sounds somewhat dated. For someone still young, like you, it seems rather strange and mysterious, as if you were born into the wrong era. But your ghazals are beautiful and spellbinding. I've not seen or heard anything as powerful, as capable of inducing such fantasies. A man cannot live a normal, peaceful life after hearing your ghazals.

'But Mr Ghazalnus, let me go back to the subject of Paradise. You and I have both given it a lot of thought, one way or another. I can tell you this: not all imaginations can create it. A thousand roads branch off from the imagination, and only one of them leads to Paradise. Your problem is that you haven't yet thought about that road. The very furthest reach of the imagination is Paradise.

'My friend, imagination is not my forte. I am a lover of poetry, books, old ghazals, cinema, architecture, paintings. I am obsessed with understanding what imagination is. And yet, I don't possess a rich imagination myself, and that's why I've chosen to work as a planner, as a manager. I need you to construct the dream district. I need you and all the Imaginative Creatures. I need your ghazals. I'm the one who wants to buy your ghazals. It's me.'

'Jawahir Sarfiraz,' Ghazalnus said, 'the furthest reach of the imagination is not Paradise. That's not the case. To me, Paradise is not peacefulness; it is not a beautiful place free from sadness. The imagination doesn't contain a road leading to it, at least from my own experience. Imagination is one of the weapons with which we fight in Hell. Building Paradise is not my concern. I've never sought it out, or even thought about such things. I walk this world with the help of the imagination, through the hidden gardens within human beings. Imagination is something that helps me to a better understanding of other people; it does not mean sidestepping the real world to reach the dream. You're mistaken. You've completely misunderstood me. The very end of the imagination is the truth, the truth at its most extreme. It might even be death, because death is nothing but the extreme truth.

'My friend, I don't have dreams. I have fantasies. I have known for a very long time that imagination breeds strange dreams in man, and dreams are often dangerous. Dreams don't stop at a specific point; they turn into floods that want to sweep away the whole world and create something new. You and I are two different creatures. You have dreams, and I have imagination. It's the biggest difference that could divide any two creatures. Don't forget, I read out ghazals. I don't build dream cities and fantastic districts. I write ghazals. Those endowed with an imagination don't run away from this world. They think about the fate of all its creatures. They worry even about the flowers and the ants. And that's what I do … really, it is.

'But someone with a dream wants to make everyone service his dream. Jawahir Sarfiraz, the world's dictators, its cruel rulers and emperors all had dreams; but the poets boast imagination. The most dangerous thing that can happen is for imagination to be transformed into dreams. Imagination should be transformative and become the means to see the truth. That's how I've come to understand the world.'

'Mr Ghazalnus, what's the use of the imagination if it can't create miracles?' said the stranger. 'It's not the duty of great imaginative minds to busy themselves with small, lowly creatures. The history of humanity has preserved the Pyramids, the Taj Mahal and the Great Wall of China, not the fate of flowers and ants, as you put it. Let flowers flourish and die, but don't let your imagination be wasted and leave no mark on Earth!

'Ghazalnus, you and I may not be friends, but I've been looking for you for some time now. I know your worth. Your imagination can be a great generator of power, the catalyst for a miracle. These beautiful creatures are a boundless force, a mighty force, and I have a feeling you hold the key to some of them. Listen, emperors, armies and rulers have been passing through these cities, villages and lands of ours ever since the Safavid and Ottoman wars. Even before then, this land teemed with poets and ghazal writers, and yet when you look around, there is no trace of the imagination. For years and years, I walked the streets like a madman, wondering, 'Where's the imagination?' It lies in ruins. Ghazalnus, sell me your books, give me those ghazals so that I can build a unique district in this city, something that will endure. This city of ours should build something, a miracle the world bows to, respects and protects.'

'Your words are beautiful,' Ghazalnus said after cleaning his glasses, deep in reflection. 'I, too, want this city to have its own legends. Yes, it's true, it is a city lacking in imagination and it's poor. I agree with you that its districts are dusty, narrow and disorderly, and its streets dirty, starved of greenery and colour. But human beings cannot combine their imaginations. They might be able to have one collective truth, but they can't have one collective imagination, because the essence of man's freedom is in his imagination.

'Just as the poems of the world's poets do not look alike, neither do people's imaginations. Picture all the poets of the world getting together to write a poem. Just picture it. The poem would probably turn out to be nothing but meaningless words, because it would be devoid of the real soul of any one of the poets. The imagination of each person is tied to his or her soul and existence. It's not something that can merge with a big dream. Go and build a dream district for yourself. Fold up your master plan and leave. You can come and travel through my imagination, but you can't take it for yourself. You can invite me and show me around your dream city, but you can't turn me into a worker in it. The Pyramids are not miracles of the imagination; they are miracles of labour, of effort. The greatest miracle of the imagination is to create a human being with a profound understanding of the world, one who can always be in love, who can always inspire. Apart from that, the imagination has no other miracles.'

'Then you reduce imagination to worthless talking in your sleep,' Jawahir Sarfiraz said, concealing the fact that he was upset. 'I've known of this serious ailment for a long time. It's an old one, and many poets and writers suffer from it. I, too, know that the imagination is a potentiality, but it must work to a map if it is to leave anything behind. You don't have that map. I do. You and I must help each other.'

Ghazalnus sat serenely in his chair, appearing still more thoughtful and wiser than usual. 'But the imagination has its own map,' he said, without looking directly at his guest. 'No one can know what the map of the imagination is. Once man knows the direction the imagination takes, it's no longer imagination – so you're mistaken there, my friend. Excuse me, sir, but you look at the imagination as some sort of décor, when it is in fact our real lives. Our imagination cannot beautify life, because it is part of life itself.

'You want to construct the imagination in the form of a city, a district, a street, just like the kings, emirs, politicians and leaders who always adorn governance with a dream, with a superstition. Every king and prince looks to a big dream when they get bored of the truth. But, my brother, you are ignoring something. Throughout history, the people who had vast, profound dreams were the very ones who doubted the existence of Paradise. Imaginative people carry their paradises inside their souls, in their imaginations, in the ishraqs they show the world. My paradise lies in my unsuccessful and failed loves. It is behind the gates of the gardens I must head towards. The imagination is power, yes. My dear brother, you are right, the imagination is power, but the imagination only ever alters the soul, not the world.'

'My dear Ghazalnus, tell me,' Jawahir Sarfiraz said patiently, 'isn't this city worthy of something that would make us feel that human beings have imagination? Is it not worthy of that? I am neither a philosopher nor a poet. I am a contractor. Yes, sir, I am a contractor. Jawahir Sarfiraz is the hunter of masterpieces, of beautiful souls and imaginations. I know what kind of city I can build, but I need your powers on my side from the outset. What do you want, oh man of the ghazals? Tell me what wealth you covet, so that I can offer it you. The realm I am dreaming of cannot be built without the poets, the ghazal writers and the great singers of this city. Tell me which mansion you covet in this city – which field, which farm, which woman, which impossible thing, tell me. Together, you and I shall build a city or a district, its map drawn by your imagination and my power. A small but beautiful district.

'Why do you look on me as an enemy? Why don't you understand the meaning of my words? If you want the world to be beautiful, the poet must descend from his tower and the king must leave his palace. They must meet halfway, and there, yes, right there, they must think about building something else. I've come to your home, to your doorstep. I hate stubbornness and arrogance. Understand me, Ghazalnus: it is dangerous to let down kings. Understand that nothing is more dangerous than a king going home angry. Put yourself in his shoes. You are a king. You want to make the world a beautiful place, and yet there is no one who will help you. Well? It's dangerous when the king cannot find someone with whom to cooperate in making the world a beautiful place. Let's shake on it, and keep our peace.'

'I can't,' Ghazalnus said. 'Humans are not given imagination to make filth, disaster and destruction look beautiful. The gardens of imagination are beautiful because they do not become mere decoration that conceals the truth. If the imagination turns into something that conceals the truth, it becomes a dangerous force. Forgive me, brother, stranger, I feel that you want us to create something that would conceal the filth and beauty of this city. If you want my imagination to come to your aid, don't try to stop us from seeing all that is ugly. The imagination is a beautiful journey, but it should not make humans forget about disaster.'

'Ghazalnus,' Jawahir Sarfiraz said, 'disasters, despair and sadness have existed throughout the history of humanity, and will continue to do so. You have to understand: it is impossible to build one huge paradise, but not to build a few little ones. No one on Earth, no leader, no king and no prince has managed to obliterate sadness and bloodshed – but something *can* be done to reduce man's feeling of suffering and the pain of bloodshed … and that is what I hope to achieve.'

'I don't know what the kings could do,' Ghazalnus said. 'I don't know, but I am sure the imagination is not there to deaden humans' feelings of sadness. The Imaginative Creatures are sad creatures.'

Jawahir Sarfiraz tried very hard to convince Ghazalnus to help him with the construction of the dream district, without success. Late that night, he left Ghazalnus's home calmly, but he felt an immense hatred in his heart – something he had rarely felt before. He wanted badly to turn back and kill Ghazalnus.

THE BARON OF CHICKENS' WIFE RECOUNTS
THE STORY OF CHINESE YOUTH

JULY 2004

I left the house of the Baron of Milk and Sugar after telling a long story about a giant elephant who moved stars from one side of the sky to the other. I was then supposed to go to the house of the Baron of Pears, to tell his daughter a new story as well. I knocked on the door of the baron's house just as I had done on previous occasions, and a young servant opened the door. I calmly climbed the stairs in the baron's mansion.

The baron's daughter's name was Rozhan. She was one of the children who always fell asleep halfway through my story, but she asked intelligent questions that made me think that all the children, even those who fell asleep halfway through listening to a story, were geniuses.

I opened the door to the young lady's room just as on any other day, but to my great surprise I saw two beautiful women there in addition to the exquisite little Rozhan, whose black hair had been plaited into two braids. I immediately recognised the Baron of Chickens' wife. She was wearing a short, tight skirt, and appeared younger and more sensual than on the night I had seen her at the party. The other woman appeared to be the Baron of Pears' wife. After a brief exchange of greetings, she and her daughter quickly left the two of us alone in the room; the Baron of Chickens' wife had evidently determined that this would be the best way to meet me without arousing suspicion.

She wore an orange shirt and had straight, highlighted hair. Her face was narrow, her protruding eyes sad. She was an extremely attractive woman, but seemed to be modelling her dignified pose on someone else. Her wrists were adorned with many bracelets, and she wore light make-up. A large brooch with a golden flower glinted on her chest. Right from the start, I detected an element of fear and shyness in her eyes, qualities rarely seen in the baronesses. When we had the room to ourselves and before she had a chance to speak, I said, 'My dear lady, I am sorry, very sorry, that the other night I so stupidly and rudely ruined your evening at the party. Believe me, I didn't mean to, but I couldn't find any other way of letting you know that I wanted to talk to you.'

She didn't meet my eye but concentrated on her hands, and asked, 'Who are you and what are you doing in Nwemiran? I am sure you're not just here to tell stories. I'm sure.'

'Madam, I have come to Nwemiran to tell stories to the children,' I said calmly. 'But I was very keen to meet you too. I work for a foreign organisation that searches for missing people. I needed to gather a little bit of information about Murad Jamil, and my search led me to you. A woman who was one of Murad Jamil's many mistresses mentioned your name, as if Murad Jamil's final secret lay with you. But truth be told, I still don't know your real name. Everyone refers to you as "the Baron of Chickens' wife".'

'My name is Sayran,' she said, looking at me now and smiling a small, mysterious smile. 'Most of us wives have practically forgotten our own names. No one uses our given names – as if they were a source of disgrace.'

When she spoke in that way, she appeared even more alluring. I detected a simplicity and purity in her that, until then, I had thought could not be found in Nwemiran. From her manner of speaking, her looks and movements, I understood that she was a woman who liked everything – but was also afraid of everything. At first these women seem impenetrable, but then, when they do open up, they go wild, breaking all the barriers.

'We called Murad "the Chinese Youth". Just as in the old stories we were told when we were kids: a young prince enters a cave and finds a picture of a girl, then falls in love with her. Later, it turns out to be a picture of the daughter of the Chinese king. Murad Jamil was the same. Anyone who saw him immediately fell in love with him. He looked like the son of a king, visiting this city in disguise, and because of that my women friends and I called him "the son of the Chinese king". His secret name among us was "the Chinese Youth".'

I hadn't heard this name before.

'"The Chinese Youth",' I said, looking at her in surprise. '"The Chinese Youth". It is a strange name, just like the ones in the old tales.'

I felt that she was opening up to me very quickly, as if the secret had created a bond of trust between us.

'For thousands of years, whenever Kurdish men talked about beauty in a story, they've said, "She resembles the daughter of a French king." Haven't they? They never really used our beauty as a reference point – isn't that so, Kak Majid? So the nickname was our way of taking revenge. We all fell in love with Murad's handsomeness; it had us all enchanted. His good looks weren't like that of the men of this city. He had a foreign air about him. Perhaps he really did come from China, or perhaps he was the son of a European king. He was something else, just something else. I think he liked his nickname a lot, too. I always addressed him as "the Chinese Youth". When I saw him for the first time, I couldn't control myself, and asked, "Where are you from, that you're so handsome?" I had never said anything like that to a man before. He looked at me, laughed and said, in that passionate voice that drove all the women crazy: "I'm from China."

'Some of the women in Nwemiran called him "the European Youth",' she said, as if reflecting on a sad memory. 'But I liked to call him "the Chinese Youth". I really liked the name. I don't know which of the women made it up. Murad knew many women outside Nwemiran. Maybe one of them gave him the name, or maybe he chose it himself. No one knows. What matters is that among us, that was his name.'

I was sitting across from Sayran Khan. I took a white handkerchief out of my briefcase.

'Khanim, do you know what happened to Murad Jamil?' I asked her.

She looked at me sadly and said, 'We all know what happened to him; all of us do. There's no woman in Nwemiran who doesn't know what happened to him – but how, when and where, no one knows.'

'I shall tell you a secret that you mustn't divulge to anyone else,' I told her, just as sadly. 'I have detailed information that Murad Jamil has been killed.'

She, too, took a handkerchief out of her bag, and wiped away some tears. She said, 'We all know he was killed.'

That night, instead of me telling a story to the Baron of Pears' daughter, the Baron of Chickens' wife told me the story of the Chinese Youth from the beginning. It is so long and so full of names that recounting it here in its entirety would be hugely damaging to public morality and our social norms, so I am obliged to sum it up as follows:

The Chinese Youth was an ordinary – but very handsome – young man. He was the son of a poor or middle-class family, someone with a divine gift denied most men in the world: the majority of women who came into contact with him were powerfully attracted to him. Obviously a blessing like that, which all men dream of, is not entirely free of risk in such a city as ours, but Murad ignored the dangerous aspects of his innumerable relationships. His vocabulary had no room for words and phrases such as 'faithfulness' or 'settling down'. He could love a countless number of women and have countless relationships at the same time. Surprisingly, no woman wanted to possess him, as if every one of them knew he was like a pearl she could not keep to herself, but could only touch or look upon once, or go to bed with once or twice.

Before the emergence of the vast Nwemiran district, Murad had been the lover of the daughter of a man who smuggled trucks, lorries and wheel loaders into Iran. Murad was a truck driver himself, to begin with; driving the trucks to the border opened the door for him to mix with people from all walks of life, including some very wealthy types. For some inexplicable reason, Murad was always able to get through customs checkpoints faster than all the other drivers. This endeared him to people and won their trust.

Before Murad began mixing with the wives of the city's aristocrats and quasi-princes, he had many relationships with girls from poor families and dejected public-sector employees, luring them in with his good looks and ghazals. That's right – ghazals. The Baron of Chickens' wife was the first to tell me that Murad had a great voice for reciting poems and ghazals.

Of course, today it is common knowledge that Chinese Youth Syndrome (as it came to be known), which spread rapidly through the female population of Nwemiran, originated with a single photograph disseminated by one Khanim-i Gulbahar, whose real name we shan't reveal for ethical reasons. Gulbahar seems to have fallen in love with the Chinese Youth in early 2000. Most of the women in Nwemiran blame her even now for spreading the ailment, a sickness more like a severe flu than love. Gulbahar showed the photo to the Baron of Honey's wife. She, in turn, became infatuated with the image – more infatuated than the folk hero lusting after the engraved drawing on the walls of the cave in our old story. She swore that the photo couldn't be real, that such a creature couldn't exist even in China, by which she meant the land of the imagination.

This prompted Gulbahar to find an opportunity to introduce the Chinese Youth to the Baron of Honey's wife. It appears that the two first met at a lingerie shop owned by a friend of Murad's. After the baron's wife – a respectable woman with no previous romantic adventures – saw Murad and listened to a couple of his ghazals, she fell in love with him. So it was with all Murad Jamil's lovers. Gulbahar, who knew she couldn't keep Murad to herself forever, selflessly and without further ado surrendered him to the Baron of Honey's wife. All the women who enjoyed Murad's love, when obliged later on to give him up for another, felt their experience had been nothing but a dream, as if they had grasped a mirage for the briefest of moments. The women developed a mutual understanding that an affair with

Murad did not constitute a breach of any taboos or tarnish their reputations.

Thus Murad became a sort of dream that the beautiful, lonely women of Nwemiran passed from one to the next. The only thing that varied in the dream was its duration, which might also have been the only thing Murad had any control over.

After quitting his job as a truck driver, he became the owner and co-manager of one of the city's large function rooms, a popular choice for betrothal, wedding and birthday parties. It was there, too, that he became a regular guest of the aristocrats and wealthy people of Nwemiran, attending their parties. In that function room, young women walked past him and fell in love with him in droves. In the last two years of his life, Murad appears to have been especially attracted to rich women, but this did not keep him from short-lived affairs in the poorer districts. No one knows exactly how many aristocratic women had affairs with Murad.

The fascinating thing was the strange stars he left behind on the women's bodies, or hanging in the air of whatever room they'd slept in together – as if he were the son of the sky or the ambassador of the stars. It was these stars that would eventually give him away. It is difficult to say how much the men of Nwemiran knew about these relationships at first. As Murad had so many affairs and frequently embarked upon new ones, no one could produce solid, long-term evidence against him. Among the women, his story was treated as a great, sacred secret that they should all guard. As a result it was not revealed, and did not become the subject of gossip.

The Baron of Chickens' wife believed the Chinese Youth appeared so angelic, so divine, that all the women treated their love for him as a holy mystery. Three times in the course of our conversation she said, 'The Chinese Youth actually smelled of the imagination.' Although I deemed myself to be an expert in the imagination, I had not heard anyone described like that before. I reckoned that even if Nwemiran's men had heard part of this story, they wouldn't have believed it. The story's sad end seems to have been occasioned by the Chinese Youth himself falling in love. This constituted a dangerous change in the game.

As I heard it from Sayran Khan herself, the Baron of Chickens' wife was the last in the series of women Murad had affairs with, but before her the Chinese Youth had taken a fancy to the wife of the Baron of Courgettes. Her name was Baran Shukur. She was exceptionally striking, very young and very rich in imagination. Her elderly mother had died many years earlier. Apart from that, no one knew anything about her origins.

After Baran Shukur, the Chinese Youth entered a relationship with the Baron of Chickens' wife for a while; but when it was her turn, he became sad in a way no one had seen before. The few occasions the Baron of Chicken's wife met with Murad were largely spent drying his tears; he had fallen in love with the Baron of Courgette's wife, and was not ashamed to weep for her. Murad could not seem to forget Baran Shukur. His sole hope was that the Baron of Chicken's wife could help him. From what she said, I gathered that she had not been at all reluctant. On the contrary, she seems to have supported both lovers faithfully. It was the first time ever that the Chinese Youth had gone backwards, becoming infatuated with a former lover. From Sayran Khan, I gathered that Baran Shukur and the Chinese Youth were in a relationship for around a year.

As I have said, it was the stars Murad left behind on the body of the baron's wife again and again that gave him away. Murad did not leave his stars only on Baran's body, but also on the walls and the bed. The Baron of Courgettes, an observant young man, was very quick to notice the stars. He himself was not faithful; it seems he had heard the story of the stars from one of the women he had slept with, and put two and two together. The Baron of Courgettes went on to tell the other barons the story. Some of them revisited their own memories and remembered that they, too, had once seen strange stars and suspicious lights on the bodies of their wives or hanging in the air of their homes. Because of this story, most of the barons began to nurture a blind hatred of the Chinese Youth.

The Baron of Chickens' wife believed not that the story of the stars was true, but that any ordinary woman would be graced with the light in question after a real rendezvous; that after profound lovemaking, any woman would believe there was a man who could take her to Heaven and would be filled with such beauty and light. She also believed that because life in Nwemiran is cold, dark and bereft of light, the stars shine stronger and more clearly there.

As far as I was concerned, women hadn't meant much to me for a long time, and the whole story seemed like a film. Truth be told, I didn't know when women should or shouldn't shine, and it didn't matter to me whether they did or not. After Baran Shukur began to shine, the Baron of Courgettes had her watched by numerous eyes until he found out that the young man his wife was madly in love with was Murad Jamil. Sayran Khan believed that the Baron of Courgettes had sent Baran to her uncle abroad, in Germany or Britain, to avoid disgrace. She was also certain that the Baron of Courgettes was not the only one involved in the killing of Murad – that it had been plotted by a large number of the princes, aghas and barons of this country.

THE MEMOIRS OF THE
BARON OF IMAGINATION

There is no one in this city with the name of 'Jawahir Sarfiraz'. It was I who visited Ghazalnus's home one night in September 2002, posing as a buyer of old manuscripts and hunter of literary masterpieces.

What I understood from Ghazalnus is that each person has his or her own dream city, but what I found dangerous was his view that king and poet cannot work together to build a city. He maintained that the poet has nothing to offer the king. His comments were not rooted in a feeling of inferiority, but of arrogance. He was described to me as a simple man, but I found him ambitious and adventurous. Now I understand that the arrogance of a poet is of a kind not everyone can see. As he spoke, I looked deep into his eyes. Very deep. I sensed that there were dangerous things in them.

The biggest question facing the city at the time was how to ensure that king and poet worked together; how they could sit around a table and think about beautifying this city, about the future of this country that had only recently begun to breathe the air of freedom. I knew that the Leader could not do it alone. I had been among the country's politicians for over a decade then, and it was clear to me that no one knew what they were doing or what they wanted. We were like a group of blind people rolling down a high mountain to the bottom of an abyss, believing we would land in a lush green field at the foot of the mountain. But I could see that there was nothing to land in but a bottomless abyss. I knew I would be dragged down with them, but I wanted to build *something* beforehand – a district, a garden, even just a street. Ghazalnus, however, worked alone. I wanted him to lend me his imagination, but he would talk to me about the truth.

After my meeting with him, I retreated to my private space for some time, reading many books about the severe ailments of the poets and the physical and spiritual diseases they often developed. I concluded from my research that all poets suffer from this dangerous disease: when asked to help build the world, they run away into their imagination and fantasies; when given permission to live in their imaginary world, when told, 'Gentlemen, you may carry on living in your colourful illusions', they return to the world, stir things up and speak out in a loud voice against the kings. This has been the trouble with poets throughout history. What is al-Hallaj's cry, 'I am the truth', at the moment of his death,[18] or Lorca's gazing at the stars before *his* death, if not a flight towards the imagination?

Many times, I brought out that dangerous towel, that daunting piece of fabric that frightened me like nothing else. I brought it out and looked at it. I concluded that to love the flowers, the stars and bulbuls, poets must hate kings, presidents, princes, ministers and fighters. If a poet does not carry such hatred, the pure blood of this evil species does not run in his veins. It is the poets' obsession, their evil obsession, to triumph over everything that is not poetry. If they put this any other way, they are lying. Even when they are talking about the filthiness of the world, it is to imply: 'Look how beautiful we are, how pure.' Let me say for the record that, on the night I went to visit Ghazalnus, I read many dangerous, really dangerous, things in his eyes. If I hadn't needed the power of his ghazals, I would have killed him. Yes, I would have killed him there and then. He read it all in my eyes but was not afraid, as if he wanted to anger me and force me to remove my mask and tell him every single word inside my heart. Yet I showed patience and remained calm. When I left, I was filled with a desire to know what was going on in that house, to know who this man was and what was he up to.

In the end I turned to Attar, and told him that I wanted to employ an agent in the house, someone to be my eyes and ears. Attar said the job was impossible, beyond him. But the man is a genius, and never lets anyone down: not long afterwards he came to tell me that Ghazalnus was looking for a maths teacher, because his children were poor in science and numeracy. Attar organised everything himself, and had Rashid Tarkhunchi employed as teacher to Ghazalnus's children. Before Tarkhunchi's first visit to the house, I asked him to come and see me. I swamped him with my generosity. He was a tall, slender, cheerful man, capable of adopting a thousand faces. I said, 'I am a patient man; at first, all I want is that you gain their affection and make sure they don't suspect you.'

Tarkhunchi visited Ghazalnus's house for several months. He sent me regular reports detailing at length how bad Ghazalnus's children were at maths, which was irrelevant to me. Fortunately, his reports also showed a great flair for description and a level of attention to detail unusual in a maths teacher. Through them, I gradually became completely familiar with the geography of the house. He accurately recorded the number of rooms, doors, lampshades, lightbulbs and curtains. He mentioned that Ghazalnus had two libraries – one open, the other concealed. He also described, in detail, the poet's taciturn, sad nature. He suspected that there might be an unspoken love between Ghazalnus and Trifa.

Tarkhunchi used several different ruses to familiarise himself with the house. He soon discovered that one of the children, Khayalwan, was prone to fainting at the smell of flowers. So he sometimes put a flower close to the child's nose and then seize the opportunity to walk around the house, eyes and ears open, until he came across someone, at which point he would would cry out and beg them to go and help the child, whom he would say had fainted out of fear of the maths book, at the sight of numbers.

Through his reports, I obtained the names of the visitors to the house. I grew very suspicious when I learned that a certain Hasan Pizo-i Gulaw, a well-known former member of the assassination squads, frequented it. I asked for a list of the people Ghazalnus received. Needless to say, it took Tarkhunchi a long time to prepare it, but I finally got the list I had been looking for all my life. It was also through Tarkhunchi's reports that I got to know Majid-i Gul Solav. This same unassuming, cheerful Tarkhunchi brought me the names of most of the Imaginative Creatures – engineers who built imaginary towers, bridges and buildings in their heads; gardeners who could grow flowers and grasses by merely looking at the land; lovers who, when they walked through a street, impregnated its walls, stones and soulless pillars with the scent of love; birdwatchers who could fill the sky with various birds with just a clap of their hands; girls who, when they walked through a garden, made water burst out of the ground and fountains shoot into the air; carpenters whose chairs made one feel as if one was flying; cooks whose tables smelled of the banquets of Paradise; shy vendors who counted among their wares items that were only useful for imaginary journeys; medicine-sellers whose powders conjured up dreams of flowers, the taste of sunshine and the texture of the moonlight … It was an endless list. I needed all of them. I needed each and every one of these creatures who visited Ghazalnus's imaginative library and listened to his ghazals. I decided that all these creatures should be mine. Just like that, I decided. Yes, they should all be mine.

AN UNSUCCESSFUL ATTEMPT TO KIDNAP
THE REAL MAGELLAN
AUGUST 2004

It was late at night. As on all the other nights, I was waiting for Afsana. I was waiting for her kisses and dreams, for the way she pronounced her words in that mysterious voice. Suddenly, someone switched off the power in the hotel. A generator supplied the electricity from evening till morning, but all the neighbouring streets were plunged into darkness as soon as the sun went down. I was grateful for the generator, and when the power went down that night I felt afraid.

Shortly after the lights went out, someone pushed open the door of my room with great force. I could hear the sound of two people's footsteps as well as their breathing as they entered the room. I sat up, my heart trembling like a bird's. Many things flashed through my mind. When I thought back to that moment later on, I was astonished that so many different things could go through someone's mind in the shortest of moments. Between sitting up and getting to my feet, one of the two people flashed the light of a torch right at me and I could no longer see a thing, though I could sense that there were others waiting outside the room, behind the two men.

In the dark, I could make out the indistinct shape of a giant. With no hesitation and without saying a single word, with all the might God had given his massive body, he pushed me in the chest and I fell sideways onto my bed. Death is often the only thing you can think about at such times, but I thought merely about escaping. I could feel the man's heavy weight against my body, but he seemed to have underestimated my height and strength. He tried to grab and bend my hand, but he couldn't see well enough in the dark; I snatched it away, turned around, seized the hand holding the torch and slammed it against the wardrobe door. The torch went out, and darkness descended again. The others couldn't see anything clearly, so I seized the moment and pushed the second man with such force that he fell against a small nightstand in the corner. I was aware that another man on the threshold was making to switch on a torch, but before he was able to do so, I made it to the door.

Pursuing me in the darkness, the giant fell on his companion and yelled out to the third man, 'Don't let him get away!' But I was too fast. I ran so quickly down the stairs and out the main gate that I surprised even myself. I was sure that unless they shot me right there outside the hotel, they wouldn't be able to catch me. Someone was shouting at the hotel entrance: 'Piece of shit! Catch him!'

Waiting in the car they had come in, apparently, was a sleepy, inattentive driver. Before he could go into action, I ran towards a narrow alleyway opposite the hotel. From there I kept going, with all my strength. I knew that if I ran fast enough, I would reach a labyrinth of alleyways where they would not be able to chase me by car. Even on foot, it would be hard for them to find me in these meandering back streets. I never looked back or hesitated – and that's how I escaped the first attempt to detain and kidnap me.

Disappearing at night is one thing, but you had better have a safe destination come morning. Throughout that night I walked from one street to another, fearful of every shadow and silhouette. The only person who could help me was Afsana. I had to wait until morning.

Luck was on my side the next day. As if prompted by her heart, she came to the hotel earlier than usual. I went back, and with great fear I recounted the story of the night before. She held my hands, kissed me and said, 'I assure you, all of this is the work of the Baron of Courgettes and Murtaza Satan.' She also said that her husband must be in on it as well. She told me my life was in real danger, and that it would be better if I went back to Europe – but I told her I couldn't possibly walk away from her, and that I would not return before discovering Baran Shukur's fate. She took my British passport out of the hotel safe, gave me the phone number of a female acquaintance and sent me to a town some 150 kilometres away. She called her acquaintance before I arrived, and they rented a room for me in a hotel. She also told me that she would find me a place very quickly and send for me, and in that new place we would sleep together freely. Then, she kissed me many times, laid her head against my chest and said: 'Go and wait for me.' That is how I came to spend some time away from Afsana and that city.

A LONG DAY IN THE LIVES OF
MAJID-I GUL SOLAV AND GHAZALNUS

Ghazalnus, Trifa and Hasan sat opposite Majid-i Gul Solav. He told them the story of the Chinese Youth, word for word. They were full of praise for the fact that he had obtained such an impressive amount of information in such a short time. When Majid finished his story, the main questions still to be answered were: What could they do now? How should they proceed? Where should they go? What direction should they take? Ghazalnus believed that the barons were dangerous, and that no one could openly enter into a war with them; that the only thing to be done was to trace Baran Shukur's story and discover her real fate. In his view, Majid should have tried to collect as much information as possible about Baran during his stay in Nwemiran.

Trifa, quiet and pale, was lost in thought. She did not say a word throughout the meeting. They all noticed that she was paler and quieter every time they saw her, and whenever they enquired about her accordingly, she would say, with a soft smile, 'It's just tiredness – lack of sleep and too much thinking.' During that period, Trifa was, on one hand, caring for the children at the house, and on the other, together with the women given shelter at her house, weaving a carpet intended to be the most beautiful carpet in the world. And all this on top of her work with the Notebook-Keepers. She spent more time reading the collected stories of death than the others. On some nights, the stories prevented her from getting any sleep, and she would weep until morning. On one occasion Ghazalnus asked her to stop reading them because they were having such a devastating effect on her that they made her be ashamed to be human; he feared they might even make her want to leave this merciless species and join another in the animal kingdom. Reading the stories saddened Trifa greatly. Her only modest comfort was weaving the carpet. Not until she was in her chair at the loom did she overcome the terrifying stories of death gnawing at her soul.

After the meeting, Majid asked Ghazalnus to have a chat with him in private.

They sat facing each other at the table Ghazalnus had worked at for years. For a while they were silent, as if they had a difficult account to settle and did not know where to start. The room contained a large library, from which Majid sometimes borrowed novels and other books. The entire room, including the table and chairs, smelled of old paper, and had acquired the colour of old manuscripts. Ghazalnus appeared more confused than ever, and like someone who cannot bear silence, said: 'Majid, I know you didn't tell us the whole story upstairs. I have a hunch that maybe there are things you would like to say just to me. '

'I did recount the whole story, Ghazalnus,' Majid replied, looking Ghazalnus in the eye. 'I told you everything I know. Except for one small part, and that's to do with you. Before I brought it up, I had to hear what you had to say. I need to understand.'

'To do with me? Maybe so,' said Ghazalnus, pretending not to know what he meant. 'But first, tell me what you have now seen or heard that makes you appear so full of doubt?'

'Ghazalnus, how long had you known Murad Jamil?' Majid asked.

As if faced with a very difficult question, Ghazalnus sat back in his chair and said, after much reflection, 'It was a few months after Mahnaz Maro's death – a time when the smell of charred women's bodies dominated my life. The first time he came, he was so handsome I thought he was a figment of the imagination. That was the first time. He was very young back then, very young.'

'The Chinese Youth read out some ghazals to the women of Nwemiran, which sound like they were influenced by yours,' Majid said. 'He seems to have been a very close friend of yours.'

'Friend?' Ghazalnus said, 'I'm not sure that I can call it friendship. We weren't friends as such. We had a relationship that is difficult to categorise. I couldn't tell you and the others anything at the outset, because I still struggle to understand it myself. I can't put a name to it. I have doubts about myself, about him, about the whole world. It's like I've seen and talked to someone in the dark many times without being sure who it is, or knowing if they are friend or foe. Is he part of yourself, or a devil that wants to trick you? Is it all pure fantasy or is it real? I wasn't sure of anything. I'm still not.'

'You knew he was called "the Chinese Youth", didn't you?' Majid-i Gul Solav asked.

'Majid, I'll have to tell you everything from the beginning. Absolutely everything,' Ghazalnus said. 'Be quiet for a while, and don't ask too many questions. Just be patient for a little bit and then you can ask me whatever you like.'

Majid nodded his assent, and Ghazalnus carried on.

'One night, in the months after Mahnaz's death, I returned home after reading some ghazals to a gathering of lovers. At that time a huge number of depressed and lonely young men who had lost all hope in this country, the majority of whom were immigrating to the West, would often invite me to give ghazal readings. I would read them ghazals for a few hours on as many occasions as my energy allowed, bearing in mind that I was younger and more hopeful then. At the time, I didn't know where to hide from my inner pain, and from the smell of Mahnaz's death. I considered joining the caravan of emigrants to make a clean break with this country, whose only wealth and masterpieces are the faces of its sad people. But a dangerous desire to suffer kept me here. I found love for the world in that suffering. I cannot help being concerned for the trees, the gardens and butterflies, so I know I am a lover, an ashiq.

'In those years, I asked myself thousands of times: whose son am I? The son of Mullah Hajar or Mullah Sukhta? Am I the son of the soul who tormented himself endlessly so that love would not vanquish him, or am I the son of the man who dedicated his life to the praise of love? Whose son am I? There was no one on this planet to answer this question. Do you know how hard it is to have your life dominated by such a huge question, and not to have someone to guide you or light the way? I am a sad person who has always walked in the dark. No one has wandered through the night and darkness of his life as much as I have. Deep inside me, two dangerous and powerful forces toy with me constantly. On one hand, I am Ghazalnus, messenger of love, poet of love, a person who has spent all his life reading, understanding and writing ghazals. On the other hand, I am a man who has run away from worldly pleasures all his life. I have made a connection between love and Hell. I have merged together love and pain. Which one am I, Majid? Which one of the two? I'm asking you, because I can't ask Trifa. She and I have decided to die estranged, without our lips ever touching. I can't ask Hasan-i Pizo-i Gulaw, because he has never been in love. I have to ask you.

'When I got back from the reading that night, I put my glasses on the dinner table, brushed the dust of this city from my beard, had a small bite to eat and hoped to get to sleep early, so that I could go on a trip to Hazarbagh at dawn. The lady who was working here at the time put the children to bed and wanted to go home. She gave me the keys; I bade her goodbye, checked on the sleeping children and then lay down in my bedroom, hoping to alleviate my fatigue. Murad Jamil appeared that night. I was oscillating between wakefulness and sleep when a young man opened the door and said: "Ghazalnus, you can't run away from me forever. You just can't. I am your real side. I

357

am what you dream of being." He was exceptionally handsome. His sudden appearance reminded me of Mullah Sukhta's when Mullah Hajar had withdrawn to his privacy, or, conversely, of Mullah Hajar's appearance in Mullah Sukhta's ghazal library.

'At first, I thought he was one of those young men disturbed by the ghazals, but he had such a clear, unusual appearance, and spoke so confidently and calmly, that I was overawed. All my life, I had been scared of people who speak calmly, people whose calm and nonchalance tell you they know what they want and what they live for. I've always been a frequenter of gatherings of the lost and aimless. Imagination is a threshold crossed by the lost; those who know their path rarely become Imaginative Creatures. Once someone knows their destination, they don't need the imagination.

'He said, "I've been present at most of your recent readings. I hear every single letter you pronounce. I taste your ghazals with my soul and body." I hadn't seen him before. I wondered if it was possible to forget such a good-looking person.

"Where could he have been hiding?" I asked. "You're not telling the truth. I've never seen you at a gathering. You don't belong to any of the groups that need my ghazals to survive, and to continue their journey full of dreams."

'There was only one chair in my room. Very politely, he asked if he could sit down. He said, with great sadness, "At all your readings, I felt that when you were reciting your ghazals, you looked only at me, to such an extent that I thought it odd you should look someone in the eye so blatantly. But don't worry, you're not the only man who doesn't see me. Most of those who know me believe I am fantastical – so handsome that they can only see me in their imaginations. When someone is searching for a beautiful appearance that isn't his own, he finds me."

'It was a strange answer. His handsomeness was such that if any man on Earth was given the option of deciding his own appearance, he would choose something like this form. It was the kind of beauty that, if found in a woman, would evoke the envy and spite of all other women. If found in a man, it would lead to plots to kill him.

'"What do you want from me? What can I do for you? You've crept into my house like a thief," I said.

'"I've listened a lot to your ghazals," he said confidently. "I have a feeling those ghazals are not yours. They can't be."

'"You're right. They're not mine," I said. "Most of them were written by Mullah Sukhta, an obscure classical poet, and occasionally I read one of my own. But people find the way I read them to be intoxicating. It helps them live in their imaginations. I've read those ghazals so much, they've become part of my being. I don't think there is anything that separates them from me. I am an extension of Mullah Sukhta. I am him, but living in a different era and form … and I pass on his message."

'He sank into reflection for a while, then said, "It's not my aim to find out who wrote the ghazals. What I'm trying to say is that they're *not yours*. They shouldn't be. You're nothing but a cowardly lover. Those ghazals are mine. I could put them to good use. I'm the one who needs those ghazals, so that I can read them to the girls and women who fall in love with me. You talk about the fantastical aspect of love, but I'm the one who is living its real aspect. I am the part of you that you have stifled. You can't cope with the real side of love."

'I looked at him in surprise and asked, "And you, can you cope with the fantastical side of love? When love becomes a bottomless sea, when it becomes a desire that draws man, whirlwind-like, into the depths of this world and of the entire secret of our existence? Can you cope with love when it becomes an endless journey through an imaginary garden that embodies all humankind's dreams and beauty? Or when it becomes an infinite trip that brings deep pain and happiness in equal measure, when its pleasure lies in its torment and infinity?"

'He chose not to answer my questions, and began instead to tell me about his relationships. Back then he was very young, and still at the start of the long journey that was to take him to his fatal end. Strangely, he insisted that these ghazals should belong to someone who could use them in real love, at the heart of life, at the height of love and lovemaking. Majid-i Gul Solav, I've always been weak before the truth, ever since the time I walked through the streets of this city and repainted the trees, the birds, the columns and the walls in my imagination. As if he knew my weakness and had managed to diagnose my main illness, he said, "I am aware of the story of Sayfadin Maro's daughter. She was a very beautiful girl. If she had loved me, I wouldn't have left her so wretched. She had a very rich imagination. It would've been enough for her if you had said the words *I love you*. That would've been enough for her – but you managed to kill her. Ghazalnus, there's something you should know. People do not set themselves on fire out of contempt for those they hate. They kill themselves out of concern for those they love."

'"Mahnaz was a vulnerable student of mine," I said. "I didn't feel that she loved me. I didn't feel it. I didn't know about it."

'"Women don't open their hearts. You can be sure of that. They really don't," he said, laughing. "They leave it like a riddle, and we have to solve it – to go into it and analyse it. What kind of ghazal writer are you, that you haven't realised that?"

'"I had to teach Mahnaz to have an imagination; that was my job," I said, in a sad voice. "She was a young girl. Even if I'd wanted to, how could I have laid hands on her? What do *you* think?"

'As if he wanted to rile me even more and deliberately torment me, he said, "You showed the poor girl an imaginary realm. You isolated her from everything on this Earth, filled her imagination with colourful gardens. You made her hate her fiancé. And then you abandoned her. You just walked away, and left her. You could've told her that you loved her, or something simple that could have helped her get a grip for a while. Love isn't a mythical, immortal, profound and complex thing that should hang around your neck like a rope until death. Love's easier than that. It's the mingling of two souls, you see. Love makes human beings each other's friends, not each other's slaves."

'"I can't be like you," I said, staring at him. "Your Western law of love doesn't fit my love-filled psyche. The head of an old, Eastern Sufi is on my shoulders, while you have the lascivious body of a European man. You and I can't become one."

'"Women call me 'the Chinese Youth', because everyone knows I emanate the scent of imagination," he said, as he looked at me with great sadness for the first time. "Everyone knows. I am an imaginative creature like you, but I experience love in a real way. You don't dare to experience love in a real way. You want to immerse yourself in the sea of truth some other way. The only real thing an imaginative creature can engage in is love."

'Dear Majid, when he called himself "the Chinese Youth", a judder passed through my whole body. At that moment, I understood that the person opposite me was part of me. I collapsed on my bed and lost consciousness. When I came around, he was no longer in the room. That night, I revisited the ghazals like a madman. I turned page after page as I searched. I was certain I had seen the name "the Chinese Youth" in those books. I was sure of it. I searched through the night. At daybreak I found this quartet:

> You come and go, you are a storm, a wind,
> You are a Chinese Youth, a lonely ghazal reader
> Stars are raining down from you, you are an undervalued book
> You resemble reality, but you are pure magic and fantasy

'I read on for several hours and came across another quartet that astonished me. The verses shed light on the enigma of my existence, and told me about my predetermined path in life.

O child of the imagination, o Chinese Youth
You live in imagination, but see the truth too,
You are the moonlight of this garden; you are a star, you are love,
You'll die on the plains, you are the son of China

'Tell me, Majid, how can anyone live in peace after a night like that? The name "Chinese Youth" originated in these ghazals. I was "the Chinese Youth", you see. It was a special name given to me by a woman intoxicated by ghazals, and she borrowed it from the ghazals. She took it from these ghazals. I both was and was not "the Chinese Youth".'

Ghazalnus had reached the end of his narrative. He appeared tired. The Imaginary Magellan looked at him in astonishment. He had so many questions.

'Ghazalnus,' he asked, 'how was he part of you? How? How was he you, and how were you him?'

'All my life, I've tried to solve that puzzle, in futility,' Ghazalnus said wearily, sitting back. 'I always started from the story of Mullah Hajar and Mullah Sukhta. My question is this: how can a human being split into two different, conflicting souls? I've asked that question for years, but never found an answer. No one can answer it. After many years, I now know what a big mistake that question is. Often, there is no answer because the question has been misunderstood or misconstrued.

'My dear Magellan, dear Sardarbashi, Mullah Hajar and Mullah Sukhta were not one soul that split into two. On the contrary, they were two souls who wanted to become one. I've mulled over this story for years. I've read their letters thousands of times. After all this time, I now understand the story better. Neither Mullah Hajar nor Mullah Sukhta could figure out for certain who they were; because they were so close to one another, they thought that their separation was the splitting of two souls into two different continents – whereas the real tragedy of these two men was to be two intimate souls who could not become one. Mullah Hajar and Mullah Sukhta were two different human beings, both attracted by the same love. Both were carried away by the same love. Love had made them similar to each other.

'As I understand it, Mullah Hajar waged a concerted war against that love, investing all his powers and energy in running away from it. For Mullah Sukhta, on the other hand, the greatest desire of his life was to live that love, to take it to its peak, and yet there was a profound desire inside Mullah Hajar's soul to be Mullah Sukhta, just as there was a divine fear inside Mullah Sukhta – and he wanted to be Mullah Hajar. Mullah Hajar was nothing but Mullah Sukhta's projected image of himself, and Mullah Sukhta nothing but Mullah Hajar's projected image of *him*self. They were two people who wanted to merge with each other.

'Everyone in this city is looking for his or her projected self. This city splits everyone in two. People in this city can only choose one part of their self and live it out. There is no one who could reveal or acknowledge his or her full being. Mullah Sukhta and Mullah Hajar are exactly what everyone else is condemned to. Everyone in this country has a projected self, an image of himself or herself that they realise through external figures. They are not necessarily in agreement with their imagined, projected half. They are often forced to hate, humiliate or kill it so they can live at peace. They are forced to seek the strength to rein it in. The two sides never meet except at the moment of death, because the truth and imagination meet only then.'

Ghazalnus took a deep breath, looked at Majid-i Gul Solav calmly for a while, then carried on: 'When I found the ghazals that night, I realised I was "the Chinese Youth". I realised that this man was part of my soul, part of my being. He was another side of me that I had, so far, been running away from. He was a dangerous part of me, and I didn't know whether to wage war on him or submit and let him play his game.'

'So you let him be. You let him live and play his game. You let him be killed,' Majid said wryly.

'He returned after a few nights,' Ghazalnus said, continuing as if he hadn't heard Majid. 'He asked me to give him some ghazals. He said they had been written to be used in life, in reality. He taunted me, depicting me as a man who can't face the truth. He said, "All cowardly people can try imaginary loves." I defended myself as if caught up in a vicious war. I said, "Even ugly, awkward men can use sweet words to deceive poor, lonely women deprived of passion, but none of them would ever reach the infinite imaginary gardens of love where the beloved becomes an ideal."

'I argued that love was not about touching the body of the beloved, but her soul, when she reaches the status of a goddess. I shouted at him, saying, "Every ignoble man in this city can lay his hands on the body of a prostitute whenever they want, but who could live a love that creates an imaginary creature of high esteem in the body of the beloved?"

'Laughing, he looked at me, concerned that I had unfairly seized all these ghazals that belonged to him and other lovers like him. Day after day, week after week, the young man planted doubts in me, making me believe he was right. At the time, Mahnaz's memory

362

was tormenting me more and more. I felt I was nothing but a lover who could love only an imaginary woman, who could worship only a woman who did not exist in this world. I was madly in love with an imaginary girl whom I would meet in imaginary gardens. He read all that was in my heart without my saying a word. One day he cornered me, and I told him about Mahnaz's garden; I told him about the birds, the big flowers, the mind-boggling colours of the leaves. He said, "Ghazalnus, you don't look for what's real in women – you are after their shadows." He wanted to hurt me with those words. I was too worried about giving him the ghazals. I said, "You are an indifferent and adventurous young man, exploiting my ghazals for your dirty, devilish desires." He laughed and said, "These ghazals were not written to die on their shelves. Open the door and let them fly. They are made for men in love to read to women. They are made to live, to be wet with tears, to be burned by desire, to be stained with blood."

'Week after week, month after month, after each battle, I yielded. After each battle, I gave him a ghazal or two. After all, he was living a life I yearned for, deep down. On some nights I forced him to recount his love stories to me, to tell me the stories of the stars he left on women's bodies. He would laugh and say, "You are a shameless man. There is stifled desire inside your soul. Beneath that Sufi-style beard and romantic glasses lies a shameless heart." I wanted to travel the world like him, but I was lost. I felt I was lost the first time I entered Mahnaz's garden. It was then that I became sure I couldn't live like him. My friend, one night we were walking together in Mahnaz's garden. I asked the Chinese Youth, "Murad, why does this girl offer me this garden? Why is she offering me this infinite tulip garden? Why does she ensure the flowers stay open for me all the time?"

'"To make you lose yourself, so that you can't connect to any other woman in the world," he said, laughing. "At the moment she chose death, she was certain she was leaving behind a huge garden, an infinite one, indeed, a garden in which you would lose your way. When Mahnaz set fire to herself, she wanted to become a mythical creature, the very thing you want. All people who kill themselves, all women who set fire to themselves, do so to show us the part of their soul they project outside. Through her garden, Mahnaz offered you what you want. She took revenge on you by fulfilling your dream. Ghazalnus, it's strange: no garden on Earth is bigger than the one we build for a tryst that never happens. Because it is infinite, it is a garden that offers you nothing but somewhere to lose your way. It is an infinite search through all the beauty of the world. You are the only person who has such a garden. Look what valuable creatures women are! If they can't offer us their beauty in life, they will do so by dying, by self-immolation."

'And he was right, dear Magellan. He was right. From that day onwards, I had to look for the beloved in the flowerbeds, inside the ghazals, inside the suffering of other people, the beauty inside their souls, their imaginations. After Hazarbagh, after Mahnaz's garden, after Trifa's love, I regard love as a long and fruitless search for the beloved inside an immense bed of tulips. But Murad, he looked in real life; what I was looking for in the imagination, he found among real women and the dusty, dirty streets of this city. All the women he slept with in reality, I would sleep with later in my imagination. What he found in reality, I lost in the imagination. The day you were looking for the names of the women Murad had slept with, I was struck dumb, not knowing what to do or say or how to hide my embarrassment and the lies I've told myself. Eventually, I chose silence. I *know* the names of all the women, and I, too, have slept with them in my imagination. When he slept with a woman, my body felt it, and it shone. He was part of me. He was me, and I was the Chinese Youth.

'Majid, I won't hide from you that he, too, liked my imaginary gardens enormously. Despite his taunts, he often forgot his own convictions and said, "Ghazalnus, take me to your imaginary gardens; take me somewhere I can forget the truths of this world." I took him along to Mahnaz's garden, to Hazarbagh. When I did, he became completely infatuated by Sabri. He said: "I'll give you all my real lovers, and you give her to me." Throughout those years, he was obsessed with getting his hands on Sabri. There was a profound and imaginative side to him. I often saw him prostrate, bowing before a flower, saying, "I am your son." Majid, Murad Jamil thought I was taking him to a flower garden, one end of which was in China and the other here. He felt that he entered life when he walked through these gardens. I've never seen anyone so conscious of their own beauty. It is a happy man who is so conscious of his beauty, and he was happy for a long time.

'One night he told me something I shall remember for as long as I live. We were wandering around Mahnaz's garden. He said, "Ghazalnus, I feel as if I've been in this garden before and was expelled by someone I can't identify, as if everything I went on to do in my life was aimed solely at bringing me back here." That left me in deep, agonising thought. I felt this was the utmost darkness of my inner aspect speaking. I felt guilty for leaving the garden every night to seek the truth. Whereas with each passing day, he believed he needed the ghazals to add a little imagination to his loves. The ghazals affected him more and more each time. All his power consisted of not getting trapped in the fantasies of love. He could be in love without being overwhelmed by it – unlike many imaginative creatures, who become overwhelmed by love without ever having experienced it. He could please his lovers and himself for a while, then move on. That's all he wished for, until finally he came across one of those overpowering loves that requires you to give up all of your soul for it.

'All through those years, arguments and instability were features of our lives. We often went on long walks together. At times we were friends, at others sworn enemies. One thing I never argued over was the name, "the Chinese Youth". Although I considered that it genuinely belonged to me, as time went by I felt he deserved it more than I did. There were many things we never reached agreement on before he died. I'd say, "Murad Jamil, I am an imaginative creature who fell into the real world, while you are a simple person who wants to add a bit of imagination to your life." For his part, he thought he was an angel who had emerged from within the poems. In a sense, he was right. His handsomeness had the same impact on the mind as the poems. He was surprised I paid so much attention to the truth. One day he said, "Your biggest problem is that you experience the imagination as if it were part of reality, while I experience reality as if it were part of the imagination." I continued to give him ghazal after ghazal, and with each one, he moved one step closer to death. A few weeks before he was killed, he wrote me a letter that said: "Love is neither a fantasy nor reality. Love is the only thing that is like death." Back then I didn't know exactly what he meant, but now I understand it all. I saw him every night. Majid-i Gul Solav, I still do.'

'Ghazalnus, I want to know one thing,' Majid said. 'Did he have the slightest inkling about those who wanted to kill him?'

Ghazalnus looked at Majid sadly. His eyes were half-tearful, half-smiling.

'Over the past three years, he became more and more caught up in each of his love stories. He was happy, like a butterfly flying blithely in a garden, but each time he gave a slice of his soul, a portion of his happiness, to someone else. I rebuked him, punished him, deprived him of ghazals, but it was all in vain. Two weeks before he was killed, he came here, all smiles, and sat in the very chair you are sitting on now. He said, "Ghazalnus, they're going to kill me."

'"Of course, they are," I replied, "I've known that for years. Eventually, a husband, a brother, a father will come from somewhere and kill you like an animal. What do you expect? To keep making cuckolds of men for good?"

'"Ghazalnus, this time they will kill me for love – real love," he said, in the same cheerful tone. I didn't know what was making him so happy that day – his profound and infinite love for Baran Shukur, or his death. He asked for a ghazal, one that "could melt a stone", as he put it. I took him for the first time to where I stored the ghazals, and let him swim freely in their sea. I let him search through them and take the ghazal he wanted. We searched for three days and nights. We read ghazals for three days and nights. When I was tired, he would simply carry on reading. His voice, his posture, his recitals were all beautiful. After three days, we emerged. In the light of a bright morning, I noticed that his skin had become a different colour; it was as if he had aged. He looked at me and said, "Now, I understand why you have dedicated your whole life to these books. Now I understand what I've missed." He left like an angel.

'I didn't see him again. It was our last encounter. A week later, he sent me a letter. On the night he was killed, I could sense everything. I sensed his death, without anyone telling me a thing. It was a strange feeling, as if half your body had gone and you went on living with just the other half. It felt like standing on one leg, seeing with one eye, working with one hand. I would shut my eyes and see his blood. I would shut my eyes and see the location of his grave. The very next night, I took Darsim Tahir and went out to the plains at the edge of the city. I found the body of the Chinese Youth three nights later.'

Before Ghazalnus finished his account, he stood and took a letter from a well-hidden section of his library.

'Majid,' he said, 'this is the letter he wrote to me before his death. You can read it if you want to. There are many things in it that cannot really be put into words, or that I can't now recount.'

That night Majid-i Gul Solav returned home and read the Chinese Youth's letter in utter astonishment.

AN EXTRACT FROM THE
CHINESE YOUTH'S LETTER TO GHAZALNUS

My dear Ghazalnus, I am sorry that, unlike you, I have no gift for writing, a gift that could enchant you. This is my first and probably last letter. The day we came out of the ghazal library, I, too, had the same feeling. A feeling I am running away from, and that I want to see as unreal; the feeling you've often talked about, the feeling that you and I have each been left with only one half of a world when that world in its entirety belongs to us. Throughout the years, whether we were friends or at odds, I always prided myself on my ability to impress the girls of this city with my good looks. I took pride in actually living the things that you only experienced in the imagination. And yet I will not hide from you that, years back, when I heard your ghazals for the first time, it was as though I was born in that very moment. Certain things have such a great impact on a person's life that they cannot be explained by the mind alone.

Certain people live and live and live – they come and go, they visit the bazaars, the streets and the fragrant qaysaris, but nothing happens in their lives. Nothing at all. They see thousands of women, but nothing happens; read thousands of books, but nothing happens; travel dozens of times, but nothing happens; listen to poetry and poets thousands of times, but everything remains the same. And absolutely nothing can disturb their peace, as if this Earth were a wave, and man a seabird unaware of the world, the world a breeze and man a fallen leaf. But it can happen that one glance, one gaze, one vague smile from a stranger, from someone you know nothing about – someone whose soul, life and body you have not understood – turns your life upside down. It disturbs your peace so drastically that nothing remains the same. You lose all certainty; such mayhem engulfs your life that only death can restore your peace and happiness. People who have not witnessed such earthquakes, such storms, may be happy, but they may also be the unhappiest people of all because they die without knowing the meaning of bewilderment.

The day I heard your ghazals for the first time, I experienced the bewilderment I am now talking about. The ghazals changed my life in the way that a woman's glance, the sight of a painting, the melody of a song, the reading of a book can turn a life upside down. Until then, I thought I was created just so the women of this city would look at me and be left bewildered. Until then, I thought I only caused bewilderment but could not experience it myself; but I was suddenly so bewildered by those ghazals that my life never recovered its old form. I was left so bewildered that I could not live without them, as if they were a set of words that had been sleeping inside me that I couldn't reach, and you came to raise them from the bottom of my heart and read them to me. I felt that every word you uttered came from the depths of my own soul.

As time passed, the feeling that those ghazals were mine grew stronger and stronger. I often thought you were right: I was so immersed in worldly love that I had lost the path between love and the imagination, which you claim is what makes for the unhappiest of lovers. To me, the important thing was the transient, worldly happiness we experience in the present moment. Ghazalnus, all my life I've felt that the richer our imagination, the sadder we are. Your ghazals made me thirstier. With each one, I felt that I wanted to go even further in love, but I never knew what going further in love meant to you. I understood it to mean giving my heart to every human being if only for a second, for a breath. Perhaps I was mistaken, but I assure you I wanted to be a good person. Like the ghazals, I wanted to bring fresh air into people's lives, even if only for a second; I wanted to be something new in the lives of others, something different from the mundane, daily repetition they experienced. Only angels and devils stop the world from repeating itself, but man is a creature who involuntarily repeats the things he is certain of. I often say that perhaps it is easier if you love the same woman forever, just as it is easier for a human being to write just one ghazal forever. And yet I can assure you that, just like you, I chose the harder path.

You and I are either an angel divided into two halves or a devil split into two. Which it is, I don't know. Let's leave it to God to decide. Until the day I heard your ghazals, I saw myself as a person who plunges into life, like a fisherman who doesn't dream about fish but sails straight out to the middle of the sea in his boat to cast his fishing line time and again. There are human beings who dream first, and others who dream at the end. I am the latter kind. I caught the fish, then dreamed about it, rather than dreaming about a fish and then going out to catch one. The day I heard your ghazals, I was bewildered. Bewildered at seeing myself as your other half, the one you've stifled inside you. I was like a child who finds out after a long time that he is the son of different parents, that the family bringing him up is not his real family. I believed I was part of you, and yet you pushed me away forcefully and drove me out.

You might ask how I arrived at that conclusion, what led me to these convictions. Don't be surprised if I say that it was not that you and I are similar; on the contrary, we are one hundred percent different from each other. We are two opposing poles, so much so that we appear to be two ends of the same soul. I felt that throughout your life, you had been running away from me and I from you. We are each aware of the other's existence, but do not dare reveal ourselves to each other. You are an imaginative lover and will defend the purity of your imagination until the end of time. You are a Chinese Youth who has never stepped out of China, yet all your imagination and desires were designed for doing just that, for falling in love outside China and tasting the European lips your imaginary lips are too abashed to touch.

Ghazalnus, after all these years, I am abandoning my obstinacy to say that we both deserve the name. Even if you feel too bashful to accept it, I give you the right to be 'the Chinese Youth'. Perhaps you deserve the name more than I do. I don't remember when I came out of 'China', when I crossed out of the realm of the imagination, but I am sure you are still there. You never left. You have not seen beyond the borders of that magical country. Now that I see you collect true stories, I understand you. You need to take a portion of truth to the imagined world in which you and those like you are immersed. By contrast, I need to blend some imagination with all these truths. When I heard your ghazals, I smelled my own homeland, I smelled the land; and, like you, I should have watered its flowers and extracted the rosewater. There came a point when I understood that I am as thirsty for the imagination as you are for the truth. When you read your ghazals, you speak about your thirst for this world, and when I hear the ghazals I speak about my thirst for 'China'.

Day after day and year after year. Something had to change. The day I met Baran Shukur, I understood that this girl would take me back to that magical country. When I saw Baran, I realised that all the ghazals on earth couldn't do her justice. All the years I spent telling you about the women who came my way, I always forgot to emphasise one fact: real love is not the desire to sleep with your beloved, but the desire to die with her. Before Baran, I had never thought about dying with any woman I had met in this world; I had only ever thought about her body, about my desire. Or, sometimes, I'd had no thoughts at all. But tell me, Ghazalnus, why did I think about death when I first saw Baran? Why was I sad before and after I slept with her? Ghazalnus, tell me, what is it that binds love to death? What?

I expect them to kill me one of these days. In fact, we both expect them to kill us. Baran's husband has known everything for a while, yet neither of us thinks about running away. This love is making me unusually sad. Tell me, why is real love always sad? I understand that a love thwarted, whether by God or man, should become sad. That's not what I'm talking about. I'm talking about love always being sad, deep down. Even if there are no external objections, even if there are no hurdles before it, it is still sad. In true love, even when the lovers meet, they still think they have not met. They have a feeling that they have not met the Beloved. Baran and I have slept together dozens of times. Every time after we made love, we had that profound feeling of a vacuum, the feeling that we were not together, that there was something we couldn't give each other, that there was a depth we couldn't reach.

Ghazalnus, the day I came out of the ghazal library, I realised that in Baran, I was looking for the beauty of those ghazals – ghazals that do not end, because they also seek a beauty they can never reach. It was as if I had put my finger on Mullah Sukhta's story, the one you told me a while ago. As long as he lived, Mullah Sukhta never stopped writing ghazals, because he was seeking a beauty he could never attain. When I stepped out of the library, I realised that love is searching for something that eludes us. Being in love is not the desire to be constantly with your beloved – on the contrary, it is to feel you will never meet them. Love is that, and nothing else.

I picked up this ailment from you and your ghazals. Year by year, drop by drop, your ghazals have been killing me. You infected me with your sickness, but I couldn't do the same to you. When I stepped out of the library, I felt I would roam around aimlessly, forever – that I was doomed to spend all my life searching in Baran

Shukur for the beauty of those ghazals, and in the melody of the ghazals for Baran Shukur's beauty. Baran is the imagined woman of your soul who was flung into mine. Now, death is meaningless to me. I wonder to what extent Baran's husband understands her, what he might know about life. Let him kill me. Killing me is not unjust – it is the distant door I have been seeking for a long time. Baran and I, as two lovers, are doomed to be kept apart.

If they kill me and Baran is left alive, please don't let her see my body; and if they kill her too, try to bury us next to each other. If you manage to find my body, wherever it may be, please bring it here and bury me in this ghazal library, near these books. What could be more marvellous than a lover buried inside a ghazal library? A lover ought to be buried in the midst of all the libraries in the world, in the midst of thousands of couplets. Dig me a grave right there among the bookshelves and manuscripts. Bury me there with Baran Shukur. Bury us together. That is my last wish. My final hope.

THE MEMOIRS OF THE
BARON OF IMAGINATION

In the summer of 2004, the Leader sent for me and enquired about the project for the dream district. He had forgotten about it for many years, yet now he spoke about it very passionately, as if he had just had a dream about it. He was so carried away by the idea that he said he hoped to build a unique dream district in every town and city in Kurdistan. He had got a bad case of the modernising-Kurdistan bug, and I had never seen him in such a state.

The Americans were evidently a major influence on his fantasies. In that period, the Leader met the Americans more often than he met us. It appeared that an American general had fed him some ideas, and he wanted to implement them swiftly. He put some designs before me and said, 'This is the start of a "Marshall Plan" for rebuilding Kurdistan.' I thought the designs lacked imagination. Clearly, after central Iraq was plunged into instability, the Americans had been infected with the same illness I had – an obsession with constructing an ingenious city – and were presenting this to the world as an example of the triumph of the spirit of modernism and the American dream.

At the Leader's request, I met an American delegation specialised in building extraordinary cities. I met with the city council, the municipal commission and the syndicate of civil engineers. They spoke about changing the basic plans, master plans and so on. I took part in all the meetings enthusiastically, joking for the reporters and smiling into the cameras. But all the while I had a strange gut feeling that without that fucking Ghazalnus, nothing could be done. While His Excellency the Governor, the minister of construction and the official in charge of special projects talked about signing contracts with Turkish, Jordanian and Malaysian companies, I chose a different path and went to see Attar. If you want to rebuild or destroy this city, you need to visit the likes of Attar.

I told the Leader this. I said, 'Sir, the issue of the city of dreams is not about architecture or engineering, but something that poets, experienced middlemen and vendors of human beings should take part in.'

The Leader's mind had been dulled by all the gunpowder that went up his nose in the capital. It now took him a long time to understand the smallest and simplest of matters. Failing to grasp what I was getting at, he mentioned the names of two untalented poets of the time and gave me a couple of poetry collections from his library. I took them so as not to give offence, and left.

I went to see Attar without prior arrangement, taking with me the names of all the Imaginative Creatures I had discovered by then. Attar did not particularly like me. Once he plucked up his courage and said, 'Mr Baron, you seem to be an ominous creature. Anything I do with you goes nowhere.' His own failures with Trifa Yabahri and Ghazalnus were the two great wounds of his life. He did not understand at all why the imagination was important, why a wealthy statesman and politician such as myself was so obsessed with it, why all the fuss over ghazals and carpets and such like.

To make sure our business went smoothly, I was obliged to explain things in plain language that even a camel like Attar could understand. I said, 'Attar, I know you are very keen to find out why I am chasing these people. I want you to know that we are living in a different world, that things have changed. Nations don't only live by power, swords and their ability to produce suicide bombers. Nowadays, beauty is greater than everything in the world. I have been to many cities and countries in the past few years. Two things have given power to nations: first, organisation; second, the imagination. Both these words have many meanings. Attar, look at the progressive nations' – I said these two words, 'progressive nations', knowing they had a powerful impact on the imagination of the people of this city, who liked to think themselves progressive even though their thoughts about progress were dictated more by their bellies and their underbellies than their heads – 'look at progress and civilisation. We have been thinking about progress and civilisation since the time of Hajji Tawfiq Piramerd and Ahmad Mukhtar,[19] but we have nothing to show for it. Day after day, our world is deteriorating. This isn't only true of the Kurds. The whole of this region is rotting, its earth decaying, its air polluted. It's a hopeless situation. Brother Attar, look what we've done. We've forced those unfortunate Americans from the other side of the world to cross oceans and skies to come here with tonnes of equipment, just to bring us an iota of awareness, just to teach us an iota of civilisation – and all for nothing. We've left the world stunned and at a loss. We are neither retreating to the past, nor genuinely building a new civilisation. And why is that, Mr Attar? Because we lack organisation and imagination.

'Look, I'm not blaming science, philosophy and the like. They're available to read and learn about in the public library. Science belongs to all of humanity, but imagination and organisation are things that are inbuilt. When any nation makes progress, it has two groups of people that prompt it to embrace civilisation and development. It has a group of people whose only job is to think. They can be found in any area – they are like queen bees in their hives, as they sit and ponder things. Their only job is to expand the horizons of their areas of expertise and to add to them. And there are people whose only job is to draw up rational plans so that people's minds, muscles and imagination work together in harmony.

'How have other nations achieved progress, Mr Attar? Our ancestors have been talking about uprisings and rebellions by the lions of Kurdistan for hundreds of years. Yes, Mr Attar, it was the dream of my father and of yours that the Kurds become a prominent, world-renowned people. That dream of progress and civilisation has been eating away at us for a hundred years, and now we've reached the point where these Islamists have emerged to tell us we don't need progress and civilisation after all. That's what they say. They say: "The Book of Almighty God and the sayings of His Prophet and his followers are sufficient." But that's not what you or I say. We need progress and that's that, because if this region remains as it is – which is to say, barbaric – and we take to devouring each other, then you and I, being Kurds, will be skinned alive before anyone else. Isn't that so, Mr Attar?

'Other nations acquired their status and grandeur because those with reason, muscle and imagination worked together; scientists, politicians and poets worked collaboratively. They worked together, you see. Not us. Here, the politician shows the poet his backside and tells him he can indulge in his own fantasies. The poets of other nations don't say, "Politicians are all bastards, and I don't even want to see their faces." The scientists don't say, "My world is all about my pen and paper and my lessons." Instead, they work hand in hand – and that's how they have created a civilisation.

'Because we don't have our own state, we haven't understood this. Yes, dear Mr Attar, the scientist thinks of and produces science; the politician draws up plans and is paid for it; and most important of all are the poets and imaginative people, who enrich the plans with their visions, aesthetics and inspiration. Nothing can be done without the latter. We're not building a prison, we're building a city where a stroll through the streets should rekindle your artistic feelings. When you see development and progress, it should make you say, "God Almighty, how beautiful it is!" Civilisation is not the dust, rubbish and dung of our bazaars. It is bewilderment, my friend, *bewilderment*. You can't separate civilisation from the creation of unique and exceptional objects. Make a beautiful object, and no one will ask how it came into being. They'll just say, "Good God, how unusual!" No one today asks how many labourers and slaves died building the Pyramids, the Great Wall or the Hanging Gardens of Babylon. Everyone just looks at them and says, "Look at that power, that beauty, that strength of will."

'Attar, history is a stupid thing. You often need to know how to cheat it. You must create something that makes people feel as if they are walking through a feat of reason, imagination and willpower simply by gazing upon it. Do you see? Progress fascinates us. You can't produce that fascination without the support of the Imaginative Creatures. Now, brother Attar, you might be wondering about my place in all of this. My job is akin to that of a project manager. My job is more dangerous than all the others. Without me, the plan doesn't work, and if the plan doesn't work, the entire machine falls apart. You see, my problem right now is not how to build walls, but how to build a city full of imagination, dreams and beauty. And that bastard Ghazalnus just won't give in.'

This time, I felt that Attar had understood me very well. He looked at me cautiously and said, 'Mr Baron, that Ghazalnus is not trustworthy. A few years ago, I arranged for him to become the private teacher of Sayfadin Maro's daughter, may God forgive her sins. He had such a negative influence on her imagination, the whole affair ended in Mahnaz Khan leaving her fiancé – I am sure you know him, poor Najo Ashkani, he's an official at the Ministry of Peshmerga now – and, finally, setting herself on fire. I feel Ghazalnus puts such fantasies in people's minds that they get out of control and can never be placated again.'

Attar was making a good point, but I had already considered that risk.

'That's what happens when the imagination operates without a plan or a map,' I said. 'Dear Mr Attar, we want the imagination so that we can use it to make the world beautiful, to build something. I want to *plant* imagination, to let it put down roots. Imaginative people themselves cannot do this. My biggest problem with this lot is that they resist the idea of putting down roots, and that makes them dangerous. Mr Attar, it is my job to prevent imagination from existing unrooted in this city. I have a feeling the youth of this city are increasingly rootless. You see, two concepts are sacred to me: the first, plans and organisation; the second, roots. Only God knows how important and sacred roots are for every human being. I want a fantasy that can attract the world's attention, that reflects development and progress. But a fantasy that cannot be tamed, that says, "I don't work on the streets or alleyways, I don't go down to the level of qaysaris and bazaars, people are worthless", is dangerous.

'Do you see? An imagination that encourages an inner desire not to fit into a particular category is a lethal game; an imagination that speaks about love in such an abstract way that I don't understand what it means, that pays no attention to the state or to the fate and progress of the nation, is deadlier than any plague. Look, there's a tradition that was established by twentieth-century Kurdish poets that the fantasies of a poet or anyone else are public property. We know this from these outstanding Kurdish poets. We don't accept it when someone thinks otherwise. That's why you've got to help me put the beautiful imaginations of these people to work.'

It was clear that no one had ever spoken so clearly to Attar before. He became ecstatic. He promised he would lend me his full support. I gave him the names of the people and said, 'I need them all. You don't have to convince them all, but, just so you know, I need them all.'

When I said that, neither Attar nor I was certain of anything. Attar could buy any human being; no one in this city was more skilled at buying and selling human beings than he was. Winning people over by offering them money was his specialty. He worked between engineers and corporations, the Land Registry and the major property owners, the ministries and contractors, the Finance Ministry and the Chamber of Commerce. He had only become involved in major deals of late, but even so had already taken against the work of the Imaginative Creatures. As I tried slowly to find my way into the beautiful imaginations of these creatures, there was no one to turn to but Attar.

At that time, I received a strange bit of news. I heard from my assistant for security affairs that Majid-i Gul Solav, also known as "the Imaginary Magellan", was in Nwemiran and had become storyteller to the barons' children. My heart immediately began to pound with fright, and my mind was flooded with concern. Majid had become Ghazalnus's closest friend in recent years. I knew he told stories to the children at the Organisation for the Blind. He was an arrogant young man with almost no friends. He was also more prone to dreaming than the others. I didn't think there was anything in the real world that interested him, and to the best of my knowledge he had no friends apart from Ghazalnus. He was a quiet, complex and unusual person – and his appearance in Nwemiran was no ordinary matter.

That same evening I found out that the Baron of Dolls was behind it. When I spoke to the baron on the phone, he said didn't know anything about the relationship between Ghazalnus and Gul Solav. I feigned ignorance, pretending not to know much either, and kept my suspicions about Gul Solav to myself. Inwardly, however, I knew the boastful, elegant young man must be in Nwemiran for a reason. I had stopped seeing Ghazalnus as a simple, ordinary type some time ago – Tarkhunchi's reports spoke of his house as a lake teeming with mysteries. I decided to unravel Gul Solav's secret. One evening, at Mir Safin's party, I summoned him to meet me. I could read many things in his eyes. I could sense the sudden fear in his heart. My informers recorded how flustered he was when he bade me goodbye. Anyone else in my position would have been suspicious of him, too. His sudden flight from the party, his panic, his trembling hands and sudden headache only strengthened my resolve to keep my surveillance in place. That night, I sensed that this young man was the weak link in Ghazalnus's little team. I was certain I could penetrate their world through Majid-i Gul Solav.

A CONVERSATION ABOUT THE MEANING OF THE CHINESE YOUTH'S BODY, AND LATER MY DECLARATION OF WAR

HASAN-I TOFAN, EARLY SEPTEMBER 2004

Only a small number of the barons frequented the Idle Murderers' Club. I learned from Shibr that the Baron of Courgettes was among the few who did. Shibr had extensive information about him.

'The Baron of Courgettes is not a real baron,' he said. 'Until 1995, the guy was an ordinary bazaar trader who started out selling courgettes. In his early days, he was so poor he worked as a porter at the wholesale fruit and vegetable market. It was the looting that followed the uprising that made him the man he is today. At the height of the gunfight between the people and the fascists, the baron – known as "Saman-i Shafa-i Shijar" at the time – stole hundreds of big cardboard boxes filled with cigarettes from a state warehouse, and hid them for a long time. It was the baron's good fortune that the price of cigarettes soared dramatically in the days of economic sanctions. That was when he struck his blow, amassing a large amount of capital by the standards of the time. Employing his shrewdness in a few deals with Baghdad's famous merchants, he redoubled his wealth by selling milk that was past its use-by date.

'Meanwhile, the Baron of Flowers died from taking too much Viagra, and by the end of 2001 his son had squandered most of his father's wealth on women, whiskey and senseless business ventures. Their mansion in Nwemiran ended up being passed on to the Baron of Courgettes for a pittance. Had it not been for this, it would have been impossible for this man to gain access to the circle of princes, parliamentarians and senior officials. Many of the rich men of Nwemiran still regard him as an outsider who got to where he is purely by chance, as someone who doesn't deserve to be in their midst. But the baron has forged a close friendship with the Baron of Porcelain and the Baron of Henna and Dye. They are his greatest backers. He is also self-promoting and audacious, and does not shy away from anything. Everyone now knows that Murtaza Satan mainly works for the Baron of Courgettes, as well as the likes of Caesar and the Sheikh of Fried Bread.'

I related Majid-i Gul Solav's story about the Chinese Youth to Shibr, and told him that our work now was to collect news and information about the Baron of Courgettes' wife, who had, apparently, also been missing since Murad Jamil's disappearance. Shibr knew nothing about the baron's wife and the Chinese Youth; this was because Shibr was an extremely high-minded man. He would not contemplate people discussing the honour of anyone else's wife or daughter.

'Hasan-i Pizo,' Shibr said when I told him the story of the Chinese Youth, 'it's likely Murtaza Satan had a hand in it. Very likely. During all the years that secret women's refuges were being set on fire, many more women were killed across the city and a few girls in Nwemiran also went missing. There has been a lot of talk that Murtaza Satan, Ismail the Jackal and their gang of stupid adolescents had a hand in it. I don't know whether there's any truth in it. But the rumours are persistent, and from what I've heard, they were started by the Nwemiran women. The clues all seem to point to Ja'far-i Magholi, whom the Party still holds in high regard. There is also talk of the Deputy Leader taking him with him to the capital, and that he might be given a very special task in the south. They say that even the Americans are certain Magholi can really get things done. Hasan-i Pizo, you and I know that Ja'far Magholi was one of the people who murdered women after the uprising. He did what you and I said "no" to at the time. The Party used him to kill dozens of women, and in many cases the reason for the deaths remains unclear ... Murtaza Satan is a close friend of the Baron of Courgettes. If the Baron of Courgettes' wife has been secretly killed, then I would say Murtaza Satan had a hand in it.'

After Shibr gave me this information, I went back to Ghazalnus to share with him what I had learned. Until then, none of my friends had even heard the name 'Murtaza Satan'. It was a strange day. Majid-i Gul Solav was there, too. The three of us sat in Ghazalnus's study. That day, Ghazalnus told me the story of Murad Jamil and himself. He said he had kept it from us because he didn't want us to feel obliged to follow up the mystery of Murad Jamil's death out of love or respect for him, for Ghazalnus. His aim was for us each to experience the story according to our own interest. He feared that if we knew that the Chinese Youth was close to him, we might rush our searches and get ourselves in a lot of trouble. I was surprised to see him cry for the first time. He wept passionately and incessantly.

'Ghazalnus,' I said, putting my arms around him to comfort him, 'we are sons of this country. This country is full of bodies. The only factory at work in this country is the one that makes and buries bodies. Don't worry that you might have put us in danger. The apparition of a corpse dwells in the imagination of each one of us, and drags us along behind it constantly.'

Majid and I were so caught up in the affair that we would have followed the story whether or not Ghazalnus had wanted us to. Murad's body was with us constantly. It had become part of our lives. 'Ghazalnus,' I said, 'the problem is that we lost Murad's body. We shouldn't have lost it. We need it desperately now.'

He did not respond. He looked at me with his tearful eyes and said, 'Now we have to focus on reality. The important thing is to find out what became of Baran Shukur.'

Ghazalnus's indifference towards Murad Jamil's body disconcerted me slightly. I don't know why, but at that moment I realised that Murad's body and Baran's mystery had acquired a significant meaning for each of us – that the real meaning I'd lost after the uprising, the meaning Majid was looking for in his imaginary maps and the profound hidden meaning Ghazalnus sought in his ghazals had all come together in the secret of those two people.

'You can't pursue a dead person unless their death becomes part of the mystery of your own life,' I told Ghazalnus. 'In the lives of each one of us, there is a dead person we want to see again, to talk to, apologise to, serve and understand. More often than not, that corpse is the body of someone close – our mother or father, someone else who was close to us and left us abruptly in the course of this cruel life. If not, then it is an imagined corpse, an imagined dead person, which could represent our own death, our own body. I've often spoken to my own death through other dead people. Often.'

'Hasan-i Pizo, the Chinese Youth was different,' said Ghazalnus with great sadness, as if he had not expected me to say such things. 'I killed the Chinese Youth, you see. My ghazals killed the Chinese Youth … he's someone who really lived … he wasn't pursuing an apparition; perhaps he was the only person in this city who wasn't. He did what you and I couldn't do: he lived in this city as if it were an imaginary garden. His Hazarbagh was no different from these streets and alleyways. For him, every woman was an imagined beloved, every alleyway an imaginary garden. I killed him … I tried hard not to give him any ghazals. I tried very hard to prevent him from treading the same street of imagination that I know so well … He himself saw the beauty of his life. He knew how majestically he lived. But the ghazals took him away and killed him.

He was the creature I dreamed about; he lived the life I wanted for myself. The ghazals didn't let him live.'

'The Chinese Youth did have happy times,' Majid said, 'but he didn't see the real life of this filthy city. Real life is not an obsession with women's bodies, but walking down these dirty streets. I don't understand how anyone in this hideous, grimy city could live an enchanted life.'

Ghazalnus threw a glance at Majid and said, after a moment's reflection, 'To start with, the Chinese Youth didn't know the distinction between the imagination and reality. Like a newborn baby, reality and the imagination were just the same. He understood the distinction afterwards, under the influence of my ghazals.'

I believed that distinction was the secret of our life and death. Personally, since the time of the revolution, I had felt myself torn between the imagination and reality. I still say that there is no one in this city who is *not* divided into two halves – but some of us are aware of this, while others die without ever realising as much.

'During the revolution, when I worked in the assassination cells,' I said, butting in, 'I felt that if we did away with bad people one by one, the world would turn into a paradise. Often, my colleagues and I were pleased when we killed someone, thinking it took us a step closer to this goal. We threw parties and celebrated. There are people who still think like that. In most people's lives, there is probably a time when they think this. From childhood, most of us were raised in such a way that we couldn't paint a mental image of our idyllic homeland without murder or a scramble over other people's corpses.

'The first night I went to Hazarbagh, I said, "The beauty that exists in the imagination does not exist in reality." I asked myself, "What do you need reality for? All the years you spent making rosewater have now brought you this garden. Rest here, and keep quiet. Today you have your own paradise. Keep your backside planted in your imaginary pants and hang on to the safe spot you've secured for yourself." When I walk past the Sebagh district during the day, I am surprised that, come nightfall, this same spot becomes such a magical place in your mind, and in the minds of the older women, and in mine as well. Just as day and night don't meet, the flowers of Hazarbagh and the dirty, dusty daytime don't meet. I'm not well versed in any of this, but I can say that it was my desire to leap out of reality and into the imagination that made me a murderer. And I wasn't the only one: many of the peshmergas of the time, part of the national struggle, harboured this idea of a leap out of this ugly world and into another.

'I was once talking to one of the leaders of the revolution. "Comrade," I said, "what are we pursuing in this revolution? I'm getting fed up of killing people." He looked at me with sadness. He said, "Comrade Tofan, we are chasing a hat swept away on the wind."

'"Comrade, what do you mean, a swept-away hat?" I asked.

'"A swept-away hat, Comrade. Something we cannot catch even if the revolution is successful."

'The entire revolution was such a fantastical event that no one knew exactly what to make of it. When the uprising succeeded, it came to a bitter, ugly end. One day, I killed a woman and looked into her eyes. That gaze changed my entire life. In the eyes of that woman, I saw the end of the fantasy. I saw the swept-away hat the comrade had talked about. My dear friends, my revolutionary comrades threw their fantasy away, and never revisited it. And no one ever asked what the fantasy of that long revolution actually was, or what became of the martyrs' fantasies. A revolution is like a dream. When it ends we all wake up, the dream fades and is forgotten. There is nothing in this world as fickle as a revolution.

'After the triumph of the uprising and the people's return from mass exodus, I looked into the eyes of my friends and saw not even the faintest glimmer of fantasy. It made me run away, go home and lock myself in. There are people who can get by without imagination, but others, like us, cannot live without it. When we tread an imaginary road and realise it is a cul-de-sac, we change our path to take another street. I won't deny that it took me a long time to distinguish between these two worlds. When I killed that poor woman after the uprising, I understood that the fantasies of the revolutionary era would not bear fruit in this land. I told myself, "Hasan-i Pizo, get out before you turn into an even more disgraceful and unscrupulous creature." In order to cleanse myself and instill something else in my soul, I withdrew into near-seclusion for six years. I believe that, during that time, the smell of my mother's rosewater took me out of this damned world, day after day …

'More recently, there's been no point in life except Murad's body. I took part in writing the book of the dead for your sake, but my dear friends, no matter how strongly you are attracted to the realm of imagination, reality will always rise up before you in the form of a corpse. We can't run away from it … imagination does not relieve us of the weight of reality. Reality is an ugly thing that will destroy us whether we like it or not. The imagination, too, is overwhelming. No matter how immersed you are in the real world, you cannot escape it.

'My friends, even though Murad Jamil lived in the real world, and the doors to real pleasures were open to him, in the end he couldn't escape the power of the imagination. Man is a delicate creature. Caught between the pressure of reality and imagination, he becomes either a murderer like me or a poet like you, Ghazalnus. Ghazalnus, my brother, I'm scared of you now, and of Majid. Don't look at me like that. I'm scared of you, Ghazalnus. You are a man of the imagination. We have the same garden in our heads, but I'm scared all these bitter truths will kill us in exactly the same way that fantasies of love killed the Chinese Youth.'

Majid-i Gul Solav usually didn't hide his dislike of my voice and manner of speaking. Whenever I talked a lot, I could see him becoming irritated. Although I wasn't all that talkative, my unpleasant voice and incoherence meant people paid little attention to my words. That evening, however, I thought I observed Majid looking at me with respect.

'Majid,' I said laughingly, 'when someone says what's in his heart, he is beautiful even if he is Satan.'

'It's a huge mistake to tear down the wall between imagination and reality,' he said with his aristocratic smile. 'It's a mistake. It's dangerous to overburden the imagination with reality, or reality with imagination. Mingling these two realms is like mixing water and fire.'

Ghazalnus looked at both of us in disbelief and, after a moment's reflection, picked up some papers from his desk; then he put them back down again, unsure what to do with himself. 'The boundary you all draw between reality and imagination is impossible,' he said. 'What killed the Chinese Youth? Have you asked yourselves that? Reality, or imagination? Man can only draw the boundary between them in a world where there is no love or murder. Wherever there is love and murder, the truth and the imagination blend in such a way that they become inseparable.

'I've been reading ghazals for many years, and with each one I immerse myself deeper in the world of the imagination; but whenever I've gone some distance into it, I've thought a lot about the real world. Have you ever wondered why, of all the people in this city, we are the only ones collecting the stories of death? Or why the Chinese Youth's body changed your life as it did? Have you, Magellan? Because no one is as thirsty for reality as an imaginative creature. The imagination itself seeks to hold our hands and set us on the straight road back to reality. The Chinese Youth came to me via the real world. Love brought him to me. I wanted him to live without the risk of murder, or being made miserable by love. I wanted to make him content with a small portion of reality and a small portion of the imagination. The sickness we suffer from is not having an imagination or thinking about reality. Everyone boasts a small portion of both. Our sickness is that we aren't content with just those small portions. When someone wants to reach the furthest end of the imagination, he must go to the furthest end of reality as well, and vice versa – that's our sickness. Other people manage to survive on small portions of each without any sense of their lives lacking something. But we are doomed to continue to the very end. As far as I am concerned, that's what I'm fated to do; the Chinese Youth left me no other option. He came and went to the end of imagination, which is death. Now I have no option but to go to the end of reality; you are free to decide if you want to come with me or not. You can leave. You each have your imaginary realms and private lives, but I am destined to carry on. I have to.'

'Ghazalnus, we have done everything together,' Majid said. 'We know this is all fraught with danger. We know someone killed the Chinese Youth, and a woman is missing, and there are unidentified people who want to make off with the ghazals – we can't just stop here and do nothing.'

That day we decided to see the game through to the end. There is no one more inept than a player who leaves the field halfway through a game, and none of us considered ourselves an inept player.

That same day, Majid-i Gul Solav and I had the most important conversation of our lives. I knew that his majestic poise and English suit, and my modest, rough nature made for an unlikely combination, yet I admired Gul Solav even more than Ghazalnus. Ghazalnus appeared to be lost between two worlds. I couldn't see any great difference between him and me – neither of us belonged to either world, in fact – but Gul Solav's belief in his imagination was strong, and that gave him a certain power we lacked.

I would remember our conversation for the rest of my days. It was the first time he unburdened himself with me. From that day on, I held him in special regard, though his swaying gait and excessive self-satisfaction in his white, black and cream suits never failed to disappoint me.

'Gul Solav,' I told Majid that day, 'the Chinese Youth's corpse is always with me. Sometimes I can see him as soon as I close my eyes. When I walk around Hazarbagh, I see him. When I stroll around the streets, I have a strong sensation that he's watching me from behind. Sometimes I even feel his breath so close, it's as if he might touch me. Gul Solav, you're younger and better educated than I am. You may not have seen the world, but precisely because of that, you may understand it better. I have a question for you. This corpse has a strong hold over me, and I'm trying to understand it. What do you think would make a man of my age fall in love with a corpse?'

'Hasan-i Pizo, I feel just the same,' Majid said. 'Ever since I first saw that body, I've wanted to do something for it. It occasionally appears in my life, too, but I won't let it rule my imagination completely. The dead are cruel if you let them in. They'll invade your life and disturb your peace.

'Do you know why I want to see this story through to the end?' he added, after a pause. 'Because reading the fate of the dead is the only thing humankind can do without any ulterior motives in mind. The dead don't return to thank us. We're doing them a favour without their knowledge, without expectations on either side. That's the utmost generosity, and it marks a man's arrival at perfection. Doing the dead a favour is not the same as doing it for the living. Whenever someone does a favour for a living person, their heart is full of expectations; obligation blossoms between them, and there are hopes of greater favours in return. The granter of the favour is pleased that others are indebted to him. Even when serving God or his homeland, man expects rewards. Look at what hideous creatures those serving the homeland have become. I often wish they'd never served our homeland at all. Look and see for yourself just what monsters those who serve God are, how indifferently they tear other human beings to pieces in the hope of reaching Paradise.

'Whereas I don't expect anything in return for serving this departed young man; it simply strengthens my belief that I have no roots on this Earth. Unlike Ghazalnus, I am not seeking the truth, and when I accompany this corpse, I give nothing to the dead man and the dead man gives nothing to me ... that's the purest kind of connection there can be between two creatures. They ask nothing of me, and I ask nothing of them. That's the most humane form of relationship, superior even to love. Love is filled with fears, demands and selfishness, but attending to the fate of the dead is free of demands and selfishness. It's a kind of relationship that can only be formed with the dead, do you see?

'No, I'm not seeking the truth. Unlike Ghazalnus, I'm seeking purity. Ghazalnus is searching for his lost half, but I want to complete a full but pure circle with the Chinese Youth. He gives nothing to me, nor I to him, and yet we are both part of the same equation, part of the same circle. You're not in love with the corpse, Hasan-i Pizo, you need the corpse more than any of us. You need to accompany him more than any of us, because he is your only guide out of the camp of the killers and into the camp of those killed.

'Look, since the moment I met you, I've wanted to tell you something. Most of the killers of this country seek political absolution. Don't accuse me of being crude. Whenever I think about you, I immediately ask myself: If a killer says, "I regret it", is that the end of the matter? If he says, "I'm ready to take my punishment", will everything be over then? If he goes before his leaders and says, "You made me a killer", is that it? Would that do even the slightest damage to the hideous politicians of this city? If he went before a court, bared his chest and said, "Kill me, I'm a criminal", would he become someone else? No, Hasan-i Pizo, he would not. What if he started reading poetry – would he become an honest person? When I put my head on the pillow at night, I think about these dangerous things.

'No killer can be exonerated like that. Those political and sentimental absolutions are merely a salve applied to a wound. To be absolved, you must cross over to the camp of the murdered; the spirit of a person who has been killed must enter your body, and only then will you understand everything. Hasan, just seeing a corpse isn't enough in itself. It's not enough to sense the presence of that person and feel he's walking beside you. On the contrary, you have to *become* him. Absolution for the killer comes only through wearing the soul of a person who has been killed, and living in his stead until death, pursuing his dreams, becoming immersed in his wishes. The Chinese Youth is giving you the chance to live on his behalf, to put on his soul and continue his story. If you want absolution, put it on and see the world for once from a dead person's perspective.

'My friend, this country of ours is the country of death. Every day there are all these corpses, their stench filling humanity's nose; there are all the women who are killed in this city, whose stories have spread to the ends of the world. Hasan-i Pizo, King of Rosewater, I believe we all need to put on the spirit of a dead person at least once and wear it around the city. I'm completely serious. Think what the Chinese Youth would do if he came back to life now. Hear me out, then make this your passion. Think about it. Then go and pursue it.'

At that moment, I believed that if the spirit of the Chinese Youth returned to this world, he would immediately set out to look for Baran Shukur. I stood up. That search was now the only thing on my mind. It was like being under a spell.

Under the influence of Magellan's talk, I was the first to declare war openly. When I decided to do this unilaterally, I had no real idea of the enormity of the battle. I don't believe anyone who went into battle with the princes and barons of Nwemiran at the time did. When we did enter the war, the Nwemiran princes had already been laying siege to us for a long time.

I attacked Murtaza Satan on 6 September 2004.

That same night, after my conversation with Gul Solav, Shibr and I sat down at Murtaza Satan's table at the Idle Murderers' Club. He greeted us with a big smile, but there was fear in his eyes. Even so, he said, 'What a beautiful night it is! What a magical, melodious night! Two of the nicest guys in this city are my guests. A man would put his life in danger for a night like this. There are people who die without experiencing such a night. How lucky I am, how happy! My oh my, why does fortune favour me so? What luck is carried on the breeze that blows through my garden?'

Shibr and I said we would be pleased if he could join us for dinner one evening.

'Your invitation is a great honour,' he said. 'It is as if I am reborn. Neither a breeze coming from afar, nor the morning's gentle air can cool my heart and soul like the respect you have for me.'

Shibr and I both knew that Murtaza Satan held the key to most of the secrets in the Murad story. The whole affair was filled with genuine peril. I didn't want Shibr involved in it; I wanted to implement the plan on my own. But Shibr refused to leave me alone in such a risky situation. Despite his disability and physical weakness, he was more cunning than I was. I started the conversation with Murtaza by talking about my own past with Ja'far-i Magholi. I told him I was a close friend of Magholi, whom I hadn't seen for more than twelve years; that I knew Magholi was a close friend of his as well, and that it would be wonderful to see him if at all possible.

Murtaza said in his flowery language, 'Magholi, well, he's really top-notch, a brave man. Dear God, how many more flowers are there in the vase of this homeland? How many buds and saplings like him can be found in the gardens and fields of our country? I should've known that a nobleman like you, that honest guys like you two, would be friends of a man of his calibre. I am lucky to live in the same era as Ja'far-i Magholi; I'm lucky to be the contemporary of unique and brave men like him. I swear by the sun's rays and the clear spring water of this homeland in whose arms you and I were raised, that man is an invaluable gem.'

Everyone knew Murtaza was lying. 'Murtaza, tell me frankly, do you get to see much of Ja'far-i Magholi these days?' Shibr asked, to encourage him to keep talking. 'I've heard he's still in Europe. It's said that he hasn't been back since he went to Holland.'

'He came back three days after the Party asked him to, after the Leader sent him a special letter asking him to return,' Murtaza said, laughing. 'Ja'far-i Magholi. Oh, how he cares about this land! Who could forget a valiant man like him? He said, "Farewell, you beautiful cities of the West, farewell peacefulness; the homeland is calling, my native land beckons; the Leader in all his glory, bearer of a sacred message, has summoned me." Ja'far is one of those who have devoted their lives to this homeland. He is indeed, brother Shibr. I do see Magholi, and even if I didn't, I'd be willing to crawl all the way to his doorstep for your sake. It's an honour – yes, an honour. You are bestowing a great privilege on me by asking me to become a junior messenger between great men like yourselves. What happiness it is for an insignificant no one like myself to serve great men like you.'

'Murtaza, we'd like you to arrange a meeting for us with Magholi,' Shibr said. 'If it is true he's been promoted to a senior position by the Party, he should remember his friends. Tell him Hasan-i Tofan and Shibr Mustafa would like to see him. He's an old friend of ours.'

'Magholi will not forget his friends,' said Murtaza, raising his hand as if he were on stage. 'The Leader would not appreciate him so much if he were not loyal, isn't that so, brothers? Throughout his life, the Leader has sought out loyal men – great men and princes, you mustn't forget this … But then there's his workload. Just imagine, serving such a ruined country as ours, carrying out your duties tirelessly, being alert to your enemies and all the people hostile to you. Just think, all the nights he stays awake protecting this country, protecting its great men. My brothers, Magholi would die for the good men of this country. If he has to guard a beautiful soul, he can go for weeks without a moment's sleep. He has not forgotten about you; he has not. But his workload, his duties in the Party …' He trailed off.

When I looked at his hands, at his smile and laughter, I was sure I could trap this fox. I was certain there was something in his heart you could catch if you hunted it down. I knew that only one game plan worked with these creatures, and that was confrontation. All the monsters created by the Party were adept at furtive games and play-acting.

'Murtaza, I am Magholi's friend,' I said plainly, entering the game. 'I'm not like him. Do you understand? I left the Party and won't join it again in my lifetime, but I will work. Do you understand? I'll work, but on my own terms. I carried a gun for as long as guns meant something, but that's all over now. Magholi isn't the son of this homeland. He is now the servant of the princes. I want to see him and ask him a few questions.

'Do you know what those questions are? Would you like to hear them? Well? I'll be asking him this: "Ja'far-i Magholi, what was your role in killing the women who were burned to death at a refuge two years ago? Do you remember them, the poor women in the Babardan district?" I'll ask: "Magholi, my friend, don't be modest now, tell me, what's your role in the killing of some of the girls and women in

Nwemiran? More than one woman has disappeared from Nwemiran in the past two years." Isn't that so, my dear Murtaza? I'll also ask: "My friend, killer of women, how many more women have you killed since I stopped?" And I'll ask: "Which agha, prince, or loyal senior cadre are you working for? Which of them rewards you most generously?" I'll tell him: "My dear Magholi, I'm an old friend; tell me, for whom do you open fire today? Apart from Ismail the Jackal and Murtaza Satan, how many more men are working for you in the bazaar and on the streets, intimidating people?" I'll ask: "How many companies do you have shares in? Tell me, my dear friend, how many dividends do you receive? For how many people's benefits do you meddle in tenders? How many people's teeth do you break every year among those who dare to open their mouths? How many journalists' ribs have you broken so far? You have investments in how many new blocks of flats?" I'll ask: "My brother Ja'far, how many people in the bazaar are frontmen for you and your baron friends? How many shops do you have? How many hundreds of dunams of land do you control near the city? How many unfortunate villagers have you forced into selling their villages, and how many of their sons have been recruited into the police, robbing them of their livelihoods? How many petrol stations do you secretly own? Who pays the expenses of the loyal men who work for you – the Baron of Porcelain, the Baron of Courgettes, the Sheikh of Fried Bread, Caesar? Who? Is it the Party? The Politburo? Their loyal friends, colleagues and cadres? Tell me, who?"'

My words were like a blow straight to Murtaza's head. For a moment, he was so shocked he couldn't utter a word. No one had ever spoken to him like that before. It was the only possible gambit with him. I knew that if we both talked with our masks still in place, the game would never end, but if one of us threw the mask off, everything would change. I knew it would take a while for the blow to wear off. Shibr, too, was shocked I had gone that far, but he was happy to see Murtaza Satan in that state. I could see the satisfaction in his eyes.

'Hasan-i Tofan, my brother, great man,' Murtaza said, giving himself a shake. 'Don't fall for the lies of our opponents. I swear by the purity of the butterflies and the apple buds, Magholi has no hand in those matters. The burned women, the murdered girls? Ha! Oh, my brother Hasan. Magholi is an honest soldier. I welcomed him the day he returned from Holland. As soon as we arrived in the city, as soon as he saw the minarets, as soon as he saw the mountains, as soon as he saw the dome, the citadel and the electricity towers, he started crying. He even tasted the soil. You don't know how much he loves this land

and its waters. He ate the grass. Yes, my friend, like someone driven mad by exile, he actually ate the grass from the garden of his house. Had you seen Magholi that day, you'd know what a gentleman he is. You would know how much he loves this country. I couldn't control myself, and started crying with him. I ate the soil with him, I ate the grass with him.'

'Murtaza,' I told him, 'all the women of this city have heard your name. Whom do you work for? They all say that you poisoned the two sisters in the Kanitoz district for Magholi, that you had a hand in beheading the runaway wife of an agha. I don't have any power over you, so why are you scared? I'm asking you about things people outside already know. Everyone knows.'

I could tell my words were slowly driving him into a rage, but he controlled himself again and said, 'Hasan-i Tofan, my friend, my sweet brother, Murtaza is a butterfly. He couldn't hurt an ant. A wicked person has misled your great and pure heart. A dangerous person has poisoned your great soul. I swear by the lives of the flowers, I swear by the sound of goodness and purity being killed, I am innocent. My heart is purer than snow, purer than water, purer than dew. You don't know Murtaza. I walk around this city day and night, telling people, "You don't know Murtaza, come and see his soul." That's right, his soul.'

'His soul?' I said sarcastically. 'His soul? The devilish soul he'll sell to any buyer. Murtaza, do you remember the night you and Caesar were tormenting a young man on the outskirts of the city? Do you remember talking rubbish, just like you are now, out there in the dark? I was there that night. I was watching you, Caesar and the other brave men beating up a poor kid in the dark because he didn't want to hand over his shop. Do you remember, or not? How many times have you guys beaten people up like that? You mentioned the soul – where's Baran Shukur's soul? Tell me, where is the Baron of Courgettes' wife? Aren't you a pure soul? If so, tell me, where is Baran Shukur?'

As if he'd been scratched by sharp fingernails, he leaped up and took a step back from our table. 'Hasan-i Tofan, you are dear to me,' he said. 'You are my lord. Everyone knows that the Baron of Courgettes' wife is abroad … the whole world knows that. Almighty God, save me from this man's evil suspicions, God forgive him. Almighty God, forgive him, because Hasan-i Tofan is my superior, my teacher; he is dear to me. He's my lord.'

As if dizzy, as if he had been struck by a poisonous arrow and was waiting for the toxins to reach his heart, Murtaza Satan walked slowly and unsteadily out of the building with the all the shame of a defeated monster.

When he had gone, I looked at Shibr and said, 'My brother Shibr, now they'll either kill us, or Magholi will send someone to silence us. Or, if the Baron of Courgettes' wife is alive, they might let her be seen in public even if she's currently being hidden in a basement.'

'No, none of your three possibilities will come true,' Shibr said, looking at me. 'They won't kill us because they assume bigger powers are behind us. That's how they reason. I grew up inside the machine; I lived between its teeth. Look at my legs and you can see where I've been. I know how they think. Magholi won't make an appearance because Murtaza Satan wouldn't dare share tonight's news with him, and the Baron of Courgettes' wife won't be seen because, I'm sure, she's not alive.'

'So what is going to happen then?' I asked.

'I don't know,' Shibr said, looking at me.

'What should we do now?'

'Now, we leave,' said Shibr, flashing me a wide smile to calm me down. 'Take a good look at this hall, because you won't be seeing it again before you die. Neither of us can come back here now. We don't need to come any more. All the time we've been coming here because we wanted to fire a shot. We just fired it. Now that we have, it would be wrong to appear again. So, bye bye, Idle Murderers' Club. Let's go. Once we're out of here, I'll tell you what we have to do.'

THE ENCOUNTER BETWEEN THE REAL
AND IMAGINARY MAGELLANS

SEPTEMBER 2004

Afsana described Zuhdi Shazaman as a man who smelled of distant trees and undiscovered seas, who carried the magic of unknown lands and secret regions, who smelled of mysterious fruits and wild leaves, whose scent could only be found on the imaginary plains. When you slept with him, you felt as if you had slept with the night's breeze; that the passer-by touching your body had touched every star in the sky before you. His fingers evoked the fantasies and daydreams travellers engage in aboard ships, and his kisses brought distant fields to mind. His intimate touch was like a key unlocking hidden treasure. When his lips touched yours, your body filled with rapid currents; at the sound of his breathing, your tense muscles relaxed, and when he spoke, it was as if a breeze was gently pressing against your breasts and a pair of thirsty lips caressed the length of your body.

Ghazalnus listened to Afsana's descriptions with astonishment. He had known her for sixteen years. In that period, she had been a loyal friend and an honest woman. Throughout those years, the woman of the enchanting whispers had regularly spoken of her hatred of her hotelier husband, her annoyance with him, but she had never cheated on him. He was sure that if she had, she would have told him. This was her first instance of infidelity. 'One day, I'll cheat on him, but with someone who is so masterful in love, someone who can so intoxicate me that if Ismail kills me afterwards, I won't care,' she had told him many years ago. When he looked into Afsana's eyes now, he was sure she had found the man she had been seeking all her life. What struck him as strange was that this knight of hers should be Baran Shukur's uncle, who had come home from the other end of the world to find her. He was surprised to learn that Afsana was aware of the Baron of Courgettes' lie. She also recounted at length the story of the stolen letters, the tale of Zuhdi Shazaman's encounter with the baron in an old house and the story of the attack, which she knew her husband had had a hand in.

393

After Afsana had recounted everything in detail, she placed her hands on Ghazalnus's and said, 'Ghazalnus, help him. Help him for my sake. He needs us desperately.'

'Afsana, my good friend,' said Ghazalnus, with the tender expression that appeared on his face while reading ghazals. 'It is I who need your help. I am now certain that Baran Shukur's story is closely linked to the killing of the Chinese Youth. Baran and the Chinese Youth had a secret liaison for around a year. The whole thing is more complicated than you think. There are many strands to the story. We now believe the young woman and her lover have been killed. You must keep away; it's likely there are big fish involved. You know what I mean. Two of my friends and I are very invested, because the Chinese Youth was close to me – very, very close. We need to bring Zuhdi back. He should be with us.'

Three days after that encounter, Zuhdi returned to the city of his childhood. On the evening of 6 September 2004, the very same night that Hasan-i Tofan and Shibr launched their first attack against Murtaza, Zuhdi dined with Ghazalnus and Majid-i Gul Solav. He sat there with all the ease of a globetrotting traveller, sporting long hair like a king and wearing a new suit. That evening was the first time the two great travellers, the two Magellans, sat at the same table.

After dinner, Zuhdi took an enormous atlas out of his suitcase. It was very old, but had not yet lost its lustre. It contained large, detailed maps on which he had highlighted the routes of his long journeys with a red pen. He circled the cities he had seen, of which there were many across the globe, in red ink. That night, Zuhdi told them about Hanoi bike-sellers; paddy fields between Macau and Beijing; making love to a young woman selling Tamil statuettes outside one of Sri Lanka's temples; getting lost between two parks in Johannesburg; the thieves who robbed him in Izmir; his nights in the arms of prostitutes in Manila; a slap in the face from a headscarved woman in Kuala Lumpur; the impudence of the watch-sellers of Kolkata; his fight with the jealous husband of a woman wearing niqab in a Tangier hotel; the story of the Moroccan girls who asked him not to use condoms; his stay with a poor family in Bogotá; the story of his arrival in the village where Che Guevara had been captured; how he had survived drowning in southern Chile, and escaped a knife fight with thieves in Venice.

He told his dinner companions extraordinary stories all that night. He talked about the difference in the taste of varieties of fish and birds; about a white whale he had seen by chance while on a passenger ship somewhere between Indonesia and Australia; about a seagull that once stayed eighteen days with him aboard a ship.

Ghazalnus and Majid listened for a long time. Majid felt a deep admiration for Zuhdi, a man who had seen most of the world. The journeys Majid made in his imagination, Zuhdi had made in reality; the waters he navigated in imaginary boats, Zuhdi had crossed on real ones. All his life, Majid had wanted to lead just such an existence, going from one land to another, from one city to another. Listening to Zuhdi, he found himself growing somewhat angry at Ghazalnus, who seemed to be paying attention only halfheartedly. With great patience, Majid wished Ghazalnus would praise his own imaginary journeys to Zuhdi, but eventually he had to do this himself. Somewhat shyly, he said, 'Most esteemed Mr Shazaman, I am called "the Imaginary Magellan". I have an imaginary map and go on imaginary journeys along its rivers and across its lands. It's a map that has no beginning or end.'

Shazaman, who didn't know what Majid was talking about, said, 'Many a night in my life, when I slept on the seashore or amid the undergrowth and tangled branches of the jungle, when I smelled faraway lakes or lifted my head to the heavens to see the stars of other lands with my bewildered eyes and to inhale the air of other nations, I told myself, "I am a Kurdish Magellan who sees the world as if I were the very last explorer. Everyone discovers the world for himself. No one can reveal a city to another person. All cities are built and lost as many times as the number of foreigners visiting and leaving them."'

That night Ghazalnus named Zuhdi 'the Real Magellan'. 'We are so caged in this city that we've never met anyone like you,' Ghazalnus said. 'Travellers and explorers rarely pass through this city. Sometimes I feel that the humans, trees and birds here all want to be lost. I am very keen to see people who, unlike us, don't live in this world through their imaginations. Dear stranger, I hope this city won't swallow you up. If they are not careful, those who stay in this city for too long lose their sense of what truth is, and their capacity for imagination becomes disabled. This is the only city in the world that wants to be neither compared to other real cities, nor measured against the cities of the imagination. It is happy to be unaware of the world. Cities that are unaware of the world do not exist in reality or in the imagination.'

Zuhdi was pleased with his nickname. Laughing, he said, 'Ghazalnus, I've seen many cities. Some decide neither to live nor to die. This is one such city.'

'This is one of those cities that once you enter, you cannot leave again,' Majid offered reticently.

'Mr Gul Solav,' Zuhdi said, looking at Majid with admiration, 'that is true. I've been travelling from one country to another for many years now. I leave one and head for another, come out of one city and go to another. Yet when I leave the gate of any city and step into another, I feel I am still here. A dark shadow from this city has always loomed over me; the shade of its walls is in my soul. Wherever I went, I was running away from this city. I feel like a total stranger here. Man is not a stranger in the cities he leaves, but in the ones he cannot leave. Man is not a stranger in the place from which he is expelled, but in the place that ties him down.'

Majid spoke in some detail about the strange cities he had entered on his imaginary map, which he had then believed he could not leave. He explained how, thereafter, wherever he went, he had a strange feeling he was still in their alleyways and streets, incarcerated and imprisoned in their winding roads. 'There are some cities that you enter, and others that enter you,' he said with some conviction and confidence. 'Those that get inside you invade you in such a way that wherever you are on Earth, you feel you are still there.'

The Real Magellan became gradually more and more impressed by the language and imagination of this young man with the table manners of a European lord. He was the only person he had seen or known in this city who ate like noblemen. Ghazalnus, with his tousled hair and overgrown beard, appeared confused to him; Zuhdi saw him as someone whose fantasies had no shape or form, whereas Majid's fantasies were unusually geometric and planned. Zuhdi himself was a lover of maps. He adored his own, the evidence of his travels throughout the world. He felt a sudden desire to see the map Majid-i Gul Solav spoke of – an imaginary map unlike the maps of our planet, a map that never ended. A realm that never ends: that was something he had often thought about during his long travels. Whenever he came to the edge of the sea, whenever he crossed one ocean and reached another, he asked himself, 'Why does the Earth end? Where is the land that has no end, through which you can walk forever? Why is the planet so small? Why can't it go on endlessly? Why can't the ground under me carry me without my needing to stop, disembark, fly or cross waters?'

That night, the three of them went to take a look at the Imaginary Magellan's map. Ghazalnus walked between the two of them. He was surprised to find himself with these two different creatures. The tall, imposing man with the appearance of a sailor whose ship had been hurled into the skies by the north wind before being dropped at random on this city now walked alongside the arrogant, elegant Gul Solav. One was lost in the real world, the other in the realm of the imaginary. Ghazalnus, bemused, listened to their marathon conversation. It went on till morning, and was like a race between reality and imagination in which they took turns speaking about their own realms. Of his imaginary map, Majid talked about fabled birds that suddenly produced hundreds of others, with each of those hundreds producing dozens more. The Real Magellan talked about the flocks of seagulls he had once seen block out the sun in southern Italy.

'If you had seen all the birds I saw, you would have thought this infinite number could only exist in the imagination,' he said, looking happily at the Imaginary Magellan. 'But it was real. I raised my head and could see no clouds, no sun, nor anything else, as if the whole world had been invaded by birds.'

Majid told him about a small village where all the stones, down to the very smallest, bore the engraved image of a heart and arrow. 'Gul Solav,' the Real Magellan said, 'one night I ended up on the shores of Spain. All along this stretch of land, I saw lovers embracing each other and crying. Not one pair, not two, but thousands upon thousands, as if all the heartbroken lovers on Earth had come to weep on these Spanish shores. I was walking alone, a bottle of beer in my hand, among all these lovers. Someone called to me in fluent English, saying: "Hey, you, Kurdish man – why are you alone? Why don't you have a woman with you, on whose shoulders you could cry while she weeps on yours?" I looked around, but saw no one. I took a few steps back, but didn't think any of the people near me had called. It was like a fantasy, like being called by a voice in my head. I walked for a long time after that, long enough to get far away from everyone. I threw away my beer, lay down and started looking at the stars. That night I said, "Shazaman, tonight the world is fleeing towards the imagination." I've often seen that. You do, if you travel a lot.'

'Real Magellan,' said an excited Majid, 'I have lived the opposite of that moment. One day, with the blind children, I happened upon a city that had no trace of the imagination. Everywhere else I had been had displayed at least a trace. Any village, town, camp or group of nomads I'd come across on my imaginary map had some trace of the imagination ... but since then, I've often encountered places that have no imagination. I don't know how it happened, as these places don't belong to the map I have created. This was a strange city. All its birds were weak and sick – they looked like the birds in this city. The trees were yellow, withered and sad. When I touched them, they seemed upset with people – just like the flowers of this city seem to be. When I touched the city's walls, I felt that they were neither happy nor peaceful. They were shy and scared, like the walls of this city. When I touched the stones, I felt them startle. The blind children picked up on this too, remarking that some of the dark alleyways they passed through resembled the darkness of the alleyways of blindness.

Its residents seemed either angry or sad and indifferent, like those of this city. There was hatred in the eyes of the young people to match the hatred in the eyes of the young men of this city. The city was too real. It was full of muddy puddles; it was full of streets swept by no one but the wind, of children washed by no one but the rain. I quickly brought the blind children out of the fantasy, and we ran. Afterwards I said nothing, but the children told me, "Sardarbashi, you sometimes get confused and re-enter our city without even realising it. Why don't you take a different direction?"

'"No matter how robust an imaginary map, a crack can suddenly appear and reality can attack us like a wild brute," I told the blind children. "In those moments, we must not be scared or become confused. We have to grasp quickly that it is the image of the real world that will not leave us alone. This city is like the Devil: it won't let us carry on our journey undisturbed. We should always be mindful that wherever we are in this world, it could attack us like a madman."'

'Although I have roamed real lands,' the Real Magellan said, 'and travelled by the atlas of the geographers, there have been occasions when I came under attack from the imagination. It's happened a thousand times that I was walking along a road and suddenly the flowers were talking to me, or the trees beckoning me. Many a time I've embraced a tree and asked, "Oh, tree, what do you want from me?" I have kissed flowers with the scent of human beings, of the tears of the girl I ended a relationship with here twenty-four years ago.

'One evening, I was standing by the seashore in western India when I suddenly saw thousands of fish leap out of the water, like mischievous children trying to out-jump one another. I said to the Dutch tourist who was with me, "Do you see all those fish jumping in the evening air and trying to fly?" I felt as if he couldn't see a thing, that I was the only one who could see them. I borrowed a boat from one of the boat owners and sailed out towards the middle of the sea. There I saw thousands of these fish jumping about all around me. Thousands, glittering like gold in the moonlight, as if they were playing for me. I thought they wanted to make me happy. I felt they were telling me, "Hey, Kurdish man, don't be so sad all the time. Laugh a little." I reached out, seized one and kissed her to my heart's content. It was as if she kissed me back, with a kiss that smelled of the depth of the sea. I still don't understand whether it was a real or an imaginary fish that kissed me on the waters of western India.'

That night, Majid opened his endless imaginary map and talked about it until morning. For every story he told, the Real Magellan told one from his old atlas. In some of Majid's imaginary stories, reality appeared strange, bitter and dark, and in some of Zuhdi's real

398

stories, imagination manifested itself so vividly as to make you suspect it was impossible for such events to have happened. Ghazalnus looked at each man in turn, and did not know whose world was stranger, more beautiful, more profound. Here were two worlds that suddenly clashed before him, and the outcome was the birth of hundreds of stories that spread through the room, colliding or colluding with each other. At dawn, Ghazalnus looked around the room and couldn't decide whether it was a room of truth or imagination.

THE SECOND ATTACK ON MURTAZA SATAN
7 SEPTEMBER 2004

Hard work awaited us the following day. It was our day to confront the truth. The Real Magellan sat down with the four Imaginative Creatures. We told him that Murad Jamil had been killed. Not wanting to destroy his hope altogether, Hasan-i Tofan said, 'We think it's possible Baran has been killed too … You should prepare for all eventualities. In recent years, quite a few women have gone missing in Nwemiran in a similar fashion, but we haven't given up hope completely. We mustn't abandon hope.'

Zuhdi felt like crying, but like many men who feel the need to weep, their throats tight and frozen, he couldn't shed a single tear. He had to stay there in that house until things became clearer.

That same day, Hasan-i Tofan and Shibr had a task to perform. The arrival of Zuhdi Shazaman, and the new information he brought with him, had been an unexpected help.

'Hasan-i Pizo,' Shibr had said the evening before, upon leaving the Idle Murderers' Club, 'in a battle, you can delay your first shot; but if you delay your second, you'll be in real trouble. With your first shot, you awaken the enemy. Your second shot has to hit him. It must create great confusion in the enemy's heart, so he is not able to recover his composure easily. You must know that the outcome of a confrontation often depends on the second volley. After the first, you still have some time for reflection, but after the second you need to know that your opponent is going to start playing his own games.

'We must not delay our second shot. Tomorrow, you and I will go to Murtaza Satan's house and continue the game, understand? Murtaza must get the impression that we know a lot, and that there are some big guns behind us. Don't you worry. I know the Party has split into too many wings; it's been torn to pieces. There is still space for two men like you and me to play our games. Murtaza has to be made to think the game is bigger than him. That's our only chance. Once he knows we're on our own – once he is certain there's nothing but the wind at our backs – we're done for. We'll be eaten up like birds within a week. We've got to make it look like we're secretly working for people who are more important than the Baron of Courgettes.

'Murtaza's a clever devil: he knows the various Party wings are caught up in a war for survival. Outwardly, the barons and princes of Nwemiran appear to be in agreement, but secretly each of them is connected to big guns in the Party. The game's so confused, and the Party wings so intertwined, that no one knows where exactly they fit in. No one knows who's stronger than whom, who is secretly working for whom. Hasan, I grew up inside the belly of the whale. I know what's going on inside the Party. The parties of this country have become like seven-headed dragons whose different heads devour each other. If we can make him believe some powers are behind us, maybe Murtaza will help us simply to save his own skin. I know that several of the barons and other people in the Party are lying in wait for the likes of the Baron of Porcelain and the Baron of Courgettes. Neither of them is loved. Murtaza knows these things. He also knows that if the boat begins to sink, he and others like him will be the first to be thrown into the sea. Do you understand? Unfortunately, that's how ugly the game is, but don't forget we're up against very powerful people. If we don't put all our intelligence to work, we're done for.'

Murtaza received them that afternoon. He was wearing shiny pyjamas, which looked highly incongruous with his crooked mug, fluffed-up hair and devilish laughter. Feigning hospitality, he helped Tofan carry Shibr's wheelchair up the stairs.

'Good Lord, what a beautiful day it is!' Murtaza said in his customary style. 'What a scent of the perfume of Heaven! What a breeze, that so resembles the rosewater of your esteemed mother! How happy I am that great people like you are so kind as to call on someone like me.'

Despite his words, Murtaza Satan was visibly afraid, confused and even pale. It was clear he had not slept the night before. His face was tired. Shibr knew that, although not a handsome man, Murtaza paid great attention to his appearance. Yet today he looked miserable in his overgrown beard. His soul was clearly exhausted. When Shibr saw him in that state, he was certain that their last blow had found a vulnerable spot and wounded him.

'You must forgive your humble brother,' Murtaza said. 'I always feel low at the beginning of autumn. Seeing all the leaves fall dampens my spirits, so much so that I feel my heart dies a little with each leaf. In autumn, my worries about trees kill me. Just think about it. Millions of trees – our friends – dwelling on this beautiful planet alongside us, fall ill, become sad and grow pale in autumn. Oh, just think. All these friends and brothers who stand next to us, stripped bare by nature and told to sleep. My brothers, I am so saddened by the season of falling leaves that my head really aches. I start praying that autumn will pass painlessly for the fragile saplings, that it will not hurt the flowers too much. Sometimes I ask why there's no autumn for us humans. Ha ha! For us worthless humans. If we were renewed once a year, if we shed our black leaves and dispelled the grave doubts that linger inside us, if we entered spring with pure hearts, the world would be different, would it not? It would be different.'

'Dear Murtaza,' said Shibr, running his fingers through his blond hair, 'if we had our own autumn like the trees do, then come springtime, men by the dozen would be denying what they'd done the previous summer. The seasons would give man an opportunity to forget himself and his sins.'

'Murtaza,' said Hasan-i Tofan, 'my worry about autumn not hurting the flowers is matched by my worry about humans not hurting one another. Last night I put you in an awkward situation, but you have to realise that you and I are forced to do this. If nature is forced to act, why shouldn't man be? We, too, are made from nature's soil. A force bigger than ourselves toys with each one of us. We, as you like to say, are billiard balls. Just billiard balls.'

'Murtaza,' Shibr said, 'we have no problems with you. We're not your enemy, and we don't hold any grudges against you. The one who sent us is bigger than you and me. He's even bigger than those you work for. Do you understand? He's more powerful than the Baron of Courgettes or even Magholi. Murtaza, I want you to listen to me. Do you understand? Neither I nor Hasan-i Tofan is here of our own accord.'

Murtaza looked at them nervously, shifting constantly, twitching his head, cracking his fingers. He would laugh, and then be quiet. He could not and did not dare be sure of anything. Since the previous night, he had wanted to go to Ja'far-i Magholi and the Baron of Courgettes several times and tell them everything, but after careful consideration he had decided against it. His life with the barons and their men had taught him to consider every little thing carefully. Hasan-i Pizo and Shibr were seasoned individuals, after all; they wouldn't open fire like two novices. Their words were part of a greater game. In bed the previous night, he had shifted his restless, asymmetrical, gnarled body all night long. With each toss and turn, he had seen the shadow of Hasan-i Pizo.

For a long time now, he had put himself at the service of the barons without much thought. All that mattered to him was finding a footing among them, but now there was more at stake. He knew that in a play like this, there would be a scene where the barons sought to devour one another. He knew that in the past few years, his name had been connected with many things – some of which he was unaware of, while others had happened right before his eyes. His greatest error had been to make himself the enemy of women. The night before, as he wriggled about in bed trying to get comfortable, he'd told himself: 'That was the biggest mistake of my life. It makes me more visible; it makes me out to be a devil who should hurry off the stage as quickly as possible!' Throughout the night he had asked himself, 'I wonder who's behind Hasan-i Pizo and Shibr? Who is it that wants me to exit the game? Who is it that wants to use me as a shield?'

Was it the disillusioned wings of the Party? The wings of the Leader's relatives? The wing of the second-in-command? Of the veteran cadres? The wing of Loyalty and Faithfulness? Of Change and Renewal? The women's organisations probably had a hand in the matter – those groups in which the barons' wives are active. Most of those women were Murad Jamil's mistresses, even if only for one day. Another possibility was the husbands of those women, men aware that Murtaza knew more than anyone else, and might talk about the honour of their wives. These men might want to silence him. It might be Ja'far-i Magholi himself, reasoning that the time had come to be rid of a defective machine.

But no. If it was Magholi, he wouldn't ask for anything, he'd just kill him straight off. He knew Magholi. He was the cruellest man in the Party, someone who still had a 1980s mentality. Magholi and the Baron of Porcelain's wing, regarded by many as the largest and most dangerous alliance between the military men and merchants inside the Party, didn't go in for subtlety. They considered themselves very powerful, and annihilated their opponents without hesitation. Magholi had worked for all of them. Whoever sent Hasan-i Pizo after him wanted to intimidate Magholi, knew deep in his heart that Magholi and the Baron of Porcelain would distance themselves from him. That if things escalated, if Hasan-i Tofan's words reached the newspapers, they would all ignore him like a dog. Hasan-i Tofan and Shibr were too clever to play such games without a powerful backer. The whole matter was far more dangerous than he thought. He woke up dozens of times that night, getting up and pacing the room. He laughed to himself sadly a few times.

At first, he had wanted to run into Magholi's arms; now he thought he should withhold the information from Magholi, the Baron of Porcelain and the Baron of Courgettes at whatever cost. He must not let the news reach those he had worked for, because if they knew he was under that sort of pressure, they'd kill him. They had a thousand and one ways of killing him. They could know nothing until he had strengthened his position and safeguarded his secrets. Meanwhile, he would have to play the game himself. Now that he saw Shibr and Hasan-i Tofan, he was pleased and scared at once – pleased to be able to find out more, but also terrified of his fate.

He knew that Shibr and Hasan-i Pizo could read all this in him. All his cunning and ability to play-act could not elude these two veteran murderers of the city. Their past was known to everyone in the Party. They had reappeared at the Idle Murderers' Club of late without anyone knowing what they were up to. Not even Tunchi or Fazil Qandil knew their intentions, and here they were, suddenly and bravely attacking him – and he considered himself one of the giants. Only someone with the backing of a much larger beast can attack an elephant. He was certain that Hasan-i Pizo and Shibr, too, knew this rule.

'Murtaza,' Shibr said, as if reading his mind, 'you and I are only bit players in this game. When war breaks out, people like us become cannon fodder. Look at me. After all my years of political struggle, I was almost disgraced. If I hadn't been vigilant and found powerful backers, I would've lost. You know many secrets; you ought not to lose out. We need to find out certain things. We, too, have been delegated to do this. We would never put ourselves through this hell otherwise. You know there's nothing in this for any of us. We're doing a job, just like you. I want you to know that we're not your enemy, that we do feel for you; but we, too, have a job to do. The one who delegated us wants information – it doesn't matter how we get it. We won't mention your name. Nothing will happen to you. Your name will stay a secret. Last night, we hurt you. You know that's how it has to be. You've played these games yourself often enough.'

'Me?' Murtaza said. 'What is it I'm supposed to know? People always suspect me unfairly. Many black hearts seeking a culprit will target me. These false suspicions have given me a bad name I don't deserve. Just because I'm ugly, with a crooked figure and Satanic laughter, because the women of this city don't like my smile, because since the days of Cain and Abel they have believed ugly men to be devils and handsome men angels, because the women of this city are mad for handsome guys and go weak at the thought of a good-looking man … because of all that, they blame me for every sin. What an injustice! I am friends with the barons. I am friends with Ja'far-i Magholi. But I haven't killed so much as an ant with my own hands. I can't. I'm not capable of it.'

'Murtaza,' Hasan-i Pizo said, 'maybe you're right, and you haven't killed anyone. I have. The Party made me kill men and women. Not all ugly men are devils. You're an intelligent man. No one doubts that. You often use your ugliness to intimidate people. Sometimes you use it as a shield. No one in this city can use their ugliness to their advantage like you. In the past, it has earned you as much wealth as being handsome would. You're the type who knows how to sell his ugliness and cash in on it. Oh yes, you are.'

Murtaza rose up, his figure bent. He unfolded as he had before, and laughed. 'The ugly ones are the Christs of this city. That's something you don't know, my brother Hasan. I swear by any heart that knows the source of beauty, by anyone who links beauty to the soul, that we are this city's Christs. We are crucified at daybreak and again before nightfall. We are guilty without having done anything wrong; we are seen as filthy because of our extreme purity. Even if our hearts contained all the gardens and light of the universe, we would still be seen as Satanic, simply because our smile is not beautiful. Even if our souls were snow-white, they would still be regarded as black. We would be dark even if our hands were filled with light like the saints'. The bigger we are, the smaller they consider us; the more cheerful we are, the baser they deem us to be. I have dragged the burden of ugliness all my life. I'm paying for an appearance I had no hand in creating.'

'Those who delegated us didn't ask about you,' said Hasan-i Pizo, who was baffled by Murtaza's words. 'You're not the one under surveillance, or whose secrets have to be revealed. My heart goes out to you, but I did see you: one dark night, I saw you with that Caesar guy. But I'd like to ask you one question: what do you know about Zuhdi Shazaman? Or do you want to deny that, too? Are you going to say that you and the Baron of Courgettes didn't steal his letters? That it wasn't you who, early one morning at about six o'clock, stormed the hotel like a madman, robbing a stranger of his sleep? You know very well that Baran Shukur didn't go to Europe to see her uncle. Zuhdi Shazaman is her uncle, and he's come back to find out what happened to his poor niece. Murtaza, will you deny that it was you who, not so long ago, switched off the generator at the Snow and Mirage Hotel at midnight and tried to kidnap the poor man? Will you say that wasn't you?'

Murtaza stood in the middle of the room, looking at his two guests without saying a word. He was so baffled, he didn't know which of them to look at. For the first time, he feared he might be trapped inside an inescapable net.

'Who killed Murad Jamil, Murtaza?' Hasan-i Pizo asked, going in for the kill. 'Who killed the Chinese Youth? Was it you, or the Baron of Courgettes? Or was it Ja'far-i Magholi? Murtaza, Ja'far and I worked together in the assassination cells for over ten years. We recognise each other's signatures; but I want to hear it from you. Who killed the Chinese Youth? Why did you try to kidnap Zuhdi Shazaman? What have you done to Baran Shukur? There are very senior people in the state and within the Party who would like to hear the answers to these questions. They really would.'

'Murtaza, think about it and think carefully,' Shibr added. 'Only Hasan-i Pizo and I can help you. If Ja'far-i Magholi and the Baron of Courgettes find out that you've been discovered, they'll kill you. They'll kill you tonight, before the day breaks.'

TRIFA IN HAZARBAGH

Trifa's phobia of invisible monsters hiding in the silence of the outside world began to define her life. Silence ruled in her rapport with the fantasised children and her work with the friendless women. Sometimes she would hold one of the young children and speak silently to him or her. The children gradually learned to communicate with Trifa this way. One after another, she would hold them close to her breast for weeks and teach them to acquire language, exchange words and understand one another without moving their lips. Month after month, year after year, her spiritual relationship with them became deeper. By the end of 2003, most of the children could see and hear Trifa even when she was not at home. Often, she would be in the room, but as an apparition that took the shape of a cool breeze, passing gently over everything like a morning zephyr.

The unfortunate women sheltered in her own sad home had the same feeling too – sometimes they would wake up at night and sense her apparition roaming about the yard or the corridors, or they would hear her voice from the cellar. These women all knew the extent of her madness, and her love for Ghazalnus. Nawras-i Gul Solav, who was then her closest female friend, was more aware than anyone of Trifa's strange, profound internal changes. Her continuous reading of the ghazals had made her believe that, in order to become Ghazalnus's beloved, she had to leave this world and become an image that could only be reproduced in the imagination. What strengthened her fixation, Nawras later explained, was her discovery of the gates of Hazarbagh.

After many years of questions, hesitation and patience, Trifa decided to follow Ghazalnus on one of his nighttime expeditions. She was not the type of person to be overcome by jealousy; she simply wanted to understand what ailed Ghazalnus, and what might bring happiness to his restless soul. She then followed him on many subsequent nights, and saw how he always slipped into the alleyways of the Sebagh district, disappearing as if kidnapped by the wind.

Night after night, Ghazalnus set off with Trifa hard on his heels. One night, she finally entered the imaginary garden, the gates of which could only be discovered by exceptionally Imaginative Creatures. She was bewildered at the sight of all the flowers, and astonished that such a garden could exist right in the middle of the city without being visible. She crossed the winding routes of the enormous flower garden and watched from afar as the black-clad women picked imaginary flowers. She noticed that Ghazalnus seemed adrift and confused; she saw him roam from garden to garden and from meadow to meadow, until finally he approached a beautiful woman ensconced in a bower. She watched as he sat before the woman and began to read ghazals, one after the other, until dawn.

Trifa observed this scene on several occasions. Every night at midnight, she followed the sad man, not knowing whether she was actually walking through the alleyways of this city or roaming Ghazalnus's imaginary streets. Night after night, she gazed at the young woman who had once been a real, living being but was now a fantasy. She became certain that this imaginary figure was the woman of Ghazalnus's dreams, and that he could only fall in love with imaginary women. To him, love meant chasing a woman who could not be caught, in a magnificent, invisible garden. According to Nawras, Trifa once came face-to-face with Sabri herself. When Trifa asked the imaginary woman why she did not leave the garden, Sabri replied that if she did, Ghazalnus's love for her would die instantly, because he could only love women who did not exist in the real world and could never be attained.

We know, of course, that Trifa was already intent on becoming pure fantasy herself. Meeting Sabri seems to have confirmed that this was the only way she and Ghazalnus could genuinely be in love with one another. And so she took this fatal process to the extreme.

Neither the story of Trifa Yabahri's visit to Hazarbagh nor her meeting with Sabri has been verified. It could well be a story that Nawras-i Gul Solav concocted to further glorify Trifa; but her desire to hide, and her metamorphosis into a living apparition, *are* true, and this story is one to which we can all bear witness.

At the beginning of autumn 2004, an exhausted Trifa stopped her work on the longest book in the world after a distressing event. It appears that her ability to endure suffering and worry on behalf of others had reached its limit. She focused instead on her many other obligations: in the mornings she would enter the world of carpet-making with the sad women, and in the evenings she would return home to care for the children. At night, she returned to the weavers. She was constantly on the move, consumed by the fear of sharp-toothed monsters whose presence she could feel around her at all times.

During that period, her love and admiration for Ghazalnus grew by the day. She fully believed that, in love, there is no such thing as meeting the beloved. In her mind, Ghazalnus took on the image of a distant, elusive love, and she could not live without that distance and unattainability. She would say to her friends, 'In love, the beloved is elevated to superhuman status. The more Ghazalnus reads me poetry, the more I realise I'll never have him. Just as no one can catch the music of a poem in their hands, so no one can catch love in their hands.' On some nights she would sit with the sad women who had fled their families and say, 'The further I move away from him, the more I feel I have reached the station or position he requires. The further he moves away, the more I feel he has reached the station I want him to reach. In love, the beloved increasingly advances to a higher station than your own, rising higher and higher until you can live alongside them only in your imagination.'

The foundations of love between Ghazalnus and Trifa were built upon columns of extreme pain.

Ghazalnus once wrote to Trifa, in a short letter: 'My love, we should have loved in the sixteenth or seventeenth centuries: distant, dusty and cold times when the darkness of Earth and nature's cruelty compelled human beings to go back to their souls. You and I are children of the ancient dervishes, remnants of a time when humans did not love their own bodies. You and I do not have bodies.'

Both of them greatly enjoyed imagining themselves as ancient dervishes and qalandars.[20] They would address each other as 'roaming dervish', 'dhikr master'[21] and 'hermit'. The story of the short letters exchanged between Ghazalnus and Trifa is one of the stranger parts of our tale. There came a point when they only saw each other during their work on the book of the dead. Each would otherwise avoid the other, shying away from physical proximity. Ghazalnus spent a long time in his study, while Trifa rarely stepped into that enclosed, distant home, which smelled of ancient manuscripts. Trifa felt that increasingly, Ghazalnus was beginning to resemble the old collections of ghazals. They now often communicated with each other through the short letters Ghazalnus regularly placed in the drawer of a small desk that belonged to Trifa, from which he also collected her replies. Some of those letters have been passed down to us. We obtained them from Nawras-i Gul Solav, while another bunch had inexplicably crept into the Security Directorate's files and reached the Baron of Imagination through Tarkhunchi. Here we present a few of them to you. Most are very short, rarely exceeding four or five lines, yet they seem to illuminate a love that, in some cases, borders on the suicidal.

> Angelic Trifa, last night was harder for me than previous nights. Thinking about attaining my own perfection led me to think about yours. Whenever I try to rise to your level, I feel that your perfection goes up another level, so that the distance between us remains the same forever.
>
> Ghazalnus

> My dear Qalandar, we do not have a single thing in common. In love, one is always on Earth, the other in Heaven; one is the offspring of Adam, the other divine.
>
> Trifa

> Trifa of my dreams, oh eternal cup-bearer at a gathering I shall not reach in time to taste the wine, I feel that slowly I need to look upon you more and more. You were not here this morning; in the bazaar, as if looking for you, I searched the ranks of God's creatures, my hair dishevelled and my face tired. It dawned on me that the world has not seen your like before.
>
> Ghazalnus

> Oh, bespectacled angel of the taverns of love, you are an extraordinary creature. When I am far from you, you are near, and far when I am near. Human beings do not fall in love with other humans. Rather, love is something born between a child of Adam and an angel. When I feel you are human and move towards you, I look at myself and notice I've turned into a fantasy, an angel. When I feel I am human and should kiss you, you become an angel and leave.
>
> Trifa

> What a bad cup-bearer you are … anything I drink from your hand turns into ghazals.
>
> Ghazalnus

I know if I have you, I will die. If my body touches yours, I will die. If I kiss you, I will die. If even the air around your hands touches me, I will die. A kiss from you would prove fatal, because it would be the last kiss of my life.

Trifa

Khanim-i Yabahri, I have lost hope. Whatever hopes the imagination offers us, we must be brave and look for in reality. But how could any hopes of yours be realised? How could your fantasies come true? Do tell me.

Ghazalnus

Ancient hermit and expert of the poetry manuscripts, I know how reality becomes fantasy, but no one has taught me how fantasies become real. You who are the master of love should know better than most – love has not taught anyone how to find themselves. Love is losing your way, nothing more.

Trifa

How can you say the two of us will not meet? For some time now, wherever I go, in whichever garden I walk, in whichever alleyway I pass through, I feel that you are with me. Yesterday I was reading ghazals for some wretched, pale women. They were listening to me like ritualists at a secret retreat. They all knew I had strayed from Sukhta's ghazals, and was writing my own. How can you say that you and I are not for each other? Day and night, I see the wind carrying my ashes to you and smell your scent wafted in on the imagination ...

Ghazalnus

Kiss? Are you saying 'kiss', Ghazalnus? You don't understand. If you kiss me, all your mystery will be gone. Your beauty and magic lie in the fact that you are now a fantasy, that you used to be a fantasy, that you will always remain a fantasy. A kiss will render us all identical ... but there are stations in love ... don't ruin with a kiss what love's toils have elevated or dragged down, don't destroy with your lips what the heart builds.

Trifa

Not a night passes in which I do not think of burning these ghazals, coming upstairs to embrace you, to experience with you Paradise in this world …

Ghazalnus

Not a night passes in which I do not think of coming to burn your ghazals, jump into your arms and lose myself in your hands … but on reflection, my fantasies would have no meaning without you. The joy of always missing you is more profound than the joy of being with you.

Trifa

THE MEMOIRS OF THE
BARON OF IMAGINATION

One day, Tarkhunchi did me a favour I shall never forget. He was cunning and two-faced, and became so caught up in the story that at times he appeared keener than I to find out everything about Ghazalnus. In the autumn of 2004, during one of his thorough searches of the house, he entered a locked room. (He had been provided with a bunch of keys that could open any door in the world, and had about his person advanced listening and filming devices.) What he found there initially gave cause for surprise: it was an enormous book placed on a table in the middle of the room, like a sacred artefact. Pressed for time, Tarkhunchi was only able to take a few pictures of the book with his digital camera.

When I saw the book, I felt nothing but astonishment. You've all heard stories of fishermen coming across some mythical creature while out at sea. Inevitably, the creature lifts its head out of the water only once, shows itself to the sailors for just a moment and then sinks back into the water, leaving behind an unresolved mystery and splitting the world into two camps: one that says yes, it's true, such creatures do exist; the other that says it's a lie, a mere figment of the imagination. You've heard the story. Well, the book looked like just such an enormous creature, making just such a sudden appearance – it was a whale of a book. It was most unusual, so big I thought it might contain all the knowledge of the world.

When Tarkhunchi brought along the first photos, I was so excited at the sight of them that I wanted to call my colleagues at the Security Directorate right there and then. I wanted to storm the nest of that king of ghazals on any pretext, take the book, go through it page by page and find out what was written in it. Tarkhunchi told me he could steal the book if I helped him. I knew that, during that period, Trifa Yabahri slept most nights at the home of the women who had fled their families. I was aware of her every move. I was also aware that she wanted to weave the most imaginative carpet in the world, the likes of which neither the ancient kings of Iran nor the Ottoman sultans had sat on. I was not an enemy of women – women's freedom was an important prerequisite of civilisation, and a key principle of my city of dreams – but if I had to intimidate Trifa Yabahri so that my pressure on the Imaginative Creatures bore fruit, I would do so. I knew for sure that a poor, rustic woman and her daughter cared for Ghazalnus's children at night in Trifa's stead.

Tarkhunchi was spurring me on to carry out the plan of stealing the book. It was a detailed plan that would enable us to navigate the house and its inhabitants with no problems at all. Ghazalnus resided in the tucked-away basement. He was constantly immersed in ghazals. The room where the whale-sized book was kept was secluded and unmonitored, according to Tarkhunchi's description – something our maps also confirmed.

'If you know how to place the key in the keyhole, you can easily get to the book,' said the ever-wily Tarkhunchi.

Before we took on such a formidable task, I encouraged him to steal into the room again and read some of the pages of the book. When I made this request, I believed it would be no easy feat; but, demonstrating his skill, Tarkhunchi swiftly returned with an odd bit of news. The entire book told stories of death – different death stories written in a very refined hand. The photos Tarkhunchi had taken were very clear. As soon as I saw them, I was certain I was on the brink of resolving the riddle of the Winged Notebooks. I was sure Ghazalnus was the culprit responsible for collecting the death stories. I had no choice but to take the book and try to understand it.

One night, I dispatched one of the most skilled and formidable thieves in this city along with Tarkhunchi, while I kept an eye on them from a distance. Around three o'clock in the morning, they left the house with that colossal book, the largest I had ever seen. It had a unique scent. This was the first time I had held a book with its own scent, which brought to mind some of the cul-de-sacs of this city. That same night, I had three people transport the book to the basement of my house, where I started reading it. I will not hide from you that I cried as I read many of the stories. The book contained as many deaths as you could find in a thousand books – just like this country, which contains as many deaths as you could find in a thousand countries. Spellbound, I read story after story. With every tear, I would say, 'Ghazalnus, why don't you want us to forget these stories? Why? Why do you look for the truth only in death? Wouldn't you rather create beauty and portray reality as thriving? Why do you pursue sadness rather than hope?'

I thought to myself that if I ever constructed my dream city, I would bury the book in the foundations of the city's main park. A dream city should be built on the demise of these dark memories. Yet the book signified something else, too. It showed me that this Ghazalnus did anything he wanted. When the effect of the words wore off, I was seized by a deep fear. I didn't know whether this man was working to a calculated plan, or whether life had simply endowed him with a vast supply of natural strength and energy. There is nothing more dangerous than a poet enjoying too much power. Every time I sat with my Party colleagues, I would say to them, 'Reform yourselves, become solicitous and far-sighted. Be reasonable. Don't just follow your whims. Make sure that power in this society doesn't fall into the hands of poets and writers, who would play with the minds of the common people as they wish.'

You mustn't assume that I have no reason for wanting to deny poets power. Don't assume I am inherently against poetry, or am a pupil of the Platonists, who have cropped up in our time in many forms. No, I do not hold any blind grudges against the poets, nor am I a Platonist; but I ask you, what would poets do with power? The very first thing they would do is rid life of anything that wasn't poetry, and this is most hazardous – but they are so eloquent that they can portray this danger as unique beauty, and leave people enchanted. To draw a halo around poetry, they would create a new type of conscience – and the conscience of a poet is not like that of judges and legal experts. I have read and reflected a lot on the profound difference between the two types of conscience. The conscience of poets rests on a distinction between the powerful and the powerless, while the conscience of the law rests on a distinction between the guilty and the guiltless. Judges work to abolish crime, but poets work to end the disparity between the powerful and the powerless. Poets find thousands of reasons to prove the innocence of the guilty party, and employ thousands of devious schemes, artistic devices and philosophical tricks to portray criminals as victims, heroes and philosophers. Stendhal does this with Julien Sorel, Dostoyevsky with Raskolnikov or the characters in *The Brothers Karamazov*, Kafka with Josef K. in *The Trial*. Josef K. keeps completely quiet about his true crimes, closes his eyes to them, does not write a single word about them; poets have done this throughout history. They would elevate the very worst person to the status of prophet if they felt like it, just to sully the image of the authorities.

When Ghazalnus's book was brought before me, I was certain he was writing it to vilify our era. To poets, conscience amounts to regarding anything that is not poetic as a crime. His obsession with the dead was an obsession with making us curse the times we live in. It's what all the great poets of the world do. Only the little, worthless poets perch politely on the seat of wisdom and say, 'What a beautiful

age this is! How generous the times are to me and to the people!'
Search history and you won't find a single great poet who has said that.
They would not have written such things unless they were hypocrites
or under duress. Do you know why they always pursue this kind
of conscience? Do you? Because when poets are born, they embody
two feelings: they believe they are unique, and that a mystery enters
the world with their births. They believe that God has singled them
out, and that they were not created in the image of other creatures.
Then, without exception, they believe they are the real masters of the
world, and deserve to sit on life's throne.

Their deep hatred is rooted in that eternal spite. This is why the
kings, queens and rulers of the world dislike poets – not because of
the poets' beautiful words, but because they know that poets are the
only ones who will genuinely fight them for the throne. The poets
are the only ones who feel they occupy the throne, even when they
do not. Personally, I wouldn't have had much of a problem with their
dangerous sentiments, if only they were more engaged with life. I'm
scared of those who do not engage, who are both lonely and powerful,
who simply sit back and yet are still able to create ripples in the
world without taking a step into it. That's right, I'm frightened of
them, especially when it becomes evident that no power can take
them out of their seclusion, when it becomes evident how indifferent
they are to what is said about them in the wider world. It is this
indifference that makes me fear the poets.

Now I feel as if my body is gradually being overcome by a lethal,
black disease. The more I hear the ghazals and become enthralled
by them, the more I want to make Ghazalnus feel he is weak, to hurt
him, to make him suffer. I have my own dream and should fight for
it, do you understand? That's my justification.

At the end of September 2004 and a few days after the book about
the dead was stolen, I visited Ghazalnus again. It was a sudden and
ill-timed visit. I took with me the towel that bore the story of the poet
and the king. At the time, I completely understood the state of mind
he was in. Trifa Yabahri was growing increasingly distant from him.
I was of the opinion that this had put him in a troubled psychological
state. I tried very hard to get to the root of their disagreement, but
without success. The scraps of paper that Tarkhunchi brought me
occasionally were of no use. In any case, I saw Ghazalnus's troubled
psychological state as an opportunity to attack. So, once again, I went
to see him in the guise of Mr Sarfiraz.

I must say that despite Tarkhunchi's accurate description and
the detailed maps of Ghazalnus's house, I had a peculiar feeling on
both occasions that I stepped into that house. I felt I was stepping

into an immense, primordial and profound world. It was eerie, as when entering the vast prayer hall of an ancient mosque or standing beneath the ceiling of a cathedral or great church while the bells are ringing. There was something about the house that drew you in. You felt you heard whispering even when surrounded by complete silence, mysterious whispering that seemed to speak to your soul. It was such a huge house that wherever you were, you felt unaware of the other rooms in it. On both occasions, I started to feel that the other rooms were teeming with sleeping creatures, peaceful ghosts who sat like yogis lost in the exploration of their inner selves.

Ghazalnus sat opposite me with his unruffled gaze and that damned romantic face. He was polite with his guests. Although I was sure he wasn't happy to see me, his eyes displayed a deep love, which I now believe was his secret love for all humans – philanthropy, you might say. No matter who you were, you were entitled to your own share of the love that was in his eyes.

He was alarmed by the sight of the towel with its colourful designs. At no time during my last visit had I seen him so observant and alert. Intense curiosity poured from his gaze. His hand gestures teemed with questions.

'Why are you showing me such a story?' he asked. 'What does this story have to do with me?'

'Ghazalnus,' I said, 'I am sure this towel is the fruit of a poet's imagination. Poets think constantly about dominion over kings. I want you to see it to find out what you make of this story. What do you see in it?'

He looked at me calmly. I was scared of his stillness.

'The poets' power resides in a realm not accessible to kings or other humans. I don't feel the poet in this story has done anything to defeat the king. He just saw things the way he naturally did. It's not as if poets are endowed with a second pair of eyes through which to look at things in a different way. Poets don't enter into fights. The world is in a quixotic fight against the poets. Through the ages, there have always been those who thought they could attack the imaginary realms in the soul of the poets. Wars waged to reach and invade the gardens in their souls far outnumber those waged to invade real countries and kingdoms. All attempts to kill poets are in fact attempts to invade, burn and destroy the gardens in their souls.'

'Ghazalnus, look,' I said, 'the whole story is about which of these two is immortal, which will come out on top. This is not the kings' question. They don't like comparisons. I am certain this whole story was concocted by a poet in order to restate poetry's triumph and superiority over a country's rulers.'

Ghazalnus inspected the images with his customary composure, turning the towel over several times and gently brushing his fingers over the design.

'Your interpretation of this story is wrong,' he said at last. 'It was the kings who wrote the story, and I am sure it is the poet who was killed at the end. If you look closely at the towel, it will tell you everything. Everything. Look, the bet is on as to who could best describe the city, right? Here, the one describing the city is the king. Contrary to your interpretation, the poet in this story played by his own rules. He wasn't thinking about life and death. A poet cannot describe real cities. The scenes on this side of the towel don't portray a city. Rather, the poet has created another city, an imagined one. The one portrayed by the poet is not the one portrayed by the king. The poet has left the portrayal of the city to the king, without hesitation and without it even occurring to him that with this choice he has chosen death. It is the way of poets to choose death unhesitatingly. It is the poet who gets killed at the end of this story, because in fact he does not take the bet or play the game. Ultimately, the poet plays by his own rules.'

'And why, in your opinion, has he done this? Why has he chosen death? So that the king lives?'

'I have never heard of poets dying for the sake of kings,' he said, laughing. 'A king's life, to a poet, isn't worth a fig. Think about this moment: there is someone who wants to test the poet's ability as a poet, someone who doesn't understand that poets don't live in the same city as kings. If you want my opinion, a huge and fatal trap was set for the poet. The young king wanted to cherish the joy of kinghood and give up being a poet. The test is fundamentally unfair and inappropriate, because poets cannot portray the beauty of a real city. They are more adept at portraying its ruins.'

Ghazalnus's interpretation of the story left me numb. Contrary to my plan, which entailed more talking, I felt I needed silence and reflection. Without saying much more, or showing any dissatisfaction, I wrapped up my towel and left Ghazalnus's house, already thinking about our next encounter. Like a prisoner released in the middle of the night, I didn't know where to go. It was one of those rare nights that I considered myself to be Ghazalnus's slave, when I forgot I was a baron and was carried away by the air of the slumbering poets inside my soul.

SETTLING INTO GHAZALNUS'S HOME
THE REAL MAGELLAN

You can tell when a human being is filled with love if, when you look into his or her eyes, you see they are thinking about your fate. In my long travels, I had seen such eyes before. Trifa Yabahri had them.

When I first saw her, Trifa teemed with angelic sympathies, and her eyes radiated concern for everything. I spoke to her in detail about my life in exile, about being lost on the endless roads of the world, about Baran Shukur's letters and my connection with Afsana. She put her hands on mine like a sister and said, 'Close your eyes and pray for Baran with all your heart, and hope she is happy wherever she is. Live in hope that she is alive, and that we shall find her.' She told me many things about her life, too. I had the impression of someone very fragile and weak. She looked pale. I was worried she might faint or be carried away by the air as she spoke. Her words were so simple, so soothing, they could wash all your suffering away.

Afsana came to see me daily during those days. We went to the house of a friend of hers several times, where we made love. Every instance of lovemaking with her was a spiritual journey for me. Afsana's body was not ordinary. It encapsulated all the magical things I had looked for since my childhood. She taught me what a long and unique journey it is to make love to a woman. Every time was like a journey into an imaginary city, the discovery of a new continent. It was as though I had been travelling all my life in search of the city that slept in this woman's body, her secret geography. Throughout my life, whatever body of water, whatever ocean or mountain peak I had visited, whatever city I had ended up in, whatever woman I had taken to bed, had left me aware of the emptiness and absurdity of life. Now, for the first time, I felt I had grasped a genuine soul. When I entered the circle of Ghazalnus and his friends, I understood that this city was dangerously split between reality and the imagination. At the same time it dawned on me that Afsana's body, her infinite womanhood, her whispering, her slightly husky voice, were the only things that remained detached from this eternal battle between reality and the imagination. The pleasure Afsana's body gave me was different to the purely physical pleasures I had experienced with other women. Her body was an eternal bridge suspended between reality and imagination. It appeared that I had been looking for that bridge all my life, where I, too, could live suspended, resisting the draw of the real world and the pull of the imagination alike. I was meant for that bridge. Afsana gave me the chance to stand there forever and make it my home.

During the period I spent at Ghazalnus's house, I noticed the love between him and Trifa. What an invisible, unspoken and fatal love it was.

What I am about to say may be a bold statement, but it is accurate. There are two types of love: one takes a human being to Hell, the other leads to Paradise. Ghazalnus and Trifa believed that love must burn us before we can understand it. It was strange for me to see those two sensitive creatures strengthen their love through constant separation. They didn't believe in finding one another, they believed in burning and seeking for each other until death.

One evening, when Ghazalnus had talked at length about his vision of love, I told him how Afsana inspired me. 'I couldn't be in love like you,' I said. 'I have a European mentality, as you put it. Love isn't pure imagination. Love isn't the transformation of the beloved into an illusion. My dear Ghazalnus, you have unfairly created a hell for yourself. Nothing can bring a man and a woman closer to each other than the merging of two bodies. Love is sucking the beloved's lips until they fill with blood; it is touching every inch of her body, rediscovering her body every night, kissing each drop of her sweat. Ghazalnus, you must understand the body of the beloved; only then can you know her soul. The Sufis love only the illusions of their imaginations. A perfect lover is neither so immersed in the beloved's reality that they cannot see the beloved's imagination, nor so wrapped up in the beloved's imagination that they cannot find them ... that's how I understand it. Real love is neither discovery alone nor search alone. It is discovery *and* search. Search and discovery.'

Afsana had a different body each time I slept with her. She changed a great deal, and was filled with colour. She was a tree; every time I reached for its fruit, it tasted different. Someone who doesn't touch the beloved's body cannot understand that the beloved alone can be the whole world. No two nights are the same with the beloved, just as fruits from a single tree need not taste the same.

'Ghazalnus, you are a strange man,' I told him. 'I have scoured the world on my motorbike, and not met anyone like you. There is no one like you to be found on the edge of any sea or in the far reaches of any jungle. What are you doing, man? Love means eating from the fruit of the tree. It means letting the beloved show you her body in a thousand colours, and you being able to do the same. That's what love is.'

Ghazalnus, Trifa and I could have talked about love every day, from breakfast until evening, but I had only been in Ghazalnus's home for five days when an important book – a large tome full of secrets – was stolen from it. I hadn't seen the book. It was said to be one of the largest in the city. Its theft changed many things in Ghazalnus's and Trifa's souls. Until then, the book had been the most powerful bridge connecting them. Its disappearance was a great mystery. It sent Trifa into a panic. She felt as if imaginary monsters were chasing her and eating her. She said she couldn't sleep, that she could feel their muzzles and fangs on her skin if she did. Often, when I spoke with her, fear was clearly etched on her face. She was certain that someone was watching her. She was certain there was someone who wanted to catch her unaware and bite into her. More than once she said to me, 'Ghazalnus's house isn't safe. Leave this place.'

After the book was stolen, I felt that Ghazalnus, too, lost his former calm. He too would have sudden moments of panic, too. They both felt that something was after them. At first, like any timid guest, I thought I might be the cause of their fear, but they reassured me to the contrary, telling me their fear was too big, too mysterious and dark to be related to me. The same fear then overtook me; I became infected with it. The atmosphere in Ghazalnus's house now hinted at imminent disaster.

One day I met the Notebook-Keepers who had collected and recorded most of the book's contents: seven angelic individuals who all shared an unusual resemblance. They were very sad, as if someone had stolen the entire history of their lives. As soon as I saw them, I had the feeling that the Notebook-Keepers were not really alive. Since arriving in this city, I had noticed people who appeared to be dead, their faces white as ghosts. That's what the Notebook-Keepers were like, too: slim, white and quiet. One day, they all sat around the now-empty table where the book had lain, and invited me to join them. That day Trifa said that she would no longer work on the book, but would dedicate herself to weaving carpets. Her announcement caused a great commotion. The Notebook-Keepers wept quietly. I didn't know where to look.

'We could start again from scratch,' said Hasan-i Tofan.

Majid-i Gul Solav put his arms around Trifa and said, 'I'll copy it all out again. I won't sleep day or night. I'll copy out all the stories in handwriting that is even more beautiful.'

'There's no point,' Ghazalnus said. 'Whoever stole the book would steal it again. We have to find it.'.

'Where should we look?' Hasan said. 'We don't have a single clue.'

Trifa felt the frustration more keenly than any of them. Talking through her tears, she said: 'The work of so many years. We can't just rewrite it. How would we even begin to write it again? How?'

'We'll continue as if nothing had happened. Nothing at all,' Majid said eventually. 'We are working on a subject that has no beginning or end. Isn't that so, Ghazalnus? We are recording the story of endless suffering. That suffering will always be there. I can work with the Notebook-Keepers on my own. I can.'

'I am sure we're being followed. I'm sure of it,' Ghazalnus said. 'But I don't know why, or by whom.'

'Ghazalnus,' Hasan said, 'it's the barons. It's got to be. They're the ones following us. They've been after us for ages. It's them.'

These words sounded alarm bells in my mind. I remembered the night I had almost been kidnapped. A shiver went through me, and I looked at all of them nervously, as if I had been found guilty and unremorseful. There had not been such upheaval in my life for a very long time, and I felt that fate had cast me into the strangest place in this country, into the fold of the most exceptional people in this city, alone in their suffering and unique in their dreams. After a great deal of weeping and discussion, their arms around each other, they decided to take a break for a while. They would take some time to consider things calmly and wait to see what happened.

The following day, Hasan arrived in a good mood and said, in his hoarse voice, 'Real Magellan, tonight Shibr and I are going to see a friend of yours.' He paused for a moment before adding, 'Sadness, like imagination, is hot on our heels.'

I looked at him without uttering a word. But in the days that followed, I came to understand clearly what he had meant.

WHEN I MET THE BARON OF IMAGINATION AGAIN, HE WAS ON THE BRINK OF MADNESS

MAJID-I GUL SOLAV

When I met Tishkan Tahir again, I immediately remembered a scene between Jessica Lange and Jack Nicholson in *The Postman Always Rings Twice*: the scene in which Jack Nicholson's character assaults Jessica Lange's character, the beautiful wife of an old Greek. He forces her down on a kitchen table. The Jessica Lange character initially attempts to resist, albeit with the type of resistance that speaks of an invitation and secret demands. The scene ends with Jack Nicholson's character placing his hand on her most intimate area. Then, things change, from a fight between the two of them to a passionate scene between a man and a woman. Every time I saw Tishkan Tahir, that scene would come to mind. Even when I saw her for the last time under difficult circumstances, when my life was hanging by a thread, I remembered it – the scene with Jessica Lange and Jack Nicholson on the kitchen table.

I had watched the film many times just for that scene. Now I couldn't believe there was a woman like Jessica Lange in this city. It wouldn't be a lie to say she was the woman of my dreams. I often looked for a woman like her when I entered a new city on my voyages. I had given up on finding one in this city. In fact, the appearance, looks, fashions and way of talking of this city's women sickened me.

When I met Tishkan again, I was so clean and spruced up I looked like the young Johnny Depp as he appeared in the 1990 film *Cry Baby* – still on his way to stardom and already being compared to the likes of James Dean and Marlon Brando. That evening, I had been telling a story about a mischievous mouse called Qirtila to chubby little Sewan, at the house of the Baron of Civilisation. Afterwards I took leave of the girl and was still thinking about the mouse when I saw Tishkan standing outside the living room. She was elegantly dressed. I was sure she'd been waiting for me, but she put on an act, pretending it was all a coincidence. She said, in a pleasant voice, 'Oh, Nice Guy, you're here! Why so smartly turned out, Nice Guy?' From the way she drew out the 'u' in 'guy', I could tell she'd grown up outside Kurdistan, which only made her even sweeter. When I heard her talking to me like that, even my soul would have died for her.

I managed to keep my cool, though, and greeted her nonchalantly. 'Good day, Khanim. How strange to see you here! I thought you lived outside Nwemiran.'

'No, I am living here, at the Baron of Civilisation's,' she said. 'I have classes in the evenings. That's why you haven't seen me.' Then she took my hand and said, 'Don't worry. No one's at home. Come with me.'

She uttered her 'come with me' in such a way that no man could have resisted.

That day she appeared more striking than on the evening of the party. Then she had been wearing so much make-up she had lost her real beauty, but today it stood out: her complexion, the delicate line of her lips, her lustrous, pale eyes, all of it would bring you to your knees. She was wearing a white skirt and dainty purple T-shirt with a white collar. They both clung to her slender waist in a way that put you in the mind of some divine design.

Tishkan took me into the kitchen of the baron's mansion. I sat on a chair and she put a chilled can of Coke before me, saying, 'Nice Guy, as soon as you go, Sewan tells me all the stories. I really liked the one about Qirtila, who, like his brothers Firtila and Mirtila, poisons himself by eating old books. It was such a nice story … Haven't you got any stories for someone my age? Stories to put a young woman to sleep …?'

Her words were so coquettish, I almost choked on the Coke.

'Why not, Nice Girl?' I replied. 'Originally, my job was to tell stories to adults, but nowadays only children want to listen to them. So I'm forced to live like this.'

'Does that mean you've told stories to women like me before?' she asked.

'No,' I said. 'As you know, this city, its customs, its people – they don't allow such things. But if someone wanted me to, I could tell them stories.'

She ran her hands through her short, glossy hair and gave me a lovely smile.

'Well, Nice Guy, I would like you to tell me such stories,' she said.

I was very pleased with everything thus far. She really was the spitting image of Jessica Lange, there before me in flesh and blood. When you are in the early stages of getting to know a woman, everything is pleasant and wonderful. The problems start when you ask, 'Now what? Where is this going?' That was partly why I didn't want to get particularly close to women; you always have to *get* somewhere with women, and I wasn't interested in getting anywhere. My favourite relationship is with the dead, because they don't ask anything of you. They become silent friends, and that's that. Women are marvellous creatures, but their worst characteristic is that they always want something from you. They believe they are constantly entitled to demand something from you, and even when they're not demanding anything, they're reminding you of the fact. (I had never dared to mention such things to Trifa, who kept saying, 'All the monsters that are chasing me in my imagination and want to eat me are male.') I had reached my conclusions from examining and analysing hundreds of films. Another problem with relationships is that you have to go step by step, and each step requires a lot of thinking, calculation, planning, fear and trembling. I like relationships where, right from the outset, everything is clear and straightforward – and such things are impossible with the women of this city. Even so, I was willing to do anything to get this Jessica Lange. Anything at all. You only meet Jessica Lange once in your life, so it would be foolish to let the opportunity pass.

'I still don't know your name,' I said, although I did.

'My name is Tishkan. I was born in Baghdad.'

'How are you related to the Baron of Civilisation?' I asked.

'I'm not. I'm just an acquaintance,' she said, lowering her head slightly. 'I live with the baron's niece on the ground floor here.'

After some more small talk, I finished my Coke and said, 'Unfortunately, I have very little time. I have to go to the house of the Baron of Bullets and Gunpowder. Delighted to make your acquaintance. Hopefully, we shall meet again.'

'Majid, I'd like to come and visit you. Which district do you live in?' she said.

When she spoke my name, she swallowed the 'i' slightly, as is customary with native speakers of Arabic.

'Aren't you afraid to come to see me in case I tell you a story, you fall asleep and I kiss you? You're so beautiful, I think it would be bad for my health to see you too often,' I said.

She laughed and, in that soft way that could kill a man, said, 'Yes. I'll come so that you tell me stories and I fall asleep; but you're a good boy. You won't kiss me.' She paused then, before adding: 'If I am not awake.'

I gave her my address. When I left, she threw me a kiss from the window and waved goodbye in the fashion of adolescent girls. I had seen such goodbyes only in films. I don't know why that goodbye made me so happy. When I stepped out of the baron's house, my brief and sudden happiness reminded me what a very sad man I actually was. How unfortunate I was, to have wasted all my life lurking in a couple of streets of this dirty city. I leaned against the wall of a house and nearly wept. I looked back at my life, and there was nothing there. Nothing at all. That little goodbye had made me so happy because my life was a vast emptiness, the life of a man who could be shown happiness with a simple gesture. This hurt my pride so much that I felt people were quite right to take no notice of me and ignore me.

That night, when I had finished telling all my stories, I wanted to go home. I was on my way towards the great gate of Nwemiran when a big, flashy car pulled up in front of me. A voice from inside said, 'Majid-i Gul Solav, get in the car.' Through the window I could see the Baron of Imagination. I tried to say no, but the baron was insistent; I was left with no choice but to join him. He looked more agitated than when I had seen him the first time around, and appeared slightly angry, as if something was getting on his nerves and making him tense. He drove me around Nwemiran fast.

'Majid-i Gul Solav,' he said, 'you are the master of imaginary stories. How do you see Nwemiran? I'm desperate to find out.'

'Baron of Imagination,' I said, 'You know I'm the son of a poor family. To me, Nwemiran is a beautiful place. It's like a dream. For a deprived and impoverished person like me who craves a pleasant life, Nwemiran is like a distant mirage that I don't want to think about too much.'

'But it is not an imaginative place, is it?' he said after a pause.

'It depends how you define "imagination",' I said, to avoid answering the question. 'Maybe for a poor man who can't pay his rent, it is an imaginative place. It's hard to say.'

'I know you are not being truthful,' he said, looking at me sadly. 'I can tell. You've seen nicer places. You've travelled to more unusual places, collecting a story from each one.'

I looked at the baron, trying to decide whether he was serious or making fun of me. I saw a hint of both seriousness and mockery in his face. 'Honourable Baron, whoever told you that is mistaken,' I said calmly, hiding my fear. 'I've never been on any trips. I've never left this city in my life. I haven't even seen the nearby towns and villages. All my life, I've walked only through the alleyways and streets of this city. I've never even been on a picnic, or seen the nearby resorts.'

I pointed to the nearby mountains and said, 'Baron, I haven't even been to those mountain peaks that the people of the city visit every week. I was here even during the mass exodus. When the state's tanks and armoured vehicles returned to the city, I was walking the streets all alone.'

I had the impression the baron was tipsy. He said, dreamily, 'Gul Solav, you travel all the time. I know that. I've been told. I know a lot of things about you. The Baron of Dolls thinks you only tell stories to the blind children. What he doesn't know is that you take them on real journeys. No one knows that but me.'

'I don't take anyone on *real* journeys. I can only take them on imaginary journeys,' I said after a short pause. 'In fact, I do nothing. I only make the blind children happy, children who can't see this world of light – so I help them see another world, the one that sleeps in our imaginations.'

'But you and the blind children can truly experience those imaginary cities,' he laughed, his voice now definitely tipsy. 'I've asked the blind children. They see everything aboard your ship. They breathe in the smell of the trees and rivers. They get to know the imaginary villages and stroll around the big cities you take them to.'

After a short while, he parked at the side of the road and grabbed my hand. 'Tell me, Gul Solav. How do you take people inside that map? I'm crazy about maps and plans. Ever since I was a child, there's been a large map inside my head, but I don't know how to create it. Can you tell me how? I've been working with the politicians for years, and now with the engineers. I'm one of the city council officials responsible for drawing up a master plan of this city. I like maps, you know, big ones that encompass the whole of life, that contain all of us. A map is like a fishing net – you weave it and are inside it at the same time. It's like a tall building with bricklayers constantly at work inside, unable to get out.

'That's my dream. Gul Solav! A map is about the whole of humanity, not just for one human being alone. Do you understand? Anyone who thinks about a map has to take all humans into consideration. I want a map that we can all create and dwell within. Humans are distinguished from the animals not by language or imagination, but by maps. Animals have both language and imagination. Science has proved that. Oh yes, what I'm telling you is entirely scientific. The only thing to set human beings apart from animals and other creatures are maps. A map suggests that you can see the entire scene, that all the world is right there in front of you, on the map you've drawn.'

As if he could read my panic, he frowned a little and said, 'Tell me, did you hate geography in school as well?'

'I don't know. I don't remember,' I said, to avoid being caught out.

'Just like you, I hate this city, I hate this world as it is now.' He brought his head close to minem and spoke in a low voice. 'Geography or history speak about the world as it is or as it was, but I'm talking about a map drawn for all of us. Look at me: what gave Westerners such huge power? The intelligent men who drew a map so large it encompassed the whole world. Isn't that so? Isn't that what made them masters of the world?'

He no longer had the serenity I had seen in him the first time. His looks, his demeanour, were different. There was something of the madman in him now. He was so ablaze with emotion on account of what he'd drunk that I was scared of him. As I never drank anything stronger than beer, I was very wary of men who got drunk. Since childhood, I'd been suspicious of them. I felt that seeing them was bad for my imagination.

'Tell me, how do you show those blind children around the world? Why don't you take me along one day? Hey?'

'Honourable Baron,' I said, rather boldly, 'I am a storyteller. If you read this city's history, there have always been storytellers. It used to be different. People would sit in the teahouses, and storytellers would tell fairytales and yarns from a raised platform. But I was born in a different time. I am an unfortunate man, born in the wrong time or place. I don't go anywhere. It's just that my stories are of a kind that the blind understand better. I am someone whose imagination can only be seen by the blind. Whether the sighted come or not wouldn't make any difference.'

'I don't want to sit down and draw the map of the world with a pencil, ruler and protractor,' he said. 'That's what the geographers do. You and I have a map in our heads, and we bring it to the world. That's the difference between us and the idiots I hate. Majid-i Gul Solav, I need to see the inside of your imagination. Just as the blind children do. I, too, want to see the inside of your imagination.'

'Honourable Baron,' I said with my frightened smile, 'just as a man can't see the other side of the moon, the nighttime of the sun or the sides of the stars that are invisible to us, so he can't fully see anyone else's imagination.'

'I want to see one of your imaginary cities,' he said, almost pleading now. 'I want you to describe them to me. I want to close my eyes, and for you to take me along with you. I want the lands that are in your imagination to be mine. Oh, how strongly I wish I had been born a few centuries ago in the West! I really do.'

'Well, of course, it would have been nice,' I said, not understanding what on Earth he was talking about. 'I sometimes have an urge to wear ancient costumes, too.'

He raised his head and, ignoring my fatuous comment, said:
'A time when there was another land – another life – man could

discover ... But now the whole world looks similar. The old Europeans, the lords, the barons and dukes were fortunate: there were other lands to invade. But we, the rulers of these countries, compared to those great men, are nothing but hunters of ordinary prey, hunters of pathetic birds. Right now, I am nothing but small fry. Gul Solav, in your opinion, what is power?'

It wasn't something I'd ever thought about; nor did I think anyone would ever turn up in front of me to ask such a question.

'Power is having big mansions and magnificent cars, being able to have some of the women you want. Actually being in power, imprisoning people you hate – that sort of thing.'

'All the barons in Nwemiran think like that, too,' he said, laughing as he looked at me. 'Yes, all the stupid barons of Nwemiran think like that. But that's not what power is. Power is something else. I came to this belief after many years of study and hard work. If you can't tame the imagination and see it bring forth fruit, you're powerless. Power is nothing but the taming of the imagination.

'Gul Solav, at times people go round and round in circles before they come to a certain conviction. That's what I'm like; but once I do come to a conviction, I can dedicate my whole life to it. I can kill and create mayhem because of it. There is nothing more dangerous or more exquisite than having conviction. Man is mad until he has one, and then becomes madder still.'

'Honourable Baron, how did you come to that conviction?' I asked shyly.

He resumed driving and was quiet for a while, but clearly he was thinking about my question. 'Brother Gul Solav,' he said eventually, 'the imagination of the world's rulers is what has created and defined human history. There are many idiots in this city who still don't understand this. There are idiots who believe that the *poets* have a monopoly on the imagination. There are such idiots in the world, and plenty of them at that. Isn't that so?'

'I don't know ...' I said, looking at him, still with fear.

'It was imagination that took the Europeans beyond the boundaries of Europe. All world rulers read about the ambitions of the rulers who came before them. Napoleon read about the ambitions of Alexander and Hannibal. Napoleon's and Bismarck's ambitions dwelled in Hitler's head. Saddam Hussein planted Hitler's and Stalin's ambitions in his head. But those kings and dictators were intent on expansion. The entire Earth was their laboratory and their home. We can't harbour such dreams in this little city.

'I have made a close reading of the history of poetry, too. At times, poets are nothing but dogs that follow the imagination of the politicians. You're lucky you're not a poet. Very lucky, even. Politicians first speak about freedom, and then the poets come and sing its songs. Fifteen years ago, it was our dream to get this far – to have the freedom we have now. Back then, our poets, our politicians and the man on the street all had the same dream. We wanted to be in control of a city, a town, and live peacefully. Those were our golden days. It was a time of beauty. We all had the same dream. Now, I want to do something similar, understand? I want all of us to have the same dream. I don't want to wipe out other people's dreams and bring mine to fruition. I'm a modern man. Do you understand? Fifteen years ago, a modern man like me wouldn't have been born in this ruin. I don't want my fantasy to replace yours, but I want to have a map which can embody the fantasies of both of us; I want to build the garden together, to build the ship together, to travel together. I want for your ship that takes the blind children on their travels to be the ship of us all, for those bright green regions to guide us all. Do you see? Do you?

'When I say these things to my old Marxist friends, they smile and say, "You're talking about utopia." I laugh and say, "No, it's not utopia, it's geometry, mathematics, the art of bringing people into the map. It's persistence and mercy."

'Yes, mercy and sympathy, but also mercilessness. The person who resists till the end, who completely denigrates the beauty of this city, its future hopes and future value, will drown in his own fantasies like a pig in shit – and I won't have mercy on him. How could we all have had the same dream fifteen years ago? Why? And why can't we today? I told my fellow barons, this isn't fantasy, it's art. At a meeting of the Princes' Council, I stood up and said aloud, "Our job is to prevent human fantasies from going to waste, but here we don't let any fantasy come out of our heads. We're all used to claiming that fantasies are dangerous, and shouldn't be allowed to emerge. We've all learned to quickly bury our dreams, like a cat covering up its shit, to dismiss them as utopian." Believe me when I say that's exactly what I told all the politicians and barons of this country ... but most of them haven't got a clue what you're talking about.'

I looked rather meekly at the baron, who was now driving his car at a ridiculous speed through the empty streets.

'Honourable Baron,' I said, 'I don't understand you, either. I'm not intent on realising my own fantasies. I'm not a revolutionary person – that's what revolutionary people think about. Honourable Baron, I've never been a revolutionary. Today's revolutionaries are tomorrow's dictators. I don't like them. I'm impartial. Children understand my fantasies better. There's no such thing in the world as the "dream city". A dream city is one without dreams, and such things could not be built in our country.'

I glanced at the baron to gauge his reaction. He was a handsome man.

'I'm not a revolutionary either,' he sighed. 'The age of revolutionaries is over, and has been since the late Eighties; but I still know some things that you don't. We Kurds are at the very bottom of the world. If a hole was to appear on this planet and it wanted to lighten its load, we'd be the first to be thrown out. In this age when the world has become one, poor nations like ours are disturbed by the feeling that we are the redundant limb of humanity, and that one day they might throw us off the ship and into the ocean. Majid-i Gul Solav, every single Kurd secretly feels this way. It's dangerous to feel we are the dregs, the refuse of the planet, but the smaller the world becomes, the bigger is this feeling in our hearts. We force-feed it to our children with their mothers' milk. The more big powers emerge in the world, the smaller we become. We only have one option: to create such beauty that humanity feels we are not redundant, to magnify ourselves with beauty, to rescue ourselves with a garden.

'I often feel that the solutions to humanity's problems can be seen better from our perspective, but what do I have to do with humanity? What's an unfortunate Kurd doing thinking for humanity? I decided not to go beyond the boundary of the local municipality in my imagination. In my youth, I was a nationalist Marxist, but now I can't even think about places beyond the municipality.

'My dear brother, I know there's something important this world lacks, that our countries lack a certain type of person. Do you know who that is? A politician who thinks poetically, or a poet who thinks politically. In the case of small, unfortunate nations such as our own, these two souls should not be set apart. The great nations don't care. The great nations can wreak havoc and still remain proudly on Earth, but we will die unless we make beauty our guide. That's my philosophy. Do you understand? I'm not a revolutionary, a politician or a poet, but a realist who knows where things are heading. I know it is only the creation of beauty that can give us the feeling that we're not redundant on this planet. We can't make rockets, machines or medicines for humanity, but we can be beautiful. If we become extinct, or die, our demise would be like the death and extinction of beauty. You, too, are like that. Majid-i Gul Solav, you are like me. Among the Imaginative Creatures, you are the one closest to me. That's why I am begging you to take my side. Side with me. Don't become an enemy of the barons. Don't waste your time on trifles. Don't think only about the past. Give me your hand, and let's step into the future together.'

'Honourable Baron, I don't know where you want to go,' I said, withdrawing my hands fearfully. 'I don't.'

'Those fucking Americans can't do anything for us, you know,' he said, enraged. 'This nation of ours used to be strangled from the outside, but now it just self-destructs. Listen to me, Gul Solav. I've met those fucking Americans. Their imagination is like that of our foolish politicians. You don't understand me? I feel as if nobody does. Who should understand me? Nwemiran's foolish barons? When I talk to them about the imagination, they remember the stories of Aladdin, the hat of Sakhri Jin, the Ring of Solomon the prophet; they recall tales of the bald boy or the winged horse.[22]

'Gul Solav, I want you to be with me when we make this world anew. Tell me about the beautiful things you see on your imaginary voyages, the unusual minarets that come your way, the sculptures of the world's unusual cities, the towers and castles made of crystal. Tell me about the huge mosques where the most virtuous of believers pray, the harmonies human beings create. The harmony between human beings – that's the real music of existence. Imagination, in my eyes, is about creating a garden that will prompt whoever sees it to say, "This is the garden that has always lived in my dreams."

'What qualifies as a "city of dreams"? It is a place where looking at the trees makes you say, "This is the tree I want to look upon forever", where smelling its flowers makes you say, "These are the flowers I want to smell till I die", where seeing lovers kiss makes you say, "This is the kiss I want to die witnessing". It is a place where anyone who walks its streets feels he never wants to reach home, where anyone who sits in its rooms feels he is swimming in harmony between humans and things, where anyone who sees its minarets feels he is close to the purity of the sky. Sitting on its carpets, he feels he is flying over the garden of intoxicated kings; reading poems, he forgets about the world. Poetry should kill the black memories inside our heads. I need poetry to take myself out of the world, not to relive old memories or disappointments even more deeply. Beauty is creating one thing and forgetting others. For us, it is creating something and ignoring this dirty world.'

The baron, I felt, was becoming completely carried away by his own fantasies. Never before had I come across an Imaginative Creature who went so far, dreaming of building such streets and alleyways. In creating my imaginary cities, I always followed one main rule: I made sure they would never become real. Imagination is the creation of something that cannot be translated into reality. Hearing the baron speak about taming the imagination, I was seized with fear. Yet his style of talking and self-expression was such that I couldn't imagine him to be a dangerous man.

I was thinking about his words when he grabbed my hands again and said, 'The poets who decorate their sheets of paper, who squander their energy on praising their beloveds and leave the world as filthy as it ever was – they are dangerous. Our nation won't be saved by a thaw between our stubborn parties, but by uniting our imaginations and producing something new. When I talk to you about a map, I'm talking about a place where the imaginations of the poet, the politician and the engineer come together and feed off one another. Gul Solav, we cannot save ourselves and rid our homeland of our enemies, but we can save our imaginations. We can't expand across the world like the old empires, but we can expand in our imagination, just as you do. We can't unify our territories again, but we can unify our imaginations. That's my worldview, and that's why they call me the "Baron of Imagination".'

He paused to look at me. There was a hint of madness in his gaze. He said, with a deep sigh, 'I am a statesman, you know. I have been for twelve years now. I've worked in a variety of fields over that time. I assure you, I was never one of those who put the Party before the state. I put the dream city before everything else … but I am all alone, Majid-i Gul Solav, all alone. I want to build a city that will house the dreams of all of us. It's my job to create it, but I am all alone. Do you think a politician can create a beautiful world? Do you?'

I could tell that the baron was growing increasingly sad and angry.

'Honourable Baron,' I said, 'I don't know what difference it makes whether the Party comes before or after the state. I can't make heads or tails of such things. I don't know how to talk about politics. Sir, I only know how to do two things really well: watch films and tell children stories. That's all.'

The baron glanced at me and laid his head on the steering wheel. He was quiet for a while; I watched him out of the corner of my eye. Throughout our conversation, I hadn't dared to look him in the eye. We sat in silence. I could sense the baron's inner turmoil … he was crying. He was crying, although I hadn't said a single unpleasant word to him. Tears flowed down his face like a child. I looked at him for a long time, but said nothing. Then I opened the door and stepped out of the car. Outside, the sound of his crying still rang in my head. When I returned home, I went straight to bed. I was at peace. I saw the baron as a good man on the brink of going mad; but I was sure we were all on the brink of going mad, each in our own way.

SEARCHING FOR YAQUT-I MAMAD

Attar set up many special-information teams around the turn of the millennium. He bought and sold information to the police and security apparatuses. He also worked for senior state and Party officials on the side. Over the course of three years, he had set up this team of young men and women whose only job was to gather news about women fleeing their families. He was an expert in faces. Most of his spies and informers were innocent-looking children. He got to secrets before anyone else because of his own skills, and those of his secret auxiliaries – so much so that anyone with a missing female relative would resort to Attar. Day by day, he became fatter. Day by day, his complexion grew darker and he sweated more profusely.

In the autumn of 2004, the city was rocked by the story of a woman known as Yaqut-i Mamad. She was the daughter of one of the renowned aghas of Spiraz. She ran away with the son of a politician from a remote town, and came to the city. The young man was coarse and boorish. No sooner had he realised that he couldn't provide her with shelter than he dumped the poor woman in the middle of the city to save his own skin. He was so unmanly that he didn't even give her any guidance on how or where to hide. If Yaqut had not come across a scrupulous old man known as Mam Harir, whose daughter worked for one of the women's organisations, she could have got into serious trouble very quickly. Two days after Mam Harir came to her rescue, Yaqut arrived at Trifa Yabahri's house. She was like a star that had just fallen from the sky, and anyone who saw her immediately fell in love with her.

Yaqut was happy to have found a home after her ordeal. When she arrived at the secret refuge, it was clear she had thought a great deal about death. The girls and women at Trifa's house welcomed her warmly. She told them her story, and they told her theirs.

Meanwhile, the men of her tribe and their armed members within the Party and the army were scouring every inch of the region for traces of her. Advisors and experts recommended the famous Attar to Yaqut's elder brother, Wusu Agha. Three nights after her escape,

Wusu Agha and their brother Chato Agha, fully equipped for fighting, went to Attar's house and placed a bagful of money and various photographs of their sister on a table in his living room. As was his habit of an evening, Attar had wrapped a big towel around his head like an Indian maharaja. He was watching an old Arabic film starring Ahmed Mazhar and Mariam Fakhr Eddine, in a lethargic state. Increasingly, he could not endure sleep deprivation or late-evening guests. Only when the Spiraz aghas said, 'You must bring our girl back from underground at any cost' did Attar come to life a little, yawning deeply. He gave the back of his neck a scratch and took a look at the photographs.

'We know you can find her for us if you want to. And if you don't find her, we'll have another little word with you,' Wusu Agha said.

Whenever Attar found himself on the receiving end of veiled threats, he would involuntarily reach for the tip of his nose and scratch it. When the threats were over the top, his ears would sweat and the tip of his nose would swell like the crop of a pouter pigeon.

'If she's still in the country, I'll find her for you,' he said after calmly eyeing up the aghas' weapons. 'If I can't find her, it means your sister has left Kurdistan and is no longer on my turf. There's no fish in this damned pool that I can't see. But if she's left the pool, she's no longer within the reach of my hooks, and you can't blame me for that. Aghas, no one threatens Attar. Attar will do what is possible, but there is no hunter in the world who can hunt all the birds. Not one. I'm a human being, not a divine radar.' For some time now, whenever he had a problem, he would say, 'I am not a divine radar.'

From the following day onwards, Attar would have to put all his skills to work if he was to find Yaqut-i Mamad. He knew that these people from Spiraz were stubborn and ruthless, only praying to God when they required help with one of their devilish deeds. He knew that anyone who fused devilish intentions with divine assistance was dangerous – very dangerous. Eventually, he would bring in Shahryar the Glass-Eyed, the boy who could see through walls. It would, of course, be impossible to employ Shahryar from the outset. He was the trump card to be played towards the end of the game. It was impossible to inspect this city street by street, house by house. First he needed to zoom in on a small area. He carried out most of his jobs successfully, but the beginning was always difficult.

To catch his prey, Attar first gave photographs of Yaqut-i Mamad to the people manning the checkpoints. They were Attar's principal support in his searches; he would reward anyone who played a genuine role in finding a target so open-handedly that word of his generosity spread quickly. He had a large network of informers among the traffic police who monitored streets and vehicles, and in the shops selling women's accessories. People worked for him faithfully, and he had set dozens of traps in the restaurants off the main roads and in the border villages. Whichever way a person moved, he or she was in danger of falling into one of Attar's traps. For the past two years, he'd accomplished most of his work using photographs and mobile phones. With the gradual spread of mobiles, his work had become faster and easier.

For Attar, there was no such thing as 'good' or 'bad' work. Human beings constituted his market. He never gave a moment's thought to the identities of the people he chased. Sometimes he felt that he had fallen in love with this job; the richer he became, the less he thought about getting married. He was in touch with one, maybe two backstreet prostitutes, and called one of them once a week to come and see him. Apart from that, he was content with the pornographic films he watched in bed, tucked under his blanket, before going to sleep at night. Sometimes he fell asleep while watching and, as long as there was no power cut overnight, would be woken the following morning by the white noise from the huge television set.

There had been a time, a few years earlier, when he had thought about getting married. A sly university student who looked like the Egyptian actress Hind Rostom had caught his eye, and a friend of his set them up on a date. He turned up to see her in his striped blue jacket and trousers, clean-shaven, wearing a heavy Syrian perfume. His ears were dripping, and the customary cunning in his eyes had been replaced by stupidity. As soon as she saw him, his gait and clothing put her in the mind of the foolish men depicted in old Arabic films. The knobble on the end of his nose was badly swollen, and his sweat-drenched face made him look like a camel-seller from the south, dizzy in the sun. After taking in his appearance, she made her apologies and left before bothering to engage in conversation. The manner of her departure was so hurtful, it left Attar frozen.

Later, she told Attar's friend, 'Damn him. He smelled like a sack of radishes from the market. I had no interest in sticking around.' His friends called him 'the radish sack' in jest for a while. *A sack of radishes from the market* ... every time he stood before the mirror and looked at himself, he remembered that comment. He had never been so hurt in his life. Since then, he had taken great pleasure in chasing women who had fled their families, in wearing his traditional Kurdish garb, in keeping his business bustling as he drove around in his new jeep – and in thinking of nothing but his prey.

On her very first night in the refuge, Yaqut-i Mamad went over to the big loom where the young women were weaving carpets – not for any person in particular, they explained, but in order to find their own souls once again. When she first showed Yaqut the huge weaving apparatus, Trifa said in her kind voice, 'The carpet we are weaving isn't for laying on the floor; it's not for people to stand or sit on; it's not for the market. Just as the birds fly in the sky, so we fly on these carpets. We travel through their designs and reach a world where there are no brutal or hard-hearted men.'

Sitting in a chair, Trifa set the hands of the girls dancing with her magical voice. As the tempo of the weaving increased, the carpet weavers became like apparitions immersed in a haze. Slowly, the young women entered another world, acquiring a different spiritual form. Yaqut sat calmly in her place like the others, listening to Trifa's instructions and words, and learned how to pick out the thin threads that were as delicate as air. She learned that every single thread, like the string of a huge saz, has its own function and sound. She slowly understood that it was not the colour or quality of the threads or the weaving that made a beautiful carpet, but the hands that produced it. Yaqut was surprised to discover that when she touched the threads of the carpet, she could not feel anything; when she clutched at them, she felt nothing in her hands; but when she lifted it she could see it – each thread a thread of light.

When she arrived, she was overwhelmed with fear. True, the house was in a tucked-away and pleasant spot; an older woman lived on the top floor as a decoy; and everything in the house lent the place a comforting ambience. But Yaqut knew the Spirazans were hot on her heels, and was sure they would pursue her to the death. When she had run away with the young man, she had been aware of the kind of person he was – but she wanted to experience running away. 'Only animals don't attempt to run away from their lives in this country,' Yaqut had thought to herself. Until then, everyone she had ever known had wanted to run away. Now, when she touched the carpet, she felt at last as if she was being transported to another realm.

Nawras-i Gul Solav had told her, 'Maybe one day a foreign organisation or someone can help you leave the country and start another life elsewhere. Who knows?' But when she sat at the loom, she thought to herself, 'I don't wish to go anywhere. Help me forget about this world, God, like these women have through this carpet.'

As if Trifa could read her thoughts, she placed her hands on Yaqut's and said, 'In the past I didn't want to use my imagination to run away from this world; but now I do. Yaqut, look at me. This world is so ugly. It's a great shame that wonderful people even live in it. A great shame.'

A LONG MEETING WITH MURTAZA SATAN

HASAN-I TOFAN, SEPTEMBER 2004

'Our power now lies in the fact that Murtaza Satan doesn't know who sent us,' Shibr said. 'He isn't sure who is behind the game. The first thing he'll do is carry out a thorough investigation to try and find out which clique in the Party we're linked to. He will dig deep to discover which official is backing us, and because we're not connected to anyone, he won't get anywhere. He can't reveal his hand to Magholi and the Baron of Porcelain. He is sure that if things take a different direction, he'll be finished. His best option is to make a deal with us. Murtaza knows this better than anyone. His long experience has taught him to assess things carefully. He isn't someone who walks around with his eyes closed. That's something only people like you and I do, because we don't give a toss about the world. When someone wants to see everything, they actually see nothing. I was in the Party, and I know that's a problem for most of them. They're all trying to see everything, but eventually go blind and see nothing at all. Hasan-i Pizo, rarely does someone remain in the Party without going blind.'

Shibr's initial plans and visions proved correct. Before too long, Murtaza paid us a visit one evening at the carpet-sellers' market. In a voice unlike his own, he said 'I want to see you, my dears. It seems that fate has sent you to put me back on the right path, to bring some light back into my worthless life.'

This play-acting infuriated me. I would often become upset hearing him speak and seeing him gesticulate that way. 'Because the man was once an actor, he lives his life as if it were the theatre,' Shibr would say, but I thought he was a devil who had learned the language of the angels. He could sweet-talk all he liked, but inside, a devil ruled his heart. At his request, Shibr and I went to see him. We wanted to keep him close, so that he couldn't get away. We started our conversation talking about his peculiar rhetoric. I called it the 'rhetoric of the angels' – not without a degree of sarcasm – after a line I'd heard in one of Ghazalnus's verses one night in Hazarbagh. He found the expression interesting.

He resumed his play-acting and said, 'I was still a pure child. I couldn't tell black from white. The substance of which I was made was not yet clear even to God. Compared to other children, I appeared demonic and ugly. My brothers, my old friends, I swear by all the clouds of the world, all the martyred and withered buds on Earth, that mine was not the only evil-looking, doglike and fearful face of that season. I swear to you. I beg you to believe me. I was born in a season that produced only ugly children. None of the children that season had an ordinary birth. I am the son of such an accursed season, in which a ravenous devil went from house to house and fucked the women of this city. I tell you this, and it is up to you to believe me or not. In no city of the world has the devil married and fucked so many women as here.'

'Murtaza,' Shibr told him, 'it appears your fine rhetoric is an attempt to rectify the mistakes your hands have made. There are many who use beautiful words to hide the hideousness in their hearts.'

'No, I don't use my words to hide my black hands and heart, but to mask my terrible face and ugly body. Without beautiful words, poor, ugly men are condemned to Hell in this life and the next.'

That night, he sat across from us in a new set of clothes. He held a cigarette askew between his fingers, neither lighting it and lifting it to his lips, nor replacing it in the pack. His hands were disconcertingly veined, bony and hairless. His forehead was extremely wrinkled, yet his cheeks were unusually smooth and unblemished. The great contradictions in his appearance made him so ugly that if you dwelled on them too much, you ran the risk of concluding that this man was indeed the result of copulation between Satan and a human being. Yet, when he stood on his feet, when I saw his curved figure in his new, beautiful suit, I concluded that he was just another ordinary man from this country – like Shibr or me, like Magholi and Tunchi.

'Murtaza, have you made a decision?' I said, interrupting him in my nasal voice. 'We don't have much time. We're under pressure from our superiors. They want to hear the truth from you. We can't let you take so much time thinking and making calculations.'

'You're mistaken,' he said, looking at me with fearful eyes. He spoke in the tone of someone whose life was at stake. 'Who am I to know everything? I am a servant, a junior attendant, Murtaza Satan, a creature loved by no one. Who is Murtaza to kill people? What is the castrated Murtaza? What is he? Nothing but a cur. When I wake up in the morning, I say to the light, "Forgive me for passing through you with my torpid body." When I walk under the sky at night, I say, "God, I pray I do not step on one of your sleeping ants in the dark, as the ant is more valuable than I am.'" I had a sense that Shibr, unlike me, was thoroughly enjoying what Murtaza had to say.

'Murtaza, who is responsible for the killing of women?' I pressed on. 'They all say you are. How long would you have kept this empty performance going? I am Hasan-i Pizo, you know. I don't have the patience to spend half this age listening to your lies.'

'Me?' He laughed sadly. 'Butterfly-hearted Murtaza; castrated, sad, loyal-as-a-dog Murtaza, with his gracious speech? Murtaza, who could not hunt an unfledged nestling? Me?'

'Oh, drop this clowning, this empty acting from your theatre days,' I said angrily as I sat back. 'We both know there are more than a few corpses between us. Gracious speech and pure words can't hide what your evil hands and heart have done. The Party has dumped people a thousand times more competent than you. There are some people who don't want the Party's name to be blackened by you and your baron friends. Who would want the majesty of a patriotic party to be blemished by your wrongdoings? The whole thing is more complicated than you think.'

My sudden anger upset him. I had the impression he was pretending to be on the verge of collapse, but then he looked at me and said in a plain and confident tone, 'I didn't kill her. I haven't killed anyone.' He sighed, then said, 'Everyone thinks I did, but it wasn't me. It wasn't Murtaza.'

'Who was it then?' Shibr said, lighting up a cigarette.

'I have nothing to do with the women who were set on fire in the Babardan district,' he said after a moment's pause, as if coming to a difficult decision. 'I swear by the bulbul's small wings as she fights with the storm, Murtaza hasn't killed anyone. Who am I? What or who do you think the unlucky Murtaza is? It was that damned Attar who found the houses of those women. Attar. The wife of the Baron of Candyfloss was at a safe house. She'd run away ten months earlier. Attar found that house. I wasn't aware of it. Oh my, oh my. How could you drag me into every story? Murtaza is too innocent to set fire to people. It was the wife of the Baron of Candyfloss who was burned in that house.'

Shibr was pleased that Murtaza was starting to talk. With a nonchalant air, he ran his fingers through his hair and said, 'But you are responsible for the killing of two other women in Nwemiran. You're not going to deny those as well, are you?'

Murtaza looked at us both with sad, fearful eyes. I saw white foam on his dry lips.

'I haven't killed anyone. I've never killed so much as an ant in my entire life. I'm nothing but a poor guardian. I can't kill people. I swear by the pure hail as it hits the grass, by brotherhood that drives away suspicion and doubt and defeats and exposes them. I haven't killed anyone.'

At this point I felt it was becoming an effort for him to speak. He stood up from his seat and said, 'You don't know who poor Murtaza is. You've given him a much higher status than he really holds. You've deemed him worthy of a branch of a tree he can't even reach. You have placed him in a garden he can't even see. I am a lowly little servant, lowlier than the ancient slaves of the royal courts screwed by the kings. I am less worthy than them. I haven't killed anyone. My, oh my. I exploit people, yes, I bring them news. I do little things to survive; but because this city has no one else with such a hideous appearance, I am held to blame for every sin. If I were handsome, if my teeth were not like those of Satan, no one would've dared turn me first into a servant and then into a culprit. What do you know about the castrated Murtaza? What do you know about his sufferings? What do you understand about being looked at like a dog by every woman and girl in this city – and for no reason? What do you understand of that? I was a theatre actor. Many years ago, I played the role of Iago. What a life I had. Poor me! When I said, "And did you see the handkerchief?", the entire audience would stand and applaud. They accused me of helping a friend of mine kill his wife. I was unfairly sent to prison. All of you want Murtaza to be the main culprit. It's what you all want. You all need a murderer to pin the crimes on … but I haven't killed anyone.'

'Who are you then, Murtaza Satan?' Shibr asked him, doubtfully. I didn't understand the question. I didn't know whether Shibr was trying to scare him or really wanted to know who he was. I stood up and looked into Murtaza's eyes.

'Murtaza, who are you? Who are you?' I said in a low voice that seemed to be coming from afar, as if I were in a play and my lines meant I had to ask that question. Suddenly, I felt great sympathy and compassion for him. I walked around the room for a while and said to myself, 'Hasan-i Pizo, don't be carried away by sympathy. Right now, the spirit of the Chinese Youth is inside your body. You have the heart of someone inside you who wants to know what happened to Baran Shukur.'

I returned to his case, all mercy gone. He had curled up in a ball on his chair, so you could barely see him.

'Murtaza, the night they killed Murad Jamil, were *you* with them?' I said.

'I shouted, "Don't kill him,"' he said, with tears in his voice. 'I swear by the cool summer wind, by the rustle of the summer breeze,

I shouted at all of them not to kill him. I asked them, "What's the use of killing this man?" It was a moonlit night. I had to talk to Murad Jamil to lure him out of his house. When he saw me, he understood everything. Believe me, he did. He was wearing an orange shirt and jeans. When we called him "the Chinese Youth", a smile appeared on his lips and he replied in a loud voice, as if responding to death. I swear to you, when I touched his hands, he knew where I was taking him. Yet, like a happy player making his way onto the field with unrivalled enthusiasm, he was cheerful and excited. It was a moonlit night. The pleasant cool of spring was in the air. The moon resembled a silver sickle. Pardon me. Pardon me, brothers. Pardon my flawed rhetoric. The moon resembled a glistening round bracket that has flown out of a beautiful book to settle in the sky. The clouds kept covering and uncovering it. My heart was like that moon. I didn't want to kill anyone. Believe Murtaza. Killing a lover has no place in my book. But the Baron of Courgettes, he was so desperate. He was so hurt. I swear to you, I completely understood him, too. He came from a poor family; he rose to become a baron and carried a great burden on his back as a result. They all hated him. They all hoped his wife would turn out to be a slut.

'I miss the Chinese Youth a lot, an awful lot,' he said suddenly, as if overcome with emotion, and put his face in his hands. 'I had been tracking his movements for more than two years. Over two years! Two years ago, the Baron of Porcelain asked me to follow him step by step and record every bit of information I could about him. I knew how many women he had affairs with. I did, I swear by the stars in the sky. I swear by the morning wind of summer, by the soul of a tree killed in a storm. If I'd wanted to commit evil deeds, if I'd wanted to play games or sow sedition, I could have done. But you don't know what a good person Murtaza is, what clean hands he has, as they say. If he has committed any evil deeds, then it was out of good intentions. If he has mistreated anyone, it was to please someone else. Oh, how I miss the Chinese Youth. For a while, my job was to list the names of the women and girls he loved. It was the first time I'd enjoyed a task since becoming a servant to the barons. Day by day, I collected the secrets of Murad and the women of this city. So-and-so's sister, so-and-so's daughter, so-and-so's wife. Good Lord. Day by day, I, too, fell in love with the Chinese Youth; yes, I too fell in love.

'Day by day, I passed the information on to the Baron of Porcelain. He was delighted. He wrote down the names of all the women Murad slept with. The Baron of Porcelain liked to know people's secrets; he liked to have plenty of information on people so he could intimidate them should they become his enemy. Until the day he realised that one of Murad's lovers was his own sister. I'd known for a while already, but I controlled myself and didn't tell him about it. I knew he would kill them both. You see Murtaza as a Satanic, merciless man, but I knew for a *year* that the baron's sister Heshu was the Chinese Youth's lover. To protect the life of the young man, I hid the secret, buried it and stifled it in my heart.

'Dozens of times, the Baron of Courgettes sent me to spy on Baran Shukur and Murad. Every time I would return in tears, telling him, "Your wife is clearer than crystal, purer than dew." I lied. I saw them together with my own eyes, but I lied so they wouldn't be killed. I lied for as long as I could, but there comes a point when the dagger reaches your own neck and you can no longer lie. When the Baron of Porcelain found out that his own sister was one of Murad's mistresses, he said, "We must kill him." I swear by all the stars at dawn, I swear by the rosewater of the untrodden gardens, the Baron of Courgettes is innocent. The baron couldn't have killed him alone. The baron didn't want to kill him, but the Baron of Porcelain egged him on.

'For a whole month, they tried to kill him. Night after night, they set a time. Every time I would lie at the feet of the Baron of Courgettes, saying, "You love this woman – why would you kill her? Why would you do that, Baron?" The baron would cry. I swear by the scent of the chaste angels, I am not lying. The Baron of Courgettes didn't want to kill her, but the Baron of Porcelain was inciting the others against him on the sly. Every day they sent him taunting letters. "Your wife's a slut," they would write. Pardon my language, but that's what they called her. "When you go home tonight, check the stars to see where they are on your wife's body." Do you understand? The Baron of Courgettes was only a kid. He was young – really young, like Baran and Murad. He had very little experience of Party life and didn't know what was happening around him. He genuinely liked Baran, but they drove him mad with letters and phone calls. They did their utmost to persuade him to kill Murad. When I became sure that the baron really would kill Baran Shukur, I wrote her two letters telling her of their plans and entreating her to run away. Almighty God, I was the one who wrote those two letters. It was me.'

Uncoiling like a snake, he rose from his chair and stretched. I was standing by the window at that point. He came towards me and said, 'The night they killed him, he was wearing an orange shirt. They had switched off the city's power supply. Not a single feeder line was on. The Baron of Courgettes and I were in the back and Ja'far-i Magholi was in the front seat,' he sighed. Then he gave his characteristic laugh. 'I told Murad, "We've hired a venue. We're planning a huge wedding.

Come and check if everything's in order and whether or not we need anything else."

'He acted as if he believed me. He said nothing to suggest he suspected anything. When he saw the Baron of Courgettes, he said, "I've been meaning to pay you a visit for ages." Magholi put his arms around him, as if he was a favourite brother, and said, "Have a look at the venue for us and tell us if it's up to scratch." Ha ha! Magholi carries out any job they want to keep secret by himself – they don't let anyone else get involved. All the way there, Ja'far-i Magholi and Murad were telling each other jokes and laughing. They talked about the Arab women who had come to the hotels. Murad was very happy.'

'Don't tell us any more, I already know it all,' I said, grabbing his hands. 'I know how Magholi killed him. I was Magholi's friend. I know everything. Instead, tell me this: how did you kill Baran Shukur?'

Murtaza sat back in his chair and rolled up in a ball again. He was such a long-legged Satan; when he sat like that, his sharp, pointed kneecaps came up much higher than the rest of his body; he looked like a giant insect. He was taken aback when I described the spot where they had buried Murad.

'No, no. That's not where we killed Murad. It was somewhere else,' he said. 'After Ja'far-i Magholi fired his last shot, he soaked his handkerchief in Murad's blood. The three of us loaded the body into the boot of the Baron of Courgette's car. We wanted to take it back to Nwemiran. What a night that was! In those days, all the bodies were taken back to Nwemiran. When we arrived, we saw that there was a heavy police presence around the entire district. The British consul and a senior American official were visiting the home of the Baron of Sugar and Tea. The area was controlled in such a way that even if Paul Bremer himself had turned up, he would have been searched three times before he got in. Magholi reversed and we reluctantly buried the body out on the plains.'

He looked at both of us and said, 'He was a handsome young man, God rest his soul.'

Shibr put out his cigarette without taking a single puff. 'You killed Baran Shukur, too. Was it that same night?'

'When we got back, it was one o'clock in the morning. The British consul and the other guests had all gone,' he said after a short pause. 'The clouds gathered and drifted along. The wind blew, then fell quiet. I swear by the dew and the buds, it was a lovely night. Apart from the business of the two killings, it really was a lovely night.'

Awkwardly, he stretched a hand round behind one knee to get at the other and scratch it. He gave us both a wide smile and then went quiet for a while, as though deep in thought. He shifted slightly, looking like a creature bracing for a huge leap. His neck was so long, he resembled a goose striving to hear a distant sound. The more you examined his appearance, the more hideous it looked. The contours of his body and his face were the epitome of asymmetry.

'The Baron of Porcelain and Magholi told the Baron of Courgettes: "We're not going to kill Baran Shukur. She's your wife. You should do it." The Baron of Courgettes was nearly crying. As God is my witness, I have never seen anyone who loved his wife as much as he did. When we arrived home, Nwemiran was completely silent – not the silence of a city asleep, but of a dead city. When Nwemiran slept, it was like the dead, and when it awoke, it was like the waking of the dead – painstakingly slow and lethargic. We opened the front door of the house. I thought the sound would be heard across the city. Oh my, oh my. To me, there is nothing more dangerous than the creaking of a door at midnight. Brothers, I stood in the yard of the baron's house, intoxicated by the smell of the spring grass. That shouldn't come as any surprise – we still smelled of blood, after all. The smell of grass: I was completely immersed in it. Magholi asked me to accompany the baron into the house and give him any help he needed, so I climbed the stairs to the second floor with him. Baran was asleep in her bedroom, lit by a dim blue light.

'I swear by the purity of all the world's honest people that this blue light bulb looked just like the one we used in our production of *Othello* twenty years ago. That bulb on stage produced the same blue light when we turned it on for the last scene of the play at the Education Department's public theatre. The very same colour. The Baron of Courgettes climbed onto Baran Shukur's bed, where she lay just like Desdemona in her marriage bed. As if she was already dead, however, as if to avoid repeating Desdemona's same words, she didn't wake up. Her beautiful white neck shone in that dim blue light, positioned just so, fuelling the baron's urge to touch her, strangle her. I swear by a child's pure breath; I swear by a feather from a dove unjustly hit by hunger's bullet; I swear by Almighty God, who created the butterfly's delicate wings and the wolf's fangs. The whole scene was like that in which Othello kills Desdemona: Baran Shukur's white clothes, the Baron of Courgettes' black gloves, the silence in the room. Yet I was not Iago, nor the Baron of Courgettes Othello, and Baran Shukur certainly was not innocent like Desdemona. When the baron took her by the throat, Baran neither flinched nor moved. I did not hear any gasping or choking. I still maintain she was dead before the baron took her by the throat. I swear by the morning wind and the cool northerly breeze before the dawn. Have you ever heard of such a thing? Have either of you seen a living person strangled remain completely still? Not a cry, not the slightest noise?

'I told the baron thousands of times: "Baran was already dead before you killed her." But he says, "I felt her heartbeat, I felt her breathing, I felt the flow of her blood." But who's to say all this is not just the delusion of a man looking for a sin to torment himself with? I know the pressure he applied to her neck with his fingers was not enough to break even the wing of a butterfly or to pluck a flower from a branch. That's why I think only heartbreak and self-torment made the Baron of Courgettes feel he was guilty.'

'Or is it that you want him to be innocent?' I said.

'I'm telling you what I saw,' he said after a short silence. 'May our Great Lord be my witness: I saw what I am telling you. That same night, I carried out Baran's body and buried her. The Baron of Porcelain and Magholi took the Baron of Courgettes away, and I didn't see him again for a week. To distract himself from his grief, he consumed nothing but alcohol for seven days straight, roaming from one prostitute's house to another. When I saw him a week later, his beard had grown, and sleeplessness and anxiety were nearly killing him. I took his mind off his misery and brought him here, to this house, to this room. For another week, I gave him advice and guidance, and gently reproached him. When he emerged, he was scared. He is still scared. Of everything. Oh, the bloody mornings of life, how can we escape you? He's young as well. He's distraught and despairing … like you and me.'

Murtaza was on his feet now, his eyes open, his teeth yellow and old. As he talked, he gesticulated wildly in all directions, as if he were tossing his words into the air and catching them again as they came down. To me, he seemed again like a snake, curling up one minute, uncoiling the next. Shibr looked at me, astonished, and then asked our enemy once again: 'Murtaza, who are you? What do you do? Why are you in the game?'

To my eyes, Murtaza was like an old, leafless tree suddenly inhabited by a spirit and now walking about, stripped bare to its branches. He turned towards me, laughed loudly and said, 'Don't assume I'm talking to you out of fear. If you do, I'll be angry with you. I'm telling the truth precisely so that I can come to reveal secrets. There is nothing I enjoy more. Nothing is more enjoyable than sitting in front of two great and honest men who want to hear the truth. What a pleasure it is! I love people who want to hear the truth. You think I'm a lying devil who hates the truth. You assume that in the depths of my heart, I have no desire to reveal truths. But you're mistaken. A person enters the sea of secrets to come out with a collection of stories. When I went down to the bottom of the well that is this city, I became obsessed with the moment when, sooner or later, I'd tell everything. I knew that one day my poor knees would give way before two men who like to hear the truth, my poor tongue would yield – ha ha! – my poor neck would droop, and I would tell everything. For ten years now, I've been waiting for a creature to ask, "Who are you?" But no one dares. No one dares to ask Murtaza Satan who he is. True, I may be a servant, but I am also a box of diseases and secrets. That's it: a box of diseases and secrets.'

He seemed physically more relaxed now. His entire face, as he watched us, was one great grotesque smile. 'And where did you bury Baran?' I asked him calmly.

'Hasan-i Tofan,' he said, 'I am not what you understand me to be. I'm not. Everyone thinks I'm an important person. Even at the Knights of the Highlands Club, they think I have a prominent status among the barons, but that's not the case. True, I serve them, but brothers ... brothers, I am nothing but the burier of their dead, a deep sea of secrets. They all think if I bury a secret in my heart, only death will take it from me. Shibr Mustafa, do you want to know who I am? I am the barons' black box. They write down all their dark secrets in my heart. I am a book, and I open my poor heart for them to write in then close it up again so no one can read a single line. They believe me to be a book that no one will ever read.

'Hasan-i Tofan, do you think I don't know who you two are? Do you really? That I'm a fool? I thought about it for a very long time. I checked you out ... I know you're nothing. No one asked you to do this. Ha ha! You think that all morning I've been telling you things out of fear. Ha! You're pleased to see me weak, miserable and scared. You're happy to be playing with a poor, pure soul like me, but I know no one has asked you to do this. You just hate the barons, that's all. You hate the Party, that's all. You hate our leaders.'

I didn't know what to say. Shibr scratched his blond hair. 'If you're so sure no one has asked us to do this, why haven't you told Magholi? Why haven't you given us away to the Porcelain Prince?'

Murtaza came alive now and spoke freely.

'Because I love you,' he said as he raised his hands. 'You are two unique flowers of this city. You are two trees in a garden that is about to die and wither away completely. Don't laugh, I mean it. You think I don't respect your magnificence. I'm telling you all this because I know you can't do a thing. I swear by the newly laid eggs of cuckoos in their nests, you can't do a single thing. You can't. Because you and I belong to the people of this city, who can't act whether we know the truth or not.

'If I knew someone had sent you, I wouldn't have revealed a thing. I swear by the spring dawns, I swear by the pure morning fields, I would've turned into solid rock and revealed absolutely nothing. I would have been like a monkey that speaks no language, a dog that runs away with its tail between its legs. But I know you are both seeking the truth. You are two butterflies who have come to suck the nectar of truth from the flower of Murtaza's heart. Forgive my poor rhetoric, dear brothers. You know that I am the garden of truth, that Murtaza is the tulip garden of truth. I know you have no ill intentions, work for no one and don't belong to any of the various wings of the Party. You are two eagles, gliding down from on high to see the truth.'

Like a dancing clown, he was moving in circles now, looking at both of us with that enormous, crazed grin. For the first time I was certain that reading this creature's face told us nothing clear about his soul. His face was there for all to see, but his heart was far more complicated.

'Don't assume that poor Murtaza is a genius, don't assume his heart doesn't fill with fear and uncertainty,' he said as he stood before Shibr. 'Murtaza's heart is sometimes like that of a terrified fledgling ... he can't sleep at night. I swear by my brotherhood, my heart, too, suffers from regrets; I, too, can be consumed by heartbreak. Many nights, I've run around the rooms of this empty mansion, shouting at the top of my voice. I don't want to take any secrets with me to the grave. Do you think Murtaza is scared you will go to the barons to tell them he revealed their secrets? You won't do it. Even if I am guilty beyond redemption, you are too dignified and too honest for that. You understand me. You know how clean Murtaza's hands are. You want the truth; Murtaza is the guardian of the truth. I know everything. Murtaza Satan can read everyone's heart. From the first night that Hasan-i Tofan humiliated me – from his tone, his anger, the way he breathed, I understood what a truthful man he is. Yesterday I said to myself, "Murtaza, shut your eyes and surrender your soul to these two angels." I said, "These are souls who want the truth." The wonderful men and women of this city want to know if the truth is alive or dead. Ha ha! They all want certainty. Last night, I danced on one leg until dawn, I was so pleased to have found you. I've seen the depths of your souls, and when you finally came to see me, I knew you wouldn't humiliate me. I just knew it.

'I, too, hate the Party. I swear to God, I hate it,' he added in a whisper. 'There's no one who doesn't. Ha ha! Even the Leader hates the Party.'

'Murtaza,' I said very sadly, 'it's not important who we are. Just tell me, where did you bury Baran Shukur?'

'I am the burier of the Party's dead, the burier of the barons' dead,' Murtaza said. 'For ages now, I've wanted to find someone to tell these truths to … I swear by the souls of bulbuls, the smell of cloves and the colour of fresh jasmine, I'm fed up with living like a book that they write in and then slam shut. Hasan, if you dare, come and open this book and look at just one page of it. If you can, come and read my heart, on which they have been writing their secrets year in, year out. Come and open my chest and see what's in there. But beware: whoever learns these secrets will become a dangerous monster. I know that one day they'll kill me … once they've written on the very last page of my heart, once they notice that it has no more blank pages left and no room for more secrets, once they see that poor Murtaza's soul is overwhelmed. Ha ha! Ha ha! Then they'll kill me, and send me and my secrets to Hell forever. Blond-haired Shibr, don't ask me who I am. I'm a living book, I am black, living evidence. Kill me, and the living book dies with me. Do you want me to die and take with me the secrets of an age? I am a living antique.'

He came over to me with an air of seriousness, like that of an experienced actor, and said in a loud, limpid voice, 'Hasan-i Tofan, could you put yourself in danger as I do? Could you? They've turned me into a dark museum that walks on two legs. For ten years, I've opened up my heart and they've written their secrets in it. Every night I tell my heart: 'O, unfortunate heart, endure this, and stay strong.' No box in the world can hold as many secrets as my heart; if you knew only a fraction of them, you'd go mad. If you take the lid off the box, you'll see enough ills and fears for thousands of cities in the world. Nothing drives a person mad quite like having to keep secrets. I laugh to stop myself going mad. Ha ha! Hi hi! I dance to stop myself going mad.'

'Murtaza, what is it that you do?' Shibr asked him. 'I don't understand what it means to be the "burier of the barons' dead". Murtaza, don't be scared. Open your heart to us.'

'Murtaza, scared? Scared?' he said. 'Murtaza is sometimes really, really scared, and sometimes he's the bravest man in the world. That's Murtaza for you. My stories start from the time of the civil war. I had just come out of prison, a sad man with no job. The Ba'athists' prison had turned me into an ugly monster. Do you think I was always as ugly as this? Yes, I was ugly, but not to this degree – like all God's creatures, I had my own beauty. Once, the heart of a normal human being beat inside my breast. Like any other human being in this world, I had my moments of sadness and happiness. There were times when my soul was filled with that compassion and love of yours. I swear by the beauty of love that someone may even have felt the purity of

452

my love, and taken a shine to me from a distance. Who knows? Ha ha! But I feel there must have been a divine, universal plan at work to distort my soul as it did.

'During the war, the Baron of Porcelain wanted to give me a hand and lift me out of poverty and friendlessness. Back then I was supported by one of my brothers, who was poor like me. I was so broke that stray dogs and cats led a better and happier life than I did. My old friends, my fellow actors in *Macbeth* and *Othello*, scorned me, regarding me as a cruel murderer of women. Whatever alleyway I walked through, women hid themselves, ha ha! Children ran from me. Murtaza Satan's scary reputation in this city goes back to those days. How could they say such things about innocent Murtaza? How could they destroy me like that without even seeing the beauty of my soul? How? Things were was so bad that whatever job I sought, the doors were shut on me. Ha! So bad that there was no food on my table. So bad that hunger, pennilessness and wretchedness increasingly drew me to the abyss.

'It was then that the Baron of Porcelain kindly found me a job. Initially, there were corpses from the civil war that needed to be hidden. They had to be lost so that no one could discover who they were, whose sons they were. There were three corpses in a cellar; the stench was overwhelming. I don't know who they were or to which party they belonged. Three youths wrapped in three black blankets. I carried away all three bodies and buried them. I swear by the truth: that was the first time I touched a dead person's hands. I dug graves for them, buried them and entrusted them to God. Sometimes I turn to God and say, "Almighty God, if it were not for Murtaza bringing You the corpses of innocent people, what would You do?" I came to understand that the Party always had a corpse to hide. The parties of this city always do.'

As if thinking about a time long gone, as if oblivious to my presence and that of Shibr, he went to the window and said, 'Back then, Nwemiran had not yet been constructed. It was a huge plot of land with no owner. The baron drew a circle in it and said, "Bury your corpses here." Ha ha! It was a huge circle drawn with chalk. I fixed the boundary of the circle in my mind, acquired a white pick-up from the baron and became a burier of the dead. Not a week has passed without there being a corpse for me. If one week the corpse was late, it was Hell for me. I swear to God, there have never been as many corpses as during the civil war. Sometimes, corpses on the battlefield would be left without any identity papers. Most of them were fighters with no relatives. After acquiring a signed paper from the Leadership Committee and the General Command of the Armed Forces, I'd go out late at night in my clean, white pick-up – my angelic pick-up – and collect the corpses and bury them. Ha ha! You think Murtaza lacks mercy, you think Murtaza doesn't love those corpses. Ha! Right here, in my heart, I have a secret album that no one can open, that no one can see … in it, I've saved a picture of each one of the corpses. Here, in my ugly head, I've saved the smell of each corpse separately. On my clean hands, I have saved the feel of all their skins. If I hadn't buried the dead, who would have?

'After the civil war, the Baron of Porcelain came to me one day and said: "Ghafur Agha of Sarmawzar needs your help." Ghafur Agha was one of the Leader's close friends. He'd say at gatherings, "Half the fat in the bellies of Kurdistan's politicians comes from the tail fat of the lambs I rear." A young woman from Sarmawzar village had gone to university, where she had fallen for a penniless nobody from the Hawar tribe against the wishes of the agha and his sons. The agha's sons killed them both, put the bodies into two big sacks and hid them in an inaccessible cave in a narrow valley. She was the first woman I buried. When I retrieved their bodies from the cave, I didn't think the corpses of unfortunate women like this would come my way again. When I buried her, I thought the lady might feel scared and bored down there among all the fighters of the civil war. I swear by the pure breath of the partridge singing, the body of that woman was the first my fingers ever touched. Ha ha! Thereafter, when any agha, tribe, Party official, security organisation, political party, wealthy person or police officer wanted to hide a corpse, to make it disappear, they gave it to Murtaza. When they built Nwemiran, they surrounded that plot of land with a huge circular wall and put in a gate on either side.'

Murtaza paused, fumbled in his deep pockets and added, 'These are the keys to the doors. These are the keys to Murtaza's Garden – the keys to the garden of truth. I plant flowers and bury human beings in that same plot of land. Ha! Everyone in Nwemiran think it's just a garden. Everyone calls it "Murtaza's Garden", everyone but the barons – all the barons know about it. Over the past decade, not a week has gone by in which I haven't buried a corpse there. I swear by the remoteness of the sky, the height of the moon, the distance of the stars. I swear by the light the mornings shine on the heart, if there was any agha who wanted to hide the body of his unfaithful wife, I hid it for him. If there was any official who wanted to give a proper burial to his opponents, I did that for him. Any trader, spy, terrorist, lover, keeper of secrets or cheat killed in recent times, I've carried them with my own hands and hidden them in Murtaza's Garden. Rare is the time I do not kiss the dead person's forehead and say, "My dear, why did you die like this?" They are all here, inside Murtaza's heart, inside the hushed and silent, tongue-less sea called Murtaza. Ha! Oh, my silent and hushed heart ...

'You think I am talking to you out of fear? No, you are the only two people who ever approached the edge of the hushed sea of my heart and wanted to hear, to listen to me, to find out what the dark sea in Murtaza's soul would say. He who listens to this ocean must fear. He who listens to the deep waves of Murtaza's heart will be too frightened to ever sleep peacefully again. So I've told you now ... I buried Baran Shukur in my garden; Baran Shukur is with me. These are the keys to the gate – here they are.'

'Murtaza,' I told him, 'I want nothing from you except that body. Give me that body, nothing else, and be assured your secrets will remain inside their deep sea.'

Murtaza looked at me, astonished. 'What do you need it for?' he asked. 'What would you do with the corpse? No corpse has ever left Murtaza's Garden. Not a single one.'

I felt as though I'd been struck on the head with a club. I looked at him unsteadily and said, 'I don't know what I need it for, but I want it.'

'Even if you offered me the whole world, I couldn't go with you,' he said, leaping up before me like a madman. 'If they find out I've revealed the secret of the graveyard, they'll kill me. I swear by the last summer bud, I swear by all the cool evenings in the world, they'll kill me. I can tell you the location of the body ... I can do that, but I swear by the morning dew, if they find out, they'll kill me. If you want to issue my death sentence, if you want to kill me, then I'm ready. Virtuous men, if by killing Murtaza your hearts will be at peace, kill him – but not like this. I don't want to be killed by them. I don't want them to kill me and bury me in my own garden, even though I'm sure that, sooner or later, that's exactly what they'll do.'

That night, Murtaza gave me the key to one of the garden gates. We took an oath that we would not mention his name at any time, under any pressure or fear. What really pleased me was that Murtaza didn't know a thing about the fate of Murad Jamil's body. Just like us, he had returned one night to the location of his shallow grave only to find an empty pit. The body's disappearance had put great fear in the hearts of the Baron of Courgettes and the Baron of Porcelain. After Murtaza told the story of its disappearance at great length, I understood that the corpse was not at their disposal. Now I knew where it was, and with whom. I left Murtaza's house elated. I sang lustily as I pushed Shibr's wheelchair, prompting him to say, 'Hasan-i Pizo, I have never seen you so happy in all your life.' That night I went to Hazarbagh and fell asleep among the flowers laughing. I dreamed until dawn about a beautiful girl named Baran Shukur running among the flowers and whispering, 'Hasan-i Pizo, follow me ... oh, Hasan-i Pizo, why are you just standing there? Follow me.'

THE MEMOIRS OF THE
BARON OF IMAGINATION

'Attar, what have you got for me?' I asked.

He looked at me, laughed his foolish laugh, took out the list of the Imaginative Creatures' names and said, 'Your Excellency the Baron, so far I've signed contracts with everyone on this list.' He showed me some of the names – imaginative engineers, bricklayers, lawyers, legal experts and gardeners. He raised his head, wiped his ears and said, 'But some of the Imaginative Creatures won't commit to any contract, to any worldly agreement. They won't commit to a project.'

By then, I had formed an almost complete picture of the dream city I wanted to build. My idea was that it should be created from a fusion of three types of beauty: first, that of architecture – buildings and gardens; second, that of life, harmony between people; third, that of the imagination, which enabled all beauty to endure.

You all know that I came up with the project after reading extensively, and visiting many countries on every continent. One night, I called a meeting of all the Imaginative Creatures who had signed a contract with that big-headed, wet-eared fellow. They were all members of Ghazalnus's army – people who wanted to translate some of their imagination into reality. When I looked at their faces, I immediately saw two types among them: the dark types, who I knew had beautiful fantasies but were more preoccupied with turning them into commodities for sale than with aesthetics, the beauty of their dreams or mine; and the bright types, who were seeking someone to support them in realising part of their dreams. Only those who genuinely understood the meaning of beauty could work with me. There are many people who have fantasies, but I wanted people who have both imagination and an understanding of beauty – and not in the sense of simply creating a magnificent bead, but of threading that bead onto a long necklace, placing it exactly where it belongs in the plan.

My first fight with the Imaginative Creatures over the meaning of beauty took place on the first meeting. Influenced by Ghazalnus, they believed that the beauty in anything was intrinsic to it and inseparable from it; but views like this drove me crazy, hysterical. They left me feeling alienated and lost.

The venue for our meeting was a room on the second floor of the Engineers' Club. I was standing in the middle of the room, Turkish bottled water in my hand. I said, 'Nothing is beautiful in itself. Anything beautiful acquires its beauty from its surroundings. What kind of feeling would a beautiful woman living among ruins evoke in us? Well? Instead of a sense of beauty, immortality and greatness, there would be sadness, meaninglessness and absurdity. When we see a beautiful woman among ruins, instead of happiness, desire and sexual arousal, we sense the absurdity of this world, the futility of this existence, the chaos of this life. One day I was walking in a park. Just like any one of God's creatures, I walked to and fro. The grass was dry and dead under my feet. Nothing about that dry grass or withered lawn drew my attention. Nothing. After walking to and fro dozens of times, I saw a small white flower, beautiful by any standard. I asked myself, 'Prince of Imagination, what's wrong with you, that you cannot see this flower?' My friends, do you know why I didn't see it? Because you can't see beauty amid a sea of wreckage. Beauty can only be seen in context, in a place that is full of beauty. If the flower had been in a great, lush meadow, I would have seen it – but I didn't, because I could see only the yellowed tulip beds and withered garden. If I had ignored those surroundings to begin with, I would have seen the flower earlier. Unless we ignore the world's ugliness, unless we ignore the withered tulip gardens, we cannot see the unique flowers. The world's ugliness must disappear for the beauty of the imagination to shine forth.

'My architect friends, fellow users of protractors, compasses and rulers, look at this city. Consider the tall, stone houses with Greek-style columns and all the serenity of the dwellings of the Olympian gods that are slowly mushrooming. What, when you look carefully, do you see, other than disorder? Nothing. *Nothing.* Despite the meticulousness of the engineers, each working to their own designs, it's still a wasteland. Any beauty you plant in a wasteland will only draw more attention to that wasteland. That's why you must forget about this city. If you want to work with me, ignore this city. Let its own people worry about it. To me, beauty is a plan. It is working according to a plan with every stone and every inch calculated. The city of the imagination is one where mathematics, politics and poetry are in harmony and work together. Brothers, that's my wish for our wounded society, as it tries to make its way back from Hell. I want to reconcile mathematics, politics and poetry. A solitary example of beauty cannot be beautiful within a sea of ugliness.'

I felt that some of the Imaginative Creatures were warming to my ideas. And yet, at the end of that meeting I realised the extent of Ghazalnus's impact upon them. They saw themselves as unique people on Earth, as alienated outsiders, and wanted to remain so. The strangest thing in man is that he can take pride in his alienation. That's another ailment the poets have bestowed upon humanity. Before the poets, no one ever wore alienation like a crown on their head. If only I could snatch imagination away from the poets. Then finally we could create a beautiful world. Poets, the fuckers, get to live inside a beautiful world, yet won't let us ignore or forget about the suffering in this one … that's my biggest issue with them.

That night was one of the most harrowing of my life. That night, I understood it was likely that some of these engineers, bricklayers and gardeners would actually support me in creating a dream city; that they might be able to bring both diversity and harmony to the project, albeit with great effort. I felt that, with these Imaginative Creatures, I might be able to build houses, gardens and roads.

But I still needed an architect who could instil harmony in their hearts and ensure they complemented one another, who could bring the souls of these people together and ensure their love for the city. I was confident the Imaginative Creatures who had signed up could provide me with beauty and harmony between *things*, but could they provide the force that makes humans love one another?

Oh, you don't know what a harrowing night it was! I had lived my entire life in fear of just such a night, when you conclude that a beautiful realm cannot be created without poets. Although I had always harboured such a view, when I looked at the faces of the people Attar had gathered, I could see the dangerous face of this dark conviction. When I was fixated on buying the ghazals, I had pondered their meaning deeply. I had compared the samples in my possession with other ghazals. I spent many a night with old masters of classical poetry interpreting the couplets in my study. I concluded categorically that Ghazalnus's ghazals spoke to the harmony between man and the universe, rather than to abstract love. His ghazals were not poems, but bridges.

One of the old teachers of classical poetry told me, 'They are bridges between the possible and the miraculous, between the living and the departed, between oneness and the infinite.'

'I'm a modern man,' I replied. 'In the language of today, in the language of the twenty-first century, you are saying, "These poems are bridges between the individual and the world, between the self and others, between loneliness and the soul of society."'

The old man nodded. 'Perhaps, they are, my son. I wouldn't know about that.'

That first meeting with the Imaginative Creatures, I understood that I could do nothing without Ghazalnus. What's the use of building beautiful cities if you can't create harmony between the souls who inhabit them? If you can't create a connection between them? If you can't guarantee that the imagination remains alive forever?

Not long afterwards, I got hold of Majid-i Gul Solav, and in passing he uttered a dangerous sentence I would never forget: 'Baron, the city of dreams is a city where there are no dreams.' I mulled this over later, and understood what a heart-rending sentence it was.

I needed Ghazalnus to help me fill my plans with imperishable dreams. My city of dreams needed the ghazals so that imagination would not die in it; it needed Trifa Yabahri's carpets so that human beings could feel close to miracles; it needed Majid-i Gul Solav's ship to make us see that reality is transient, and imagination eternal. The residents of the world's beautiful cities have all understood that the only thing able to protect them from demise and decline is the imagination. I needed Ghazalnus to create harmony between people.

The night I met the Imaginative Creatures, each of them was living in his or her private world, and as far as I am concerned there is nothing more dangerous. The very idea of human beings each immersed in their own imaginations is anathema to me. Private lives, private imaginations separating people one from another – those are the weaknesses of our nation's Imaginative Creatures. That night, I understood that I needed to graft the poets onto the world. This is my job, and my hope. It is my sacred message, one that God has chosen me to deliver. Without the poets, the architects are nothing; if the magic of poetry is not grafted onto the fingers of gardeners, their flowers will be no different from thorns; love without the breath of poetry is a kind of war; without Ghazalnus, the city of dreams would become a city devoid of dreams.

That night I tossed and turned in my bed incessantly, shouting, 'God, what a magical force is the imagination!'

But when the poets seized hold of it, it set them on the wrong path. It was my job to put an end to this nonsense. Any poet who refused to graft his soul onto the trees and buds must be condemned to Hell. Any poet who refused to mix his wine with ours must be punished. On that first night we met, I told the Imaginative Creatures, 'You belong to me now. Go and fill your souls freely with imagination and beauty, but wherever you go, know that you will be moving within my plans.'

My aim was for Ghazalnus to know that, slowly and gradually, I would invade his empire. Everything I did was geared towards obtaining his ghazals and support. I couldn't just leave him in peace – I wanted to tame him. When poets are at peace, they simply stay in their rooms; they withdraw from beautifying the world and from realising their dreams. At this sad moment in history, the poets had to work; they needed to come out of their rooms and work alongside us. No, don't say I am blind. I can see the beauty and significance of all people. But I hate the poets anyway: they are the only type to hide away in their rooms and their books precisely when the world most needs them, their beauty and imagination.

One night, I knocked fearlessly at the door of Trifa Yabahri's secret house. I wanted to lay siege to Ghazalnus from all sides. I wanted him gradually to become so frightened that he would realise what a massive force he was up against. Time after time, I played stronger and stronger cards to put pressure on him, without letting him know who was behind it. He *would* become my ally. I hate poets who live their lives as if there were no king on Earth. They want kings for the sole purpose of cursing them. No, don't believe that I was his enemy; he was his own enemy.

When I knocked on Trifa's door, an old woman opened it. She looked like someone out of an ancient tale. I did not know whether life had made her old, or she had made life old. I said, 'My dear, I'm not a bad man, and I haven't knocked at the door to hurt anyone. My name is Jawahir Sarfiraz, and I've come to see Miss Trifa Yabahri.'

When I saw Trifa, she was pale from fear. I paused for a moment and just looked at the deep dread in her eyes. She invited me in. It was a quiet house, with no signs of any other residents. I assumed she must have hidden the others in a different part of the house, because for a long time now I had sensed, even if only from afar, that there were other people there.

I said, 'Lady of the Magical Carpets, I am the man who bought the carpet factory a few years ago because of the power in your hands. Now I have come to take you and set you at a loom worthy of your imagination. I don't want to hurt anyone. I don't want you or your carpet weavers to tremble in fear. All I ask is that you listen to me, like a sister listens to a brother or one human being to another. I desperately need your imagination. My job is to save beautiful figments of the imagination and not allow them to be wasted, to make something out of them all, something that will live on. I want to take your carpets to their proper place, to lay them where the beauty of the columns, windows and walls match that of your carpets, where those who walk upon them appreciate their magic, where people have the capacity to understand and love them. Trifa Yabahri, consider me a powerless brother. No one's imagination can reach perfection on its own. You can't weave a carpet to replace all the beauties of the world. The fantasies need to complete one another. Beauty must hold hands with beauty. Hold my hands, sister, and come with me. I want to build a new city. The Leader has assigned me to do this. So have the Americans. A city can't be built unless Ghazalnus fills it with love, unless it has an enchanting carpet weaver like you. When visitors come from every corner of the world, they need to know they are walking on a carpet made from the essence of the imagination. Trifa Yabahri, we have always been a nation of daydreamers. Give me your hands and come with me.'

I felt that the more I spoke, the more scared she became, but it wasn't the type of fear that sought to run away and hide from me. On the contrary, she reached out her hand and placed it on mine. God, her touch was sheer magic. For a moment, it filled my heart with a certain coolness I hadn't experienced before. Her touch was like a salve that would immediately take the heat from a branded wound. It takes the touch of such hands to let a person know how wounded his body really is, how badly in need of a salve.

She looked at me with her hollow eyes and sad gaze, and said, 'Brother, don't build your city of dreams. Help the people of this city to escape even more sadness. We fantasise to forget our suffering. Imagination acts as a shield in this city. Come closer, brother. Let me whisper something in your ear. Imagination is like love: it lives only when it eludes everyone, when it is without form. Come closer, let me explain it to you. If there's a dream city on this planet, it's the one we are travelling towards, but will never reach. You're rich. You have power. First, heal the real city. Heal the city of disease, of danger and self-immolation. Build a city for the women who have nowhere to hide from monsters. Don't mix your work up with that of the poets. Brother Jawahir, imagination is not your abode. My dear, believe me, it's not. Leave the carpets of my imagination alone. Don't invade them, too. If you want to serve the imagination, make the real world beautiful. If you can, help the unhappy so that they no longer suffer. Set up a charitable organisation to help the hungry and the vulnerable. Do that, focus on that. Let *us* save the imagination in this hell. My brother Jawahir, I have worked non-stop for sixteen years, ever since I was young. Listen to me, when reality is wonderful, its happiness spills over into the imagination; when it's bitter, so does all its poison.'

Though I tried not to show it, I was hurt by Trifa's words.

'Imagination isn't something a person should imprison in his or her head,' I said. 'Imagination isn't a shadow we're always chasing but failing to catch. Imagination is power, just like any other kind of power – like willpower or the power to reason. Trifa Yabahri, my dear sister, give me your hands so I can kiss them. I know everything about this house of yours, but I am not a traitor, nor am I someone who could ever utter a bad word about others. Give me your delicate hands. I am a politician. I have been since I emerged from the egg. Politics is will – will without imagination, without a mind – while imagination is a force without will, without plans. My dear sister, put your hands here so I can kiss them. I have will. I can make sure your carpets live on; I can make sure Ghazalnus's ghazals create Imaginative Creatures generation after generation. I could make sure each of your carpets is hung in the royal chamber of a legendary city as a symbol of our triumph, of our ability to survive. If our fantasies don't survive, then neither will we.

'I don't want to surrender to death. Our politicians, who lack imagination, have given up and surrendered to death. Don't say that imagination is beyond our reach. There is a time for each nation to take hold of its own imagination and capture it. I know the imagination is difficult to catch, like a house sparrow, but it's not impossible. There's a moment when we can tame that house sparrow and summon it to land on our hand. I want to build the city of dreams. That's the Leader's order, but the Leader doesn't know exactly what the city of dreams is. Not once has he thought about the details the way I have. The city of dreams is the place where my will and your imagination meet, each of us feeding off the other's expertise. Trifa, give me your hands so I can kiss them. This is not how the politicians of this country think. I'm the only one who thinks this way. We have a great opportunity to create something beautiful, something that embodies the forgotten harmony of our people's soul. I won't let anyone take this opportunity away from me or kill it. Trifa, I am talking on behalf of the spirit of a people whose harmony has been disturbed; the city of dreams is the reconstruction of that harmony. Lower your hands for me to kiss them, my dear sister. The district I want to build isn't one that shuns the poor, only available to a handful of wealthy men with wads of money. It's a place for you and me, for all of us.'

'My dear brother, what a good heart you have,' she said, as if taking pity on me, as if looking into the eyes of someone who was going mad. 'You want to reconcile our imagination with the world. You want to reconcile us with all these fears, flights and sorrows. Brother, my imagination can no longer be reconciled with the world. You are a good man, a very good man. Go back to your wife and children – if you have them. Go back to the Leader and tell him, "I can build beautiful cities." So that he doesn't hurt you, be quick to add that the imagination has been so estranged from this city that no one can reconcile it with the world. Before you are thwarted, tell him: "Your

Excellency, the Imaginative Creatures cannot be reconciled with the world." Before you spend any money and ruin your reputation, tell him that what is disturbed cannot be rebuilt or reassembled.'

My friends, no one had ever given me so clear an answer as Trifa Yabahri. I spoke at length with her – I threatened her, I tempted her with wealth. I said I'd expose the women she was hiding, I wept. But all the while her response was to place her hands on mine and say, 'Your job is to fix the world. Leave the imagination alone.' She said, 'Your ambition is to incarcerate our souls, not to make the world a beautiful place with us.' She said, 'If you want to become an Imaginative Creature, go and look at all the failures, disappointments, blood and suffering in this city. That will take you to the realm of the imagination.' She said, 'All imaginative creatures are disappointed, unfortunate and lonely. All of them.' She said, 'Politicians create fresh hells, not dream cities.' Finally, she said, 'Brother, my imagination is estranged from the world. I want to escape from the world, rather than re-enter it. I don't want my imagination to engage with any plan. I like to transform it into a magic carpet and take flight upon it. My dear brother, imagination is not a path, as you would have it. Rather, it is a secret door we run through when our houses are set alight.'

No, friends, no. Nothing was of any use. Ghazalnus had entered the souls and minds of some of these imaginative people so strongly that no force could change their way of thinking. That night, I left Trifa's house with my eyes full of tears and my heart full of hatred. I drove to one of the mountain peaks on the outskirts of the city. There, I bit my clenched fists. There, in tears, I spat at the world with all my strength.

GHAZALNUS'S STORY OF CREATION AND THE RELATIONSHIP BETWEEN THE DEVIL AND BOOKS

MAJID-I GUL SOLAV, EARLY AUTUMN 2004

Four days after the night I had snuck out of the Baron of Imagination's car, Tishkan Tahir came to see me. She knocked on the door one evening, and my mother showed her to my room.

'Well, hello, handsome,' she greeted me, before taking in her surroundings and adding, 'What a nice room!'

Never had I thought she would just turn up to see me.

Looking at the map on the wall in amazement, she said, 'Heavens! You have your own world!'

She was wearing a plain black shirt and a pair of striped beige trousers. She had on make-up and a subtle perfume that wafted through the room like a cloud. I've always liked women with short hair, but hers was something else. It was enough to make a man say, 'Khanim, for God's sake, let your hair grow a little longer so it doesn't get us into trouble.'

She glanced through my film collection and said: 'Oh, so you speak English, too.'

I said, 'A bit; enough to watch the new films that don't come with Arabic subtitles.'

She paused for a moment, looked at some of my books and then said, 'So, handsome boy, do you have any Bulen Bulen CDs?' Bulen Bulen was a trashy singer, the kind who limits herself to aping Turkish pop stars – all waving arms and swaying head. I wasn't surprised Tishkhan liked Bulen Bulen; she was a simple girl who didn't know much about the world.

'No, Tishkan,' I said. 'I don't like Bulen Bulen and her ilk. Sorry, I don't have any of those CDs.'

She looked at me flirtatiously and asked, 'You're not annoyed that I came, are you?'

Although I had longed all my life for a girl like Tishkan, deep down in my heart I believed any relationship would end in disaster. But even with this feeling, I said, 'Listen, Tishkan. I don't think there is any man on Earth who would be unhappy if you came to see them. I really do like you a lot … but I don't want to keep anything from you, and I don't know what would happen if people in Nwemiran found out you'd been to see me.'

'No one in Nwemiran knows I'm here with you,' she said. 'Do you really like me?'

'What I mean is that no man in the world could *not* like you,' I said, correcting myself. 'You're a beautiful woman, and you deserve all the love in the world. I'm sure lots of people must have fawned over you before me. Tishkan, I might not be very experienced, but I'm not a fool either. I know the world you have come from.'

Perhaps to avoid getting into that conversation, she yawned gently and said, 'I've come so that you can tell me a story to send me to sleep. Come on, Mr Nice Guy, I haven't had a good night's sleep in ages.' She came to my bed, lay down slowly and said, 'A good story, mind. Suitable for a girl like me.'

I lay down next to her and gently caressed her hair. I told her a long story about the daughter of a baron who owned vast palaces, dozens of homes, hundreds of orchards. The palaces contained all that is beautiful: gold, rubies, coral and hundreds of maids and servants. Princes from every corner of the world came to the royal court to ask for her hand in marriage. But she was an unhappy creature. She was rich enough to have anything she desired, but her enormous wealth meant she didn't know what to like, and she wept constantly as a result. One day she left home in search of something difficult to find: she longed to find something in the world that she wasn't allowed to have, something she couldn't buy or possess, just to taste the pleasure of acquiring something hard-sought, unique. She visited many towns in many lands. She bought whatever she liked the look of, and recruited anyone whose company she enjoyed as a servant.

One day, she came to an isolated residence at a crossroads. From outside, she could hear the voice of a melodious nightingale. When she entered the house, she saw a handsome young man standing by a window, singing – like a nightingale. The woman, who was used to buying anything she liked in the world, asked the young man, 'May I buy the singing nightingale from you?' He invited her in, and they sat down. Softly, he told her his story. He explained that the nightingale was the only thing in the world that could not be bought or sold, because it was nothing but a fantastical nightingale that, after years of work, he had created inside his head, throat and soul. Immediately, the baron's daughter fixated on the idea of possessing it. She started bargaining with the man, offering him half her palaces, then three-quarters of her palaces, then all her wealth and assets – but it was futile. She offered herself to him: again without success.

Finally, when the woman was about to go out of her mind, the young man said, 'Khanim, for years I have known that one day you would come looking for something you could not have. To avenge all my poverty, I created something you cannot lay your hands on, buy or possess. That's the difference between my wealth and yours. I have something that you cannot own, but you have nothing that others cannot own. Khanim, you cannot buy fantastical things, nor can you own them. There will always be something in the world that you cannot appropriate. That is the wisdom of my fantastical nightingale. It will kill you, and still you won't own it.'

And so it would be. The baron's daughter contracted a deadly illness. The sound of the nightingale ate away at her from the inside wherever she went. It echoed inside her head. Madness and yearning sapped her energy, and finally, after months of suffering, she died, never having listened to the magic nightingale again.'

When I told Tishkan this story, I didn't know it would lead me into deadly waters. She pretended to be asleep, but I was certain she was thinking about the story. I wanted to kiss her desperately; I knew I could put my lips on hers and kiss her, but an invisible inner force held me back. I knew Tishkan was waiting for the touch of my lips, that her lips were waiting for a long kiss, that her body wanted something special from me. I also knew that once a woman expects you to kiss her and you don't, she becomes a dangerous enemy. Perhaps if I had kissed Tishkan that day, everything would have been different. But I don't know, perhaps it wouldn't. For all my lack of experience, I'm sure a kiss can sometimes change the course of a person's life. When Tishkan eventually left without being kissed, I felt I had made a huge mistake.

On the evening of the same day, Hasan-i Pizo told the Real Magellan, Ghazalnus and me everything that had happened with Murtaza Satan. Back then, we hardly saw Trifa. Our gatherings had gradually become men-only. They lacked a woman's presence to soften this otherwise rough environment. The absence of Trifa's smile, and her gentle outbursts, disheartened me. Whenever I noticed her absence, I missed her fury and harshness – this woman who was like dew to the entire world, but very unkind to me. And I blamed myself for any wound she inflicted on me.

That night Hasan assigned me the most difficult mission in my life: to accompany Darsim Tahir to Nwemiran and exhume Baran Shukur's body from behind the walls of Murtaza's Garden.

467

'I feel it's all we can do to bring some happiness to the young couple,' Hasan said. 'It's the only thing we can do to bring some happiness to Mr Shazaman, so he doesn't think that, after twenty-four years, he has set foot in a jungle where there are no humans. We should rebury the bodies next to each other. Isn't that right, Ghazalnus? We're neither beasts nor the Devil. We should still have enough energy to fulfil their last wish.'

That was one of Ghazalnus's profound and never-ending nights. We had been friends for many years, and confided so much in one another – things that can be said only between two friends – that we found each other's imaginative side entirely normal. Yet that night, he was a completely different being. For the first time I realised the difference in our ages was a difference of wisdom and reason too. When Hasan-i Pizo narrated the full details of the Chinese Youth's killing, when he put his hands on the table and said, 'Ja'far-i Magholi killed him', it was as if Ghazalnus had been relieved of a heavy burden … as if he had come to a truth more important to him than all the imagination in this world.

He looked at us calmly and said, 'Pizo, you've done a great job. You have all revealed the mystery of a death that is the mystery of my death, too. I am very grateful to you all, to you and Majid. That body is my body; the body of that woman is my body.' He gazed sadly at us all, and put his hands on the shoulders of the Real Magellan, who was weeping for his niece.

Ghazalnus said to him, 'Baran liked my ghazals a lot. I, like the Chinese Youth, admired her. The more he loved her, the more ghazals I wrote to her. Anything the Chinese Youth loved, I loved too. But I ran away from his worldly love. His Baran lived inside a real palace in this city, a baron's wife. But my Baran lives in an imaginary garden. Dying together was their overriding wish. They had been together for around a year. They had tried all the pleasures of the world. Those who live life to the full can look death in the eye, unafraid, and not shrink or cry out in the face of it. They were not the type of lovers who long to die because they cannot be united … Baran and the Chinese Youth lived fully that year, and yet felt they were not one. They wanted to journey into the imagination. The garden was their only hope.' Lowering his head sadly, he said, 'I made love so difficult, remote and unattainable that the garden might have been their only hope.'

Ghazalnus had begun our meeting by reading out some of the ghazals the Chinese Youth had read to Baran. They were more profound and beautiful than any of his own ghazals that I had heard.

That same night, he asked us to join him for a long walk as he read ghazals out loud. It was a moonlit autumn night and the air was becoming chilly; there was an abundance of light but few souls, a huge silence versus the faint whisper of the universe. The stars were happy, but we ourselves were sad.

As we walked, he read out ghazal after ghazal. I still don't know how or just when we entered the land of his imaginary garden, whose name, address and location I wouldn't reveal in any book. He dragged us through a magnificent flowerbed that was unrivalled by anything I'd seen in my imaginary cities and forests. He led us to a garden that will remain forever beyond the reach of either my visions or the Real Magellan's maps. That night, I understood that the essence of imagination in Ghazalnus was more colourful, far-reaching and profound than the essence of the imagination in me, or of the real world in Zuhdi Shazaman. The more we walked, the more we were overwhelmed by beauty, so much so that Hasan, Zuhdi and I felt certain that, for the first time in our lives, we were travelling through a poem.

The long, white-haired Real Magellan said, 'Ghazalnus, this place you've brought us to isn't a place at all; it's the depths of a poem.' He was right. Ghazalnus had taken us into the limitless depths of a poem that could be endlessly reflected upon, beauty not to be experienced on Earth with our normal senses.

Ghazalnus pointed to an endless garden in the far distance, saying, 'Look what boundless beauty there is in ghazals.' He led us from one garden to another, astonishing us with each flower. Somewhere in that sea of splendour, he stopped in the middle of a stretch of grass and led us to a mound with a tombstone on it. Written upon the stone were the words: 'Here lies the Chinese Youth, asleep forever.'

One night, after we first exhumed the Chinese Youth's body, Ghazalnus had gone back to the same spot and exhumed the body again. He had carried it on his shoulders to these boundless gardens, and buried him at the end rhymes of these blossoms and buds.

When we raised our heads, we found ourselves surrounded by blossoms and an infinite array of bookshelves. I looked up to see where I was; the full moon was above my head. I reached out to the flowers to see if they were real or imaginary. And they were real. I reached out to see if the books were real or imaginary. And they were real anthologies of ghazals. It was a place that smelled of farms, of gardens, of libraries.

The Chinese Youth was buried in a small, narrow grave among the ghazal books and the beautiful flowers of the garden. Standing in a ray of light, surrounded by the buzzing rhymes of the ghazals and the scent of the rosewater from the garden, Ghazalnus put his hands on the grave and said, 'This is where I lie dead.' He looked at the three of us. We were all pale, exhausted and bewildered. We looked like three prisoners of war who had fled through a dark forest and been led astray by flowers, trees and moonlight to a strange place that we wouldn't be able to find again.

It was the first time in my life that I couldn't tell whether I was in imagination or reality. But I understood that the aim of Ghazalnus's journey was to bury the two lovers inside an imaginary garden. He was infatuated by imaginary gardens – his soul constantly roamed within them. His real life was divided between the ghazals and the gardens. In this particular garden, he had hidden his ghazals. It was his secret library. He had one odd and foolish belief, which underscored every myth, fantasy and wish of his life: he believed that lovers do not die – they turn into books or flowers.

That night, he showed us around that library of ghazals for the first time. He said, 'The ghazals written after me will come and find this library; the same way, Majid-i Gul Solav, that the imaginary travellers who come after you will complete your map; the same way, Hasan-i Pizo, that the gardeners who come after you will unlock the doors of the secret gardens; the same way, Real Magellan, that the explorers who come after you will see what you have not seen.'

He looked at us and said, 'Anyone who looks deeply enough into a ghazal will reach this garden. Reaching a beautiful garden is man's greatest goal. Living in a beautiful garden like this is man's oldest dream. Paradise is the relationship between God and man that takes the form of a garden. The ancient kings built vast gardens to show what power they had over beauty. The kings always want to be kings of beauty, too. All kings in the world want to build beautiful places, to design ornamental gardens that will defeat and devalue the imagination. When kings build beautiful gardens, it is to kill the bird of the imagination, rather than for human comfort.

'The kings' gardens are different from those of the ancient poets who named their anthologies after rose gardens, because poetry is the awakening of the soul – as is a garden. It doesn't matter whether people have imagination; what matters is that imagination brings them to the garden, that the ghazals bring them to it. A perfect human being is a creature who draws everything to the garden. Wake up the human soul, and all the gardens in the world will awaken with it. All poets will eventually come to a garden unlike any other. There are two types of paradise in the world: the paradise God gives to man, and the one that man gives to God. He who cannot give a paradise cannot receive it.'

On the way back, the Real Magellan asked, 'Ghazalnus, why don't you give these anthologies to the city's public library? Why don't you put them where they'd be accessible to everyone?'

Ghazalnus said, 'Magellan, these books *are* everywhere. This garden has a door onto each and every alley of this city. Open any beautiful book in the world, and it will take you to these flower gardens … as long as people look for them. I don't hide my books. When have I ever hidden my ghazals? I simply keep them for those who are looking for them. First, a person discovers a great book in their soul. Only then does he or she read it.

'I am letting you in on a secret. It might be the last and greatest secret of my life. After all the years I spent reading and writing ghazals, I concluded that God devoted the eighth day – which is sometimes mentioned in the creation story – to writing all the beautiful books in the world. The Sufis' old debate as to whether God's books are eternal or written by humans is futile, because God devoted the eighth day of Creation to writing books; but who knows how long that eighth day lasted?

'Don't be taken aback if I tell you we are in the eighth day now. The eighth day never ends. In seven days, God created all the truths in the universe, and then He rested. After a short rest, He thought about creating something that would never end. God is a creator, and a creator cannot simply sit and not create. People commit the greatest blasphemy when they say God completed everything in seven days. There is no creator who could complete all of Creation within seven days and then sit idly by forevermore.

'In the first seven days, God created only the truth, the whole truth and nothing but the truth. Truth is the simple, imperfect, primitive aspect of being. God created books on the eighth day, and to create books, He had to create imagination. The Almighty was surprised that the creation of man was a simple, finite job, that the creation of birds, the Earth, water and waterfalls was completed with great ease. He was surprised by how quickly the day of creating the angels and the Kingdom of Heaven sped by. Everything was done, everything happened quickly and easily, until the eighth day. On the eighth day, when God created the imagination and then books, He understood His own infinite and eternal side. The eighth day never ends.

'On the eighth day, God *ordered* Adam to eat from the Tree of Knowledge. You see, God never once prohibited eating the fruit of those trees. Humans have had the story back to front for years. The Tree of Knowledge is nothing but the tree of imagination. The fruit Adam eats in Paradise is not the fruit of knowledge as we understand knowledge today; the tree is not the tree of mathematics and physics. It's the tree of imagination. Humans dwell on Earth to learn to imagine, to learn to write books. That was God's hope.

'Just as humans settled into a final form, just as the stars and the sun are fixed in their places, just as the animals and trees have assumed their final shape, so, too, were books to be confined within a finite form. But God saw that with each book, Creation returns to the first hour of the eighth day. He saw that the gardens and strange creatures humans create in their imaginations, that books and dreams, have no finite form. God felt the imagination was the only thing that held the secret of Creation's infinity. From that day on, God has helped humans and humans God, so that Creation lasts forever in books and the imagination – and it will continue in the most beautiful, magical form.

'And it is here that the Devil enters the game.

'It is not for nothing that the Devil refuses to bow down to Adam. The Devil is the creature who, contrary to humanity's wishes and the will of God, wants the eighth day over and done with. He knows that Doomsday will come when humans can no longer write books rich in fantasy. He wants the process of Creation over, so he can walk away, rest and sleep.

'All the wars the Devil wages, all the plagues and diseases he sows upon the Earth, are not acts of disobedience but an attempt to bring the process of Creation to a close. It is the Devil who writes bad books, books about the death of the imagination. It is the Devil who burns books, who defiles and debases them. He gives them to people who don't understand their true meanings, who strip books of imagination and make them slaves to petty dreams and obsessions.

'The Devil is a creature who robs books of imagination and magic, rendering them worthless by tossing them to the pavement. He mixes their contents into this old, exhausted, simple world so that they, too, look simple, old and exhausted, as if they were utensils, goods or fruit; as if they were one of the many weapons of war – an axe in the warrior's hand.

'The Devil comes and finds other games for the books. He weaves them into dangerous plots. He wants us to forget how lethal this world is, to forget the truth. Once we forget the truth and become happy and satisfied, we stop searching for other gardens, we no longer run after the beauty of the imagination. A 'perfect human being', however, is always thinking about prolonging Creation, about prolonging the eighth day. As soon as he forgets about the truth, the Devil incapacitates him, preventing him from thinking about the withered flowers. And as soon as he forgets about the imagination, he is cast out of the garden.

'The Devil is not the enemy of imagination for its own sake. He wants imagination to come to an end. Through his deceptions and lies, he wants to show us what appears to be a beautiful world, so that we say, 'Dear Lord, if Earth is so beautiful, what do we need imagination for?'

'It was the Devil who stole the book of the dead from us. He blinds us so that we forget the filthiness of the world. He's the one who wants to take away these ghazals, to empty them of meaning; the one who kills their magic in order to deprive the real Ghazalnuses who will be born of them tomorrow. Real Magellan, thank the sky and the stars that brought you here to see this garden – whoever wishes to prolong being and Creation will come to this garden.

'Only perfect human beings reach it. Anyone who wants to touch the power of these ghazals can do so. No real Ghazalnus would seek to possess ghazals; he needs to be possessed by ghazals to get here. A ghazal is a pact that a human being signs with the gardens of life.'

Ghazalnus's views were new to me. Though I said nothing, I continued to think about them. Now I understood why his fantasies always ended in a garden, while mine were full of dark recesses; why his imagination was full of flowers, and mine of unknown powers, dangerous spaces, dead ends. Why he always walked through gardens while I journeyed through forests; why I travelled only with the blind children, while he wandered the whole world. When I looked at his eyes, when I listened to his voice, when I contemplated his words, I knew that I would never be capable of ridding my imagination of all its darkness and forests, its strange and unknown routes. Ghazalnus was a pure lover: he accepted love with all its headaches and its pains. I was not in love, and couldn't write one line of a ghazal. To me, his fantasies seemed clear and simple, while mine were difficult, complicated, overwrought.

We walked for a long time in silence. Then came a long conversation between the Real Magellan and Ghazalnus about the importance of the body for reaching the essence of Creation. I was too immersed in my own thoughts to pay much attention.

When we reached Ghazalnus's house late that night, the carer had already put all the fantasised children to bed. The four of us walked through the rooms and looked at them. One by one, we kissed the children, beautiful and pure as angels. We were all certain that imagination was the only genuine way to prolong Creation. That night, for the first time, I noticed how the children's smell was like that of the flowers, how their purity was like that of the ghazals.

When the time came to say our goodnights and part ways, an argument broke out over who should go to Nwemiran to retrieve Baran Shukur's body and take it to the imaginary gardens. Hasan-i Pizo, who felt the Chinese Youth's spirit had entered his body, believed that as he'd been the one to get hold of the key to Murtaza's

Garden, he was best suited to the task. The Real Magellan, as Baran's uncle, maintained that as he had come back from the other side of the world to find her, he should exhume the body of his unfortunate niece. Ghazalnus, who regarded himself as her lover, said, 'I started all this. No one else should have to put themselves in danger.' While I said, 'I am the only one who can easily visit Nwemiran. That's why I, and no one else, should carry out this task.'

I insisted I was the only who could do it. It wouldn't be easy to take any of them with me, and would increase our risk of exposure tenfold. I had become familiar with Nwemiran by then, and had a plan in mind for exhuming the body. I just needed Darsim Tahir to help me open the grave.

After a long, unsettled night of heated argument, I said, 'Brothers, what we are doing is very dangerous. Can't you see? You don't know the world of the barons as well as I do. This short period has taught me that our task is extremely perilous. You must listen to reason, not emotion. I know that if it weren't for Hasan-i Pizo, none of us could get to Baran's body. No one but he could have secured the key to the garden and found the site of the grave. I know that Ghazalnus feels personally entitled to see this through to the very end, and that we won't ever be able to understand the extent of his secret connection to the two lovers. I know the esteemed Zuhdi Shazaman has travelled a great distance, and would like to give some meaning to his journey and his sad return. But I am the only one who can do this job, the only one who can take the body out of Nwemiran.

'In two nights' time, it will be the wedding of the daughter of the Baron of Wheat and Barley to the son of the Baron of Digital. It is going to be a very, very big wedding, with all the mirs, barons and aghas of the area invited, and many people coming from neighbouring cities and towns. Rumour has it that some members of the Governing Council will be there too.[23] I've been invited, and can take two other people with me. That night is the only opportunity to smarten up Darsim Tahir, bring him to Nwemiran and take advantage of the alcohol-induced insanity to get into the garden. Brothers, it's our only chance. So, please, let's not waste it on pointless squabbling. Over the next two days, I'll explore all the possibilities. On the evening of the day after tomorrow, we'll meet here again before Darsim and I leave for Nwemiran. You need to find a car before then to transport the body.'

What I said seemed reasonable. In fact, I thought it would probably be our last chance that autumn. If we lost it, I didn't know how I would get to the garden or exhume the body. Eventually, the others relented and agreed to go along with my plan.

First I would need to check the moon; if it was a moonlit night, I might not be able to do anything. I consulted lunar-based Arabic calendars and established that the moon would be at its weakest. That was encouraging. A full moon would not be good for my imagination on a night as important as that.

The following day I found Murtaza's Garden with the help of the maps he had given to Hasan-i Pizo. It had a high, white wall. Without the key, it would have been almost impossible to get in. I drew up a firm plan and determined that I would refuse to let sentimentality get the better of me. The garden was in the northern part of Nwemiran and had two gates, one at the front and one at the back. Leaving through the back gate, I would have to walk some two hundred metres behind the enormous mansions before reaching the district's outer fence. Then I would need to cut a hole in the wire fence and scramble under it to get out of Nwemiran. With some luck and a degree of caution, the task seemed safe enough. But it wasn't completely free of risk. I didn't know what would happen if they caught me with the corpse. But it didn't matter. Nothing did.

This was the first time I had felt I was doing something real, something that smelled of life and danger – something to give me a sense of living in the real world, full of people who face death day in and day out. Actually, it was a horrible, tragic feeling.

I had never been anywhere except my own city, and yet I saw myself as more foreign and alien than you might imagine. To have lived in a few cities and feel alien in some of them is normal, but to have lived all your life in the same city and still feel alien is truly dreadful. And as this was the city of dangers, you had to have been through real danger yourself if you were to live in it and not feel alien.

I wanted to look danger in the eye just once. During all those years I spent copying the book of death or watching foreign films, I had longed to confront a vast and treacherous force like the men who drowned in the Aegean or the women thwarted in love who set fire to themselves … or at least like Tom Cruise, Bruce Willis, Will Smith or Tommy Lee Jones. Ghazalnus didn't have the faintest idea how much I needed that. To understand the meaning of life, each of us must come face to face with immense danger once in our lives. That was something he didn't understand.

THE MEMOIRS OF THE
BARON OF IMAGINATION

I met with the Imaginative Creatures twice more in the space of a week. Both times, I came away deeply frustrated. At the first meeting, I understood that imagination and poetry cannot be separated. At the second, I realised that poets are the source of inspiration for any Imaginative Creature, regardless of their walk of life. It doesn't matter whether a person is a politician, an engineer, a physicist, a thief or a lover, they will all pay a visit to a poet's home when they want to create something new. If the poet's voice inside a human soul is muted, that person can no longer bring anything new into the world. For someone like me, intent on taming the poets, turning them into obedient employees, ending their isolation so that they don't become alienated and a threat to the world, this was a heartbreaking conclusion. Whenever I felt that the poets were stronger than us, I would become spiritually and mentally distressed. On those days, I would be seized with an uncontrollable rage and turn into a wild, dangerous creature. What scares me in the poets is not only their dominion over imaginary lands and waters, but also their sheer lack of concern regarding their enemies. I knew Ghazalnus was aware that I was slowly buying up his army and taking away his warriors, but he looked upon it all with immense indifference. I tried very hard to find out if he would try to discourage any of his friends and followers, whether or not he would call anyone and warn them about working in the city of dreams. Yet all the information I received from Tarkhunchi and others suggested that he really couldn't have cared less. Ghazalnus looked like a weary warrior for whom nothing mattered but the fixations of his own mind. He fought very carelessly, no doubt confident that anyone who needed to think deeply about imagination in that city must first pay a visit to his home.

I had to make one last effort and do my utmost to bring Ghazalnus and the ghazals into my plan, which is not, in fact, mine alone. I am merely a servant of the plan, just as he is a servant of the ghazals. On the night I went to see him, it was with the good intentions and kindness of someone whose only wish is to make life better, to beautify a city and strengthen a nation. I didn't want to play hide-and-seek with him anymore. I wanted him to understand his importance to this city, to understand that if dreams were realised without poets, they would become dangerous nightmares. He was the only one who could keep my obsessions and imagination from turning into harrowing terror. I went filled with optimism and hope, with no animosity. When I arrived at his house, I felt free and self-assured. I knocked on the door, and the little old woman who cared for the children showed me to Ghazalnus's study.

His face was still inscribed with the same infinite depth, confusion and loneliness. Over the years, I had investigated the faces of poets at length. I often went to a teahouse and sat in a corner, quietly studying their faces, young and old. They all came across as lost creatures in search of something invisible. I compared, too, the gazes of hundreds of world poets, from Rimbaud, Lautréamont, Baudelaire, Mallarmé and Byron to major poets of the twentieth century such as T. S. Eliot, Derek Walcott and Octavio Paz. They all seemed to have lost something suspended in the air, or to be looking at a flying house sparrow that we couldn't see. I compared the gazes of Pushkin and Dylan Thomas, and those of Sohrab Sepehri and Badr Shakir al-Sayyab. I compared Goran's smile with that of Nâzim Hikmet. They were all the same, all looking at that flying sparrow the rest of us couldn't see. When I went to see Ghazalnus, he had that very same gaze.

'Ghazalnus, why is it that all poets are looking at something invisible in the air, at a flying house sparrow or a dove?' I asked. 'Why don't they look life in the eye?'

Ghazalnus invited me to a small table adorned with beautiful autumn flowers.

With a sad, absent-minded smile, he said, 'Because life doesn't give us its meaning directly … No, my dear. Kak Jawahir, my friend, the poets are not looking at a flying house sparrow at all, they are contemplating their lost souls. I believe that anyone who wants to see beyond his own time must betray his place and his home. Whenever you look at the lost gaze of a poet, be assured: he's not looking at a flying dove, but is absorbed in his own exile.'

I felt that, as a prelude to the night ahead, these sentences were fatal. I sat by the table and eagerly breathed in the scent of one of the autumn flowers. The whole house had a lovely, autumnal smell. I imagined myself in a huge garden in autumn, magnificent trees shedding their leaves around me. Everything in the room was imbued with a pale, sombre yellow. I said, out of deep conviction, 'Poets are the architects of their own exile. At a time when the city needs them, they all remain within their own cities. Public employees work, politicians work, doctors and engineers work. It's only the poets who create an artificial exile and lose themselves in it.'

As if Ghazalnus had been expecting this, he said, 'It is the poets' job to reside in exile and look at life from there … it's what they do.'

'Ghazalnus, I want to bring you back so you can look at life from here,' I said with a quiet laugh.

He said, sorrowfully, 'My brother, Kak Jawahir, there's something you haven't taken into account. Go into exile once, and you will be in exile forever.'

I looked at him seriously and said, 'This city has a great job for you. We need the beauty of your ghazals. Let me be honest with you: I'm tired, Ghazalnus. I've been trying for too long to sow imagination in this city, to make sure it *doesn't* go into exile, to make sure that those gifted with imagination can work, that they become part of our lives and our world. I'm being honest, here, Ghazalnus. My name isn't "Jawahir Sarfiraz". My entire story is a lie. I am the Baron of Imagination … I'm the one who has been buying your Imaginative Creatures. I have to start building the city of dreams very soon. The Leader and the Americans have assigned me this task, but it's my dream, too. Do you understand? My dream. If it wasn't, I wouldn't care what the fucking Americans said.

'If you don't join me now, I'll have to pull out of the whole project. I'll have to burn all my plans. I'll have to return the entire budget to the public coffers and assign the project to a group of engineers, who will reduce the city of dreams to houses with multiple bathrooms and hot and cold running water. I'll have to hand it over to these engineers, who think the city of dreams is a place where human beings eat a huge amount of food and shit very frequently. Ghazalnus, if you don't come with me, I'll have to put that massive budget at the disposal of men who would dust off this city's ugliness and sell it to us at the price of a brand-new item … There's a beauty and a harmony between the human souls of this city and its various locations. If you don't help me, I can't do it. Do you understand? I want to build a city where poets *aren't* obliged to go into exile.'

'It doesn't matter who you are. It just doesn't,' he replied, looking at me very seriously for the first time. 'It doesn't matter if you buy the Imaginative Creatures or not. I don't own any human beings. Some of them are my friends, others are acquaintances. I won't be upset if they work for you. But my dear and respectable Baron, every city in the world is initially built with the intention of its being a dream city. And any city already built will have people come along at some point who want to transform it into a dream city. When a ray of hope is seen in any nation, there are people who want to take advantage of it and build a huge human settlement. Listen to me, Your Excellency, the city you are building has nothing to do with the imagination. Your city owes its construction to the fear of death, or a sense of victory. You and the other barons want to feel that you're successful, whereas imagination – deep imagination – exists to ponder suffering.

'Your Excellency, the imagination always wants to be close to the great suffering of humanity. You want to foster a celebratory imagination, one that inspires beauty, so that you can build a neighbourhood unlike the other districts of this city … This is what matters most to you and the other barons – to create a district that does not resemble the others. Isn't that so, sir? But I don't want to do that. I want to know why the people of this city are so sad. I want to know where the doors to the gardens of their souls are. I want to know this: when wonderful people die, where do their dream cities sink? When they are burned, what kinds of flowers are lost with them in the flames, and what kinds of gardens live on in their ashes?

'Your Excellency, the city you are building is a replacement for the fantasies killed by the other barons, for the dreams that perish in our hearts every day. The gardens you want to plant are replacements for the ones that wilt and wither away every night in this city. The lovers you would like to see walk along the streets of your dream city are replacements for the lovers condemned to burn and to die, to perish from grief and sadness. The ghazals you want in order to create beauty and imagination in your dream city are replacements for the ghazals we should be reading here among the tormented souls. You are an odd person, Baron, I don't understand you. Imagination is nothing but unrealised potential. It's unfulfilled potential that becomes imagination. Life itself is the greatest fantasy. Reorganise life, and you have a dream city.'

With these words, Ghazalnus showed me the evil soul inside all poets of the world, a soul that blames contemporary politicians for all humankind's great errors since Adam and Eve, and holds local rulers responsible for all crimes of humanity since Cain and Abel. But I chose not to respond, because I didn't want to upset him so early on.

'Ghazalnus,' I said, 'just assume the worst about my past: that I'm an offspring of all those who have wreaked havoc on Earth, that I'm an offspring of Satan. But listen to what I'm trying to tell you now: I want to reorganise life, to forget the hideous things that have happened and make a new start. To do that, I need you. Without you, nothing can be done.'

'This city has become a huge wasteland,' he said, interrupting me. 'Baron, your biggest weakness is that you want to go leave this city behind, build a number of large, beautiful buildings and wide roads and call this new place 'the city of the imagination'. But building a real city of the imagination doesn't mean running away, it means waking up the sleeping potential of *this* place, awakening its slumbering beauty.

'Baron, look at me. Imagination isn't a picnic resort we can just build next to the city, it's our own lives once we've come to see which bits of it have been killed. Someone who can't bear the truth can't bear the imagination either. Your dream cities are worth nothing to me. Your mansions and engineers give nothing to my soul ... you, your leaders and barons create these cities because you can't bear to look at the real city, whereas I can arrive at the gardens of imagination precisely because I dare to look upon all this sadness. You can't look at the hideous streets or the troubled people in them. You can't look at the withered gardens with their dead flowers. Your Excellency, I don't need your dream city, I have my own. And my own imaginary garden. I have walked the streets of this city for thirty years. *This* is my dream city.

'To understand the imagination of the people of this city, you must know which parts of their souls have been killed, and by whom. To reach the dream city, you have to be able to see the real one right in front of you. Inside the soul of every deprived person on these dilapidated streets, there's a great garden that will only open once you understand it. You can't see anyone's imagination without seeing the truth, but you, Your Excellency, wouldn't dare do that. You call your running away imagination. You call your fear of the truth imagination. You're not the only one. The majority of honest Imaginative Creatures do the same.

'Sir, have you any idea why the people of this city are running away in droves? It's because they can't bear the beauty inside them, and so they call it imagination ... Do you know why the young women of this city set themselves alight in such great numbers? Because they can't bear the beautiful gardens inside them, and call them imagination ... human beings call the beauty within them that has been killed "imagination".'

His words were lethal. Like daggers plunged into my soul – cruel and dark.

'So, Ghazalnus, that's why you wanted to collect the death stories,' I said, fixing my gaze on him. 'Your imagination only works when it pokes its nose into the fates of other people. It only works when it portrays this city as a wasteland or a huge graveyard. Your imagination only works when you have all the death stories in front of you. To you, imagination means being adept at looking at tragedies. Is that so? To you, it is understanding what garden has been killed, or what flower, what has been left to fade. Is that right? Only then you can really create fantasies.'

Ghazalnus was too intelligent not to understand. He looked at me and said, 'Your Excellency, you took our big book; I know you did. It's of no use to you. We laboured over it. Those who come after us must understand how the people of this city lived and died; they must. Give me back the book. I know you took it.'

When he said that, I felt I'd come to the end of the road with him, that he would hate me and I would hate him forever. I told him: 'People die – they are killed, drowned and burned everywhere, in every country on Earth. How can you say that with each death, a land disappears or a garden vanishes! Rather than the force that makes this world beautiful, the imagination in your eyes is a long walk through a graveyard.'

'Imagination is tied to love and respect for that which has been created,' he said, looking at me nervously. 'There is a great lover inside every human soul. Imagination works on that great lover, on the crazy artist in our hearts, the restless traveller who never reaches home. I can only protect the ghazals within the human soul. I spent several years on the move, writing ghazals. My only hope is to stop them dying in our hearts. I've reached all the troubled people of this city even in their times of seclusion. My only job was to prevent the Ghazalnus inside each one of us from dying. My job is not just to sit in Paradise. It's to make sure love doesn't die in Hell. That is why, Baron, I can't play your game. I can't.'

Livid now, I exploded: 'To you, imagination is man untamed and in conflict with the world, thinking there's a great fire beneath his house and that he's got to run away! A dangerous storm is raging, and he has to run away! That's what imagination is to you!'

He was silent for a long time. Finally, he let out an enormous sigh and said, without looking at me, 'Imagination is one thing; lies are quite another. For thousands of years, man has confused the two.'

Those were his final thoughts. I felt as though he wanted to expel me with his words. My face was bright red with anger. I understood that the only thing left between Ghazalnus and myself was death.

'If people cannot forget about death, they cannot be happy,' I fumed. 'If the imagination doesn't help people forget, they can't live happily. Why don't you want people to forget about death? Why have you dedicated your life to remembering it?'

Ghazalnus rose and continued to speak without looking at me. 'Baron, this city is like a lake full of pirates and sharks. The only ship that can cross it is one we have created with ghazals and imagination. But as soon as a ship like that appears on the lake, all the pirates on the surface of the water and the giant beasts beneath it launch themselves at it to try and sink it. If you're taken in and leave the ship, you'll never be able to get back on board. You might have good intentions, Baron, but you're seeking an impossible dream. Poets and kings can never play the same game – and ghazal writers and barons can't share the same dream, the same ambitions or the same fantasies. You're testing your strength against a weak creature like me. Baron, I don't have anything you could tame. I am alienated in your city. I am sad. There is nothing I can do for you.'

Just then, I could have killed him. There was an old pestle and mortar on one of the shelves. I could have brought it down on his head with all my strength and killed him. But I restrained myself and said, 'You've decided to remain a rootless human being until the very end … to glory in your alienation.'

Ghazalnus looked impatient. It was clear these would be his final words.

'The city you're building would become just another habitat for pirates and sharks. The genuine Imaginative Creatures would die of sadness on its outskirts. It will become a city inhabited by people without fantasies or dreams. Perfect human beings will not enter it. Perfect human beings will not betray the truth.'

I understood then that the man before me was a tenacious soul. I left his house with a heavy heart and headed to Ja'far-i Magholi's. When I knocked at the door, it was one o'clock in the morning.

THE PARTY AND THE CORPSE

THE EVENING OF 11 NOVEMBER 2004

On the evening of 11 November 2004, Majid-i Gul Solav and Darsim Tahir went to Nwemiran. It was a night when each soul chose its destiny.

The party was enormous, the vast hall abuzz with the sound of music and human exhalation. Darsim was afraid of anything and everything. He had never heard such loud music or met such people before. To deflect attention away from him, Majid steered him into a sea of chairs, children's commotion and mingling families. The party was so big, and the hall so packed, it wasn't easy for people to find one another.

Beat, oh, music. Beat, oh, hearts. Dance, bodies, dance. Dance away, sad women. Stir yourselves, you sorrowful hearts.

Majid felt out of place, and nearly ruined the entire plan right from the outset. He wished he could go to his blind children and board the ship – *open up, oh, you waters, open up, you endless darkness of the imagination, open up, you formidable closed maps of the soul* – to go away with the children and never return.

He looked across the hall and saw a chilling market of flesh, feelings and imagination. He was astonished to find himself in a place like that on account of the corpse of a woman he had never met. The meaning of his life was now reduced to doing something for the dead. When he took in the excitement, smelled the heady mix of perfumes and noticed women lewdly eyeing up his body, admiring his hair and eyes, he knew he could establish a strong relationship only with the dead.

Right from the moment he had entered the hall, he had felt that his presence could be sensed, that he had created a great wave of whispers among the women of Nwemiran. He could hear them say, "That's him, that's the one." The name of the Chinese Youth rang in his ears a few times. Some of them avoided him as if they were afraid, while others were all over him. What made them think he was the Chinese Youth? From the night he had seen the corpse, he had felt the body of the murdered man to be his own. Now he was at the mercy of these women's gazes, their whispers echoing inside his head. He sat alone at a table. He felt that each and every woman of Nwemiran was passing in front of him and looking at him, each of them eager to know for sure whether the man they saw was the Chinese Youth or not. He was sure he could hear them say, 'He hasn't been killed. It's a lie. He's not dead.'

Majid asked himself, 'What games are you playing with me, ghost? What games are you playing?' He felt the dead man close to him, with him. Still, they filed in front of him, stealing covert glances and whispering. The whispers reverberated strangely in his head. He felt isolated from the world around him. He felt that the sound of the music, the noise of the children, the women's whispering and the men's indifference towards him were all a dream, that he was trapped in a very tight space between life and death and couldn't go back. He went to the toilet twice and stood before the mirror. He said, 'I am not the Chinese Youth. I am Majid-i Gul Solav.'

And yet he was aware that all his life he had wished to be someone else. He knew that every time he boarded his ship, a real day of his life was wasted. His ship was nothing but a vessel in which he constantly moved away from himself. It was feasible for him, too, to live like the Chinese Youth. Surely it was. He was just as handsome, attractive and charming. Now, as he looked at himself in the mirror, he was certain that the Chinese Youth was his murdered half, just as he was Ghazalnus's murdered half, the murdered halves of all the Imaginative Creatures – but it was too late to go back. He had to live as the Imaginary Magellan for the rest of his life, as a captain who boards his ship and sails through realms and rivers only in his imagination.

When he returned to the party, he remembered one of Ghazalnus's couplets: *The heart that's estranged from him yearns for you / he thinks all the kind-hearted are his lovers.*

The murdered woman had suddenly become his mistress. As he walked through the revellers, he became certain that only in that spirit could he arrive at the grave of the woman buried at the bottom of Hell. He saw his descent into the city like that of the Greek mythological heroes to Hades. As he moved through the scent of the women's perfume and their hungry looks, he felt as though he were walking down the long halls of Hell to the restless ice of its frozen pit, in order to recover a secret from its guards – from those who had lost their way – and bring it out. He felt very out of place, and wanted the night to pass quickly. He couldn't help thinking about Baran Shukur. He couldn't help thinking that had she not been killed, she, too, would have been here, among the revellers and dancers.

At ten o'clock, the party would reach its peak. At that moment, he and Darsim would leave the hall separately. Once outside, he would use the pretext of finding somewhere to change Darsim's deliberately stained clothes and get lost in the streets of Nwemiran. Just before ten, Darsim spilled a drink onto his clothes, and Majid left the hall with him. It was an unhappy night, quiet and clear. When the noise of the party and the racket of the dancers had subsided in his head, he was astounded by the silence. He looked at the stars and felt the universe to be solemn and peaceful. He was certain that this peace and silence were his true abode.

It seemed that all of Nwemiran was at the party. He held Darsim's hand as one holds a younger brother's, and the two of them walked through its streets. A gentle autumn wind began to blow through the mansions and yellowed gardens. Darsim, unafraid, was now leading the way. All they could see was darkness, until they came to Murtaza's Garden. On this night, Majid was not in the mood to tease Darsim about his nose, and Darsim was not the type to initiate a conversation. The area around Murtaza's Garden was deeper in darkness than anywhere else. The lights from the nearby mansions were all out. Without fear or hesitation, they opened the back gate. It was a garden, a real one. There was no sign whatsoever that underneath these trees and flowers lay a huge number of corpses. Darsim started suddenly – his nose had sent him a secret signal. He could feel that the soil under his feet was packed with the dead. Bewildered, he looked around the garden and gave a sad sigh.

Their instructions were to dig up Baran's remains from the earth two metres to the left of a tall cedar tree in the third circle of the garden. Although the world was bidding farewell to the last autumn leaves, a smattering of tiny flowers that had grown on her grave in the summer months could still be seen there. Darsim dug through the soil with extraordinary speed, a sign of his expertise and power rather than fear and panic. He came upon a piece of Baran's shirt in no time. Lord, six months after her death, Baran's body was still intact, as if she had been buried the day before. She gave off an unusual scent of flowers: she smelled of the gardens.

Darsim was overcome by the scent. 'It's lovely ... really delightful,' he whispered. After lifting her body out of the earth, they both heaped the soil back into the pit – but the marks of their digging were too obvious to be covered up properly. They retraced their steps to the back gate, and from there they headed towards the outer boundary of Nwemiran. Everything went smoothly. There was no one around to instill any doubts, hesitation or fear in them. Majid-i Gul Solav, who had lifted Baran's body onto his shoulders, walked across the flat, even ground on that dark autumn night. He was happy. He felt himself returning from the restless depths of Hades and up into the world of light.

Darsim cut through the barbed-wire fence of Nwemiran, and together they carried the body out. The Real Magellan and Hasan-i Pizo were waiting in a black pick-up truck. In the dark, quiet side street, the Real Magellan took the body of his niece from Majid. She smelled of the imaginary flowers he had smelled in Ghazalnus's poems; Hasan looked with great bewilderment at the face of the dead woman resting in Zuhdi Shazaman's arms.

'Almighty God, Pride of all Creatures ... she's the spitting image of Sabri,' Hasan whispered.

'Who is Sabri?' Zuhdi asked.

'The lover Ghazalnus goes to see in Hazarbagh,' said Hasan, with the same bewilderment.

The Real Magellan laid the body on the ground, pushed his hair back off his face and for the first time saw Baran Shukur clearly by the light of a torch. A stifled sigh escaped his throat. He could feel both his hands shaking. He put his head in his hands and said, 'She was so young ... so very young.'

Majid shone the light on Baran's face again and looked at her carefully. He, too, said to himself, 'God, she was so young ... so very young.'

MY SECOND AND LAST STORY FOR TISHKAN

MAJID-I GUL SOLAV, 12–13 OCTOBER 2004

We buried Baran's body next to that of the Chinese Youth in the big imaginary garden at the end of the sea of ghazals. All four of us carried the body from garden to garden, ghazal by ghazal. We buried Baran in the middle of the vast library, its shelves entirely covered with books of ghazals. Standing beside the grave, Ghazalnus said, 'Just as ghazals are a way to be born, so they are a way to die. Some enter life through ghazals, but cannot return through them, while others do not enter through ghazals but do return through them. All those who love the imagination are born with a line of a ghazal etched into their chests. The mission of those people in later life is to complete that line, and make a poem from it ... but those who can live with that line and complete the poem are few and far between.' Later he said to us, 'The real map of this garden is with you. Keep the secret inside your hearts.'

We left the Chinese Youth and Baran inside that garden, convinced they would dwell peacefully in their sea of ghazals forever. I felt our story had ended there – a minor victory in a great battle. I told myself that if this story were ever published in book form, the people of the future and the Imaginative Creatures of the future would be proud of me. They would be proud of one Majid-i Gul Solav, who, in the dawning years of the twenty-first century, exhumed the body of a lover from a garden in enemy territory and carried her to an imaginary garden and, like a true hero, feared nothing. I was certain that in the future, I'd enter the history books. I felt that the task I had carried out had a more profound meaning than many a long and dangerous war. Man has taken part in thousands of wars in history without knowing why; but I knew the importance of transferring Baran's exquisite remains from a dark, obscure and neglected garden to an imaginary one filled with ghazals.

Even so, the sense of triumph was short-lived. When I woke up the following day, I saw Tishkan Tahir outside my room. I heard an internal voice saying, 'Gul Solav, don't just throw words around. Don't go too far, don't be rash. The war's not over just yet.'

Standing there in a short skirt on the threshold of my room, Tishkan said, 'Hey, Nice Guy, you don't mind me coming in, do you?'

'Tishkan, even if you'd come to kill me, I wouldn't mind,' I said with a long yawn. 'Come on in.'

'Last night you didn't even look at me,' she complained. 'I don't understand why you didn't look at me all throughout the party. Why was that, Nice Guy? Then you just vanished.'

'Oh, last night. Last night … Last night,' I said. In fact, I didn't know what to say. She hadn't crossed my mind the entire night.

'Last night I was so sad, I was worried my sadness would disturb your beauty,' I said. 'When I'm sad, I don't like to bother people who are dear to me.'

She sat next to me provocatively 'Nice Guy, I miss your stories. The one you told me the other day was really very nice. I miss your stories.'

I knew she was lying, but didn't want to know why. She stretched out on my bed. When she lay down, her skirt rode up so high I was embarrassed to look at her. To avoid seeing her slender white thighs, I sat next to her and stroked her blonde hair.

'Do you really like my stories?' I asked her.

'A lot. Believe me, Nice Guy. A lot,' she said.

Her eyes were so stunning that when I think about her appearance even now, I miss them.

'Which story would you like?' I asked.

'Whatever you like,' she said, slowly shutting her eyes.

I let out a sigh and said, 'Listen, Tishkan, I'll tell you a sad story today that you must never forget.'

'I never will,' she replied.

'Even if I die one day, don't forget it,' I said.

'I won't.'

I didn't know why I was saying this, but I had a feeling they were going to kill me.

'Once upon a time, there was a very skilled horse-tamer in a town somewhere out in this wide world. He wanted to own all the beautiful horses that existed. He was very skilled at breaking in wild horses. He could tame even the wildest, and put reins on them. So skilled was he at putting reins on horses that no one in the world would have dared to doubt his abilities; if anyone had done, he would have told them to bring him the wildest of horses to tame. People with unbroken horses that were thought impossible to tame would send for our horse whisperer. No horse had ever proved more than he could handle.

'One day a friend – another expert like himself – came to see him, and told him about the predicament of one of the country's best-known horse owners: the man had acquired a horse that could not be controlled, a horse that pawed the ground in anger and could not be calmed. The news pleased the great horse-tamer. The master believed this would be a great opportunity to test his art and prove his abilities. He set out for the field where the wild horse in question was kept, confident that he would soon return with another medal celebrating his achievements.

'When the master reached his destination, he saw a headstrong white horse with a thick, silky mane. No sooner did the horse catch the scent of its would-be tamer and his human breath than it began to paw the ground, leaping maniacally around, kicking and neighing. The horse expert spent many weeks attempting to gentle the horse, unsuccessfully. The difficulty of the task and the beauty of the horse enthralled him so much that he decided to dedicate his life to taming it. He bought it from its owner for a large sum of money, and moved it with great difficulty to his own field, where he set it free. Years went by, but still the man failed to tame the horse despite using all his skills as well as those of other experts.

'After many years of hard work, he concluded that some horses can never be tamed; that there are some horses that no one can ever saddle or put reins on or force to follow instructions. Deeply frustrated, he took out his gun and shot the white horse dead. This expert tamer, with his abundant love of horses, believed that killing the horse was the only thing he could do to ensure that his life and efforts had meaning. Horses that cannot be tamed, must be killed.'

Tishkan, having failed to understand my story, rose from my bed after a short nap and left quietly. I was sure she was going to see one of the barons. After her departure, I felt miserable. I knew she would never visit my room again, that I had lost my Jessica once and for all.

That morning when I went to see the blind children, I was sure it was our last day together. 'Today,' I said, 'we're not boarding the ship. Today I'm just going to tell you a few things. There will come a time when I will leave you … but I know the map that guides us will not end, for as long as life and the universe exist. The journey is long enough for us all. Now, each one of you has just such a map in his soul. You can look at the darkness inside you and carry on with your journey. Each of you has become a young Imaginary Magellan who can discover fabulous realms inside his or her heart. Each of you has a ship you can steer along rivers, and down running waters and across dangerous lands. If one day you should feel that life is hard, and that you need to travel to another world, look into the depths of your souls, at the beauty in your hearts. There you will find maps that are more intricate, unusual or beautiful than mine. When, one day, you reach the farthest end of beauty, the farthest reaches of the imagination, a realm you regard as the home of your dreams, build a small garden there and call it "Sardarbashi Gul Solav's Garden" or "the Imaginary Magellan's Garden".'

The blind children were very sad, but I had no choice. I was sure I needed to prepare them for a new era, a different time. They had to learn to make their own maps and travel alone through their imaginations, to discover the hidden and destroyed continents of their souls. We had no other choice.

THE MEMOIRS OF THE
BARON OF IMAGINATION

The Baron of Porcelain gave me the news. Never before had I seen him so confused. He epitomised a type of man of which there were too many in the twenty-first century: brave and daring, but stupid; the kind who associates power only with fear and awe. I had known him since becoming a member of the Princes' Council. I had given up engaging people such as the Baron of Porcelain in conversation a few years earlier, but Party affairs and the day-to-day routine of politics kept bringing us together. Although not exactly friends, we were on cordial terms. Two years ago, when the Leader became obsessed with his own political future and wanted to prepare himself for a new phase, he delegated many tasks, giving up a lot of the minor duties he had willingly performed until then. As the Leader treated me as his own son, he was kind enough to delegate some of those minor duties to me. (Most of them were nuisances.) One day he summoned me along with the Baron of Porcelain, the Baron of Yoghurt Drinks and the Turkish Baron. Addressing us together, he said, 'The four of you are like beloved sons to me. From now on, there will be many things that you must do on my behalf.' It was His Excellency who secured our election to the High Council of the Princes, which some people called the 'High Committee of the Barons'.

After the Baron of Porcelain and I had been unanimously voted onto the Princes' Council and put in charge of security in the Nwemiran district, there came a night when he told me the story of the garden in north Nwemiran built on the remains of people killed in separate incidents, and for different reasons. The issue came up because I had designed a plan to erect a great monument in honour of the women killed in Anfal[24] in that very garden. I was serious about the project. To me, building this monument would send a clear message that our authorities respected women.

The day before I brought in the diggers, the Baron of Porcelain came to see me in person and calmly explained everything to me. With the smile of a man who is content with the world, he said, 'This city always has a body to hide. It has always been so, since the olden times, and that isn't going to change. So drop your project, Baron. God knows how many dead bodies would be dragged up in just one scoop of your digger. Listen to me, your brother, and drop it. The place is full of human remains. Even the body of Abdulaqadir Niya is there. You might remember him – the owner of the carpet factory? So, Your Excellency, leave it. Do not open the gates of Hell.'

Not keen to dig into the identities of the dead, I said, 'Baron of Porcelain, the presence of such a cemetery in the middle of Nwemiran requires us to always be vigilant and to guard its secret. The story of the cemetery must remain among ourselves. If a story like that leaks out, it will disgrace us all.'

'The cemetery's guardian is the soul of discretion,' he replied. 'He would die rather than reveal the secret.'

Once he had reassured me so emphatically, I was happy to go back to my own concerns. I spent those years, when the stories of the Chinese Youth's love affairs were on everyone's lips, mostly reading poetry books and studying the essence of the poets' evil. I was trying to understand the endless magic of poetry and poetic fantasies about humanity. Every time I saw the Leader he would say, 'Hey, Baron of the Imagination, what have you been up to? How's it going?' And I'd say, 'Prince of All Princes, Chief of All Barons, I'm busy thinking how to tame poets and make sure they join us in building the country.' The Leader didn't know much about the power of poetry or the dangerous role of imagination in history, so he would always give a wide smile and say, 'The efforts you are putting in with the poets look like my efforts with the Americans.' One day, I decided to show him the big towel so that he would understand how threatening the situation was.

'My son,' he said, 'you've completely misunderstood the story. Whoever helped you make sense of this did a bad job. The plain, colourless, soulless side of the towel is the poet's story. Poets are not materialistic. They see the world as poor, colourless and unsatisfying. Unless a poet comes from a noble family, my son, he is too ungrateful to appreciate what has been and is being done for him. God made them in such a way that they can never see the good around them. Have you ever known a poet to see all the colours in his own city or the world around him? When have poets been so optimistic as to see their world in colour? It's the king who sees his city as beautiful and colourful. Baron, how could you be afraid of a towel like that? We're the ones who've won the contest. It's the poor poet who will be beheaded. Poets are a species that sees only plights and plagues, never prosperity.'

After the fashion of a soft-hearted father, the Leader put his hands on my shoulder and added, 'Poets are nothing to be scared of. I'm more scared of wasps and bald-faced hornets.'

There was a worrying indifference to the Leader's words. I explained the roots of my fears in detail, saying, 'Your Excellency the Leader, poets wear masks. They are often dangerous, chameleon-like creatures. During the French Revolution, people like Rousseau and Voltaire were poet-like souls, but still, they furtively toppled the king from his throne. Pushkin and Lermontov eroded the foundation of the Tsar's regime. First come the poets who denigrate the regimes, and only later, well, along come other people to topple them with just a little push. There are clear examples among our own neighbours: the Shah of Iran fell the day he hanged Khosrow Golsorkhi.[25] Any system the poets don't recognise will be denigrated. Sir, just look to history. In the end, history listens to the poets more than to the public or their leaders, and the trouble is that they never take part in the game, so their beauty and purity are kept intact.'

The Leader was a very optimistic man. He donned a solemn smile and said, 'If one day I think they're a danger, I'll put their severed balls in a sack for you to carry on your back and empty into whatever lake you like.' He paused for a moment before adding, 'And we'll come up with something for the women poets too.' I looked at his face and saw that he didn't understand anything about this world.

That day, a panicked Baron of Porcelain came and whispered to me, 'Mir Sahar, something dangerous has happened. The Baron of Courgettes visited his wife's grave in Murtaza's Garden yesterday. When the poor man arrived, he saw that it had been opened, and her remains exhumed. Nothing like this has ever happened in Nwemiran before. The poor Baron of Courgettes is devastated. He's in a terrible state.'

I knew very little about the story of the baron's wife. I had heard from most of the informers that he had killed her under mysterious circumstances, but I hadn't thought the story worthy of attention. That day, the Baron of Porcelain told me the entire story of the Baron of Courgettes and his wife as we drove from the Office of Economic Affairs to the Office of Civil Society Affairs. The Baron of Porcelain was very angry about the incident. He said: 'Whoever did this has to be killed. If the secret of the garden leaks out, God knows what might happen.' I understood his fury. His eyes went so red, I was terrified.

He said, 'All this city's secrets, plus half the secrets of the princes and the friends of the Party, are buried in there. Some of them will create personal problems, some political problems and some, huge tribal problems. Whoever lifted the lid on that garden would be lifting the lid on every scandal of the past fifteen years. Baron, you and I are in charge of security; if this issue leaks, we'll be the first to pay for it with our heads.'

When the Baron of Porcelain said that, I paused and said, 'Your Excellency, I might know who's done this. I just might.'

'Who, Your Excellency?' he said, giving me a baffled look.

'If you promise not to kill him and to hand him over to me, I'll tell you,' I said, without giving it much thought.

'Your Excellency, I don't understand,' he said. 'What do you mean "hand him over to you"? This is no laughing matter.'

'Leave his punishment to me. Swear that you will,' I said.

'I will, Baron, I'll leave it to you ... but tell me, who is it?'

'The only people who want to lift the lid off the dead are Ghazalnus and his friends. The person who disturbed the peace of the dead is Majid-i Gul Solav. You know, the one who tells stories to Nwemiran's children at night.'

This was a golden opportunity to bring the Imaginative Creatures to their knees. I was sure that for as long as Ghazalnus lived, for as long as this group of Imaginative Creatures was free, they would produce human beings constantly, dangerously looking elsewhere for beauty. These words had been playing over and over in my head for days now. As I sat next to the baron, and as he told me the story of the Baron of Courgettes' wife, I recalled the reports my loyal men had written about a secret connection between the Chinese Youth and Ghazalnus. Back then, I had considered the story of the Chinese Youth to be the most trivial thing in the world and had no interest in listening to gossip about the honour of other men's wives. Now, though, everything had been turned upside down. As I listened to the story of the Chinese Youth and his countless affairs with the poor girls and women of Nwemiran, I became convinced that he had been dispatched by Ghazalnus to plant imagination in the hearts of our women, to disturb the peace of mind of the respectable women of this district leading happily married lives.

That day, I held the hands of the Baron of Porcelain and didn't let go of them until we were on the threshold of my private room at the Mirwari Club. Several phone calls and a couple of hours later, we had collected plenty of video footage from the party. We looked at Majid-i Gul Solav from every angle, video after video. We saw him enter the hall with a small, plump creature with a big nose. We saw his confusion, giddiness and hesitation. We watched him hide his teenage friend with the big nose in the crowd and the hustle and bustle of the night. We saw how, come midnight, the big-nosed creature spilled a can of Coke on his clothes, and how the two of them left the party for an unknown place. We called the guards at the main gate, and they informed us that they had not seen the master storyteller leave Nwemiran that night. We set off for the place where the incident had occurred. We saw the gap they had made in the outer fence of Nwemiran, and the traces of two pairs of footsteps on the soft, damp autumn soil on the other side of the fence. The following day, we asked our informers and spies to establish the existence of that giant-nosed creature. In the evening, Attar, his nose dripping, came to me and said, 'It's Darsim Tahir. He's an expert in locating and digging up graves. There's no one in the world who can open a grave more quickly. I passed him on to Ghazalnus a few years ago with my own hands. He's been living in his house with the other children ever since.'

After Attar's vital insight, everything became clear. The big nose of that ugly creature became our key for arriving at the truth.

The Baron of Porcelain, who had not yet understood the bigger picture, said, 'Your Excellency, let me kill the storyteller. This isn't a simple matter.'

I put my hands on his shoulders and said, 'Killing Majid-i Gul Solav isn't important. You have to be careful. Killing Gul Solav would rekindle the issue of the Baron of Courgettes and his wife, too. It would bring utter disgrace upon the Party and Nwemiran. Gul Solav is not alone. You know our brothers in the National Democratic Party are lying in ambush for us. Our own colleagues in the 'Cleanse It and Reform It' wing are after just such a bit of news. On the streets, in the bazaar, in the meetings of the Party's organisations, they are speaking out against our chief, badmouthing him. The Baron of Butterflies, from the 'Consume it Patiently' wing, would pounce on the information, and his candidates would sweep the board in the western region. Even the randy Prince of Nighttime Copulation from the 'You Can't Have It Until I Do' wing would enter the game, and God knows how many tens of thousands of dollars it would take to shut him up. The Baron of Mules from the 'If We Are Going to Have It, Let's Have It Quickly' wing would enter the fray frantically, saying, 'Colleagues, what about my share?'

'Gul Solav is a small, weak creature. You've grown up in the Party – you know that other methods are needed to silence such creatures.'

The Baron of Porcelain put his hands on my shoulders and said, 'It's because of this wonderful mind of yours that the Leader loves you so much. But, Baron of Imagination, what do you want to do to him?'

'Don't worry,' I told him proudly. 'Tomorrow night I'll tell you what I'm going to do to Gul Solav.' As I spoke, I looked at him. He had a wide, ruddy face, a big head, a broad chin and curly, salt-and-pepper hair. Unless he was about to visit Dubai, he always wore a reddish rankuchogha, the traditional Kurdish suit for men. That day, his belt was so tight, he could barely move. I looked at him and said to myself, 'Oh Leader, how can you not see the difference between this idiot and me? How? How can you rate this beast and me in the same way?'

The baron was pleased that we had reached a conclusion swiftly.

'Baron of Porcelain,' I said, 'tomorrow, I'll show you a supremely dangerous book. A giant tome that's very much linked to this story.'

MY INTERPRETATION OF THE STORY
OF THE KING AND THE POET

MAJID-I GUL SOLAV, MID OCTOBER 2004

That evening like any other, I went to Nwemiran. I smartened myself up more than usual, and walked naturally, with a solemn air. I didn't come across anyone or feel there was anyone watching me. I told the Baron of Sadness's son the story of a magical ball that makes friends with a young child and helps him avoid defeat in games. For the plump daughter of the Baron of Fat and Tail Fat, meanwhile, I made up a story about a well-behaved girl who talked to the moon at night and asked it about the sparrows that live on other planets. When my journey led me to the house of the Baron of Civilisation, Tishkan was sitting on the bed in little Sewan's bedroom. I had the impression that she had been crying before I arrived; I could read something dark and unusual in her pale, mesmerising eyes. She was wearing a thin green tunic. Its collar looked as if it had been torn open, revealing her beautiful breasts spilling out of a tight bra.

'I wish you hadn't come,' she said quietly.

'Why? What's happened? Where's Sewan?' I asked. I loved those children more than anything in the world.

'Nice Guy, please forgive me,' said Tishkan, even more quietly. Before I could say a word, she began screaming a woman's high-pitched scream, loud and relentless – the shriek of a woman who has just been assaulted. I stared at her and stood as still as a statue in the middle of the room. I didn't know what I was supposed to do or say. Hands over her ears, she carried on screaming, looking right at me. She screamed and forced herself to scream even more loudly. I felt as if her cries were echoing throughout Nwemiran. Her shrieks were like the sound of a wounded animal running through a dark forest. To make matters worse, as she kept up her cries and shrieks, she reached for her collar and tore it even more. For weeks afterwards, I'd wake up, day or night, with the sound of her screams echoing in my ears. I heard men climbing up the stairs as the shrieking continued. From the speed and force of their tread, it was clear they were coming in response to her cries. I stood where I was, smiled and said, 'My dear, they'll still hear you if you scream a little less loudly.'

At that very moment, the door flew open and the Baron of Civilisation and the Baron of Popcorn burst in, accompanied by two guards. Both barons pretended to panic when they saw the scene in front of them. Tishkan quickly covered her chest, curled up in a ball on the bed and said in a hoarse voice, 'He attacked me. This man here, he attacked me.'

'Dog!' The Baron of Civilisation slapped me across the face and pushed me against a wall. 'You son of a bitch!'

The next few hours were the darkest of my life. The barons' guards hit me with their weapons several times, there inside the room. I fell and stood back up each time. The Baron of Popcorn dragged me over to the wall and repeatedly banged my head against it. The Baron of Civilisation kept kicking my kneecaps. Then they pinioned my arms behind my back and took me off to the security office in Nwemiran. Wounded, my clothes soaked in blood, I was dragged away groaning in pain, my hair falling into my eyes. I felt as if all the children of Nwemiran were staring at me from their windows, and as if the women of Nwemiran had come out to watch me, saying, 'It's him, the Chinese Youth … that's him.' I didn't say a word the whole time. I was sure there was no escape. On my first night in Nwemiran's security office, I slept on a thin blanket, my body still drenched in blood. I dreamed that they would kill me in the morning and bring me round again before bedtime. I dreamed that a baron with a face like all the barons' faces combined peered into my forehead and wrote down my dreams. He wrote down the imaginary cities in my head, one by one. I wanted to do something to prevent him seeing them. I woke up dozens of times that night, but as soon as I closed my eyes, I plunged back into the same dream.

In the morning, they gave me a paltry breakfast, cleaned me up a bit and took me to another room on a higher floor. The Baron of Imagination was waiting for me there. He looked at me reproachfully and said, 'Why, Gul Solav, why? How could you encroach on someone else's honour? Why would you lay your hands on beauty that doesn't belong to you?'

The sight of the Baron of Imagination calmed me down somewhat. I thought I could speak with him openly. I sat on a small iron chair and said, 'Baron, I have not laid my hands on anyone. Your Honour knows very well that everything is going according to a plan you yourself have devised – you or one of the other barons are masterminding the whole thing. You forced the woman to do that. Why, Baron? Couldn't you have gone for a better, more honourable method?'

He looked at me and said, with the smile of a man confident of his powers, 'Gul Solav, I'm not a liar. There are two schools of thought inside the Party. One believes in silent murder: you kill your prey and distance yourself from it. They might even attend the funeral and weep loudly. The other believes in dishonouring its victims and allowing them to live with their shame, forcing them to agonise over their inevitable disgrace. Wherever you go, whatever jobs you do, even if you get married and have children, when people mention your name they will talk about the night on which you were disgraced. It is crucial for the Party that no one's honour be purer than its own. That is a law. Any idiot who lives in this country and doesn't understand this law will find it tough going.

'I am the only person in the Party who is still ambivalent. Sometimes I belong to the first school, sometimes to the second. I don't know what to tell you, Gul Solav. I would really like you to live. You're young, so much younger than Ghazalnus or me. If other people don't get to the Leader first, if more senior or powerful people than me don't poke their noses in, I won't let them kill you. I want you to live. A dishonoured man is better than a dead one.'

His words were a mixture of mockery, torture, explanation and threat. He paused for a moment, and then his expression changed slightly. He let out a sigh and said, 'You will be sentenced for sexual assault, according to the law on the protection of honour. You will spend many years in prison. Even so, you're lucky. The prisons aren't what they used to be. They're cleaner, and in better condition. But it won't be easy. I know you'll really miss the blind children … The barons won't forgive you, ever,' he added, looking at me from the corner of his eye.

'Am I allowed to know how I've upset the barons?' I asked quietly.

'Do you really think you can dig up a corpse in the middle of Nwemiran, hoist it on your shoulders and take off with it, and no one will find out? What sort of logic is that?' he said.

'But you are not upset with me because of that, I'm sure.' I looked at him. 'That corpse has nothing to do with you.'

He was quiet for a moment. 'Majid-i Gul Solav, what did you need that corpse for?' he asked, as though asking a friend a perfectly ordinary question.

'So that I could bury her side-by-side with the Chinese Youth,' I said casually, not looking at him.

'But what do you have to do with the Chinese Youth?' he asked loudly, his voice curious. 'What do you have to do with such a womaniser and adventurer? I don't get it. You're anything but that kind of guy.'

'Your Excellency,' I said, looking at him now, 'around eight months ago, when I found Murad Jamil's corpse on the outskirts of the city, I decided to do something for the dead man. The dead are friendless people. I wanted to do something to make him happy, so that he wouldn't feel he had no friends.'

'Majid, where did you bury the body? I want you to take me to the location of the bodies,' the baron said.

'Baron, you can't go near those bodies. They are in a remote garden, a garden that can only be opened with ghazals. Ghazals alone can open its gates. It has no other keys. You must be able to walk through the flowerbeds and tulip beds of poetry to get there.'

He looked at me angrily and said, 'Ultimately, you and Ghazalnus wish to have a garden that is beyond our reach. Isn't that so? It's your wish.'

I touched my wounds cautiously and said, 'There are gardens that are unreachable of their own accord. They have their own keys. The keys to one garden can't open another. Your Excellency, the gardens of this world don't even look alike, and yet you want to find a key that can open them all. You treat your back garden and the ghazal gardens in the same way. That simply won't do.'

He sat back across from me and said, 'I didn't realise what a danger you were until I heard the stories you told Tishkan. Last night, I listened carefully again to both your stories. I think you are the most dangerous man to have visited Nwemiran, even more dangerous than the Chinese Youth. Much more dangerous, in fact.'

I said with a defeated smile, 'So you even recorded my stories. It appears you have been very thorough, Baron.'

'Only God knows how many dangerous stories you've told to Nwemiran's children – the kind that stay in their imaginations forever; stories of kings, emirs and sultans who can't tame the Imaginative Creatures. From day one, I knew you hadn't come with good intentions, but I didn't know what you were up to. I didn't figure it out until very late. Your stories are more evil than those on that damned towel, more than the story that has ruined my life – the one I can't get to the bottom of,' he said.

The baron took out a silk towel from a cupboard and placed it before me. It was exceptional, a masterpiece. He recited the story of the images in detail, coolly, then asked, 'Gul Solav, how do you understand this story?'

I looked carefully at both sides of the towel. It was a wonderful tour de force of embroidery and imagination. 'What can I say, Your Excellency,' I said. 'I'm not gifted in these matters. This was handmade by a brilliant master of the imagination, some sort of embroiderer from God only knows what age. I don't know what to say ... as I understand it, these two images are of two different worlds. I see the entire story differently. I don't believe the proud king had come to invade the real city. He wasn't seeking to dethrone anybody. Rather, his incursion sought to invade the imaginary city in the poet's mind. I believe that when the triumphant king entered the other king's city, he found it cold, grey and colourless. He must have wondered what the point was of being king of a city that lacked imagination and beauty. Then, he must have said, "My dear poet, I've come from afar. I have travelled through thousands of villages, farms and orchards to reach the imaginary city inside your soul. I destroyed ramparts and high walls to come to the threshold of your imaginary garden. If you now open the door of your imagination to me, I shall give up this city, these sad and wretched alleyways. Let the king rule over his cold, soulless realm." Then, I think, the poet would have opened the door to his imaginary garden. Both poets would have entered the garden and never left it again. That's what the story of the towel says ... This side is the king's journey through the soulless city of the kings, and this side is the king's journey through the colourful city of the poets.'

The baron gave me a strange look and said, 'It's an unusual interpretation. It doesn't resemble any of the others. But, Gul Solav, tell me, in your opinion, how could this king enter the beautiful world inside the imagination of the captive poet, while the princess of your story who wanted to catch that sweet-voiced bulbul, or the skilled trainer who wanted to tame the wild horse both failed? Why is that?'

'Because the triumphant king was a poet himself,' I said after a short pause. 'Both sides of the towel tell the story of a battle that occurred inside the poet's imagination. It is a triumph of the poet within the king over the king within the king. The king could enter the poet's garden because he had killed the king within himself. It is impossible to be both a king and a poet at the same time. The king didn't kill a rival king at all, but the king inside himself. That's the story. That's how I read it. Look here, Your Excellency. All the gardens, colours and images that you see on the reverse side of the towel, all the beauty you see here, can only be observed by those in whose souls the poet defeats the king.'

I didn't realise that with this interpretation, I would make matters worse and cause complete chaos.

The baron, his finger in his mouth in the manner of a man contemplating something very serious, said, 'So you think that in this story, the poet killed the king? You believe the poets will ultimately triumph?'

'Yes, Your Excellency,' I said, looking innocently at the extraordinary towel.

'And your understanding is that king and poet can't live together?' he asked.

'Yes, Your Excellency, that's exactly how I understand it,' I said, not knowing what he meant. 'They might be able to live together, but they can't enter the same garden together.'

For a while, he paced up and down the room then said, 'Hmm, and they can't harbour the same dream?'

'Never, Your Excellency,' I said. 'Never. Each of them would have a different dream right to the very end.'

'Like the princess who can't reach the imaginary sweet-voiced bird?' he said, after a pause.

'That's right; just like the princess, the king can't reach the sweet-voiced bird,' I replied in the same simple manner that I used to answer Nwemiran's children.

'Do you believe those two worlds are so very different that they never meet?' he asked unhappily.

'They are two different worlds that will never meet,' I said.

'Never?'

'Never, Your Excellency.'

He looked at me fearfully and said, 'Gul Solav, why did the unlucky trainer in your story kill the horse at the end?'

'Because he could neither tame him, nor get him out of his mind. He had to kill himself or the horse,' I said.

'And why didn't you let the white horse win?' he asked, dejectedly.

I touched the wound on my forehead and winced. 'Because it's what most people who become very powerful do – they kill whatever they can't tame … There are some, like the gentle princess, who let them die a natural death, and won't destroy people's lives; and there are others, like the horse trainer, who can't endure defeat, and would rather kill to erase the story from their own and other people's minds.'

He gave me a sharp glance and said, 'When you were telling the two stories to Tishkan, did you know that they would reach me?'

In my eyes, the baron appeared hot and out of sorts; I thought he might be running a high fever. 'Your Excellency, I knew they'd reach the barons. I didn't know which ones,' I said.

'Were you saying that we cannot see the imaginary gardens of your soul, cannot tame you or get close to your world? That you live in one world, and we in a different one?' he asked.

'Although I don't have "imaginary gardens", as you put it, yes, Your Excellency, that is what I wanted to say,' I answered unhesitatingly.

A CARPET MORE BEAUTIFUL
THAN ANY OTHER IN THE WORLD
18–19 OCTOBER 2004

On the evening of 18 November a group of heavily armed men, helped by Shahryar the Glass-Eyed (who could see through walls), found the house where Yaqut-i Mamad was hiding. That night, as on every other night, Attar was with them. At around ten o'clock in the evening, ten men – among the cruellest in Spiraz – stormed into Trifa Yabahri's house in search of Yaqut.

Through painstaking efforts and the accumulation of complex information, Attar had discovered where Yaqut had taken refuge. The Spiraz men were positively glittering with bullets and guns. If anyone saw them, he would have thought they were on their way to conquer a city that had eluded many great heroes before them. Before they entered the house, the boy with the beautiful eyes said, 'They're in there, I can see them.' The young men from Spiraz didn't even consider knocking at the door; they vaulted the walls and entered the yard instead. They searched every room in the house. They smashed down the basement door and went inside. It was empty. They searched the upper storey and the attic, but found no one. The house was empty, devoid of a single soul.

Wusu Agha, the commander of the gunmen, turned to Attar and the boy. 'Attar, you've brought us to an empty house, a house without a single human being inside. You've filled us with empty anticipation and tricked us at this time of the night for no reason.'

Shahryar fixed his gaze onto the wall again and said, 'They're there, sir. I can see them – they're weaving.'

Wusu Agha returned to the house, inspected room after room and storey after storey, but did not find so much as the shadow of a human being or hear the murmur of any creature. There was a grave silence, and nothing more – a silence that scared Wusu Agha and the disappointed gunmen.

Back he went again and said, 'Look, Shahryar the Glass-Eyed, I, Wusu Agha, am not someone you can poke fun at. That house is empty. Come and see for yourself. Come and show me the women you can see.'

The boy got out of Attar's car and joined the agha. At first, everything appeared normal, but as soon as he stepped into the house, he felt a cool breeze blowing towards him, bringing with it the scent of a tulip bed in spring. He heard a lovely song coming from all the rooms, as faint as though it were the sound of an angel coming from the remotest part of the Kingdom. He felt that he could see the shade of flourishing leaves, and the intense scent of flowers came over him. He was also aware that Wusu Agha and his gunmen could not smell the garden or hear the song. As if the scent of the tulip bed had made him dizzy, the boy put his hands to his forehead and leaned against a wall. He had suddenly experienced a spiritual awakening, an abrupt intoxication. He paused for a moment, threw a glance at Wusu Agha and his gunmen and said, in a sick, tired voice: 'Let's go.'

In just a few slow steps, he led them to the attic. There, too, he felt the same scent and cool breeze. He inhaled the scent several times, lifted his head to the cool breeze and went down into the basement after everyone else. It was there that he saw the extraordinary scene he would remember to his last day, the one that would live in his memory forever.

He saw a splendid garden and, in the middle of it, a group of very beautiful women weaving a great carpet. It was being woven in a thousand colours he had never seen before, from shimmering, imaginary threads. It seemed to be constantly changing colour. Every inch was replete with images of endless gardens and magnificent birds that the glass-eyed boy had never seen before, not even in his dreams. It was as though the birds were flying, horsemen urging their steeds into a gallop, the flowers opening and then reverting to buds once again. The carpet's suns seemed to rise and set, its moons to wax and wane, its clouds to gather and drift away. It rained; he saw the wind begin to blow, and a storm play in the trees on the carpet. He saw thousands of gardens and fields, thousands of peacocks, doves, rabbits and people. Blue angels gazed at flowers by the sea: innocent children who slept in a swing made of leaves. He could feel the wind on his face. He saw poets in the carpet, their heads encircled by haloes, deep in thought as they radiated light. He saw child engineers building imaginary, invisible cities, colossal churches bathed in light and tall minarets composed of shafts of light.

Shahryar the Glass-Eyed had never encountered such unusual and magical sights in his life. He didn't know where he should look, or at what. For a moment, he shifted his gaze from the carpet onto its pretty weavers. He felt as if all the women were looking at him and smiling.

They were the most beautiful group of women – thin, transparent and white, as if made entirely of mist. He was now sure that he was the only one who could see their massive, otherworldly loom.

Quietly, he took a step and said, 'I'm sorry, Wusu Agha, I'm sorry. I made a mistake. There's something wrong with my eyes, my head.'

He took a few slow steps back. As if drugged, he paused on the stairs, dazed, and heaved a deep sigh. He had been working with Attar for many years, but had never experienced such feelings before. As if suspecting there was something unusual going on, Wusha Agha said, 'Hey, Glass, what's got into you? What is it? Tell me. Maybe you can see something we can't.'

Shahryar the Glass-Eyed lifted his hands to his forehead and said, 'No, sir. It's just that every year, as winter approaches, I start to imagine bad stuff, and don't see things as they really are.'

Wusu Agha, in his large turban, shook his head, mumbled something and made his way up with his gunmen. This was Shahryar's last night with Attar. The sight of that carpet, with all the brilliance of the world in miniature, changed the boy's life. When I began to look for Shahryar to gather more information for this story, I heard that, soon afterwards, he had left Attar and went to southern Iraq, where he worked with the Americans. He was an active member of the special inspection and search team that looked for Abu Musab al-Zarqawi and Abu Omar al-Baghdadi.[26] Until his final days, he hoped to return to the north and see the carpet again; but in early 2006, he was ambushed by Sunni terrorists who beheaded him and buried his severed head along with a few others in one of the burned and yellowed orchards of the Balad district.

Today, when we look at the history of these events, we know that the boy's severed head was the first to see the carpet, with its beauty of mythical proportions.

The following evening, Trifa returned to Ghazalnus's house, clad in a graceful white dress so unusual it might have been woven from the imagination. She went first to the children's room, kissing them all one by one and clasping them to her chest. Then, she went to see Ghazalnus, who was discussing the interpretation of a couplet with his older son Khayalwan, now sixteen, a shy and quiet child whose thoughts about the world were not known to anyone. Trifa kissed him and said, 'Dearest Khayalwan, I need to have a few words with Ghazalnus, if you could excuse us for a moment.'

When Khayalwan left the room, Ghazalnus, in agony over their lengthy separation, was on the brink of tears. Trifa appeared dreamier and more ethereal than ever that day. Never had he been so struck by her great beauty; her black hair and clear pupils filled with sparkling light. They had rarely talked together of late, but their love was growing stronger. Unlike on any previous occasion, there was a heavenly note to her tone of voice. Ghazalnus told her, in a few words, the latest news of Majid-i Gul Solav's situation in prison.

Trifa said, 'That baron is mad. He's to blame for most of our miseries. Ghazalnus, I've come to tell you that I'm leaving, too. Last night, we all should have died. Those searching for Yaqut found our house; they discovered her whereabouts. The friendless women and I can no longer stay there. We've decided to become displaced: to roam this city, to wander the world. Attar and the jealous husbands and brothers won't let us live.'

'Trifa, why is it that you and I never meet? Why?' Ghazalnus asked, as though he had not heard a word of what she had just said.

'Ghazalnus,' Trifa said, placing her hands on his, 'it took me a long time to reach the high station of perfection you wanted me to. It really did. I am there now, in the imaginary gardens … I am where you wished me to be, the place frequented by all your lovers, the place a person has to reach if they are to reach your heart, too. My dearest, I'm there. I am waiting for you in that eternal garden. We can be together in those gardens forever.

'Ghazalnus, I am now weaving a fantastical carpet every bit as beautiful and infinite as your ghazals. I have a garden, woven from the souls of the sad women and my own, from souls filled with dead designs, stifled seas and mystical images. Out of the sleeping flowers in our hearts and the sleeping birds in our souls, we are weaving a carpet that will never end. It's the carpet of the world we have always dreamed of, but never lived in.'

Ghazalnus held Trifa's hands and said, 'Trifa, why are you so cold and distant? Why do I feel like I'm seeing an apparition when I see you? Where do you and your sad women want to go? Trifa, I fear the day may come when the gardens of imagination are the only place left for humans to hide in.'

'Ghazalnus,' she said, 'what matters is that we weave a carpet we can travel through, a carpet teeming with winding roads, vast gardens and luminous stars. What matters is that we weave something we can lose ourselves in. Your love prompted me to want to reach that place, to head to the restless bottom of the sea where my existence fuses with those of other humans, birds, flowers and stars. Day after day, when I immerse myself in your love, I feel I am immersed in the whole world, in the wounded souls of flowers, children and women. When I melt into you, I melt into the world. Imagining is to melt into you.

To dissolve into you, I must first become the gardener of the stars, a wayfarer who creates the paths she treads. Like you, I have to become the creator of the flowers and their buds.'

'Trifa,' Ghazalnus said, 'wherever you are in the world, in whatever garden, I will be there. Whenever I write a ghazal, I will be thinking about you. The further away you move from me physically, the closer I draw to you in the sea of ghazals and the magic of their rhythms.'

Trifa held his hands and said, 'Now I am nothing but a deep sigh of yearning, a shadow on a fantastical carpet. I have to go back to where I came from, to where your mother and my mother came from, to the gardens of yearning, to the tulip beds born of unfulfilled dreams and despair. You and I are children of despair, and will return to the unearthly realms it creates. The carpets I weave are my infinite path; they are my ghazals. I have never woven a carpet without thinking about your ghazals, without my imagination being fixated on your gardens.'

Ghazalnus looked at her angelic eyes and said, 'You and I do not meet in the same way as the world's other lovers. For as long as there are gardens, you and I will meet in their buds, their scents and the imaginations of their gardeners. You are not my dream alone, you are the dream dreamed by all gardens, by all imaginative gardeners.'

Trifa said, 'I have to go. I must. I am nothing but a deep and constant yearning for you. Wherever I am in the world, I will be that eternal yearning.'

That day, Trifa and Ghazalnus reminisced on all their memories together. They talked about the night they first met at Sayfadin Maro's house. They both remembered everything, from the colour of the curtains and vases to the perfume Mahnaz had been wearing. Together they would shut their eyes, and as if time was nothing but a recurring lie, they saw themselves once again in Shams's elegant living room. They revisited their memories of Mahnaz and Najo, and wept. Step by step, they revisited their own suffering, and that of others. They were more certain than ever that this eternal yearning, this ardour, this not-meeting, was love.

That day, Trifa checked the entire house as Ghazalnus and the children looked on. She went through all the rooms, through every corner. She went into her own room, to the study and the bedroom in which she had slept alone for so many years. She smelled some old ghazal manuscripts, the children's clothes and their small books, and wept over little memories. She wept over kitchen items as well, and the small, white vases. Before stepping outside, she said, 'Ghazalnus, this house was the largest garden you offered me. It's where I listened to the most beautiful creatures of the world and the saddest stories of this city. Thank you for all the generosity that flowed from your heart.'

Ghazalnus looked at her sadly, but said nothing. Those were the last words that would ever pass between them.

That same day, a few hours after Trifa's departure, Hasan-i Pizo arrived with some strange news. On a street close to Trifa's house, police had found the bodies of fourteen women who had been killed and mutilated beyond recognition. That afternoon, Ghazalnus and Hasan, together with most other residents of the city, rushed in confusion to see the bodies: the fourteen women had been murdered; all fourteen wore white; all fourteen had mutilated faces. The police would not allow anyone to touch the corpses. All Hasan's and Ghazalnus's efforts to get through were useless. A long wait proved futile, and in the evening they went to Trifa's secret house. They saw that the door had been smashed in, the windows left open. When they stepped inside, they saw a green and infinite garden. The whole house was a thicket of trees, foliage and birds, an endless garden with large, colourful flowers that had spread through all the rooms. It stretched from the basement to the end of the world, and from the attic to the end of the Heavens. It was an infinite sea of imagination and flowers.

Realising exactly what had happened, Ghazalnus gripped Hasan's hand tightly, and they left. They returned through the city's main streets on foot. It was a cold and crowded evening. A group of people had gathered near the central square, talking about a miracle inside a small park.

A sunflower-seed seller said, 'A group of very beautiful women who look like angels are weaving carpets in the park.'

Indeed, a group of fourteen striking-looking women – so thin and transparent the entire garden could be seen through them – were weaving, as if in a deep trance, an immense carpet that appeared to be suspended from the sky. No one had ever seen such gorgeousness before, even in their imaginations. Ghazalnus recognised Trifa Yabahri among the carpet weavers.

The carpet shimmered in the evening darkness, and the gathering crowd was keen to see the extraordinary sight glimmering with dreamlike images: a herd of running deer, seagulls flying beside ships, stars circling in great orbits, gardens whose flowers were calling people by name, women in love gazing into the distance at the endless horizon of life from garden benches. Ghazalnus saw fantasised children in the carpet; he saw Majid-i Gul Solav's imaginary ship transporting the blind towards the light; he saw the Real Magellan and Afsana walking along a spring path; he saw Hasan-i Pizo among the black-clad women, in the eternal tulip bed of motherhood, looking at the flowers. Oh God ... He saw himself with Sabri in an endless garden, sitting opposite one another, reading a book of ghazals together. He saw the Notebook-Keepers, their heads buried in a large book as they examined death's secrets.

A vast crowd had gathered around the imaginary women; all those who could see the carpet weavers were so enthralled that they stood frozen to the spot, unable to take their eyes off them. As though waking from a deep sleep, one by one, they would then regain consciousness, only to realise that the carpet and its imaginary weavers had gone.

All that night and into the following morning, and for days afterwards, the entire city talked about the magical loom operated by a group of white-clad women whose work was never complete. All those who had looked into the carpet had glimpsed a fragment of their own lives. From that day on, people – in public parks, distant streets and roundabouts – would gather frequently to share their stories of having seen the imaginary weavers.

For a long time afterwards, people's lives were taken up by the story of the wandering carpet, which was forever popping up in different places. Many dismissed the whole story as a mere hallucination induced by a few warped minds, while others become so taken with it that they took to walking around the city in the hope of happening upon it again. The story of the carpet weavers quickly spread across the country, reaching other cities and towns. To this day, those who claim to have seen the carpet are unable to escape the vast outpouring of imagination brought about by the sight of the infinite world it contained.

That night, Ghazalnus was in an odd frame of mind, his happiness fused with sorrow. He told Hasan, 'All my life, I've tried to fit the entire universe into a single ghazal, and I couldn't do it. But that's what the carpet is. Hasan, Trifa is free forever. Nothing can put limits on her imagination anymore – it is imagination that never ends. No one can interfere with it, or tamper with its purity. I'm sure Trifa is no longer scared of any demons or monsters.'

Hasan and Ghazalnus were restless. They returned to the hospital to see the women's bodies, but were denied entry by hard-hearted doctors, police and hospital staff. They were like roaming madmen, unable to settle anywhere. They went to Mahnaz's garden, where once again they looked at the phantasmic flowers. Standing amid them, Ghazalnus said, 'Hasan, women didn't gift me their bodies, they gifted me the gardens inside their souls. Come, let's walk in those gardens together.'

They strolled for hours in Mahnaz's garden, smelling the flowers. Later on, they headed to the garden left behind by Trifa and her women: new and lush, it glistened with immense dewdrops, and filled with the melodies of singing bulbuls not seen in any other garden or forest in the world.

'You're a lucky man,' Hasan told Ghazalnus. 'Women rarely gift the gardens of their souls to anyone. You are the luckiest man in the world.'

Ghazalnus said, despondently, 'But a woman's body is also a garden. The Chinese Youth spent many nights telling me about the magic and beauty of a woman's body. I know a woman's body is like the garden of her soul. You cannot know what their buds are until you touch them.'

Hasan picked a flower and said, 'Ultimately, a woman's body, just like her soul, leads to a magical garden. I am sure of that.'

They ambled around the garden all night. It was limitless, like Hazarbagh.

THE MEMOIRS OF THE
BARON OF IMAGINATION

I first met Tishkan Tahir at a house of ill repute in the capital. She was a young, beautiful woman. Anyone who saw her became infatuated with her shiny blond curls, bright eyes and slender figure.

Watching as she washed herself with a white flannel after we had slept together, I said, 'Tishkan, why don't you come with me to the north? I'll rent a house for you and send you to university to study whatever you want. I'm worried you may die in this hellhole of the south.'

I said this knowing that I could conquer the strongest fortresses through this young woman. I knew that, like all the politicians on this planet, I would one day need a prostitute in my political and social life. I also knew that, in times of great difficulty, a loyal prostitute would come to my rescue more effectively than hundreds of political allies. Besides, most of the barons at the time had their own prostitutes. In this regard, I was the least gifted and most hopeless of them all. The others had such an excess of prostitutes that once, at a major conference, the Leader threatened to make some of them wear chastity belts and keep the keys himself. In the Party, I was known for my propriety. At gatherings of the barons, they called me 'the Baron of Morality' to get a rise out of me. In fact, that image really did upset me, and made me feel inferior.

That day, as if surrendering to fate, Tishkan looked me in the eyes and, without so much as a pause, said, 'Baron, if you will have me, I'll come with you.' Her quick, painless acceptance pleased me, and rather than make me suspicious, it endeared her to me. At first, I rented a small house for her and another young woman, a petite prostitute with blue eyes whom the Baron of Civilisation had brought along from another city. I made a couple of phone calls that summer and secured Tishkan a place at one of the colleges, where she became a student. Many nights, when I was troubled by my fantasies and fed up of thinking too much about the fate of our homeland, I'd visit

Tishkan and her white, slender body would help me forget about the suffering of this world.

One evening I visited her, but she wasn't at home. The Baron of Civilisation's diminutive, blue-eyed prostitute was there. The Devil encouraged me to ask her to sleep with me. A wily, opportunistic woman, she agreed readily. I knew that some of the barons treated their prostitutes as their private property and would be angry to discover that someone else had slept with them. The Baron of Civilisation was one such man. I slept with her a few times, pleased to have tricked him behind his back. When he sat opposite me in the Princes' Council, I looked at him with a sly smile and thought to myself, 'Poor you, you haven't got a clue. You have no idea I've slept with your little blue-eyed prostitute many times.'

Eventually, the baron wormed the secret out of her and lost his temper with me. You can't imagine how upset and bitter he became. I was at the Mirwari Club one night, reading about the world's lost cities, when he stormed in and said, 'Baron, I won't forgive you for any of it! I swear by our fraternity, if you hadn't done this in secret, I would not have minded, but now God alone knows how upset and hurt I am. Your only choice is to give Tishkan to me right away. I swear by God, that's the only salve that will heal my wounded heart.'

I knew that once the baron had laid eyes on something, he would not give up until he had it, even if meant risking all his wealth along the way. I was sure that whether I agreed or not, he would take Tishkan from me. I wanted to survive with minimal damage, so I said, 'Baron, Tishkan is yours, provided that whenever I need her, you give her back to me.' He agreed to this minor proviso.

When the baron brought Tishkan to Nwemiran, no one knew about my long history with her. Tishkan was very upset when I presented her to the Baron of Civilisation, but I swore to her that I'd do my best to take her back again. I kept in touch with her all the time she was in Nwemiran. The Baron of Civilisation introduced her as the daughter of a friend of his, but everyone knew he was lying. In fact, in Nwemiran, no one cared who was lying or what lies they told; all they cared about was that life carried on as normal.

When I first heard the news of Majid-i Gul Solav's arrival, I knew this young man was too quiet and deep to let himself be trapped by ordinary means. That very first night, the Baron of Civilisation and I agreed to put Tishkan in his way. Tishkan was very useful in Gul Solav's arrest, but it left the poor woman feeling very sad. She felt she had been very unfair to Gul Solav, whom she considered the most handsome man in the world. I swore to her that I wouldn't do anything to him or let him be killed or imprisoned for long.

I swore dozens of times by her beautiful hair, her eyes, until she believed me.

I wanted to understand the workings of Gul Solav's mind. It was I who ordered Tishkan to ask him to tell her stories. Everything went according to plan. I dispatched Tishkan to him on the evening of the party. When she returned with the tapes of the two stories, I realised what a dangerous man he was. I listened to them once, twice, a dozen times, growing more scared every time. When I listened to them, I saw the kind of devil I was dealing with. I understood what secret messages he was sending me through her. Tishkan had no idea at all about the codes in Gul Solav's stories. I was sure that he, like his friend Ghazalnus, was dreaming about a power higher than that of a king; that he was dreaming of a fortified castle, the kind that rebels of the olden days would have built on a rugged mountain peak or in the depths of a dark forest. But today's rebels had moved the castle to a distant and inaccessible location: they had moved it inside the mind, into the imagination, into dreams.

If this had been the era of sultans and kings, I would have amassed an army to reach the inaccessible castles and towers; but when the rebels take their subversiveness into the gardens of the imagination, I am powerless. There is nothing I can do. The only solution is to tame their souls and hurt their stubborn hearts so that their bodies get no peace in my realm. When they stole the corpse, I felt they were telling me that they had dominion over reality *and* the imagination. The most dangerous thing in an Imaginative Creature is that he or she is not only an Imaginative Creature. I told all the Imaginative Creatures I bought and signed contracts with: 'You are not entitled to interpret reality. The interpretation of reality is a job for other people, not for you.'

When the Baron of Porcelain saw the book about the dead, he went crazy. I showed him the book page by page, with its thousands of death stories and their secrets set out in great detail. I read him some of the pages on purpose. I interpreted it for him word by word, deliberately.

'My friend, we've been caught napping. They know everything. They know everything there is to know about this world of ours, Your Excellency. Understand? They are not as simple as you make them out to be. They have the key to your damn graveyard, too. I know it's full of other dead bodies. They have a much greater understanding of everything than the idiot barons of Nwemiran.'

'And yet,' he said, 'you won't let me kill them. Do you know how dangerous that is?'

I feigned a look of surprise. 'Won't let you? Me? I only talked to you about Majid-i Gul Solav, not Ghazalnus. I know how dangerous

Ghazalnus and his imaginary gardens are. I do.' Then, dropping my voice to a whisper that reached his soul and echoed in his imagination, I said, 'The person behind this book is Ghazalnus. The mastermind behind the plot to steal the body is Ghazalnus. He's an evil man. It was he who stole the body to bury it in a secret location. We don't like killing people. Gul Solav is in our hands now. No matter what he says in his defence, people won't believe him ... Baron, if you're looking for the culprit, well, it's obvious who that is. I had to go through pain and terror to acquire this book. I stole it from his house.'

Rage was gradually turning the baron's ruddy face an even darker shade of red. He was an impatient man, and when he sensed a threat he became many times more brutal.

He looked at me and said, 'Baron of Imagination, come with us one evening and show us the way.'

I said, 'My dear friend, don't worry, I'll get him out of the house. I'll say to him, "Friend, let's go out and look at the stars." Every fucking poet in the world likes to look at the stars.'

The following day, I was plagued by apparitions of demons, dark creatures and terrifying faces. I didn't leave the house that morning. My head was filled with bizarre sounds and distant noises that seemed to reach me from another world. I felt the need for something to calm my soul. I reached for one of Ghazalnus's verses and read it. The more I read, the more distance I felt between us. This quatrain gave me pause for thought:

> It is a city drowned in blood and flowers,
> Hell its outward show, though Paradise its heart
> Its alleys are dismal, bereft and full of regret
> Its soul is a flowerbed, its interior full of gardens

I felt that the gardens he was speaking about were beyond my reach. I asked God: 'Why can *he* see the gardens, while I can't?' I felt that Ghazalnus had a thousand secret gardens in this city that I could neither see nor enter. That afternoon, I got in my car and drove like a madman around the city. I wanted to look one more time for his beautiful gardens, the ones he spoke about in his ghazals, but I couldn't find them. I saw nothing but dirty streets and filthy people. I was surprised that he had found his imaginary alleyways and roads in this squalor, that he didn't want to come with me to build another city far away from these swarms of flies and filth. I had to kill him before he killed me. All through the previous night, I had dreamed of the white horse killed in Majid-i Gul Solav's story. From the day I heard the story until this very moment that I am writing these words, every night in my dreams I kill a galloping white horse. Every single night.

I visited Ghazalnus on a starry autumn night. I had already made all the arrangements with the Baron of Porcelain and Ja'far-i Magholi.

When I entered his house, he appeared bright and dreamy. He was bending over a book of ghazals. As if he had been expecting me, he looked at me and said nothing. I walked calmly into his room and said, 'Ghazalnus, one of your ghazals brought me here. I've been driving around this city like an insane person since this morning, asking myself why it is that the beauty of the gardens of poetry cannot be found in the gardens of life.'

This was the first time I saw him take off his glasses – the small, elegant glasses I have kept to this day as a souvenir. He stroked his beard for a while, then said, 'Baron, you're mistaken. The beauty of poetry drinks from the beauty of life.'

I hadn't gone there to talk. I told myself, 'The days of talking are over, heart.' Out loud, I said, 'Ghazalnus, I was outside just now. I enjoy going for walks on nights like this … I'd like us to look at the stars together.'

My mention of the stars immediately made him weak at the knees and sapped his will, as it would all the poets of the world. They can't resist that sort of thing. I swear, there isn't a poet out there who doesn't go soft at the mention of the stars. Just as the word 'prostitute' has an incredible impact on the barons, so the stars have a ridiculous impact on these damn poets.

He put his glasses back on without saying a word, took my hands and said, 'Baron of Imagination, let's go and look at the stars.'

As his bad luck would have it, it was as though the sky had borrowed thousands of stars from God that night.

I asked him one last time, 'Ghazalnus, why don't you take me to one of your gardens? It doesn't matter which. Take me to the very smallest one. It really doesn't matter.'

Ghazalnus said, 'Baron, how about you take me to where I belong on the plan? My real place. I, too, have my own place in your plans.'

I said, unhappily, 'Ghazalnus, you no longer have a place in the plan. Only your friends do – the ones I signed contracts with, the ones who are working for me. I've already employed many of your female and male Imaginative Creatures in my world. We'll build a masterpiece together.'

When he spoke next, it was clear he was trying to conceal his sadness. 'And are the Dulbar Brothers with you?'

I laughed and said, 'Last week, I took them to Nwemiran for the first time. They are supposed to build a big garden for us there, and to plant greenery on the peripheries of the district. They are unusual young men. They can plant beautiful trees even in the dark and shade; they can make gardens grow in absolute darkness.'

Ghazalnus looked at me and said, 'Yes, they are two unusual young men.'

I could feel that he loved them a great deal. We walked in silence for a long time. It was evident that he was cold in the autumn chill. He was wearing a thin, olive-green jacket.

I said, 'Ghazalnus, what do you think of death?' I knew that he understood why I was asking.

He smiled and said, 'Humans are finite, gardens are infinite. Death and buds are eternal.'

'Baron of Poetry, if you died tonight, what would you leave behind?'

He was surprised to be called 'Baron of Poetry'. He looked at the sky for a moment and said, 'Whenever I die, I'll leave behind an imaginary garden for the fantasised children, which they can find and enter when they grow up.'

With a heavy heart, I said, 'Ghazalnus, you and your friends have treated me very badly. I promise to forgive you if you take me to one of the gardens. I swear by anything at all that I'll forgive you … but, please, take me to one of your gardens. Take me just once, and all the problems between us will be over.'

With an evil smile, the kind poets put on for the world, he said, 'Whether you go to the gardens or not isn't up to me. It's up to the gardens.'

I had been expecting this kind of answer. I insisted. 'Ghazalnus, give me your anthologies. I will pore over them all my life until I find the code that will take me to the imaginary heavens, I promise. I can't get any closer or bow any lower before you.'

He stroked his beard thoughtfully and said, 'Baron, whenever you leave Nwemiran, whenever you give up your dream of taming the imagination, the gardens themselves will open their gates to you. He who wants to tame the imagination wants to kill it. Leave the ranks of the barons, and the complexion of this world will change before your eyes of its own accord … and then I can give you all my ghazals.'

It was the one demand I couldn't meet.

'If I stop being a baron, how can I build the city of dreams? Who would look at me or respect me? I wouldn't be worth a bean to the Leader.'

He didn't let me go on. 'Anyone who wants the codes to the ghazals of Mullah Sukhta and to my poems must think about nothing but ghazals, love and gardens. A perfect human being thinks only about gardens, the light of flowerbeds and the everlasting scent of rosewater. Baron ... Baron, you can't offer human beings Hell and still bring gardens to this city.'

Ghazalnus and I couldn't find a single point of contact. As I stood opposite him and listened, I wondered: if this man were left to live, how many more people would he convince to transform their imaginations into impregnable castles? How many people would he force to turn their backs on Nwemiran, and this country, in search of the beauty of the imagination? I had tried my best. As God is my witness, I did all I could. In return for one journey through one of his imaginary gardens, I was ready to forgive him, to forgive Majid-i Gul Solav, to release all of them. But he wouldn't meet me halfway. Now, as I revisit everything carefully, I'm sure he wanted to die. He felt that he had completed his long journey through the imagination and reality, and it was time he slept forever.

At the top of the bazaar, where a long road stretches out towards the university, a traffic policeman was asleep in his booth. Nearby, there is a large bakery, an old barbershop and a grocery, its proprietor elderly and weak. The Baron of Porcelain, Ja'far-i Magholi and Murtaza Satan were waiting in a shiny new 4 x 4 on the first side street after the roundabout.

I said, 'Ghazalnus, get in the car with me. It's a friend's. He'll take us for a short drive. On this cold and starry night, a quick drive around the city isn't such a bad idea.'

I am sure that from that moment on, he fully understood where we were taking him. As if he had already seen the night's events unfold in his mind's eye, he asked, 'The Baron of Porcelain, Murtaza Satan and Ja'far-i Magholi are in the car, aren't they? That's right, isn't it?'

I looked at him and said, 'Ghazalnus, how do you know who's inside?'

'Baron, you've forgotten that this is the second time I am to be killed.'

At the time, I didn't know what he meant. I didn't understand, but took his hand and said, 'Ghazalnus, if I don't kill you, I'll hate myself forever. I'll spend the rest of my life waiting for something I won't be able to reach. I'll be thinking about a journey the routes of which I can't take, about a garden I can't enter. God only knows what a catastrophe it will be if the poets defeat the kings, if the kings die and the poets live. Otherwise, for as long as I live, the barons will hate me; every dream that enters my mind will take me to your doorstep and enslave me to your magic. Ghazalnus, ultimately, you and I are two billiard balls hitting each other; it's the fate of each of us to move the other in a direction he doesn't want to take.'

I felt that Ghazalnus hadn't yet fully grasped what I was saying. I felt he loved life very much. He was quiet as he got into the Baron of Porcelain's car. He threw me a glance and said, 'If it wasn't for the Chinese Youth, I wouldn't have come.'

Later, this last sentence made me want to try and understand the whole of his life. It threw me into a veritable storm. I felt I truly didn't know anything about this man's soul. The profound feeling of alienation that came between us at that moment made me even angrier and more anxious, but later helped me embark on a thorough investigation of the story of his life and childhood.

Several weeks after that fateful night, His Excellency the Leader requested my presence in order to reprimand me for having withheld information from him. He asked me to gather detailed intelligence on Ghazalnus. The Leader was known for this. Whenever anyone raised something about someone, he would order that 'detailed intelligence' be gathered about them. Numerous media outlets and the Party's network cells were engaged in collecting information about people. No one knew where it ended up, or who read it. For my part, I used his orders as a means of achieving my own goals.

Anyway, that night I didn't understand why that one sentence made Ghazalnus such an alien person, an enemy. In the car, we all fell silent. Every now and then, Murtaza Satan would say to the Baron of Porcelain, 'I swear by this beautiful night, you are driving very fast, Baron. Very fast indeed.'

We were all panicking – even Magholi, who otherwise never did. But just then he appeared confused and fearful. The baron took a long route around the city, approaching the plains and the desolate landscape on the outskirts several times before finally driving out of town. Around half a kilometre away from an area dotted with the small, unfinished houses of cash-strapped junior civil servants, we stopped near a big gully. The smell of algae on the banks of a stream filled the night air. The others got out of the car, but I stayed behind on my own. I couldn't bring myself to join them.

From where I sat, I could hear Murtaza saying, 'I swear by all the beautiful ghazals, I've never seen a night like this before. Baron, look, it's lovelier than even your wedding night. The air is clear, it really is. The city merges with nature out here. What a wonderful night it is, sir, a wonderful night.'

I blocked my ears so I wouldn't hear Murtaza's voice, and rested my head on the seat back so I wouldn't hear anything. I was sure he felt great fear now. I didn't want to meet his eyes before his death. I was sure that if I saw his final gaze, it would haunt me until my own death.

I sat very still, and started counting a number of imaginary flowers I could see in an imaginary garden, but my chain of thought was suddenly interrupted. Still, I sat motionless, and soon enough began to count a number of large house sparrows I imagined flying overhead, but to no avail – the thought of Ghazalnus insisted on returning. To take my mind off him, I began to think about the bodies of the women I had slept with. I said to myself, 'None of them had beauty, vigour or charm to match Tishkan's. I was about to start picturing all the details of Tishkan's body, from her neck to feet. I was about to lose myself in a purely erotic fantasy when I was shaken from my reverie by the sound of the first shot, and Ghazalnus's first groan.

I held my breath, and – as if I had been shot at myself – shrank even further into the seat and covered my ears more tightly. I was so firmly wedged against my seat that I couldn't leave it. I was aware that the baron had opened the door and called me, but I didn't move a muscle.

The Baron of Porcelain said, 'Your Excellency, curling up like that doesn't sit well with your usual poise.' He called me several more times, but I paid no attention.

Later, he and Magholi dragged me out of the car with great effort. They sprinkled water on my face and stood me on my feet. Murtaza Satan took me by the hand and led me over to the dead body, saying, 'Baron, look. He died a beautiful death.'

Ghazalnus was lying in a pool of blood. I saw nothing special, nothing divine in his face. In his bloodied olive-green jacket, with his long beard, he looked like a dead dervish. I shook my head and began to come to my senses. I saw Magholi soak a handkerchief in Ghazalnus's blood and put it into a special container. When I saw that, I took a towel from a bag in the boot of the baron's car – the towel I once bought for a stupendous amount of money. I took off Ghazalnus's glasses and put them in my pocket. I wrapped the towel tightly around him and said to the others, 'Bury him here.'

The Baron of Porcelain and Murtaza wanted to take the corpse back to Nwemiran. Murtaza said, 'It's not right, my supreme Baron, to deny me such a beautiful, important body to go with the other bodies I have gathered in my secret graveyard.'

I had a splitting headache. I said, 'If this corpse comes back to Nwemiran, I won't be able to sleep. I won't be able to live there. Do you understand?' I spoke furiously, my heart pounding. When they saw how adamant I was, they said nothing more. Murtaza started digging a large hole. I could hear him striking the ground with a pickaxe as I got back into the baron's new 4 x 4. Its thud echoed through the night and rose above the city and the distant graveyards before fading away, its destination unknown.

JA'FAR-I MAGHOLI AND PIZO'S ROSEWATER

HASAN-I TOFAN, LATE AUTUMN 2004

It took us ten days to find Ghazalnus's body. For ten days, the Real Magellan, Darsim Tahir and I set out very early every morning and came back late at night. We scoured the fields on the outskirts of the city, inch by inch. We found the bodies of a murdered woman and two infants. Darsim sniffed around all the plains, foothills, ditches and ravines on the outer limits of the city until, in tears, he finally unearthed the body we were looking for near the site of an old sewer.

Like me, the Real Magellan felt great sorrow. For ten days, he had worked tirelessly alongside us. To alleviate our fatigue, he told us tales of his long journeys. I felt as if he grew even taller with every day that passed; Darsim and I were small by comparison. When we disinterred the body and wiped the dirt from its face, all three of us recognised the handsome, dervish-like looks, the bright open eyes still looking at the stars. He was wrapped in an unusually beautiful silk towel, soaked in his blood. I unwrapped it and carefully turned the body over. Nothing was there but the traces of two bullets, the same two bullets Magholi always fired at his prey. I lifted Ghazalnus's head onto my lap in the autumn moonlight, looked up at the sky and swore to avenge his death. I asked myself what the use of gardens and ghazals was if we were all to be killed in so cowardly a fashion.

That night, the Real Magellan carried Ghazalnus's body on his back and only put it down when we reached Ghazalnus's house. Darsim and I walked behind him, weeping. We announced a memorial service for him the following day. No one came to the men's service save for a few Imaginative Creatures, several gardeners and two or three booksellers. But at the women's service, the yard and corridors of Ghazalnus's house were overwhelmed. The forlorn women came, as did the black-clad women. The children swore they had seen Trifa Yabahri at the service.

For a whole week, the fantasised children, the Real Magellan and I visited Ghazalnus's grave early in the morning. We paid our tributes and returned home. The black-clad women of Hazarbagh brought so many flowers to the grave at night that they nearly drowned the entire graveyard: it was an endless sea of imaginary blooms picked from different gardens, giving unrivalled beauty to Ghazalnus's plain grave in its small, tucked-away graveyard. Even now, when I dream about his grave, I picture it in the midst of an infinite ocean of flowers.

In the days that followed, I drew up plans to kill Ja'far-i Magholi. It was the one and only thing left for me to do. With Shibr's help, I obtained Magholi's address in Nwemiran. The night before I set out to kill him, I took the bunch of keys and went to Hazarbagh. That night, the gardens I saw had already changed a great deal. The tulip beds and rose gardens seemed vaster. All night long, I unlocked door after door, leaving the gates flung wide open. I visited all the delicate flowers and watered all the withered ones. I had never seen Hazarbagh so enormous and limitless.

I looked for Sabri for a long time among the flowers, but couldn't find her. It was as if her existence had been tied to Ghazalnus's imagination, as if she'd been a flower spun from his fantasies and fixations. By the end of the night, I understood that Ghazalnus and I had travelled through each other's imagination for years, and that at some point our gardens had merged. After his death, he had left his gardens to me, his lonely pal with no other joys in the world. That night, I contemplated the flowers and fantastic lawns for as long as I could, and left the gardens in sorrow.

I spent the whole of the next day with Shibr. Before leaving him that night, I entrusted him with the bloodied towel that had been wrapped around Ghazalnus's body, saying, 'Oh, noble and sad peshmerga of this homeland, keep this blood-stained piece of silk forever.' Then I placed the keys to the gardens of imagination before him and said, 'Keep these keys safe, and never ever give them to anyone. They are the keys to a number of imaginary gardens. One night, a group of black-clad women will appear at your doorstep and say, "Blond Shibr, saddest war veteran in the world, the flowers are close to withering; it is time they are watered." Then you must go and open the gates for them.'

Shibr took the keys from me and said, 'If it weren't for this wheelchair, I wouldn't be letting you go. I would kill him myself.'

We kissed one another goodbye and I headed to Nwemiran, armed with my pistol.

It was raining by the time I slipped under the fence and into Nwemiran. I followed a map Shibr had been given by a friend of his.

Ja'far-i Magholi had numerous enemies within the Party and outside it, but because he had been leading a peaceful, even complacent life for many years now, these days he lived without fear like a man with no worries. It was nine at night when I rang his bell. One of his private guards opened the door. He was about the age Magholi and I had been when we joined the assassination cells twenty-five years earlier.

'Tell Magholi that his friend Hasan-i Tofan is here to see him. He knows who I am.'

I hadn't seen Magholi for thirteen years. When he came out, he was as small, thick-lipped, wide-nosed and ugly as ever. The world had changed a great deal, but Magholi was still the same, only fatter, with chubbier hands and thicker arms. Otherwise, his look was the same look, his voice, the same voice and his soul, the same soul. He tried to appear jovial and friendly, but by the light of the faint bulbs above the doorstep I detected great discomfort and hesitation in his face. I could see doubt assailing him, but finally he invited me inside.

At first he thought I had come to ask for a favour. He welcomed me and said, 'Hasan-i Tofan, after all these years, you must have come to my doorstep to ask me for a favour or to pull a string for you. If that's the case, don't be upset when I say that it's almost certainly not in my power, that I can't do anything for you.'

I was too caught up in admiring the chandelier, the lights and big vase in his room to reply immediately. I was happy to have reached him. I wanted to take a close look at him before reaching for my pistol and shooting him in the chest from a distance, just as I would have done all those years ago, to avenge the Chinese Youth, Ghazalnus and the rest.

'Don't worry, Ja'far,' I said. 'I'm not here to ask for any favours. I know all you have to offer are your services as a murderer. Apart from that, you're good for nothing.'

These were harsh words by way of an introduction – I knew what a dangerous man he was. But he merely said, in his pleasant voice, 'So why are you here?'

I looked at him and said, 'Ja'far, why did you kill Ghazalnus?'

He threw a glance at me and asked, 'Was he your friend?'

I was about to answer. I was about to reply and engage in conversation; but a powerful force blocked my throat and stopped me from doing so. The two worlds that had been severed forever were not allowed to reconnect. Magholi was my dangerous half, the half of me the gardens had obliterated, the horrifying half numbed to sleep by reason, conscience and ghazals. This half was outside me, far away from me. It was my enemy. It had to remain distant, invisible and silent forever. I had no desire to listen to him and his talk; his voice did not reach my ears. He lived in the mansions of Nwemiran, I in the gardens of imagination.

When I looked at his expensive chair, desk and chandelier, I was sure that all he had acquired in life, all the fancy furniture he was given by the Party, was not worth even a bud from my gardens. I looked at him and became certain that I wanted nothing but death to bring us together. What is separated by gardens and ghazals cannot be reconnected by anything else. When I looked at him, I saw an old, indolent apparition, a filthy monster that had slipped away from me and gradually turned into this hideous brute. He had to be quiet forever. He had to remain silent and unable to speak.

Without answering his question, I stood up and took out my pistol. It was an odd moment. In thirteen years, ever since the day I'd killed the innocent woman, I'd never aimed that pistol at anyone. Just like the old days, I wanted my target to have no time for hesitation, worry or fear. I wanted to spare him the interval in which one thinks about death. But from the moment my hands touched the pistol grip, from the moment I took aim at Magholi, a terrible din arose in my soul, something akin to what had happened a few years ago at the Idle Murderers' Club. My head was suddenly full of the sound of old shootings, of repressed memories of gunfire rattles and explosions. I could smell the gunpowder from the bullets Magholi and I had fired. I looked at my hands and could see the steam of a dead age and a bloody century coiling between my fingers. I staggered and nearly fell onto the coffee tables. I wanted to pull the trigger and come to my senses, but a torrent of smells assaulted me. The smell of Pizo's rosewater called to me from afar. As if under a spell, I closed my eyes and walked towards Magholi. I wanted to straighten my arms and fire the shots, but instead I twisted, faltered and fell.

When I regained consciousness several hours later at the security office in Nwemiran, the Baron of Imagination was standing over me, laughing.

THE FINAL DESTINATION:
WINTER 2007

When they brought the Real Magellan to the prison, he had nothing with him except for his old world atlas. When his long-haired, long-limbed frame emerged through the prison door, such was his presence that all the prisoners fell quiet and stared at him for a good, long time. He looked like a great leader defeated in battle, who had ended up somewhere unworthy of kings. He reassured me from the outset that he had handed over the fantasised children to Afsana, and that they were in safe hands. I enquired keenly about the giant-nosed boy, and he said, 'Afsana has sworn she will do all she can to make him happy.' Hasan and I were very concerned the children might end up on the street, but he kept reassuring us of Afsana's reliability and big heart.

He touched the walls of the prison fearfully and said, 'Majid, my friend, I've been running away from these walls all my life, but when you've been sentenced, no matter how long or how far you run, eventually you will come back and serve your time.' All his life, he explained, he had been pursued by a fear of one day ending up in prison again. 'I've spent my life roaming free under starry skies so that when I end up in prison again, I will be able to endure the walls,' he said. During the time we were held together in prison, my regard and my love for the Real Magellan grew constantly.

He was held in Block Six, charged with the murder of Ghazalnus; Hasan-i Pizo was in Block Five, charged with the attempted murder of Ja'far-i Magholi; and I was in Block Eleven, charged with sexual assault. Hasan and I also faced charges for being involved in writing a book that brought the country and the state into disrepute. One day, the public prosecutor had summoned me and shown me the stolen book of death.

'Majid Abdulrahman Gul Solav, are you connected to this book?' he asked.

'Sir,' I said, 'I wrote every page of the big book that is before you in my own handwriting.'

The judge recorded my statement in full and said, 'Alas, my son, I've not yet seen an offender as idiotic as you. Woe is you, for you are deeply implicated in this. My heart goes out to you because you are young.'

Although I was indeed strongly implicated, the arrival of Hasan-i Pizo and the Real Magellan had somewhat eased my worries. From the very first night, the Real Magellan took out his map and started to tell the prisoners stories of his journeys. His tales gave me the strength to recount my own imaginary journeys. Eventually, the entire prison would gather nightly to listen to his or my travel stories in turn. His travels, real as they were, were also long journeys through the imagination, and my travels, fantastical as they were, also teemed with reality. He and I were two sides of the same creature; we were two worlds, two halves. No one in the prison knew our real names – we were both Magellans, one real and the other imaginary – but the two of us together formed one image of the world for the prisoners who, in their dark and terrible confinement, lived far from both imagination and reality.

In that prison, we spent dozens of wonderful nights telling stories about other, colourful worlds. In that prison, reality and imagination were, for the first time, genuinely reconciled in our stories and coexisted side by side.

One night, the Real Magellan ran his hand through his hair and said, 'Majid, only incarcerated people or those who are truly free can reconcile reality with the imagination. No life is more horrible than that of a person who is half-incarcerated or half-free.' He placed his hand on my shoulders and said, 'When I die, don't forget this: either be completely incarcerated as we are now, or completely free. Don't accept anything else.'

I badly miss those nights now. When darkness fell, the entire prison, the guards and the prison warden included would gather around us as we narrated our magical journeys for them. The warden was a plump, dark-skinned, cheerful young man. Although we were not allowed to have visitors, he did once let Afsana come and see the Real Magellan. When she arrived, she drove the prisoners mad with her alluring whispers. She had finally left her husband in order to marry Magellan. She gave us news of the fantasised children, and said they were well and being cared for with the help of my sister, Nawras, and a few other women.

The Baron of Dolls visited me twice in that period. On his first visit, he strongly reproached me and said, 'I told you: Nwemiran is a sea, wrapped in waves of secrecy. Even if you take out a drop of the secret, you won't learn anything about the sea. How could you be so brainless as to open a grave and steal a corpse? How could anyone understand this country by understanding just one corpse?'

Then he spoke at length about my guilt. In his flowery language, he talked about a universal force that had made me into Gul Solav, incarcerated and without a future, while making him the Baron of Dolls, majestic, free and happy. According to the baron, had I heeded his advice from the beginning, I would never have come to such a pass.

'Your Excellency is right,' I said. 'I didn't fully understand your words, and must now accept this punishment – the consequence of my own recklessness.'

He stroked his shiny, white beard and said, 'I told you that this city is no Thebes. I told you that the Sphinx standing on the doorstep of Nwemiran kills those who know the answer to the riddle, not those who don't. In Nwemiran, the one who solves the riddle gets killed. Did you forget that, or what? I told you on the first day … the very first day. You solved part of the riddle. That's enough to render you disgraced and unhappy until the day you die. The whole country is on the wrong course. Not even the course of the stars is straight as they pass over this city, and as for the moon's rays, they fall aslant on our doomed streets. But I told you no baron would accept your game, and nor will I. You embarrassed me, and made me regret what I did for you.' The baron was genuinely concerned about me, but I knew there was nothing he could do; and even if there had been, he wouldn't have dared. The others were far too powerful.

When he visited me the second time, he brought a letter from Tishkan. 'She gave it to me in great secrecy. Be careful. Don't show it to anyone else.'

The letter was short:

> I genuinely loved you. You were not like any of the men I had met.
> You were not like the barons. Your stories were very nice. You are
> a very nice man. You are a very handsome guy. But if I hadn't done
> it, the Baron of Imagination and the Baron of Civilisation would
> have taken me out of university and kicked me out on the street.
> My only hope is that you forgive me, and don't hate me.

I knew that Tishkan's words were the type of eternal lies girls tell after making huge mistakes, and it was because of these very lies that I hadn't wanted to fall in love. It was a rainy day. I tore the letter up in the prison yard and surrendered the pieces of paper to the torrential winter rain. When I went back inside, soaked to the skin, I remembered the scene from the Jessica Lange film; I remembered the fatal beauty of a girl about whom I knew nothing – not who she was, where she was from or why she had treated me so badly.

We spent the whole winter of 2005 in that prison. There was no word of our trial. Finally, in early spring, the Baron of Imagination's ugly face appeared before us once again. One April day, he summoned the three of us to a special room. He said that if we were put on trial, we would receive very heavy sentences, so he had begged the Princes' Council and the Leader to hand us over to him. Then he spoke at length about abandoning the idea of building a dream city. He no longer harboured such hopes and fantasies, he explained. He told us instead about a ruined village where his grandfathers had once lived – a village set in the midst of rugged mountains, at a point where all the mountains of the region met. Behind it sat important Turkish army bases, and to the east were large Iranian army bases. He wanted to rebuild the village in that same spot.

The baron appeared tired and impatient. He had initially taken part in the investigations against all three of us with great energy, but now he seemed thinner and more dejected. We all three hated him; we knew he was behind Ghazalnus's murder. On one hand, he wanted to isolate us from the entire world, concerned about the stories we told that brought the prison to life at night, concerned that tomorrow an army of Imaginative Creatures, impossible to control, would emerge from behind bars; on the other hand, he wanted us under his supervision forever.

Hasan believed the baron wanted to make us work for him at any cost, that it was his way of killing our imaginations. One of his baron friends had suggested that he force us to work because when people are physically tired, their imagination dries up. The baron's meeting with us wasn't a consultation. He simply wanted to pass on the decision. Before leaving, he brought out a sheet of paper to show us that the top Party organs all agreed that we should be at his mercy; he had instructions to help us become rehabilitated. 'The Leader would be pleased to hear you have become loyal and patriotic citizens,' he said.

Two weeks later, we were woken early one morning to find the baron and six guards ready to take us to the remote mountains. It was so early we had no time to bid farewell to our fellow prisoners. We were driven for four hours in a military vehicle, then forced to walk up a rugged mountain for nine hours from there. It was the first time in my life I had been in the countryside. Despite being a prisoner, I was excited to experience nature and the grandeur of the mountains.

We finally arrived at the village late in the evening. The baron had, apparently, given a lot of thought to this before resolving to dispatch us to this inaccessible spot from which no one could escape easily. It was situated in a perilous ravine within a rocky landscape. We were surrounded by such glorious peaks, sheer mountain slopes and tough, rocky terrain that not even the nimblest of mountaineers could navigate them. We were flanked by unusual rocky outcrops; even now, the sight of them strikes fear into my heart. There was a police checkpoint at the access to the only road, our sole link to the rest of the world.

The baron was a shadow of his former self, tired and despairing. Something in his face reminded me of Ghazalnus; he might have been his evil, imagination-free half, displaced and roaming the Earth. That evening I looked at him carefully, up close, and thought, 'Good Lord, how could I not have seen the resemblance between him and Ghazalnus this whole time? How could I have missed it?'

For a moment that felt like insanity, I saw all human beings as a series of mirror reflections of each other; as each other's opposite halves and completion. I imagined the first human being as a single tiny sperm that split into millions of parts in a massive explosion, just as one day the Big Bang had split the universe into millions of stars from a minute particle. I saw human beings as a monkey constantly jumping from one mirror to the next and trying out a fragment of life in each one.

Oblivious to my agitated mind, the Baron of Imagination said sadly, 'This is the site of an old village, the ancient home of my grandfathers. When you complete the reconstruction of this village, you will be set free. Work; put some effort in. Dig day and night, and put all your strength and thought into it. Each day you work brings your release a day nearer. The more fascinating the results of your work, the more kind-hearted and merciful I shall be. And should it occur to you to escape, that way is the Turkish border and this way, the Iranian border … I won't be particularly bothered if you escape in either direction – fleeing your homeland is also a kind of death. I no longer care about my own death, either. Every month, write down what you need and give it to the guards. Everything will be provided, except imagination.'

We haven't seen the baron since then. The guards say that he sometimes comes and looks at our work from a distance. They say that once every few months, he peers down at us from the peak through a pair of binoculars. However, we have not seen the Baron of Imagination in person.

Now we work in this village day and night – three men with dishevelled beards covered in dust. My sister Nawras and Afsana of the enchanting whispers write to us occasionally. Our captors read every word of the letters we send and receive. Our letters contain nothing but routine greetings and customary enquiries. During the first few months, we lived in a small tent until we had built our first house. By the day Tarkhunchi arrived, we had completed twelve such houses. If we maintain this momentum, by 2009 we will have completed a large chunk of the basic plan that the Baron of Imagination supplied us with at the outset. His main concern is that we follow the plan strictly, and do not use our own imagination.

The Real Magellan is our great bricklayer. I look at the man who was afraid of walls all his life and see a skilled, meticulous bricklayer. We start our working day at eight in the morning and finish at eight in the evening. We have two one-hour breaks in between. Since we started living together, we have developed a great ability to read each other's imaginations. Our wishes and interests are so intertwined that we often have the same dreams. On many a night, as we lie exhausted on our beds, I imagine boarding the old ship again and sailing along the rivers. Many nights, I miss the blind children so much that I cry under the blanket. One night I was crying bitterly for the children, and had the feeling Hasan-i Pizo was crying with me.

'Hasan,' I said, 'why are you crying?'

'Because like you, I miss the blind children.'

That was the moment I became sure the others felt whatever I felt. I know the Real Magellan greatly misses Afsana … he's forever thinking about her body. When I look at him, I can see the full, naked figure of that whispering woman. Many a night, in his imagination, he spends the whole night with her. He sometimes rides his fast and unstoppable motorbike, travelling through cities and farms, now beautiful, now sad. These days he understands better that being a Kurd means building walls forever. The day he abandoned his motorbike and returned to his city, he knew the walls would lay siege to him.

At work, he constantly repeats a sentence I don't understand. He also says in his dreams: 'Oh, heart, what a big leap you made into the darkness … what a leap.'

When he's tired and his body aches, he tells himself, 'Be quiet. You had to come back and build the walls of your own prison. You can't run away forever; you can't.'

He often talks to himself, but his sense of awareness and intelligence are still keen. I have travelled so often through his imagination that I have become familiar with all the countries he has seen, all the women. I feel that he, too, has travelled so much through my dreams that he knows by heart every inch of the imaginary map in my head.

Hasan thinks less about women and travelling. If I want to smell flowers, I enter his dreams. He is always to be found with a group of black-clad elderly women in an infinite garden. That garden is his only true home. He has nothing else in his life. Since we moved here, Shibr has written twice to Hasan, who says, 'I don't write back so that he won't think about me anymore.' I try to make him change his mind, but he says, 'He must live for himself and forget about me.'

Every night, all three of us spend a long time thinking about Trifa in unison. We are all in agreement that we will call the village 'Trifa's Village'. Nawras said in one of her letters that she had seen Trifa and the other carpet-weavers with her own eyes, but that, because every word of our letters was being read, she couldn't say any more. I sometimes think about Tishkan, and wonder what she might be doing. But I don't think about her a lot. It isn't good for my imagination.

None of us even thinks of running away. If any of us tried, it would prolong the others' prison terms. Hasan doesn't want to leave this country; the Real Magellan wants to spend the last years of his life with Afsana; and I can't escape alone. In the beginning, it was different: I thought a lot about running away. But slowly I dropped the idea, and got on with the work.

On many nights, Hasan makes a dreadful hash of reciting some of Ghazalnus's ghazals in his awful voice. I correct all his mistakes in my head …

So here we are, working day and night. If we continue at this rate, we'll have everything finished in a few years' time. If we aren't able to get out of this village until 2010 or 2011, I don't know what will have happened to our imaginations, but to be honest, none of us knows just when we might leave. I think that in future, this village will become the residence of the Baron of Imagination and his guards. Our work is very difficult just now. Two days a week, we transport the materials on mules; these are the toughest days of our working week. The nicest time is when the three of us lead the mules to water.

I am slowly coming to realise that too much work is taking its toll on my imagination, but I have to do it. Since the day I started recounting our story to Tarkhunchi, I feel a bit more at peace. All three of us know what Tarkhunchi is here for. One night, the three of us sat him down and said: 'Tarkhunchi, you've come to extract the secret of the ghazal anthologies and imaginary gardens; but you won't hear it from us, as long as we live.' We said: 'Tarkhunchi, write down our words and memories line by line. The secret of the gardens, their keys, the location of the ghazal anthologies and the path to the imaginary libraries are between the lines and words of our stories.'

He was a thin, tall man with many faces. I liked to say to him, 'Tarkhunchi, if the Devil were to see you, he would be happy and proud to have a son like you.'

He is too shameless a man to be hurt by insults or humiliation. Despite all his wickedness, however, we still regularly tell him the stories of our lives. Our only hope is that our story somehow finds its way out to the people of this country. Like a dog loyal to his master, he writes it all down, line by line. I am always telling him, 'Tarkhunchi, make sure you get it all down accurately. Read it with insight, and then you'll understand where the gardens of imagination are. You can learn how to find the gates to the gardens. I mean it; I'm not lying. I'm sure that anyone who reads this story carefully will be able to reach the gardens. Read it, once, twice, three times, and look inside your soul. Inspect your secret flowers, look at the hidden tulip beds in your heart and you will understand what doors will slowly open up to you.'

During the day we work around the clock, and Tarkhunchi watches us. He uses every trick in the book to get to the bottom of our secrets. He is a cross between a mathematician and a policeman. I regularly tell him, 'Tarkhunchi, I know all your tricks', but still he looks at me with his odd, vague smile – the smile of a man who can solve problems both in politics and advanced mathematics – and laughs.

All three of us now know everything about Tarkhunchi. We know that he wants to examine our souls and read the depths of our hearts. All the same, we would like him to find the gardens in his own heart. Every now and then, he starts speaking about the secret, hidden beauties of his soul. The three of us believe him, because we know that every human being has a beautiful garden that they can find if they so wish. Yet I am still deeply suspicious of people who are very engaged in mathematics. I might be mistaken, but my impression is that they hope to reach the gates of the imagination through calculations and by solving sets of equations. I often see him at night, engrossed in long mathematical equations. Hasan doesn't like him. His smile, deceit and strange gamesmanship mean he is always viewed with suspicion. But I don't hate him. I regularly sit him down and say, 'Tarkhunchi, write it down, write it all down. Only through these pages, only through a deep understanding of these letters, words and stories, can you reach the gardens. Write it down, Tarkhunchi, write it down, write it down. Tarkhunchi, write it down. It's the only way … writing is the only path we can take that does not end in death. Writing is the only path the day can take never to meet the night.'

FINAL WORDS IN THE MEMOIRS OF THE
BARON OF IMAGINATION

The story on that damned towel was my story. I was the one divided between poet and king in my heart of hearts. I have now killed the poet inside my soul, and can be at peace.

On the day I accompanied the Leader's aides to see the plots of land allocated by the municipality for the construction of the city of dreams, it dawned on me that the poet inside my soul had died forever. When Ghazalnus was killed, I felt absolute peace, but a dreadful emptiness also came to prevail in my life. For a long time my soul was at peace, every ounce of it rejoicing in the stifling of the nightmare poets. After Ghazalnus was killed, I went to Europe for three months. The Americans secured me an open visa, and I went on a majestic tour of beautiful cities. I went to Stockholm, Copenhagen, Hamburg, Barcelona and Prague. When I lay my head on my pillow at night in these beautiful cities I was very happy, though I couldn't explain why. There is no joy greater than that of not having a poet in your heart to make you hesitant and wake you up at night.

From the moment I killed Ghazalnus and arrested Hasan-i Tofan and Zuhdi Shazaman, I decided to live like a king. I felt the war was over, the poets and fantasists defeated and punished for their arrogance. When I returned, I decided to send my three prisoners to a place where, through hard work and suffering, they would slowly forget their fantasies. Day after day, I grew more hard-hearted. I decided to create a city devoid of imagination, a city filled with royal majesty and prestige, full of long roads and tall, multi-storeyed buildings, with only the walls of other buildings visible from their windows. I forced the imaginative engineers, bricklayers and workers to transport stones from morning until midnight. I forced the Dulbar Brothers to make the trees green for my baron friends and me. I had planned everything so strictly and discreetly that not even rival parties and sharp-eyed journalists suspected anything. I employed people whose only job it was to gather the flowers, which, astonishingly, rained down on Ghazalnus's grave at night. As far as I was concerned everything was going smoothly – until the evening I drove home, alone, on my way back from the Office of Reconstruction Affairs. Out of nowhere, I observed a scene that was to renew my obsession with the imagination.

I was driving along contentedly when I saw the female carpet weavers. They were weaving a heavenly carpet in a small, withered garden. I could see a number of youths nearby, watching them intently, all bewildered. At first I thought I was seeing things – tiredness, no doubt – but on closer inspection, I made out a number of slim, lovely, translucent women sitting at a big loom, weaving a divine carpet.

Anyone who saw that carpet must have believed it had descended from the very heart of the Kingdom of Heaven. It displayed all the magic of this world, all the beauty of this universe: golden doves, violet partridges, golden francolins, crystal seagulls, deer running over rocky ground, trees as tall as the moon. No words or power could speak of the beauty of that carpet, the depth of that imagination and the impossible dream it represented.

And then I saw Trifa Yabahri. It was there I understood that I had never managed to kill the imagination; what I had killed was the poetic half of my soul, which had pursued me since childhood. That day and the days that followed, I was like a deranged man – I paced the city, alleyway by alleyway, district by district. My only hope was that I would see the fantastic carpet again on another street, in another alleyway, but it was not to be. I felt as if seeing the carpet had shattered my pride. A few brief moments in front of it were enough for me to understand how absolute my defeat was, and how small and insignificant the victories were that I had won.

I started drinking heavily. One night, I sent for Tarkhunchi and asked him to bring me the secret of the gardens. I dispatched him to the remote mountains for a whole year, where he discovered many great secrets for me. During that year, he recorded every word, every expression, every story. He brought me thousands of pages to read. He told me that the secret of the gardens, the keys to them, lay in these stories, fantasies and anecdotes. I stayed up until dawn, night after night, reading the recollections and memoirs of Hasan-i Pizo, the Real Magellan and Majid-i Gul Solav, but I did not discover the keys to the gardens supposedly inscribed in secret code within the stories. I approached wise men and mystics for help, but it was no use. I sat with experts on classical and contemporary literature, but we got nowhere. I discussed it all with university teachers of physics and mathematics, but it was futile. I read Rashid al-Din Watwat's *Magic Gardens: On the Nuances of Poetry* in its entirety, but it did nothing to help my cause. With the aid of a brilliant Persian speaker, I spent many weeks reading and examining Sharaf al-Din Rami's *Truth Garden*. I didn't stop there, but read his *Lovers' Companion*, which he wrote in Maragheh, as well. Yet I found nothing that could remotely take me back to Ghazalnus's gardens. By this time, I didn't even understand what the word 'garden' meant. It left me even more angry and frustrated. I collected everything that had been written about gardens since the Babylonian age, but it was pointless. I became convinced that I didn't know what the word meant. I didn't know, and it made my suffering all the more unbearable.

I've really taken to drinking a lot of late. Sometimes when the Party's satellite TV station invites me to explain world politics to their viewers, I'm drunk when I go on. Drunkenness and sadness prompted me to open my heart to everyone. Like a man possessed, I told everyone: 'I killed Ghazalnus.' I told the entire story from start to end, dozens of times, certain that my fierce opponents and enemies in the Party were recording it all, word for word.

In the early spring of 2007, having failed to complete his mission, Tarkhunchi left the mountains and never went back. To reward his efforts, I appointed him editor-in-chief of one of the newspapers so that he could continue his services, offering praise and loyalty to the barons and myself from his new position. Now, despite my excessive drinking and bad behaviour, internal changes within the Party are promoting me higher and higher by the day. The Leader has me firmly under his wing, and I am well protected. He treats me as a loyal son, his own offspring. Yet, despite all this prestige and these senior posts, my thoughts still dwell on that gang of friends – as if the horse had never been killed, as if he were still pawing the ground outside my house.

The stories and memoirs Tarkhunchi brought back from the mountains opened my eyes to many things. It was under the influence of those stories that I awoke from my slumber feeling as mighty as a pharaoh. I instructed my informers to bring me any child born with a couplet engraved on his or her chest, and instructed Attar to do the same. If it hadn't been for the memoirs, I would never have got to the bottom of that particular secret. After just one week, they brought me a child. One of the informers had spotted her at the maternity hospital. She was such a tiny little girl. When I first saw the lines of verse, I couldn't believe my eyes. I said, 'Oh, guilty eyes, go blind. Don't tell me such lies.'

But I will never be able to forget the two couplets clearly written on her chest:

Child of the angel of land and sea, daughter of imagination and adventure
Bearer of love's miracle, babe of fate's vessel,
Your heart is a melancholy wanderer, your sight full of tears.
May ghazals protect you from evil, imagination from the Devil.

Bewildered, I snatched away the swaddled baby and headed to the Leader. I entered his office unannounced and, like a disturbed man, declared: 'There is a generation of these children – the products of the imagination – being born. A generation of these dangerous people is entering the world, and you are asleep. These people will pose a threat to whomsoever is in power. They will weaken them with imagination, poetry and ghazals.'

I unwrapped the swaddled baby and showed him her chest.

The Leader was, as always, optimistic and naïve. He said, 'What is this, Baron, you're scared of a line of poetry on the body of a three-day-old infant? Are you crazy? Have you lost the plot? I don't pay attention to dozens of poetry books and here you are, terrified of a single line on the chest of an infant. Take this as a warning: you're losing your manhood and your courage.'

I was sure the Leader had no idea what I was talking about. Oblivious to his indifference, I told my loyal people that, should they find any infant with such inscriptions, they were to enter the names on their birth certificates in a different colour. I was doing a favour to those who would come after me, who would have to fight these imaginative beings. After all, even when kings are enemies of one another, they remain brothers against the poets.

Despite all these developments, my obsession with reaching the gardens of imagination never fades. Nowadays I struggle day and night to put it out of my head. I visit the construction site of the city of dreams every day and ask the engineers to make the windows smaller, to make the gardens smaller. I say, 'Build me a robust structure, something the imagination cannot access.'

Last night, when I was drunk, I called a meeting with the engineers and told them: 'You must build me a mansion in an unassailable spot, in the middle of a big concrete city that cannot be reached by the imagination; I want to be able to walk its corridors without thinking of ghazals or magical carpets.'

Almighty God, help my soul, assist me in virtue and in vice. Judge me not for my virtues and vices, but understand me through your greatness and wisdom.

THE END

Now that everything is over and we have come to the last pages of this book, and while I would like to take my leave of you quietly, there are a number of facts you really need to know – things you need to be aware of. My real story with this book started on the day I went to see the hotelier to help him spy on his wife. Back then I was out of work, and would have done any job assigned to me. I didn't have much choice. That's how, one day in September 2004, a senior politician and distant relative of mine introduced me to Attar and told him that I was an alert young man to whom he could assign difficult surveillance tasks. So, Attar sent me to the hotelier and said, 'Find out what's wrong with his wife.'

To begin with, I was a junior worker for Attar, merely another member of his large army. I kept a close eye on Afsana: whatever she did, I was on her heels. I quickly established that she was cheating on her husband by having an affair with a tall man with long hair, but something told me I shouldn't reveal the secret. Every time I saw Afsana, with all her beauty and charm, I felt I couldn't hurt her. At the same time, I couldn't give up scrutinising her life or the dark, hidden side of her relationships. I took great pleasure in being aware of every detail, large or small, of her illicit relationship. I won't pretend that this sort of scrutiny, pondering other people's illicit relationships, hasn't always been one of my greatest obsessions. Attar had masses of people like me, each with the sole job of looking at and revealing the secrets of people's lives.

One day, after reading a poem, I began to see Attar as a filthy man, and the game we were playing as hideous. I had no choice but to go to that beautiful woman and say, 'Khanim-i Afsana, your husband has hired me. I've been following you for a while now. I am one of Attar's assistants, and know a great deal about your relationship with your man. Please be careful, for your beauty's sake. As of today, I'm giving up the job, but I'm sure your bastard of a husband will hire someone else to follow you. God knows who or what kind of person it might be.'

She thanked me in her marvellous voice, and said she would never forget the favour. Later, my warning played a major role in her separation from her husband. Meanwhile, I was also very curious about the globetrotter with whom she had fallen in love. Just as I had done with Afsana, I started following him. After watching him for a while, Ghazalnus was killed under mysterious circumstances in the same house where Afsana's lover lived, and the long-haired man was arrested for his murder. I knew the whole story was a fix, that the man was innocent. I once visited the prison where he was being kept on the pretext of visiting a friend, and saw him there. I didn't reveal my identity; I greeted him as if I was a stranger. My great curiosity to understand Zuhdi Shazaman and prove his innocence brought me into regular contact with Afsana. Soon enough, I became her voluntary assistant at the house where she cared for the fantasised children.

I have worked in Ghazalnus's old house with Khanim-i Afsana since the winter of 2005. The house has a blended scent of flowers and books. If you shut your eyes and walk around, you sometimes feel as though you are walking in a secret garden, while at other times everything smells of old manuscripts. Being close to Khanim-i Afsana and helping her – all the while unable to access her bewitching beauty – has created a spiritual longing in me that has made me love my job. When she's busy, I take charge of the children. Khayalwan is going to university this year. The young man is quiet, and writes poetry in secret. I often see him with an old anthology of poems in hand, but I don't know where he gets them from. I don't ask either, because I know he won't tell me.

In these two years, Afsana has often sat me down and talked to me about the society of forlorn women. She tells me that they meet regularly, even now. They weep and dance. They talk about the hopes or despair of the women of this city. They still take flowers to Ghazalnus's grave. She occasionally brings new infants whom we swaddle together, and both of us, astounded, read the ghazal lines on their chests. We've hung a big chalkboard in Ghazalnus's old room. Whenever a new baby arrives in the house, we write down their name, the ghazal on their chest and the day of their arrival in fine handwriting. Afsana says most of the societies with imaginative members are dying out, except for the society of the distressed women, which just keeps expanding. I sit opposite her and listen to her whispers. I listen, and never tire of them. Many nights, as we sit together, she tells me of her love for Zuhdi Shazaman – a man who smells of the stones, trees and seas of this planet. I listen to her, and am never bored.

It was also through Afsana that I first got to know Shibr Mustafa. Shibr occasionally drops by to ask her for news of Hasan-i Pizo. When he placed his archive of memoirs and stories in front of me for the first time, he said, 'I can't make anything of these papers. I need your help.' They contained all the memoirs Tarkhunchi had compiled for the Baron of Imagination over a whole year in the mountains, along with numerous small cassettes containing all the baron's conversations. Someone had stolen it from the Baron of Imagination to sully the image of the Party's main wing. All the files had reached the desk of the former security chief, who had stored them in a basement to avoid fuelling the conflict between the Party's various wings and to protect himself from blame.

Later on, when there was a reshuffle and the security chief was moved to another post, one of his close aides knew that in his distress, he had left everything behind. He pulled out this and a few other important files and stored them away in a safe place. One day he became curious, and started going through the files. In one, he found a batch of photographs that must have been taken with Tarkhunchi's camera. The images of three long-bearded workers covered in dust caught his attention. Wearing thick gloves, the men are positioning a steel frame to support the concrete roof of a new building; they appear to be working in the winter cold, and are surrounded by inaccessible, snow-capped mountains. He recognised Hasan-i Tofan – the brave, isolated peshmerga of this homeland, the man regularly seen pushing blond-haired Shibr in his wheelchair. The young man placed all the files in a big cardboard box and took them to Shibr at once.

Shibr and I spent an entire five months rewriting, correcting and editing the story. During that period, I tried hard to find my way into Nwemiran to see for myself the great book of death, which the Baron of Imagination is said to have stored there, locked away in a special box. But I have neither the ability nor the bravery of heroes like Majid-i Gul Solav. All I could do was to go one night to the Idle Murderers' Club on the pretext of looking for a close friend, and there I saw Murtaza Satan drinking and dancing on a table. He was so drunk I couldn't really talk to him.

Afsana and I tried very hard to reach the Baron of Imagination, to beg him to let us see the prisoners for a few hours; but the baron sent us a message through one of his aides, warning us not to harbour such ideas and to abandon such wishes. A few days ago, a group of creatures with strange appearances and souls came to see Afsana and me, saying, 'We are the Notebook-Keepers.' They asked us to help them resume their writing of the infinite book of death. Afsana and I looked at each other, uncertain about how to respond. I said, 'We should think it over carefully.' Since then, Afsana and I have thought a great deal about the Notebook-Keepers. We think about them day and night without managing to reach a decision. I occasionally visit Shibr, quietly pushing him in his wheelchair down the streets, alleyways and bazaars of the city. We sometimes bring out the bloodied towel and look at it. We both think it still smells of warm, fresh blood.

Shibr is now much calmer than before. On some of the nights that he comes to see me, he brings the scent of big, infinite gardens. When he comes to Ghazalnus's old house, the children climb onto his lap and push him in his wheelchair, and he tells them stories, one after another, until they all grow tired and fall asleep around the wheelchair. Today we have completed our work, but Shibr says that we should store this book in a place that cannot be reached by the barons. I look at the young children who have fallen asleep around him. Both Afsana and I share this view. And you, too, who have entered the garden, it does not matter how you came by this book, but please, do us one small favour: don't let it fall into the hands of the barons … Please don't let it fall into their hands. The peace of all of us depends on it.

NOTES

1 The ghazal is an ancient rhyming poetic form with roots in the pre-Islamic Middle East. It was used most famously by classical Persian and Arab poets, and popularised in South Asia from around the twelfth century. Ghazals often express the pain of loss and separation as well as the beauty of love despite the pain it brings.

2 *Gulistan* (*The Rose Garden*) is a landmark thirteenth-century epic poem by the renowned classical Persian poet Saadi. (It is therefore also known as *The Gulistan of Saadi*.)

3 Hafiz ('memoriser') is a term derived from Arabic and used in Kurdish typically to refer to a blind person who knows the Qur'an by heart.

4 Jarir ibn Atiyah and al-Farazdaq, two Arab poets from the seventh and eighth centuries, are known especially for their satirical poems – a dominant form at the time.

5 Ishraq, often translated as 'illumination', is a key term in Sufism. *The A to Z of Sufism* explains it as 'a way of describing how God works in the hearts of the spiritually advanced, and the name given to a school of Persian Muslim philosophy associated with Shihab-ad-Din Yahya Al-Shurawardi "Maqtul".' (John Renard, *The A to Z of Sufism*, p. 165, Lanham, Maryland: Scarecrow Press, 2005.)

6 A religious ritual often translated as 'invocation', 'dhikr' in this case refers to the rhythmic repetition of one of the names of God.

7 In Iraq under Saddam Hussein, mustashars were mercenary chiefs in charge of paramilitary units, which were often used to fight against fellow Kurdish guerrillas.

8 A qaysari is a covered labyrinth of alleyways with a myriad of shops, normally located at the centre of the old section of the bazaar.

9 Kurdish fighters and working-class men often wore the traditional baggy trousers called 'sharwal' on the street and when at home, so as to be ever-ready for action. Wearing pyjamas was seen as a habit of educated, urban people.

10 A bilwer is a wooden tube attached to a cradle, which collects and carries the child's urine into a separate container – often a glass jar.

11 Kurdish women wear special cotton trousers called 'darpe-i kudari' under their traditional garb.

12 In the 1970s and '80s, the Iraqi government built centralised towns and villages in the vicinity of major towns and cities. Known as 'collective towns', they housed rural populations displaced by the conflict between the Iraqi army and Kurdish guerrillas, who controlled large swathes of rural Iraqi Kurdistan.

13 Las and Khazal are two legendary lovers in Kurdish folklore.

14 The names 'Waqwaq Island' and 'the peak of Qaf' are commonly used to denote very remote or inaccessible places.

15 To 'make one's wealth in the shade' is a Kurdish expression implying that someone has acquired his or her wealth with little difficulty – the suggestion being that toiling under the blazing sun is the lot of hard-working people. The Kurdish word 'sebar' – the baron's nickname – can mean either 'shade' or 'shadow'. Hence the two explanations offered by the Baron of Dolls.

16 'Sa'ol' and 'Khila' are derogatory diminutive name forms. 'Ba Ron' means, literally 'in oil': the Baron was considered so poor that his main staple was bread dipped in oil.

17 After the end of World War One, the victorious powers divided Kurdistan into four, allotting a portion each to Turkey, Iraq, Iran and Syria. As a result, many Kurds consider these states as invaders and occupiers, and do not have strong attachments to the countries in which they live – and in which they have often been treated as second-class citizens by the respective ruling ethnic/national groups.

18 Mansur al-Hallaj (c. 858–922) was a Sufi mystic and poet who was executed publicly in Baghdad for his heterodox ideas. During his trances, he was said to utter, 'I am the Truth.' This was taken to mean that he was claiming to be God, as 'al-Ḥaqq' ('the Truth') is one of the names of God in Islam.

19 Piramerd and Ahmad Mukhtar were prominent early-twentieth-century Iraqi Kurdish poets. In their poetry, they advocated secular values and expressed admiration for the role of science and technology in Europe.

20 The term 'qalandar' was originally used to describe an itinerant, mendicant dervish unattached to any particular institutional framework. (John Renard, *The A to Z of Sufism*, pp. 236–37, Lanham, Maryland: Scarecrow Press, 2005.)

21 The leader of a dhikr ritual is known as the 'dhikr master'.

22 The 'hat of Sakhri Jin', which features often in Kurdish folktales, is a magical hat that makes its wearer invisible. The 'bald boy' is another folkloric figure; born into a very poor family, the bald boy rises to success by dint of his goodness and bravery, and goes on to either marry a princess or become very wealthy. The 'winged horse' appears in different cultures under various names, e.g. Pegasus in Greek mythology and al-Buraq in the Islamic tradition.

23 The provisional government of Iraq from July 2003 – June 2004, set up by the US-led Coalition Provisional Authority, was known as the 'Governing Council'.

24 The 1988 al-Anfal campaign of genocide against the Kurds, conducted by the Iraqi state under Saddam Hussein, saw at least 50,000 and possibly as many as 100,000 people (mostly civilians) killed. Thousands of villages were also razed.

25 Khosrow Golsorkhi (1944–74) was an Iranian leftist poet and journalist who was executed following a televised trial, during which he was accused of plotting to kidnap the Shah of Iran's son.

26 Al-Zarqawi and al-Baghdadi were two senior al-Qa'ida leaders in Iraq. They were killed in 2006 and 2010, respectively.

Quies
Rocks

Jack Collett

Troubador Publishing Ltd
Unit E2 Airfield Business Park,
Harrison Road, Market Harborough,
Leicestershire. LE16 7UL
Tel: 0116 2792299
Email: books@troubador.co.uk
Web: www.troubador.co.uk

ISBN 978 1805142 676

British Library Cataloguing in Publication Data.
A catalogue record for this book is available from the British Library.

Printed and bound by CPI Group (UK) Ltd, Croydon, CR0 4YY
Typeset in 11pt Minion Pro by Troubador Publishing Ltd, Leicester, UK